The Boy Genius

A Tale from the Realm of the Blind

William Wilkin

I0561406

Bell Street Publishing

Published by Bell Street Publishing, LLC,
7360 Middlebrook Cir
Nashville, TN 37221-6545

ISBN: 978-0-9903164-7-3

First Published in the United States,2019

Cover Art: W. Wilkin
Graphic Design: Matthew A. Stone & William Wilkin

Contents

Acknowledgements

I owe an immense debt of gratitude to several people who have contributed substantially to this book's artistic integrity.

There are my two sons, James Wilkin and Matthew Stone.

James and Matthew contributed a number of graphic design suggestions that are incorporated in the cover design and interior of the book.

They exhibited attention to detail and artistic consistency far beyond my capabilities.

My wife, Lou, contributed in both obvious and subtle ways to the completion of the book. She is a Spanish teacher and has extensive experience editing and correcting texts—both student and professional. Any remaining grammatical and spelling errors must not be accounted to her. They proceed from my eccentric ideas about the value of deviating from standards occasionally to accurately portray a state of mind or emotional content. A subtle way that she supported the completion of this book was her endless patience with those eccentric ideas.

In addition, she was willing to endure the many, many times that I worked into the early morning hours pursued by my characters who insisted on telling their stories at the most inconvenient hours.

She has always been emotionally constant in the shifting winds of our lives throughout the long thankless years of the struggle to bring these stories to print. Bravo Lou!

Prelude

For those of you who have not read any of the preceding books, I will warn you that this preface contains spoilers. If you want to learn about the story line to the point where this book begins, you could read the stories in sequence—*In the Realm of the Blind, The Chessmaster, The Spare Wizard,* and *The Ministry Witch and Other Tales of Perfidy.* However, reading the first book by itself would give you a good grounding in the Realm of the Blind. Another alternative, which I prefer, is to read *Wandering with Wizards* after *The Ministry Witch* but before reading this book. The events in *Wandering* happen simultaneously with those of this book, but they provide more context for the events in this book. Also, the events of *Wandering* add tension to the events of this book.

This story takes place in the universe of the Realm of the Blind where Hogwarts School for Witchcraft and Wizardry exists. It is a residential finishing school for magical youth.

The main character James Wendt is an English Literature Professor and Muggle (non-magical). He has been hired by the Headmaster Albus Dumbledore to bring diversity to the school and the slightest touch of liberal arts education to an institution that is basically a vocational school. Dumbledore has been assassinated by Severus Snape who is now the Headmaster of Hogwarts. Wendt was last seen attempting to flee England to the United States.

Wendt and the Assistant Headmistress Minerva McGonagall are "an item." However, the astronomy Professor Aurora Sinestra seems to have designs on Wendt.

The would-be despot Valdemort has a gang of followers who call themselves Deatheaters. Valdemort was permanently separated from his body but survived as a disembodied spirit. He had recently been gifted a new body and threatens the magical world order as he once had done. He and his followers are determined to enslave the Muggle population. Thus, Muggles like Professor Wendt are on their *persona non grata* list. They have been trying to kill Wendt for several years because of the effrontery of a Muggle in choosing to teach at one of the premier schools of magic.

The magical government of England was led by Minister Fudge who wished to deny the survival of Valdemort. He has recently been replaced by a new Minister of Magic who recognizes the obvious—the return of Valdemort. Harry Potter is now a wanted man—the number one undesirable. Every relative of Potter is now in danger. They would be used by the Deatheaters to reach Potter. These relatives include his cousin Dudley Dursley, his aunt Petunia Dursley, and his uncle Vernon Dursley.

Other teachers at Hogwarts include Rubeus Haggrid (Professor of Magical Creatures), Severus Snape (formerly Potion-Master), and Professor Flitwick (Professor of Charms). Other staff at Hogwarts include the Janitor, Filch; the Librarian, Ms. Pinz; and the Nurse, Madame Pomfrey.

This story brings to a close the parallel lines of narrative of James Wendt and Harry Potter. Everything that follows opens completely fallow ground in the saga of Hogwarts.

Preface

In the Soviet Union in a certain era, it would have been called a black Mariah. I was sitting in one. I was being pursued by the most dangerous man in the world, possibly the most dangerous ever to walk the face of the earth.

I was breathing in rapid shallow breaths, thinking frantically. Why didn't I have another 24 hours? If only I had those 24 hours, I could be on the boat. I'd be on the sea, putting fifteen or twenty more nautical miles each hour between me and trouble.

I took several deep breaths and tried to understand what had happened. What did I know for sure? Well, really, nothing. This arrest had come completely from the blue. All the officers would tell me was that I was wanted for questioning under the Official Secrets Act. What official secrets did I know?

I felt the cell phone in my jeans. I could call Her. SHE could get me away from these officers easily enough.

But what good would it do me? I couldn't board the cruise ship that was going to sail the Atlantic on a re-positioning cruise. I was back on the grid. Beside that, it would only put her in more danger—as if her current danger weren't enough. Even if Minerva pulled me out, the police would be waiting for me at the dock. Even if they weren't, they'd have been alerted, and I wouldn't have been allowed to board.

That reminded me of visiting a bank to withdraw all that money. I'd withdrawn about 100,000 pounds. I'd not paid close attention to my account, but I found that I could make that withdrawal without straining it. Amazing. More amazing had been the feeling of carrying out a valise with 10 neatly banded stacks of one hundred pound notes. Each banded stack had a hundred bills in it. I don't think that I'd ever had in my hands at one time a tenth that amount.

Now, it was of little use to me. I'd hidden it away in my garret apartment. I suppose no self-respecting thief would have spent more than fifteen minutes finding it. On the other hand, what self-respecting thief would have been caught dead burglarizing such an inauspicious attic—for that was what my apartment was.

As I reviewed my situation, I realized that I still had hope. Maybe I'd be released after a few hours and permitted to take the boat. I could still avoid my pursuers, who would much less imagine escaping pursuit by cruise boat than the average citizen would. All that I had left to do was wait—and hope. But, in my heart of hearts, I thought that escape wouldn't happen.

The SAS

We arrived at a police station that I vaguely remembered from the time I'd been there years before. We walked up to the 2nd floor and went to the 3rd door on the left. The name on the door was Chief Inspector Morse. The DI Lewis opened the door for me, and I entered the office. The inspector was neatly dressed. A small pair of speakers attached to a CD player was playing what sounded like an aria from a classical opera, probably something by Mozart. He got up, shook hands briefly but firmly, re-introduced himself—no first name, and started in. "Mr. Wendt I'm glad that we found you so quickly. There's been a disappearance. When you were identified as one of the last persons to see her, they've been trying to find you for almost a week. It was known that we'd had dealings with you before, so Lewis and I were requested to be involved." He turned to Lewis and said, "Please go get the two gentlemen." There was the slightest hesitation between the word "two" and "gentlemen" that led me to believe that Morse didn't necessarily think that they entirely merited the word "gentlemen". Lewis left the office, and I asked the inspector, "Inspector Morse, who was it that disappeared?"

He hesitated a moment again, obviously embarrassed by what he was about to say, "I don't know. This was all very fast, and they haven't told me—other than that it was a woman. Do you have any idea who it might be?"

Then it was my turn to hesitate. I was trying to decide whether it would be a good idea or not to suggest whom I had in mind, especially if it weren't Minerva.

The two men who entered the office at that moment along with Lewis were pretty nondescript. They wore conservative suits and were average height and weight. The slightly shorter one began, "Mr. Wendt, I'm Robertson and this is Stone. We're with MI5, and we'd like to ask you a

5

few questions about the disappearance of a middle-aged woman with whom you were seen a week ago."

I stopped listening when he said MI5. I started asking questions, "What are we talking about? MI5? What could you have to do with a missing person?"

"If you'll just come with us, we can explain all of that."

I turned to the inspector. "Inspector Morse, I refuse to go with these," and here I definitely paused before using the word, "gentlemen, until I've had a chance to speak to the American Consul. I'm an American citizen If military intelligence is involved in some way, I want someone official at the American embassy to know that I've been detained."

Morse had a wry little smile on his face. "Well, gentlemen, I really don't think that we can deny his request, do you?"

"Mr. Wendt does it make a difference that the woman who disappeared was Minerva McGonagall?" My heart sunk to the soles of my feet.

"Are you sure?"

"Yes. We have the disappearance on video."

There didn't seem to be any choice. If these people could help recover her—and that I doubted seriously—I really needed to work with them. "OK. I'll go with you."

We left the building in complete silence until we were in their car. "When was she last seen?"

Stone said, "At 3:07 PM last Monday."

Robertson shot him a glance and said, "Let's save all that until we get where we're going."

"Where are we going?" I was over the initial shock and was beginning to think again.

"Sorry. I'm not at liberty to tell you that."

"Thanks." That was not encouraging, but I still didn't see that I had much choice if I wanted to help Minerva.

We arrived at a warehouse somewhere among the old docks along the Thames. Robertson went first followed by me and then Stone. We entered the warehouse and were immediately in a brightly lit large room with desks and computers and people working them. They were separated by low partitions that were about waist-height. Most were in some sort of military fatigue, but there were a good number of people in civilian clothing. We crossed the room and entered an area with enclosed offices and meeting rooms—apparently. We entered meeting room 600. It was about 40 feet long and had a long table with arm chairs and a projector at one end. It was on and focused on a white board on the far wall. There were about half a dozen people waiting in the room—a couple in fatigues and the rest in casual civilian dress. Robertson spoke, "This is Mr. Wendt. " He pointed at various people around the desk and said names, Major Stevens, Lt. Colonel Parker, a couple of unranked civilians whose names I couldn't remember and a couple of non-coms.

No one offered their hand except the Colonel. He spoke, "Well, Mr. Wendt you are quite hard to find, you know."

"No, I didn't know."

"Oh, yes. We identified you 5 days ago, but the 2nd best intelligence service in the world hasn't succeeded in finding you until today."

"Well, I've certainly not been trying to hide."—a mostly untrue statement but certainly true with respect to MI5 or whoever these people were.

The major turned to one of the non-coms and said, "Bring in his piece." He walked out and returned with what looked like my Glock. "Mr. Wendt can you identify this firearm?" He hesitated a minute, and when I didn't answer, said, "Don't bother denying that it's yours. We found it in your room and identified three of your fingerprints on it."

"Well, I guess I might as well not try lying to you, gentlemen." Again I used the hesitation. "Do you think that I had anything to do with the disappearance of Ms. McGonagall?"

"Please take a seat. I'm sure you're wondering what the SAS has to do with missing persons." I glanced around as movement out of the corner of my eye informed me that my escorts had moved. They had left the room without any further announcement.

"Oh, so that's what you are. Well, that was the 2nd question I had in mind. The first, you just answered."

"We wouldn't ordinarily get involved in missing persons, but this disappearance is so strange that we suspect the involvement of . . uh . . 'foreign forces'."

I decided that I would let them do as much of the talking as possible until I understood what was really going on. Even then I didn't want to do any talking. "Yes."

He turned to one of the non-coms, asked him to turn down the lights, and start the PowerPoint. The screen lit up with a video of a woman whom I immediately recognized. We were embracing and "snogging". After a few seconds we broke, and I apparently said something to her. She nodded and backed away from me, ours hands continuing to touch for a moment. Then we parted, and she disappeared. I couldn't recognize the location, but the time that Stone had told me allowed me to. I couldn't decide whether to play coy or be open about the incident. So, I didn't say anything.

7

"Would you mind commenting on this 'disappearance'?"

I tried to stare inward and think as hard as I could. If I told them even a tenth of what I knew about that disappearance, I'd be in a funny farm so quickly that I would never know what had happened. I'd been in a funny farm before. It wasn't pleasant.

"I don't see any particular reason to comment."

"Don't you think that what we just saw was rather strange?"

"Strange, . . perhaps, but I didn't see anything illegal or even unethical. What should I comment on?"

"Like explaining how that could happen."

"No comment."

"Look, under the war powers act, we could lock you up until you decide to talk and keep you a long time after that. We don't have time to 'convince' you to talk. Where's your public spirit?"

"I'm an American citizen. I keep my public spirit in Ohio."

The Lt. Colonel spoke for the first time. "Major, go ahead. Give him some more information, but first, I'll set the stage.

"Mr. Wendt, are you aware that there are a lot of UK citizens who are disappearing and dying. By the way, not in such pleasant ways as your Ms. McGonagall did. Show him slide ten and eleven." The non-com running the laptop hit a couple of buttons, and the image of Minerva and me snogging was replaced by two men that I didn't recognize. One swept his hand, which seemed to hold a wand, and the other crumpled. That video was replaced by another where it seemed to be three to one but with the same result.

"We were 'lucky' to get these videos, but there are hundreds of people, who knows, perhaps thousands who are dying or disappearing like that. We thought it was Al-Qaeda or some related terrorist organizations until we got these videos. Then we began to put two and two together and got about a million. Major, go ahead and show him slides 2 thru 10 and comment."

The Major took over, and as the non-com advanced the slides, I saw a series of videos where people either singly or in groups disappeared. "You see, over the last few years videos like these have been recorded by public surveillance cameras around the country. Nobody noticed them until recently when the rash of murders and disappearances became impossible to ignore. We hoped that we would find the criminals in the videos. As you can see, we did in a couple of cases, but we couldn't identify anyone in the videos. Even the bodies weren't identified. They had died, officially, of 'heart failure' or variations on that, but the coroners have never identified a real cause—even when the corpses were quite fresh.

8

"In the course of searching for videos of the murders, we found these other bizarre disappearances, none of which seem to be under duress. So then we started looking more broadly for strange things—and believe me we found them. Private, go to slide 25." What appeared on the screen was a street scene that I recognized. It was the faux department store that housed the Ministry of Magic. I'm afraid that my surprise showed on my face because the Major said, "I see that you recognize the place. It's very strange. I can't tell you exactly where it is, but I can tell you where it isn't with great precision."

I thought really fast, and I decided that they'd seen enough bizarre things that they might just believe some of what I could tell them. I took a deep mental breath. It just might be my last free one. I said, "They call that 'unplottable'. It means that you can't put the location of the place on a . . ." I was interrupted by the Major who said with a good bit of tension in his voice,

"I know exactly what 'unplottable' means. It means that you can't place it on a map. I know; we've tried. We've also tried to break into the place."

"No luck, eh?"

The man's lips were tight. I could see he'd had some difficulty explaining to senior officers precisely why he'd not been able to get into the place. "No, we've not had any 'luck'. We've tried everything that anyone could think of, including having a truck 'accidentally' collide with the building. The driver just kept missing it.

"It sounds like you might be able to shed some light on this 'phenomenon.'"

"Well, I'll try, but before I do, you'll have to give me a signed, notarized statement that you won't commit me to a mental institution when I've finished."

Parker spoke. "Look, this whole operation is dedicated to figuring out what's going on. We've completely run through all sane theories—including aliens—and we're now ready for completely insane options. It would be nice though, if it had some internal consistencies, eh."

"Oh, yeh. The real explanation is internally consistent." I took another deep breath.

"OK. I'm going to trust you. Let me start with Ms. McGonagall."

"Your girl friend?"

"Yes. Her disappearance is called, in the group she belongs to, 'disapparation'."

The major commented, "A reasonable name for it."

"Yes. The people who can do it, can disappear from one spot on the surface of the earth and appear on just about any other within a radius of say three, four hundred miles. Now, here's the key—provided that they know it and can mentally describe it in some sort of way. They don't have to have been there before. They just have to provide some sort of description of it—it could be a mental image. It could be map coordinates. It could be a name of a location."

One of the non-coms, commented, "Like Google maps."

"Yes, like Google maps. If you can describe it, you can get there—usually."

The major again said, "What kind of people could do that?"

I seemed to be taking lots of mental deep breaths lately. I took another. "Witches and Wizards."

The major seemed to have had the limit that he could stand. "Don't kid with us. This is serious."

Parker intervened, "Stevens, we asked for crazy answers. We can't very well blame him for giving us one.

"Just what sorts of things can these wizards do besides 'disapparating'?"

"I don't know all the things that they can do, but I can list a few. They can fly on brooms." One of the non-coms burst out into laughter briefly and excused himself.

"I know, it'd be funny if it weren't so serious. They can do about a million little things like peel potatoes at a distance. They can unlock doors without a key in a few seconds—any lock, any door. The better ones can make themselves invisible. They. . . hell. . . I sometimes wonder if there's anything that they can't do. They can modify people's memories. You guys are lucky that you still have your memories."

"We've been very careful that no one suspects that we know about these 'wizards'."

"Good.

"Now, I'd like to talk a little about the murders. There's a group of wizards who are on a systematic program to take over the world." The Major looked ready to interrupt again, so I tried to forestall him. "Look, Major, I really wish I didn't have to say these things. Just imagine yourself saying them, and you'll realize just how stupid I feel.

"Anyway, they're mostly murdering other wizards and witches who are standing in their way. That will probably change sometime. Oh, yeah. They also have a prejudice against Muggles and people of Muggle descent." The Major looked ready for another outburst. "Major, you've really got to develop some patience.

10

"Muggle is the wizarding name for non-magical people. They've been killing and imprisoning people who are wizards but have Muggle parents.

Parker had been quiet for some time. He asked me the question of the hour. "How do you know all this? Are you a wizard?"

"No, I'm not a wizard. although I have a lot of wizard friends. I've been a teacher at a Wizarding school in the far north of your fair country, your realm, your England. I've gotten to meet several people on both sides of this little war that's been going on. The Black Hats are led by a guy who seems to be effectively immortal. He's referred to as "He Who Must Not Be Named". His real name is Thomas Marvolo Riddle. He's taken up a *nom de plume* that I won't repeat. It just gives him more honor than he would ever ever have in a just world."

Parker, "So you've met him?"

"Are you kidding? No, I've never met him, and I hope that I never do. I saw him once for a few seconds. His followers call themselves 'Deatheaters', because they hope to destroy death—for themselves anyway."

"How about the other side?"

"The other side has an organization that calls itself the 'Order of the Phoenix'. Their leader was the most powerful wizard, possibly excepting Riddle, in the world. His name was Albus Dumbledore. He was also my Headmaster at school."

A frown had grown on Parker's face. "I've got a feeling I'm not going to like the reason you keep using the word 'was'."

"You're right. He 'was' alive. Now, he's dead. He was killed by one of Riddle's agents."

"I knew I wasn't going to like it. Who's in charge now?"

"Depending on how you look at it either nobody or a 17 year old kid who is currently hiding out who knows where."

Parker was silent for a long moment. The he said, "I guess it's just a measure of the 'crazy' factor here, but I think that I'd rather that you were in charge. All right, I'll bite. What's the kid's name and how do we get hold of him."

"Unfortunately, I don't know how to get hold of him. His name is Harry Potter. But I could help you get in touch with at least one member of the Order of the Phoenix."

"Well that's a start anyway. How do we do that?"

"You could get me a piece of paper, envelope and pen."

"Don't these people have telephones?"

"I'm afraid not. They consider them barbaric."

"What do they use instead?"

"Well sometimes they use owls."

Parker couldn't help himself from interrupting me. "I don't want to know. Don't tell me. Would you take me to their home or place of business?"

"You're really not going to like what I'm going to say."

"Why am I not surprised?" the Major asked.

"Well, the places they work and lots of places they live are unapproachable by Muggles."

"But the Post Office can deliver letters to them?"

"No, but there's a mail drop that I know where Muggles can communicate with Hogwarts."

'OK. I'm tired of being the straight man, but I guess I've got to. What is Hogwarts?"

"Hogwarts is the school that I teach at."

"Lieutenant, get the man paper, pen, etc."

"Yes, sir." He returned after a couple of minutes with letter writing materials.

I started to write while the Major stood over me and read aloud as I wrote, "Dear Minerva, I need to talk with you. I've been detained by some people who might like to lend support to the Order. The thing is I'm not sure that I can trust them, so I'd like you to choose a meeting place and time where you, I, and a man named Parker can meet to discuss the possibilities like civilized people. Please choose a place where it will be easy to see if he and I are being followed. Return your answer to the return address on the envelope. Just in case things don't work out, I will always love you. James."

"I can't deliver that. We choose the place."

"No, you don't. Not if you want help. Believe me, you desperately want help. You don't have a chance in heaven of winning this war without lots of inside, willing information. And believe me, no matter what you think about how easily you got hold of me, wizards are a whole different thing. If you alienate the ones who are inclined to want to help you, you're dead—we're all dead."

Parker looked away from me and said, "Shit! I just knew you were going to say something like that. I've got to talk this over with my superiors. We weren't exactly expecting something like this. Major, see him to his cell."

"Cell?! What happened to habeas corpus?"

"Surely you didn't expect us to respect the niceties of English Law?"

"I suppose not. The Wizards don't. Why should you? Let's go." They accompanied me past the offices, out into the open warehouse, and then to some cells that were obviously added to the original warehouse structure. The next couple of days they were pretty decent to me. Then, I had a visitor other than the guards.

"Well, Parker, what brings you to my humble abode? You can have the stool, and I'll take the cot. OR we could break tradition for prison movies, and you could take the cot, and I'll take the stool."

"Drop the humor. You want to mail the letter?"

"Sure. I pulled it out of my pocket and wrote an address on the letter. Then I handed it to Parker.

"Don't you want to deliver it to a post office yourself?"

"Why? I trust you. Even if I didn't it wouldn't make any difference. I'm sure that you could pry the back off a postal box, get it out, and 'fix' it if you wanted to."

"Aren't you interested in getting out in the open air?"

"Well, let me put it this way. I'm a whole lot more afraid of Deatheaters than I am of you guys, and I think I'm safer in here than out in the open air."

"You make it awfully hard not to believe you. I work really hard to convince myself that the spooky picture you paint is not true, and then you go and say something like that."

"Look, the quicker you stop convincing yourself that you're safe, the closer we all are to being truly safe."

"Thanks for the address. We'll get this in the mail right away."

"Good. Oh, and don't try to barge in on this address. It would be awful to lose our one contact with the wizarding world."

"Yeh, contact with the wizarding world—our most important product."

The Sign of the Yellow Unicorn

The next few days, I spent a lot of time exercising. There wasn't much choice. It was about the only thing they let me do, besides eat and sleep. The Warehouse, as I'd begun thinking of it, had a kind of open air courtyard that was completely enclosed. When I asked for some exercise, they put me out there, and I jogged around it clockwise until I got bored with that direction. Then I took anti-clockwise. I was joined occasionally by an off-duty guard who thought that it was funny that I, who obviously had never exercised a lot, suddenly was interested in exercise. On the 2nd day of our silent jog together he introduced himself as Albert. That day I started a conversation with him, "Albert, where'd you grow up?"

"In Sussex near Handcross."

"You play soccer when you were a kid?"

"Sure. If you mean football? Never on a regular team. We played on the school yard field. There weren't any nets. We had more arguments about whether a ball went through or behind the goal."

"And you?"

"Where I grew up no one had ever heard of soccer, but they'd heard of football—US football."

"Weird game—US football. Uniforms with pads and helmets. How do kids ever afford the equipment?"

"Did you kids have soccer shorts and Nike soccer shoes and shin pads?"

"Are you kidding? We were lucky to have shoes with soles."

"Same here."

Over the days, the morning jogs got to be a regular feature. One morning, Albert asked a question, "I hear that you have a girl friend who's a witch."

14

"Well, you could say that, but I don't think your boss thinks that there are such people as witches."

"What's it like? Aren't you afraid of her—you know, afraid that she'll turn you into a rat or something?"

"Well, do you have a girl?"

"I used to, until I got this assignment. She didn't like the fact that I'm always on the job, and I couldn't talk to her about it."

"Weren't you afraid that she would slit you throat in the night or something else?"

"Are you crazy? NO. I loved her, and I thought she liked me, she wouldn't do anything like that."

"Exactly, I love Minerva, and I trust her completely. I'm just afraid that one or both of us is going to get killed before this is over."

"But hasn't she already done something to you? I mean, I've seen her in that video. She's OLD. I mean, no offense."

"None taken."

"But she must be 10 maybe 15 years older than you."

"I think that she might just be more than that."

"Well, see. It's just not natural."

"I don't blame you for thinking that. But, I'm going to bet you two things."

"Go ahead. A fiver on each?"

"Sure."

"First, someday you're going to meet someone, and you'll end up having a conversation very much like this with a friend about your new girlfriend. Maybe it won't be because she's older than you. Maybe it'll be because you are much older than she. Or maybe it will be because she doesn't match the traditional ideal of beauty. Or maybe it will be because she's from someplace strange."

I went on, "OK, and the other thing is that you'll not be able to explain to anyone why you love her."

"And here, I thought that you had a serious bet in mind." He shot back quickly.

"Oh, they are serious bets and ones that I'm going to win. The only question is how long it will take before I win them."

"Well, how about giving a shot at explaining why you love this Minerva?"

"OK." I thought for a minute. Trying to explain years of history together in a few words, I said, "Let me answer that question with one of my own.

"Have you ever known a woman who laughs at all your jokes?"

15

"No, but maybe you're a great comedian."

"I don't mean that literally. She doesn't laugh at all of my jokes, but her face does light up when I'm there. You can't imagine how exciting it is to have a woman who just can't help smiling when you're around. You really feel great when your woman always is smiling at you—not just at special occasions, but all the time. It really makes you feel wonderful—able to do anything—able to love her. And you find yourself smiling back too."

"Hmm. Never been there."

"Too bad."

I later discovered that he was humoring me when we jogged together. He was much faster than I, but he slowed down to stay with me. As time went on, I began to challenge him.

□

On the fourth day, Parker sent for me. "We're going for a ride."

"Anywhere in particular?"

"How about to meet your girl friend?"

"Sounds good to me." By this time we had reached a small side door through which we exited. Parker accepted a little salute from the guard there. I noticed a video camera inconspicuously placed as well. A driver was waiting with a Mercedes limo.

"Where are we going?"

"You ever heard of Godderick's Hollow."

"No, I don't think so. Where is it?"

"In the Southeast. It's got a population of around three, four hundred. You've really never heard of I?."

"Got me."

"It's a good three hour drive. You might as well settle back. That's where your fancy lady wanted to meet us."

"Great."

It was a pretty day for a change—warm, fairly cleara few high clouds. I decided to enjoy the trip and try to memorize the route. It occurred to me that it was interesting that Parker didn't seem to care that I knew how to get home. Was that ominous? Or encouraging?

As we drove along I asked Parker about his life, "Where did you grow up?"

"In Bath. I was a typical kid. Played football, cricket."

"Did you ever play Rugby?"

"No. Are you kidding? Rugby players eat their dead. I was just a soft-spoken, pick-up football kind of player. What about you?"

"Oh, I was never much for team sports. I played a little organized baseball, but mostly just neighborhood pickup. I got kind of serious about swimming, but not competitive—except competing with myself. Never for speed, just distance. I remember once swimming for 3 straight hours in a crowded public pool. I don't know how far I swam. I just thought I wanted to keep on swimming forever."

"Do you swim any these days?"

"No, there aren't many pools where I used to live."

"Hogwarts?""

"Yeh. They have a big Loch, but it's cold for my tastes."

"Ever think of swimming the Channel?"

"Again . . ." Parker finished with me in unison.

"Too cold."

Parker asked, "Have you ever been where we're going?"

"No. I'd never heard of it before today. I don't know where Minerva found it. I hope they've got a good pub."

"We're not hanging around there. I want to talk with her somewhere that I'm happy." Parker didn't look very happy.

"I don't blame you, but we're not leaving Godderick's Hollow. I'm sure of that."

"We'll see. In a way, I wouldn't mind stopping by a pub myself. Are you buying?"

"Very funny. I haven't seen any of my money since you picked me up."

We had been progressing from freeway to good highway to winding country road. Now we turned a corner and went over the rise of a hill to see a town laid out before us that seemed to have about ½ dozen streets and a town square with some sort of memorial stone and a church overlooking the square. The houses were generally pretty well kept except for one that seemed to be pretty ramshackle. As we got closer we could see that that house had fallen in on one side. Strange. Why would the owner leave it like that? Why not at least sell the property if you weren't going to do something with it?

We parked on the town square and waited for about 10 minutes.

I finally lost my patience. "Do you mind if I get out and stretch my legs. I'd like to look at that memorial.

Parker said, "I don't think that your lady friend is going to show. Go ahead."

17

I got out and walked over to the memorial. It was a WWII memorial. There were a long list of people who had fought and, I supposed, died in the war. I touched the surface. It was as cold as it was dark.

I started to turn back to the car, but my hand was still on the stone when someone took my free hand. Startled, I swung around and practically walked into the arms of Minerva. She kissed me just as I was about to whisper into her pearl-like ear, "Disapparate. Now." But I didn't have to. I felt the familiar pressure that seemed to want to shove me into a sphere. After a moment it released. "Well, this is the way to make the medicine of disappartion go down in such a pleasing way. Where are we?"

"Turn around." I did and saw that I was standing in a bell tower of a church overlooking a town square with a World War II memorial. "Nice. Nice view. I see that our friends are pleased as punch. Why did you disapparate? Don't misunderstand; it was exactly what the doctor called for."

"I thought it would be good to establish from the offing the relationship here. We don't have to put up with anything that we don't want to. We can both disappear at will. So they should be respectful. Somehow I've got a feeling that they've not been entirely hospitable to you."

"Oh, they've not been awful. But it's a good idea to set the stage properly. Yes, I'm very glad that you sent us for a little trip to start with. When are we going back?"

"Personally, I've got a little lost time to catch up on." She demonstrated what she meant by catching up, repeating the totally enjoyable greeting that she'd given me when she arrived. After a couple of minutes, I backed away and let myself take in her beauty. "I'd forgotten how very much I like spending time with you."

She asked, "How much more time do you suppose we have before they get totally disgusted with us and leave?"

"We really should get back to them." But against my words she closed and we kissed again.

"Now I'm ready to go back." And the pressure returned that I had long ago decided was the force of the atmosphere that we were displacing out of the way as we insinuated ourselves into the space which had once been occupied by air. We re-appeared next to Parker.

"What . . . Bloody . . . Hell . . . were you doing?"

"We just wanted a little privacy for our first meeting in weeks." I replied mildly.

She had a slightly different take on it, "Oh, yes, and I wanted you to know in no uncertain terms that we are here because we choose to be—not because you've any power to force our attendance."

"Well, let's go. I want to get back to London."

I said, "No. We're going to have our first little conversation here—or not at all." I was determined that he would get the idea completely clearly.

"I could arrest you both."

"Now, that's no way to get started with a new friend, and believe you me, you DO want Minerva to be your friend. How about dropping by the local pub and having a pint or two as we talk over old times?"

Parker's lips pursed, and worry lines appeared as he tried to decide how to take some victory out of this standoff. "Fine, but you're buying."

"Minerva, you didn't happen to bring along some Muggle money did you? I'm temporarily short due to the hospitality of our new friend."

She was still miffed with Parker, "Do you steal candy from babies too?"

"Yes, and I kick widows when I get a chance. It's standard procedure to provide safe-keeping of property for prisone . . . guests of the state."

Minerva looked over to me and said, "You really must be more careful whom you keep company with. Yes, I brought some Muggle money, but really . . ."

Minerva apparently knew this town because she led us off the main street to a side street where there was a pub called the "Yellow Unicorn". There was a plaque over the door with an ancient weathered painting of a unicorn. The color could just be made out in good light.

□□

We went in. The place was pretty quiet. It was still a bit early for dinner. I only saw one man sitting at the bar sipping what must have been the local brew. We took a table in the corner. I got up and asked what everyone wanted. Parker wanted a pint of bitters. Minerva asked for a glass of white wine, and I decided I'd take whatever the barman had that wasn't bitters. Minerva handed me a twenty unselfconsciously. I just hoped that I looked equally unselfconscious as I took it.

The barman asked me what brought us into town as he filled glasses. I tried a pretty close approximation to the truth. I've decided that if you have to lie, you should come as close to the truth as you possibly can. "I'm having a job interview with the other guy. My old lady's along because she doesn't entirely trust me. We decided to come here so that we wouldn't run into my current boss. So, I'd appreciate it if you'd keep quiet about it."

"Job interview, eh. Good luck. But you're crazy if you ask me, bringing along the wife."

"You might be right." I took the glasses in one trip. I had the handles of the 2 mugs in my left hand and the wine glass in my right.

"Here's to you." I took a good swig of the beer, which was not bad. Considering that I don't like beer, that's saying something. Parker didn't touch his—living up to the part of the job interviewer.

He started the conversation. "Let me speed things up by giving you the condensed version of what I already know."

Minerva shrugged.

"OK. There are real wizards and witches," he said the last word with a little hesitation that showed that he was finding this distasteful already. "They've been around for a long time. They are powerful, and they have kept their existence secret for a couple of hundred years. There's currently a bad internecine war going on between two factions—the Deatheaters and the Order of the Phoenix. The leader of the Deatheaters wants to 'rule the world'. There are a lot of norm. . . uh Muggles getting hurt because the Deatheaters are nasty people who enjoy hurting Muggles—especially Muggle relatives of wizards and witches," again there was a hesitation. "The Deatheaters seem to be having things going pretty much their way at the moment. Does that pretty well sum it up."

"Yes, that's the Reader's Digest version," Minerva agreed. "So, what do you want from us?"

"Well, help. Speaking as a Muggle, I think that it's your responsibility to keep the lid on these Deatheaters, and if you can't do it, we'd like to . . uh . . help."

"I wish you could, but—to be blunt—I just don't see a way that you could be helpful."

His voice quivered a little, and he struggled to keep his voice down. "Look, I've got a crack unit of anti-terrorist troops who are the equal of any such unit in the world, including the Israeli's. If I can't help you nobody can."

Minerva's voice started to quiver a little itself, and her Scottish brogue showed through a little, "You may be good at Muggle terrorists, but you've never had to face dementors or Giants or . . ."

I had to interrupt here, "Wait, wait, wait. Minerva, I think that there are things that they can do to help us. Do you know that they know where the Leaky Caldron is and the Ministry of Magic itself. They may be unplottable, but they know that wizards go in and out of both those places on a daily basis. They even have some nice photos of some of the clientele."

She looked at me with a screwed up expression on her face, and I quickly added, "I'm not talking about you, of course."

"Oh, of course."

"To start with, I think that we can exchange intelligence. They could keep surveillance on wizarding places like those and the homes of known Deatheaters to find possible new recruits and fellow travelers. We could provide them with a list of the names and locations of known Deatheaters." I took a deep breath, "I don't think that this is something that we'd want to do on a regular basis, but they could probably give you some tactical assistance in special circumstances. I think that it'd be best if 'You Know Who' doesn't have any idea that Muggles are assisting us. So we don't want to do anything that could tip the Deatheaters off to Muggles working against him, but there may come a time when we'll need any and all help we can get."

Minerva was leaning on an elbow and running a finger through the hair behind her ear, which would be very distracting under normal circumstances. I was just happy that she was thinking about what I had to say.

Parker's face had relaxed some, and he warmed to the topic. "Yes, my lads are very good at surveillance, and we have the latest in video cameras and other sensors. We can pick up conversations in a house from the outside across a street. We could maybe even bug some of . . ."

I said, "Maybe, but I think that'd be a bit dangerous until we know a lot more about the Deatheaters."

Minerva was clearly thinking this through. Her eyes were looking somewhere out the window of the bar. I suddenly had a bad feeling and looked out the window myself to see if she'd seen something out of the normal out there, but I didn't see anything.

She seemed to come back to us. "Yes, I agree. I think that it's a good idea to exchange information. The next time that we meet, I'll bring a list of everyone who we think is associated with the Deatheaters."

"Do you have photos of any of them?"

"Yes, we do. I'll try to collect as many as I can. But I'll have to get other people in the Order involved to do that."

I added, "Minerva, please make sure that none of them know whom you're doing this for."

"Do you think that I'm a troll? Of course, I wouldn't."

"OK. OK. You're the smartest troll that I know." With that comment she kicked me in the shins. That was actually welcome. It had been far too long since it had happened.

"How do we get in touch with you to set up our next meeting?" Parker wanted to know.

"I'll get in touch with you. Just like this time, I'll tell you where and when we meet."

I interjected, "I think that we should meet about once a week."

"That's a long time to wait for that list." Parker said.

Minerva said, "It'll take me at least that long to compile that list, but we can give you some names and a few addresses right now. Honey, I'm surprised you haven't given them any names yet."

"I wanted to be sure that I could trust them to not just walk out and try to arrest them right away. I figured that you could do much better convincing than I can, dearest." The last word was said close to her ear and as softly as I could.

Minerva proceeded to give Parker a list of Deatheaters, mostly the list of usual suspects that I'd known about—the Malfoys, Roquewood, the current Minister, the Crabbs, the Goyles, etc.

"Well, it's about dinner time. Can I offer to stand you dinner? Since it's not my money, I'm feeling generous."

Parker laughed, the first smile I'd seen him crack since we arrived in town. "If the lady will permit, I'd be happy to pick up the check for dinner. After all, I've got an allowance for these things."

We all agreed. The barman had a limited menu, including fish and chips and steak and kidney pie. Minerva & I had the F & C and Parker, the steak. The fish was actually pretty good, lightly battered and the chips were a little too good, I ended up hesitating over whether to order another order of chips to go. After we'd finished, Parker said that he'd like to spend a few minutes letting his food digest and suggested that Minerva and I might want to go outside to admire the war memorial.

I thanked him for his consideration. Minerva and I went out to the far side of the memorial. She put her arms around my back and lifted my right hand to her face and hair. I brought my lips close to hers but said, "I've missed you so much that I can hardly bear to have you leave now." Our lips brushed, and then I felt a loud pop as she disappeared. I turned and went back to the Unicorn where I found Parker talking with the barman, "Yes, I've decided to hire him. He starts immediately, and it was the lady who turned the trick for him."

"OK. Boss, time to go isn't it?" We left the pub and returned to the car. The driver had apparently made himself a sandwich and dinner from the things he'd bought at the grocers nearby. We drove back to London, and both of us were silent on the trip. I was thinking about Minerva. I guessed that Parker was trying to decide what to make of what he'd seen and heard that day.

As we neared London, Parker asked if I were a football fan. I admitted that in a small way I was, but "I don't really follow any teams."

"Well my boss has season tickets to Liverpool; I'll have to see if I can get them sometime."

"That'd be great."

"We'll see."

We got back to the warehouse that had become home and my cell, but the door wasn't locked. No one said anything. It just wasn't locked. I began escorting myself to the loo and the lunch room and the exercise yard. The next morning, I went out at the normal time to the exercise yard, and my running buddy showed up as usual. He was hardly letting up on me at all (I think). I was curious about his experience. "How long have you been in the anti-terrorist business?"

"Well, it's not exactly a business."

"OK. How long have you had anti-terrorism as a hobby?"

"I stand corrected."

"Well, how long?"

"I've been in the unit for 2 years plus some."

"How does it work?"

"Luck mostly. Let me give you an example. A German motorcycle cop stops a guy who's speeding—10 klicks over the speed limit. He decides on a whim to search the vehicle. He finds 10 pounds of C. They arrest him and interrogate him. He drops a name. The Germans are feeling kindly to us and they give us the name. The guy turns out to be in England. We find him and put surveillance on him. We watch him for 10 weeks and find out who the rest of his cell is. We watch them and find the drop where they exchange info with the next link in their system. That takes us back to Germany. The Germans surveil the guy and find out who's in his cell. They trace his contacts back to Pakistan."

"What happened then?"

"You've got me. I don't know."

"Maybe you will this time."

In the afternoon Parker sent someone to bring me to a meeting. It was in his office. There was one other person in the room. He introduced him as Brahms—Nicholas Brahms. The way I got it, he was a programmer of some sort or another.

Parker was directly to the point, "I want Brahms to work on surveillance of these terrorists. Tell Nicholas how they get around."

"What do you mean?"

"How they disappear. How hard it is to follow them by conventional means."

"Thanks. OK, Nicholas. Here's how it is. Either you believe me or not. If you're not going to believe me, you should just leave the room now."

Nicholas laughed, "What's the big idea. I haven't said anything."

"You will be saying something."

"OK. Go ahead and let's see."

"OK. First a question."

"Go ahead."

"Have you ever seen Star Trek?"

"Sure."

"You know matter transporters."

"Sure."

"These terrorists can transport themselves. Anywhere in a five, six hundred klick radius. They just disappear. Parker's got videos if you want to see examples."

"I've seen them. It's a trick."

"If you think that, it'll get you killed."

He looked at me carefully. "You're not kidding are you?"

"Look, it's happened to me. I've been squirted through space and landed a hundred miles from where I was. You just disappear one place and end up in another in 3 blinks of an eye."

Parker said, "OK. These terrorists can do that. It sounds like you can't surveil them. You can't follow them. They disappear, and you don't know where they go. What can you do?"

I looked at Brahms and asked, "Yea, what can you do?"

Parker said, "If you're a good programmer, you can program a network of computers to look for sudden changes in the visual field of the network of public cameras that are on just about every street corner these days. You can coordinate the times of disappearances and arrivals. You can direct the video scenes that are affected by these to analysts who can verify whether the sudden change was a person disapparating or a piano falling from the 3rd floor of a building into the visual field of the camera."

24

Nicholas looked at him quizzically. "You keep looking at me when you say these things that are nearly impossible to do."

"That's why you're here. You can do the impossible. You've told me that before."

"Yea. I exaggerated."

"Jim's your expert on this. If you need more information, ideas, or even a demonstration, Jim can arrange it, right?"

'Yeh, I can even arrange the experience for you if you're crazy enough to want it."

The session ended, and I returned to my room. I'd decided to call it my room, since it wasn't really a cell any more. But it was kind of hard to accept the lack of privacy now that it was my room.

The next day, after exercise, Parker himself came to get me. He led me to a distant part of the warehouse and led me through a door into an office. No one was there, "Well, how do you like it?" He asked.

"Oh, it's fine for an office. I like the leather sofa. Who are we meeting?"

"Nobody. This is your office now. Open the upper left drawer in the desk."

I did and I found my personal "effects". Also, there was a ring of keys that I didn't recognize. "Thanks. I was wondering what happened with my stuff. What are the keys?"

"Well if you've got an office, you've got to have keys to the door, the desk, the front door, don't you?"

"Yes, I guess so. So, I can go if I want to?"

"Anywhere you like. You don't have to return if you don't want to, but the office will always be here. By the way, the sofa folds out, and there's a bathroom behind that door over there."

I went over and jumped onto the sofa. It was very firm and smelled like leather. "Nice. Thanks, and you know very well that I'm not going to be walking out on you for a whole slew of reasons. I'm scared to death of being found by Deatheaters. I like to eat, and the Cafeteria has decent food, seemingly for free. I want to fight the Deatheaters, and you're my ticket. First and foremost, I want to keep seeing Minerva safely. You're my ticket to that, too."

"Yea. I know."

"I suppose the chest of drawers has my clothes in it."

"You've got it."

I spent the afternoon getting acquainted with the office. I found it to be just too, too much fun. There was a computer on the desk with high speed internet access! I thought about what I could do with that.

Nukes in the News

The next several days were quiet. However, there was lots for me to do. I had never seen a computer up close, and though I knew about the Internet in theory, I had never actually "browsed" it. There were manuals in a bookshelf along one wall. I read voraciously about "Windows" and the "World Wide Web" and "widgets". Why was it everything having to do with computers starts with a "W"?

I still ran with my guard buddy, but more and more we ran outside the Warehouse. Sometimes we ran along the Thames. One day while we were running, he stopped and turned to me. He looked up at the cloudy sky. "How would you like to learn to do something useful with the muscles you've been developing?"

"Useful? I'd like a definition of that before we go overboard, here."

"Useful, as in self-defense. Is that useful enough for you?"

"Does this involve me in getting hurt a lot, and you not very much?"

"It starts that way."

"I suppose it was inevitable, 'Give a mouse a cookie'."

"What??"

"Oh, nothing. Just a bad joke. Maybe I'll explain it some time. OK. Let's get started."

"We'll start with pure defense. Put both hands up in front of your body about shoulder height. Palms out. Now, I'm going to throw punches at you and you block them with the flat of your palm."

"OK. That seems easy enough."

It seemed easy, but he was quick and could almost always get past my palms. After about a dozen body blows, I was beginning to hurt in a serious way. "OK. You've proved your point. I'm completely incompetent. Let's move on to something else."

He didn't hesitate, but just kept throwing the fists. "This is the practice. It develops your eye hand coordination, and getting hit gently a few times gives you incentive to do well."

"This is gent. . ." I didn't finish the sentence. He caught me in the solar plexus, and I crumpled.

"Come on, get up. We've barely begun. And if I wanted to hurt you, I wouldn't be as gentle as this."

I could see that it was going to be a long session. By the end, I was able to block about 1 in 7 punches. This sort of thing made you long for simple running. We took a short cut home, and I nursed my wounds for the rest of the afternoon.

□

A couple of days later, Parker phoned me. "I want to come over and talk with you. Are you busy?"

"Are you kidding, I'm never busy these days. Come on."

He arrived about 5 minutes later. He had a rather serious grimace on his face. After closing the door, he got right down to business, "Well, Wendt, we've got a problem."

"I knew the last couple of days were too good to be true. What's up?"

"My boss has a brilliant idea."

"You know, bosses should just leave the thinking to people who can do it and stick with writing reports."

"Look, this is serious. He's getting pressure from 'Above' for results. He wants to do something dramatic. He wants to attack the Ministry of Magic."

"He's crazy. It's not possible. Even he should be able to figure that out."

"No, I'm afraid that he's got an idea that just might work."

"OK. What is it?"

Parker started to turn around and stopped. I had the feeling that he was about to look over his shoulder. "He's going to nuke the Ministry."

"You know, my hearing's been going funny lately. I've been taking too many punches to the head. I could have sworn that you said. . ." I hesitated. I couldn't quite bring myself to say it.

"Yes, nuke as in thermonuclear device, as in blast and radiation and Armageddon."

"Oh, come on. Even he couldn't be that dumb."

"He can make a pretty good case—at least on paper."

"How can he do that? Is he a complete moron? A nuke in downtown London? Even a small one would surely kill thousands of people if not tens of thousands. How could he possibly think of doing it?"

"Oh, he makes it sound plausible. First, he'd use a very small one, around 1 or 2 KT. Second, there are actually 'shaped' nuclear charges that can direct most of their force in one direction and create very little radioactive debris. His idea is that we could demolish the Ministry and probably only kill a couple of hundred innocent bystanders."

"That's crazy. Even if you could, how would he explain using a nuclear weapon on his own country—in London, no less?"

"Oh, he wouldn't. We'd blame it on terrorists. You know there are terrorists trying to get nuclear materials."

"But, don't nukes create radioactive debris that can be traced somehow to who made it?"

"Oh, yes. Sort of. We've already bought some plutonium from Russian agents. It was made in Russian reactors for the Soviet nuclear weapons program. The cover story will be that the Russians sold it to terrorists."

"This is crazy! Even if all that worked, you'd kill hundreds and hundreds of innocent Muggles and wizards. That alone would be bad enough, but there's worse, far worse."

"Oh, great!"

"Look, this Tom Riddle who's the organizer of the Deatheaters hates Muggles and is trying to convince wizards that Muggles are really evil and should be suppressed. Maybe a tenth of a percent of wizards are Deatheaters. And only a few percent of wizards are fellow travelers. On the other hand, far less than half of wizards are kindly disposed toward Muggles. The rest are pretty much neutral. If something like this happened, most of the uncommitted would be having 2nd and 3rd thoughts about Muggles. Even if Tom Riddle somehow disappeared from the scene, we'd still be stuck with a wizard population that mostly hated Muggles. That's something you really don't want."

Parker's face looked miserable. "Is it really that bad?"

"Well, look. Even if the public buys the terrorist story, which seems to me unlikely, the way wizards would see it, terrorists are just a different group of Muggles. That cover story doesn't help at all with the people that really matter."

"Great. Frankly, I don't know how to talk Gen. Davis out of this. He's really determined to do something. I've already tried everything I could think of."

"How about letting me see him? It couldn't hurt. . . . Could it?"

"I suppose not. He's in a hurry to do it. I'll try to get an appointment for us to see him in the next day or two."

"Is that soon enough?"

"Oh, yes. They haven't used the Russian Plutonium to build the bomb yet. That will probably take a couple of weeks. We have some time, but these things start to develop momentum of their own, so we really need to get that meeting set up soon."

□□

A day or two later we were sitting in the General's office. My stomach would have been turning inside out if it weren't that it was empty already. Parker looked as calm as I was nervous. Gen. Davis was frowning and looked grim.

Parker started off smoothly. "Well, it's nice to see you again. I hope that you had a good breakfast this morning."

"Passable."

"That's too bad. A good breakfast is the start of a good day."

"I'll bear that in mind. Now, I hear that you're here to talk me out of defending the country."

I gulped and broke in. "Not at all, sir."

"You're Mr. Wendt." It was a statement, and it put lots of emphasis on the MR. as in not military.

"That's right. I am."

"We'll, we're burning daylight, young man. What would you call it? I've got a plan to attack a threat to this country. Nobody else seems to have any ideas. I'd like you to tell me just why I shouldn't do something before the country is lost to these. . ." He hesitated, looking for the right word. "Terrorists." The word came out sounding a lot like a spit.

The reason that I had been so nervous was that I had an idea. The idea was extremely crazy, but I kept telling myself that Davis didn't know just how crazy it was. Only I had the slightest idea how stark raving mad it was. I tried to sound as smooth as Parker and said casually, "You sound like you'd like to make these 'terrorists' hurt."

"You bet I would—don't you?"

"Yes, I would. But, I'd like to do something that would really make them hurt."

"And a nuke in their headquarters wouldn't hurt?" There was a sound of smug self-assurance in his words that made me begin to think that I might just have a chance.

"Yes, if it were their headquarters, it would."

"We know where their headquarters are. We see hundreds of them go in and out every day. What are you talking about?" There was the slightest quaver of doubt in his voice.

"Yes, hundreds do go in and out every day," Parker said with all the confidence that I lacked, "but thousands of people go in and out of Tube stations every day. Does that make the Underground the headquarters of MI5?"

"You're saying that you know that there's some other place that is the headquarters?"

I said. "I know that none of the people whom I've seen go in and out of the M.O.M. are the top people in the organization." That was a little bit of an exaggeration, but not much. "I also know of a way to strike these terrorists that will really hurt them."

"Well, why don't you tell me about it?" There was pessimism and doubt in his voice, but not outright rejection.

"The terrorists have fortresses. Some we know about. Some we don't. One that we know about is a prison or maybe concentration camp would be a better term."

"And you know where it's located."

"Yes, we do," I said with all the confidence that I didn't feel, hoping that we could find it.

"Who do they keep in this 'concentration camp'?"

"They keep dissidents—people who disagree with them. Sort of like Jews in World War II. These are people who would be natural allies to us."

"Hmmm. And what do you want to do?"

"I would like to attack the prison and release these prisoners and give them sanctuary."

"A very humanitarian goal. How does that help us?"

"First, it would be thumbing our nose at them."

"That's a start."

"Second. These people could be the basis and beginnings of an army."

"An army. But we have an army already and it hasn't done us any good."

"Yes, our army is pretty powerless against these people." I hesitated. "But an army of these wizards would be different. They know how to attack the Deatheaters effectively. They have powerful motivation to fight them. It would be effective."

"Hmmm. We would attack this prison and free the captives. Hmmm. That's an interesting idea."

31

"Where would we keep these escapees?" That was Parker's contribution. He always seemed to have a way of bringing things down to earth.

Davis looked introspective. "Do we have to keep them anywhere?"

"I'm afraid so." I said. "They got into prison because they were picked up. We've got to provide them with a sanctuary, and, of course, if we want their help in fighting the terrorists, we'll have to train them as well."

Davis smiled. "How about a military base. We've got a couple of old bases that we're ready to de-commission."

I had visions of someone disapparating into London and being seen. "No, it has to be remote—really remote. So remote," and I looked over at Parker, "that they can't go AWOL and be seen anywhere in England."

Davis asked, "Is it really necessary to get them out of the country?"

Parker agreed, "Yes, I'm afraid that Wendt's right. It has to be out of the country and, I suppose, out of Europe." He looked over at me with a question in his eye.

"Yes, I agree. As a matter of fact, I think that out of the British Empire or what is left of it would be best."

Davis, "Oh great. You mean that I'm going to have to ask the Americans for help?"

I brightened at the idea. "Yes, that would be really good. Put an ocean between them and our refugees. It would also make going AWOL less likely. Yes, really good."

Davis turned business-like. "Good. How soon can we put this raid together?"

Parker answered quickly. "First we've got to get our sanctuary lined up. We've also got to put together a team and put them through training. And, most important, we've got to start forming up a leadership team to do all that."

Davis was really warming to the idea. He had a bright smile on his face and enthused, "If you need any help from the Royal Marines or regular services, just say the word. I'd really like to have a hand in this."

I groaned inwardly, and I'm sure that Parker did too, although he was as bright as ever. "We'll have to put together the team, but if we need any man-power or diversion or whatever, we'll think of you first."

"But how soon do you think that we can start?"

Parker looked over to me. He had a way of doing that when there was bad news to deliver.

"Well, as I see it, it will take at least a couple of weeks to put together a team and start training. In the mean time, we can be finding a location in the States—I hope. I'd think that that would be the hardest part. It might take a month to find a suitable base in the US and get approval. Then there'd be more time to prepare it. Arranging transport there might not be too easy if we have to avoid going through customs with them. I really think that it will take at least two months if not three to be ready for the raid."

Davis was not so happy. "Look. We've really got to get going on this faster than that. We'll give you all the manpower that you need."

"I appreciate the offer, general, but this has to be a really special team with special. . . uh . . . talents. Of course, if we find that we can't find the people we're looking for, we'll be very glad to send you a list of talents that we need."

Davis said gruffly, "Be sure you do. I want to get regular reports on progress."

Parker admonished, "You know these operations require the tightest security. We'll keep you generally apprised of progress, so don't press us much on this."

"Well, then get out of here and get going. We're burning daylight."

We left, and I gave a sigh of relief. When we were in the car on the way back to our base, Parker looked over and asked, "Is there really a prison like you described?"

"Sure there is. It's called 'Azkaban'."

"You're not shitting me?"

"No sir."

"How are we going to put a team together to attack it?"

I had to do what I was really hoping that I could put off until the next day—think. I sighed a lengthy sigh to give me a little time to do some of that thinking. "As I see it, it's got to be a wizard team. By the way, it has been done successfully. Azkaban was broken into, and there was a mass break out."

"Who did that?"

"Riddle."

"I was afraid that you'd say that."

"How are you going to find a team to do that? I doubt that the Deatheaters are going to line up to volunteer to do that again—even for the fun of it."

"When you're right, you're right. I've got to get in touch with my wizarding buddies and see what I can put together."

"You do that. And don't waste any time."

Well, I did the best I could. I used the letter-drop at the Leaky Caldron to send a letter to Minerva. The key sentence was, "Minerva, do you happen to know anyone who might be interested in breaking into a certain high security prison."

A couple of days later, a letter, addressed to me at General Delivery, the main London post office showed up. It was brief. "Meet me at our favorite pub, the Yellow Unicorn—Saturday, 2 PM." I had to think a few minutes, and then I remembered Godderick's Hollow.

Godderick's Hollow Revisited

That Saturday was clear and cool—a perfect football (American) day. I arranged to arrive at the Yellow Unicorn at 11AM. I ordered a tap ale and picked a table near the front window, but in a corner. I had a decent view out the window, and I knew that there wasn't much of a view in. I had brought the Saturday *Times* and started working the crossword. I sat and sipped (very slowly) the ale and worked the crossword. At about 1:15, the door opened and a couple of familiar faces entered the room. They walked over to the bar and both ordered something. I couldn't tell what. They sat there for about ten minutes with their backs to the bar, seemingly talking together in a leisurely fashion. I did my best not to notice them. After about 15 minutes they walked over to my table and invited themselves to join me.

They were hard not to notice with their flaming red hair. George took a seat opposite me and Fred next to me. Fred said, "Your sweetie will be along in a few minutes, but we thought that it would be good to check out the pub first, just to make sure it wasn't too rough."

George chimed in, "Yeh. It just wouldn't be right to get into a fight with DE's while she's around."

I looked at them and said, "You're a sore site for sad eyes. I suppose that you're hoping to get a piece of the 'action' that Minerva and I are planning?"

Fred smiled and said, "Yeh. We've been getting tired of lying low while you guys have all the fun."

"Fun is not exactly what I had in mind when I invited Minerva here."

George smiled a sly smile, "Oh, come on, don't tell me that you aren't going to have a happy little re-union later."

I had to laugh, "I suppose that's a possibility, but you're a little young to be talking about those things."

Just then Minerva walked in. She strode over with a big smile on her face until she saw Fred and George. She sat down and drilled them with her hardest stare. "I think that I distinctly asked you two to show up a half-hour AFTER two rather than BEFORE two."

George answered, "Sure, but we thought we ought to come in a little early and check out the pub to be sure there weren't any undesirables here." He looked significantly at me and said, "Like this Yank."

Minerva's gaze didn't weaken one whit, and she said, "If you insist on butting in where you're not wanted, then you should be prepared for the consequences." Then she reached across the table, stood, leaned over the table and drew my head toward her. I kissed her passionately. The two brothers said, "Yeewww", in unison to which I replied, "You asked for it. You're getting your just deserts."

Fred answered, "I always thought my just deserts would be chocolate mousse."

George chimed in, "Yeh or maybe spotted dick."

I said, "As much as I'd like to continue this little discussion that Minerva and I've started, I really think it wouldn't be as much fun on opposite sides of the table. I suppose we should get started. These are your experts, I suppose, Minerva."

Minerva was still gazing at me and started suddenly to life. "Yes. I was looking for real criminal types for this break-in, and I couldn't think of anyone who enjoys crime more than these two."

George stood, bowed, and gallantly said, "Guilty as charged."

"Let me explain what we want to do."

Fred said, "Well, go ahead."

"Well. . . . We want to break into Azkaban."

"Oh. Yeh. Nothing easier. Why don't you ask for something hard, like flying to the moon or the bottom of the sea?" George said.

"There's no way. . ." Fred started off

I answered, "The Deatheaters did it."

"Yeh. The Deatheaters didn't care how many people they killed or what happened." George said

"AND they had a team of people who had done lots of fighting over a period of years." Fred chimed in.

"OK. Then you think it's impossible?"

Fred said, "We didn't say that, did we George?"

"No. We didn't. It'll be hard, and we'll have to do a lot of training."

"Yeh. Training."

"Yeh. A team of trained wizards."

"Then we have to start training first?" I asked.

"No, there's already such a team." Minerva's statement surprised us all.

"Really, where?"

Minerva started chuckling and said, "Yes. The DA."

I asked, "DA?"

She answered, "Yes. Dumbledore's Army."

Fred chimed in, "I and even George were members."

I remembered. "At school, right?"

"Right."

"Where are they?"

George said, "Well, we're in luck. Some of them are already in Azkaban."

I groaned, "Great."

"Yes. But some are still at Hogwart's."

George went on, "And the rest are on the run, trying to stay out of Azkaban."

I thought about it. "Do you suppose that the ones on the run would like to find a safe haven?"

"Well, yeh. But where would they find a safe haven?"

"Oh, we're putting together an army, and we're working on a place to train that army—a very secure and therefore safe place."

"There isn't any place in England that's safe."

"Precisely. We're working on someplace across the Atlantic."

Fred whistled, "Realllllly? Just where?"

I smiled. "Maybe sunny Florida."

George smiled. "Maybe we'd be interested ourselves."

I was thinking fast, "Maybe we'd be interested in having you as. . . as . . . instructors."

There was general silence for several minutes. George said, "I don't know about my brother, but I think that we should do some thinking about this. Sorry, brother, I know that we have a general rule against hard thought, but I think that we really need to do some."

Fred answered. "Yes. We've got to be really careful about these precedents, but when you're right, you're right."

I said, "Think fast. It will take a lot of time to set this up. Time is short."

Minerva said, "Well, gentlemen, you've got your assignment for the next lesson. Toddle along now. There you go." The boys were clearly not interested in leaving just yet.

George said, looking at me, "We've been thinking, and we'd like to see how a smooth operator like you handles yourself in this situation."

Fred went on, "Yeh. We figure that anyone who can charm an old. Er. Uh. That is, a charming lady like Ms. McGonagall, who has a no nonsense attitude toward life, must have a few lessons worth learning."

"Yes, that's really a good point. Perhaps you'd care to give the boys a lesson," Minerva said with an arch smile on her lips.

I looked daggers at them and said, "This is hardly your style boys. I thought you guys preferred extendable ears.

George said, "Oh, that's fine for hearing secrets. But you need visual information for real understanding, don't you Professor Wendt?"

Minerva broke in, "Boys, you're not prepared intellectually or emotionally for the lessons that Wendt can give. Go work on your homework before I decide to give you a lesson of my own."

Both Fred and George jumped up quickly and said, "Yes, ma'am. Have a good afternoon." They left the inn quickly. Minerva pulled her wand, silently spoke a spell, and said, "There, the room's sealed imperturbably."

I said, "That's all right. I really don't care if they hear a few endearments that I intend to say to you."

"But I care if Deatheaters or other wizards hear what I'm going to say to you and show you. I brought along some files on Deatheaters" She pulled a large bundle of file folders from her small purse. I'm always amazed by the way that large things can be pulled from small boxes and bags—like the troop of clowns that parade out of a small two-seater car at the circus.

"I got these mostly from a source in the Ministry."

I had a pretty good guess as to who that source might have been. I took it, unwrapped the string, and thumbed through the various folders. Each folder had the name of a Deatheater and things like known associates, home addresses, relationships to other Deatheaters and so forth. There were about three dozen. I said, "This is great. I'll get the intelligence boys working on this right away. As soon as they have some results, we'll have to get together again to share."

"I'm counting on it. The Order would like to have files on the rest of the Deatheaters that we know are out there but that we don't know." She took a sip of her drink. "The person who got me those took a big risk. The fact that we have them had better not leak out."

"I appreciate the issue. We'll do our best."

"Now. We can have a pleasant talk."

"Good. I'd suggest that we have lunch and then perhaps retreat to a previously prepared position."

"Do you have a previously prepared position?"

"I've got a suite reserved at a location in London. Just to show my generous intentions, I don't care if we disapparate there."

"What about your boss? Won't he be concerned if you just 'disappear'?"

'Oh, he can just stuff his concerns. We're going to have a good time whether he likes it or not."

So, we ordered a simple lunch of salad and soup and talked about old times at Hogwarts. I asked, "How's our old buddy Filch?"

"Oh, he's in a fine state. He doesn't know whether to be delighted that the administration finally approves of some of his more interesting discipline techniques or terrified that he's working for Deatheaters. He's deathly afraid that the Deatheaters will decide that he's not a pure-born because he's a squibb.

"So, he tries to stay out of all the Deatheaters' sight, but it's hard to do that when the headmaster is a Deatheater." She chuckled dryly and said, "I almost feel sorry for him, but really, he's just getting what he deserves. His ideas on discipline are just what the Deatheaters love. Oh, well. It's hard to be too mad at him. He's such an institution at Hogwarts. Since Haggrid fled into the mountains, he's about the last institution that the old school has."

I asked, "What about you? Aren't you as much an institution as he is?"

She looked at me crossly, "Are you suggesting that I've been around as long as he has?"

"No." I spent a few minutes trying to come up with a retort but found I was stuck. So, I ended by just smiling. She returned the smile.

Eventually we finished the leisurely lunch, and the conversation turned to where we would disapparate. Minerva said, "I've got a place, too. But I'm not going to tell you. We'll just go there, and it'll be a surprise."

"OK." I paid for the meal with my credit card.

Minerva gazed at the small parallelepiped of plastic and asked, "I've seen you use that thing a number of times. I've even used it some, but I still don't understand its magic. How does that work?"

I signed the receipt and put the card back in my pocket. We walked out the front door. Minerva gazed around. A casual passerby would have thought she was looking for where she'd parked her car. I knew that she was looking for a quiet corner from which to disapparate. But I answered her question, "Do you really want to know how the thing works? Or are you just making conversation—not that I'm opposed to idle conversation with you—ever."

She finally spotted a shaded alley, and we started walking there, "No, I really want to know. It just seems impossible that anyone would accept such a thing as payment and not even keep it."

We reached the alley, walked in, and looked around to make sure that no one was looking directly at us. She suddenly took my hand, and we were gone. We appeared in a loo. I commented, "You picked the right place. I think I might just throw up."

"Oh, don't be such a wuss."

I looked around and said, "Yeh. I see that this is the lady's loo. Let's get out before I get in trouble. You were right about it being a surprise." We found the door and left quickly. I looked around and realized where we were—the British Museum. I took her in my arms and kissed her. Then I said, "This is a pleasant surprise. Do you have time to do a little touring? I never get tired of the British Museum!"

"Yes, I thought that you'd never ask." We walked off in a random direction and continued our conversation about credit cards.

"If you're really interested in knowing about credit cards, I'll explain."

She said, "Yes, I am."

I stopped a moment to think how to proceed. The idea of credit was something that the wizards had never developed as we Muggles had. They had loans and mortgages and they ran tabs at bars but the idea of a line of credit that a wizard or witch could tap at will was something that they hadn't fully developed yet.

Minerva broke in, "That's what I thought. It's not possible to explain. It's not logical."

I frowned at her and said, "Oh, I can explain it. It will just take a few minutes."

"Go ahead."

"OK. You know about running a tab at a bar, right?"

"Sure. I've never done it. It's a vulgar habit."

"Right. But you understand the idea?"

"Yes, the barmaid knows a regular customer and just lets him order as much as he wants within limits, and at the end of the night, she collects from him."

"Right. Does a barmaid ever let a tab extend over more than one night?"

"I suppose so. Yes, sure. I knew some students, sixth and seventh years, whom Madame Rossmerta let run up a tab across a term, and she'd collect from the parents when they visited Hogwarts."

"OK. Credit cards are basically the same thing. A company, usually a bank, gets to know a customer very well and decides to let him run a tab for a month at a time. They call the tab a credit account."

"But that wasn't your bank back at the inn that accepted that credit account thing."

"You're right. The banks convince businesses that anyone who has one of their credit cards is a good risk, and the business puts the customer's bill on the bank's tab."

"OK, but how does the inn get paid?"

"The bank immediately pays the inn when they present the receipt that I signed. The bank keeps track of all these receipts and bills me once a month for the tab that I've run up through all the businesses that I do business with."

"It sounds fishy to me, but it obviously works. I just can't believe that the banks can convince all those business to go along with this."

"It took some time, but they developed a reputation for paying for the receipts promptly. Once the inn across the street accepts my credit card, if your inn doesn't as well, then you'll have a hard time convincing me to come in and buy ale at your inn."

"I suppose it could work that way."

We continued strolling the exhibit halls, occasionally stopping to look at a painting or statue more seriously. Finally, we decided that we needed to head on to my previously prepared position. Minerva wanted to disapparate there, but I convinced her that a cab was a better way to get around in the crowded London streets where it was harder to find a secluded spot to disapparate.

We checked in at the hotel. My lavish tips from previous visits had established us as customers worth remembering. We spent only a moment or two at the front desk, and the bellboy who accompanied us to our room was not disappointed.

We were quickly in our two room suite and took our time getting comfortable. Minerva showered, and I pulled out of my pocket a small shaving kit that I took along on these outings. I shaved and joined her in the shower to help her scrub her back. We had a strict rule in the shower that we only were there for ablution. A disastrous incident had occurred early on in our relationship when we'd tried to do more than wash in the shower. It had convinced us both that showers were for showering. We finished and dried each other off. That was far safer and more pleasant than trying anything unusual in the shower.

Clad in towels, we went to the front room of the suite and sat in each other's arms. I'd turned on the classical music stations of the Cable TV in the room. Fortunately they were playing some Chopin piano music. We had been there when you could only get Shostakovich symphonies on the channel. It was a very comfortable time being in each others arms, partially clad in towels, gazing into each others eyes.

After an indeterminable period of time, we had somehow lost the towels and were enjoying each other's bodies.

Suddenly, for no apparent reason, Minerva stood up and declared that she had to leave. I'd seen that happen enough to know that there was no appeal—either logical or physical that could keep her. I complained about the fact that we'd paid for a night and it wasn't even close to midnight.

She kept talking as she dressed. I always enjoyed watching her do her hair up after one of these trysts. She finally finished dressing, and I knew she was just moments from disapparating. I took her in my arms, and we kissed one last time before she left. I asked, "When can I see you again?"

"Not for a while. This was a long time for me to be gone. We don't want the Carows to be curious—not to mention Snape." She hesitated. "You know, Snape is funny. He's smart, and he knows that we are, well, close, but he's never asked about where I go when I have these lengthy absences from the school."

I was anxious to keep her as long as I could, so I suggested a provocative theory, "Perhaps he knows where you're going?"

She gawked at me, "You can't mean it. Even if he thought that our rendezvous were innocent." I gawked at her in my turn, "Well, innocent of Order of the Phoenix implications anyway, he's no friend to Muggles. I can't believe that he would condone a witch and a Muggle cavorting." She chuckled at the word, which was so appropriate to what we had been doing.

"Perhaps you're right, but what's the alternative? You don't believe that a Deatheater wouldn't try to find out what the Assistant Headmistress was doing on long absences from the school, do you?"

"I suppose not, but . . Hey, you're trying to keep me here with all this talk of Snape." She smiled none-the-less.

"What in the world makes you think that?"

"It's easy. I just think about what we've just been doing. If I were in your shoes, I'd be doing that myself."

"You too can be in my shoes if you want to."

Then I took her in my arms again and said, "You be careful with Snape —he's as serious as death. And, come to think of it, maybe our death if we aren't very careful."

She touched her forehead to mine and nodded with it, dragging my head into a nod as well. "Yes, I will. And you be careful out there too."

Then she fell away from my arms that were encircling her. It was the most bizarre sensation that I'd ever felt—a person completely encircled by your arms getting further away from you even as your held her tighter. And she was gone. The sense of emptiness never lasted long, but it was always intense. I had the sense that I would never see her again—that she had disappeared down some rabbit hole where I could never follow her.

Now that she was gone, there was no point in staying longer. I made sure that I had the scant belongings that I'd brought and walked out of the room, leaving the key. I stopped at the front desk and checked out. I knew the man at the desk. His name was Herbert. He asked, "She's gone, isn't she?"

I just mumbled a "yes".

"If you'll pardon me sir, why do you let her do that to you?"

I was confused, "Do what?"

"Turn off and leave so suddenly."

"I don't blame her. She does what she has to. Even if it were only a few minutes, it would be worth it."

He nodded. I turned and left the hotel.

My Favorite Brunette

I got up late the next morning and made it down to the Cafeteria just before it closed.

Suddenly, I realized that I wasn't alone. Someone had sat down opposite me. She asked, "Do you mind if I join you?"

"Not at all. I'm sorry, how long have you been sitting there?"

"I just sat down." She extended her left hand, "My name is Sally."

"I'm James. What do you do here? Or do you have to kill me if you tell me."

She laughed for about 2 seconds, more of an expulsion of air than a real laugh. "Oh, I run the commissary. How do you like it?"

"Is this a customer survey?"

"NO! I've seen you around a bit. I can usually figure out what the pecking order around here is by how everyone treats everyone else. You, I can't figure yet. I know that you were in one of the cells, and now you've got the swankiest office in the building."

"How do you know it's the swankiest?"

"I'm one of the few people who've been in all of them. Remember, I deliver meals when people can't leave the office or cell, as the case may be." She had a little sense of humor herself.

I tried to look serious. "I would have to kill you if I told you where I stand in the pecking order."

She didn't say anything or laugh.

"I was just kidding, Sally. I don't know where I stand either. I do know what I'm doing here, but if you don't know already, I can't tell you. So perhaps we can start with other topics. Have you always worked here?"

"Are you kidding? Even you must know that this place hasn't been in operation for a long time. And I'm not exactly just out of the egg."

"You're right, you're not. But other than saying that you're not 20 something, I can't guess how old you are. Have you always been in the food service industry?"

"Industry?" She puffed out of the side of her mouth. "I managed a Starbucks before I got into this 'industry'".

"Really, I used to work in a Starbucks. That was 7 years ago. Where was your store?"

"In Manchester."

"Nice place?"

"Manchester or the Starbucks?"

"I know what Starbucks are like. I don't know Manchester."

She shrugged. "It's a city."

"That good?"

She chuckled. "Yes. That's why I was desperate and took this job."

I nodded. She asked, "What have you been doing for the last 7 years?"

"Teaching. At an exclusive finishing school."

"Really? What's that like?"

"Well, let me just begin by saying that it's nothing like 'Mr. Chips'. It was in the far north. Pretty desolate. Sometimes I wondered if they put it there to discourage kids from trying to run away to join the circus."

"Were the kids really that bad?"

"Most of them weren't. There were a few whom you couldn't turn your back on."

"Didn't you have any support from the administration?"

"Actually, they were pretty good at running the school. It's just that the school was sort of a special needs school in reverse. Everyone had some special talent, and some of them let it go to their heads. Those talents could sometimes be turned to pretty nasty practical jokes. But, most of the kids were OK, and the administration always punished the ones who got out of line."

"They were all smart?"

"No. It's hard to describe, and I really won't try to describe them."

"Or you'd have to kill me?"

"Well, yes. I'm here because some of the graduates of that school have been doing some nasty stuff, and I guess I'm sort of an expert on their . . . uh . . . psychology."

"Were you out late last night?"

"Well, yes. How do you know?"

"You always come in at the same time. About an hour before the Cafeteria closes for breakfast. Today you came in really late for you."

"Yes. I was out late last night."

"Was she pretty?"

"What makes you think that I didn't just go to a late cinema—on my own?"

She looked me up and down. "You look . . . uh. . . . distracted—like you were thinking about something you'd done last night."

"Such deductive reasoning deserves to be rewarded. Yes, I was out with someone last night."

Her eyes narrowed as she regarded me. "Was she pretty?"

"You don't deserve to be rewarded that much."

"What does it take to be rewarded that much?"

"I don't know. The question has never come up before." I was working my way through the bagel and jam that I was breakfasting on. It was a far, far cry from Hogwarts breakfast fare. I paused to swallow the last bit. "I'll think about it and let you know sometime.

"For now, I've got to get to work."

When I got back to my office, I decided that I really needed to get off my rear end and do some proactive work if I didn't want a mushroom cloud over downtown London. So I decided to call a meeting myself for once. I found a phone directory of local phone extensions in the top drawer of my desk and I started studying the names and working groups. There were a couple that looked interesting. There was a group called "experimental interrogation", which I decided I'd stay clear of. But there were also a group for "Surveillance" (I knew a little about them), "Background Research", "Plumbers" (I thought they might be good for something other than loosening clogged drains), and "Pseudo Identities". I looked up Parker's phone # and punched it. A male "administrative assistant" answered. I asked him to set up a meeting with Parker for later in the afternoon. He hesitated but gave in. I was to see Parker at 4PM for half an hour.

I had begun to have an idea about how to make some headway in this war that we were starting to fight.

When I arrived at his office, the outer room was pretty bare bones—a desk with the "admin" and a couple of plastic chairs. There was a small end table with an ash tray that looked like it had never been used and bare walls. The desk didn't have a name plate, so I introduced myself. The "admin" gave me his name—Charles Conners. I tried not to laugh. I asked him if he liked Western movies. He said that he preferred comedy, like Benny Hill. That was the end of my attempts at humor with him.

Parker came out of the inner office and waved me in. "I've got ½ hour for you if you can use it."

"I think I can use it. I've been thinking about how we might start off. We already have some names of Deatheaters, and pretty soon we'll have more with photos and some biographical information when Minerva sets up the next meeting. I think that we should try to find all their associates. We can't very well follow them to see whom they meet, but we can set up surveillance on their homes to see who comes to them. We get photos, try to identify them, and set up surveillance on their homes. Pretty soon we can deduce not just whom they're working with but probably something of the hierarchy."

He rolled his eyes. Apparently, this was not a new thought to him. "Yes, we have something like that in mind. We'll burglarize them and . ." I interrupted immediately.

"No, we won't! That's way too dangerous. We can't take a chance of their finding out who we are or even that we are at all."

Parker was beginning to get exasperated. He started speaking a little faster with more volume and emphasis. "Well, if it's too dangerous to burglarize them, isn't it too dangerous to put surveillance on their homes?"

"I don't know. It might be, but we have to start somewhere, and I can't think of anything that we could actually do that would be less dangerous."

"All right. No burglary—for now. What else can we do?"

"I'd like to start having people watch the live video from random spots in London. We might catch someone while we're waiting for the computer geeks to automate surveillance of those cameras."

"Ok. That sounds doable although I hate using a lot of valuable resources."

"What did you say?"

"I said I didn't want to use lots of valuable resources to watch cameras that will probably never show us anything useful."

I said, "When you say resources, you really mean "people", right?"

"Yes, so?"

"Well, I'd never heard of people referred to as "resources" before. It kind of strikes me as bizarre or maybe even 'bad'."

"We do that all the time here."

"Yeh, I've been getting that idea."

"Well, what else could we do?"

"We could research the background of Deatheaters that we know of. Then we could find out what their likes, dislikes, weaknesses are and so on."

Parker drawled, "Yeh. We'll do that for sure, but I've got a feeling that we may find it kind of hard finding people that know these people."

I agreed,."I think you're right, but you never know what we might turn up under some rock."

"Well, this is a start anyway. I'd like to have a planning meeting to kick this project into high gear. I'll get the heads of the departments that we need and you can give them an overview of what we're up against and what we'd like them to do. Would the day after tomorrow be too soon to get everyone together?"

"I almost think I could do it now."

"You haven't been thinking hard enough. You need to put together a nice tight presentation:

- Whom we're up against.
- What their capabilities are.
- What the dangers are.
- What information we can get.
- How we can get it."

Parker went on. "You should probably meet with each of them first to find out how they like to operate, how many resources they have—oh, sorry—how many people they have, and what they can do. Then you can make some intelligent suggestions in our main meeting. You should include Parkinson from Surveillance, Peters of the Plumbers even if we're not going to use his group right away, Jergens from Background, Tarkin of Renditions, and probably Bogart of Interrogations"

"I don't think we'll ever get to interrogate anyone."

"It doesn't matter. If he's not involved, he'll make a stink, and we'll end up having him sit in anyway. Is that enough to keep you busy?"

"Too much."

"Good, maybe you won't pester me so much. Say, would you like to see a football match on the weekend? ManU is coming into town."

"It would be a pleasure to get away from this place. Yes. When?"

"The game is at 2PM on Saturday. They're starting a little late for Telly. I'll see if I can prise the tickets loose from the General."

□

I got hold of the various department heads. The first was Parkinson. I went to his office and found it to be pretty much standard, nothing special except a framed photo of him in a team, a cricket team. I asked him about it, "You were on a cricket team?"

"Yes, I was. I played for Eaton. It was my greatest joy. Did you play sports?"

"Yea, I was on a baseball team as a kid. Never anything like playing for Eaton, but I enjoyed it."

"What did you want?"

"Well, Parker and I are working on the beginning of a surveillance plan, and we want all the department heads together to discuss it. I want to find out what . . uh . . *resources* you have. How you work—not in detail, just generalities."

"Have you got the correct clearance to hear this?"

"Well, uh. . . "

"Oh, bloody hell, Parker wouldn't have sent you if it weren't OK.

"Here's the way we work. I've got 53 men who work for handlers. Each of them is really good at ghosting, languages—they all have at least 5 languages, and are decent assassins if they have to—guns, knives, hand to hand if it comes to that. They can tail anyone in city or country without being detected (several are Sikh's). I have a team of another 50 or so who work for the handlers. They work in Control Rooms that are connected to the internet, our intranet of personal information databases, the network of government video cameras, and who knows what else?

"There are 5 managers who manage the handlers. I have about 100 floaters who can go on any team that needs more backup. I get daily reports on all activity, but I can get them minute by minute if I have to."

"What's your rank?"

He got up from the desk. It was the first time that he had since I'd entered the room. He said, "Haven't you figured out yet that rank is just a technicality here. Anyone regardless of rank gets what he needs in this unit. You don't have any rank. But you've got me, a Major, at your beck and call." He reached his hand across the desk and smiled—for the first time. I hadn't realized how tall he was when he was sitting behind the desk. He must have been 6' 5". I saw for the first time a scar on his neck.

A thought struck me, "Did you work your way up through the ranks in this unit?"

"Why?"

"Well, it just seems to me that you would have a hard time following somebody and not being noticed."

"A good question. No, I was never in the field tailing people. I was an 'intrusion' expert. I would have made a decent burglar in a different life. Who are you thinking of tailing?"

I scratched my nose and pondered how much to tell him. Finally, I said, "I could tell you, but there's not much point. You'll hate me when I do. And I really don't want somebody with as much 'pull' as you have hating me any sooner than necessary. Besides that, you'd probably not believe me."

"Oh, I don't know. I've seen some pretty bizarre things in this assignment."

"I hope so. You've got your work cut out for you. We'll probably be getting together tomorrow. You'll get all the bad news then."

"Yeh, well you don't have to be in any hurry."

"Talk to you later."

"Right."

I went on to my next appointment—with Jergens. His office was pretty much the opposite of Parker's. He had photos of what I guessed were family, two wall calendars—one with photos of military airplanes, the other with a picture of what might have been the Grand Canyon, all sorts of bric-a-brac, and who knows what else?

After introducing myself, he said, "Yes, Wendt. You were born in Circleville, Ohio, went to Ohio State University, where you majored in English, did graduate work at Stanford. You were never much into organized sports, although I think you played on a baseball team one year. You spent a couple of years bumming around here in London, and then you dropped off the grid for 7 years.

"Oh, not completely off the grid. You show up every now and then—usually around Holidays, Christmas, the Summer, Easter. Your girl friend," here I interrupted.

"What do you know about my girl friend?"

"You went out with or maybe mostly stayed in with her for 2 or 3 months, and then she doesn't hear from you for months on end except for occasional letters. You have no 'visible means of support' but you seem to have money when you are on the grid. Oh, and here's an interesting late development. You just withdrew 100,000 pounds from your CREDIT card, and they went along with it. Just how do you have that kind of credit and, just as a matter of interest, what happened to the money? We've not found it yet.

"The few people who know you claim that you say that you have a teaching job, but can't say with whom or where it is. There are very few people who can drop off the grid completely, and those few who can are usually working for a foreign intelligence service or are criminals. Which is it?"

"OK. You're going to learn anyway. I might as well tell you now. I can't believe that you don't know already. I've been a teacher at a school for wizards and witches—the real thing, magic, flying brooms, wands of power, you name it. I get paid in gold—yeh, just like the real spies. My current girl friend is a witch, which is pretty scary if you stop to think about it. I don't."

His eyes focused for about 25 seconds on a spot on the wall behind my head, then he looked at me very, very carefully without saying a word for about a minute. "I think that you're telling the truth—at least, the truth that you understand. And you wouldn't be here if you hadn't convinced some smart people that you knew what you were talking about.

"Well, I suppose that would explain a lot of things. . . . Yes, why we can't learn much about the people that we're trying very, very hard to learn things about.

"What can I do for you?" He finished his tirade with the simple question.

"You've already done it. What I wanted to know was what you do and what your capabilities are. You've pretty much demonstrated them. But who have you been trying to get background on?"

His face relaxed, "I suppose you've heard of someone whose name is Sirius Black?"

"Yup."

"How about Draco Malfoy?"

"Sure."

"Greg Goyle?"

"Senior or Junior?"

"Senior."

"Yup."

"Would you care to fill in some detail on them?"

"Another time. Oh, I will tell you this now. Sirius died about a year ago. He had nothing to do with our problems, besides being stuck like us in them. You haven't been operating that long have you? And where did you get Sirius' name?"

"Almost right. And his name was given us by a very high source who thought he had something to do with our problems."

"No, he was wrong. That is, the prime minister was wrong."

"How do you know it was the prime minister?"

"He's the only Muggle . . uh . . normal person who knows anything about wizards outside of this building."

"OK. Wizards. Yeh, we're going to need luck."

"Right."

I'd had about as much of interviewing people for a while. I considered them as strange as I was, so I decided to call it a morning and have some lunch.

51

The commissary was really pretty decent. It had 2 or 3 main entrees each meal and lots of miscellaneous sides. The food went through cycles, but I hadn't figured out yet what the frequency was. I usually ate by myself in my cell or office but had decided now that I was part of management. I could show my face in the "caf" more often. I didn't see anybody in the room that I recognized, so I sat at a small table by myself. As I ate, I thought about Minerva. I realized that talking with Jergens about a little slice of life at Hogwarts had made me home sick. I thought about Minerva and tried to imagine what it would be like to see her. I'd been doing more of that sort of day-dreaming lately.

Sally walked over and sat down at my table.

"Do you never take time off? Have you been here all day?"

"Of course. You can't run a food service if you're not around at all the meals."

She stopped for a moment and then picked up where she left off in the morning, "Where are you from?"

"The States—a place called Circleville in the state of Ohio."

"I guessed you were American."

"Decent of you not to mention it before now."

"Yeah, right. What was it like?"

"It's a small town. Twenty, Thirty thousand people. The main industry is wood pulp. The place stinks of Sulfur compounds most of the time. You get to the point that you don't notice much."

"Sounds like Manchester."

"Is that where you grew up?

"Yeah. Decent of you not to mention it before now."

This time I laughed. She said, "I shouldn't stay away from the so-called chef for this long. It's been interesting talking."

"Yes, it has. Don't you eat your own food?"

She'd risen, and so had I. "I eat my food. I just don't eat the chef's food."

'You could have mentioned THAT before."

"I want you to keep coming back. I shouldn't have mentioned it at all."

"Oh, I'll come back. You've got a captive audience in me."

"We'll see." She walked off to the kitchen.

Email

I went back to my office and decided to learn something about computers and the internet. One thing that I knew about, well short of, was email. I decided to do a little research. I sat down at the PC and opened a web browser. It opened to yahoo. I decided to search for people I knew. I searched for Ferguson. Well, there were a lot of Ferguson's but none that seemed to fit. Oh, well.

I then started out to setup an email account. I'd never had one while I was working for Hogwarts, there being no ekeltricity as Mr. Weasley would say. I'd almost signed up for one when I thought I was going to leave England so that I could communicate secretly with Minerva. There were a lot of free email sites on the web. Even Yahoo had one. But you had to register. I decided that there must be an email that the SAS used so I decided to see if there was any help in this computer. It turned out that there was a program called Outlook that would send emails. I started the program and after trying a variety of buttons I finally found one that actually seemed to do something useful. It opened a window that had a place that you could key in a message. All I had to do was find the email addresses of the people I wanted to send an invitation to a meeting. I pushed the button titled TO, and I got a list of people. It was a short list, but it had all the people I was interested in. The department heads all were on the list. And now they were all on my TO list. My first email message was simple:

"I'd like to meet you at Parker's office tomorrow to figure out how to beat these bastards. When can you be there?"

The answers started coming in. The last one was back in about an hour. The concensus was just after lunch. So I had to start thinking about what it'd say. I decided to write myself an email with my ideas. It was the hardest letter that I'd ever written.

The next morning when I went to breakfast, I was still thinking. I grabbed a bowl of cereal and milk leaving the cooked items alone completely. I had figured out how to use the printer and had brought my note along. I was scribbling corrections on it and hoped that I could read the scrawled notes when I got back to the computer.

I had forgotten to get a glass of OJ. I went back to the lunch line and found Sally on the serving line. "You decided that you wanted something decent for breakfast?"

"I decided that I wanted some orange juice."

"Don't break my heart. The chef slaved over these scrambled eggs."

"Don't break my heart. Don't you know those things are full of cholesterol. Where's the OJ?"

"It's at the end of the serving line—just like it always has been."

I found a glass and filled it from the dispenser. I found my way back to my table, and so did Sally. "I never found out yesterday what you taught."

"Oh, English Literature."

"Really, you don't look like English Literature to me."

"OK, what do I look like?"

"Maybe French."

"Now you're making fun of me." She could hardly hold back the laughter.

"No, I'm . . . not." The giggles kept leaking out.

"I notice that you're not eating any of the slave labor eggs."

"I've already eaten. What are you writing? A paper on <u>Pride and Prejudice</u>?"

I had forgotten that I had my presentation notes with me. "Yeh. It's a discussion of how it's the greatest novel ever written in any language."

"Sure you are. Can I see?" She reached across the table, and I snatched the papers away.

"You really are cruisin' for a bruisin' as we used to say in Circleville. You'd be in so much trouble if you saw what's on that sheet of paper They'd probably never let you out of here."

"'Cruising for a bruising'. That's pretty good. Did you make it up all by yourself?"

"No, the English department of OSU all worked on it."

"Seriously, I suppose you can't talk about it."

"Seriously, I can't."

"OK. Just promise me that when all of this is over, if it ever is, that you'll let me know what was on it." She hesitated a moment. "It's about some new kind of terrorist, isn't it?"

"I can't tell you that. What makes you think that there's some new kind of terrorism going on?"

"Oh, I was around when this group was the main IRA anti-terrorism group. They were about a third the size, and we worked out of an ordinary office building.

"You can't get into or out of here without passing about four checkpoints. Haven't you noticed? And I think that there are snipers on the roofs of every building for a couple of blocks around. And the garage has half a dozen armored personnel carriers with Bushmasters. And at least once, I could swear that a Harrier landed on the heli-pad."

"Well, if you were right in your observations, I think that your deduction would be considered valid by any logician."

"That's what I'm afraid of. Aren't you?"

"Let's just say that I don't think that you're scared enough."

"Shit."

"Yeh. Eloquent. Did you make it up all by yourself?"

I had finished my cereal and OJ by then, and I got up to go, "Oh, yes. I didn't say that. By the way, have a nice day."

"Thanks."

The Staff Meets

I decided not to have lunch so that I could stew over the meeting. I practiced my presentation about 5 times by the end of the morning, and I still wasn't happy. Well, I decided, it would have to do.

His assistant had brought about 6 extra chairs into Parker's office. I hoped that no one would have to stand—other than me. They entered in groups of two and three, talking about lunch, their kids, the latest football scores. How was I going to turn this from the mundane to the bizarre and keep their attention?

Parker started the meeting, "You've almost all of you met Mr. Wendt. I think that we should just get started, eh?"

I was up. "Yes, I've been trying to come up with a joke to start this off. But the only joke I can think of is the spot we're in. We're adults met to talk about how to deal with the monster hiding in the closet.

"You've had enough experience with this that you're desperate. And you should be. You're up against people who enjoy torture. They'd just as soon look at you as kill you, and they have the power to do both in their hands. They intend to enslave the human race. And they probably have the capability too. Their leader is as close to immortal as you can be in this universe. They make the Nazi's look like amateurs and the Viet Cong look like Sunday school teachers.

"They call themselves Deatheaters, and they have all the powers that you've heard attributed to real magicians and much more.

"I lived for seven years among these people—wizards and witches, some of them the kindest, most generous people I've ever know.

"How can we defeat these monsters? The only way is to make allies with their enemies in the wizarding community. They do have enemies. The enemies have an organization—The Order of the Phoenix. They've been fighting them for over a decade."

One of the listeners, someone I didn't know, interrupted. "Why Phoenix? Is it named after the mythical bird?"

"It might be named for the tutor of Achilles from Greek myth. But I think you're right. It's named after the bird, which, by the way, is not mythical. I've seen one."

"Come on now!"

"I'm afraid so.

"Our goal is giving the Order something that everyone fighting terrorists needs desperately—information. You can do what you do well. Trace conspirators, find their meeting places, and identify their sources of information and support. With that information the Order can act in ways that we can't."

"Why can't we act? We're pretty good at that." This was Peters. A few agreed.

"Let me back up and give you a better idea of what we're dealing with." I looked over at Parker. He smiled at me and nodded slightly. He was giving me the go-ahead to read everyone fully in on the situation, and incidentally, make a fool of myself if I weren't careful.

"I see that there are some people whom I haven't briefed on what's been going on, so I'll take some time right now to do that.

"First, the people we're up against. These people are, well, uh," This was getting easier and easier but it would never be completely easy. Just keep an even voice and look people in the eyes, I told myself. "They're magical. Magic is real. It works. There are people who have the power. There are principles that can be learned, discovered about magic. They know them. They've discovered them." I hesitated, waiting for objections, questions. There weren't any.

"I used to work with them. I was a teacher at one of their prep schools. No, I didn't teach magic. It was English Literature. I got to know a lot of them pretty well. A few, I knew. . ." I hesitated because there was a catch in my throat. "I knew them very well.

"They've gotten along very well with Muggles (their name for non-magicals) for hundreds of years. But now there's one of them who quite literally wants to rule the worlds—both magical and Muggle. He's probably the hardest target you will ever have. He's effectively immortal. He's got the ability to bend people's wills to his. He's got a following of people whose wills he doesn't have to bend to get them to hurt, torture, kill. They're magical like him and almost as powerful. We're in a bloody lot of trouble.

"Now, tell me how we get a line on him and his followers."

Nobody said anything.

"OK, I'll start you off.

"Let's see, 'Are you crazy?', 'Who could believe such crazy stuff?'. You can probably come up with better."

Tarkin looked around the table and smiled. "If we find him, I'll get him and it doesn't matter if he is immortal. When we're finished with him, he'll wish he were mortal. He'd be a perfect subject for experimental interrogation, don't you think Bogie?"

Bogart smiled. "I only wish we could get him."

I had expected something like this. "You have no idea how much I wish you could do that, but there's one little problem. You'd perhaps manage to get him here, if you were unlucky, but then things would come apart. In the first place at any time he wanted, he could disappear and come back with a gang that would make you all wish you had never found him. Or, he could use the *Imperious Curse* to make you do his bidding. That would be good. Lead him right here, and that would be the end of this little operation."

Jergens spoke for the first time, "But surely wizards have to have their wands for those sorts of special effects. And we surely would disarm any wizard we wished to capture."

My respect for Jergens went up a notch or two. "How do you know about wands?"

"I read your various reports, unlike some people in the building."

"You're right. If you could disarm most wizards, then you'd maybe be able to hold them. However there are several problems with the idea:

1. Disarming a wizard is a lot harder than you think.
2. Even if you got him disarmed, all wizards are able to do some magic without wands.
3. Tom Riddle, the leader of the Deatheaters is no ordinary wizard. He can do quite a lot without a wand. And much more with one."

Parker broke in, "Let's start with the assumption that we're just going to be an intelligence gathering group until we learn a whole lot more about wizards. Let's discuss what we can do along those lines."

Peters spoke, "Can I assume that we can enter any of their homes or offices to collect information.

Parker turned to me, "Well?"

"No. Wizards have ways of securing their homes that even I don't know much about. We need to stay at a distance and observe. I think we'd have a really hard time even getting in, let alone knowing what was significant and not."

"Well that lets my department out." Jergens said disgustedly.

Bogart asked a question that was so different from what I'd expected that I didn't understand it. I asked, "Excuse me?"

Bogart's mouth turned up slightly at one corner, "I said, 'Follow the money.'"

I shook my head, still unsure that I'd heard him right, "What do you mean?"

Bogart's smile widened, "I thought so. It's a common technique. You get hold of financial records of the subjects of your investigation. In our case, we do it by fair or foul means. The paper records usually lead you to interesting places. It's also called the paper trail.

"We can do that pretty well."

I sighed in resignation and started what I was sure was going to be a lengthy explanation of why that wasn't really feasible.

"Well, you see, here's the deal. Wizards mostly don't have paper trails. All transactions among wizards are performed using specie."

Parker interrupted, "What do you mean? You mean they use coins and bullion?"

"Yes. Well, really only coins. They have small denomination coins but mostly they use gold coins that they call 'galleons'."

Jergens asked, "But there are wizard banks, aren't there?"

"Sure, but wizard banks are 95% safety deposit boxes. Wizards either put galleons and other valuables into their safety deposit boxes or withdraw them. Wizard banks loan money on occasion but only their own money—not depositors' money. They don't strictly speaking have depositors."

Parker swiveled his chair nervously back and forth. He seemed to be trying to come up with an objection to reality.

Meanwhile Bogart asked, "Don't wizard businesses keep records—write receipts for purchase and so forth?"

"Sure. But if you think that we can do a plumbing job to get access to them, remember our conversation about burglary of wizards' homes?"

Bogart was not to be denied, "But what about wizarding government. Can't we get a writ or something to search business records?"

"Oh, no. The writ might come from Her Majesty's government, but it would have to be served by the wizard Auror's office. We USED to have good relations with them, but now that Riddle's in charge, all you'd get would be blank stares—at best."

Parker had apparently found his objection and turned to me. "Do you mean to tell me that wizards don't have any idea of credit or credit cards?"

This was really going to be hard because I would have to admit that they did. So, I took a minute, stood and began to pace. There was a white board in the office. I walked over to it, as though I needed to use it to answer. I longed, as I occasionally did, that I had acquired the vice of smoking cigars or, better, a pipe, so that I could spend time cleaning and loading and lighting it to give me time to think.

I drew it out as long as I could and began, and all heads turned toward me. "OK. The thing is that wizards recently have started to use credit. But it would do us no good to search those records."

Bogart was mentally sharpening his knives, so I quickly went on, "Please let me explain.

"In the last couple of years, wizards have started using credit cards. Wizards occasionally have Muggle credit cards. They mostly use them for personal and business purposes when they're dealing with Muggle businesses.

Bogart couldn't restrain himself. He was leaning on Parker's desk and burst out, "Then we've got them!"

I shook my head, "No we don't. In the first place, wizards only use credit cards when dealing with Muggles. There's nothing that the people we want to trace need from Muggles.

"More than that, they despise all things Muggle. They wouldn't be caught dead dealing with Muggles or using a Muggle invention like a credit card."

Bogart wouldn't be denied, "But you'd be surprised what innocuous seeming transactions lead us on a trail to terrorists. Even if these Death Beaters or whatever they are don't deal with Muggles, they probably deal with wizards who deal with Muggles."

Parker interrupted here, "Maybe he has something there. Just how do wizards deal with Muggle banks to get a credit card?"

"They go to a wizard bank. As a matter of fact, there's only one wizard bank that handles these transactions—Gringotts. Gringotts applies to a Muggle bank—like Barclay's on their behalf. Barclay's issues the credit card and delivers it to Gringotts which delivers it to the wizard."

Jergens asked, "Then, the statements go to the wizard?"

I shook my head again, "No, they go to Gringotts. Gringotts forwards them to their client. The client has Gringotts remove gold from their safety deposit box to pay Barclays."

Parker nodded, "Then we need someone on the inside of Gringotts."

I was getting tired of this, but soldiered on, "No, the people who run Gringotts are not human."

Parker laughed, "Well, some people might say that the people who run Barclay's are not human."

"No, no. I mean literally not human. And, even if you could somehow get in touch with one, you'd find that they're unbelievably loyal to their race. They wouldn't help you voluntarily, and you couldn't force them."

Parker asked, "Doesn't Barclay's have records of the transactions?"

I shook my head sadly, "No. Gringott's is very secretive about their client's privacy. They insist that all printed receipts be sent to them. They do all the accounting. Barclay's only passes through those transaction slips."

Parker wouldn't let go, "But what about electronic records?"

This was becoming really tedious, but I kept going. "Barclays prints all those as paper records, which are sent to Gringotts. The electronic records are destroyed immediately when two printed copies are verified as good. Gringotts insists on it. Both copies are sent to Gringotts."

Parker asked, "But the businesses retain records, don't they."

That forced me to pause and think. I began talking through an answer, "Well, yes. I suppose they do. You're thinking of going to every business in England and rummaging through their records." I paused again, and said, "You'd have to get some kind of court order. How many businesses are there in England?"

That stopped conversation as we all rummaged through our minds for ideas.

Bogart's eyebrows knit in concentration, and then he asked, "Just how do you know so much about Gringotts?"

Now things would get really sticky. I decided that I couldn't tell them that I'd been on the board of directors of Gringotts for one meeting—maybe I technically still was. So, I told them a partial truth, "I invented the technique of using Muggle credit cards. My credit card is one of those."

There was a moment of stunned silence around the table, and Parker said, "You're our man inside Gringotts."

"No, I'm not. I just patented the technique, and they license it. The moment that I walked inside a Gringotts, I'd be picked up by Aurors and shipped off to Azkaban or worse. The Deatheaters have tried killing me more than once, and they'd be happy to get another shot at it."

Parker temporized, "OK. OK. But surely there's another way. How do they transfer money and receipts back and forth between Gringotts and a Muggle bank? They sure don't use wire transfers. There must be a courier."

I thought a moment. "I don't think there's much hope there. I'll tell you what I know happens."

□

Ponsonby was reviewing the Gringotts settlement account. His office in the foreign exchange department of Barclay's was small, but he had walls that went to the ceiling and a real door. He was happy to have it. The picture of his wife and two kids on the desk was the only personal decoration that he had. The bank discouraged personalizing one's office— unless one were at the V.P. level.

His current concern was the current month's settlement of accounts between Gringotts and Barclay's. Gringotts insisted on settling every month and doing it by transfer of either specie or English pound notes. This month, Gringotts owed Barclay's a little over two million pounds. He'd have to draft a note to Gringotts and put it in the mail himself. Gringotts insisted that only one person have access to the information. That meant that he had to use his computer to write the note rather than the office secretary. At least Gringotts didn't insist on lots of detail.

He started the letter using the previous months letter as a model. The only things he changed were the date and the body of the note. "Dear Sir,

"Since our balance of trade this month is in Barclay's favor by 1,235,089 pounds and 15 pence, I request that you send a courier with that amount in pounds sterling and or specie to this office on the fifth of the month, which is the first Monday. Please reply with the amount of specie and pounds that you intend to send and the time that you wish to make the transfer."

He printed it on his personal printer. He got out of his lower left hand drawer two envelopes. One was a standard business envelope, and the other was a larger manila envelope. He addressed the manila envelope first: Robert Stanhope, POSTE RESTANTE, Islington Post Office, 116 Upper Street, London N1 1AE.

Then he addressed the smaller envelope: Gringott's Bank, Diagon Alley, Attention: Settlement Accounts Department. He slipped the letter in the business envelope and sealed it. Then he slipped that letter in the manila envelope and sealed it. The blasted Gringotts wouldn't even let him send it with a secretary to the post box, but he had to do it himself.

He took it out at lunch and dropped it in the post box on the corner near his favorite chip shop.

When he got back, there was a courier waiting for him from the special print room. Ponsonby unlocked his office. The courier and he entered.

62

The courier opened his briefcase and took out two envelopes. Ponsonby accepted them, signed the receipt that the courier offered, and sent the courier on his way.

Ponsonby got out the log book and wrote in it what he found printed on the outside of the envelopes where an address would ordinarily be. One envelope had a count of computer generated credit card receipts and a total amount in pounds and pence. The other had a count of conventional credit card receipts and a total amount in pounds and pence. He closed the log book and returned it to its drawer in his desk. He locked the door and then checked the seals that were on the envelopes. Each was intact. Each was the image of a stylized lion in purple that was Barclay's logo.

He then proceeded to the one scary part of his job. He unlocked a different drawer in his desk and pulled out what looked like an over-sized drawstring coin purse. It was partly open in what appeared to be a negligent way as though the owner had simply not taken the effort to draw it tight.

He shoved the two envelopes into the purse. It looked barely large enough to fit the two envelopes in, but somehow, it didn't bulge when he pushed the envelopes in. There were already more than four dozen envelopes in the purse, but it didn't look any fuller than it had at the beginning of the month.

He stared at it for at least five minutes as he contemplated just how frightening it was. It was always an effort for him to pick it up after he'd put envelopes in it. Before he'd done that he could almost believe that it was just another purse, but after shoving the envelopes in he could no longer believe that fiction.

Of course, there was the one other thing that scared him even more than the purse. Thank God it had only happened once on this job and should never happen again. His mind traveled back in time to his first day on this job.

□□

Ponsonby had arrived for the job interview fifteen minutes early like the recruiter had insisted that he do—not any earlier, not any later. The secretary had immediately taken him to the Conference Room where he would have the third and final interview for this position.

He was not sure where to sit at this long Conference Room table. It was certainly not at either of the ends. Maybe it would be best near one of the ends—the one nearest the door to the Conference Room. He chose a seat that left once chair between him and the head of the table. He didn't want to intrude on the interviewer's personal space.

As he waited, he wondered who the interviewers would be. He was pretty sure that one would be from H.R. Would the other be from the "C" suite? He didn't know whether to hope for that or not. They'd told him that this was a very responsible position. Did that warrant a "C" suite interviewer?

The secretary opened the door for the interviewers. The first to enter was a woman. He knew she was the head of H.R. He'd been introduced briefly at the first interview. Would the other be from the "C" suite then?

The next person to enter was a disappointment. He was tall and wore a knit woolen sweater and a dress shirt with a tie. He was wearing jeans and were those sneakers? He must be some techie from a back office somewhere in the bowels of the building. Well, at least Ponsonby needn't be nervous with him.

Ponsonby immediately rose, and the H.R. introduced them all. She first re-introduced herself, "I'm Abigail Penrose, head of H.R" She then turned to him and pointed with an open palm at Ponsonby, "This is Ponsonby Rickaby-Hackaby. He's the job applicant." Then she turned to the stranger and introduced him.

Ponsonby hadn't realized how tall the other man was until he himself was standing. He was almost overwhelmed by the shock of shocking—no, flaming—red hair that he had. His first reaction was that this man would have been a natural for the 'Red-Headed League' that John Watson had immortalized. This reflection kept him from catching the last name, but he had caught his first name. It was Bill or Will. Well, he'd use Bill and hope that the other fellow wasn't bothered by first names.

He wasn't. The first thing he said was, "I hope you don't mind if I use your first name. It's intimidating enough without tacking on your last, and you may simply use 'Bill' for me."

Ponsonby breathed a sigh of relief.

Abigail opened the conversation by saying, "Well, to relieve your mind, you've got the job." She hesitated and added, "If you want it."

Ponsonby was so relieved that he started to say, "If I want it! Of course, I want it." But something about the hesitation in Abigail's statement made him stop with the word "Of". He tried to figure out a way to proceed. He could, of course, say what he thought, "Is there a reason I shouldn't want it?" However, he didn't have time to say that because Bill immediately picked up the conversational thread.

"Uhm. Let me begin by assuring you that you have a position, regardless what you decide about this position that you're applying for."

That was so bizarre a beginning that Ponsonby glanced over toward Abigail who was nodding judiciously.

Bill was going on. "The only thing left for you to do is to take an oath in the form of a non-disclosure agreement."

Ponsonby breathed a sigh of relief. He'd signed non-disclosures before. They were usually couched in scary terms like, "termination of employment", "disciplinary actions", and the like. They were usually terrors for children, but both Abigail and Bill seemed to be really serious.

Bill went on, "Let me emphasize that at any point, you may back out and change your mind—before, during, or even after taking the oath. Whatever you do will not result in a black mark on your record, will it Abigail?"

She nodded more vigorously.

Bill went on. Also regardless what you do, you'll be offered a comparable position. Abigail was still nodding.

Ponsonby couldn't hold back the question that was screaming in his mind, 'Well, what is the problem with a non-disclosure?"

Bill gave a sigh of relief, and Abigail seemed, if anything, more up-tight. He went on, "The 'problem' is the penalty if you break the non-disclosure. If you do, you die."

Ponsonby couldn't prevent himself from laughing. It was preposterous. Was he going to work for the Mafia? Still, he noticed that neither Bill nor Abigail were laughing with him. He quickly stopped laughing and asked nervously, "What happens, does your cousin Vinny show up at my house and shoot me?" He quickly added, "No offense intended for your cousin Vinny."

Bill leaned back in his chair and scratched his chin that had the slightest hint of flaming red stubble that looked a little like flecks of blood. He seemed to make a decision, and then he leaned forward. "I don't actually know exactly what will happen. I do know that if you decide to take the oath, you will believe that what I just said will happen."

Ponsonby looked from one to the other of them. He tried to imagine a way that they were playing a practical joke on him. He just couldn't see it. He asked, "How can you know if I say tell my wife, if she doesn't tell anyone." He actually couldn't imagine his wife not telling her twin sister something that struck her as interesting.

Bill said, "Oh, you don't have to worry about me or any other human being finding out."

That had Ponsonby really bothered. Was he actually in Crackerbox Palace imagining this conversation? He pinched the inside of his thigh through his best suit pants. He was awake and not crazy.

Bill went on, "Take your time and think it over. It's as serious a decision as you are likely to make in your life."

He did think for a minute on it. Then he asked a question, "And if I do decide not to take the oath, I still get a good job?"

Bill shrugged and said, "Sure. No harm, no foul."

Ponsonby made a snap judgment. "I'll take the oath."

Bill said ominously, "Don't forget that you can back out even as you're taking the oath."

He reached into his sweater. Ponsonby expected him to pull out a pen or maybe a document for him to sign. Instead, he pulled out a wooden rod. He couldn't help chuckling. It looked like a magician's wand. No document appeared. No pen.

Bill stood and said, "I'm going to recite the oath that you'll take. Please listen carefully and decide if you want to take it."

He then waved the wand, and a small sheet of paper appeared out of nowhere. It landed on the table in front of him, and he read, "I Ponsonby Rickaby-Hackaby swear that I will never attempt to learn the contents of any credit transaction to be sent to Gringotts, nor will I ever reveal the contents to anyone if I accidentally learn them."

Ponsonby stared at the paper as he read the oath. He realized that it was not ordinary paper. He didn't know what it was made of. It was heavier and darker than any paper that he'd ever seen. Then he looked up at Bill and asked, "Is that it?"

Bill's expression didn't change, but he asked Ponsonby, "You want more?"

Ponsonby said, "No. No. I just thought there would be more to it."

He asked "Are you ready to take the oath?"

Ponsonby nodded.

He looked over at Abigail and said, "Please clasp hands with Ponsonby."

She had been watching the two in rapt fascination. Then she realized that Bill had addressed her. She said in a sort of muffled squeak, "Me?"

Bill nodded, 'Yes, you. Somebody has to be a witness to the oath. You do that by clasping hands."

She hesitantly reached her right hand across the table toward Ponsonby. He clasp her hands as if about to shake it. Bill examined the contact of the two hands and nodded. "Fine. We'll start."

He said, "Ponsonby. Please repeat after me word for word exactly as I say them."

Ponsonby nodded. Bill pointed the wand at the clasp hands and said, "Now, remember. You can stop at any time, and you're off the hook."

Ponsonby nodded again. Bill began reciting the oath, and Ponsonby repeated at the pauses. As he spoke an insubstantial cord extended from the tip of the wand and wrapped itself around the clasp hands. As the oath went on the cord wrapped more and more around the two hands and seemed to tighten.

Ponsonby felt the pressure increase more and more. When they reached the end of the oath, it was briefly almost unbearable and then suddenly ceased.

Both Ponsonby and Abigail released held breaths. Abigail massaged her hand and stared at it—seemingly in disbelief.

Bill was speaking again, ". . . said, you can still back out. The oath will still be effective, but if you don't take the job you won't have an opportunity to break the oath."

Ponsonby just shook his head.

Abigail seemed to come to herself and asked, "If he backs out, and I don't honor the promise to get him a job, will anything happen to me?"

Bill stared at her and asked, "Are you thinking of backing out on your pledge?"

She hurriedly assured him, "No. No. I was just . . . curious."

Bill smiled and said, "I don't know."

Abigail gulped and then seemed to regain possession of herself. She said, "Well then, let's take a tour of the special print room."

She stood and led them out of the Conference Room and down a hall to an elevator. Inside the elevator, there was a card reader, which Abigail inserted her picture ID into. Then she pushed the button for the 4th floor.

They arrived and exited. She led them down the hall to a door with a glass window. Inside there were two people and what looked like two printers and two machines that might have been printers, but Ponsonby was pretty sure they weren't.

Abigail pulled a small piece of paper out of her purse and handed it to Ponsonby. She said, "Memorize the number on that paper. It's the code to grant access to this print room."

He unfolded it, glanced at it, and handed it back. "I've got it."

She nodded and said, "Use it now." Then she added, "Bill, please turn so that you don't see this."

Ponsonby keyed the number into the small pad beside the door handle. There was a click, and the door opened a hair. He turned the knob and allowed the other two to enter before him.

Abigail took the lead. She walked first to one of the printers. "This printer creates duplicate credit card images from electronic credit transactions. It puts them in envelopes that are sealed. They look like this."

She picked one up out of a hopper at the base of the printer and handed it to Ponsonby. It had a seal that looked like a stylized purple lion's head. He was reluctant to take it but did.

She went on, "Don't worry. These are tests. The two printers ensure that there will always be one working printer available to print the receipts."

Ponsonby nodded and asked, "If a printer failed, couldn't you just re-run the print job to create new copies?"

"No. We had to agree to keep the transactions in volatile memory and destroy the data as soon as possible."

Ponsonby asked, "What are the other machines?"

She nodded. "Just going to go over that. Transactions also come in on ordinary paper receipts. They are sorted by these machines. The ones that you're interested in come out in similar envelopes. The machine both sorts and calculates total pound value. It stamps those numbers on the envelope."

Ponsonby took up the narrative, "So, these get sent to my office. What do I do with them?"

Abigail nodded. "Yes. Let's go up to your office, and I'll show you."

They left the print room, walked to the elevator again, and traveled up to the fourteenth floor. There, she led them to an office. She took a key out of her purse and handed it to Ponsonby. "Your office. Don't make a duplicate of that key. If you loose it, report it, and we'll have a new lock installed and give you a new key."

Ponsonby unlocked the door and led them into his new office. It had a desk, a couple of chairs, a credenza, computer, and so on.

Here Bill picked up the narrative. "So, each day, you'll get some number of sealed envelopes. If any seal is broken, report it immediately. If they're intact, record the amounts on the envelope in a log book that you'll find somewhere in your desk. Then put the envelopes in this."

He reached into a jeans pocket and pulled out what looked like a large coin purse with draw strings. He loosened the draw strings and widened the mouth of the purse. "See if you can put those envelopes into that purse."

Ponsonby did.

"Good. That's what you'll do with all the envelopes that are delivered to you. Don't attempt to open the purse wider or retrieve any envelopes. You won't be able to. If you have forgotten to record the numbers on the envelope, you won't be able to find out what they were. Just record the fact that an envelope was delivered and put question marks where the amounts would normally go.

"Once a month, I'll be by to pick the envelopes up and either deliver money or pick money up for Gringotts."

Ponsonby looked the question, and Bill answered it, "Gringotts is the name of the bank that I work for."

Ponsonby asked, "Why would you pick up money?"

"We do more than handle credit card transactions. Money changing happens too."

Ponsonby was having cup o' during his morning break when he heard a tap on his window. It took a minute to realize what it was. It was the stupid homing owl that Gringotts insisted on using to deliver messages. He supposed that it was probably more secure than the normal post, but why didn't they just use FEDEX like any other self-respecting business?

He opened the window. Then the owl leapt into the air, flew around the office twice, dropped a standard business envelope on his desk, and flew out the window.

It was addressed, as usual, Mr. George Ponsonby, etc., as a normal letter would be but then at the bottom there were the additional lines: thirteenth floor, fourth office from the southeast corner. As if the bird could read that and figure out where to drop it!

He slit the envelope and read it. There was the usual boiler plate and then the key part. "We agree to the date. Our usual courier, Mr. Weasley, will present himself at your office at 1:23 in the afternoon. Please do not fail to be present alone in your office. We will settle with 500,000 pounds and 67 pence sterling and 1,154,215 galleons, mostly in hundred galleon coins."

It was such a bother dealing with specie! He would have to give the armed guards a call to be ready outside his office to tote it all down to the vaults.

Bill Weasley made one trip a month into the deepest of vaults at Gringotts. It was always on a Monday, and it was always to retrieve galleons and pounds or deposit them, depending which way the transfer was going. Today he had brought two brief cases—one for the pounds and one for the galleons. The ride down on the rail car to the vault had the usual unpleasant features—going through the waterfall that washed enchantments away, the crazy roller-coaster sense of weightlessness from time to time, the especially unpleasant goblin that accompanied him. They passed the vault with the dragon. They reached the Gringotts vault. The vault was seemingly innocuous, but he knew that if he attempted to take a brass knut or a pence more from the vault than was written on the parchment, he'd be crushed on the sill of the vault by the massive door swinging shut.

He'd never seen it happen, but he'd heard stories of a wizard who had miscounted the silver sickles by one. There was still a faint red stain inside the vault that could never be eradicated. It was all that was left of the bloody pulp that had been the wizard.

The Gringotts' goblin had used his finger to key the door open. They stepped over the threshold. Before them there was a long gallery with niches containing stacks of coins, pounds sterling, American dollars, French francs, and so forth. Weasley stepped into the alcove that contained wizard money, raised his wand, and said, "Enumero 11,542 hundred galleon coins." Several neat stacks of hundred galleon coins glided across the smooth stone floor and placed themselves at his feet. The same happened with the galleon pieces and then with the Pounds Sterling. He loaded the wizarding money into one brief case and the Pounds Sterling and pence into the other.

The galleon brief case weighed over three stone. Without magic, it would have been hard, but possible to carry. The pound brief case was not as heavy but it was bulky. A strong man could have managed them. With magic, it was easy. A curious bystander on Picadilly might have wondered why a business man was carrying two brief cases, but he would never wonder that they were heavy. Of course, it would never come up because he would never be on Picadilly.

Instead, he got into the rail car again and took the long ride up to the public level of Gringotts. When they reached that level, a couple of guards joined them and accompanied him out onto the street, where Bill promptly disapparated.

The water closet that Bill appeared in was rarely occupied when he arrived. But even if it had been, no one would have wondered at someone coming out of a stall. He flushed the toilet just before he left, to establish his bona fides for being in the WC. This time he was alone.

He walked out and down the hall to Ponsonby's office. He knocked and was admitted. As usual, when Bill had closed the door behind him, Ponsonby picked up the phone thing and requested that the guards come up. In the mean time, Ponsonby dragged the brief case with the galleons in it to the machine that had been modified to count galleons, sickles and knuts. He scooped part of the coins in. Then, when the brief case was light enough, he picked it up and poured the rest into the machine. A few stray coins fell to the floor, but Ponsonby retrieved them and tossed them in the hopper.

After a couple of minutes the coins had been sorted and the count appeared in red lighted numbers on the front of the machine. Ponsonby checked them and then turned to the other brief case. This was the one that Ponsonby hated. He pulled out the neatly banded stacks of one hundred pound notes. He counted them one at a time, tallying on a piece of paper. There were five thousand of them and he repeated the count. He then counted the sixty-seven pence. He'd already prepared a receipt for the money. Both he and Weasley signed it. He gave Weasley a copy and kept two for himself and the bank.

Ponsonby and Weasley exchanged purses. Ponsonby got one that he presumed was empty. He had no way of knowing whether or not it was. Weasley got the one that was full of envelopes. Once they had become confused which was which. They had pondered for five minutes on how to know which was which. At the end of that time Weasley had slapped his head and just opened one of them and looked inside. He'd declared that that was his and left.

They shook hands, and Weasley opened the door, letting the Barclay guards in while he left. He returned to his favorite WC and went in. No one else was there. That was good. If someone had been there, he'd have to enter a stall, close the door, and wait until everyone was gone. But since it was empty, he simply raised his wand, began to spin, and disappeared.

"You see, what could you gain? You could intercept the letter at the post office, I suppose, but you'd never know exactly when the wizard was coming. You wouldn't know how he was going to arrive. You couldn't even know where he'd show up."

Bogart was dogged, "We could find that from Barclay's with a court order."

"Sure. And that would be all that you'd find. You couldn't do anything besides find out when the courier was to arrive. You could try to arrest him. Notice I say, 'try'. We're stuck."

Jergens asked, "Why didn't you invite that computer nerd. What's his name, Bach or Beethoven or whatever. We could get him to put a trap door in the Barclay's software. Then we could get all those electronic transactions anyway."

I didn't like it. "We could get Ponsonby killed if any of those transactions were picked up by us."

Jergens shrugged, "So what."

I looked around the room from one to another of the people who off and on I thought of as felons—especially now. I looked at Parker, who was the sanest of them. "Will you tell him?"

Parker sighed, "OK. I'm not sure what Wendt is thinking of, but one problem for sure would be that Ponsonby wouldn't be the last clerk to die. Everyone who replaced him would. That would be the end of credit transactions."

Jergens muttered under his breath, "Frigging goblins, frigging Gringotts. They're worse than the frigging Swiss banks."

Parker answered, "For now. But we may not be out of that game forever."

Parker looked unhappy. "Well, I suppose that puts me up to bat. Let's go back to the Deatheaters. Do we have addresses for these 'Deatheaters'?"

I answered, "We have some addresses, and we'll have more soon."

"Then we can set up surveillance on the houses, see who comes and goes. I suppose that you're going to tell me that we can't 'tail' them?"

"No. Probably not.

I went on. I ticked them off on my fingers as I spoke, "The ways that they get around are:

- "Disapparate—sort of like teleportation, but it has limits. I don't know precisely what they are but probably less than five or six hundred Kilometers. No way to follow them. Not all wizards can disapparate, but all the ones that we're interested in can.
- "Floo network—you". Someone interrupted with "what the bloody hell?" I answered, "Yes, it's crazy but true. You get into a chimney with some 'floo powder', say the

destination chimney that you want to go to, and throw the powder at your feet. You disappear in flames and almost instantly appear at the chimney that you were aiming for. I've traveled that way. It's uncomfortable, dirty, and I've no idea why they do it. Well, maybe because it's a lot easier than disapparation.

- "Port Key. This can be any sort of object. It has a fixed destination and usually a fixed departure time. It is intended to be inconspicuous, especially to Muggles. They are usually common everyday items, like a tire iron or an old boot."
- "Flying carpets—these are much like brooms but have been forbidden in England for a number of years—apparently due to some sort of trade dispute.

Somebody, I think Jergens, interrupted, "And flying broom."

"Yeh, Another means of travel that I simply can't understand. Even in the best weather it's cold and you're lucky to do 80 or 90 miles per hour. As you can see, there's really not too much that you can do to trace people when they travel that way." I reconsidered and added, "Well, maybe radar or visually, but wizards don't travel that way much."

Parker was surly, "What you're saying is that we might as well give up."

Jergens answered, "Not at all. Just because we can't follow them doesn't mean that we can't figure out where they went. Usually people travel to visit other people or to places of business, etc. We just have to put surveillance on them all, and then we find out where they went. We develop travel patterns on them, and then we're in business."

Parker, "Yeh, where do we get all the people to stake out—that's what you Americans call it, right—all those places?"

"We don't. We use surveillance cameras and monitor them from here. We're already doing that on a small scale."

Parker finished that line of discussion, "We're working on automated ways to monitor surveillance cameras, but until that happens, we need to get a lot more video feeds into this building and a lot more monitors. I'll get that started. Jergens, I want you to start working up a list of all places that we want video feeds from and people to monitor them. Try to figure out how many monitors one person can watch without missing anything. I want everyone else to put your men on that detail for the time being. We need to get photos of everyone who comes in or out of any of the subject houses. Jergens, you need to get your people going on identifying all these people and learning everything we can about them. You know the drill at this point. If Wendt can think of anything useful for any of you to do, do it. Questions?"

No one had any, and no one seemed very happy either. The meeting broke up, and I went for a little early dinner. The Cafeteria was informal. At regular meals the staff made a menu up. At other times, you could just walk behind the serving line and eat anything you could find. I was looking for a sandwich or at least things to make a sandwich with.

What I found was Sally. She was talking with the cook about dinner. I said, "Don't pay any attention to me. I'm just going to make myself a sandwich."

She said, "People who eat between meals put on weight"

"Thanks mother."

"Don't you have a sense of humor?"

"Usually not when I'm hungry. Turn around, and you won't have to watch me putting on weight"

She said something under her breath which sounded like, "I rather" or maybe "rather not".

Computers

Nicholas Brahms, whom we'd begun calling the "Boy Genius" because of his general intelligence in addition to his specific computer skills, called me on the phone and asked me to come down to his secret laboratory. I didn't think about him or it that way at the time. I'd met him, but I had never been in his sprawling work space. He had been given a corner of the warehouse that was about as far away from me as you could get. He had to give me detailed instructions on how to get there. The warehouse was not one large room, but was divided by fire walls into several sections. I'd never been able to figure out a pattern to the design. Maybe it had just grown into the way it was over the decades. A section added on every decade or so. Anyway, there were several turns and firewalls to traverse to get to his corner. I went through a firewall and found a large open space with rack after rack of, well, of black boxes with smooth fronts and thousands of wires sticking out the back. I guessed that must be the back. Surely no one would call those sprawling random masses of cables the front of the thing. I'd had to step up to the floor that was raised about a foot above the real floor underneath. The space was pretty well lit by fluorescent lamps. There were desks scattered about at random and lots and lots of computer monitors everywhere. There were a bunch of people in t-shirts with cute mottos on them. One guy had a picture of Einstein on the front of his t-shirt. Another had a t-shirt with a spiral of numbers that I recognized when I had a chance to look at it closely. It was the number pi.

The Boy Genius reminded me that he was Nicolas Brahms—which was lucky for me. I couldn't remember his name. He wasn't a boy. I guess he was a few years younger than my age. He was a genius though. He wore an izod shirt and jeans.

He began bluntly. "I hear that you want to find magicians."

"Wizards." I corrected.

"OK. It's important to keep the terminology straight. Tell me how you know a wizard when you see one."

"You don't—unless you happen to see him appear out of nowhere or riding a broom."

"I thought that was witches."

"Oh, witches ride brooms too."

"Really? No kidding."

"No kidding.

"Are they good looking or do they have warts the size of avocados on their noses?"

"It depends. I've seen a few avocado warts. Mostly they look a lot like your average Brighton housewife."

"Ugh. I'm sorry."

"No. That was meant as a compliment. I know a couple of witches who make me wish I were a wizard every time I see them. Oh, by the way, I've seen a few Brighton housewives that made me feel the same way."

"You have strange tastes."

"Yeh. I get a lot of that lately, but you didn't invite me here to discuss the theory of beauty."

"No. I invited you here to discuss the theory of finding . . . uh . . . wizards and witches." He had this habit of walking around the giant room and looking over people's shoulders as he did. Once in a while, he'd notice something on a screen of computer code. He'd stop talking and point at it. The programmer would make a change on his keyboard, and Brahms would move along

"Good. Do you have any ideas?"

"No. I was hoping you did."

"I was thinking that you'd invited me here because you have some special skill or technique that might be helpful."

"Well. I've been working on optical recognition systems for a long time.

"You have strange tastes."

"Yeh. I get a lot of that lately. But I didn't invite you here to discuss the theory of beauty. Well. I've been working on optical recognition systems for a long time."

I pointed out that he'd said that already. He just said, "Yeh. Your boss Parker thought that we might be able to automate what your people do when they watch security tapes and feeds."

"OK. Let's start on that. I think that you could recognize it if a person suddenly appeared out of thin air. What do you think?" I watched as he

76

presumably thought. His eyes seemed to stare off into the distance. Then they glanced up and to his left, still staring in the distance. Then his gaze strayed to his right, still looking someplace above my left shoulder. Then he looked directly over my head. I'd once seen the movie, *Full Metal Jacket*. One of the characters described a look that came over war-worn soldiers that he called "The Thousand Meter Stare". That was Brahms. Finally, he returned to earth.

He looked me straight in the eyes and said, "Yes. We can do that.

"Actually, it is pretty easy in theory. We want to search for sudden changes in the Fourier Transform of the visual field—particularly in the high frequency spectrum—a sudden change in intensity there."

He laughed a short, choppy chuckle that was almost not a laugh. It was strictly a private joke. I couldn't see anything funny in the situation. He went on, "Of course, we'll have to do something about falling pianos. We don't want lots of false alarms from pianos." Here he paused to laugh a laugh that was almost real, and then he went on, "Yes, we want to avoid pianos falling from the 4th floor triggering a 'red alert.'"

I didn't quite see the humor in that, but I let it pass. "This is all fine, but I just don't see that it's worth the effort. Even having computers scan endless hours seems pointless. How often would you catch a wizard apparition? I mean, only newly licensed apparating wizards actually do it every few minutes."

He shook his head sorrowfully as though he were dealing with a particularly obtuse student. "Oh, I think you underestimate the possibilities. You would not believe the network of security cameras that are all around. And we've been quietly collecting the video feeds centrally for quite some time. There are literally hundreds of thousands of cameras around and not just security cameras. Every joker with a webcam seems to run it continuously and expose it on the internet. It's a pretty random collection, but there are amazingly few places that don't have some sort of camera surveillance that we can tap into.

"The real problem is having the artificial intelligence to scan it all looking for what you want."

I harked back to my physics days to come up with an objection. "But, surely all that video would choke any communications network that you could build, wouldn't it?"

"You'd think so, wouldn't you?" He got up and got that thousand meter look again. "Actually, that's not as big a problem as you'd think. The feeds would come into local nodes in the network. We'd do the heavy lifting there in a distributed way. We'd filter that down so that we throw out. . ." He paused here to look to the left at eye level and then went on,

'Oh, say, by a factor of a million and then aggregate what's left to here." He paused again and then said, "No, probably regional centers. There, we do a little more filtering. Maybe exclude people we know about already. Then aggregate to here."

"It sounds like a good way to throw away a lot of money to me."

"No no no no. This could work." He became animated for the first time. He stood up and started pacing back and forth. Every now and then he made a comment, sometimes directed at me, sometimes not.

"You. Can you get me some test data?"

"What do you mean, 'test data'?"

He looked at me for the first time in a while. "You know. You've got to have good test data. I need examples of people apparating and disapparating in all sorts of situations, outdoors, indoors, in the rain, in the snow—if we could get any. Oh, yes, we'd also need all sorts of lighting situations, broad daylight, cloudy, twilight, moonlight, the dark."

He stopped for a second, and then chuckled his little mirthless chuckle. "And of course, we'll need some false positives. You don't happen to have a few spare pianos, do you? You know, to drop off the top of some building."

I didn't smile. I was beginning to think about dropping one particular person off the top of a building. He went on, "Come on over to our 'war room'. We'll have a little meeting with the team." He walked down the rough aisles between stacks of electronic equipment, stopping now and then when he passed another human being, and inviting them to a meeting in the "war room". We finally reached a room that had walls of glass on 3 sides with a door facing the center of the larger room. He'd collected about half a dozen people as we went. In the transparent room there was a large table with about room for a dozen or so people to sit around it. There was a strange triangular device in the middle with a phone cord coming out of it and snaking across the table down to the floor over to an outlet in the floor. We all sat down at the table. I sat next to Brahms, and the rest of the people sat on the opposite side of the table.

There were muted conversations going on between a couple of people. Brahms started talking, "Fred, let's get started." He paused for a moment while the conversations died away. He went on, "This is our new user. His name is." He stopped to look at my ID badge. "James."

I interrupted. "Please call me Wendt. All my enemies do." There was a little tittering.

Brahms went on, "He's our new user rep. He's given me an idea about how to approach this thing. He's suggested looking for sudden disappearances or appearances of objects in the visual field. I think we could do something with the sharp edges of a person appearing from nowhere. Maybe high frequency intensity of the Fourier spectrum."

A short woman that I guessed to be in her 30's interrupted, "Could we have introductions?" She was about 5' 6". She had hair that was either brown streaked with blonde or blonde streaked with brown—I couldn't decide which. It was a little longer than shoulder-length.

"Oh, sure. Go ahead and introduce yourselves."

The woman started, "I'm Joan. My field is graph theory." I filed that information. I was going to have to find out what graph theory was.

The rest were men, and they identified themselves going around in counter-clockwise rotation about the table.

"I'm Fred. Networking."

"Jasper. I'm a programming gopher. I know a lot of languages."

"John. I know a good bit about mathematical transforms."

"Manuel. Nothing special."

"Dick. I know hardware."

Brahms went on, "Our user is going to get us lots of test data." He hesitated as if he didn't like to say the next word out loud if there were more than one other person present. "Wizards. Apparating—appearing out of nowhere."

Joan cut in, "OR disappearing? Yes."

Brahms said, "Yes."

Dick asked, "Anything else that we can use as an identifying mark that would help to identify" again the hesitation, "wizards."

Joan's words sliced into the turgid stillness that was filling the room, "or witches". She turned to me and went on, "right?"

"Yes, you're right. There are witches—about as many as there are wizards."

"I thought so. What are they like—do they wear anything distinctive? Tend to wear their hair long, short, what?"

I thought for a minute. "Well, both witches and wizards tend to wear outlandish clothes when they go dressed as 'Muggles'."

She cut in again, "What in the world are 'Muggles'?"

"People like you and me—you know, non-magical."

"What do you mean by outlandish?"

"Well, would vermilion pajamas on Piccadilly strike you as 'outlandish'?"

"Yes."

"I've seen that, believe it or not.

"But they typically don't disapparate in Muggle clothes. They usually wear what they call 'robes', which are like a university Don's—only less ornate."

"I see."

John broke in, "I don't think that clothing style will help us much. But I just had an idea. Since we're keying off this 'apparation' thing, maybe we should use a three-dimensional Fourier Transform. That could give us a very distinctive signal to look for."

Harold picked up the idea. "Yes, there may be something there. I think we should break up into 2 working groups—one running the conventional 2-D transformations to ground, and John can lead the other following up on the 3-D approach."

Jasper—"I'm on John's team."

Joan answered, "That's just because he's smart. I'm on the 2-D team."

The rest of the team chose up sides.

Brahms exclaimed, "The winning team gets a kegger party."

Joan asked, "What does 'winning' mean? Is it getting a working solution first or is it the team with a solution that gets adopted."

Brahms said, "Both, we'll have 2 kegger parties—one for each winning team."

There was a visible stir in the room. The tension was there. People seemed ready to get up out of their chairs and start right now.

Manuel asked me, "Wendt, when can you get us test data—you know, videos of people disapparating?"

I stopped and thought for a minute. Say a couple of days to get hold of a wizard, probably Minerva, and a couple of days for her to put me in touch with someone who could safely spend a few days with us. Give him a day or two to actually do the videoing. I answered, "I'd say about a week, more or less."

Joan laughed, "Get with the program man. We're going to be working through the night on this. How hard can it be to get a half-hour or so of video?"

"Well, actually, it is pretty hard. I've got to find someone who is willing to be seen with me. I'm kind of a *persona non grata* in the wizarding world. That person—and I—would probably be dead quicker than a cockroach in the restaurant of the Ritz if we were seen by. . . uh. . . any 'Deatheaters'."

Joan asked the obvious question, "What's a 'Deatheater'?"

"A close assistant to the leader of the wizarding equivalent of the IRA."

"Oh. . ." She trailed off. "Is this place safe?" The air seemed to suddenly have chilled.

Brahms asked me, "We're going to beat them, aren't we?"

I looked at him and wondered how honest I could be with him—especially in front of his team. I flipped a mental coin and said, "With your help, yes." I tried to put conviction into my voice without sounding obviously forced. I looked straight into his eyes and tried to convince him that I thoroughly believed that.

"Now, if you want some 'test data', I've got to get going." We broke into 3 groups: the 2-D and 3-D teams and Brahms and I. He walked with me back to the entrance to his demesnes. He looked around briefly and asked, "You are going to get us those videos in a couple of days, right?"

"Sure. I'll let you know as soon as I get them."

I left him and headed back to my desk, composing in my head the letter that I was going to send to Minerva. I wondered to myself how I could manage to work this into a visit with her.

Late in the afternoon I walked out of the building to the Tube station and found a post box. The letter was simple. It said, "Dearest M.; I need someone to help me do some research. All they have to do is disapparate a few dozen times as I photograph them. Can you suggest someone? Love, Jim oxoxoxoxoxoxoxoxo"

The day was cold and rainy. I like walking, but this was just not the day for a walk. The only thing that made it tolerable was the thought that I'd had a reason to write to Minerva. It was hard to justify doing it just for the pleasure of writing to her. You never knew if a letter would be intercepted, and it might be the tipping point for sending her to Azkaban or something even worse.

□

The next day I was down to breakfast at the normal time. Sally was behind the serving line. She said, "We've got a special on the oatmeal today. Why don't you try some?"

"Is it *specially* bland today?"

"There's no pleasing you is there?"

"Not with oatmeal, there isn't. I'll splurge today and take a bagel."

"Cream cheese?"

"No. Do you have any jam—blueberry jam?"

"I'll go back to the vault and see if we've got any. I'm pretty sure the only thing we've got on the serving line is grape jelly."

"There's nothing too bland for this Cafeteria, right?"

"You have such a bad opinion of us." She leaned over the serving line. "Is there nothing that we can do to redeem our good name?"

"Go back to the vault and see if you can find some jam."

I checked out at the end of the line and found my usual table. I liked one by the wall—by myself if possible. That gave me time to read *The Times*. Usually. Today, Sally came over to my table and dropped into the chair across from me. "We didn't have any jam, but I did find some orange marmalade."

"Thanks," I said with feeling. "I like orange marmalade. It's worth its weight in gold here."

"You're welcome. Any good news in the paper?"

"No. There were three people found dead in their apartment on the West side. No signs of a struggle. Plenty of valuables lying around, untouched. A couple of hundred pounds in the man's wallet."

"Do you think. . ." She trailed off.

"Who knows? I don't recognize the name. That doesn't mean much. This could be terrorism."

"This is spooky. I'd like to help. Sitting in the kitchen and making up menus for lunch just doesn't meet my idea of being proactive."

"You want to help? I'll ask the boss to see if he can get you cleared for tippity-top secret. Then you can help me with a little research I have to do, and I can at least tell you what it is you ought to be afraid of."

"You mean it's not some new IRA group?"

"I don't know, maybe it is."

Sally pouted and frowned at me, "You are absolutely no help."

"I'm not kidding. I'm going to try to get you cleared to hear so much you'll wish you'd never met me."

"Have a good day too. Back to lunch planning."

"Yeh. Have a better one."

I went back to my office and wrote a note asking for clearance for Sally. And then I wondered what I'd tell her if she did get clearance.

Brahms called me. He asked if I'd made any progress on test data. I put him off.

I went down to lunch a little early. I scrounged around in the left-over bagels, looking for a whole wheat one. Sally was nowhere to be seen. I sat at my usual table, and she showed up. "I see that you are going on a bagel diet."

"No, this is my bagel day. I hope you have some left tonight for supper. Tomorrow is my English Muffin day. I hope you save some for lunch."

"I think you may not be kidding. That's not exactly a balanced diet. I'll be sure that I throw whatever's left away before supper."

Just then there was a screech coming from outside in the hall. A bird flew into the Cafeteria pursued by an MP with his service pistol drawn. The bird roosted on the table between Sally and me.

She asked, "Are you Dr. Doolittle?"

"No, it's an owl."

"Yeh. I can see that."

Just then the MP reached our table and was stymied—not knowing just what to do.

I looked at his name badge. I said, "Private O'Sheah, the bird's OK. You can return to your post."

"But sir, this bird is unsanitary, and we're not supposed to allow anything in that doesn't have clearance—especially owls."

"It's OK, really."

The private was reluctant but left eventually.

Sally asked, "Is this your pet?"

"No, but I was half-expecting an owl."

She cocked an eye at me and asked, "You were?"

"I can't explain it."

"That's for sure."

"NOW."

She still looked quizzical.

I went on, "Please leave. I have some private business with the owl."

"OoooKaaaay. I'll see you at dinner. If you and the owl are done with your private business."

"We will be." She went back to the kitchen. I took the small note that was tied to the owl's leg off and unrolled the parchment. It read, "Got your guinea pigs. Meet them on the upper floor of the British Museum tomorrow at 2PM. They'll be in the Mesopotamia room. Return note with owl if rendezvous is OK. All my love, M."

I turned the parchment over and wrote, "Perfect. Can you come? All my love, W." I tied it to the leg of the owl and gave it a little scoot. It just sat and stared at my bagel. "OK. Owl, you can have some bagel." I tore off a little piece and laid it on the table. It stared at it and back to me. "OK. A bigger one." I tore off about a quarter bagel and put it on the table. The owl took it in its beak and took off. "I thought you guys were carnivores," I shouted after it.

That evening I had something other than bagels for dinner. I had the usual visit from Sally. She sat down with me, unbidden as usual. "Have you finished your business with the owl?"

"Sure, he got disgusted with me and went on back home. He wanted to sell me life insurance, but finally decided I was too bad a risk."

She guffawed and asked, "What was that really all about."

She had me over a barrel. If I told her it was none of her business, she'd figure it somehow had something to do with what we were doing here. Of course, she'd be right. The other alternative, lying wouldn't work either. I just couldn't lie effectively. So, I just didn't say anything.

"Well, be that way, if you must. I'll see you tomorrow."

"I wait with bated breath."

□□

The next day, I started getting together equipment for the experiment: video camera, videotape, gadget bag, weather forecasts (there was rain predicted for Bath this afternoon). I made a list of the different types of disapparations that I wanted to video. While I was collecting equipment, Parker intercepted me.

"What have you been doing? You are the hardest person to find that I have under my command. Your buddy has her clearance. You can read her into the game."

I was overjoyed, "Just in the nick of time. I have a little job for her. I wasn't looking forward to it, but she can take it."

At 11AM, I went down to the Cafeteria. It was early for lunch, but I didn't want lunch. I walked into the kitchen, looking for Sally. I found her at her desk. She was working on something, probably trying to come up with a new boring menu for next week.

I said, "Sally, you wanted to find out what this all about, get a top-secret clearance, know what's going on?"

'Yes, what about it?"

"You've got your clearance—provisionally, but if you're still interested, you're invited to a little outing this afternoon and evening."

"How could you possibly get me a clearance in such a short time?"

"Well, I said that you were essential to my work, and you had to have a clearance for that."

"Why in the world did you do that? You're going to get in trouble."

"No, I couldn't really get in more trouble than I am.

"As to why I did it, well, I think you deserve to know what's going on here. If you look at the people who are here risking their lives on this project, you find that about half know what's going on. Then there's another third that are in the service and have signed on for dangerous situations. Then there's another few who are crazy and don't care whether they're in danger. And then there's you. You're here voluntarily, and you don't know what you're up against. I think you should. You might decide to move on. And then again, you might not. But it should be your decision."

"Wow. Well, yes. You intrigue me. If I go along, what am I getting myself in for?"

"Well, nothing really dangerous. You'll have to operate a video camcorder. Do you think you can do that?"

"Sure. I've never done it before, but I'd sure try."

"Good enough. It's easy. The manual says so."

"You've not done it either?"

"Nope."

"Hmmm. I'm game. Will this really take all day? If so, I've got to talk with the cook to give him instructions. I think he can manage on his own one afternoon."

"Great. Be quick though, we've got to get going quickly."

She went after the cook, and I twiddled my thumbs. She returned, and we left. She started asking questions as we left the building, "Well, where are we going?"

"Oh, we'll start off at the British Museum."

"Really?"

"Sure."

"What is this, a Mystery Tour—a magical Mystery Tour?"

I frowned and made sure she couldn't see my face, "It just could be."

"What are we doing at the Museum?"

"We're going to have lunch, if you'll eat at someone else's establishment."

"Sure, but it's not in my budget."

"It doesn't have to be. This one's on the expense account."

"How is that possible?"

"Well, this is all in the line of duty."

"And this isn't dangerous?"

"Not much more dangerous than eating in your Cafeteria."

"Ouch. That's not a nice thing to say."

"Oh, but it's dangerous eating at your place not because of the food but because of where the Cafeteria is."

We took the Tube and got off at the museum just before noon. We went in and went directly to the restaurant on the upper level. We were seated and looked at the menu. Sally took a look and gasped. "This is expensive."

"It's lucky we're on an expense account."

85

"Have you ever eaten here before?"

"Once. I had a guest then as well."

"On expense?"

"No. It was purely pleasure."

"A lady friend?"

I smiled. "Yes. A very close friend. I don't get to see her very often. It was a really pleasant day."

"At these prices, I'd hope so. What do you recommend?"

"We had vegetarian pasta. It was pretty good. But then, I like what I have at your Cafeteria."

"Really. I've never heard that before."

"You never asked."

We were served and ate for a while in silence. Sally finally asked, "What happens next?"

"We meet my contact, and then, well, I'm not exactly sure what happens then. I don't expect them until two, so we could do a little touring while we're here. Do you like art?"

"I don't know a lot about art. I like realistic painting."

"We should try the European rooms then on this floor." I paid for the lunch, and we went out to the European Rooms. I was hoping we might find a Vermeer—foolish of me.

She asked, "You took your friend here?"

"Sure. Why not?"

"Oh, I've never been here before. I always hoped someone would take me somewhere like this."

"Well, now you've here. I hope it lives up to your hopes."

She studied the floor carefully and said, "Your friend is lucky."

"I think so. Do you have a friend?"

"Not at the moment."

"The world is a strange place, isn't it?"

She studied the floor again and asked, "What do you mean?"

"It's full of impossible things that should never happen, but do. It also has lots of very possible things that really ought to happen but don't."

She was really drilling the floor with her eyes now, "Like happy endings for girls like me."

"You're a long way from the ending. Socrates warned about judging lives' endings before they come."

"She's very lucky."

"I wouldn't go that far. But you can if you insist. Well, it's time to make our rendezvous—almost. I must warn you that the person we're about to meet is likely to be a little uh 'eccentric'."

"Why is it that I'm not surprised?"

We left the 19th Century Room and returned toward the Court Restaurant. As we walked through the Mesopotamian Room I heard a voice that I recognized.

"Well, if it isn't our favorite Muggle." I turned and saw not one but two Weasleys approaching. They were wearing Lavender suits with red ties and black shirts.

I said, "I see that you boys haven't learned much about fashion since I last saw you." I turned to Sally and said, "Allow me to introduce the brothers Weasley—Fred and George. They're twins, if you haven't guessed." She held out her hand, and they took turns. Fred shook it, and George raised it toward his lips but didn't kiss it. He smiled broadly as he said, "Charmed."

Fred cast a slightly jaundiced sideways glance at him.

I turned toward Sally and said, "Well, we've reached the point that I've been dreading. I have to explain what we're doing. Let's get going, and I'll explain on the way."

Fred said, "Good. We've got a nice quiet place in mind that we can disapparate to. Let's go into the Men's Room and. . .'

I interrupted him, "Wait a minute, Fred. You were thinking that we would disapparate there?" I asked.

"Sure, it's the fastest way. What's the problem?"

Sally broke in, "What do you mean 'the Men's room'?"

George broke in, "Well, you don't expect us to disapparate out here in the open with all kinds of Muggles around to see it."

Sally asked, "What's this apparate thingee?"

I decided that we needed to get some order in this. "Wait, wait, wait. We've got some talking to do before we go anywhere. Let's go into the restaurant and get a cup of tea and."

George broke in again, "and biscuits?"

"Sure."

So we went back to the restaurant and got ourselves seated at a table by a wall well away from anyone else. After the waitress was heading off for tea, I started, "Well, we need to bring Sally up to date. These two estimable young men," they both smiled and waved at Sally, "are wizards."

Sally chuckled softly, "What kind of magic tricks do you do?"

I interrupted swiftly, "Don't you dare give demonstrations here."

Fred answered, "You do us a grave injustice."

I answered for them, "No, they're not that—not magicians, not illusionists. They're the real thing. They can do <u>real</u> magic. As a matter of fact, in a few moments you'll see just how real. This anti-terrorist unit that we both work for is going up against the most dangerous, most insidious terrorists anyone has ever faced—people who can do real magic. We've brought the video camera along to do videos of one particular . . . uh . . . magic feat that is common. It's called 'disapparating'."

George began as I paused for breath. "Yes, lovely lady, you are going to have the pleasure of disapparating with me. Disapparating is being transported from one place to another in a moment, in the twinkling of an eye." At that, he winked at her.

"Is he kidding?" Sally had turned to me and asked me point blank.

"No," Just then the waitress brought tea and biscuits. Both Fred and George were quick to stuff their mouths with cookies.

I continued after she left. "Are you a Sci-fi fan?"

"I've seen a few movies, so?"

"Well, Disapparation is just like the Star Trek transporter, only there isn't any hardware—no computer, etc.—running it. It's just, well, magic." I ended weakly.

"Yes, and you're going to be one of the few Muggles to experience it." George added.

Sally looked over at me again.

'What he says is true. Now's the time to bail out if this makes you nervous or scared."

"No, but this is crazy." Her voice rose and almost broke.

I'd done this so many times that it was becoming second nature to convince people that the impossible is indeed possible. "Look, we're either all crazy or not. If we're crazy, you take the hand of one of these guys. Yeh, yeh, I know, but there's no other way." She had made a face. "And then either you suddenly find yourself 100 miles away or you're just standing there with an embarrassed look on your face."

She was silent for a moment while she looked at each of us in turn hoping, I suppose, that someone would laugh and say, "The jokes on you. We had you going there for a while." But that didn't happen. We just stared back at her. Finally, she said, "OK. I know that this is some sort of elaborate practical joke, but, what the heck, I'm a sucker."

George and Fred said in unison, "Great, let's go!"

Nobody was laughing. I said, "OK. I have to explain something first.

"This is not a pleasant process. Don't believe what these jokers tell you. It feels like you're being stretched out, then you feel like you're falling for a second, then you're squeezed like an orange in your orange juicer, and then suddenly you're disoriented because nothing that you see around you is familiar in the least."

"And you guys do that all the time."

George and Fred said in unison, "Every time we can."

I answered, "I agree completely. I don't get it, but I do know that shortly after they qualified to disapparate, they were doing it dozens of times a day. They made real nuisances of themselves. Well, once you know them you'll probably ask how that's different from any other time, but . . ."

Sally asked, "OK, how do we do this?"

I answered, "They're right. We can't just do it in a crowded museum. I suppose that the Men's room is OK to disapparate from, but we've got a lady here to accommodate."

Fred looked at me and said, "It's easy. George and you go in and scout out. If you find someone, just hang around until they're gone. Then when the coast is clear, you signal Sally and me to come in, and we disapparate."

George broke in, "Wait one minute, I was thinking that you and Wendt could scout out the Men's room, and Sally and I could come in and . . ."

Fred was getting excited, "Why you and Sally?"

I said, "Wait, wait. The only way to do it is for Sally and me to stay out. I came with her. That would seem less unnatural. And I'm running the show, so that's what we're going to do."

Fred and George grumbled.

I went on, "When we're all inside, I take Fred's hand. You take George's and hold on for your life—because you are holding on for your life. Don't let go for any reason. When we arrive, we'll sort out things."

Sally had been listening intensely and said, "Sounds too easy."

"Just tell me that after we arrive."

Sally asked, "What are we waiting for?"

We all agreed that there was no reason to wait. I paid, and we left. George and Fred went in the Men's Room. They immediately opened the door and signaled to us. We walked in. I took Fred's hand, and George took Sally's. I was reminded why I hate disapparation so much. After the gut-wrenching trip, we found ourselves in a forest clearing. The first thing I heard was a small gasp from Sally.

She said, "This is for real!"

"Yes, I very rarely kid."

She asked, "OK. What now?"

"Do you know how to use a video camera?"

"No. . . Why don't you show me?" I walked over and held out my hand for the camcorder. Sally misunderstood and took my hand in her free hand. I gently released her hand and reached for the camcorder. I slowly went through the operation steps. I recorded George for a few seconds, rewound it, and played back the recording.

I said, "George, do you want to see yourself in living color?" He perked up and came over to look over my shoulder. He smiled as he saw himself.

"Gee, it's just like magic."

"Well, duh. . . Yes. I should hope so. There's nothing great about that." Fred guffawed.

"No, no. Come here and look at this."

"I don't need to. I see you every time I look in the mirror."

I interrupted. "OK. OK. We came here to get some work done. Sally, record Fred and let me see the results."

She recorded Fred, but George insisted on getting into the picture. They had a little duel while she taped them.

We reviewed the results, and I pronounced her an old pro.

"We're ready for business. I want to record you two disapparating. First one disapparates away, then back. Then the other does it. Then both away and back at the same time."

So we started a marathon video session. We recorded disapparation in broad daylight and in the shadows—two at a time and one at a time. As the day wore away, and it cooled, we took a break.

Sally asked the brothers what it was like growing up as wizards.

George answered first, "It was strange."

Sally laughed and said, "No, really??"

"No, I mean it. Every young wizard and witch has this time when they begin to be able to do magical things, and their parents have to get them to cool it and not do anything when Muggles are around. It's like when parents bring kids to a nice restaurant and have to keep them from running around making noise and all that. The kids don't understand what it's all about."

"Yeh," agreed Fred. "You'd want to play a fun little trick on your brother—like making his hair green, and the parents are constantly trying to keep you in line and turning your brother's hair back to red before the waiter notices."

George went on, "And there's the time when your parents finally tell you the facts of life."

Fred agreed again.

Sally frowned slightly, "But every parent has that embarrassing moment."

George asked, "They do? You mean every parent has to tell his kids that not everyone can do magic, and you have to not do magic around people who can't?"

Fred went on, "And that you mustn't look down on the poor Muggles who can't tie their shoes without bending over?"

Sally broke out laughing, "You two are awful. No I was thinking about sex."

Fred and George said in unison, "Funny, I was too."

There was an awkward moment of silence as Sally turned beat red and said, "But I didn't mean . . ." and sort of trailed off.

I saved the day by putting us back on track. "I'd like to find someplace that's cloudy, maybe even drizzling to do some more videoing."

"No problemo." Fred held his hand out toward Sally. George got up and fairly leaped to her side. He said, "Allow me, mademoiselle."

I was beginning to get tired of this jockeying for favor and took Fred's hand. "Let's just go and be done with it."

George said, "Inverness?"

Fred answered, "Sure." Then the world turned inside out, and I picked myself up off the wet ground. The rain was coming down, and I was glad I was at least wearing a jacket. Sally had a small folding umbrella out of her large bag. We went through an abbreviated set of recording like we'd done in the much more pleasant clearing.

Despite Sally's umbrella even she was pretty well soaked before we were done. She was apparently getting a little disgusted with the rain. "Can we go somewhere dry and warm?"

"I'm ready." I said.

Fred said, "I know a nice little pub in Bath. How about that?"

George added, "Oh, yeh. That's good. I know the one that you're talking about."

I had my doubts. "I'm not sure that anyone else in the world has the same idea of 'nice' that you two boys have. This is OK, isn't it, for mixed company?"

George asked, "Mixed company?"

"Yes. You know. Sane and insane."

The two answered together, "You cut me to the quick, James. You know I wouldn't suggest anything but the best establishment."

Sally chimed in, "Anything would be better than this."

"OK. But you don't know these young men's tastes, my dear." We took hands, shivering and re-appeared in an alley behind a pub. Fred and George led us around the corner and into an establishment that even I had to admit was decent. We gathered more than a few puzzled stares as we shook the rain off our clothes and hair before going beyond the entryway. We took seats at table in a dark corner. There was loud rock music playing, and we didn't really have to worry about anyone hearing us. We could hardly hear ourselves.

After a waitress had taken our orders for drinks, I asked Sally, "Well, do you still want to work for us?"

Before she could say anything George said, "This is nothing. You should be along when we have some fun. As a matter of fact, I'd ask you out next week if I weren't being chased by Deatheaters."

Sally stared at him for a second and asked, "It's really too loud in here. I thought I heard you say that you were being chased by 'healthmeters'."

Fred and George both broke into gales of laughter. Sally, looking confused, asked me, "What did I say?"

I was having a hard time keeping from laughing myself. I could only shake my head and tell her that it would have to wait until we were someplace that we could actually hear ourselves talk. We ordered some food and spent most of the meal silently listening to the music. We really didn't have much choice.

After we left the pub, I suggested taking the train back to London and that the lads accompany us so that we could talk in a quieter environment. I bought tickets, and we waited at the station. The next train for London wasn't leaving for another hour, so we had time to sit in the lonely station and talk.

Sally went back to 'healthmeters', "What were you saying about being chased by . . by . . well whatever it was?"

Fred answered, "Deatheaters. Don't blame me. I didn't make up the name. They invented it for themselves. They're a band of. . ." Here he hesitated and said, "terrorists. Wizards and witches who want to take over the world. We're on their top 30."

Here George interrupted, "Top 20."

Fred went on, "Top 20 list of undesirable wizards who just want to save the world for free enterprise."

Sally looked at them for a minute and asked, "Are they Communists?"

"No they're worse."

Fred said, "Yes, much worse."

George asked, "What are Communists?"

I answered, "People who don't believe in free enterprise. What the boys are trying to say is that the Deatheaters don't believe in democracy. They want to establish a world where Deatheaters are on top, and wizards 'lord it over' Muggles."

Sally said, "It's funny how there are so many people who want to do that."

"Yeh. Wouldn't it be great if we could take up a collection and get them an island of their own where they could entertain each other to their hearts' content?" George asked.

I elaborated, "Well, anyway, it's another group of terrorists who think they are Masters of the Universe. Only they've got a real chance of becoming Masters of the Universe. Anyone who stands in the way is in a real danger of being. . . oh, I don't know. . . . tortured to death to get whatever knowledge they have of the opposition.

"The salient question for you Sally is 'Do you want to keep being mixed up in this kind of thing?'"

Fred and George exclaimed, "Oh, please say you do! Please?" They tried their best puppy-dog look.

She looked at both of them and then at me. "Have you got a desire here?"

I frowned and said, "Look. You are one of the few bright spots in a dismal job that I have. How could I not want you to stay on? But, I like you. How could I wish you to keep risking yourself?"

"You are definitely not a help."

She finally sighed, "I'm tired, and this has been way too full a day for me to decide anything. I'm going to sleep on it. We can talk tomorrow."

I nodded. We waited for the train. We were all pretty done-in and spent the remaining time waiting silently with our thoughts.

We arrived at Paddington station. I hailed a cab and put Sally in it. I told the cabby, "Take her wherever she wants." I handed him a couple of 20 pound notes and said, "Keep the change."

Sally objected, "That's way too much money."

"Don't worry. It's expense account money, and I don't mind in the least spending Her Majesty's money on you. You deserve it a lot more than they do."

George bent over and stuck his head through the door on the other side of the cab and said something to Sally. I don't know what he said, but he had a big smile on his face after he closed the door, and the cab drove off.

Fred said, "Well, another adventure successfully completed."

I looked at the two of them for a moment, shook my head, and said, "Yes, we bravely took a picnic, flirted with a pretty girl, and flitted around England by disapparation."

"Can you find your way home by yourself? We could always disapparate you wherever you want to go," George asked.

"Thanks. I'll take the Tube or a cab or walk before I'd do that with you."

"Suit yourself." Then the two of them disappeared. I had the camcorder, so I went down the stairs to the Tube.

Refugees

The next day I dropped down to see the Boy Genius. He was in the big room. He was delighted with the videos that I'd brought him. He called all his staff in, and we watched the videos on a big monitor. They walked through the videos one frame at a time to see if there was any moment of partial transmission. All the disappartions were a single frame with nothing in the field of view and the next frame full of people. The twins were sometimes in motion and somewhat blurred, but there was no sign that they were only partially there. The Boy Genius was sure that he could capture these disapparations by computing.

I asked him, "You don't need any further videos?"

He was beaming, "No. No. This is great. Just give us a couple of weeks and we'll be in full swing. We've been setting up the network and installing servers in the routing centers to do the early stages of filtering. We'll fine tune our logic with this data and will probably be finding wizards every day. Heck. Maybe we'll find them every hour."

He paused a moment thoughtfully and said, "It's really too bad we don't have any wizards ourselves. This 'disapparating' would be a real boon to military science. Just think what we could do!"

As he said that I had an inspiration, "That's brilliant! That's just what we need!"

He looked a little confused and asked, "Yeh, I know it's brilliant—I said it. But just which bits were the brilliant ones?"

I was rapidly trying to think through the implications of the thought that I'd just had. I turned and started to trot out the door. He called after me, "What was the brilliant part again?"

"No time to talk now. I'll see you later." I was on my way up to Parker's office as quickly as my little legs would carry me. I ran into the waiting room and breezed past Connors, "I've got to see the colonel right now."

He just had time to get out, "He's not to be disturbed," before I entered his office. He was on the phone. I made waving motions with my hands and made signs for him to hang up the phone. He was not buying any. So, I sat down and waited. He finally finished his call and swiveled his chair toward me.

"What's so damn important?"

"I just got a brilliant idea about recruiting wizards to our side."

He looked at me quizzically and asked, "Go ahead. I could use a little good news once in a while."

"Well, we've already started with the Order of the Phoenix. They're not lots of them, but it's a starting point. Second there are the people who are being repressed by the Deatheaters. I don't know how many there are, but they've got to be out there. Anybody who's got Muggle sympathies or who has relatives who are Muggles have got to be on our side and are probably being discriminated against or worse. We just have to find them."

Parker harrumphed, "Do we put adverts in *The Times of London*? I can just see it—'Tired of Tom Riddle running the roost? Sign up with the Muggles—see Colonel Parker at . . . '"

"No, no. Of course, not. But I know that the Order of the Phoenix must keep in touch with them. They must know who they are."

"OK. Let's suppose that we can find them. What do we do with them —hold parades down Picadilly?"

I stopped to think. Just what would we do with them? Then an idea occurred to me. I tried to seem smooth as I slowly drawled out, "We smuggle them out of the country. . . . They go to a camp in . . . in the United States. You know, we talked about this."

Parker sneered, "I thought that was just a ploy to get General Davis off our backs."

I was beginning to feel really good about the idea. "No. We train them there, and they're a force ready to fight when the time comes."

"The United States? Why the United States? Why not Germany or Spain?"

"Riddle has lots of contacts on the continent. But I've never heard of him having contacts in the United States. He even has contacts in Russia, I believe."

Parker said, "Hum."

"The US is a friendly country. We should be able to convince them to turn over an old Air Force or Army base to us. It would need an airstrip for flying people in and out in case quick movement is necessary."

Parker's 'Hum' lengthened, and his gaze turned inward. "It might just work. My superiors are putting pressure on me to have some kind of actionable plan in place. This might just be the thing." He hesitated again. "You'll have to sell this. Put together a more detailed plan—how many recruits we'd have. How large the base would have to be. How you'd smuggle them out of the country. Everything that's important to you. I'll get us an interview with the PM and critical Army officers. How long will it take you to finish the plan?"

"I'll have to get in touch with my contacts in the Order and meet with them. Let's say a week."

"Let's say two weeks."

"OK. I'm on it."

I left and headed for my office to start making notes.

I spent a couple of hours filling several pages of a legal pad with ideas. I went down to the 'caf' just before it closed. I brought my legal pad and pen, worked my way absently through the serving line, and picked up a wilted lettuce, soggy tomato, and rubbery bacon sandwich. I sat and continued scribbling when I finally noticed that there was someone else at the table.

Sally asked, "A pence for your thoughts."

I felt disoriented for a moment and then answered, "I'm writing a list of 'to-do's for the next couple of days."

"Let me see." She reached for the pad. I pulled it back.

She had a whiny look in her eyes. I'm not sure how to describe it other than that. I'm sure you've seen it and probably recognize what I'm talking about. If you haven't, then you'll have to imagine that she drew out the word 'see' in a long whine.

"Not yet."

"When?"

"Maybe never. I'm busy. Go peddle your papers somewhere else and let me finish my wilted lettuce and soggy tomato sandwich."

"Well, if you came down sooner than 2 minutes before the close of lunch, it wouldn't be wilted."

"I promise I'll let you see it, if your name shows up on it."

"Fat chance of that."

"Well, you never know."

I went back to the legal pad. I was writing a letter to Minerva. I wanted her to meet with me so that we could talk about someone to lead a group that required a wizard. I didn't want to go into a lot of detail, but I wanted to make the request intriguing so that she would want to take some time off to get together with me.

After lunch, I went out to drop the letter off in the standard postal drop that I always used and returned to the office.

□

The next day, an owl showed up in the lunch room. I'd like to know why they always came at lunch hour. Sometimes I thought that it was a little joke of Minerva—arriving at the most embarrassing time. This time there was a table of guards nearby. They dropped by to look at the owl.

One of them said, "That's a pretty nice pet you've got there."

"Yea. Has it got a name?"

"Yes. But it's never told me what it is. I think it's here to keep the guards on their toes. You obviously let it in without proper credentials."

"You've got the wrong blokes. We're on lunch break now. I'll tell the guys on duty that you've been 'dissing' them."

I hadn't taken the message off its claw, and it began to get irritated. I didn't want to expose myself to more ridicule. But the owl started pecking me. It obviously had better things to do than wait for me to get around to relieving it of its message.

One of the soldiers noticed as they were leaving the table. "I think your friend was sent here to get you to show some respect for the staff." I frowned, and after they'd headed for the exit, I finally took the letter off its claw.

"All right, just be patient. I may have an answer for you." Just then Sally came up and joined me.

"Is that a love letter from your friend?"

"If people would leave me in peace for a few minutes, I would find out."

"Don't let me stand in your way."

"Thanks." I stared at her pointedly, but she didn't get the hint. I opened the envelope and read the brief note. It said, "Same place and time as Romulus and Remus. All love. M."

Sally reached over and snapped up the letter. "What does this mean?"

"That's for me to know, and you not to find out."

She stuck out her tongue at me, got up, and went back to the kitchen.

I took the scrap of parchment that the note was written on and turned it over to write an answer. I simply wrote, "It's a date. XOXOX." I tied the note back on the bird's leg. I could never understand how wizards did that. I struggled several times trying to knot the small leather cord that Minerva had used to tie the note on It was finally secure, and I told the owl to vamoose the ranch. It flew off out the Cafeteria door and on.

The week seemed to drag on and on. I was polishing up my document that I would use for the presentation, but it was dull work. I much preferred to speak off the cuff, but this was one presentation that I needed all my points lined up and ready to go without any "hems" or "haws" as I tried to win over the skeptics in the crowd.

□□

Finally, Saturday arrived. I was up at the crack of dawn. The crack of dawn that time of year in England didn't come until almost 8AM. I stopped in the Cafeteria for some breakfast. Weekends, the food service was pretty rudimentary. Breakfast was cold cereal, cold bagels, cold muffins, and cold milk. The only warm thing was hot water for tea—that came out of the spout of a really hot water faucet—70 degrees C. Lunch was cold cuts, bread, condiments, and whatever else you could scrounge out of the large refrigerators in the kitchen. Supper on Saturday was actually cooked and served by human beings. But again it was simple, and anyone could have prepared it—even I. Sunday night you were strictly on your own.

I like bagels, but I don't like the things they call bagels on Saturday morning at our Cafeteria. I usually had cold cereal and cold milk. I usually had raisin bran. Anyway, I usually took my time over Saturday breakfast. It seemed like a luxury. I usually had the Cafeteria to myself, especially this time of the morning on Saturdays and Sundays. I usually read *The Times* and make a stab at the crossword. I usually get no more than10% or 20% of the boxes filled in, but I like an impossible challenge. I don't feel bad when I don't fill in the last 3 squares or 300 squares.

This morning I didn't fill in 5% of the squares. I was too keyed up to concentrate. It was in one sense the worst of all possible combinations. I had to convince Minerva of something that I wasn't sure that I completely believed in myself. I also was nervous because it was Minerva and not people whom I'd never see again—like the PM or Army officers. And there was, of course, the nervous energy of knowing that I was going to see Minerva at all.

I decided that I'd go to the museum early and get in some casual browsing as though I were an ordinary tourist. So, I left immediately after breakfast.

I arrived at the museum just before opening time and picked a gallery at random. I actually lost track of the time and was almost late after all. I had to run up the last flight of stairs to arrive at the stroke of 1PM outside the ladies WC. The door opened, and . . . a matron walked out. I turned, lowered my head and started to pace.

Then I knew there was someone standing behind me. A gentle hand touched my right arm, and a smile shone on my face. I knew without having to look in a mirror. She was wearing an ankle-length deep purple dress that looked like it might have passed for a robe had she been at Hogwarts. Her hair was up on top of her head as usual, but I couldn't help thinking that it was the most beautiful hair-do that I'd ever seen.

I took her into my arms, and we kissed. During the kiss, Minerva stiffened and broke the kiss. I drew back slightly, and her eyes moved to the left. I turned my head that way and saw Sally.

"Well, what is this?" I asked.

She said, "A co-inkydink." Then, she smiled, looked expectantly at me, and said, "I figured out where and when you were going, and I was hoping that maybe the Weasley brothers might be meeting you."

"The Weasley's. I don't know that anyone exactly looks forward to seeing them. They're not here. But I suppose that I should make introductions." I turned to Minerva and bowed, "I have the honor to present Sally Harker. She is on the staff where I work.

"Sally, this is Minerva McGonagall." I left it at that.

Sally looked, almost stared, at Minerva.

Minerva said, "Go ahead. I've heard everything you're thinking and probably more."

Sally glanced down at her feet and asked, "Well, you do seem a little . . ."

"Old?"

Sally gave a short burst of laughter that was more a sigh of relief. "Yes, you do seem a little old for Wendt."

"Wendt, eh. . ." Minerva looked over at me, and I could see a lengthy discussion coming. "Well, I agree. It's just kind of hard to convince him of that."

I asked Sally, "Well, do you want an explanation—something that will make you understand how I fell in love with an 'older woman'?"

She didn't say anything.

"I don't have one. I don't think anyone has an explanation for their loves. They just happen—like this one." I turned to Minerva, "Do you know when I first began to love you?"

She looked at me with a wry smile on her face. "I know when I knew I loved you. Do you remember when we first took the flu network to Hogwarts from London?"

"That was it?"

I turned to Sally. "Now, Minerva and I have business. Enjoy the museum. I'll see you Monday."

She looked down and turned. Then she took a step. Then she turned quickly and blurted out, "Miss Minerva, do you know the Weasley twins?"

Minerva smiled. "Yes, if you can know those two by having them in class for 7 years? And I sometimes see them now."

"Well, would you say 'hi' to them for me? Uh, . . . and tell George, I enjoyed talking with him."

"Ohhh. Sure. I see them pretty frequently. I'll say 'hi' to them, especially George."

"Thanks. Thanks a lot. I hope you enjoy your day."

We went into the restaurant. We took a table at the edge of the room. We ordered tea and looked at the menu.

I slipped my loafer off my left foot and ran it up her leg. She looked up, slapped her menu down on the table, and looked at me with a grim smile on her face. I had the feeling that if I'd been one of her students, I'd have had a wand slapped across my knuckles. But she didn't. Nor did she move her leg.

Finally, she asked, "What's this 'date' about other than shenanigans?"

I looked her directly in the eyes. This had to be good because I was trying to convince myself as much as I was trying to convince her. "I had this idea."

"I know about your ideas."

"This is different. I want to recruit a wizard army. I guess sort of like Dumbledore's army, but adults and trained full time."

"How are you going to do this recruiting?"

"There must be lots of wizards who aren't happy with the way things are—maybe even being persecuted?"

"Not just persecuted, but. . ." She hesitated and then said, "I suppose that you don't know. They started sending Muggle-born and half-Muggle-born to Azkaban. There are lots more that are just waiting to be sent for to be tried. Even some pure-blood are being summoned. There are stories about people wandering alone, hunted."

"Is there any way to get in touch with them? My idea is to send them to a military base where they'd be trained, drilled, and formed into the army."

101

She asked, "Where would this base be? I can't imagine anywhere in England that you could keep anything like that from, well, from 'You Know Who'."

"It wouldn't be in England."

"In Europe?"

"No."

She smiled for the first time. "I hope you're not going to tell me that you've got a spot in Antarctica."

"Definitely not Antarctica, and don't ask me any more. I'm not telling anyone who doesn't absolutely have to know, and you don't absolutely have to know."

In a soft voice she said, "That's what you think."

"What I need is a way to get in touch with all those people who might be interested in this army. But more important, and I suppose this is impossible, 'You Know Who' can't find out about it. Oh, yes. One other little matter—I need a leader for this army. Someone who can train or recruit trainers. Do you have any ideas?"

She looked at me speculatively. "What do you think about two leaders?"

"Who do you have in mind?"

"Well. Don't jump to conclusions and hear me out."

"Sure. You know that I'm not a precipitate man."

"We'll see." She looked at me long again. "How about the Weasley twins?"

I silently started counting. When I reached 6, I said, "Are you serious? I know they're good at business, and great good fun at parties—if you consider sneaking 'Fainting Fancies' into the punch good fun. But somehow I just don't consider them in the same class as General Swartzkopf."

"Who?"

"Don't you ever read the papers?"

"You mean the *Daily Prophet*?"

"No, I mean real papers like *The Times*. Oh, never mind. Surely there're some better people around. What about Kingsley Shaklebolt?"

"He's guarding the Muggle Prime Minister."

"Oh. What about Lupin?"

"He's doing undercover work with the werewolves."

"What about," I had saved my best hope for last, "'Mad-Eye'?"

Her face fell. I knew there must be something awfully wrong. "What about 'Mad-Eye'?" I said with some 'edge' in my voice.

A tear rolled down her right cheek. She gasped. It was the kind of gasp that people do when they're trying to control their emotions so that they won't break down and sob. Her voice was shaky. "He. He." She stopped again, her face turned more determined, and she said simply, "He was helping Harry escape from the Dursley house. 'You know . . .'" She seemed on the edge of losing control but continued, "Who'".

I broke in and offered, "Tom Riddle"

"Yesss. Tom Riddle killed him. We never found the body. He'd fallen from a broom at pretty high altitude."

"Shit. All right, I know when I'm beaten. You wouldn't have offered them if they weren't the best available. They're not so bad, I guess. Awful in class. I could never get them to see the virtues of Shakespeare, but I guess that's not something to hold against them. Would you get in touch with them for me? How soon do you think that they could start? I suppose they're up to their eyes in work keeping their business going."

"Actually, they lost their business. They were part of the team that sprung Harry from the Dursley's. They've been 'undesirables' ever since. Their business was seized."

"Oh, I'd like to have seen that happen. I'll bet that whoever came to take over the business had a rude awakening."

Minerva smiled, "I don't know, but I've heard that they had to close down the block they were on for a week getting the fumes cleared out of the shop."

I smiled too.

"I'll get in touch with them and arrange a meeting. It'll probably be sometime next week. They're not doing anything at the moment besides hiding out, but it's not that easy to get messages to them."

"That's OK. It'll probably take me at least a week to get approval to go ahead with this idea of mine. And, of course, I might not get approval at all."

Minerva turned her head a little to one side and looked at me out of the corners of her eyes. "Have you got any more business?" I almost jumped as I felt something on my right foot and realized that it was a stocking-clad foot.

"I definitely don't have any more business."

Blackhawk

The phone rang on a typical dismal November day in London. I was trying to think of a way to crack open the problem of how to go on the offensive. When you can't even find your enemies, how do you attack them? It was just one interruption too many. I was ready to bite his head off, regardless who it was. "Yes, Wendt here."

I recognized the voice right away. It was the Boy Genius. Now, what was his name Braught or Braum or, "It's Brahms. Come on down to the 'pit'. I've got something that might interest you."

"I certainly hope so."

"Oh, you'll find this interesting."

"So, what is it?"

"Just come down and see."

Well, getting up and moving would take my mind off my troubles, wouldn't it? I got up and decided to trot down to the 'pit'—the seeming maze of computers and monitors and cables that should have been buried in the floor. This was nothing like everyone's image of a computer room —bright, spotless, white walls and floors, rectangular ceiling high boxes. It was a mess with cables everywhere. At the center was a semicircle of monitors—floor to head height stacked on top of each other. The only unobscured lines of sight were between the monitors and a couple of tables with computers on and under the tables. As I entered this 'pit' there were a couple of techs seated before the computers talking to Brahms who was standing behind them. He was short, had a short beard, and wore wire-rimmed glasses. He was scratching his left ear with his right hand. Usually a sign that he was deep in thought. As I came into sight and then got close, he looked up and smiled—uncharacteristic. He rarely smiled these days. This time he was smiling broadly.

"Good. Come here. I want you to see something." He looked down and said to one of the techs, "Fred, cue that video up to the beginning."

I walked around to the other side of the table where I could see the monitor that he was watching intently. He smiled at me again; he was almost chuckling. This must be good.

"Take a look at this video."

The video was frozen, and Fred started it rolling. I looked at the monitor and saw something that would have startled most people, but I'd seen it so many times that I was pretty blasé. One instant I was staring at a scene with two people standing in front of a large gate. Then, suddenly, there was a third figure. He turned around slowly, apparently scanning the surroundings. As his face became visible, I started as if I'd never seen a man materialize out of nothing.

Brahms picked up on it right away. "What did you just see?"

I was momentarily frozen as I watched the figure briefly looking almost directly at the camera and continue his scan around 360 degrees. His face disappeared. He walked up to the gate, which distorted as though it were seen in a "funhouse" mirror, and an opening appeared in it. He walked through and disappeared from view as the gate undistorted.

I said, "Shit."

Brahms asked, "Who was that?"

"Play it again." They did so. When the face was pointed almost directly at us, I said, "Pause it." They did. I stared at that face for two or three minutes. I don't know how long.

"Well?"

"I think that might have been Tom Riddle. I've only seen him once before and that under poor lighting, but I've heard descriptions. Are the eyes red? I can't quite tell."

Brahms said, "Give us a close-up of the face."

The face expanded till it almost filled the screen. It was a little blurry, but it was still quite easy to see. The eyes were slightly shaded. "Can you increase contrast or brightness or something? I want to see the eyes clearly."

Fred was fiddling with the mouse, and the scene got brighter. There was definitely some red in the eyes, though I couldn't be sure if the pupils were actually red or just blood-shot. But there was one unmistakable thing. "I've heard that his pupils are vertical slits, but somehow I just didn't believe it. I thought that it was just a way of saying that he was snake-like. Yes, it's got to be Riddle."

"Bango! I told you, you wouldn't regret this investment."

"Where is this?"

"The camera?"

"Yes, the camera."

"It's outside the Malfoy residence."

"It's got to be him."

"Is he still there?"

"As far as we know."

"He hasn't been seen since that video was taken."

I frowned. "Where's your phone?"

Brahms pointed to the adjacent table. I finally saw that it was surrounded by piles of sysout listings. I picked up the receiver. I dialed an extension that I knew by heart. Parker answered the phone, "Yes."

"Wendt. We've got HIM."

"You don't mean... Oh what's his name Tom... Tom... uh."

"Yes, Riddle. He's at the Malfoys'. Perhaps even still there."

"Yeh. We've got a unit up near there. They set up the Malfoy cameras a few days ago, and are working on a few other Deatheaters in that general area. Hummmm." He paused and asked, "If we could kill him, would you advise it."

"Forget it; you'd only make things worse if you tried.

"Would you like to go up and see it? Maybe you could eyeball him in person."

I thought long and hard. "Yes. Yes. I suppose so." I didn't really want to, but I guessed that I had to.

"Good. Go down to the exercise yard, I'll have a helicopter there shortly."

"Yes, sir."

I walked slowly down toward the exercise yard. I wondered what would happen if I saw him. Would I be scared shitless? The last time I'd seen him I hadn't been, but then I was really trying to kill him, and I supposed, myself.

I reached the exercise yard, and I decided it would be better to exercise than not, so I set off at a jog around the yard. In about ten minutes I heard a helicopter. In less than a minute, it appeared above the opening to the sky. It came down quickly. It was very thin and long. I wondered if there were room in it for more than two abreast.

There was a pilot and co-pilot. The pilot got out and opened the rear door for me. He shouted over the noise of the idling helicopter, "Get in and put on a pair of headphones. It's an intercom. You can talk then."

I got in. The pilot shut the door behind me, and I saw the headphones. I put one pair on, and after a few seconds the pilot spoke. "We're going to fly directly up to this Malfoy's. I've got the coordinates. Have you ever flown in a Blackhawk before?"

"No." I wondered how many people had ever flown in a Blackhawk.

"You're in for a treat." After a couple of seconds pause, "Do you like roller coasters?"

I wasn't so sure that this flight was going to be a "treat". "Usually."

"Good, we like to stay close to the ground. It cuts down the probability of being seen."

"Good." I had a sinking feeling in the pit of my stomach.

We rose quickly to what must have been a couple of thousand feet. We were well above the London skyline. We headed roughly North, perhaps a little East of North. The first part of the flight was pretty easy. We were high and making pretty good time. We passed the last suburbs and were over pretty open country, but stayed at altitude. Then, suddenly, without warning, the bottom seemed to drop out of the helicopter. We seemed to be in freefall. I must have made a sound because the pilot came on the intercom. "You OK back there."

"Yeh. You just caught me by surprise." We were still dropping pretty fast. "Are you planning on landing?" I asked feebly.

"No... Oh, yea, I guess it is a little startling when I drop like that. I'll try to warn you in advance if I do that again."

"Thanks." The helicopter was still dropping precipitously. I wondered if the pilot had gone crazy or fainted or something, but finally we leveled off just above ground level. The pilot gave a little whoop.

I asked, "Just how high are we off the ground?"

"Oh, normal cruising altitude—about 25 meters."

"OOO...KKKay. Just for curiosity's sake, how fast are we going?"

"Oh, maybe 140."

"140 klicks?"

"No, 140 mph."

"Great."

We were bouncing up and down with the ground contour. I kept telling myself, "Look in the distance. Look in the distance. Don't look down." But it's hard not to look down when you swoop over a hill and suddenly drop off the edge. They say the flight lasted a little over 2 hours, but it seemed to me to be about 2 days.

After a while I was able to look down as we swooped over the countryside, passing whole farms in a matter of seconds.

Toward the end of that endless flight the pilot came on the intercom and said, "You want to see the Malfoy estate?"

"Yes, sure." I was really happy because it must mean that we were close to the end of the flight.

"In about a minute we're going to be there. I'm going to fly by it to the East. Be looking out the port door. I'll give you the word when we're there."

We didn't slow down at all. We were coming up a wooded hillside, and the pilot said an elongated, "Now" with final emphasis. At the same time I had about a 2 second view of a mansion surrounded by high iron fence in a clearing in the woods near the crest of the hill. Then it was gone. We kept going straight for about a minute, and then the pilot turned the Blackhawk in a tight curve decelerating as he did. There was a clearing ahead, and we slowed enough to make a graceful landing. I had forgotten that I was buckled in and tried to rise. I unbuckled, and the door was open. There was a HumV and several men in camouflage standing near it. They came over to the helicopter as soon as the rotors slowed. The lieutenant in charge came up and saluted. I fumbled a salute wondering why I warranted a salute.

□

A young man and his father were standing in the yard of their estate. The young man looked up suddenly. The father noticed his son look up, and he asked, "Draco, what is it?"

"I don't know. I thought I saw something flash just above the trees, but I saw it out of the corner of my eye, and by the time I looked up, it was gone."

The older man looked up and said, "I don't know. Perhaps."

□□

"Sir, we were expecting you. I understand you want to see the Malfoy place." It was a statement.

"Yes, Lieutenant Stevens." I read the name on his uniform. How do we get there?

"Sargeant."

"Yes, sir." A tall dark-skinned man approached.

"Please take Mr. Wendt to the observation post."

"Yes, sir. Come with me." He was carrying a camouflage flack jacket. "Here, put this on. We don't want to be noticed."

He walked off toward the Hum,V and I trotted to catch up.

108

He turned and said. "We are trying very hard to keep our presence unknown. Please observe total silence and follow me as closely as you can."

"Yes, sir."

He looked me up and down. I was wearing kahki pants, sneakers, and a wool pullover over a long-sleeved shirt and now, the flack jacket. "It's good that you're wearing athletic shoes. I'll try to take an easy path though."

We walked up a hillside that quickly turned to woods. It seemed like we were going by no discernible path, but somehow there wasn't much brush in our way. We struggled up one hill and down another. Then we repeated that. I was breathing a little hard and started to ask for a break. As I opened my mouth, he turned and looked at me as though I'd committed an unpardonable sin. The question that I had died on my lips, and we continued in silence. After about an hour, he slowed and turned to me. He approached slowly and bent a little so that he could whisper in my ear. "We're going to come to the top of this hill, and when we do, I'll bend down. Do the same, and we'll go to hands and knees to enter the observation post. When we get there, we can talk a little." I nodded. He turned and started off again. We were about 5 minutes reaching the point where he went to his knees. I followed him. Suddenly we were in a small clearing with some electronic equipment behind a tree and a slight rise with a sniper rifle pointed toward… the mansion about a kilometer away on a hill opposite us.

He sat beside the rifle and motioned me to join him. "You can talk if you keep your voice down." He whispered.

"Is this as close as we get?"

"It's as close as you get."

"Have you been closer?"

"Yes, but the going gets really tough from here on."

I looked down the hill. It didn't look much worse than what we'd just spent an hour climbing through.

He saw the query in my eyes and said, "It's not the terrain. It's…" He paused. "I'm not sure what it is, but it just gets hard to keep going. You keep thinking that you've got something else to do, but of course, you don't."

I nodded. "Yes, it's a 'charm' to ward off Muggles. But it doesn't work with you?"

"It's hard, but I can get quite close."

He smiled and said, "Why don't you look through the sniper scope. It's quite good. You can get a real close-up view without fighting off the 'charm'."

I smiled and went prone so that I could pick up the gun and aim it at the mansion. I looked through the 'scope and swung it around trying to find the mansion. It was quite a powerful 'scope, so when I finally found the mansion in it, I could only see a little of it at a time. I had to steady the gun with one hand on the barrel and the other grasping the gun at the trigger. When I got the hang of it, I slowly started scanning the mansion up and down. I couldn't see anyone on the grounds. The windows were mostly dark although there were a couple that were lit, and I could even see a few details of furniture in them. I was slowly scanning on the top floor and had just passed one window when I noticed a bit of movement in the window that I'd just passed. I swung the scope back a bit, and my finger convulsively squeezed the trigger. It happened even before I realized what I was doing, or that I was seeing a person. I then realized what...who I had seen. At the same instant, the gun was snatched from my fingers, and the sergeant made a violent hand sign down the hill that we had come up. He started off. I couldn't believe that he was moving as fast as he was over that uneven terrain. I stumbled after him as quickly as I could. He was obviously moving just fast enough that I could barely keep up with him. This went on for 40 to 45 minutes. Then after topping a hill and starting down the other side, he swung around on me, grabbed me by the shoulder, and forced me to look directly into his face.

"What kind of bloody bone-headed trick was that you played up there?"

I'd been thinking about what had happened when I'd instinctively squeezed the trigger. "You mean that twitch on the trigger?"

"Twitch. You moron, if we'd had a live round in the barrel, you'd have blown everything for us." I'd never seen such a composed face deliver such a stinging blow so calmly.

I took a deep breath. "First place—it was instinct. It happened before I realized what was happening."

"What the hell could you have seen through that scope that would cause you to want to pull the trigger instinctively?"

It hadn't taken me long to reconstruct the view that I'd glimpsed. "I saw someone who murdered one of my students." I paused. "Back when I was teaching."

"Murdered him," I thought. The phrase doesn't really apply to that. I said, "He was just an innocent bystander. He was at the wrong place at the wrong time. He was in a school competition, and then he was in a grave yard. It turned out to be his grave yard. He was one of my best students. He was one of the few that didn't think that a Muggle teacher was an oxymoron. He was brilliant, hard working, a good kid. He was a brilliant chess player—maybe world champion class some day. It's so unjust that I almost wish there had been a round in that gun."

"Who did that? Did you see him in one of the windows?"

"Yes. His name is Peter Petigrew. He's a coward who kills people because he's afraid. He's afraid of Riddle; he's afraid of ordinary wizards. Heck, he was probably afraid of me."

"I see." He turned and went on. I thought about it. These incidents teach you things about yourself. Like that you could be a killer. It just required the right inducement. I think if I'd known that I would see him in that window and that I'd be holding a rifle with a sniper scope in my hands with his head in the cross-hairs, I'd have made sure that there was a bullet in the chamber and the safety was off and my finger was on the trigger. It's a funny world, and I don't mean that there are lots of good honest laughs in it.

He looked at me for a minute. "OK. Let's go. Unless you want to see more."

"No, I think I've seen all that I can stand." I suppose that the trip back was as fast and stomach turning, but I spent a lot of time thinking about the person I'd seen at Castle Malfoy. I thought about the inevitable end— the inevitable point when guns and wands would be pointed, and I'd have to decide if I could really squeeze the trigger. Despite what had happened this day I wasn't so sure about pulling the trigger if it were a stranger in the cross-hairs. I wished that I could see Minerva. Minerva. Why didn't I have a nickname for her? Somehow Minee or Nerva or whatever just didn't catch her. She was far too grand and elegant for a nickname like that. Of course, she could be earthy too. But that part of her needed no nickname.

We landed at headquarters, and I took leave of the Blackhawk crew. I would try to remember to avoid Blackhawks in the future. It was close enough to dinner time that I headed for the Cafeteria. Maybe I could get something to eat a little early. I walked up the concrete steps to the Cafeteria. When I got there, I hoped that Sally wouldn't be too mad if I just popped in a little early at the Cafeteria rather than go back to the office.

I went into the kitchen. I saw the cook working over a pot and Sally chopping some veggies. I walked over and asked, "Sally. It's so close to dinner that I thought I might just sneak a little taste—an indicator of whether I should waste my time here or go out to grab fish and chips at the corner pub. But what are you doing here?"

"I like to do manual labor in the kitchen every now and then to keep my hand in."

"And, you don't have to have a taste to tell that. My kitchen is always better than the corner pub." She leaned over the work table and looked up into my face.

"I wouldn't dare argue that, but don't you have any mercy for a man who's not had a bite to east since breakfast."

She shook her head and said, "I have no mercy for someone who works through lunch when he could have it with me in my kitchen."

"You are unjust. At lunch time I was bobbing over the countryside at 250 and couldn't have held down a bite of chocolate."

"How did you happen to be flying over the countryside at 250 km/hr? Do you think really that you can take advantage of a simple girl with stories like that?"

"Oh, really! Simple girl! Take advantage! It's the truth. I was in a Blackhawk helicopter with a madman in the pilot's seat. He insisted on being able to put his foot out and touch the ground while he flew."

"Really, what happened? You were in the Video Room with that programmer. What do you call him, the mad scientist?"

"Boy genius."

"Well, we started there, and I ended up in the North country by lunch time. Then we slogged over miles of wooded hillsides and . . . and I saw someone I hated more than. . . " My mind's eye reviewed that scene again, trying to get the image of that rat face clearly in my memory in case I saw it again. "Well, that I hate a lot. Then we did more slogging, and I flew back. Now I'm starved."

"Well, there's nothing to sample. Just go up to your desk and come back at the real dinner time, and I'll give you a real treat... I'll join you for dinner."

"Yes, a real treat. There isn't something little that I could have before."

"Oh, I wish! But you'll just have to wait like everyone else."

"Thanks." I tried to put as much sarcasm as possible in my voice, but I'm not good at that sort of thing.

I trudged on up to my desk. There was a note on it. It was from Parker. He wanted to see me immediately. I detoured to Parker's office. His secretary had left for the day. I knocked on the door and entered without being asked. "What can I do for you?"

"I talked with a Sergeant Stevens. I hoped that you would give me your side of the story.

I knew that I was in for a long session.

□
□□

After that dressing down, I trudged up to the Cafeteria. Surely by now, it'd be open. There were a couple of people who had worked through the lines. There was no one in line. Since it was a Friday, I wasn't really surprised. I had the eggplant surprise. I found a table by myself and sat.

Sally carried a tray and joined me. "Have you tried the eggplant surprise yet?"

"No, I'm hoping the surprise will be that there's no eggplant in it."

"You are crazy. I couldn't call it eggplant surprise if it didn't have eggplant."

"Sure you could. It'd be a pleasant surprise."

"You try that and tell me that you don't want any eggplant in it."

I took a bite hesitantly and then another more enthusiastically. "Yes. This is not half-bad. As a matter of fact, it's more than half good."

"I told you." She crowed. "What did you mean earlier about seeing someone you hate?"

"I said that I saw someone that I hate, and that's exactly what I meant. I saw a man that I hate."

"That's hard for me to believe. You hate anyone?"

"Oh, you think that I've never met a man I didn't like?"

"I don't know about that. But I know that you couldn't 'hate' a fly."

"You think not? If you'd seen your best student after he'd been killed dead without warning and no way to get revenge, you might understand about hating.

"And, let me tell you something else." I was warming to my topic. "There's a woman that I met once. I would like to get my hands on her so that I could tear each limb from her body. She doesn't kill. She tortures people to insanity.

"If I could, I'd send them both to the worms. He killed a young man— not much more than a boy of seventeen. He did it without the slightest hesitation. I knew that boy. I'd taught him at Hogwarts. He was as fine a man as I knew there. I taught him Shakespeare. He was smart and talented. All that is gone now. Never to be recovered. Yes, what I feel about the man I saw today goes way beyond hate."

"Wow, I've never heard you talk this way. What subject did you teach your student?"

"English Lit. He was in a school production of *The Tempest*. He played Caliban. Never a case of casting against type more than that one. In a way, it's why I'm in this. I used not to believe in violence. And here I am at Spook Central for Violence."

"Oh, it's surely not that bad. Nobody here is bad."

"Sally, what have you been smoking? Tarkin kidnaps people. Bogart. Well, I used to hate what he does. Now, sometimes, I just wish we could interrogate a few of the people we're up against. And I hate that in me."

"You've had a hard day, haven't you?"

"Yes. I saw someone that I would have killed—could have killed if there'd been a bullet in the long rifle I had in my hands."

"I'm sure he deserved it."

"Oh, he really deserved it."

We worked on our eggplant for a while in silence. Then she said, "You know, I really don't know much about how you got into this."

"Boy, I don't know where to begin. I was a teacher looking for a job, and I answered an ad that looked innocuous but led me to the ultimate Crackerbox Palace. It is a school where they train people to use magic."

"I'm probably one of only a very few non-magicals who knows details about them. That makes me the most important Muggle in the world right now. I've also become the trigger for every counter attack that we've got. I think I could probably call up a nuclear strike and the PM would say 'OK'."

"You're not kidding are you?"

"No. It does make me sick sometimes."

She looked around and then put her hand on my forearm. "How do you keep from going crazy?"

I answered, "Are you sure that I'm not."

She squeezed and said, "Would you like to go to see a movie tonight?"

I squeezed out a little laugh, "Are you feeling sorry for me?"

"The last thing in the world that I would feel for you is pity. I think you can handle all this bloody shit."

"Really."

"Sure."

"I'll tell you what. Let's find a Starbucks, and I'll buy you a cup of coffee."

"Tea."

"Fine. Tea."

"I've got to clean up here, and get things buttoned down for the weekend. Give me an hour."

"You can have all the time in the world if you need it."

"Oh, an hour will be just fine."

I finished my eggplant and then took a walk through the largely empty complex. There were always people in the Monitor Area watching all the video displays. There were a few guards walking around in their random watches of the night. The old warehouse was way too clean to be a real warehouse. There were no oil stains on the floor, no odds and ends of packing material in the odd corners, no dark corners, come to think of it. It was already pitch dark outside and the stark contrast with the interior was spooky. After wandering around for a while, I returned to the Cafeteria and found Sally leaning against the door. "Well, you sure took your time."

"You said an hour." I glanced at my wrist and saw that I had been gone about an hour and ten. "OK. So, I lost track of time. I'm sorry. As a matter of fact, I'm really sorry. You are someone who should never be stood up."

"Bloody right."

"That's enough swearing. Let's go. I've got a particular Starbucks in mind." She reached out her hand, and I found myself taking it. It was at that moment that I realized that I was getting into something more than just a cup of coffee. "Shit." I thought.

I decided that I would try to keep this light—a nice light meaningless evening. After all, we were just going for coffee. Sally was talking about how to get there—"Tube", bus, or splurging on a taxi. "What do you think?"

I was knocked out of my reverie. "Oh, I guess whatever takes the longest time."

"What? Are you serious?"

"Yes, sure. It will give us time to talk. Frankly, talking would be better than thinking."

"Oh, yeh. Your little adventure today. Hey, if you don't mind talking about it, tell me more about magic. Flitting around with the Rover Boys shows me that it's real, but I don't understand it."

"No, I don't mind. Though, if I tell you, they'll never let you leave the building."

"Sure, they will, I'll just start screwing up lunch, and they'll throw me out so fast, your head will spin."

"OK, what do you want to know?"

"Everything. How you got mixed up in this, what magicians look like, everything."

"Sure. It's a long story."

"That's why we're taking the 'Tube'".

"OK."

We walked down the street and approached the closest Tube station. "I hope that you won't hold my story against me."

"Oh, I don't see how it could be any crazier than what you told me this afternoon."

"Good. Well, I'll take the long boring stretches out. I came here from the States. I bummed around a while working for Starbucks, and then I decided to try to get a job working as a teacher—English Lit.

"I found... Well, it would be better to say that I was found by the Headmaster of a school for wizards and witches. Oh, yeh. They don't like being called 'magicians'. The word implies that the 'magician' is an illusionist—it's not real. They call themselves by words that imply that magic is real—and, believe me, it is."

"Where is it located?"

"That's a good question. I wish I could answer it. The school is what they call 'unplot-able'. You get the idea?"

"You can't put its location on a map."

"Bingo. It's somewhere in far north Scotland."

"Pretty wild country."

"Oh, you can't begin to guess. There's a forest next door that contains giants, unicorns, centaurs, festrals..."

She interrupted, "What?!"

"Festrals. I've never heard of them anywhere else. They are... Oh hell, I can't begin to describe them. They're sort of like unicorns that are carnivorous and can fly."

"You're right. This is a whole lot crazier than what you were talking about this afternoon."

"You want to stop while you're behind?"

"No. I'll take a chance on a little more. How do they dress?"

We were waiting for the next train that was just coming down the tunnel.

"OK. Let's see. They wear robes, you know, like Oxford Dons are supposed to dress. They wear pointed hats."

"You've got to be kidding me."

"No. When I was at school, I wore the uniform. Except, I never wore the pointy hat. It reminded me too much of my days at school."

"What??"

"You know, the dunce cap. I..."

She chortled, causing a couple of old ladies waiting with us a few feet away to stare at us.

"Anyway. So you taught at a school for witches."

"And wizards.'

116

"OK. And wizards. What did you teach? How did you get the job?"

"I taught English Literature."

She laughed, "At a magic school! You're kidding."

"I think that I told you that you wouldn't believe me at some point."

"OK. OK. I promise not to heckle. But it does seem a strange subject for that kind of school."

"Now, you are wrong there. As a matter of fact, I'd say that English Literature is a subject that is right for every school."

"It's good for technical schools?"

"Yes.'

"And college prep school?

"Obviously."

"For people majoring in Physics or Chemistry."

"Undoubtedly."

"For people majoring in Dental Hygiene."

"Probably more important than for the physicists."

"OK. Convince me."

We had boarded the train, and just at that point, we were coming to a stop on the line. I said, "We've got to get out. Let's go."

"But why? This isn't our. . ." She had suddenly stopped speaking, "Oh, shoot. We've gone past our stop." She got up, and we got out of the car, went over the flyover and got ready for the next train going the other direction. Fortunately, one came along in a couple of minutes. We boarded and resumed our conversation.

"This time, you don't start talking again until we've gotten off at our stop." She said. She steadfastly refused to listen until we'd reached our stop. We got off and found the Starbucks. It was in a mall with a sort of food court where you could buy food from several places and eat it in a common area. We got coffee, and she led me to a patisserie where she recommended the almond croissants. We ordered a couple and found a table for two. Then she finally said, "Go ahead, you were saying."

"You're lucky that I have a memory like an elephant."

"You mean fat and gray?"

I ignored the comment and went on, "Well, first, I think that every school should be concerned with two things. Students should be able to communicate well. That's true whether you're a dental hygienist or a computer programmer. Second, every student should be challenged to develop an idea of what living a good life is."

"What do you mean 'a good life'?"

"There you are." I said and gestured broadly around.

"What do you mean, 'There you are'? Where am I?" She was obviously getting a little miffed at my obscure approach.

"I mean." I hesitated to think my way through the explanation. "The fact that you want my answer to that question shows that the answer isn't obvious or, at least, shouldn't be. One of the two main objectives of education should be to give students the intellectual tools they need to figure out their own answer to that question—not somebody else's, even somebody as canny as Socrates."

"OK." She said, "Just how does English Literature do that?"

"Let me give you an example. Do you know the American novel, *Huckleberry Finn*?"

"Oh, it sounds familiar. Written by Mark Twain?"

"Right."

"I think I read it in 2nd or 3rd form, but that's been a long time ago. I don't really remember much about it other than that it happens somewhere in the American West."

"There, you see. You should have read it in 6th or maybe 7th form. You were too young to really benefit from it."

"Oh, I remember, it was very funny. Two boys getting into all sorts of crazy adventures."

"I rest my case."

"What do you mean, you rest your case? I haven't heard a case. All I've heard is a criticism of British education."

"My point is that you need to be older to be able to understand the real questions about life that Twain poses in this story."

"OK. So, how do you teach it?"

I stopped for a minute to think about how to condense a week of study of that novel at the 7th form into ten or fifteen minutes. Then, I began.

"First let me remind you of the story. The main characters are . . ." Here Sally interrupted. She had been warming to the topic as she tried to remember details.

"There are two boys. One is Huckleberry Finn."

"Bravo!!" I applauded.

"Oh, shove it. The other was Tim. No. No. Just give me a sec. " She closed her eyes, actually squeezed them tight. "I've got it. Tom." She announced triumphantly.

"Right. There was a third main character, Jim."

'I suppose he was the leader. Although I can't remember a character like that."

"You're right, there wasn't.

"Tom was the child of a respectable middle class family. The story's set shortly before the American Civil War. Huckleberry is the son of an alcoholic ne'er-do-well who beats him regularly and barely keeps the dysfunctional family in shelter with food.

"The two go on an adventure on the great Mississippi river along with an escaped slave, Jim."

"I didn't remember that Jim was a slave."

"Oh, yes. It's very important. Jim is one of the challenges to Southern middle class assumptions about the world and how it works that happen in this story. One of the first things that happens is that there is a debate about the morality of taking Jim along and thereby abetting a very serious crime—theft of property. The property is Jim."

Sally nodded wisely, "Oh, yea, the Civil War was about the abolition of slavery in the US. We had abolished it about 30 years earlier. You colonials were always behind on things."

"The war was really about a different question—whether the national government could impose the morality of the majority of the country on the individual states. It was just that slavery was the main moral issue that happened to be at hand at that moment.

"Regardless, the point is that this book is a model for how young people can begin to figure out for themselves what makes a life good. Tom and Huck do it by going on an adventure on the Great River. Not everybody can do that. But, at least, when they're off on their own Great Adventure, they can have thought about what figuring out what the 'good' means and how to do it. *Huckleberry Finn* gives the reader lots of examples of Tom and Huck being faced with various moral dilemmas about the world and muddling through to answers."

"What about communication skills?"

"Well, Twain gives examples of good writing—learn by example is a very good way to learn. But he also gives negative examples of how communication fails. When I first read *Huck*, I almost gave up after the first couple of chapters. Huckleberry was speaking a southern slang that I almost gave up hope of understanding. After a couple of chapters Huck is speaking nearly standard American English most of the time. The point is that the value of good, clear communication is very apparent."

She took on that 1000 meter stare for a moment and said, "Yes, I see your argument. Hmmmm." She looked down and realized that she had a cup of coffee in front of her. She took a sip and made a face. "Now I've gone and let this get cold. And it's all your fault!"

"Mea culpa! Mea maxima culpa!" I took a sip of my tea and found it cool as well. "Well, there's probably a microwave around here someplace."

She made another face and said, "Don't be gross! Let's get another and throw this bloody mess out."

We did and this time paid attention to our drinks. Finally, we decided that we couldn't hang around any longer and since we were close to her flat, we walked there. When we arrived, she got out her keys and hesitated. She said, "Would you like to come up for a cup of tea or something?"

"Not a third cup of tea."

"Really only the 2nd."

"No. I've got so many reasons that I can't. Not the least of which is that we both work together."

"Come on! It's not like I work for you or" she added for emphasis, "you work for me."

"Oh, bloody hell. I'm in a relationship that I want to keep going."

She stared for a second and said, "I see. Well, someday, if that relationship doesn't go anywhere, there MIGHT be an alternative available. Remember the words 'might be'."

"I could hardly forget it. I have daily reminders." I smiled, and she leant up, so I kissed her good night.

On the way home, I thought to myself, "Well, here's another fine mess that you got yourself into."

Downing Street

I was standing in front of a mirror pacing and practicing the finer points of my rehearsed speech. I suppose that I'd never be satisfied with it, and really, I didn't have any time left. Parker would walk in the door of my office any minute now and announce that we were off to Downing street. That moment came, and from then on time seemed to really fly. There were three cars outside the warehouse. We got in the center one. It was a HumVee. The one in front was a normal car or at least looked like a normal car, as the one behind us did. The driver was military, though I hadn't seen him around the warehouse. There was another military type, though he wasn't in uniform beside him. He seemed to be carrying a short-barreled automatic rifle of some sort. Neither of them looked very friendly.

Parker and I were the only people in the back. We pulled away from the curb, and I idly looked around. I heard a helicopter that seemed really close. I asked Parker, "One of ours?" I looked up suggestively toward the roof of the HumVee.

"Of course."

"Isn't it a little obvious?"

"I don't care."

We spent the rest of the trip in silence. The front and rear cars veered away as we entered Downing street, which like most streets in London is really short. There was just enough room for our HumVee. There were several guards in the street. Our chauffeur waited with the car. We were led into a small sitting room. After several minutes, three men entered the room. I recognized one, the PM. One wore a uniform that I didn't recognize. The 3rd seemed vaguely familiar to me, but I couldn't place the connection. He was tall, black, and seemed to be the most self-possessed of the three. He didn't sit but stood behind the PM. The rest of us sat.

Parker began. "I've brought Mr. Wendt to see you. He's the contractor that has proposed talking the Americans into letting us use a military base to train an elite anti-terrorist unit."

The PM was not smiling. "Let's cut to the quick here. I know about 'magic'. I know that there are 'bad' wizards and that they are making mince-meat of this country. There's a bloody wizard standing behind me —here to protect me from them.

"We can't even protect the highest office in the land from these bastards." He turned his gaze on me. "Just how do you propose to do something about this bloody situation?"

It's a good thing that I'd had some practice with Minerva, who is only a little more intimidating than the PM when she wants to be. I held his gaze steadily with some effort. "We have to use the methods of the wizards to combat them. There are lots of disaffected wizards, who'd like nothing better than to stick it to Tom Riddle. I just want to collect as many as I can of them, offer them and their families sanctuary, and organize them into a fighting unit that can turn the tide in this war."

The PM smiled. It was a wan smile, but a smile anyway. "Riddle, eh. I've never heard a name before—just 'He Who Must Not Be Named' or, even better, 'You Know Who'. Kingsley, why haven't you or someone of your people told me his name?"

Kingsley smiled, seeming relaxed. If he was relaxed, he was the only one in the room who was. "You never asked."

The PM snorted. He turned to the uniformed man. "How's our relations with the Americans? Even more important, their military? Can we get them to turn a base over to us without much of an explanation?"

The unidentified general looked the PM square in the eyes. "Pretty good. They owe us for the cover we've given them in some of their Middle East adventures. This is a pretty big favor—asking for a foreign military base on the American mainland. If we can convince them of the importance, I think that we can pull it. It would be good if we could give them a plausible reason." He turned to me, "Can you convince them that there really are wizards, witches, all that. I'm not entirely sure that I believe it—even though I've seen a lot of strange things."

This was a question that I could handle with confidence. I'd done this already with a couple of pretty skeptical people. "I have a couple of friends—wizards—whom I'd like to take along. I think that they could convince anyone. Probably scare them stiff as well, if that would do any good."

The PM glanced between Parker and me. He was silent for at least two solid minutes. No one said anything. If you don't think two minutes can seem like an eternity, you should try sitting in a small room with 4 other people, not say anything for two minutes and see if it doesn't seem like an eternity. Finally, the PM got up and said to no one in particular, "We'll be in touch."

We all had risen. He and the other two left the room, and presently an escort took us to the front entrance and our HumVee. After we'd gotten in I asked, "OK. What happened? Good? Bad? Indifferent?"

He answered, "I don't know. That's the only time that I've ever been in the same room with the PM. I have no idea what he's like in private or whether that was a good interview or not."

We drove back to the warehouse, and we didn't hear anything for the rest of the day. At the evening meal, Sally sat down with me after I'd started eating. "Heard anything from the Weasley's?"

"No. Although I'm supposed to shortly. Would you like to come along when I do?"

"You bet. I was afraid you wouldn't ask. By the way speaking of asking, I've got a question."

"Go ahead."

"Just how did you and Miss Minerva get hooked up?"

"Just call her Minerva. I think that we're all on first name basis now.

"Anyway, it was strange. You've disapparated. You know that there are all sorts of strange sensations when you do that. I couldn't tell if what I felt when we first did that was due to the disapparation or something else."

"Oh, I know."

"Yea, I suppose you do. Anyway, we were both teachers at Hogwarts, and I spent the first year trying to figure out how to get along as the only Muggle in a world of wizards. At the end of the year, I went back to Ohio to visit family and maybe get a summer job.

"When I returned for my 2nd year at Hogwarts I was overjoyed to get back, and part of that joy—a big part—was getting to see her again. I thought at the time that was just all part of being back at a job where they valued my contribution. I thought that the source of that joy was earning a place where lots of people didn't like me very well, and the rest mistrusted me.

"When the Christmas Holiday came during the 2nd year, Minerva invited me to spend a few days with her sister and her between Christmas and New Years. What filled my heart with joy was the thought of seeing Minerva again sooner than I expected. In that moment, I suddenly realized that I was madly in love with her and really had been for some time.

Sally asked, "But how could you have been in love with her for a long time without realizing it? It's usually pretty obvious."

"I think that it was the age thing. I think that I just couldn't get over the stigma of having a lover that was a good bit older than I was. The idea of having all the jokes—you know—'she's robbing the cradle', 'you're robbing the grave', and so on ad nauseam had just made it impossible for me to see straight up what was so obvious.

"From that moment on, I could not get her off my mind. I had to wait more than a week from the time I left school until Christmas. Anyway, it seemed endless. I tried all sorts of distractions—watching TV, reading— nothing worked. I finally gave up and just sat back and let joyful thoughts of being with Minerva wash over me.

"Well? What happened when you met?"

"Finally, she showed up. There must have been something different about me that she sensed even without our having a chance to talk. When we saw each other, we both kind of hesitated. I certainly didn't know what to do. I didn't know whether to shake hands or just say 'Hi' or take a chance and hug her.

"Well. You can certainly be cruel. What happened?"

"We kind of simultaneously made a decision. We both decided to hug. I took her in my arms, patted her on the back, and let my lips brush in the lightest possible way her right cheek. At least I think that I did. I may have missed completely and just didn't realize it.

"Whatever happened exactly, we were both different. It was a while— a long while—before I got up the courage to say something more than talk pleasantries or talk shop with her. But that's another story—one that I'm not going to tell you today or maybe ever."

Sally looked at me for a long time and finally said, "You don't seem like the kind of person who's shy. But that's a shy story you told me."

"I know. The truth is that I am shy. I know how to act non-shy, and the act almost becomes the truth, but if you scratch deep enough, you find someone who is really shy."

She got up and said, "I've got to get back to work. Don't forget your promise about the Weasleys."

"Don't worry. I won't. And you'll probably live to regret it. Once you get to know them, you'll discover how truly irritating they can be when they put their considerable talents to work at it."

She walked back into the kitchen, and I finished my dinner.

□

The next day I got the word from Parker. He came to my office. He'd been doing a lot of that lately. He said in a flat deadpan manner as though it happened every day, "I just heard from Whitehall. They've decided to go ahead with your plan. They've given you a budget of one billion pounds."

I had a hard time picking my jaw up from the floor. I didn't know what to ask about first. "One billion pounds? Where did they get that number? I don't remember mentioning any number."

"Oh, they do that sort of thing all the time. You go to them with a very carefully itemized budget, and then they send you back a budget that doesn't have anything to do with your request. I often think that it doesn't make much sense to offer a proposed budget. They'll just come up with a number out of their heads."

"OK. How in the world do I spend anything near that much money?"

"You'd be surprised how it all mounts up. A million here; a million there. Before long it begins to add up to real money. I think that was Disraeli who said that."

I corrected him, "Dirksen."

"Whoever. They're both D names."

"OK. Look I'm going to need help managing that kind of money."

"Of course, do you want us to find you an executive secretary?"

"Uh, actually, I have an idea myself of a good candidate."

He looked over with some interest for the first time that day, "It has to be someone with 'Top Secret' clearance, AND with real organizational ability."

"Oh, she has the clearance. I got it for her. I think she . . ."

Parker interrupted, "You mean the Cafeteria woman?"

"Well, yes. I know what I'm doing. I got her the clearance because I value her opinion."

"Are you sure you aren't being . . uh . . unduly influenced by her . . uh . . youthful enthusiasm."

I looked at him, and if looks could maim, he would be trying to walk on busted knees.

"OK. OK. You've been pretty sensible so far. I'll trust you on this one."

"Thanks. You be careful. I'll call her over right now and see if she'll take the job." I picked up the phone and dialed the extension for the Cafeteria. The so-called chef answered,and I asked for Sally. She answered finally. I asked her to come over to my office. She said, "OK."

She arrived, and when she saw Parker, she turned around. "Come on in. This concerns Parker. You should all be here. Pull up the final remaining chair."

She sat on the edge of her chair. I smiled and said, "How would you like to take a demotion?"

"How can there be a demotion from what I am?"

Parker contributed, "Well, technically you're a department head, although," and here his voice dropped, "we never invite you to the department head meetings."

"So," I went on, "going from being a department head of the Cafeteria to executive secretary administering one billion pounds is a demotion."

She gasped. "Why?"

"You are smart. You took the shock of disapparation like a trooper. You tolerate the Weasley's. You can hardly have a worse trial by fire than that. And you came out smelling like a rose. You're the best prospect that I've got. What do you think? Oh, yes. I think we might be working with the Weasleys a lot from now on."

She smiled a loopy smile and said, "I was sold before I came in. You don't have to ask twice."

"OK. Let's get started. Parker, can you get her any training she needs for the budget stuff?"

He smiled a wan smile. "Sure. She already knows the basics because she's a department head. You should talk to my secretary. He does larger budgets. I'll get the letters of introduction off to the right places. Do you think that you can replace yourself quickly?"

She looked internally for a moment and said, "I have a friend who graduated with me. She's pretty good, and I think she'd be a good replacement. I might be able to talk her into coming here. I don't know if she'd pass the security checks.

"Oh, yea. I could probably help out until somebody replaces me."

I interrupted, "Oh, no you don't. I need you full time. You're working for me, not providing meals on wheels for the 'Boy Genius'."

"Who?"

Parker said, "You don't know his nickname? He runs the computer lab."

"Oh, you mean Brahms? The Boy Genius, eh? Yeh, I guess he does fit the description, sort of.

"OK. I give in. I'll try to get my assistant, Jeanie, to take over my spot for a couple of days and if she doesn't go along, I'll give up the Cafeteria."

The next several days at the Cafeteria were pretty rough. The 'chef' was on his own, and no one would eat his personal concoctions although he always included a dish or two on the menu that were more conventional. The first day, at lunch, I heard the screech of an owl just seconds before it showed up on my dinner tray.

I addressed the owl. It was the same one as always. I guess it must be Minerva's rather than a school owl. "Owl, I've got to have a name for you if we're going to keep meeting like this. What do you think of the name, 'Beeker'?"

The owl looked at me silently. He shook his head negatively. "OK. I'll be serious. What about Robert?"

The owl didn't do anything. "OK." I drew out the sound to see if there was any reaction, "Robert it is. Now, Robert, let's see your message." I took the parchment off its leg. It read, "The Weasleys will meet you at Albert Hall on Thursday, 1 PM. They say, 'please bring Sally.' I don't blame them." I copied the message onto a legal pad that I had along with me so that I could make notes to myself when I ate. Then, I turned the parchment over and wrote my reply, "Good. XOXOOXOOOXX." I tied it back on Robert's leg and tossed it into the air.

I returned to my office and found that Sally had had a computer installed in my office at a make-shift desk she was using. I folded the legal sheet into a paper airplane and threw it at her from my desk. She caught it and started to ball it up to throw in the waste basket. I stopped her, "If I were you, I'd read the message. It came in a bottle carried by a bird." She quickly un-balled it and pressed it out as flat as possible. She read it.

She asked, "Is this for real. They really asked for me?"

"Sure. I couldn't blame them."

"Thursday. That's tomorrow. I've only got started setting up bookkeeping for us. I'll never be done if we keep having these interruptions."

"Then you're going to stay home and work."

"Not on your life!"

"Good. I don't know if I can take them for long on my own. We'll go down and have lunch at your old stand and then. . ."

"Not on your life. I could just barely keep the mad chef in check when I was there 24 x 7. I don't want to step in that lunch room if I've not been there holding him down."

"OK. Let's go to a real restaurant. It's on the 'Mouse'."

"What do you mean, 'on the mouse'?"

"I once knew someone who worked for Walt Disney. When he took me out to dinner once, he said that—'it's on the Mouse'. He meant 'Mickey Mouse'. This is on the PM."

Thursday came and we went to Albert Hall after lunch. We stood outside. Sally asked, "This is too good to believe."

I said, "This is too 'real' to believe." And then the two walked around the corner of the building. They were wearing conservative (for them) suits with double-breasts and a subtle purple shade. I thought of gangsters from the 40's. Maybe that idea wasn't that far off.

They walked right up and took my hand in a firm handshake that had me shaking with fear for what might happen. They hugged Sally. George gave her an especially lengthy hug. I finally said, "I'm glad to see you've finally overcome your shyness."

He let Sally go and I said. "Let's talk. Albert Hall has a restaurant. Let's go in and have some tea or something."

We got ourselves seated and I outlined what I had in mind. "The key points are that we want to provide sanctuary for the refugees from Riddle's reign of terror and give them the opportunity to fight back. So, how do we find them? How do we recruit them? Who can train them? And, I suppose, most importantly, will this idea work at all?"

Fred said, "I really like the idea."

George added, "Yea. There are lots of wizards out there scared shitless because they have Muggle parents or a Muggle parent or they ever said anything bad about Riddle or some Deatheater just happens to take a dislike to them. There are people who have relatives who are in Azkaban. There are a few wizards who are wandering around trying to avoid being arrested and taken before the Wizengemott. They'd all probably join up if they had a way—a way of keeping their families safe."

Fred asked, "But you couldn't give that many people refuge, could you?"

"I've got a big budget. How many people do you think we could get—tops?"

George answered, "Maybe 3, 4 thousand. Surely not more."

I thought hard. How far would a thousand million go? Surely 20,000 per person would be covered by it, wouldn't they?

Fred disagreed, "I don't think that many, maybe 2000 tops."

"OK. Yes, we can certainly handle that many." Sally looked at me hard. "OK, Sally, what do you think?"

She said, "I don't have a guess whether we can or not, but we've got to, don't we."

"Yea, I guess we do."

Fred asked, "Do you Muggles have radio?"

Sally broke out laughing, and I had a hard time keeping a straight face. She finally calmed down enough to say, "Yes, we Muggles have radio."

I added, "Now, you two should know that if you ever listened to your dad. I seem to recall that he tried to get a broken Muggle radio working. And didn't he have a collection of radio tubes?"

George answered, "Now that you mention it, I do remember dad ranting about how clever the Muggles were. They had radio after all."

I nudged us back toward the point, "OK. Is there a point to this story?"

George said, "Oh, yea. Sure. Fred and I have a radio show on wizarding radio."

"Really? You mean that Riddle lets you have a radio show!"

Fred exclaimed, "NO! We broadcast at irregular intervals secretly."

George added, "Yea. You have to have the password to listen."

Sally brightened up and exclaimed, "Just like Pirate Radio!"

George scratched his chin and asked, "Well, is that Radio run by Pirates? I like the idea of that."

Fred agreed.

Sally explained, "Not exactly. It's called Pirate radio because they broadcast from ships at sea where they're not subject to national laws. They can do all sorts of things: Do news shows that the authorities don't like. Play whatever kind of music they like. You know—all sorts of stuff that the 'powers that be' disagree with."

Fred said, "Sure that's exactly what we are and do. We're pirates of wizarding radio."

George agreed, "And the best thing is that we change the password every show, so you have to catch them all to keep listening."

Sally asked, "What do you call you show?"

George said, "Potter Watch."

Sally asked, "What's a potter?"

Fred looked at her sidewise and said, "You don't know who Harry Potter is?"

"No."

George looked at me and asked, "How can you let her live in such ignorance?"

"Well, I'm sure that she'd like to have personal instruction from you on that topic?"

He looked at Sally and asked, "Really?"

She colored a little and said softly, "Sure."

I interrupted the little tete-a-tete, "Well, you can do that offline. But right now, what about Potter Watch?"

Fred said, "The next time we broadcast, we can announce that anyone who wants sanctuary can show up—well, where would they go?"

I answered. "We don't know where they're going to go. As a matter of fact, we don't know yet if there will be a place for them to go. That's what this meeting is about. We need to go to talk somebody into giving us a military base to house them.

"I need you guys to come along and help with the argument, if you will accept the position of leading the, well, army that we're putting together."

"What do you think, Georgie-Porgie?"

George did a swaggering salute, "Why not? I always wanted to be a General."

Fred and George replied in unison, "Sure, we'll do it."

Fred expanded on that, 'Sure, what have we got to lose? Whether we lose or just don't do anything we'll end up in Azkaban."

"OK, then we'll have to get moving quickly. We need to put together a presentation and go do it."

George asked, "Just where is 'there'? Somewhere on the continent?"

"No. It's too close. I think Riddle might find out where they are."

"Asia?"

"America."

George asked, "The 'States'?"

I answered, "Yes. They're pretty far away. They've a big country with a lot of backwaters to get lost in. And they've got lots of military bases."

Fred asked, "Then we're going to go to New York."

I answered, "No, Washington D.C."

Fred moaned, "Too bad. There's a neat community of wizards in the Big Apple."

George was enthusiastic, "Great. We'll pack and be ready to go."

I answered, "Not so fast. We've got a few things to do first."

George asked cautiously, "Like what?"

"Like getting you some real Muggle clothes. You've got interesting tastes that almost pass for Muggle, but I think that you need some bona fide Muggle clothes."

Fred was indignant, "We have very good taste in clothes. Or at least I do. Nobody stared at us when we came here."

Sally answered, "There's a difference between being polite about and favorably impressed by someone's clothes."

George whined, "Sally, you're beginning to sound like mum."

I broke in "Oh, yes. Do you have passports?"

George asked, "What are 'past pores'?"

"Passports. Most wizards don't have passports."

"No. Whatever passports are."

"Passports are. Well." I was dumbfounded. "We'll go into that when we get them for you. We need to get together tomorrow to start doing those things. Let's meet here tomorrow morning. About 10AM."

Fred said, "Fine by us. See you tomorrow."

We parted then after finishing tea. I asked Sally, "Which do you want to do—help them get Muggle clothes or work on passports and other IDs?"

Sally thought a moment and said, "Hmmm. I don't know what's likely to be harder. I'll take the clothes. How hard can that be? They are sort of natty dressers in a bizarre way."

"That's a good question. How hard can that be?" I asked.

"Somehow, I don't like the way you say that."

"I think that you should get each of them a business suit. It doesn't need to be conservative. It just has to be recognizable as a business suit and not be too cheap."

"How about casual dress? We'll have a hard enough time getting them into suits one or two days. We need something that's comfortable for travel and times when we're not meeting with . . . just whom are we meeting with?"

"I haven't heard, but I'm sure that it'll be military types and probably a couple of civilians. I agree about casual. How about a couple of dress shirts and a couple of pairs of jeans? Again, let's avoid conservative while staying away from wild."

"You trust my judgment on what's 'wild'?"

"Here's my advice. Pick out things, and if they agree, then it's too wild."

"Sounds like good advice."

□□

The next day, I accompanied Sally to the Royal Albert Hall. She left with the boys. We agreed on a meeting time—1 PM at our offices. They went off to Harods, and I went back to work.

I went down to the main entrance about 12:45. I wanted to make sure that they had a welcoming committee when they arrived, but I also brought some work just in case they were late. It was after 2PM when they finally arrived.

George was talking animatedly with Sally when they came in. I went to the door to greet them. I said, "Welcome, gentlemen. Come over here."

We went to the desk. The guard had the visitor book out. "You'll have to sign in here." George leaned over the desk and signed his name. After he signed the book, the guard gave him a badge.

"Well, what's this?" George asked as he pondered the small rectangle of plastic with a small number on it.

"It's an ID badge. Mine," I pulled it up from where it was hanging around my neck, "will let you into almost anywhere in this building. Yours, on the other hand, will keep you from being shot to death."

"Blymie, you guys are serious here."

"Just as serious as Riddle. Follow me. We have to get some more ID for you." The four of us walked down to a section of the building that I'd not been in much. We entered a room and found a short balding man waiting. The room looked like a photography studio where you'd go and find a family of five getting a portrait with the kids standing beside their seated parents. I introduced everyone.

"These two young men are the Weasley twins—Fred and George."

"No, I'm Fred and he's George."

I looked at them for about 5 seconds. They asked, "What?!"

"You know you can't do that any more."

"Why not?" they asked in unison.

"You are such . . . " I answered.

"Anyway, this gentleman is our local artist, Robby."

"Artist?" The boys asked, genuinely confused.

Robby answered, "I used to be a paper hanger."

George and Fred said in unison, "What?!"

I answered this one. "He counterfeited money. I guess he took a deal from Her Majesty's government to work for us rather than spending time in a prison somewhere."

"Right you are, guv. I can make your mum think that you're from the USA."

"But I am from the USA." I said.

"See, even you think so."

I laughed and said, "OK, maestro. Work your magic on these two reprobates."

Robby looked at them and asked, "How'd you lose your ear?"

George answered, "I was flying on a broom stick, and a Death Eater blasted me."

Robby rolled his eyes and said, "OK. Everyone has their secrets. You don't have to tell me.

He said to me, "But you do have to tell me what countries you want passports for,.

"Well, let's start with the UK." I said.

"What, don't you want something hard, like China or Sumatra?"

"No, just the UK."

"OK. What names do you want?"

"Well, their names."

"What about addresses."

"Gentlemen," I nodded to them.

"We both live at 'The Burrow', Ottery St. Catchpole."

Robby paused a minute. "No numbers in the address. I like it. But why don't you just apply for a regular passport for them."

"It has to be fast. We're leaving the country in a day or two."

"They can do it fast."

"But I don't want any special attention that speed would attract."

"I have to take some pictures. Sit down over there." He indicated the chair that stood in front of a blank wall. It was well-lit and plain. George sat down and turned his head slightly so that the earless side was prominent.

Robby shook his head and laughed, "I like your cheek, but the Foreign Service likes nice plain simple boring pictures. I don't know that I can ever make you look boring, but I'll do my best. Look straight ahead" He took several shots and finally was satisfied.

Fred sat down and did his best to make the pictures 'interesting'. He tried sticking out his tongue and hiding an ear with his hand. He finally settled down, and we got some good pictures.

Robby asked, "Do you guys speak any foreign languages fluently?"

Fred said, "Are you kidding? George doesn't speak English fluently."

Robby snorted and said, "OK. I'm making you guys US, Canadian, Indian and . . ." He hesitated and asked, "Do you know what a 'Shirley" is?"

The two looked at each other in a puzzled way, and Fred asked, "Do you mean Temple?"

Robby shook his head again and said, "OK. No Australian passport."

I said, "I don't think we need any others."

"Oh, you never know when you're going to need a spare passport. I'm throwing them in at no extra charge. Why don't you three go up and have some tea, and I'll be up to your office with the passports in a few hours."

As we walked up to the Cafeteria, Fred and George ogled everything on the route. The interior was pretty strange; there were sections of the old warehouse that were the traditional high ceiling open areas. Beside them were the equivalent of small buildings with 2 or 3 stories. My offices were in one of those. The Cafeteria was in another.

Fred said, "This isn't quite like Hogwarts, but it has its points."

"Yeah, "said George, "you never know what you're going to see at the next turn."

They were disappointed at the Cafeteria. "This is not the Great Hall."

I answered, "I know, and this is certainly not the food that you'd find in the Great Hall, but they have tea."

Sally came in with us. "Well, gentlemen, you know that the Cafeteria is closed until supper time. How're things going, by the way?"

"Oh, we've been making pictures. We should all go up to my office to see how they came out."

We went up to my office and waited. George was funny, as usual. "What kind of office is this? Dumbledore had a much cooler office."

"Sure, there aren't any cool astrolabes or memorals or clocks or God knows what they are," said George.

I smiled. "Yes, all I have is a desk, a bookshelf, a few chairs. . ."

"What's that thing on the little thingee." George started to ask.

I broke in, "Credenza"

"Oh. Credenza, then."

"It's a personal computer."

"Yea, George, don't you know a personal computer when you see one?" Fred sneered.

"Oh sure. I thought it was an impersonal computer. What's a personal computer?"

"It's a machine that can do calculations automatically." I said.

"You mean it can figure out how much George owes me."

"Oh, come on, I just borrowed a couple of galleons once and even that wasn't so much a loan as a gift."

Eventually Robby showed up. He was carrying a shoe box. He reached inside and pulled out 2 handfuls of documents. "Well, here you are, George." There were 5 documents. One was really a plastic card the size of a credit card. It had George's photo on it and his name—"George" in large font and "Weasley" in a small font. Then there were 4 passports.

George looked at the passports first. He opened the British passport first. "Wow. Fred, did you know that I've been to Ja-mai-ca?" He stretched out the second syllable like a Rastafarian.

"No, George, but did you know that I've been to Switzerland?"

George opened another passport. "Oh oh. Fred, who's Runnl Waslip?"

"Who??" Fred exclaimed.

"Runnl Waslip. It's spelled 'R U N N L W A S L I P'"

"I don't know. Wait a minute! That name sounds familiar. I've heard it somewhere before. Haven't you?"

"Yessss. I've heard it before, but I can't place it. Where did you see it?"

"It's the name under my picture in this US passport."

"Where'd you get that name, Robby?"

He looked up and said, "I found a quill pen that you'd left from filling out the forms and started to write 'Robby Wendt.' This was what came out."

"Then that was one of our 'spell-check quills'. The spell must have been running out."

George asked, "Who are you Fred? I mean on the other passports."

Fred answered, "I'm." He hesitated, "Let's see. Bill Hazelett. Albert Speer. James Thomas."

"I'm also Quentin Durwood and Edward Collier. Uh, in addition to Runnl Waslip."

Robby looked them over back and forth. "Well?"

"Oh, yeh. Pretty good. They're the best fake passports that we've ever seen." George exclaimed.

"Definitely. Premium. Real gold." Fred added.

"Oh, shut up you two." I addressed Robby, "They've never seen real or fake passports in their lives."

Washington DC

The next day I spent a lot of time working on the presentation that I would make to—well, to people whom I'd never heard of before, and whom I would probably never see again. The Weasleys were practicing wearing really normal Muggle clothes, and Sally was practicing making fun of them.

The day after that we met early in my office. "OK. Weasleys, I want you to try to not make jokes all the time during this trip because when you make jokes, you reveal way too much of what you really are. I want to get into the States without being thrown into jail three times."

"Why three time?" asked George.

"Once, "I held up one finger, "when we go through security at Heathrow."

"Twice, "I held up a second finger, "when we go through customs at Reagan National airport."

"What's the third time?" asked Fred and George in unison.

"Third," I raised a third finger, "when a sky marshal on the plane arrests us as terrorists."

"Don't you worry your little head. We'll be good as gold galleons."

"Oh jeez. Just try to keep your mouths shut." Sally said.

Having prepped pretty well for the trip, we left for the airport. We went to the nearest Tube station and descended the stairs.

Fred asked, "OK. I know the Tube is a way for a Muggle to get about London. But just how does it work?"

Sally answered, "It's really simple. You just buy a card, and you can travel as much as you like for a day or several days, a week, or whatever."

"OK, and I suppose I have to use Muggle money."

Sally smiled and said, "Of course."

"It's those funny little paper paintings, right? Dad showed us some of them once."

"Funny paintings?"

"Yes, you know. They look like paintings. I can't understand why you Muggles trust them. Anyone could paint their own, and then how do you know that they're real?"

I broke in, "You're right, you can't be sure that a pound is real. There are good 'paper hangers' who can counterfeit them, but most of them are perfectly good."

So we went down, bought some cards, got down to the platform, and waited for a train to arrive. A train pulled up, and Fred and George jumped up, ready to go. I said, "Slow down. That's not our train."

"How do you know?"

"Look at the destination on the front of the train car—not Heathrow."

Then the right train did come. We got up, and we waited for the doors to open. George asked, "What is the 'gap'?"

"What do you mean?"

"Well, those signs all say, 'Mind the Gap'."

"Oh, well look at the door of the train. There's a gap between the platform and the bottom of the door. If you don't step up, you'll end up with your foot. . ."

"Under the train. Yeh, I get it."

We boarded the train and found a couple of vacant benches. We rode for a few minutes without comment, and then Fred looking pretty sheepish asked, "And you're sure there's no other way to get to America besides flying? We couldn't take a boat?"

"Yes, we could take the boat, but it would take a week to cross the Atlantic. Even then we'd probably have to wait a week or so for a boat to be leaving."

Fred pursed his lips and clearly wanted to say something else but didn't.

"OK, fellows. When we get to the airport, we're going to get our tickets. They call them boarding passes. We leave our luggage with the airline people. They put them in the cargo hold of the airplane. Then, and this is important, we go through a security check to make sure that we're not carrying guns or bombs or dangerous stuff on board."

"Why would we want to do that?"

"I don't know. Why do Deatheaters always want to kill and torture people?"

Fred grimaced, "I take your point. OK. So what do we do at the security check?"

"You take all the metal things out of your pockets and put them in little hampers that go into an X-ray machine and then . ."

"X-ray?"

"I'm sorry I mentioned it. It's hard to explain. Call it 'magic'."

"Now, we know 'magic'. Let's call it something else."

"OK. Call it Muggle magic. Anyway, they X-ray them, and then they give them back to you."

"Does X-raying make them safe?"

"No, if they find something that's not safe, they send you to the slammer."

"'Slammer'?"

"Oh. It's American slang for jail. Anyway, we then go to a place called the 'gate', where we wait for the airplane to be ready for us. When it is ready, they ask us to board. You have to get in line and give up your ticket, and then they let you board. You find your seat, sit down, and don't make a nuisance of yourselves."

Sally added, "That last part—about not making a nuisance of yourselves—is really important."

I looked over to her and said, "I see that you're getting the right idea about how to deal with these guys."

"Now, that's not nice." George said.

Sally looked at him really intensely, and he just stopped talking and looked stunned. Fred said, "It's pretty spooky. You know you remind me sometimes of mum. Doesn't she George?"

George turned a couple of shades of red and looked at his shoes.

We finally got to Heathrow, and for once the boys were content to follow Sally and me up to the ticket desk. We got our boarding passes, checked our luggage, and then headed for the gates. We reached the security lines, and we started through. I wanted to be sure that Sally and I went before the twins so that we could model behavior for them. We got through. Then they started through. They had some galleons in their pockets and a few sickles, which they obediently put in the hampers. They went through the security scanner and I breathed a sigh of relief. But when Fred went through, he bent over to pick up his boarding pass. One of the guards noticed something and asked Fred to come to the side. I sighed and wondered what would happen.

The guard took him aside and had him stand next to the wall. "What's in your inside pocket?"

Fred looked puzzled and then he said, "Oh, you mean this. He pulled his wand out of his inside jacket pocket."

"What is that?"

He looked at it and said, "It's a wand."

"A what?"

"A wand."

I decided that it was time to intervene. "Uh, excuse me sir," I said to the security person, "It's really a pointer."

The security man's partner turned quickly to me and said, "We weren't talking to you."

I took a big breath and said, "We're traveling together, and he's a lecturer. He just has a thing about having his favorite pointer with him." Of course, the ironic thing was that what I'd said was basically true. He was going to use his "pointer" in a lecture on the power of wizards.

They looked pretty doubtful. I said, "Well, if you want, you can keep it." Fred looked over at me with daggers in his eyes. I shook my head at him briefly. He frowned and said with a little whine in his voice, "But that's my favorite pointer."

One of the security guys took it and had them pass it through the X-ray machine. He came back, "There's nothing in it. It looks like it's just a wooden, uh, pointer."

The two went off and had a little conference. They returned and one said, "OK. It looks safe. But from now on, please pack that thing in your checked luggage, please."

Fred nodded and said nothing.

We found our gate and sat. We had spent so much time with security that almost immediately they started boarding our flight. Since we were in first class, we were near the front of the line. The four of us completely filled one row. George and Sally sat on the starboard side. Fred and I were on the port side. As the stewardesses started talking about safety, I felt Fred put a strangle hold on my forearm. He said through clenched teeth, "Do we really have to fly?"

I looked at him and saw that his jaws were locked and his other hand was clutching his armrest. "Look, I know that it's kind of a scary idea, but it's really not dangerous."

"You know I never realized how brave Muggles were. It's really scary. Do you see how thin the walls of this airplane are?"

I looked with him trying to communicate incredulity. "You, who fly on a broom, with nothing to hold you on the broom are afraid to fly in an airplane, where you have a seatbelt to hold you down to the seat. You're surrounded by metal walls. You have pretty stewardesses to serve you meals. You don't have any of that on a broom."

He gaped at me. "When I'm flying on my broom, I'm in control. I know exactly what's going to happen. I know when I'm going up and when I'm going down. I know when I'm going to speed up and when I'm going to slow down. I don't know any of that here."

I smiled and said, "I suppose you're right. But millions of Muggles fly every day and hardly anyone is killed."

"You're not making it easier for me."

"OK. Just suffer through the flight, and I'll make it up to you somehow."

"You bet you will."

It was a long flight and most of it was spent with Fred squeezing the juice out of the armrests. I was trying to do the talking for the both of us. Neither of us enjoyed the great food that they serve you in first class on British Airlines. I glanced over and noticed that Sally and George were having a great time talking throughout the flight. We finally landed. There was a light cross-wind, and the airplane swayed back and forth a little as we got close to the ground. Fred had his eyes locked on the wall in front of him, and I was just glad that he wasn't squeezing my arm. I wanted to use it sometime in the future.

As we left the terminal, we found a limo waiting for us. They had a sign with my name on it. We got in, and they drove us to a hotel in the Watergate complex. We checked in and went up to our suites. The twins had one. I had one, and Sally had one. I was ready for bed even though local time was before 9PM.

Someone knocked on my door. I went to the peephole and found that the other three were outside the door. I opened it and invited them in, regretfully.

George had a book under his arm. He asked, "How about going out to a club tonight?"

"How about us getting some sleep tonight?"

Sally looked at me reproachfully, "Come on. It's early. We have time."

I frowned. Did I dare let these three loose on an unsuspecting capital? I temporized, "George, what's the book? That seems out of character for you."

He handed it over. It was *The Wandering Wizard's Welcome - Washington DC*. I thumbed through it. There was a chapter titled *Washington Night Life*.

He smiled and said, "We found all the hot wizard clubs."

"I was afraid you'd say that. OK. But we have to be back before midnight."

"Of course. No problemo."

Fred took my wrist and said, "Here we go." Between the "we" and the "go", we disapparated to someplace. We were on a street outside a blank wall. Fred kept my wrist and said, "Just hang on. You need to be in contact with me to get in." So, the four of us walked through a blank wall. Inside the music blared. The lighting was indirect and low. There appeared to be a dance floor that was pretty crowded. We found a table, which I considered a small miracle, as crowded as it was. Fred got up and said that he was going to get drinks. "What do you want?"

I answered, "Pumpkin Juice."

Fred frowned and said, "Come on. You can try something stronger than that."

"Pumpkin Juice."

He left. George and Sally got up and went to the dance floor. Fred returned with drinks and said, "I'm going to look for someone in a skirt. No offense?"

"None taken."

He left, and I nursed my pumpkin juice. The music was vaguely familiar. I'm sure that I'd heard it at Hogwarts, but I couldn't identify the song or the band. After a while I noticed a woman sitting at a table nearby with a couple of other young women. She appeared to be staring at me. When she noticed that I'd noticed her, she got up and walked over to our table.

"Hi. Can I join you?"

I'm way too polite. "Yes, but my friends will probably be back in a few minutes."

"Don't worry, I'm friendly. How about dancing?" she asked

"Oh, I don't know."

Just then Fred and a partner that he'd acquired came by. He was smiling slyly, "How about coming out and joining us?"

"Oh, I don't know. I'm really not much of a dancer."

The lady said, "Sure, anyone can dance." She reached out, took my left hand, and dragged gently.

Fred gestured over to George and Sally. They came over, and he said, "Are you going to come out and dance?"

It was getting pretty embarrassing, so I stood up and said, "I guess I just have to prove how awful a dancer I am." I took a step away from the table, and suddenly my stomach wrenched. I knew that I was going to end up someplace else. The air pressure squeezed my chest, and my vision cleared. I found that we—the unnamed lady and I—were standing outside a more conventional club. It had a door that I could see and a marquee that announced that tonight there was a band called "The Belton Big Band" that was performing there.

"I thought we were going to dance at the other club."

She looked at me sidewise and asked me why I wanted to be a boor.

Well, it did look a lot more 'normal' to me than the place we left. "Oh, very well. The Belton Big Band probably will play music that I'm more comfortable dancing with anyway."

"That's the spirit." We entered the totally conventional door and found ourselves in a totally conventional club with an eight piece orchestra. They were playing something slow that I could probably really dance to. She went over to the bar. The "keep" came up and asked her if she wanted her usual. She said "Yes." She turned to me and asked if I were having anything?"

I asked the "keep", "What is she having?"

"A gin and tonic."

"I'll have one too."

He was back in a minute with two gins with tonic. I sipped it and didn't gag. She took out her purse, pulled a twenty out, and put it on the bar. The 'keep came back with two singles. I stared a minute and asked him, "Isn't eight-fifty a little stiff for a gin and tonic?"

He was taken aback but recovered quickly, "Sure, wasn't that a five and a single that I gave her?"

I decided to play it cool, "Oh. Sure, I must just have been thinking that both the bills were ones."

After the "keep" left she asked me, "How do you know so much about Muggle money?"

I asked her in turn, "How do you know so much about Muggle clubs?"

She answered, "I like to get away from wizards and witches. You know, I'm just average, but when I'm around Muggles, I feel special."

I dropped back a half-foot and looked at her for a second. She was attractive, at least by my standards. "What do you mean, you're 'just average'?"

"Oh, you know. I was never good at school—the only 'owl' I ever got was in numeracy. It took me half a dozen tries to pass my disapparation exam. Half a dozen! I'm a secretary at my uncle's factory."

I thought a moment. "Did you see the twins that I came in with?"

"Sure. So what."

"They're barely 19 and are really successful businessmen back in London. They hardly got an 'owl' between them."

"Really?"

"Sure."

"Who are they?"

"Fred and George Weasley. I doubt that you've ever heard of them."

"The Weasleys. The Weasley's Wizard Weezes Weasleys?"

"I'll bet you can't say that three times fast."

She laughed. "Well are they the same Weasleys?"

"Sure. How do you know about them?"

"My younger brother went to London with my parents and came back with a suitcase full of stuff from them. He could hardly stop talking about them for a week."

"Well, yes. They are the same Weasleys."

"And they hardly got an 'owl' between them?"

"You bet."

She was quiet for a minute. Then she asked, "Let's dance?"

"Sure." The band was playing something especially slow, which was my speed.

We went onto the dance floor, and I dragged her around through the song. Then the band played a 'swing' tune, and I begged off until the next slow song. We went back to the bar, and I sipped the gin and tonic.

She asked, "How do you know about how many 'owl's they got?"

"I was one of their teachers."

"No. You don't look nearly old enough to be a professor."

"I'm not a professor. I was just an instructor. And I'm not even an instructor any more. I got canned."

She looked at me hard for a minute. "You know, you're really not at all the way you look."

"What do you mean?"

"First, you don't seem really very magical. Are you a . . ." She was ashamed to say the word.

"Am I a 'squib'?"

"Well, yeh. I'm sorry. I don't mean to embarrass you, but it just slipped out."

I thought for a second. She must have taken it that I was embarrassed as well. That was good.

"Yes. I'm a squib. You don't need to be embarrassed. I'm not. It's just what I am."

"But most people would not admit it."

"Most people don't have integrity."

"But you don't seem very British either. You don't have much of an accent."

'You are perceptive, my dear. I'm not really British. I was born in Ohio and grew up there. I went to Britain after school."

"Why?"

"Well, here's another potentially embarrassing fact. I went to a Muggle school—Ohio State. I studied English Literature, and I figured that it'd be a good idea to go to the home of English literature."

"Oh, but how did you end up teaching wizards?"

"I ended up at a wizarding school where the Headmaster thought that wizarding schools ought to be more than just trade schools."

"Stranger and stranger."

"Yes, I suppose so."

"How about dancing again?" The band was playing something slow again. I agreed, and we went out on the dance floor. It wasn't so bad this time. We got back to the bar, and I noticed that her drink was just about gone. I asked, "Want another?" as I pointed at her drink.

"Sure."

I signaled the "keep". He came over, and I handed him a five. "Another G & T for the lady, please. Keep the change." He nodded and went off to make the drink.

"That was pretty smooth. You really know Muggle stuff. I never have gotten the hang of Muggle money. Something else. You really aren't bothered by the fact that you're a. . ." she hesitated again, "'squib'?"

"No, I'm not."

"Are you, uh, single?"

"Yes, but don't let that fool you. I'm taken."

"The world is pretty strange, isn't it? I brought you here because I wanted to be the most magical girl in the building, and I was trying to impress someone who was even less magical than me."

"You're right. It is a strange world. You know, if I weren't committed." I stopped for a second and thought about what I'd just said. "Yes. 'Committed' is just the right word. If I weren't so committed, I'd find you pretty appealing."

She gulped and said, "The really crazy thing is that if you weren't 'committed', I'd probably really be hitting on you. Who'd have guessed that I'd be in danger of falling for a squib?"

I asked her, "Would you like to dance?"

"Sure. Let's make a night of it."

We spent the rest of the evening talking and dancing. Around midnight, Fred, George and Sally showed up.

We were sitting at the bar. They came to us, and George asked, "Well, you know, I thought you were a shy wallflower. So what happened to you."

Sally asked, "Now, now. Courtesy first. Please introduce us."

I suddenly realized that I hadn't gotten her name. So, I gaped for a second and was about to begin to explain that I didn't know her name when she took the initiative, "I'm Elizabeth, but you can call me Beth."

I recovered myself enough to introduce the Weasleys and Sally.

Sally took Beth by the hand and suggested that they have a little "girl talk", which left me to deal with the Weasleys. Fred and George said in unison, "Well?"

"Well, Beth wouldn't take 'no' for an answer, so when I declined to dance with her, she disapparated me here. How did you find us?"

George said, "Oh, it was pretty easy. Sally had noticed Beth come over to our table, and later when you two had disappeared, she was pretty disturbed. She started interrogating everyone at the club trying to find out who Beth was."

Fred added, "She eventually found someone who recognized her description. She told us that Beth sometimes frequented Muggle clubs and that she'd said that she did that because she likes a kind of music that she called 'Big Band'."

George went on, "So, Sally started . . uh . . what does Dad call it, Fred. You know, it sounds like Teflon."

Fred answered, "You, know, uh. . . uh . . . Oh, yes, Tephelone."

I corrected, "That's telephone. So, she started telephoning Muggle clubs until she found one that has Big Bands?"

"Right."

By this time the 'girls' had returned to the bar. I asked if I could buy anyone a drink.

Beth remarked "You just wanted to show off how good you are with Muggle money."

I laughed and said, "Well, it's about the only talent that I have."

Sally said, "We should all get back to the hotel. But, I think that Beth can get you back there, so the three of us should go."

Fred and George showed no sign of moving, so Sally firmly took George by the hand and said, "I think it would only be polite if we," and she emphasized the "we", "left and let them get back when they can."

She firmly squeezed George's hand. He winced and said, "OK. I can take a hint. Let's go Fred."

They walked out the entrance, and Beth said, "Jim, do you want to go too?"

"How did you know my name? Oh, Sally told you."

"Of course."

"I really should get going. I've got an important meeting tomorrow, and I want to be ready and rested for it."

"Is there a chance that I can see you again?"

"I really have got a previous commitment to someone."

She answered, "You know, this integrity business must be contagious. I've got to admit that I don't really care if you've got a previous commitment, and I'd like to see if maybe I could become your 'previous commitment'."

I took a minute to think that over. "Yes, if you want to have lunch tomorrow, we can try that. But understand that in the interest of integrity I have to say that despite your beauty and intelligence, I wouldn't put much hope in becoming my 'previous commitment' if I were you."

"Why would you see me then? Don't you think that if you had integrity you wouldn't see me?"

"I'm not engaged to my 'previous commitment'. I can't believe that anyone else would supplant her in my heart, so I feel that she's pretty safe. However, if you did kick her out, then I can't really have been that committed to her."

"You are strange. If I were her, I'd be spitting mad if you'd seen me."

"Really. Then why didn't we get engaged?"

"Hmmmm. Good point. You mean that you offered that to me er her, whatever?"

"Yes."

"And she didn't take it."

"No."

"OK. Then it's a date. Where do we meet?"

I thought a second. The Pentagon surely has Cafeterias and maybe even restaurants. "Meet me at the Pentagon station of the Tube. . er. . Metro."

It was her turn to pause for a moment. "I've never been on the Metro. But I'm sure that I can find it. What time?"

"Noon."

"OK, let's get you home. Where are you staying?"

I told her. We walked outside and disapparated.

□

The next day we all met at the breakfast bar in the hotel and talked about the upcoming meeting. I summarized things, "OK. This is our one shot at getting a base here in the States. We've got to convince these people that:

1. We're not crazy.
2. There really is magic.
3. It's in their interest to help us.

"So, we first of all need to be respectful. 2nd, we need to look sharp. 3rd, we need to convince them that we're not just importing terrorists into the States."

Fred asked, "Isn't that going to be a little hard, if we actually do magic. You know, there's something undignified about a general floating in air upside down." George laughed at that, and I stared them both down.

"We won't use 'levicorpus'. I was thinking of something more like 'Petrificus Totalis' or some transformation. Like converting a coffee cup into a mouse."

Sally offered, "I always thought that disapparation was pretty impressive. Maybe we could disapparate one of them into the lobby of our hotel and back?"

"That's a pretty good idea. I'll pick one of them while we're in the meeting and signal you. One finger is 'Petrificus'; two fingers is transformation, and three fingers is disapparation."

George said, "Are you sure that Fred can count that high?" Sally laughed and then controlled herself.

"That's just the kind of remark that I want you to stay away from. We don't want them to think that we're not serious."

"But, we're not."

"Well, try to be for one morning. After our meeting, I've got a date for lunch. You can find something to eat on your own."

Sally winked at me and said, "We can take a hint. Or at least, I can."

Fred looked over at Sally and said, "I resemble that remark."

She answered, "You certainly do, Olly." Their gaze held for about a second too long for either George's or my comfort. I reflected. Had Sally just mistaken Fred for George, or was there something going on that I didn't understand?

"Well, our limo will be here for us in a few minutes. Let's get out to the lobby." When we arrived, the driver was waiting for us. We got in the back of the limo and were headed for the Pentagon. It took us about a half hour to make it to the Pentagon in late rush hour traffic. We drove into an underground delivery dock.

The limousine pulled up beside a truck. We got out and were met by about a half-dozen heavily armed guards in flak vests and carrying assault rifles.

Fred said, "Well, George I see that your reputation has preceded us."

George said, "I think it must be Fred's 'rep'."

An officer behind them said, "Let's see your passports."

We all pulled them out and held them out.

The officer said, "Place them on the limo hood and back up to the far wall."

We did so, and he picked up the passports and examined them. "They seem good. He stared at us one at a time and compared with the photos in the passports. "All right. Get in the elevator. Move to the opposite wall of the elevator and keep your hands in view at all times."

I asked, "Do all your guests get an honor guard?"

The officer replied, "You'll have to talk about that to the people up at reception."

We got in the elevator, which turned out to be a large freight elevator. We moved to the far side of it, which turned out to be another door. The guard followed us, and someone started the elevator. We went up a couple of floors, and the elevator door in front of us opened.

Our guide said, "Walk out, turn right, and walk slowly down the aisle to the reception desk." We did so. A couple of men in business suits were waiting for us. Their tailors must have had a challenge fitting them. They had plenty of muscles and were at least 6 feet tall. One of them walked over to the officer in charge and asked for the passports. He looked at them and smiled. "I see that Mr. Weasley and Mr. Weasley couldn't be bothered to get real passports. No matter. All of you please sit down in the chairs over there, and we'll make you IDs to use here."

Fred said, "I know what this is. You're making picture IDs."

"Yes. I see you're an old hand at this."

I returned to my earlier question. "OK, I bet not everybody who comes in this way gets the honor guard?"

Suit # 1 turned toward me but didn't look directly at me. He said, "We were told that you folks were probably the most dangerous people we would ever meet."

I was incredulous, "Did they tell you anything else about us?"

"That we probably shouldn't look at you directly."

Fred laughed and said, "You never know where superstition will pop up, do you?"

George answered, "The next thing you know they'll be getting out the garlic and guarding against the evil eye."

Fred was the first to have his picture made. We all took turns, and by the time that they were done with me, Fred and George had theirs. They hung them around their necks like most of the people there did.

The suit who'd done all the talking asked us to follow him. We walked down the hall and eventually reached a door that led into a large Conference Room. It had a table that would seat at least a dozen and a half people. "The people you're meeting with will be along in a couple of minutes." None of us sat down. I walked around the room. One wall was narrower than the opposite one. It had windows in it that looked out on the central mall of the Pentagon.

Sally remarked, "Kind of inhospitable, leaving us here to wait alone."

I chuckled, "Oh, I doubt that we're really alone."

George looked around exaggeratedly and asked, "Who's here with us, Gnomes?"

"No, there's probably video cameras watching us, and who knows what else."

Fred asked, "Vid he oh?"

I asked, "Have you heard of television?"

"Is that something like telphelone?"

"Oh, yeah, something." I volunteered.

"Boy, I can see why you and Dad really get along well."

"Yea, I suppose."

As promised, in a few minutes, the door opened, and a couple of officers with lots of battle ribbons came in followed by a couple of more people in business suits. Then after a moment, a tall blue-eyed genial man came in. He greeted everyone there by name and came over to me. "You must be Jim Wendt."

"Yes, Mr. President. This is an honor indeed. I didn't expect to see you."

"This is a strange request. I thought it would be worth the price of admission to see you and your friends. Why don't you tell us what you've all been doing the last couple of years? You see, my intelligence people don't know, and they make it a point to know everything that I might want to know—right George?"

George stepped forward and said, "Yes, Mr. Wendt, you are all curious people. For example, Ms. Sally started off with a degree in nutrition, but the last couple of years she's been running a Cafeteria in an SAS facility. She's the most straightforward of you. But your mission doesn't seem to have anything to do with nutrition. I'm wondering just what you've been doing in this mission.

"Then, Mr. Wendt, you are a real curiosity. You drop off the 'net' for months at a time and even when you do re-appear on the 'net', you show up here, there briefly, and then are gone suddenly. What do," he emphasized the word, "you do? And how did English Literature degrees from Ohio State and Stanford prepare you for this mission?"

"And the estimable Mr. Weasleys. You have never been on the 'net' since you were born. Are you really who you say you are?"

149

I asked, "Do you want us to spend a few days filling in the holes in your dossiers on us, or do you want to get down to business?"

The president said, "You're right. You're here to ask us for help. As I see it, we should all sit down and discuss it."

The president led us over to the table, and we took chairs. He drawled, "Well, le'ses get acquainted. We'll go around the table and introduce ourselves. Each will tell what he does and one thing that nobody knows about you."

We all introduced ourselves. Fred, said, "I'm Fred Weasley. I run a 'joke shop' in Diagon Alley, London. And my brother only has one ear."

George responded, "I'm George Weasley. I run a 'joke shop' in Diagon Alley. My brother has two ears."

The president asked, "I suppose there's a story around that missing ear?"

I broke in, afraid that one of the Weasleys or both would invent some story that was even crazier than the truth. "Mr. President, although we'd enjoy regaling you with war stories, let's just leave it that it was . . uh . . a magical accident."

"Which brings us to the point, doesn't it? Our cousins in London tell us that they need help because of a really bad magician. Now when I hear that, I think about someone who can't pull a rabbit out of a hat, but instead gets a rat. But you're here to convince us that 'magic' is real and a national security issue." He and everyone else around the table were looking expectantly at me.

I looked around the room. Besides the people at the table, there were several Secret Service people standing at strategic points in the room. At least I thought they were. I got up from the table and took a slow walk around the room looking at the various people in the room trying to decide who could take a 'joke'."

I decided nobody sitting at the table were good candidates. As I walked around I looked at the Secret Service agents. I was looking for someone whom I might catch smiling a little. Finally, I decided on one. I asked him, "What's your name?"

He looked in my direction without quite looking me in the eye. "Agent Fredericks, sir."

"Mr. Fredericks, if something very strange happened to you, do you think it would disturb you?" I quickly added, "Nothing that would hurt you. Just something very startling."

Fredericks looked briefly over to the president, who nodded slightly. Then Fredericks answered, "No, sir."

"Good. I'll give you warning when it's going to happen."

"Thanks, sir."

I went on, "All right. I'm going to have one of the Weasleys do something to Mr. Fredericks that is going to be pretty startling, but it's not at all dangerous, with your permission."

The president's drawl disappeared completely, "Get on with it."

"OK." I turned to Fredericks and said, "It'll happen in the next couple of seconds." And, without looking away from Fredericks, I unfolded one finger from my loose fist, the index finger. For a moment, nothing seems to have happened. Then slowly Fredericks leaned forward and his stiff body fell, accelerating as it dropped head first to the floor. There was an infinitely long 2 seconds of perfect silence, then about two dozens things happened all in the next 5 seconds.

Two of the agents pulled guns. Another raised his right hand to his mouth and said something quietly into his cuff. The door flew open and three troops dressed in battle gear burst into the room. I was knocked to the floor by someone I couldn't see. Out of the corner of my eye, I saw Fred and George snatched out of their chairs and thrown to the floor. I couldn't see what happened to Sally.

I heard the president giving a sharp order, "Let go of me. I'm not leaving the room."

"Sir, you've got to, we can't take a chance."

"If you want to have your job this time tomorrow, let me go."

The president seemed to have won the argument. I could still hear his voice, though I couldn't make out quite what he was saying. That could have been because I was concentrating on the hard barrel pressed in the middle of my back. Finally, the president said, "I'm going to have you released. I suppose that you can do just as much harm where you are as you can seated around the table."

Just then, a man said, "I don't know what's happened to this man. He's paralyzed, but still breathing. I suppose a nerve poison could do this. Did it happen suddenly?"

I said, "Fred, release him."

By this time, one of the soldiers was helping me up, and I could see that Fredericks was slowly getting up. The EMT was trying to keep him from getting up, but Fredericks was protesting that he was perfectly OK. He was too imposing to resist.

Everyone was standing, and there were a couple of people who'd been in the room who were gone. The president gave some orders. "OK. Calm down everyone. Everyone leave the room except Secret Service." And then as we were being hustled out, "Except for our guests."

When the room had cleared, the president sat and said, "shall we pick up where we left off?"

"Sure", I said.

He went on. "I think you've made your point. I suppose that you could have done something much more. . ." He hesitated a minute considering the proper word and finally settled for, "impressive."

I answered, "Yes. If your Secret Service knew the limits of what we could do, I suppose we'd not have gotten into this room with you at all."

"Hmmm. OK. Let's see. You want me to let you bring hundreds, maybe thousands of people like Fred and George into the country?"

George asked, "Quite an honor, what?"

The president frowned at him and said, "How do you put up with him?"

"Oh, you get used to it after a while." Sally said, "As a matter of fact, they rather grow on you in time." She gave Fred a big smile, and he turned a pastel shade of red only slightly less intense than the red of his hair.

I went on, "But the truth is that there are already thousands, at least, probably more like tens of thousand in your country."

"Somehow, I thought you might be saying that sooner or later. Well, if you're going to have all of these Brit magicians in the country, I'd like to have an American magician or two overseeing the army base that we give you."

"First, the proper word is not 'magician'."

"And what is the proper word?"

"'Wizard' or 'witch'", Sally said.

"And it's not politically incorrect to use the term, 'witch'?"

"It's perfectly OK."

What the president said caused me to start thinking. I said, "I think, we can help you with that."

"You do that. But for now, I've had as much excitement as I like before it's time for dinner cocktails. You go tell your bosses that we'll give you a base."

I thanked him, and he just said, "You take care that you leave it in better condition than you found it."

"We'll try our best."

The president got up to leave the room, and I said, "Thank you, Mr. President", and one of the Secret Service people stayed behind to escort us out to the reception desk. The two suits were still there, and one of them went ahead of us to call the elevator.

I said, "Do you mind if I go back via the Metro?"

The two suits looked at each other, and one said, "Sure, I'll escort you out to the Metro entrance."

Sally said, "I hope you have a good lunch." Then she winked at me so that only I could see it.

I smiled and said, "It won't be as good as yours are, but we'll suffer through."

"I know you two will."

Fred whistled.

The rest went back down to the garage level and left in the limo. My escort and I walked down a couple of flights of stairs and through what seemed like a mile of corridors and finally reached the Metro entrance. He said, "You could go a couple of stops down the Metro and get out at the Mall exit. Or you could go into town and eat on the Mall."

I thanked him and waited at the Metro entrance. Suddenly, I felt a hand on my right shoulder and a familiar voice said, "Were you waiting long?"

I turned and said, "There are some people that you'd spend an hour waiting for and it would seem like a moment."

"Well, aren't you the charming one? Have you got an idea where to eat?"

"I thought it might be nice to eat on the Mall. Maybe we could find a hot dog vendor. It's a nice day."

"In the sun it's not bad. Hmmmm. Why not? Sure. How do we get there? Would you like to disapparate?"

"Have you ever ridden the Metro?"

"Are you kidding? Would you take the Metro, if you could disapparate?"

"Like I said, 'Have you ever taken the Metro?'"

She gave me a sidewise look that said, "Are you kidding?" and actually said, "No."

"Well, then you're in for a treat. Let's go ride the rails."

"This is revenge isn't it? You don't like disapparating, and you want to give me a taste of my own medicine."

"How can you say a thing like that about me?" I said with mock outrage. Then in a softer tone, "You should have a variety of experiences. Don't prejudge an experience before you know anything about it."

"Oh, I know something about it. It's underground and it's run by Muggles."

"Now, now. You see what I mean about prejudice."

"OK. I'm just teasing a little. Sure, let's 'ride the rails'."

I showed off my expertise with Muggle money by buying passes from a machine, and we entered the subway station. We went through the turnstile, which was an interesting process. She had a hard time getting the card into the slot. I finally had to take her hand and guide it to get the card in the slot. After it went in, she looked up with a sly smile and mouthed, "Thanks." I wondered if she really found it so hard to work the card. We waited by the track. We didn't have to wait long because all the trains were going to the Mall and points beyond. We got into one of the middle cars of the first train that came. There were some empty benches, so we picked one and sat. I let her take the one next to the window, though of course there wasn't much to see while we were underground. But eventually we came above ground to cross the Potomac where we got a good view of the river and the Capitol.

Beth admitted, "This is a nice view. It's too bad that we have to go back underground." But when we swooped down into the ground, I noticed that there was a smile of appreciation on her lips.

"We'll get off at the next stop."

"Well, it's not as fast as disapparation, but I admit that it does have its charms—like you."

"Right."

We arrived at the next stop, and I had to urge her out before the train started off again. We worked our way through the crowd and up the escalator. She faltered a little getting on and slipped back onto me. "Sorry. I don't see how Muggles get the hang of this."

We reached street level and walked a block to the Mall. We started walking across the Mall looking for a street vendor. "It's amazing to me how the walks across the Mall are mostly paved in gravel. But it's beautiful." I said.

"Yes, you're right. Beautiful."

It was warm, almost an Indian summer. There were a number of vendors out. We picked a vendor. Beth ordered a Chicago style, and I ordered a bratwurst. She made a face when I ordered the "brat", and I suggested that we trade.

"You've got to be kidding. Brats are so uh . . . Yuckky."

"You've never had one, have you?"

"Well, no." she said hesitantly.

"Then how can you judge them?"

"I can see them. They look Yuckky. They're fat and grey. Yuch!"

"What if you couldn't see what you were eating?"

"How could that happen?"

"Close your eyes."

She reluctantly did so.

"Open your mouth."

154

She opened it stoically. I took the hot dog and put the end in her mouth. She bit in and practically gagged. "I told you. It's awful."

"Open your eyes."

She did and saw what she had in her mouth. "That's unfair." However, the scowl slowly turned to a smile. "All right. Give me the brat. I'll try it with my eyes open." She did and chewed slowly, contemplatively. "I guess it's not half-bad." She kept eating.

We found a bench in a little grove of trees near the Lincoln end of the Mall. She stopped between bites and asked, "OK. You've got me in a secluded spot. What now?"

"Well. I got you here on false pretenses. Sort of."

She looked at me out of the corner of her eyes and said with an upward lilt to her voice, "Ohhh."

"Yes. I want to offer you a job."

She turned full face toward me and her jaw dropped. "What?"

"Yes. But before I offer it, I need to talk to you about politics."

"Well, you've come to the right place. This is about the most political place in the country."

"What do you know about wizarding politics in England?"

"Really not a lot. Oh, we get news from England, of course. But it's so confusing. One minute, 'You Know Who' is the worst thing since Splatter Gout. Then it's this Potter kid that's Public Nuisance #1 or whatever they're calling him."

"I and my friends are of the' Tom Riddle is the worst person in the world' persuasion."

"Tom Riddle?"

"Yes. 'You Know Who.'"

"He's really bad?"

"I'm afraid so. His gang—they call themselves 'Deatheaters' killed one of my students."

"Students?"

"Yes, I used to be an instructor at Hogwarts."

"I thought you were a . . . a . . ."

"Actually, no. What I really am is a Muggle."

"But how can you teach at Hogwart's if you're not magical at all?"

"That's a long story. Someday I'll tell it to you, if you really want to know it. But for now, let's just leave it that I was a teacher there, and one of my favorite students ended up on the wrong end of an "Avra Kadavra" spell." I stopped short suddenly realizing what I'd just said. "I guess, come to think of it, there isn't a right end of one of those."

"And what do you want to hire me to do?"

"Well, first, do you swear that you won't tell anyone what I'm about to tell you?"

She hesitated and asked, "Is this illegal or immoral?"

"I don't think so."

"OK. Yes."

"Would you swear that as an unbreakable vow?"

"I don't know. That's pretty serious."

I looked at her, trying to decide what I'd do if she wouldn't. Finally I decided that the reason that I wanted her for the job was that I thought she was an honorable person as well as a competent one.

"I'll take your personal word."

She released a breath that she'd been holding. "OK. Yes, I won't tell on you."

"Thanks. My friends and I are not here as tourists."

She sarcastically said, "No. You're kidding."

"OK. I guess I should have expected you to figure that out.

"Here's the deal. Boy, this is going to be hard to explain."

"Pick a spot at random and get started."

"OK. Let's stretch your credulity to the breaking point. We're here to get the US to loan us an old military base to be used as a sanctuary for English wizards and witches who are trying to evade Riddle's gang."

"Hmm. Yes, that's pretty hard to buy I've got to admit. Why would the Muggle US government go along with that?"

"Well, the Muggle British government is helping. They've got a pretty big stake in it. I don't know how closely you pay attention to Muggle news, but there's some pretty awful things happening in England to Muggles just now. The PM and probably some of his cabinet know what's going on and are trying to do something about it. So they want to play ball with us."

"Just who is us?"

"Well. I can't give you names of other people. That would possibly endanger them. But have you heard of the Order of the Phoenix?"

"No."

"Well, it was a resistance movement first formed when Riddle had his first go at world domination. Its head was Professor Albus Dumbledore."

"Really. I've heard of him. But why do you say 'was'?"

"He died recently.'

"Oh" The 'oh' trailed off as she realized what that meant.

"Anyway, I don't work for the Order. But I do have close relations with them and try to coordinate what my group does with theirs."

"Your group?"

156

"Well, I guess it's not exactly my group, but I work for it."

"How did Dumbledore die?"

"He was killed by a Deatheater—a former friend. Which raises an important issue. This is not exactly a safe occupation. Most of the action is happening in England, but I can't guarantee you that you won't be a target."

"This is not exactly a good recruiting technique—informing the applicant that she may be dead in a few days. So what exactly do you want me to do if I get the job?"

"If we get the military base, I need someone—preferably a US citizen and wizard or witch to be in charge of the base. Mostly, I think that it would involve working with the US government to set up the base with supplies, a maintenance staff, liason between the US government and us. It's probably a twenty hour a day seven days a week job."

"Let's see. Dangerous job, long hours, I suppose the pay is pretty bad too?"

"That's one thing that is good. I've got a large budget, probably a thousand million pounds if I need them."

"Pounds?"

"Yea. It's the English currency."

"What's the conversion rate to galleons?"

"I think it's running about 6 Pounds to the galleon at the moment."

She whistled. "Do you really have that kind of money?"

"Yes."

"You've got yourself a liaison person—if you'll have me."

"We'll have a 2nd interview with the rest of my team, but as far as I'm concerned you've got the job." We finished our lunch.

Sally said, "This is the strangest lunch date that I've ever had. I came expecting a little light romance over lunch and went away running an army base."

"Is dinner tonight OK for the 2nd interview?"

She paused a moment to consider and said, "Sure, why not. It's not like I've got a heavy date tonight. . . or anything tonight."

"Meet us in the lobby of our hotel. I'll be in touch if anything comes up that would keep us from meeting."

"OK. I'll see you then." We were in a secluded corner of the Mall, but Beth looked around to see if anyone was paying attention to us. I was looking a different direction when I heard the soft 'plop' and I knew that she was gone. I went back to the hotel via Metro.

When I got there, I found everyone in our suite. I noticed that everyone was all grins. "OK. I can see that something's happened. Who did it? George or Fred?"

Fred assumed a hurt expression, "Now why are you so untrusting? You've only been gone a couple of hours. What could have happened?"

"I don't know. I'm not sure that I want to know."

Sally, beaming, said, "I think she'll be great for the job."

"Yes. And what makes you think that she's going to have the job?"

"Well, there are several subtle tell-tale signs. You look pleased with yourself. You're teasing the boys. . ."

George interrupted, "Here, here now. We're not boys. We've been 'of age' for more than a year now."

She went on, unperturbed, "And Fred spied on you and told us that you'd offered her the job."

I turned on Fred, "What was the idea of spying on me? And how did you do it. We were careful to be sure that no one was around."

"Oh, you're altogether too trusting. I used a disillusionment charm so that I could get reasonably close without you're seeing me, and then I used extensible ears so that I could hear you from a distance. I was behind the big oak tree in the little lover's nook that you were in."

"I thought that she would be able to detect any wizards lurking about."

"They've never seen extensible ears here in the States. It's no surprise that she didn't know how to detect them."

"Well, I suppose that you know that we're going to meet her for dinner so that you guys can interview her."

"Why would we want to interview her? We trust your judgment, and Fred has already heard her interview with you," Sally declared definitively.

"I suppose that this will turn into a party instead of an interview then."

George enthused, "Yea! Party! Now you're thinking."

□□

Later that day, we got a call from the Undersecretary for Defense in charge of base closings. He wanted to meet us the next day to choose a base. He wanted us to bring along the liaison person that he'd be working with. I temporized and said that we would make the meeting, but the liaison person might not be able to make that meeting. I didn't want him to think that we had just hired her, and she might not be able to get off her day job to attend.

158

That evening we met Beth in the lobby, and we debated where to go for dinner. Fred wanted to choose the place. He had his "*WWWDC*" with him, and he wanted to show off how he was cosmopolitan and could find a great place on his own.

I said, "Look Fred, we've got a local expert. Why not trust her?"

He scowled and finally relented, "I suppose so, but do you know any place that has 'bangers'?"

Beth asked, "What are 'bangers'?"

George interrupted, "Oh, don't pay attention to him. He's just mad because you're getting to choose the place for us to celebrate your new job. Oh, yea. 'Bangers" are sausages."

Beth asked, "What is it with you people and sausages? Jim got me to eat a bratwurst for lunch, and now Fred wants sausages for dinner."

We finally decided on Beth's favorite Muggle watering hole. They had a grill that was fairly decent. My favorite bartender was there. After we'd been seated at a table, he came by and said, "Well, are you people going to become regulars? Should I learn your favorites?"

I answered, "A good question. I don't know if we will be really regular. If you hadn't guessed, we're not from around here."

"Let me guess, English?"

George asked, "Well, blimey. How'd you ever guess that!"

"Are you working for an embassy?"

"No, we're on holiday." Sally filled in the gap.

The bartender said, "Well, if you do decide to become regulars somewhere, make it here. I'll take good care of you. The drinks you just ordered are on the house. By the way, the chef's done a good job with the rockfish tonight."

After he left, I told Beth, "Now that you're officially 'on staff', you can start tomorrow morning. We've got an appointment with Undersecretary for decommissioning old army bases, Jim Blain, to talk about a good location for us.

Beth perked up, "That's OK. I gave notice today."

"Wow, you were pretty confident weren't you?" Fred was amazed.

"Oh, I noticed you snooping on us at lunch. I figured that if you'd not been happy with me, I'd have heard pretty quickly. Besides, my uncle owns the business."

Fred was still nonplussed and persisted, "How did you notice me? I used a dis-illusionment charm. It was pretty good!"

Beth snorted and said, "Yea, the dis-illusionment was pretty good, and I'd probably not have noticed you if it hadn't been for that stupid ear that you dropped next to our park bench. You should really do a better job of disguising that as something other than an artificial ear. Like maybe it could be a cockroach or a pen or a bowling ball."

Fred was getting really frustrated. This was the 2nd time tonight that Beth had given him a hard time. He excused himself to go to the WC.

I went back to the original topic. "So, you can join us tomorrow at the Pentagon? 11AM?"

"Sure, no problem. Just don't make me ride that stupid Metro again."

"No problem. Can you meet us at the hotel at 10:00 AM? A limo is going to pick us up and take us to the Pentagon."

"Do I have to? You and your Muggle conveyances. It would be so much faster to just disapparate."

"Look, we intended to impress them. But we don't want to carry it too far. We don't want to rub it in."

"OK. We'll ride the limo. By the way, what is a limo?"

"It's a large automobile. The one that we've been picked up in could probably accommodate 8 people pretty comfortably."

The food and drinks came, and the rock fish was good. We danced a little to a real jukebox that took quarters. George was impressed by it, but he was disappointed that it didn't have any "Weird Sister" songs.

Fred jeered, "Come on George, don't you want to hear Celestina Warblelux?"

George gave him a squinted glance as if to say, "What world did you come from?" He actually said, "I thought that she was Ron's and your favorite."

We ended the evening and split up outside the bar. Then we disapparated our separate ways.

Alabama

The next morning, when we came down to the lobby, we found Beth waiting for us. The limo driver showed up about ten minutes later, and we drove in luxury to the Pentagon. Beth was impressed by the reception we got, even though it didn't include the honor guard with assault rifles.

This time we went to a different floor. We all had our badges and only Beth had to get one. The twins were old hands at the badge-making and showed off their deep knowledge.

We were shown into a large office with leather sofas, arm chairs, and a large video projector on the ceiling.

The owner of the office was leaning against the large mahogany desk when we entered. He approached us and introduced himself. Jim Blain was about 6 feet tall, had a balding spot on the back of his head and wore wire-rimmed glasses.

He identified each of us, except for Beth. "I'm supposed to give you any help you need. I'd like to come up with a couple of candidate bases that you can use, and my superiors will make the final decision."

"That sounds reasonable. What have you got available?"

"First, tell me what you're looking for, and we can talk about what I've got."

"OOOOKKK." I drawled, "We would like it to be large enough to accommodate at least a couple of thousand people on base. It should be completely self-contained—food services, laundry, meeting halls, offices, athletic facilities."

Sally added, "I suppose that you'll have barracks, but a lot of the people will be families with children of all ages. It would be really nice if it had individual family housing/apartments for at least half that number."

Beth asked, "I don't know too much about the weather in England, but I think that you wouldn't want to be stuck in North Dakota or Minnesota in the winter?"

George added, "You're right about that. Have you got anything in California?"

Fred said, "Now, George, you're not going to find any movie stars at an army base in California."

I frowned severely at the both of them.

I went on, "We'll need an air base that can accommodate a large cargo plane."

Jim asked, "Do you want a naval base on the ocean?"

I thought about it a minute and said, "I don't think that we need that." The ladies nodded assent.

Jim thought a minute and said, "OK. Here's what we have available right now or within the next month." He started the overhead projector and a projection screen came down from the ceiling. As it warmed up, an aerial photo of a military base surrounded by pine forests slowly appeared on the screen.

"There's an army base in northern Alabama. It's about 100 miles from the Gulf. It's got an airstrip where you could land a C130. It's not a fancy airstrip. As a matter of fact, we don't have ground control there. It would be a real 'theatre' operation to land there, but quite do-able. It's pretty remote and doesn't have a large town within 40 miles.

"We've got an air base in West Texas. It's really remote—at least 100 miles from the nearest town of any size. It's got a great airstrip—ground control and everything. You could land a Concorde there."

Beth asked, "What's a Concorde?"

I answered, "A large passenger airplane. They only land at a few airports."

Blain went on, "It's pretty dry and hot in the summer. Well, I suppose the Alabama base is pretty hot too in the summer, but not dry.

"We've got a naval air station in Kansas."

Fred interrupted, "Isn't Kansas where Dorothy was from?"

Blain, not seeing the relationship was dumbfounded.

Beth answered, "You mean Dorothy of the Wizard of Oz?"

"Of course."

"Yes, she was from Kansas."

"Well, isn't Kansas really far inland?"

Blain answered, "Yes, so?"

"What's a naval base doing so far inland?"

Blain smiled in relief, "Oh, sure. It's a naval" he emphasized the next words, "air station. Naval airplanes are . . or were based there. They did training too. It's really a pretty nice base. They have on-base housing for a lot of families. The only problem with it is that it's close to a fairly large town, Lawrence, Kansas. There's a university there too.

"What's your preference?"

We looked at each other, and Blain asked if we'd like some privacy to talk. I answered, "I don't think that we could be confident of perfect privacy in this building—even if you are earnest. We'll go ahead and discuss this a little right now."

Beth looked at everyone, and since no one was saying anything she started out, "Well, I don't know what you're thinking, but the Naval air station sounds good to me. I know that we want to be remote from people, but we can put spells on the base to keep random Muggles away. I don't know about west Texas. It's pretty wild out there. I don't have anything against the Alabama base, but I don't have anything for it either."

The rest of us looked at each other and shrugged. I said, "Why not. They'll just pick what they want to give us anyway." Then I turned to Blain and said, "Why don't you give us the naval air station, if you can?"

He asked, "Would you like to visit them? We could probably put together a little junket in a week or so to go see them."

I was definite, "We don't really have time for this. We've got to get this program ramped up quickly. We'd really like to start sending people there within a month. Is that possible?"

"OK. I'll pass that on up to my superiors, and we'll see what we can do."

"When can we expect to hear back from you on your decision?" I asked.

"I'd think within a week. We probably have to do a little negotiation with the community involved, but none of the bases were going to be used for anything other than rust.

"I can work with Ms. Lawson to nail the details if that's OK with you."

I nodded vigorously, "That would be fine."

"Do you know of any reason for us to stay in the States longer?" That was Sally. She was antsy to get back to England.

"I don't think so, if you trust Ms. Lawson's judgment on the details."

"Yes, we do." I said determinedly. She smiled.

We finished off with some pleasantries, but we were done. The limo took us back to the hotel. When we got out, I asked Sally to get us some tickets back to London and asked Beth, "How can we communicate securely across the Atlantic? I know that owls can cross it, but that's pretty slow."

"Well, we can use owls for ordinary correspondence. If we really need quick communications, there's port-key courier service. That can be a couple of hours."

"No, I want something that can't be traced magically. Could you learn to use the telephone?"

Beth made a face like when she was eating the hot dog. "I suppose if I absolutely have to."

Fred said, "That would be great! My dad would love it—using a Muggle tephelone."

I corrected, "That's 'telephone'."

"Whatever."

Sally got us tickets on a flight the next morning. Since we had some time, we decided to do some sight-seeing. We bickered about where to go. I wanted to go to the National Gallery. The twins wanted to go to some bar on the "WWWDC". Sally wanted to go to see Congress. Beth pointed out that there was a Quidditch game that evening. I suggested seeing an ice hockey game that I'd seen was going to be played in Baltimore. Nobody was interested. Sally had never been to see a Quidditch game and wanted to see one.

So, we went down to the street level and found a dark corner (for the sun had set). We all took hands because only Beth had been to the Quiditch stadium. I was holding Beth's left hand and Fred's right hand, and Sally was holding George and Beth's right hand. The three wizards were all mutually holding hands and we two Muggles were holding the joined hands of the pairs. Apparently the game was in Pennsylvania somewhere close to Hershey.

After I defeated the temptation to wretch, I looked around and found that we had landed in a deep valley. There were stands built on three sides of the Quidditch pitch. There was a gate and a ticket stand with half a dozen booths. From a sign above the stand, it appeared that the Stanton Trolls were playing the Roanoke Centaurs. It hadn't occurred to any of us that we would need Galleons to get into the game. No credit cards, no Pounds, no dollars would do. Luckily between Beth and the Weasleys we had enough Galleons to get in with a couple of Galleons to spare.

Of course, I'd seen many Quidditch games as had the Weasleys (not to mention playing in them) as had Beth, but Sally had never seen one. She was gasping and 'ohing' and 'ahhing' at the wrong times. When the teams flew in it was quite thrilling, and I could understand her gasp. Seeing people, seemingly without support, flying around like airplanes in a "dog fight" is pretty startling. It's hard to follow the progress of this chaotic game. It's rather like watching ice hockey in three dimensions—if hockey had four pucks, one of which is practically invisible. Sally sat between George and Fred. She was paying a whole lot more attention to Fred, but I cleared up a few points that Fred thought were so obvious that he couldn't conceive of anyone not instinctively understanding.

For example, at one point Sally was trying to work out the strategy of Quidditch. She was stuck on the scoring system. She asked, "If catching the Snitch ends the game and is worth 150 points, then surely a team that is down by more than 150 points has to try to not catch the Snitch?"

Fred answered, "Well, duh. Sure, so?"

Sally pressed on, "But that's just crazy. It's crazy to want to not do what the object of the game is, right?"

Fred was exasperated and said, "The object of the game is winning. I know I said that the object of the game is to catch the Snitch, but that's just the main way to win."

They were both unhappy for another minute or two, but that passed. Beth was sitting between Fred and me. She seemed to be amazed that I understood Quidditch as well as I did. She had the idea that a Muggle could never really understand the sport.

"Oh, Beth, give it a rest. Admit that I know Quidditch inside and out. I've been watching it for years and years."

Beth wasn't satisfied, "OK. How about this one? When can the game not end in a tie?"

I answered resignedly, "All tournament games must end in a win. If the Snitch is caught and the score is tied (it happens about one in a hundred games), there is a penalty shoot-off mano a mano between a chaser and the keeper. Each side gets 5 shots. Each player has 30 seconds to maneuver and shoot. The keep can maneuver freely. Then if they're still tied they repeat until they're not. Satisfied?"

Beth looked at me hard, and then laughed, "I didn't know that. True?"

"Sure, would I kid you?"

She drawled, "I don't know. Would you?"

"You just never know do you?"

She turned to Fred, "What about what he said, is it true?"

Fred said, "Beats me. I've never played in a tie game. Would you look at that beater? He almost got the keep with that hit."

The game ended, and we all disapparated back to the hotel and tried to get some sleep in before our flight the next day.

□

The flight back to the UK left from Reagan National. Sally and I managed to talk all the wizards—including Beth—to go there by Metro. Fred was the hardest to convince, but Sally took Fred's hand and said, "You know Fred, I really would like to take the Tube sometime with you. This is just good practice."

The twins were seasoned travelers that day. They went through customs and security like pros. When we got out of customs at Heathrow, they suggested that we go into a deserted hall.

"Why?" I asked.

George and Fred looked at each other and then said, "Well, we don't fancy just disapparating back to London in front of all these Muggles." They looked around meaningfully. Beth nodded and started off.

I said, "Well, I don't fancy disapparating back to London in front of Muggles or no Muggles."

Fred insisted that it would grow on me with practice.

"What grows on you is holding hands with someone when you disapparate. Oh, yes, I don't want it to grow on me. Let's take the Tube."

Fred said, "You are right. I don't want to get used to riding the Tube. I might start to want to ride it on my own."

George went on, "Yes. That could be the beginning of a long string of sneaking out on the odd evening for the guilty pleasure of riding down to Paddington Station on the Tube."

Fred scowled, and I smiled. We walked down to the platform, and I bought tickets.

What-if

I was sitting at my desk. I had my feet up on the desk (with shoes removed). Sally entered our office and asked if I were taking the day off.

"No, I'm thinking."

"Are you sure it wasn't napping?"

"No. Thinking."

"It looks to me like you're taking a nap."

"Not really, I'm putting my head below my feet so I'll have more blood flowing to my brain."

She gave me a look that said, "You can't kid a kidder."

"No, really, this is the way I do my most profound thinking. I've gotten some of my best ideas this way."

"Such as?"

"Just be quiet and let me think."

I turned ideas over and over in my head. Finally I said, "Yes, even I can see through a wall if I stare at it long enough. We need to get in touch with Fred and George and see when we can start advertising our sanctuary program. I suppose you can get in touch with Fred when you want to?"

"Oh, yes." She opened her purse and pulled out a galleon. "If I rub this galleon, thus." She put the galleon between left thumb and forefinger and rubbed, "a similar galleon that Fred has turns green."

"And then he gets in touch with you?"

"Right."

"Well, get him and George and. . ." I thought a moment. "Yes, and Lee if possible to meet us for lunch or dinner or something as soon as possible."

"Will, do boss."

"In the mean time, let's talk about what we will suggest to them.

□

She arranged for us to meet the next day for dinner at the Green Man. Sally and I got there first. We got a table in a quiet corner and waited. The three arrived in about ten minutes. We all stood and shook hands. I commented, "This is old home week. I think the four of us have not been together since Messieurs Weasley made their dramatic exit from Hogwarts when the frog princess was the Headmistress.

"Oh, you mean our old buddy Professor Umbridge? Fred and George gave her quite the send-off from Hogwarts." Lee laughed at this memory.

"Oh, I'm sorry, I need to introduce Sally. Sally, this is Lee Jordan. Lee, this is Sally Harker."

"Who was this Professor Umbridge? Did you say the frog princess?" She seemed fascinated, but it seemed that she would be about anything that Fred was involved with.

Fred answered, "Oh, she was a flunky from the Ministry of Magic who was sent to suppress rumors that Riddle had returned. She briefly threw Dumbledore out and replaced him." He turned to me and asked, "You know, I've always wondered how you kept from being sacked yourself during that era."

"Oh, it was really easy. In the first place, no one paid any attention to me because I'm a Squib. In the second place, the only reason that she could sack someone was insubordination or incompetence. She visited my classes a couple of times to grade me, but she had the misfortune of not knowing anything about English literature. I never did anything the least insubordinate—at least, openly. She didn't know anything about English literature, so she couldn't suggest anything stupid like she did with the teachers of magical subjects.

"I saw her evaluation of me. It was pretty much blank with hardly anything written on it. You have to know something about a subject to critique practitioners of it.

"She was just too lazy to make up something bad about my teaching. She had much bigger fish to fry than me. She had Potter and Dumbledore and Haggrid and, well frankly, you guys."

"Yes, we did enjoy getting her goat," said Fred.

"You mean her cats," added George.

Sally asked, "Cats?"

I answered, "Oh, she had a thing for cats. Her office walls were covered with photos and cross-stitch work. The subjects were always cats. Frankly, I never wanted to know where that fetish came from."

Fred asked, "Do you know what she's doing now?"

"No." I answered.

"She's back in the ministry, doing trials of wizards and witches who are Muggle-born. She's sent quite a lot of them to Azkaban."

I answered, "Well, we've come to the subject that I'd like to talk about with you three. Lee, I'd like to smuggle wizards and witches who are on the run or enemies of Riddle out of the country to give them and their families sanctuary. What do you think about the idea?"

Lee said, "That sounds great. I suppose you think they'll make good recruits for the army you're supposed to be putting together. How are you going to do it?"

Just then our waitress came to our table to take our drink orders. Lee asked, "I'll have a pumpkin juice, please."

The Weasleys asked for butter beer. The waitress looked at them like they were speaking Japanese and said, "What are you talking about?"

Lee answered, "You have pumpkin juice don't you?"

"No."

"Well, then I'll have a butter beer."

"Look, we've got Porter and Stout on tap, about a dozen varieties of foreign beers but we don't have butter beer."

"Well, what do you have besides those?"

"We have coffee, tea, Coca Cola products, the beers, and I can get you a mixed drink from the bar. So what will it be?"

Grumbling, everyone picked hot tea.

Lee grumbled, "What kind of restaurant is this?"

I smiled slightly and said, "A Muggle restaurant. You've never been to one before, I suppose."

"And I never will again."

Sally said, "Just hold your judgment until the main course arrives. Anyway, imagine this, Lee. You will publicize my offer to give sanctuary to any wizard or witch that is an enemy of Riddle. We'd set up a meeting somewhere, probably to be named at the last moment. They'd meet us there and we'd take them on from there."

I asked, "I just see one problem. How do we be sure that there aren't any Deatheaters among them?"

Lee said, "Don't you realize that our programs can only be heard by people who have the password AND know when they're happening."

I was impressed, "Really. You can do that?"

Lee was clearly pleased, 'Sure. Guaranteed."

"That's nice, but what happens if one shows up anyway? How do we know, and what do we do about if?"

Lee was less happy, "I'm telling you, no one but Phoenix supporters listen."

I asked, "Come on, Fred, George. Would you make a suggestion about what to do? I just can't risk people's lives and freedom on this."

Fred hmmmed and wrinkled his brow in thought. George didn't change his stare. No one spoke for a while. Then suddenly both Fred and George looked at each other and they said, in that strange sort of unison that they sometimes had, "The Unbreakable Promise. Yes!"

Sally asked, "Fred. What are you talking about?"

George said, "The Unbreakable Oath. You can't break it."

Fred added, "And if you do, then you're dead."

George took over, "We insist that everyone who wants sanctuary has to make the Unbreakable Oath not to tell anyone not in the sanctuary where it is"

Fred, "or what they're doing. If they refuse to make the oath, we wipe them out with a memory charm and send them someplace interesting."

Sally said, "You wouldn't." She looked from one to the other of the twins and their gleeful faces convinced her otherwise. "No. I see you would."

I was thinking. I said, "Yes. That could work, couldn't it?"

"Work? It's as easy as pie."

Lee was nodding slowly. "Yeh. This could be fun."

Lee asked, "So, how do you get to this sanctuary."

I smiled and shook my forefinger at him, "No. Sorry. No one who hasn't taken the oath can be told."

Lee feigned surprise, 'But, it's me. You've got to. You can trust me."

"No. I don't have to. And I'm not."

Lee looked over to George, "Come on, it's me. You can tell me."

George shook his head, "no."

Lee frowned but asked, "When?"

"When what?" I asked.

"When do you come on the show? When do you issue your invitation?"

"We've got a lot of stuff to set up: Transportation to the sanctuary. The sanctuary has to be ready. We've . . ."

Lee said, "Easy. You just Disapparate and pop into the sanctuary."

I answered, "Too far. And not safe, anyway."

Fred asked, "What about a port key?"

George said, "You know, we don't have the ability to set up a port key. And the Ministry can always find out about those things anyway."

Lee asked, "What about broomsticks."

Fred answered, "Be serious. Have you ever flown hundreds of miles on a broom?"

"OK. OK. Then, it's got to be," and he shivered involuntarily, "You've got to take Muggle transport."

I brought us back to the present. "Fred will get in touch with you when we're ready."

We had a good meal, and even Lee admitted that the Muggle restaurant was pretty good. As we were leaving the restaurant, I pulled Sally aside. She said, "What is it, do you want a good-night kiss?"

"No, I want you to set up a meeting tomorrow with Parker. We need to get planning the transport to our sanctuary for these droves of people who are going to flock to our offer."

"Will we need one bicycle or two?"

"I'll leave that up to you. Do you want company getting home?"

She looked at me a second and said, "I'm going to be home way before you are courtesy of disapparation."

"But, you won't enjoy the trip as much as I will."

Wizard Radio

The owl found its way into my office pretty easily. I had convinced Parker to have one window in the building that was always open. They were going to get in anyway. It was always watched by a guard with an assault rifle—just in case something other than an owl came through. As a matter of fact, I'd instructed the guard to down any eagle owls that came through. I didn't know any wizard who used one other than Riddle. I also had an owl flap built into the wall of my office near the door.

I didn't recognize this owl, but I rarely do. As a matter of fact there was only one that I ever recognized—Minerva's owl, Endora. I had taken to calling it Robert until Minera had told me its real name. This one wasn't Endora. I untied the message and read it. "We're ready to broadcast on Wizard Radio. We'll do your spot on the 2nd Wednesday in November. We need to plan what you'll say."

What I'd say? We definitely needed to get together to work on the plan. Sally had come over and was looking over my shoulder. "Are you going to become a radio celebrity?"

"I certainly hope not. We need to get together and plan how the escape plan will work for whatever refugees show up. Is the American base ready for us yet?"

Sally shrugged. "The last owl that we had from Beth was that they had inspected the base and made sure that utilities, food deliveries, etc. would be ready in a couple of weeks."

"We need to put together a meeting with Beth and the Weasleys and Parker to plan this out as soon as possible. How soon can we get Beth over here?"

"Well, assuming that we can get her to go onto an airplane again—I don't think she liked the first trip very much—and over here, it would probably be two days. Does she have a passport?"

I said, "Oh, I'm sure she doesn't. Our American cousins can surely get her one quickly if we ask nicely."

Sally laughed, "We're way past asking nicely. The last time I asked nicely for something was when I needed them to get Beth an office in the Pentagon. I finally threatened that somebody would turn into a toad if they didn't get a move on."

Sally sat on the edge of my desk to make reading my note easier.

"Did you really say that?" I asked.

"Yes, in an email. I hinted that it might be somebody that sits in the cabinet." Sally had an absolutely straight face as she said it.

"You didn't?"

"Well, I was getting pretty mad about them dragging their feet. By the way, can we do that?"

"Do what?"

"Turn somebody into a toad?"

"Good question. Skilled wizards can turn themselves into other things and I guess that maybe they could turn somebody else into something else. I really never ran into the situation." I stopped to think about that. "Well, come to think of it, I knew a dark wizard who turned a kid into a ferret. Why not a toad? Now, I know for sure that we could turn somebody into a Newt . . . Gingrich—at least for a few hours. Do you think that's a good threat?"

"I don't know anything about American politics. Is a 'Newt Gingrich' bad?"

I didn't answer that but just made a face.

"Well, let's assume that we can get her over here by Friday. Send a note back with the owl asking them to meet us here Friday morning."

"You bet boss."

"Thanks." Then I added, "And don't call me 'boss'."

"Sure, boss."

She turned the parchment over, wrote on the other side, and tied it back on the owl's foot. "I don't know why I always have to do this."

"You always have to do this because you're a lot better doing that fine manipulative work with your fingers than I am."

I had been working out an outline of the script for this broadcast, and I was anxious to see if the pro's would think it was unworkable.

□

The Americans had no trouble getting a passport for Beth, but it turned out not to be necessary. They were anxious to get this going, and they put Beth on a military transport. She landed at a British airbase. The Brits drove her down in a HumVee. They checked her into a nice little hotel off the beaten path—small, exclusive, elegant.

The Weasleys were anxious to get going as well. They arrived at 8AM Friday morning brandishing their ID badges. They had Beth with them. They had volunteered to pick her up. I don't know how they got the idea that she needed picking up.

I first realized that they had arrived when I got a phone call from the main entrance where the guard had stopped Beth from entering.

I answered the phone, listened and answered, "Yes, she is perfectly welcome. She works for us—just like the Weasleys.

"Yes, I want her to have an ID badge. Send her along to Robby.

"Yes, right now. She's due for a meeting. . . Immediately."

They arrived about half an hour later. Beth was looking none too happy. She launched a small tirade as she entered the door. "Do you realize this has been the worst 24 hours in my life? First, I have to ride on a dangerous, jumpy 'aeroplane' for 6 hours getting here. Then I have to ride a dangerous bumpy auto for another 6 hours to get to London."

Fred interrupted, "That was a pretty posh hotel that we picked you up at."

She smiled and chuckled, "Well, yes, I have to admit that you had pretty nice accommodations for me. But then when I came into this musty warehouse, I'm stopped and embarrassed by being badgered. Then when they let me in, I'm constantly watched by men with guns as we came up here to your office."

I was shocked, "What! You saw the guards who were watching you?"

"Well, certainly, do you think that I'm blind? There must have been two or three who were paying special attention to me."

I was relieved, "Oh, whew. I thought that you might have seen them all. If you had, I'd have to have some people reprimanded. There were actually at least a dozen snipers who should have been watching you as you traveled through the building."

Parker was the last to arrive. He brought along an SAS officer that I'd not seen before. He introduced him as Major Foyle. Foyle sat down at the corner of my desk and quietly listened through most of the discussion.

I started off with a review of where we were, ticking off points on my fingers, "Well, we've got a base assigned to us in America. They're well along in preparing it for our refugees. We have a way to communicate with them and can tell them how to make a rendezvous."

"Now, we have to have transportation from the rendezvous point to the air base, an aircraft ready to transport us, the base truly ready for them, a tentative date, time and place for the rendezvous. Anything else that we need?"

Beth spoke up. "I'll have the base ready to receive perhaps a hundred or so in 10 days, two weeks tops."

I was pleasantly surprised, "Great. Let's schedule the rendezvous for two weeks. What about transport?"

Parker spoke up, "I've been working with the Americans. They've agreed to keep a military transport plane ready for us on a day's notice. It's located at an air base in Europe. How do we get them from the rendezvous to the air base?"

Foyle spoke up, "I'll take care of that. I have plans, but I'd prefer not to reveal them. The fewer people who know details, the better. I don't want to know the rendezvous point until the last minute."

I asked, "What about security? There's a fair chance that the Deatheaters will get wind of the rendezvous and may show up."

Foyle volunteered, "I'll handle security. I'll have a unit of snipers in place. We'll need a dress rehearsal before hand so that everybody will know what to expect. I don't want them hitting any of our people by mistake."

"Good. Who will be on the ground to 'greet' the refugees?"

Fred answered, "George and I'll be there. We've seen a lot of Deatheaters and can probably identify most of them."

I said, "Me too. I want to make sure that nothing goes wrong."

Beth spoke up, "I don't know why I'm doing this, but I'll be there too."

Parker was exasperated, "You can't all be there. We've got to have somebody running the operation. And I don't want you all being killed if things go 'South'."

I answered, "Sally can run the operation. She's perfectly capable and knows what I'd do better than I do."

It was Sally's turn to be exasperated. "If you think that I'm going to play it safe while the rest of you risk your lives, you're crazy. I'm going to be there next to you."

Parker's mouth was hanging open. It closed and opened again. Finally, he said, "Look, I'm in command here. Fred, you're going. Sally you're not. Wendt, I hate to do it, but I've got to let you go. George, you're out. You two are interchangeable, and I'm not going to risk both of you. Beth, you don't have enough background yet to be useful there. You don't know any Deatheaters."

Beth said, "You can't keep me away, and you know it."

"Or me," said George.

Parker answered, "I can't, you're right. But if you want to be in this operation, you've got to play by my rules."

George mumbled under his breath, but didn't protest. Beth was clearly unhappy, but didn't say anything either.

I finished up the meeting, "Well, now that everyone is happy, let's get to work on the details. Foyle, we need to set up a rehearsal. Whenever you've got your team together and are ready, we'll do that.

"Fred, George, when can you get me a rehearsal on Wizard Radio?"

George said, "We'll have to get in touch with Lee Jordan. You know, he's producing Wizard Radio."

"Yes, he was always the announcer wasn't he?"

"Announcer?" asked Beth and Sally in unison.

Fred answered, "Yes, he used to announce the Quidditch games at Hogwarts."

George said, "We'll get in touch with Lee and let you know when you can practice. We should be able to get you in soon."

I was a little worried by the sound of that, "What do you mean, 'when you can practice'?"

"That's what you want isn't it. You want to put on a public service announcement about the refuge for the enemies of 'You Know Who'."

"Well, I thought one of you would do that."

The twins said with gusto in unison, "No. We want to hear you on the radio."

I grimaced. I'd never been good at public speaking. "We'll talk about that after you've got a time from Lee;"

Foyle said, "I hate to interrupt this mutual admiration society, but Wendt, we need to get together to plan the details of how my people are going to cover you."

"Sure, when you're ready, give me a call, and we'll get a meeting going."

"It'll be a couple of days."

People left. Then, with Sally and me left alone, I grumbled, "Well, there's another fine mess that I got us into."

She looked over and asked, "Us?? I don't remember anyone volunteering me for Wizard Radio."

"I didn't either, but if I have to be on it, you get the honor, too. See what you can do to influence George and get him to do the announcement."

"I'll see what I can do, but you know, nobody's got a lot of pull with Fred.

I looked up rapidly, "Fred? I thought you and George were like this?" I twisted my index and middle fingers together.

Sally gave me a look and said, "You are behind the times. Anyway, the two of them can be pretty cantankerous when they have a joke in mind."

"No kidding," I agreed.

A couple of days later, an owl arrived. Sally had earned the right to open all the owl post that arrived. They seemed to be more cooperative with her than with me. It was a letter from the twins:

"We've got an appointment with Lee. Meet us at the Green Man tomorrow at 6PM. Look for someone with an ear missing. That'll be my brother.

"You coming, Sal?"

"You couldn't keep me away, but, I'm still not going to be on the radio."

"That's what you think."

□□

The night of the meeting we arrived at the Green Man a half-hour early and got a table. The twins and Lee arrived about 10 minutes late.

"Well, boys. Sally and I, who can't disapparate, were here a half-hour early. And the three of you are 10 minutes late. What does that tell you about Muggle transport vs. wizard transport?"

"It tells us that you two are gits," said George.

"Well, just Wendt," said Fred.

Lee said, "It's a pleasure to see you again, Mr. Wendt. How have you been? Sally and I have not yet been properly introduced. What does she do?"

"Lee, I've been good. Sally Harker is my personal assistant."

"Secretary." Sally interrupted.

"It's a pleasure to see you again, Miss Sally. I can see why Fred is so keen on you."

"That's a pleasant comment. Thanks, Lee. Just plain Sally will be fine."

They sat, and we got down to business. Lee started, "Fred and George tell me that you are ready to announce that you'll provide refuge to the people that 'You Know Who' is sending to Azkaban."

"That's right. I need to get the word out and announce when we're going to be meeting with people who want to use our service. We also want to keep word of this from the Deatheaters. That's a major advantage of the "Potter Watch" show."

Lee nodded. "We're going to broadcast in a couple of days, sooner than the Wednesday that we talked about, but I'll always find a spot for you. Would you tell me what you're going to say?"

"Sure. I have several points to make. First, we're offering sanctuary for people who are fleeing Riddle and the Deatheaters. 2nd, it's free and anyone can join us. 3rd, we won't tell you where we're going for obvious reasons, but it is out of the country. 4th, once you go, you've got to agree not to return to England until, well, until Riddle is defeated. 5th, it's not required, but any competent wizard who wants to fight Deatheaters will be trained and can take part in our army."

"Whew! That's quite an offer. Any limit on how many can take it up?"

"In the long run, no. But in the short run, we can only accept a limited number of people. I can't promise that everyone who shows up the first time will be accepted. I know that's tough, but we have no idea how many to expect, so we might have more volunteers than we can handle."

Lee pondered a moment. "That IS tough, but it's a good offer. I think lots of people will respond."

Sally said, "I hope so. We've been going to a lot of trouble to set this up. I'd hate to just have a handful show up."

"Miss Sally, I" Lee began, but a cross look from Sally forced him to start over, "Sorry. Sally, I think that it will be a good turnout."

"Do you want to see a script of what we'll say before the show?"

Lee laughed a broad, good-natured laugh. "Oh, oh. . . Do you suppose Fred and George ever provide a script?" He was still having some trouble catching his breath. "You've already given me more than they ever did.

"I will need your code name so that I can introduce you."

I asked, "Code name?"

"Sure. We don't' want to put people in more danger than they already are. What do you want your code name to be?"

I thought a second and on a whim picked an unusual name that I'd heard once. "How about 'Quiller'?"

That seemed to puzzle Lee. Finally, his expression cleared up, and he said, "I get it. Sure. That's really good. 'The Quiller'. The Writer. That's what you are. Or at least that's what you teach—writing."

I was aghast. "What are you talking about? You don't want to pick a code name that gives people hints to your identity." I pondered a minute. "I still like 'Quiller". It's 'Quiller'. Not 'The Quiller'. Not 'Mr. Quiller'. Just 'Quiller'."

Lee looked at me in puzzlement and said, "OK. Whatever you want."

"Thanks."

"What about Sally's code name."

Sally cut in quickly, "NOOOO. No. No. I'm not going to be on the radio. I don't need a code name."

"Oh, Sally," I said, "You need a code name. How about 'The Chef' or 'Chef" or 'The Chief?' Oh! Oh! Better still, 'Le Chifre'?"

Fred said, "No, better, Aimee."

Sally flushed and looked down at her feet.

I said, "We've still got to work out some details before we're ready to broadcast."

Praxis

Major Foyle had sent me an email requesting me to be ready for a rehearsal that day. I wasn't sure what he had in mind, especially because he had adamantly refused to tell me any details. All he'd said was that I only needed be ready to take a trip in the country today.

He showed up at 8:30 AM. He stuck his head in my office door and signaled for me to follow. I got up and left, telling Sally that I had no idea when I'd be back. She just said, "You've got a cell phone. Let me know if it'll be later than quitting time." I agreed to, and we left.

On the way down, he started to explain to me what we were doing.

"We're going to do a little dress rehearsal. I've gotten hold of our friends the Weasleys, and we're going to the rendezvous point to go through the routine.

"You'll announce at your next broadcast where we'll rendezvous with the refugees. The Weasleys will disapparate you there about an hour in advance of the rendezvous time."

I asked, "How did you get in touch with them?"

"Who, the Weasleys?"

"Yes, who else?"

"You don't think that you're the only Muggle who knows about owl post."

"I suppose they have been in touch with you by owl."

"Right you are."

By this time, we'd reached the ground floor, and we were headed suspiciously close to the heliport. "You know, I'm getting a little sick of traveling by helicopter. I don't want you to tell me that we're flying to this rendezvous."

"OK, I won't tell you."

I thanked heaven silently that the helicopter that waited for us was not a Blackhawk. It was a larger transport 'copter. We got on board and donned the usual headphones. Foyle explained, "We're just flying by helicopter to the nearest military base where we'll take an executive jet to an airport near the rendezvous."

"And, I suppose, back to helicopter for the final leg."

"Oh, no. We're going to drive from there in a truck."

I thought, "at least things are looking up."

The flight was much less stressful than my previous helicopter rides. We switched to a small jet that was actually pretty luxurious. There was seating for about a dozen—no stewardesses, but there was a wet bar. I had some peanuts on the ninety minute flight to an unnamed military base. We were hustled into a nondescript military lorry and bounced along in the back end without any real view of the countryside that we went through.

Foyle was explaining in detail what would happen when we got to the RV spot. "I've already positioned snipers there. If things go sour, I want to put the hammer down hard and fast before any of the bad guys figure out that anything has gone wrong.

"Do you expect that the Weasleys will know all the real refugees by sight?"

I shook my head, "I doubt it. They probably will know a lot of them. The wizarding community is pretty tight and small, but I doubt that they know everyone or anywhere near everyone."

Foyle considered that a moment and asked, "Then do you think that they'll know any bad guys that might show up?"

"I think that the chances are better, especially now that the Deatheaters are acting a lot more openly. We have dossiers on a lot of them that we've been collecting lately, but I wouldn't want to bet my life that they know every one of them."

"I was afraid of that. Well, we'll just have to fly by the seat of our pants and hope that any bad guys that they don't recognize will do something that distinguishes them quickly enough to let us act."

When we got 'there', I finally got a look at our location. It seemed to be a small town. From what I could see driving in, the town square was perhaps ¼ mile from outskirts to town center. We parked on a side street. Foyle said as we got out, "Your buddies should be here any minute." Just then, the two appeared in front of us.

George said, "Fancy meeting you here. We just can't seem to get away from you. Are you following us?"

Fred added, "Yeah."

I stared at Fred, "Is that all you have to say."

He thought a moment and said reflectively, "Yeaaaah."

Foyle filled in the gap with commentary. "Ok. I've already got snipers in place. What I want to do is practice how this is going to work. Here's how I see it.

"These refugees are going to start disapparating in. You three are going to be on the ground to greet them. But you're also going to be ID'ing them. Deciding whether they're friendly or not. We need hand signals that the snipers can see that will identify friendlies from the enemy. But it's got to be subtle, we don't want the Deatheaters getting suspicious. Do you have any ideas?"

Fred asked, "How about this. If we see a Deatheater, we come over to him and start beating him with a bludger? Do you think that's subtle enough?"

Foyle frowned, "I was thinking of something more like scratching your ear."

Fred said, "Yeah that's a great idea. I could scratch my left ear with my right hand."

George chimed in, "And I could scratch his left ear with my right hand too."

I could see that Foyle didn't have quite the temperament for dealing with these two on a long term basis, so I suggested, "How about doing this?" I pointed my left index finger at Fred with my thumb cocked like the hammer of a revolver and the rest of my fingers making a fist.

Foyle liked that, "That sounds good. Do you think that the two of you could manage that."

"Oh, definitely. Easy as pie."

Fred said, "And you think that these snappers of yours won't be found by real Deatheaters?"

Foyle asked, "Why don't you try to find them?"

George said, "Easy as pie." He got out his wand and pointed it slowly around the town square, mouthing something as he did. His smile turned mushy and then turned into a frown.

Foyle had a smile on his face though. "Not as easy as you think, eh."

Fred asked, "Did you do a revealer spell?"

George answered, "Yeah, and I don't get it. I didn't find anyone."

Foyle answered, "Right. You didn't know what to look for, so you didn't find what you weren't looking for."

George muttered, "That's easy for you to say."

Foyle went on, "Here's how we're going to practice this. I want you, Fred"

Fred interrupted, "No, I'm George."

Foyle frowned again and said with special emphasis, "I want you, Fred to disapparate in and out as fast as you can. You'll walk over to one of our people." At that point about two dozen men in various civilian clothes walked into the square. "You'll go over to one of them and either point at him with the special hand sign—or not. My snipers—not 'snappers'—will take note of him. After you've marked—or not—everyone, my boys will shoot the ones that you marked. We'll keep going through the exercise until they've got it perfect."

So, the afternoon started. Fred disapparated in and out about once a minute. He walked up to a hatless man at random and then disapparated out after signalling. It took about half an hour the first time. When he'd done the last, there was a rapid fire succession of the men hit by what turned out to be a sophisticated version of a paintball. It was so rapid and unexpected that the twins and I jumped out of our skins. I hit the ground and the two of them disapparated. They returned, pretty quickly, but around the corner and came out only after looking around carefully.

The two of them went around examining the ones hit by paintballs. Finally Fred said, "You got two or three of them wrong."

George expanded on that, "Yeah, two had green paint and the other purple."

Foyle pulled a radio out of his pocket and said, "Green, you got a couple wrong and purple had one wrong. Let's do it again."

We spent the next couple of hours working through about three or four more dry runs. Everyone had paint on them, including Foyle and me. We looked like escapees from a junior high paint-ball party. In the last one, Fred had marked George and George returned the favor.

Finally, Foyle asked me, "Assuming that we all survive this little exercise when we do it for real, do you have instructions ready for the refugees?"

I slapped my head, "No. I really hadn't thought about it."

"Well, these people are going to want to know what's going to happen to them and some may even want out when they do know what's going to happen. You get to work on your speech. We need it ready tomorrow."

We spent the night at the air base, and the next day we went back to London.

Sally met me the next morning and asked what had happened.

"Oh, you know, practice. We practiced killing Deatheaters."

"You had some, did you?"

"No, we were all playing Deatheaters."

"Did you kill many Muggles?"

"Oh, yes. I killed a nosy Muggle by the name of Sally."

"You say that now. But you'll find it hard to do it when it's time to play for real."

"Now, for real. I've got a question for you."

"Go ahead."

"Let's suppose that you were a witch."

"OK. By the way, are you completely sure that I'm not?"

"Oh, I know real witches very intimately. I assure that I'd know if you were. But now, for my question, 'If you were a witch that was trying to get away from Tom Riddle, what would you want to know from complete strangers that wanted to help you get away?'"

Sally wrinkled her brows and looked up and to her right. She hummed and said, "Well, first off and certainly most important why are you, a Muggle, helping me, a witch?"

"OK. First, I'm helping you for my own safety's sake. Tom Riddle is as much a danger to me a Muggle as he is to you as a witch." I started pacing back and forth.

"2nd I've got a score to settle myself. He ordered the death of a good student of mine at Hogwarts—yes Hogwarts. I used to work there, and I've got lots of good friends that are threatened by the Deatheaters.

"Finally, I will oppose oppression regardless who's doing it." I must have been pretty intense by the end because Sally was staring at me with her mouth agape.

"I didn't realize that you felt quite that strongly about this business."

"I guess I do. You know it's pretty spooky, but I almost have been hoping a Deatheater or two would show up and get clipped by the guys upstairs."

She looked puzzled and then her face cleared, "Oh, you mean the snipers up. . ."

"Yeah."

"Well, when you've got your little talk worked up, you can practice it on me."

"Good idea. I will."

The Broadcast

The twins met us at King's Cross station as planned at 8AM.

George asked, "Do you want to take the Hogwart's Express?"

Sally asked, "What's that?"

Fred answered, "It's the special train that goes to Hogwart's school. Wendt, you always took it, right?"

"No, I frequently got to Hogwarts by floo powder or disapparation or some other disgusting means of travel. Never went by broomstick though. I sometimes went by the Express."

"Oh, really? Did you always find it disgusting disapparating with a certain lady who will remain nameless but whose initials are MM?" asked George.

Sally asked, "Do you mean Ms. McGonagall? Is that how you got to Hogwarts? Did you have to pay for the transportation?"

I grimaced and said, "Whatever do you mean? Ms. McGonagall was always very generous."

"I'll bet she was!" Sally replied.

I looked from one face to another and didn't find a sympathetic one in the lot. "You all are determined to find the worst possible interpretation for anything that Minerva and I do."

Sally smiled gently, "Not the worst—the best possible."

I asked, "But I thought that the Hogwart's Express always went to . . . well, Hogwart's. That's why it was named the Hogwart's Express, right?"

Fred answered, "Oh, the Hogwart's Express goes to all points between here and Hogwarts. Today it's not going to Hogwarts, but we can have it stop at Waddling-on-the-Tyme."

"Is that where the transmitter is?"

"Yeh, Lee's house is there or actually it's his parents'.""

"Do they know about the pirate radio that he broadcasts?"

"Know? Sure they know."

"Good, I'd hate to get him into trouble." Somehow, Fred's assurance didn't assure me much.

We had been walking along the platforms and saw a sign for track 9 and then 10. Fred announced to no one in particular, "Well, here we are. Track 9 ¾ , last one through is dragon's tail." He started to sprint off.

I tried to stop him, but he was running too fast for me. George pulled out his wand and shot out a 'leg lock' curse that caused him to trip. We caught up, and George said, "Not so fast, bro. You forget that we've got Muggles with us. How are we going to do this?"

Sally asked, "Do what?"

I shook my head. "It's got to be seen to be believed."

Fred answered, "Well, to get to the train, you've got to walk through that wall that separates tracks 9 and 10."

Sally sniggered, "Easy as pie."

Fred sidled over close to Sally and said, "Actually it is. You just take the hand of your local friendly wizard, and then we trot through the wall," as he took her hand in his.

Sally was looking doubtful although she wasn't exactly fighting to get her hand back from Fred. She suggested, "Why doesn't Fred take me through with him after the two of you?"

George enthused, "Brilliant. I couldn't have said it better myself."

Fred agreed, "You've never said truer words, bro!" So I took George's hand and gritted my teeth. He said, as we broke into a trot approaching the wall, "Close your eyes, it's easier that way." So I closed my eyes just as we reached the wall. The first thing I felt was something stiff but soft, giving some and suddenly I was pushed back and fell on my backside. I opened my eyes and found that George was nowhere to be seen. I had a sore backside to boot. Then George stuck his head through the wall. He said, "Why don't we try that again slowly."

I grimaced and said, "You know, I never thought that I'd find some mode of transportation that I like less than disapparation, but this could be it."

George stuck his hand and part of his arm through the wall and extended it toward me. "This time we'll go slow and easy. Just take my hand, and we'll be off."

I grimaced again, reached out, and let him pick me up off the ground. He slowly pulled me up to the wall, and then slowly my arm disappeared into the wall. It felt like I was pushing my way through jello, but this time all of me went through. I closed my eyes again because I really didn't want to see anything in the wall as I went through. I'd once seen a movie called *Buckaroo Bonzai*. It had someone drive a car through a mountain without the aid of a tunnel. There were all sorts of strange things stuck to the car after it emerged from the mountain.

When I was through I looked myself over—half expecting to find some crumbs of bricks stuck to my clothes or something else disgusting. But I didn't find anything out of the usual. I had to comment, "With Minerva it was a whole lot easier."

Then Fred and Sally trotted through at a nice clip. I looked around and found that there was a track with a sign indicating Track 9 ¾. I walked down the platform looking into the cars. There were a small number of wizards in various forms of outlandish dress. I'd never gotten used to the variety of clothes that wizards somehow found appropriate when mixing with Muggles. There was a man wearing a bright purple pair of trousers and a pink shirt. I wished that I had a pair of sun glasses along. There were several people wearing jeans and a variety of shades of tops.

The Hogwarts Express Train looked a lot like Thomas the Tank Engine. I wouldn't have been surprised if it had talked. Fred passed out tickets to us, and we chose a car. We went onboard and found a set of seats. We reversed one of them so that we had two benches facing each other. We took them.

We slowly left the station. I looked to see the route. I'd ridden out of King's Cross station a number of times in Muggle trains. We seemed to be taking one of the standard tracks and went through the city. However, shortly after we left the city, I couldn't identify the country that we were traveling through. A conductor entered our car and began punching tickets. I heard him comment that one couple was going to Worchester. When he got to us, George announced that we were going to Waddling-on-the-Tyme. I asked him how long it would take to get there.

The conductor pulled out a small piece of paper which he slowly unfolded till it was about 3 feet long. He consulted it, slowly scanning down the names of stations, mumbling their names as he went. Finally he said, "Ah, yes. Waddling-on-the-Tyme. That'll be an hour and a quarter." He folded up the paper and put it back in his pocket.

We thanked the conductor, and he went on to the end of the car, punching as he went.

After an hour, the conductor announced, "Waddling-on-the-Tyme coming up in 10 minutes. Please prepare to exit the train when we reach the station. Don't leave any parcels or personal belongings. The train will not be responsible for items left by passengers."

We disembarked after the train came to a halt and stood on the platform for a moment, staring about like tourists. The station was small, and I could see a small parking lot at one end of the platform. As we headed there, an old Ford Anglia pulled up to the parking lot. It parked, and someone got out. It was Lee.

He rushed up the steps to the platform and shook hands with us one at a time. "Welcome. We've not had a lot to talk about on the 'Potter Watch' show in the last couple of weeks. I hope that you've got something good for the program."

Sally answered, "Oh, we'll knock the socks off your listeners."

Lee opened the front door for Sally, and that left George, Fred and I to open the back doors ourselves. We all got in, and I asked, "Didn't the Weasley's used to have an Anglia?"

Lee laughed a deep throated chuckle and said, "Yes, they did. As a matter of fact this is it."

I was surprised, "Surely that's not true. I thought that it had gone to live in the Hogwart's Forbidden forest for good?"

"Oh, when I graduated from Hogwarts, it drove right up to me and practically begged me to take it."

"Interesting."

□

We were in the living room of Lee Jordan's parents. The last time I'd met them, we hadn't much of an opportunity to talk. This time they wanted to talk. It turns out that his mom was from South Africa. She had gone there to work right after graduating from Hogwarts and had met a charming South African witch doctor. She was a short fortyish woman with short raven black hair. She introduced herself as Leena and her husband as Burl, who was at least 6 ft. 5 and had a muscular lean body.

She told me, "We had no idea what you were up to, but now. . ." Her voice trailed off.

Burl asked skeptically, "How do you know that Muggle-borns are being put in Azkaban. There's nothing in the *Prophet* about wholesale imprisonments."

"Oh, dad, you know that it's happening. What about the Osbornes? They disappeared, and their close friends say that they were last seen going to an inquiry in the Ministry."

Burl frowned and seemed to be totally unconvinced.

I volunteered, "We don't know how many Muggle-borns are in Azkaban, but I have friends in Hogwarts that know. They tell me that

Azkaban will soon be full. And not full of Deatheaters. What they'll do after Azkaban is full, I hate to consider."

Burl, still frowning, asked, "What are you really offering these people?"

Sally, who had been holding something back throughout this conversation, couldn't hold back further, "We're offering them a place where they can stop running. Where they don't have to wonder where the next meal is coming from. Where they don't have to be afraid of being hounded to the ground."

"Just where is this 'where'?"

I answered, "I can't tell you. I can't tell them. I can't even tell most of the people that I work with. It would just be too big a tragedy if, after promising them safety, we let them down, and they found that we'd ended up rounding them up for the Deatheaters.

Fred interrupted, "It's almost time for us to broadcast. Let's get ready."

Lee led us to his room, where the radio equipment was set up. It looked like a cross between the old crystal radios of the beginning of the century and a mad scientist's idea of a rocket launch console. Lee pointed his wand at the radio and said something inaudible. The crystal radio lit up and there was some feedback, which Lee toned down by rotating his wand counterclockwise. He tapped on the oversized microphone. He cleared his throat as we sat down around the old wooden table that the radio set was sitting on.

"This is *Potter Watch* and I'm River reporting tonight. We have several special guests here tonight. Lee was speeding up. He was obviously getting excited about it. "We have some of the usual contributors as well. First, let's start with Romulus & Remus. I'll start with our usual question for our frequent guests, 'Any idea where Potter is?'"

Fred answered, "No one knows where Potter is. We've been staying out of the way of whatever he's up to. And he's not shown his face as far as we know."

"What about you Remus—any ideas?"

"Romulus said it. There's nothing we know about where he is. Whatever you're up to out there, Harry, go, go, go!"

Lee went on, "Do you think he's still alive."

George answered, "I'm sure of it. If he weren't or if he'd been captured, it would have been all over the *Prophet*, River."

"Well, I think that tells it all. In the meantime, is there any word of other resistance activity?"

George said, "There are rumors that the climate control in the Ministry of Magic is always going bad. It rains in the courtyard or snows in the

Wizengemot chamber or the temperature is in the 100's in the Auror Office."

"We have some owl post mail to read in tonight's show. Our first letter is from 'A Concerned Neighbor'. She asks, 'An old friend of mine—a Muggle-born named Freda Clemons—hasn't been back to her cottage for several days. Do you think that she's in Azkaban?'"

"Well, Concerned, we don't know, and none of our usually reliable sources know. I think that it's a good bet that she's either left the country or is in Azkaban. Let's all pray that she made it out of the country before the Deatheaters came for her.

"We have another letter from an irate investor. He writes, 'I was down to Gringott's a few days ago to get some gold out of my vault. I spent three hours in line, and when I finally got to the end of the line, I was 'patted down' by a security troll. After all that, the bank closed before they let me get to my vault. What's happened to common courtesy in this country?'"

"Irate, you know that the Ministry has imposed really stringent security rules on Gringott's. They're hoping that Harry Potter will show up in disguise to get gold out of his vault. This is just another little irritation courtesy of the Deatheaters in the Ministry of Magic."

"Well, we'll come back to that later," Lee smiling broadly, "but I'd like to introduce our special guest speaker, Quiller, and his associate, La Chifre. They're here to talk about their offer to help wizards and witches on the run from Deatheaters. Tell us about it."

I too smiled, "Well, let me start by telling you that we're ready to announce date and time of our first rendezvous. We're offering sanctuary from the Deatheater. It's tomorrow at 1 PM at Stoker-on-the-Rhyme. Everyone who's interested in our offer should arrive not earlier than 1PM and not later than 1:30PM. If you disapparate, arrive at least 1 mile. out of town and walk in. We want to get a good look at people before they arrive."

Lee's parents were intently watching us now. Lee asked me, "Quiller, what can you tell these refugees to expect?"

"First, I can't give a lot of details, because we don't want the Deatheaters figuring out what we are doing or where we're going, but I can give you a few general points:

1. We will accept anyone who comes in good faith.
2. We will be smuggling people out of the country. I won't tell you where we're going—not even the country.
3. Everyone who accepts the offer has to agree not to return to England until 'He-Who-Must-Not-Be-Named' is

overthrown and not reveal anything about our sanctuary program..

4. However, no one has to go to our final destination. There will be a point outside England where they can leave our program."

"Good. What is this refuge like that you'll take people to?"

"It's on a large estate. There are barracks for single adults and families will be in small bungalow-like buildings. We're trying to be as self-sufficient as possible. There will be a Cafeteria where volunteers will work to provide meals. Maintenance and cleaning will be provided as well by volunteers. We'll try to organize classes for kids."

Fred broke in, "There'll be a Quidditch Pitch."

I followed on, "Yes, we'll have teams."

Lee asked, "What about fighting back against the Deatheaters?"

"We plan on having self-defense classes. These may turn into military training if things go well."

George added, "Bloody right they will. We'll have Dumbledore's army going in no time."

Lee asked, "How will you keep all this from getting out."

"We'll be located in a relatively remote area. Everyone who goes to refuge will have to swear to not leave until they're granted permission and not to tell anyone about the camp."

"How will you enforce that?"

"We'll require that people take an unbreakable vow."

There was an inrush of breath on the part of all the wizards in the room.

Lee said, "Wow, you guys really are serious."

"Yes we are."

'Will people be able to get in touch with the outside world?"

"We'll bring in copies of the *Prophet* and any other periodical that will give us reporting on the internal affairs of England."

Fred added, "We'll have our own newspaper published in the camp."

I hadn't heard anyone suggest that yet, but it was a good idea. I agreed, "Yes, as soon as we can."

Lee asked, "How many people do you expect to show up tomorrow?"

Sally signaled me and I let her speak. "We don't know, but we'll take however many show up—even if it's only one. This is terribly important, and we'll succeed at it."

Lee went on, "How many times will you repeat this offer, La Chifre?"

"We'll keep doing it until we get caught and killed." You could tell from the look in her eyes that she meant every word of it.

Fred looked at her with some wonderment showing on his face and said, "This is going to be fun."

Lee asked another hard question, "What should people do if they don't have the nerve to take your offer?"

Sally didn't hesitate, "They should resist in any way they can. They should give shelter to Muggle-borns that are being suppressed. If they can't do that, they should contribute money to them. IF they can't do that they should give them a cool drink of water. If they can't do that, they should hang their heads in shame and not come out in the light."

Lee was surprised by her intensity, "Well, . ."

I rescued the quiet that had descended on the studio, "La Chifre, you know the recipe for making people think. 'He-Who-Must-Not-Be-Named' would probably choke on your soufflé."

She turned her hot eyes on me for an intense moment. I glanced at the door where Lee's parents were standing. His mom was standing with mouth agape, but his dad was looking at Sally with a calculating look.

Lee was still stunned. Finally he said, "Well, that's Potter Watch for tonight. Keep tuning in. Next time we'll report on how this developing story turns out. Don't forget the password for the next show is 'Quiller'. See you next Tuesday at 8 PM."

The tension in the room slowly ebbed. Even the Weasley's were subdued. We left the Jordan home and disapparated to Cotswolds where I had reserved rooms at an inn. It was an ancient building with half a dozen rooms. The dining room was a dark paneled room with old dim stained glass windows that let hardly any light in. We had a meal there. The dining room was only occupied by us and an elderly couple who sat in the corner and shared a meal quietly. We on the other hand had a table near a fireplace that had a roaring fire. The twins were joking and boisterous— more than usual. I think they were excited about tomorrow—what would happen? Would there be Deatheaters? Would anyone show up at all?

I was just trying to forget that tomorrow we would be facing the first really dangerous encounter of what I had begun to think of as "the program". It worked something like this:

1. We establish a training camp to train an army to fight the Deatheaters. Done.
2. We recruit the army. We start that tomorrow.
3. We train the army.
4. We pick a target to attack to begin the war.
5. We win? Right?

But I didn't want to think about any of that tonight. I wanted to have a good meal, get to bed, and get a good night's sleep.

Sally was hard to figure. She seemed to be her usual self. She showed no signs of disturbance or unease. She joked with the Weasleys—especially Fred, as usual. As the night wore on locals started to filter into the inn, and the room was filled with the soft buzz of many conversations blending. The twins had joined a small group of locals and were animatedly arguing the virtues of the local brew. Sally turned to me and asked, "What's going on with you this evening?"

"What do you mean?"

"I mean, you usually hold up your end of the conversation. What's going on? You haven't put two sentences together the whole evening?"

I looked her straight in the eyes and said, "Look, I'm scared shi . . , well I'm pretty darn scared."

"Of what?"

"Of what? Don't you realize that we're stepping out of the shadows, and we're going to put ourselves into the middle of the spotlight? I can't believe that only the good guys heard that broadcast. I've got a bad feeling about tomorrow. I can just see the Deatheaters pouring out into the town square tomorrow and turning the day into a blood bath."

"Well, aren't you the cheery one. Remind me the next time I'm going to the dentist and can use some cheering up."

"Oh, I'm happy to help at any time."

The evening finally ended, and we retired to our rooms. Or I should say that we retired to our rooms, and the twins were still whooping it up with the locals when I last saw them.

□□

The day was overcast and pitch black at 5 AM when we got up to leave for our rendezvous. It was a cold windy day. We were met outside the inn by an armored HumVee. Foyle was in it with a driver. The four of us got in the back and we took off. We bumped along back roads.

Fred said, "Wendt, is this your wonderful Muggle transportation method?"

George said, "Yes, this is soooo much better than disapparation."

Fred, "Oh, no question! You just don't want to travel any other way."

I was feeling better now that THE day had begun. I just wanted to get it over with one way or the other. "Yes, you're right. I wouldn't travel by any other means. It's a lot less bumpy than traveling by floo powder."

"Oh, I give you floo powder all right." They said in unison.

Foyle turned around and faced into the back seat area. "Here take these and put them on your good ear".

Fred asked, "What are these things?"

I recognized them. "They're two-way radios, right?"

Foyle said, "You're up on the latest technology, I see. I thought that you'd been out of touch for years."

"Oh, I try to keep up."

George was fumbling trying to put one on his non-existent ear.

"Funny." Foyle said, "Try the other ear."

George answered, "Oh yeah. I keep forgetting."

Foyle went on, "They all work on the same frequency. We'll all be able to hear each other speak, but no one without one will be able to hear."

Fred exclaimed, "Wow, it's just like, like 'magic'."

I sneered, "Oh, give it a rest."

Foyle continued, "If you see any Deatheaters, just say so, and we'll pick them off."

George asked, "What do you mean, 'Pick them off'?"

Foyle, "We'll kill them or at least try to."

I said, "I just hope it doesn't come to that."

Foyle said, "So do I."

We drove at high speed over the single lane road, but finally came out on a larger road and passed beside a field that had a number of military trucks parked in it. There were also a couple of helicopters on the ground beside them.

Foyle said, "That's our transportation for the wizards if any show up."

Fred said, "Great. They'll be thrilled."

Foyle answered, "They'll be thrilled to be getting out from under Riddle's thumb if they've got any sense."

Sally said, in her best school-marmly fashion, "Now, boy, boys, no fussing."

Fred answered, sweetly, "Yes, mother."

I looked out the rear window when I heard a helicopter start its engine and whir into life. As I turned back, Foyle caught my eye and asked, "What have you got stuffed into your belt."

I could feel my face turn hot and red. I silently pulled out my Glock and displayed it for Foyle. He held out his hand, and I gave it to him. He made sure the safety was on and released the clip. He took a look at its contents, returned the clip into the handle of the Glock, and handed it back to me. "Do you know how to use that thing?"

"Yes, sir. I've been trained by the SAS."

He looked at me searchingly for a moment and said, "Well, I suppose you can keep it. I just don't want any 'friendly fire' casualties."

"Believe me, I intend only to use it on Deatheaters;"

"Make sure you do."

We went back on the road and proceeded for a while. We turned the corner around a hill and found our village nestled in the side of the hill. We drove to the town square, passed through it, and parked on a side street a couple of blocks down the main street of the town. We got out, and Foyle said, "We've got a couple of hours to spare. There's a café on the town square. Let's go in and get some tea."

No one objected, so we walked to the square and found a little café called "Jane's Java Jolt." We were waited on by Jane herself. There were a couple of locals already in the café sitting at tables and talking animatedly over cups of coffee? Tea? We ordered tea. Sally ordered a cucumber sandwich. I'd never gotten the taste for them. Fred and George searched the menu looking in vain for pumpkin juice and finally settled for tea.

I asked Sally, "I don't see how you can eat anything. My throat is full of my heart."

She sniggered. "This will be exciting."

"Yes, that's what I'm afraid of."

She laughed.

Foyle harrumphed and got up. He excused himself by saying, "I want to check out my boys. I'll be around. If you need anything, just shout out." That left the four of us. Fred and George were speculating about how many Deatheaters that we'd see. George opted for five and Fred was guessing an even dozen.

"What about you, Wendt? How many do you think?" asked Fred.

I pretended to think hard and to be calculating on my fingers. Finally I smiled as if I'd come to a decision. "By my precise", I put emphasis on the words 'precise' and 'calculations'". I hesitated and then said, "None."

George stuck out his tongue at me and said, "Spoilsport."

We'd spent about 20 minutes or half an hour eating and drinking, and I was getting restless. I tossed a twenty down on the table and said, "I'm going to go out on the town square. I just need some air." But it wasn't just air that I needed. This was the first time that I would be in a real combat situation. It might not happen, but it might too. There was a fountain on the town square. I crossed the street, walked over to the fountain, and sat down. There were a couple of pigeons perched on the lip of the fountain near me. I sat and stared at my feet for a while. I listened to the pigeons come and go. I heard one land near me and then was surprised to feel something peck on my forearm. I tried to brush it away with my hand and got another peck for my troubles. Finally, I looked up and saw an owl next to me. It had a parchment tied to his claw. I untied it and read the address, Fountain in the Square, Mill-on-the-Rhyme. I unsealed it and read, "I've been thinking about you a lot in the last few days. Really, ever since I heard that you were going to take in wizards on the run from the MOM today. Good luck! Get those poor people out of harm's way, and I'll try to get a weekend free. And be careful!"

I pulled out a pen and wrote a quick note on the parchment, "I'll be careful, but I won't be free this weekend. Maybe next week." I addressed it to McGonagall. I'm not magical but I had no trouble knowing where to address it—Hogwarts School of Magic and Wizardry. I tied the note to the owl's leg and sent it on its way. After that it was not so hard waiting. Eventually, the rest of the party came out and joined me about 30 minutes to 1 PM.

They sat down next to me on the fountain, and I reached behind my back to feel the hilt of the Glock. It had a hard cold reassuring feel. It made me feel hard, ready for anything. It was about 25 minutes to The Time. After a minute or two, I began thinking about how serious this was. Anything could happen. We, sitting at the fountain, could all be dead in a few minutes. I felt the temptation to feel that hard cold assurance at my back. I thought to myself, "This is bad. It isn't the gun that makes me safe. I've got to let it just be there and not be handling it all the time." So, I held back on the temptation to reach back. But as the minutes ticked by, the temptation was stronger and stronger. I had to fight it. Finally, I told myself that all I had to do was feel it one more time, and I'd be all right. I started to reach back and almost had reached it when Fred asked, "What's up Wendt? You have an itch?" I deflected my hand from the gun and scratched my rump. I answered, "Yeh."

George chimed in, "There's nothing like an itch that you just can't reach to scratch. Is there?"

Fred said, "No there isn't."

I didn't say anything. Now I really couldn't reach back and touch the Glok.

A few minutes later, I heard a dim "WhumpWhumpWhump" in the air, softly as from a distance. Fred noticed it too. He asked, "Do you hear that?"

George answered, "Yeah, I do. I was wondering what that was."

Sally answered, "That's a helicopter, isn't it, Wendt?"

"Yes, I think it's our friends back at the base camp. I suppose they've got one or two in the sky to help with surveillance."

"A Hepicober? What's that?"

196

Sally laughed and said, "A Hel-I-cop-tor" speaking the word slowly and exaggeratedly.

"OK, what's a hepicobler?" asked George.

"It's like a mechanical broom. Except that they're large enough to hold 4, 6, even a dozen women."

"Well, they'll never replace brooms. Brooms are silent, and there's no feeling like swooping among the clouds with the wind blowing in your face. You feel like you're completely free—part of the sky," Said Fred.

Sally asked, "Would you take me flying on a broom sometime?"

Fred perked up, "I am at your service always, m'lady. Name the time."

George seemed to be working up a snappy saying when our earphones crackled to life for the first time since we'd arrived. I'd forgotten that I was wearing it. Everyone else gave a little jump. Everyone's earphone said, "We've got incoming. We just spotted several wizards disapparating at the edge of the town. They're heading toward you from the west. They should be to your location in about 5 minutes."

I asked the air, "Men, women, kids?"

Foyle answered, "Yes, some of each, I think."

I stood up. My right hand was twitching slightly as I resisted the temptation to reach back. Then a group of three people turned the corner into the town square. I looked around at Fred, George, and Sally. "Well, this is it."

I started to walk over to the group. Fred said, "I don't think I know any of them."

George added, "Me either."

As I approached them, a few more turned the corner and my heart started to race. I told myself, "I've got to pay attention. Listen to their names carefully. Repeat them three times so you won't forget. First impressions are important."

I walked up to the first who was a thin man—thin hair, thin face, thin body. He was wearing a weathered black robe that was obviously expensive but had seen a lot of exposure to the weather. There was a woman with him who seemed to be in her 30's, maybe late 30's. She had long strawberry-blond hair that was matted and dirty. The third was a teen-aged girl who had the same hair as her mom. I said, "Hi. I am . . . ." I hesitated. I'd forgotten for a moment my 'code' name.

But he interrupted me, "You're Quiller."

"Yes. I am." The girl looked at me dis-interestedly for a moment and then her eyes widened and she said, "You're Professor Wendt." Then I looked more carefully and realized that I'd seen her somewhere before. Then it hit me. English Lit last year. Her name was Melissa. Melissa what? Well, maybe I'd remember later. So, I simply said, "Melissa. I'm sorry to see you here." Then, I had an inspiration, "I don't think that I've met your parents. Please introduce me."

She blushed faintly and said, "Mom, Dad, this is Mr. Wendt, my English Lit teacher for the last 5 years. Mr. Wendt this is my dad, Robert Trent and my mum, Jane."

"Pleased to meet you Mr. Trent, Mrs. Trent. I'm afraid I wasn't expecting to see a former student here. I didn't recognize her at first."

Robert shook my hand again with more vigor and said, "Why are you here?"

"I got sacked for my Muggle leanings. Why are you on the run? I vaguely remember that you are both magical?"

"Ah, right, laddie, but we too have Muggle leanings. We are what some folk call 'Muggle Lovers'."

"Yes."

Memory

It was the third time that I was standing in a town square waiting for the wizards on the run to show up. I was almost relaxed. The Weasley's were joking and Sally was laughing at (with) them. Foyle announced that the first wizards had disapparated and were walking toward the town square from the South. The Weasleys quieted and turned toward the street entering the square from the South.

We walked over, introduced ourselves, and suggested that we all gather around the statue on the town square while we waited for more wizards to show up. They did by two's and three's, five's and six's. We finally had about 45 wizards and the time was already close to 2PM, so we were ready to call for trucks.

Foyle said in my ear, "There's a group of five more wizards heading your way from the South. They should be with you in about 7 minutes."

I turned to the group and said, "We expect there will be a few more wizards along in a few minutes, so we'll wait before starting the next stage of your trip."

Shortly, the group entered the town square and headed over toward us. When they were about fifty feet from us, a voice sounded in my ear that I didn't recognize. "Wands! Alpha group choose targets. Beta, prepare to take misses."

"Bob, I've got the tall one."

"Thomas, I've got the one with wand in left."

And so it went. In the time that it took the group to close the distance to us, all the wizards were accounted for. They were quite clear about having wands out. The one in front seemed to be the leader. He said, "Well, boys, we've got a fine crop here.

"All you, just don't do anything sudden if you like having all your limbs about you."

Fred came to the front of our group and said, "You and what army."

The leader of the other group laughed and said, "We and the Deatheaters. Just put your wands down and don't make trouble."

Somehow, this made me angry in a way that I'd never been before—even with Cedric's death. I don't know why. I just found myself running to the front, apart from Fred. I shouted, "Wands down."

"Who is this?" the leader asked and raised his wand toward me.

I looked over to his cronies standing beside and behind him, I whispered, "Listen to what I say to these and do what I say."

The voice in my ear said, "Yes, sir."

The leader said, "You trying to convince us you're crazy, talking to yourself?"

I looked him straight in the eye and shouted, hoping that the men above could hear it clearly, "I'm going to count to two. Anyone with a wand in his hand after that is dead."

In my ear the voice said, "Heard, Understood, Acknowledged."

There was a delay of only a second between when I said 'dead' and I thundered, "One."

All seven dropped their wands at that sound.

Without taking my eye off the leader I said, "Fred, George, we need to have a quick discussion."

"I think that we should limit ourselves to modifying their memories. Do either of you know how to do memory charms?"

I could hear the glea in George's voice, "Oh, we've never done."

Fred continued, "But we've always wanted to experiment with them."

One of the group begged, "No, don't do that. We'll never bother you again."

The leader sneered, "Shut up. They wouldn't."

I looked at him and said, "What reason do we have to let you keep your memories? If you remembered something useful to us that might be another matter."

A third one of his group said rapidly, "What do you want to know?"

"Shut up," the leader hissed.

"How did you follow these people here? You can't follow people who've disapparated."

One of them said, "They said the name of He Who Must Not Be Named. The Deatheaters can know where someone is who names that name. They told us where you lot were."

I was stunned. That meant that the Deatheaters knew where we were. I said to the Weasleys, "Stun them." Their leader dropped to the ground for his wand. He grabbed it in his hand, but there was a sharp crack. The leader went limp. I ran to him and pulled the wand from his hand that was as flexible as a wet rag. Then I noticed the warm dark red stain on his robes over his upper back. I felt for a pulse. There wasn't one. All I could say was, "Shit."

I said to Foyle, "We've got to get these people out of here fast. Do you have enough helicopters to move, oh. 45 or so people?"

Foyle was on top of it. "I don't know. We've got four helicopters. They're on their way now. Should be there in 5 minutes."

I turned to the Weasleys who had stunned the others. "Can you get these." I hesitated because I'd almost thrown up. My throat burned with what had come up it. Then I forced the words out, "out of here by disapparating, Including this one?"

George was just staring down at him. Fred nodded silently. It took a moment before I realized that he was nodding. I just said, "Go." I could hear the helicopters. I suddenly realized that there were about 4 dozen other people that I had to do something about. I turned to the crowd and forced my voice to be loud enough to be heard—after a couple of tries.

"Look, we didn't plan this. We've got to get out in a hurry. We're bringing Muggle transportation–sort of large, mechanical flying brooms. I know this isn't easy, but if we don't get out of here RIGHT NOW." I tried to give it plenty of emphasis, "Deatheaters could be showing up any minute." I looked around and suddenly realized that it was only Sally and I to get this going. I looked at Sally,and thank God, she nodded.

I went on, "OK." I took a minute to try to figure it out. I said to the man in my ear, "Alpha leader can you send down 2 men to help load these people on helicopters and go with them to the rendezvous point."

Alpha leader said, "Yes, sir. Robert, George get cracking. Leave your pieces up here."

"There was a chorus of 'yes, sir's"

I put my attention on the crowd again. "Everyone, we've got to divide you into 4 equal groups. Families stay together. Each group will have one of us to accompany them." Just then there were two men in battle fatigues who showed up on the square running faster than I'd ever been able to. They ran up and were not even winded. They reported.

"You two go over there and separate. Sally go over there. Now, divide up into groups. Each goes in a helicopter." I added to myself, "I hope."

Two helicopters landed on the square at opposite corners. Apparently more couldn't land at once. I turned to the two soldiers. "Each of you take your group to one of the helicopters and get off the ground."

They herded their people over to the helicopters. It was clear that no one was happy about getting into the helicopters, but they didn't exactly want to hang around either to see how many Deatheaters showed up. The 'copters got off the ground and headed off to the south. The other two landed. Sally and I took our groups to the helicopters. Everyone got on, but there wasn't room for either Sally or me.

One family had a little girl who wouldn't get on. Her dad finally picked her up even though she must have been 9 years old kicking and trying to scream. No one could hear anyone but the pilot shook his head when I started to get on, and I didn't really have to hear to understand. I gave him the thumbs up and ran back away from the rotors. It took off. When I was far enough clear to be heard over the noise, I said, "Foyle, Sally and I couldn't get on the helicopters."

He answered, "I'm on my way. I should be there in three minutes."

"Good."

Just then another voice in my ear said, "There are 3 wizards, wands out, heading your way."

"How long?" asked Foyle.

"My guess, maybe eight minutes. Should we take them out?"

Foyle asked me, "Well, Wendt?"

"Don't unless they get here before we get away."

"OK."

The Hummer squealed around the corner going about 90 KPH. It shuddered to a stop beside us. Sally and I jumped in the back and we were going 60 before I had the door shut. Foyle turned around to face into the back seat and said, "You guys OK?"

"Yeh."

He then asked, "What do we do?" as we accelerated into a side street.

I thought for about 6 seconds. "Keep going. If this street dead ends into a field, go cross country." Just then the street turned and there was a rail fence that ended the lane. The driver turned to Foyle, who nodded. The driver said, "Brace yourselves." About 2 seconds later there was a big lurch and the sound of wood splintering as we went through the fence.

The driver asked, "Where to now?"

Foyle asked, "How about that stand of woods over there?" It was at the top of a small rise in the ground.

I answered, "That's OK if you keep going. Don't slow down if you can avoid it." I saw the driver grimace in the rear view mirror. We were bouncing as we went over little clumps of weeds, and the driver said, "You might want to put your seat belts on; it's going to get a little bumpy in a minute."

His idea of a little bumpy was amusing if you weren't in the Hummer. I personally don't see how he kept the Hummer on the ground. We were bouncing around like a pinball played by the Pinball Wizard.

I kept staring backwards out the rear window to see if anyone showed up. After an interminable ten minutes or so, we suddenly went through a low hedge and found ourselves crossing a road. The driver stopped and regained the road. "Which way?"

Foyle was consulting a military map. "Go south. When you reach the next road turn right. That should take us to the A5. Then we can rendezvous at the port."

Since things seemed to be under some amount of control, and we weren't all dead, I tried to size up the immediate surroundings. I discovered that Sally's hand was in mine. We seemed to make the discovery at the same moment. We both let go quickly, and I said, "Sorry."

"Don't be." She looked out the window.

I leaned back and tried to make sense out of what had just happened. The first thing that I could think of was the little tidbit that we'd picked up about saying The Name. "Sally, we were amazingly lucky that we decided to always use "You Know Who's" real name."

"Do you really think it was luck?"

I thought a second, "Let's not go there. Let's just tote it up to 'plumb dumb' luck. And I do mean 'Dumb' with a capitol 'D'."

"Whatever. We have to get that news out to everyone. NEVER use his name. Always use 'Tom Riddle.'"

"I agree with you there."

She looked out the window for a long while and finally said, almost to herself it was so low, "I wish I knew where Fred was."

We drove on through the lengthening shadows as late afternoon turned to early evening. The countryside slid by. Foyle got on the radio and contacted the helicopters carrying the refugees. They had arrived at a remote open field not far out of the port that we heading for. The trucks were supposed to arrive there in half an hour, and we'd probably be along in about an hour. So far nobody had been attacked by Deatheaters, so we thought that we'd lucked out. As far as we knew, no one had been seen by them.

We arrived at the point where the trucks had met up with refugees. There were still a couple of helicopters on the ground, and you could hear one or two cruising at a distance. The trucks were parked in an irregular pattern. There was some light from what I guessed were gas lanterns. People were milling about. We found a parking spot, and everybody got out. Foyle went off to find some food, and I found a sergeant who seemed to be unoccupied. I asked him, "Have you seen the Weasley's?"

He, in his turned, asked "Who are the Weasley's? What unit are they with?"

Sally answered, "They're not with any unit. They're with us. They are young, tall, and have flaming red hair."

His eyes brightened, "Oh, them. Haven't seen them today."

I turned to Sally. "How are they going to find us?"

Her lips were tight with tension, but she said, "Oh, you know them. They'll make out OK."

I didn't say anything, but I was a little worried. They knew the port we were going to, but we were pretty far out. I began thinking about all the things that I could have done that would have helped us in situations like this. I could have taught them how to use public phone boxes. I could have given them our cell phone #'s. I could have . . .

Shortly, Foyle caught up with us and gave us rations. They were cold. It was hard opening them and eating without much light, but it was food. Besides, we hadn't eaten properly since breakfast. The wizards and witches were grouped in small knots talking quietly. I knew we had to get moving pretty soon, or we'd get badly off schedule. So I asked, "Sally, what do you think we should do? We can start without Fred and George, but we can't get very far. We need them for the oaths."

She had her mouth full, swallowed some coffee, and then answered, "I guess you get started with your speech and hope they show up before we end."

I said, "You're right. Is there any chance of finding someone else who could fill in for them?"

She gave a short explosion of laughter that didn't seem like it was motivated by mirth, "You're the guy with all the wizard contacts. What do you think?"

I looked around for Foyle, I wanted his opinion. "Sally, I'll be back in a minute. I want to consult with Foyle's." I started to walk around to see if I could find him when there were two distinct "pop"s, and Fred and George appeared out of nowhere.

Sally ran up to Fred, looked him straight in the eyes, and said through clenched teeth, "Where have you been? Why didn't you give us an idea of where you were? What's happened to you two?"

George said, "I'm glad you are so concerned about the two of us". The emphasis was on the word "two". Sally didn't catch the meaning. That was probably good.

Fred answered, "It took us a little time to decide what to do with those 'snatchers'. We decided to. . ."

But I interrupted him, "We don't have time for details now. I want to get on with my speech, and we need you two ready for your part."

George said, "Hold on to your knickers. We'll be ready when you are."

I said, "Good, let's get on with it. Would you three round up the people? I'll talk to them over at that truck." I went over to the truck and asked some soldiers to bring lanterns over so that we could see what we were doing. I climbed up into the back of the truck and tried to compose myself for the speech that I was about to give. I'd done this a couple of times before, but it always seems to go differently each time. The Weasleys had collected everyone together behind the truck that I was in, and I started my speech.

"Witches and Wizards, I want to give you an idea of what's going to happen in the next couple of days, answer your questions, and start you thinking about a big decision that you've got to make in the next 24 hours.

"I'll start with what happens next. We're going to cross the English channel this evening. We're going by boat. When we get to France," Just then I was interrupted by a tall, fairly comely blond witch who was standing at the front. She seemed vaguely familiar, but I couldn't put my finger on where I'd seen her before.

"Why are we going by boat? Boats are dangerous. Why not disapparate?"

I was not really surprised by this question. Some variation of it came up every time. I could give the answer during the talk, but people want to ask questions. It gives them the feeling that they've got some control of the situation, and it's good to feel that you do have some control.

I answered, "Well, we really don't want anyone to know where we're going. If you disapparated, you'd know and then, if you were ever captured by Deatheaters, they'd know eventually where we went. The less that you know about routes and destinations, the better for everyone involved." She seemed to think that over a bit. It was clear from her knitted brow that she wasn't entirely satisfied, but at least she was thinking on it, which was better than not.

I went on, "After arriving on French soil, we'll be picked up by trucks, which will transport us to a special train. Then back on trucks to the airport." This always occasioned questions.

Someone in the back blurted out, "What's an 'air part'? "

George laughed. So, I turned to him and asked him to answer the question.

"An airport is a place where Muggle flying carpets land and take off. Their flying carpets are made of metal and are much larger than real flying carpets. They're noisy and shake when they leave the ground. You'll all get on to one of these flying carpets, and we'll travel for hours on end, getting to where we're going."

Someone else blurted out, "What happened to the 'snatchers?'"

I was afraid this question would come up. Especially since I didn't know the answer to the question, I wasn't anxious for everyone to find out at the same time. It was out of the bag, so I decided to let George and Fred answer. George looked over to me for guidance.

I said, "Go ahead Fred, George, open the bag and let them know what happened." It was a big risk, but in this kind of enterprise, there are some things that you just have to be open and honest about—completely.

George said, "We disapparated them to a cliff on the English Channel near Lands' End. We had to do it two at a time. We tossed the leader off the cliff. The others we released one at a time."

Fred went on, "Yea, without wands they weren't so tough. We were thinking that we might have to use the *Imperious Curse* or something to get them to talk, but they were pretty willing to talk on their own. Of course, the fact that we were holding them over the cliff with the levi-corpus spell, might have had something to do with it."

George continued, "Yes, they all told pretty much the same story. They got a lead on where we were because someone used Tom Riddle's fake name, Lord You Know Who. So, the lesson here, folks, is never use that name. We never do. We much prefer Tom Riddle or just Riddle."

I picked up the discussion, "After we land in wherever it is we're going. . ." I hesitated a moment, "We get on Lorries there."

"Now, comes the hard part."

Someone sniggered in the back of the crowd. "Yeh, as if we've had nothing but fun and games so far."

I answered, "Judge for yourself. Before we get to the airport, you're going to have to commit to this project or go your own way. We've got the 4 rules that you have to commit to:

1. You promise not to communicate with anyone who's not part of the camp about the camp, who's there, where it is, what it's about. Zero. Zilch. Nada. Ever or until we release you from the promise.
2. You promise to never leave the camp without permission of the senior person in charge at the camp.

3. You promise to never knowingly aide Tom Riddle, any Deatheater, any Snatcher, or anyone associated with any of those.
4. You promise to respect the rights of all other camp residents.

"You have to make this promise as an unbreakable oath."

Everyone had been pretty quiet until I made the last statement. Then there was a collective gasp and a lot of whispered talking. Someone asked aloud, "Blimey, the unbreakable oath. That's pretty hard. There's a lot there to remember."

"Not so much. They're things that everyone should find easy to remember. Don't help Riddle or his buddies, don't talk to people outside the camp, stay in the camp, and finally respect your neighbors. Easy to remember, easy to do—at least, until you fall into the hands of the Deatheaters.

"In any case, you've got until tomorrow to decide what you'll do. If you decide to do it, the Oath will be administered by one of the Weasleys. If you decide not to, we part company tomorrow. You get a hundred galleons and the freedom to go wherever you like. Questions?"

A ruddy-faced man with dark black hair stepped forward and asked. "When do we get to fight Vold . . . uh . . . Riddle?"

"If you want to be trained in Defense against the Dark Arts, we'll have classes. We're planning on putting together a militia to fight Riddle. You're welcome to join. I don't know when we'll see action, but I can almost guarantee that it'll be sooner than most of you will feel comfortable with."

We went through a number of other questions—pretty much the usual lot. What kind of food would we have? Who's going to be in charge of the camp, and so on. Finally they petered out, and we got people into the trucks to take us to the boats.

Sally asked how many boats we were going to use. I wasn't sure, but I thought it would be three or four. We got to the wharf and found three boats waiting for us. Sally, and Fred Weasley took one boat and George and I took the other ones. We had a couple of people who had to be "encouraged" to board ship. One spunky old lady refused point blank to enter a boat. Finally Sally sidled up to her and took her arm gently. She asked, "What's your name?"

"Elspeth."

"Elspeth. Hmmm. That's a lovely name."

"What's yours?"

"Oh, it's very plain—Sally."

"That's a nice name. Where did you grow up?"

"In Hartlepoole."

"I grew up in Hyde Park."

"How, lovely. Why don't we sit down and have a nice chat?"

"That would be nice."

"Let's just step down and sit on that bench."

"You're very clever, young lady. But I suppose that we've got to go on those boats. Yes, it would be lovely to chat with you." They clambered down into the boat with the help of one of the crew members. They found an empty section of bench and sat down together. Sally looked up at me, and I nodded and mouthed a silent "Thanks." She nodded back.

I picked one of the other boats and helped various people down into the boats. One of them was the blonde from earlier. She stared at me hard and finally asked, "Who are you? A squib? You're not magical."

I said, "I guess we ought to have introductions. I'm Jim Wendt. And you're. . .?"

Her eyes widened for a moment, and she exclaimed, "I know you. You're no squib. You're a Muggle. You used to teach at Hogwart's. You taught. . ." She hesitated, "Oh, I can't think of it. It was one of those Muggle things. Arithmetic or Art."

"Wrong. What I taught was not a 'Muggle thing'. And it wasn't arithmetic or art—even though those aren't 'Muggle things' either. It was something all English should know—English literature. Who are you?"

"They're all the same. Art, Literature, Math, Molecular Biology."

"No, they aren't all the same, and they aren't Muggle things either. And what is your name?" I was getting seriously bothered by this know-it-all know-nothing.

"Oh, OK. I'm Rita. . ." I interrupted her at that point, because I had just realized why she looked vaguely familiar. I'd seen her picture many times in the *Prophet* besides having met her briefly early in my career.

"Yes. Your'e Rita Skeeter, aren't you?"

"Of course, dear boy. I thought everyone knew my face."

"Unfortunately, yes."

"Why unfortunately?"

"Well, where to begin? Such a multitude of material to work with! Let's see. You're the one who did the hatchet job on Dumbledore." Fred had overheard some of the conversation and had drifted over to overhear the rest.

Fred asked, "Yea. What are you doing on this boat? What are you doing with legitimate refugees? I thought that you and old Valdee must be like this." He twisted his forefinger and center finger of his left hand together. "It must be 'I love Rita', the way you toadied up to him with that exposé book you did on Dumbledore."

Rita swung around toward him, and a flush of anger flashed across her face quickly before she mastered the emotion. "My dear boooy, I had no choice. Valdee, as you call him, or actually one of his Deatheaters gave me the choice of writing the book or taking a one-way trip to Azkaban."

I could feel my anger rising, "Look, I read that 'book' of yours—at least as much of it as I could stand. There was way too much joy in that book to have been a forced thing. You really enjoyed doing character assassination on him."

George was warming up too, "The way you hacked Dumbledore reminds me of your job on Harry when he was in the Tri-Wizard tournament. I say that we kick her out."

I looked over at the devilish expression on his face, "You mean right here, right now in the middle of the channel?"

"Well, it's really the middle of the harbor, but yes."

"No, you two don't. I'm a legitimate refugee. I deserve to get political asylum. "

I was really getting warmed up. "You should pray to God that you don't get what you deserve. Fortunately for you, we can't deal that out. And, really, you're probably right about being a legitimate refugee. Give me a minute, to discuss this with Fred."

I pulled Fred aside, and we walked to the prow of the boat, which had cast off, and was beginning to make weigh out to the Channel. "Look, George, we've got to do something. Maybe she's trustworthy and maybe not."

Fred looked out toward the open water. We really couldn't see much. The sky was mostly overcast. Occasionally a bright star showed through the inky blackness. There was a raw wind blowing off the channel, and it was a miserable evening overall. But I hardly noticed any of it. Fred answered, "Why don't we give her the oath right here and now. If she takes it we should be OK. If she doesn't then we get to throw her overboard."

I thought about it. We'd be administering it to the rest of the people who were serious about wanting sanctuary when we arrived on shore in France. Why not have her do it early here? The more I thought about it, the better it sounded. So I said, "I can't come up with a better idea. I suppose so." We went back to Rita and invited her to join us at the prow. No one came to the prow because the wind was bitterer there, and you were away from the lights, such as they were, on the deck further back.

"Why can't we talk here?"

"We have something special to tell you. Don't you want an 'exclusive'?" George taunted.

She reluctantly agreed, and I started the standard spiel. "Ms. Skeeter, there is an oath that we administer to all who seek sanctuary. We talked about it before. Now's your turn to decide. Will you take it or not? If you don't, you have to leave right now. You can disapparate to the shore and find your way home."

"I don't have a home. I don't have any choice."

That peaked my curiosity. "Why don't you have a choice? Why don't you have a home?"

"Well, I refused to write any more 'exposés' on resisters to 'You-Know-Who'."

"Who did they want you to write about?"

"Oh, you should be able to guess—everyone who is opposed to 'You-Know-Who' and has any notoriety—former Minister Fudge, the members of the Board of Governors of Hogwarts who are opposed to 'reforms' at that school, and so on."

"Doing that sort of thing before didn't seem to bother you much. Why now?"

"It's a world of difference, darling, between doing it by your own choice and for your own reasons and being a hack who will write anything about anybody."

"And where did Dumbledore fit in that continuum."

"Oh, just leave it alone. I'm here. I'm. . ." She took a large gulping breath of air as though she had to swallow some medicine that didn't taste all that good, "sorry. . ."

"OK, then either take the oath or don't." Fred said.

She nodded her head mutely. Fred got out his wand and instructed us, "Clasp hands at the wrists."

Rita asked, "Is that really necessary?"

Fred snorted and said, "You know perfectly well it is."

"But he's a Muggle." It was almost a whine.

"He's the only person available. I have to pronounce the spell."

"All right." She took my hand at the wrist and I took hers. Fred smiled at the two of us. Rita was obviously uncomfortable.

I asked, "Are you afraid I have cooties?"

"Oh, just get it over with."

Fred said, "We really should have a photo of this."

"Get going, or I'm finished."

Fred said, "OK. OK. Just listen to Wendt and say your 'I do's".

Now, I was a little uncomfortable, but as I said the words that had become second nature to me, I relaxed and said, "Do you solemnly swear to not communicate with anyone who's not part of the refugee camp about where the camp is, who's there or ever has been there, or what its purpose is?" I looked her in the eye as I recited.

Rita said in a clear but soft voice a repeat of what I'd said, substituting "I"s for "do you"s. A rope of fire encircled our wrists and tightened to bind us together. I could feel the pressure of the strangely cool but bright and fiery light. There'd always been the two Weasley twins to administer the oath and say the words. I never realized that both participants of the oath were so strongly affected.

"Do you solemnly swear to never leave the camp without permission of the senior person in charge of the camp?" I went on. The words again seemed trivial compared with the seriousness of what I felt as the words were spoken, and the fiery rope tightened further.

In that same gentle voice with some steel in it she repeated what I'd said. Another strand of cold fire surrounded our hands and wrists. This time the pressure of the strands was very noticeable.

"Do you solemnly swear to never knowingly aide Tom Riddle, any Deatheater." I faltered. The air was full of electricity, and I gasped down a breath of air and continued, "Any Snatcher, or anyone associated with any of them."

She repeated it and each word seemed to ring through our two bodies as the new rope of fire tightened around our wrists further. The bands of fire became intensely hot, and I could swear that the hair was standing on end on my head.

"Do you promise to respect the rights of all other camp residents?"

She finished the oath.

Suddenly it all evaporated—the ropes of fire, the tolling of the words, and the electricity in the air.

Rita's eyes suddenly broke away from mine, and she immediately looked down at her feet. "Well, that's it. I've sealed my doom. I'll either break my oath and die, or the Deatheaters will kill me." She looked her age. I hadn't really thought about how old she must be. She tried to maintain the fiction that she was on the sunny side of 30 or maybe 35, but she must really not have seen the sunny side of 40 in some years.

Fred told her, "Look on the bright side. We'll all go down together in the biggest party of the decade."

She looked up with a wan smile on her face. "I suppose you're right." She turned to me and asked, "What do you do when your only hope in the world is to keep writing? You write and write. You look for the next story

211

that will amaze the public. And eventually there is that time when there is no true amazing story. You bend the truth. Oh, only a little! And then there is that next gap. You twist the truth a little more. Eventually you reach the point that you don't recognize the straight truth when you see it. You only know the 'truth' that sells copy. And the world is full of ambiguity, so it's easy to convince yourself that what sells is the truth; that the real measure of truth is what the reader will pay for. Finally, you wouldn't know the truth if it spat in your face.

"So, I ended up writing the chop job on Dumbledore. Sure it was mean, but he was dead and I didn't want to be." She looked out across the black waters of the Channel. "Well, now I'm the next closest thing to dead. Where are we going?"

She turned to me and looked me full in the face again. I returned the gaze and said, "We're on our way to France."

"And then?"

"And then, we find out who else is staying with us. After we've separated the serious from the not so serious, we'll tell you with the rest where we go next."

She kept watching me, "But, I've taken the impossible oath. You're safe with me."

"You don't get any privileged information before anybody else." It occurred to me that you can take the reporter out of the newspaper, but you can't take the urge for an exclusive out of the reporter.

She kept her gaze on me and then said, "So, you're mister pure?"

I had to laugh. So, I did—a breathless chuckle that I had to force out. "You know, I'm so far from being Mr. Perfect that it's a laugh."

"Well, do you suppose you'll need a journalist wherever we're going?"

"I don't know. How do you feel about starting from the bottom? There isn't anything lower than where we're going."

"And you won't tell me where that is?"

"Right. You just have to wait like everyone else."

She shivered and looked out over the waters. I asked her if she were cold. She chuckled and asked if I cared about a scum-bag like her. "Sure. I'm sure we can scare up a blanket if you'd like one."

She looked up again and said, "Yes, that would be nice." I left to see if any of the crew on the fishing boat had one. They didn't but the planners of the mission knew their stuff. There was a box of blankets back at the rear of the boat. I brought her one, and I was ready to go back to the back. She said, "How about keeping me company up here?"

"Why up here? Are you a glutton for punishment? It's lighter, warmer, and less windy in the back."

"And it's full of people who really don't like me. You and the Weasleys don't like me, but you are decent. I don't think most of the people back there would stoop to pick up a blanket for me."

'I suppose you're right. In that case, hold on for a minute, and I'll get a blanket for me. Then, we can freeze together up here." She chuckled at that. I went, got the blanket, and returned. She was seated now. I sat down as well, and she was silent for a long time.

Then, out of nowhere, she started to talk. At first it was soft, I wasn't quite sure if I were really hearing it, but it slowly became easier to hear. "You know, I didn't throw everything I knew at Dumbledore. There was something else that I could have said about him."

I shook my head. Even in the dark, I guess she sensed that I'd done that. She asked, "Oh, yes. Did you know him very well?"

I sensed some sort of trap, but didn't see its jaws. "I don't know, really. There were certainly lots of things in your book that I knew nothing about. Maybe I hardly knew him."

I could sense her smile. "Well, then you probably don't know that he was gay."

I'm sure that she could sense my surprise. She went on, "Oh, yes. Gay. I'm surprised that a smart cove like you didn't figure it out on your own."

"Why should I have figured it out myself?"

"Did you get to the part of my book where I talked about his student days at Hogwarts and just after?"

I cautiously admitted that I had.

"Well, then, didn't it strike you as interesting that his best friend and he were going to tour the world together. And later that he fell in love with the Dark Wizard of his time—Grindelwald?"

I thought about it a moment. She was right. The description of their relationship might have been a description of love. The letters, for example—could they have really been love letters? Could Dumbledore have been blinded by love to Grindelwald's evil? What else could have caused this gentle, good man to agree with such heinous schemes?

I thought about it. A strange thought occurred to me. I spoke it. "Look, Rita. Can I tell you something strictly off the record?"

She barked a bitter laugh. "Why not? My career as a journalist is over. Maybe it's been over for a long time. Sure. I promise. You don't need the unbreakable oath."

"OK. You know, I think I might actually have been on a date with Dumbledore."

She laughed a real laugh—spontaneous, unforced, open, full of humor. "Oh, why did I never interview you for the book? But surely you're joking. From everything I've heard of you, you're as straight as an arrow. You've got two girl friends who feud over you like dogs fighting over a steak bone."

"Well, I didn't realize it was a date at the time—or, at least, not the sort of date that you're thinking. I ran into him one early summer day in Hyde Park by chance. Anyway, we are . . . er . . . were both fans of chamber music. I invited him to a concert of a well know chamber orchestra group at Albert Hall. We attended the concert together."

Rita asked, "Who paid for the tickets?"

I had to think a moment, then I remembered, "Oh, you know, I'm pretty sure I did." Then with more certainty, I said, "Yes, of course, I did. Dumbledore didn't have any Muggle money with him when we bought the tickets just before the concert."

She became more serious as she asked the next question, "Are you sure that meeting in Hyde Park was chance?"

I thought a moment. Could I really be sure that it was by chance? It certainly wasn't planned by me. Finally, I answered, "I didn't plan it. That's for sure." She nodded.

Then she asked, "What did you do after the concert?"

I was relieved to be able to answer that we had separated. "Dumbledore offered to take me home, but I lived close and decided to just take the Tube." Since she had vowed to keep it secret, I added, "On the way home, I was waylaid by a couple of Deatheaters. I guess I was lucky to come away alive."

We both fell silent as I thought over how strange the world was. If I'd decided differently and chose to let Dumbledore give me a lift, would I have ended the evening by being propositioned by him rather than Deatheaters? I didn't have a clue. It might have been a completely innocent evening—just two friends getting together for a concert. But who could know?

We were silent for a long time. Finally, she asked how long it would be until we got to France. I looked at my watch and said, 'We've got about two hours left."

She stopped looking forward toward the dark oblivion ahead of us and faced me. "It's funny. This is the safest I've felt in a long time. It's good to be hidden in the dark where 'You Know Who' can't find you."

I nodded but didn't say the obvious—that there didn't seem to be any place like that.

We got to the small French fishing village finally. We got off the boats and boarded a couple of French military lorries—or at least they looked like French lorries. Rita stuck close to me in the back. I announced that we had about an hour's ride to a train station where we'd be boarding a special sleeper car there. We bumped over the roads and eventually reached a train station. The crowd walked out onto the train platform and then up into the special train. We herded them into the dining car, and I announced, "OK. This is the moment of decision. You either take the oath that we talked about here and now, or you leave. We stop the train, you get off, and from there you disapparate wherever you want to. We also give you a hundred galleons for your trouble." Fred jingled a bag of galleons.

"If you do that, there's no 2nd chance. So, line up, and after the oath you can go pick a sleeper compartment and catch some rest."

Rita held back, and everyone chose to take the oath. After everyone had left, Rita and I were the only ones left in the dining car. She alternated looking at me and the floor. Then she said, "I hear that you sometimes look twice at older women."

"I can't imagine where you heard that."

Being coy, she played ignorant, "Well, my sources say that you and another older woman at Hogwarts have been seen together enjoying each other's company. Please notice that I haven't written a word about that in a very long time, even though it would have made good copy."

I looked at her quizzically, "Why in the world would that be? Surely you don't have scruples? That would be a prime story."

"Well, you're right. It's not because of my scruples." She took a deep breath and said, "It could be that I want to keep my options open." She stared at me as if she were looking at the village idiot. And then she said, "Minerva's not the only witch who has a weakness for Muggles."

Her hair was bedraggled from the long boat and lorry rides. She was haggard and her face was drawn. She was more approachable at that moment than when she had been utterly in control—in every way, perfectly quaffed hair, perfect dress, perfect makeup.

I tried to smile gently, "Do lots of witches have a weakness for Muggles?"

"Yes, lots of witches have a weakness for Muggles. I bet lots of witches have a weakness for you."

"Are you sure?"

"Oh, I'm quite sure." What had started as a subtle smile had widened slowly to a definite smirk.

She had somehow gotten much closer to me without my noticing. She had clasp my wrist in a way that reminded me of the unbreakable oath. It was very hard to pull away.

She could tell that and pressed her advantage. "We could share a compartment, couldn't we? Maybe we could figure out what witches find so interesting about you." She had managed to find my other wrist with a hand.

I shook my head, and said that I was going to find a compartment to sleep in. That was not so easy as I thought. As a matter of fact, there was only one unoccupied compartment on the several cars of the train.

Rita smirked, "See, it was Karma."

That remark woke me up in a hurry. I took another quick look up and down the aisle. There just were no unoccupied compartments. I stared for a moment with such intensity that anyone looking on might have thought that I believed that I could create an empty compartment by sheer dint of will. Then I scowled and turned to her. I said, "OK. But I'm sleeping on the floor!"

The smirk grew to a wide smile." She yawned a wide expansive yawn that was clearly fake and said, "You can sleep anywhere you little heart desires." The word "anywhere" was said with special emphasis.

I didn't say anything, but opened the door to the empty compartment for her to enter.

Inside, I quickly pulled down the foldup bed for her. She was still smiling. She said nothing but pulled up the covers that were on the bed and lay down leaving lots of room—just in case.

I picked the second pillow off the bed, tossed it on the floor near the door to the compartment and lay down with my head on it. I asked, "Are you ready for the light to go off."

She said, "Of course."

"No, teeth to brush or hair to brush?"

I couldn't see the frown, but I could hear it in her voice. "I lost those long ago soon after I went on the run."

"Too bad. You should only brush the ones that you want to keep. You'll get toothbrush and floss when we reach the end of the line."

I half-way expected her to ask me to come up with her and help her with her teeth, but it didn't happen.

I carried a small tooth brush in a case in my breast pocket next to my pen. A length of floss was wound around it. I got it out and started brushing.

She was quiet for a long time. I was just beginning to get to sleep when I heard her say in a very quiet voice, "I'm not going to bite. Why don't you come up here and share a warm, soft bed."

The floor was hard and actually pretty cold. "OK. Just remember about biting though."

I worked my way up to my knees in the cramped compartment and then rolled into the bed. She spread the blanket over me and snuggled close but didn't make contact except to put her arm over the blanket. I was facing away from her.

Sometime during the night, the train went over a curved bridge. The car rocked violently, and I woke. I found that we'd both moved during our sleep. I was laying on my back, and she was laying on her stomach beside me. She apparently was wakened too. However, she was only barely awake. She just kissed my shoulder and said fuzzily, "Go back to sleep dear." That woke me up completely. However, I did eventually go back to sleep.

When we arrived at our destination, the whistle blew, and our train rolled to a stop. I woke up and found that her arm was across me again. She caressed my arm and asked, "Do we have to get up now?"

"I'm afraid so. We get out here. " I stretched and uncovered. The air was cool, and I wished I could just get another half hour of rest. I turned on the light. Rita's head was buried in her pillow, and she just mumbled, "Oh, no."

I took a quick glance in the mirror of the compartment and decided that I didn't look too rumpled.

I warned Rita, "I'm going to help get everyone else up."

She groaned, "Do you have to?"

The question answered itself as far as I was concerned. I opened the door of the compartment a bit and tried to leave without exposing the interior much.

What I found outside were the Weasleys. I asked, "Of all the days for you two to get up on time why did it have to be this one?"

George glanced inside the compartment and said, "Take a look Fred."

Fred muscled me aside and glanced inside. Then they said in unison, "Ooooooo!"

I told them to shut it and went down the aisle knocking on doors.

Later in the confusion as people found their way outside the train, a very smiley Rita approached me and didn't say anything.

I said, "Well, you have to know that I'm devoted to one particular witch."

"I supposed that was true. But if you ever get tired of Ms. Goody Two-Shoes Good Witch of the North, and you want something more interesting, the Wicked Witch of the West will be available"

"I'll remember," I said.

She reached out and took hold of my wrist again. I put my other hand on top of hers, and she released it. "Keep on." I said.

I ran into the Weasleys again. Fred had a frown on his face and said, "I see you've gone over to the dark side."

"You have no idea what I've done."

George chimed in,"Well, whatever you've done, she deserves some time in purgatory. I hope you intend to let her have it."

"Oh, believe you me, I have plenty of reason to want her to suffer. And considering that the crowd is a pretty pro-Dumbledore group, I think that she'll suffer plenty."

Fred chimed in, "And if she doesn't, we'll always be there to lend a helping hand."

I shook my head and said, "Don't try too hard, everyone deserves a second chance."

George and Fred raised their eyelids and said in unison, "Everyone? Even Riddle?"

I have a certain obstinate strain in me, so I said, "Yes, even Riddle. And I'd give it to him—if I could figure out how to do it safely." They shook their heads and we parted. There were several Air Force MP's waiting for me at the entrance to the lead railroad car.

They introduced themselves as sergeants McBean and George. They didn't know much, just that they were to conduct about 50 people by truck to the Darmstadt Air Force Base Hangar D12 where a C-130 was waiting for us. We had to waken a good number of people who seemed to be thoroughly enjoying getting a good night's sleep in a dry, warm, private railway car. We had arrived about 7 AM local time. It was pitch black out, and nobody really wanted to get out and walk to the trucks—especially in the cold, but they did it. We helped people on board. The interior was pretty rude with simple bench seats. People grumbled, but thankfully the drive was short.

There was little to see. We stopped once at the gate of the Air Force Base and overheard bits and pieces of conversation:

"Your papers seem to be in order, but I'd like to see the . . ." The conversation waned as though the speakers had turned away.

"There's not any reason . . . ."

Finally the rear door of our truck opened briefly, and a soldier shown a flashlight over the rear of the truck and closed the door. Shortly after that we started off again, and somebody lurched against me. A child was whimpering, and most of the adults seemed to be trying to get some sleep. I knew that it was a hopeless attempt because we were inside the air force base now, and it would be a matter of a few minutes before we arrived at Hanger D12. And, indeed, it was only a few minutes.

The doors opened, and we started pouring out onto the tarmac. An officer strode up to us and asked, "Who's in charge here?"

The Weasleys and I spoke up. The officer snorted quietly. Then he said, "All right, I'm Captain Arthur Keenaugh. They told me that I'm to ferry about 100 people to the States. You don't look like 100. Are there more on the way?"

I had stepped toward him as he spoke, and when he finished, I said, "I'm Jim Wendt. This is everyone. We can get going."

Keenaugh signaled for us to follow him. We walked toward the large hanger. As we walked, he turned around, walking backwards, he gave us some instructions, "All right. We're going to go onboard right away. Find a seat quickly. If anyone needs to visit the 'can', do it now. We've got a 6 hour flight ahead of us, and we're not stopping in the middle of the ocean for anyone. One of the crew members will show you where the WC's are in the hangar. It's a bumpy ride, so stay in your seats, buckled in. We'll warn you when we're about to land, when you'll really need to stay in your seats. Questions?"

He waited about 2 seconds and went on, "Good. Use the WC, and let's get into the air."

The plane was bathed in sodium vapor light and looked unearthly. Almost everyone followed a couple of enlisted men into the hangar. It was almost 8 AM when we were all seated, buckled in, and accounted for. Fred and George walked around checking the count and identity of people.

Rita found a seat next to mine. She spoke quietly to me, "I don't think I can stand being with all these people who hate me."

"How do you know they hate you?"

"Do your friends claim that every empty seat around them is being 'held' for a friend?"

"Well, make yourself useful." I looked around and found the kid who had been whimpering off and on throughout the night. She was about 8 years old and was sitting beside a woman who was also holding a baby. She seemed to be un-accompanied by a husband or significant other. I said, "Do you see the little girl who's been whimpering throughout the trip."

"Yes, really irritating isn't it. Why can't the mother control her?"

I looked at her askance. Then I said, "Well, make yourself useful by entertaining the kid. Go over there, introduce yourself to the mom and BE POLITE. Then ask if you can sit next to them. If she lets you, although I can't imagine why she would, then sit there and introduce yourself to the kid. Then talk to her."

"The kid? What would I say?"

"Well, you could pretend that you're writing an article about this family. You should be able to handle that. You know—where did you come from? What do you like to do? If she likes to play games like 20 questions or anything that you can do without equipment, play it with her. Just keep her distracted, especially when we take off."

"Take off? What take off?"

"This is an airplane. We're going to leave the ground and fly across the Atlantic."

"The Atlantic? Ocean?"

"Yeh. What did you think we were going to do?"

"Well, I didn't know." She said plaintively, "Who's going to distract me?"

"The little girl. You'll distract each other. Now, get over there before we take off." She reluctantly got up and walked over and sat down beside the mom and started talking. I watched them for a few minutes and saw the mom's mouth drop and could read her lips say, "You're Rita Skeeter?"

There seemed to be a lot of lively discussion going on. Perhaps Rita found a fan. But the engines started cranking, and we shortly started moving. We slowly gained speed, and there was a big bump as the landing gears came up into the body of the plane. That occasioned some worried musings, "What happened?" "Are we going to crash?"

I got my voice revved up and said with as authoritative a tone as I could make at the top of my voice, "Everyone. Listen up. That's a completely normal sound. Everything is fine. If there's something to worry about, I'll let you know."

Somebody shouted, "Sure you will."

The rest of the flight was uneventful—at least, to the seasoned flyer. We went though some bumpy air at one point, and there was grumbling. It occurred to me to wonder that I hadn't heard any whimpering from the little girl. I looked over and found the little girl, the mom, and Rita in animated discussion. I looked over again later and found Rita holding the baby while the mom seemed to be catching some sleep. Her head was lolled over on Rita's shoulder, the baby was resting on Rita's left breast, and the 8 yr old was leaning against Rita's left side. I had to laugh to myself. I caught George's eye and pointed over at Rita. He shook his head in disbelief, but was too far away to comment. He made a face that was somewhere between an expression of distaste and humor. Rita noticed us and stuck her tongue out. Almost everyone else was napping fitfully and didn't notice our exchange.

We spent the rest of the flight peacefully if not comfortably. The pilot came on the intercom and announced, "We're about ten minutes from touchdown. Please be sure your seat belts are securely fastened and stop wandering around the cargo hold." I unbuckled, got up, and walked around the cargo hold making sure that everyone's seat belt was secure. When I got to Rita, she said, "Well, you came over here to gloat?"

"No, I came over here to make sure that everyone is safe. Is your seat belt tight?"

"Yes, but I could loosen it up and you could join me." She had an impish expression in her eyes.

"Just check the kiddos, and we'll talk when we're on the ground."

I walked around, tightening a couple of seat belts of wizards who were sound asleep and getting a couple of others to do it for themselves. I regained my seat and swung in as the plane noticeably swooped. Sally grabbed my arm to steady me. I thanked her and buckled up myself. About a minute later we touched down and taxied to a stop outside a hangar. The crew came out and let down the ramp. We were met by a couple of enlisted men who said that they were there to drive us to our destination. I helped make sure everyone had an opportunity at the WCs, and we got onto the USAF trucks that were waiting for us. It was a warm morning. There was just a hint of light in the sky.

The woman with the babe in arms and Rita came by, and the woman asked me, "We're awfully hungry. Is there anything we can eat?"

I replied, "Not yet. We're about an hour or two away from our destination. I guarantee that you'll have breakfast there, and that it'll be a good one. The 8-yr old looked up at me plaintively and had her arm around the back of her mom. I added, "It's really going to be OK soon." I got down to my knees and talked to the 8-yr old, "What's your name?"

"Edwina."

"Do you like pancakes?"

"Yes." She said it slowly and cautiously as though it were a trick question, and I'd force her to eat nothing but pancakes for the rest of her life if she answered, "yes."

"Well, good. I know that's on the menu for breakfast." I got up and helped people on the trucks. We drove off. Sally had switched to another truck with Fred. George was in this one with me. We drove off with a lurch, and I heard a few suppressed curses. I just hoped that none of them were for the driver. The sky slowly lightened. We didn't have a window to see through, but the interior of the truck got steadily brighter. Finally we arrived at the base. We slowed at the gate and waited for them to open the gate. Then we entered and drove up next to the mess hall. I hurried off first and called for everyone to assemble outside the mess hall doors.

I gave a brief speech. "Everyone, attention please. We've arrived at Fort Dumbledore. This will be your home until we've defeated Riddle. Some of you will have the opportunity to join the DA and fight directly. But even those of you who remain here and support the war effort from this base will be contributing significantly to the overthrow of Riddle. In a minute, you'll enter the mess hall for breakfast and have the opportunity to meet other people in the resistance. But first, I want to introduce you to the base commander, Ms. Beth Lawson. She's the nearest thing to the Queen for you as long as you are here. Here she is." Beth walked up. Her height didn't seem intimidating until she started to talk. Then she spoke, and everything changed.

Beth began, "Welcome to Camp Dumbledore. We are all here to escape tyranny, resist the evil, and work for the freedom of all wizards. We have a few simple rules here that worked for you in Kindergarten, and they'll work for you here if you use them." She ticked off on her fingers the rules:

"Be respectful to everyone.

"Keep your property safe. We have magically secured safety deposit boxes if you have valuables.

"Obey the people in charge. That would be me, the Weasely's, the house prefects." At the incredulous looks of most of the new recruits she repeated, "Yes, we have house prefects. We call the houses, barracks, here. If you'll be in the DA, you'll have lieutenants and sergeants to obey.

"Now, come into the mess hall and have breakfast."

We all entered and worked our way through the line. I held back to the end of the line because I like to take my time in the food line, so that I don't have people behind me pressuring me to make my choice and move on. Beth joined me at the end of the line and asked how this one went.

I answered, "It was a near thing. A group of snatchers showed up."

She interrupted me to find out what snatchers were.

"They're bounty hunters."

"What. . . are . . . bounty hunters." She apparently hadn't heard the term before.

"They're people who hunt anyone who has a reward posted for their capture. The Deatheaters pay a bounty for people who turn in Order of the Phoenix members and Muggle-born wizards. It's a new phenomenon. Anyway, they showed up and then we ended up killing one and capturing the others."

She gasped and asked, "You didn't?"

"Well, I personally didn't, but one of the snipers who were protecting us did."

"My God!" She was temporarily struck speechless. "How could you allow that?"

"Well, it wasn't exactly something that I had a lot of control over. Anyway, we had something even worse happen."

"What could be worse than that?"

"Some Deatheaters showed up and almost caught us all."

"What did you do to them?"

"Actually, nothing. We were able to get away before they showed up, but it was a close thing. We had to evacuate people by helicopter."

"By what?"

"Helicopter—you know, a Muggle flying machine that . . "

"You don't mean those infernal machines that make so much noise and blow you to bits with all the wind?"

"The very ones."

"Sometimes I have my doubts about you. Why not have people disapparate?" She had begun to show her temper by the short clipped sentences she spit out.

I was close to loosing my temper as well and snapped, "Well, we'd never get them all together again. It was hard enough setting this rendezvous up."

She glared at me a minute and asked, "What did you do with the Snatchers that you didn't kill?"

"The Weasleys disarmed them, disapparated with them to a remote cliff, and questioned them. Then they wiped their memories of the day and let them loose—without their wands."

"I suppose they tortured them?"

"No. No!" I thought for a moment and went on. "Well, it's hard to tell with the Weasleys. The difference between good-natured fun and torture is such a fine line with them. I've been on the edge of that line with them myself on one or two occasions."

A smile broke across her face and she relented, "You're right there. They do seem to have a sense of humor that borders on the uh the uh, well, the terrifying. What's the rest of the family like?"

"Well, let me just say that the mom, bless her heart, is the only person they're afraid of."

"She must be pretty formidable."

"Yes. She reminds me a lot of a dog I once knew. She—the dog—was owned by a friend of mine. If you were the dog's friend, you couldn't want a better companion. But if you weren't part of the 'pack', you were her worst enemy. Anyway, the family with the dog had a couple of kids. One of them played keep-away with it, using the dog's toys. That dog made growling sounds that would have convinced you that it would take the kid's leg off, but nothing of the sort ever happened.

"Then, the Weasleys have got a sister who is sort of like the mom in miniature. There are a couple of other brothers. One of them is along with Potter—wherever he is. The dad is fascinated with everything Muggle. They're all crazy in their own particular way."

Later we ran into Fred and George. Beth commented that she would like to meet their mom. Fred cautioned her, "Just don't tell Mum what we've been up to. She thinks that we've been doing Wizard radio and stuff like that."

George added, "Yea. If she got wind of our flying in Muggle contraptions and the like, we'd be in so much trouble, you can't imagine."

Beth promised to remember.

The next day, Sally and I left by Muggle contraption for the Atlanta airport where we caught a flight back to London.

B1B

It was a clear, bright, early December day—a change from the overcast and gloom. I was sitting on the embankment of the Thames. I wasn't thinking of the nice weather or the view around me—the pretty women from the offices that had come down on this nice day to have lunch—or any of the traffic moving on the Waterloo bridge. I was thinking of the dubious honor of visiting at Downing Street. It wasn't going there that was the problem. It was the fact that I was going to have to go there and eat my words from the last time that I'd talked to upper brass. I was worried about it, and I was trying to think of a way that it could be less than totally embarrassing. No ideas were coming to me.

I guess that I was not paying much attention to my surroundings. Someone tapped on my shoulder. I swung around to see who it was. I recognized one of the soldiers. He said, "Sorry to disturb you, sir. You're wanted by Colonel Parker."

"OK. Let's go."

He signaled to a car that was pulling up. It stopped, we got in, and took off. We pulled in a truck loading dock and walked in to the warehouse by a route I'd not taken before. He accompanied me to Parker's office. When I went in, I found that Sally was there already. Parker was sitting on his desk, chatting her up. When I entered the room, he stood and asked, "What are you doing taking a long lunch hour. We've got to leave for #5 in less than an hour, and you've not practiced what you're going to say."

"Oh, I've practiced it. I just haven't practiced it with you."

"Well, I want to know what you're going to say."

"You read the paper we sent ahead of us. That's what I'm going to say."

"I want to hear it with my ears. I just want . . ." I never found out what he was going to say.

I interrupted him, "You just want to make sure I'm not going to say something impolitic."

"You're bloody right. I want to make sure that you don't say something 'impolitic' or worse."

"You mean 'true'?"

I turned to Sally, "You've heard this a couple of times already. You don't need to stay."

She answered, "Oh, I think I will. I always enjoy watching you 'eat crow'. You make such interesting faces when you do that."

"Nice." So we started.

□

We were all in the limo driving in early afternoon London traffic. We went in a different entrance to #5. Strictly speaking it wasn't an entrance to # 5 at all. It was across the street. We actually went through a tunnel to #5. We went up to street level and stopped in what would have been a living room in a normal home, but this one had several large monitors that were dark at the moment. We waited by ourselves for a few minutes, and a couple of uniforms came in followed by the PM and a couple of civilians. We had all met before except for the uniforms. It turned out that one was a rear admiral, Burnes, and the other was an RAF general, Richardson.

We all sat for a moment, and the PM said, "Let's not waste time re-capitulating your paper. I've read it. Let's get down to the hard questions right away."

I looked over at Parker. I gave him one of the funny looks that Sally seemed to enjoy so much and said, "There's nothing I enjoy like 'hard questions'."

The PM gave me a funny look and asked, "Do you remember the last time you were talking about this. You did a pretty good job of convincing my staff that we should never resort to nuclear weapons. So, is that just when other people propose them?"

"Well, actually, yes. When people who don't understand what they're dealing with, propose using them, it's dangerous to act."

"Convince me that you 'know what you're dealing with'. Why is it OK when you say it's OK?"

I took a deep breath. I counted to 5. This was one that I couldn't muff. "First, let me start with some recent history that has just come to the surface.

"There is a prophecy that, strangely, both Deatheaters and the Order of the Phoenix believe. It says basically that either Riddle will kill Potter or Potter will kill Riddle."

The PM was concentrating on me intensely. He asked, "Do you believe that and why or why not?"

"Yes. For two reasons. First, the fact that almost all wizards believe this is significant—especially the Deatheaters. They normally view Riddle as invulnerable but they're nervous about Potter.

"Second, Potter is the only person who has survived a direct attack by Riddle. Potter was only a year old, and Riddle was a mature, powerful wizard—quite likely the most powerful wizard in the world. And yet, Potter not only survived, but the killing curse that Riddle used on him only left Potter slightly scarred. It rebounded on Riddle and virtually killed him. He disappeared for 14 years, and didn't return to power until he'd gotten help—very unwilling help from Potter. That's pretty good phenomenological proof that he could kill Riddle."

The PM frowned and said, "So far you're doing a good job of proving that we shouldn't change our minds about nukes. We should just let Potter kill him. What's our backup plan if Riddle kills Potter"

"Just the problem. We need a backup plan."

The PM looked over at Parker. "We know where Riddle is right now, don't we?"

Parker gulped and said, "Well, right at the moment, we don't know where he is." He quickly added, "Most of the time he's at the Malfoy residence and we know when he comes and goes." He finished weakly, "We just don't know where he goes when he leaves."

The PM asked, "I thought that we had surveillance on all Deatheaters residences?"

Parker smiled wanly, "We do. At least, all known Deatheater residences, but he doesn't disapparate when he leaves the Malfoys'."

The PM was showing some signs of irritation. His voice was becoming strained, "What does he do?"

Parker made a face that would have amused Sally, "Well. He flies."

The PM was really showing restraint, but his taught voice betrayed him, "How does he fly? Broom? Flying Carpet? Red-nosed reindeer?"

"No, sir, he just rises into the air and, uh, zooms into the clouds."

"Well, when he is at the Malfoy's, can't we just have a sniper pick him off?"

I decided it was time to intervene. "Maybe that would work. But if it doesn't, and I personally don't think that it would, it would be our first and last chance. He'd go to ground so thoroughly that we'd never have another chance. If we reach that god-forsaken spot where we have to try to kill him ourselves, we've got to give it the very best shot possible. That will be the end of civilization as we know it if we don't succeed.

"And that's not all."

The PM leaned back and stared at me with disbelief, "That's not enough?"

"I'm afraid not. Even if we do succeed beyond our wildest dreams, I don't think that Riddle will be any deader than he was after his original encounter with Potter. He came back from that encounter. But the key point is that he had to have help from his Deatheaters to do that. We need to get as many Deatheaters as we can along with Riddle."

"Go ahead."

"Well, this brings me to my next big point. We are in luck, I think. Riddle will want to have all his Deatheaters there when he kills Potter."

Richardson wrinkled his brows, "Just what makes you think that?"

"Several lines of reasoning:

"First, most dictators like to show off their power before their followers. It's good propaganda if you can humble your implacable foes before killing them.

"Second, he's already established the pattern."

Richardson followed up quickly, "But the first time he attacked Potter he was alone, wasn't he? And he was defeated. Surely, he wouldn't want to take a chance of a repeat?"

"I think he doesn't have much choice from that perspective. If he simply killed Potter alone, in a dark alley with no witnesses, there would always be doubt whether he'd really done it strictly by being the more powerful or if he'd had help.

"In the next encounter he tried to have all his Deatheaters present, but they weren't all there. In their next encounter most of them were present. In those encounters he made a point that no one should help him but all should witness. By losing three times, he's dug himself a deep hole that he can only get out of by killing Potter with lots of witnesses in single combat. I don't think he's got any choice.

"And that gives us a prime opportunity. It virtually guarantees that all of his Deatheaters will be present, and since they have to have time to get there for the duel, there will be time for us to prepare as well.

"If Potter loses, we might have time to get a weapon onto the field that will take them all out—Riddle and all his followers. Even if we trusted snipers, we'd be very hard-pressed to get them all simultaneously so that none could Disapparate and get away. It has to be a weapon that is all-encompassing and instantaneous, no-miss.

The admiral said, "Yes, just so. That's why if you're really going to use a nuclear weapon, it should be delivered by a missile, from close at hand."

Richardson interrupted, "Something like a Trident missile, fired from a hundred or so mile range. Is that it? Neat, the way you guarantee that your service gets the honor. How about a cruise missile launched from twenty or thirty miles?"

I broke into this internecine debate. "Neither would work. At least not the weapons either of you is thinking of."

They choroused, "And why not?"

"Simple. Neither of your services currently has a nuclear weapon powerful enough for this purpose."

"What!" they both shouted, "Isn't 100 Kiloton's enough!" They were so much in sync that I wondered for a second if they were channeling the Weasleys.

"Not really." I turned to Parker. "What kind of weapons are we planning to use against wizards?"

I took Parker by surprise. He was drinking some tea, and he choked on it. Probably it was not a real gag reflex. He was probably looking to gain some thinking time. "Well, we have snipers of course. And we have small munitions." He paused and thought a moment. "Actually, our munitions are completely mechanical. There are no electronic or even electrical components in them. We had the deuce of a time getting our contractors to go back to pure mechanicals—timers, fuses, detonators. It was all feasible. They just hadn't made any in a dozen years or so. They had to find old employees who had retired to help them re-tool for that kind of explosives."

"And why did I insist on no electronics?"

Parker nodded wisely. "Because electronics don't work in the vicinity of magic. It's sort of like EMP suppression." The PM had coughed, and Parker had taken the hint. "That is, Electromagnetic Pulse suppression of electronics. Except that that effect usually only lasts tens of minutes while magic seems to work continuously."

I carried on. "Right. The largest community of wizards is close to Hogwarts School. We've tested it. As one of the Weasleys would put it, you can't get ekeltricity to work reliably within three or four miles of Hogwarts. The weapon we use has to be able to kill with 100% certainty at a range of at least five miles. That puts us in the multi-megaton range. Something quite beyond the capability of submarine launched missiles or even normal bomber launched cruise missiles. General Richardson, does the RAF have anything in its arsenal in the multi-megaton range?"

Richardson cleared his throat and almost whispered, "No."

"What's the largest warhead you've got?" asked the PM.

He hemmed and muttered, "Maybe 300 or 400 KT."

The PM said "Bloody Hell. Who does have weapons that large?"

Burnes said, "Well, to the best of our knowledge just the Russians and the Americans."

The PM said, "I suppose there's not much chance of the Russians helping us?"

Richardson said, "Their attitude these days seems to be, 'we'll do anything for a ruble', but somehow I don't think that extends to detonating a nuclear weapon somewhere in England."

The PM asked, "And our cousins across the pond?"

Parker was happy to say something positive and confident for once, "We've actually got quite good working relations with them on this issue at the moment. I think that we'd have to do a selling job, but I think that they were pretty impressed by the Weasley twins when we went over there. I think that we could talk them into it."

The PM leaned back and looked up into the air contemplatively for a moment. "Yes," he said, "we'll start talks with them. I hate to get us indebted to them like we already are, but this is not a time for half-measures."

He went on, "But just where would we be likely to detonate this thing. We can hardly control where Potter and Riddle decide to have their set-to."

I answered, "I've been doing some thinking about that. It seems to me that there are two likely locations. The more likely is Hogwarts School, located in northern Scotland."

The PM asked, "Just where is that?"

I grimaced at what I was going to have to say, "I can't tell you."

The PM said, "You know, I do have pretty good security clearance."

"Oh, it's not that. It's just that I can't tell you. I literally am not able to tell you."

"But you used to work there. Surely you know how to get there?"

"Well, I never got there on my own, and even if I had, I'd not be able to tell you. You see, it's unplottable. That is, it's impossible to mark it's location on a map."

The PM's cheeks were getting red, and his mouth was set in a hard thin line. I went on, "It's a magical effect."

"Then how can you possibly attack them if you can't plot them on a map?"

230

"We can plot a location close to Hogwarts. That would be the target. That's another reason that we can't use a small nuclear weapon. We don't know exactly where to target it."

"Great. Can you show me the 'approximate' location of Hogwarts on a map?"

"Yes, we can do that. General, can we get a map of Scotland up on one of those monitors."

He picked up a phone and spoke into it briefly and quietly. The monitor warmed up, and a map of England showed up and zoomed in to Scotland. I got up, walked over to the monitor, and pointed at a spot on the northwest coast. "It's about here, close to this Loch. It's called Loch Dubh. Hogwarts itself is on another Loch that doesn't show up on this map."

Someone asked, "Are there many people up there?"

"Well, our authorities think that a low altitude multi-megaton blast would be shielded by the mountains around it, and except for Hogwarts itself and the community next to it, there would be no direct blast-caused fatalities and probably not even any serious injuries. Of course, the fallout would force us to evacuate the entire area."

The PM was clearly not happy about attacking his own people, but he was controlling his unhappiness pretty well, "And the other location?"

"It's the Malfoy residence, which is in the Lake district."

"Oh, bloody hell. How many casualties would we have there?"

Richardson seemed to be doing some quick calculations in his head. "I think direct blast, we're probably talking ten or twenty thousand and fallout—probably in the multiple tens of thousands." He hurriedly added that those would probably not happen for years.

The PM mumbled something under his breath. "If I'd only known what was coming, I'd never have gone into public service." He looked around and around the room, seemingly hoping that someone would suggest something. His hopes were dashed. Then he asked, "And this is not as bad as having Riddle around?"

No one said anything for a long couple of moments. Then I said, "Imagine that Adolph Hitler had won World War II and put an SS general in charge of England. That rule would be kind and benevolent compared to having Riddle as king of England."

The PM sighed and said, "Thanks, that's just the way you want to start your week—a choice of doing things that make Josef Stalin look good by comparison or letting Idi Amin become PM."

A moment later, he said, "Get the hell out of here. I'll let you know what my decision is. Soon."

We left without any further urging. On the way to our limo, Parker asked me, "What do you think?"

"Oh, I think there's a good chance that he'll go along with us."

'I don't know, he seemed pretty, well, unhappy with us."

"That's why I'm sure that he will. He wouldn't have been nearly so unhappy had he been completely decided not to go along with us. He's unhappy with himself for being convinced."

Parker only stared at the sidewalk and said, "Hmmfh."

As we neared the limousine, a man and woman approached us. The woman had a hand-held microphone and the man had a video camera perched on his shoulder. She had a sharp, angular face and was wearing a grey skirt with a pink blouse. She stuck her microphone in my face and asked, "You've just been seeing the PM. You're not on the official visitor's list. What were you talking with the PM about?"

Our driver jumped out of the limo and ran over, apparently to shoo them off. I shook my head at him and looked straight into the camera and then to her. "Have I?"

She was taken back for about 2 seconds and then went on confidently. "Sure, you were taking the back entrance. So, you must have been meeting about something juicy. Give."

"Well, we were talking about Riddle and magic."

She gaped for a moment. "Riddles and magic. Who are you kidding? You don't get in there without having something important to talk about."

I smiled and said, "Well, believe me or not. That's your problem. See you on the evening news." We walked over to the limo and got in. When the doors were closed, and we were on our way, Parker said, "That was pretty cheeky. How do you know she won't figure out something?"

I frowned and said, "In a way, I wish she would. But she won't. We don't fit into one of her neat categories. We're not foreign. Or at least, you're not. They may figure out who you are, but they'll never learn who I am. If she gets as far as you, she'll just figure that we're here about the IRA, and I'm some obscure deep cover mole in the IRA or something."

"I hope you're right. If she ever got a hint of why we were really there, there would be hell to pay."

We weren't followed, and we got back to the warehouse district and into our mole-hole. Sally was hanging around the office waiting to quiz me. "Well?" She asked.

"Don't you have anything better to do than waste your time here when we don't have anything to do? Go look up Fred and have a good evening."

232

She walked up to me and stuck her face in mine. "Not until you tell me what happened over at #10."

I knew that I'd have to tell her something sooner or later, so I said, "Sure. We had a friendly meeting and told the PM that he was going to have to be prepared to flatten the Lake District. He used some words that I can't repeat in polite company or even to you. Then he said something like, 'Oh, well, I didn't really like this job anyway.'"

"You mean he's going along with you?"

"Well, he wasn't that specific, but I think he probably will."

"I'll be darned." She spun around and walked briskly back to her desk, and said over her shoulder. "That's a good idea about Fred. Would you like to join us for dinner? I think he's over being miffed about not getting to meet the PM."

"Oh, I don't think so. I've got some correspondence to work on. You two go ahead. Fred will enjoy having you to himself."

"Yes, he is a bit of a fool over me."

"Right. And the feeling's not mutual, of course."

"Well, a girl's got to keep her options open."

"Yes, you go keep your options open. I do want to do some writing."

Resignation

I sat at my desk and pulled out a sheet of paper and started, "My dearest Minerva, I know that you find it very hard to get away from Hogwarts, but something big has come up. And no joking about how it's always up. I really need to see you. Please tell me when you're coming. Whenever it is, I can get away. I will get away. I'm always yours. J." I worked it down to owl-size and put it in a little leather pouch. Minerva had told me that only the person to whom you sent the pouch could open it. I hoped that she was right. Now, all I had to do was to wait for the next owl to come my way. You could never tell when that would be, but it was never more than a couple of days. Someone was always sending me letters by OP.

It was two days later. In the morning an owl found its way in from America. It was a progress report from George about training Dumbledore's Army. They'd gotten enough usable wands together to be able to do regular training. Apparently, there weren't a lot of wand-makers in the US. They'd had to go to Canada to find a couple who were willing to make some without knowing what they were for.

I quickly composed a letter back to George and gave the owl two addresses. First, Hogwarts and then the US. I sent it off just before lunch. Just after dinner a big hoot owl showed up with an answer from Minerva. "If you think this is really that important, I can get away for a couple of hours tonight. I'll go out to the Three Broomsticks and Disapparate. I'll appear in one of the women's loo's at Victoria station at 8 PM. Buy me a drink, and I'll show you a good time."

I arrived at Victoria about 15 minutes in advance. I stationed myself outside one of the ladies' loos and looked like any of a number of husbands/boy friends waiting for their spouse/girl friend. She showed up about 10 minutes after 8. "Well, I thought you were never going to get out of there," I chided as I took her in my arms and kissed her enthusiastically.

"Well, if I'd known that you were that impatient, I'd have done my business quicker." She winked at me.

We walked out of the station, and I suggested the "Kings Arms", a likely looking pub across from Victoria. She agreed. We went in and found an empty table. A bar maid came over and took our order. I said, "This place is too quiet for me. I'm going to plug the juke box."

She laughed and asked, "What in the world is a Cuke box, and does it have a leak that you have to 'plug' it."

"You know, I never know when you're serious and when you're just making fun of me."

"Well, if you knew which were which, how would I ever keep your attention? Hummmm."

"Oh, I've no doubt that you'd have some way of holding my attention." As I said tha,t she pulled off her cloak and revealed a lot of left leg. "No sooner said than . . . . " She chuckled throatily and looked up into my face. After a long silent moment, I said, "Get up, and I'll show you how to plug a juke box."

I led her over to the juke box and explained how it worked. "There's a list of songs that the juke box can play. You thumb through the songs and decide which ones you want. Then you put your coins in through the slot and key in the code for the ones you want to hear." She nodded as she watched the actions.

I asked, "Is there anything you want to hear?"

"Oh, do they have the Weird Sisters?"

"No, I don't think so."

"Good, I don't like them anyway. I really don't know Muggle songs. You pick some."

As I worked my way through the list, I saw one that I liked, "Did you ever hear 'Band on the Run'?"

"No, did the crowd hate them?"

"That's a song. No, the crowd usually loves that one." I kept thumbing through and picked a couple more. I was mainly picking loud ones because I didn't want us to be overheard. "Band on the Run" started to play.

"Ok, let's go back to our table." The bar maid had left our drinks. I caught her eye to see if she wanted to be paid right away. She came over. I asked.

She said, "No, you and your mother look respectable, I'll run a tab for you."

"Right. You've just about blown your tip with that crack." I remarked. She frowned.

Minerva said, "It's a reasonable mistake. Don't be cruel."

"I suppose you're right." I was not in the mood for jokes about Minerva at that point, but I had to admit the justice of what she said.

When the bar maid was out of earshot, I took both her hands in mine. She said, "Oh, my. You're not going to do something foolish like propose to me again?"

I choked down a lump in my throat and said, "Oh, if I thought you'd change your mind, I would in a second. No, I have something more important to ask you."

"Something more important than wedded bliss?" She had a wry smile on her face.

"I'm serious Minerva. Look. There's something that I want you to do. Besides marrying me. I know that's hopeless." I added under my breath, "for now."

"What is it? I'd do almost anything for you."

I looked into her face with all the earnestness that I could muster. "Look. I can't tell you why I want you to do this, but it's really important. It's really serious." I hesitated.

"OK. OK. I got it. It's really important to you. What is it?"

I took a deep breath. I knew that this would be a sales job that would make the one that I did with the PM a few days before look like stealing candy from a baby. "Please, please, please, please. Leave Hogwarts. Resign your post. Go to. . . Oh, I don't know where to tell you to go. Go to your sister's. Go to Bath. I don't care where you go, just leave Hogwarts, please?"

She was matter of fact, "You know that I can't do that. Don't be a silly boy. Or, at least, don't be a sillier boy than you already are."

"Yes, you can. It's perfectly easy. I'll write the resignation letter for you. It'll be easy. Snape won't care. He'll be happy to replace you with a Deatheater."

"Oh, Jim. You know that's why I can't do it. I can't leave those poor students at Hogwarts completely at the mercy of Snape and the other Deatheaters. Please don't ask me again."

I screwed up my courage again. It wasn't easy pressing her so hard for something that I knew that she not only didn't want to do, but felt was a dereliction of her duty to do. "Minerva, please, please. Don't resign. Don't even go back. Just disappear, please."

"You know, Jim. I used to think that you were an intelligent man. I thought you could figure out when you were pressing a lost cause."

"Minerva. If you leave Hogwarts, I won't ask you to marry me again. Ever."

"Oh, Wendt. This is serious." A tear appeared in her right eye. "What is it? I know that you wouldn't promise that if you weren't deathly serious. Something's going to happen, isn't it? You know that something's going to happen, and you won't tell me what."

I suddenly realized that I was grasping Minerva's hands very tightly. I loosened my grip and told her. "I don't know that something's going to happen. It just might. I don't want you anywhere near there if it does. I don't want you in Hogwarts or anywhere up there."

She shook her head "You know that there isn't anywhere that's safe. I could leave Hogwarts just to fall into something worse. I can't leave my students. I won't." She sobbed and then arranged her face into a tight smile. "Now, you've got me away from Hogwarts for something that I can't help you with. Isn't there something that I can help you with?"

I knew that I had lost for the moment. So, I put it out of my mind for the moment. I slid one of my hands down her arm and gently pulled her closer over the table. She completed the motion, and we kissed.

We were interrupted by the bar maid. "Do you two need fresh drinks."

I could tell from her inflection that it wasn't a question. I just about had my fill of being thwarted by women. I put the best smile I could on my face and looked straight into her eyes. "If you can just let us nurse our drinks, I'll give you the best tip you've ever had in your life."

She looked at me, then at Minerva. She shrugged and said, "It's your money, but I don't know why you're wasting it on her."

I smiled a real smile this time. "You're right about that. You don't have the foggiest idea why I would spend my time and money the way I do." She turned her back and walked back to the bar.

I looked speculatively at Minerva. "Now that we're finally on our own, how about my just moving this chair over toward you." She smiled and twisted a little so that I could put my arm around her. Her left ear was inclined slightly toward me. I leaned over and put my right arm around her waist. I then inclined my mouth to her ear and whispered an endearment into her pearl-like ear. The bar maid didn't disturb us again, although we eventually did buy another drink. I calculated what a good tip would be for half a dozen drinks for both of us and gave her a tip that would be generous even for that. I don't know if she appreciated our generosity. After we left the pub, I accompanied Minerva into Victoria and saw her to her loo. She walked in and after a moment, I walked away knowing that she was a couple of hundred kilometers away already.

□

The next day Parker showed up in my office. I asked, "What are you doing here? Why not call?"

"It's too dangerous talking on the phone."

"You think that Riddle has our line bugged?"

"Don't be funny. Our friends have agreed to your conditions." He added, "In principal."

I asked, "Buttttt?"

"But he has the final call on whether to use the . . uh . . device."

"That's reasonable. I didn't expect anything else. So, when do we find out what the Americans think about the idea?"

"They're going to have a high level diplomatic set-to with the Americans, and we should know in a couple of weeks."

"None too soon."

After Parker left, Sally sidled over to my desk and asked, "How was your little rendezvous last night?"

I tried to keep a straight face. "What rendezvous?"

She shook her head and said, "Do you really think that there's anyone who can't tell when you've had a good night?"

"Parker didn't say anything, did he?"

Sally laughed, "Parker wouldn't notice if he walked in on the two of you playing house. No, I mean every woman in the building knows that you had a 'wonderful' time last night."

"I guess that I'm lucky that there aren't many women in the building."

"No, you're lucky that she puts up with you."

The Green Man

I was finally getting comfortable with the idea that I might have the "go" code for a nuke when I got a call from Parker. He told me to come see him. I left my office and walked through the warehouse to Parker's office. When I got there, there was a small party going on in his waiting room. There were a couple of uniformed people that I'd never seen before. I hadn't become familiar with Brit uniforms, but they were clearly not SAS. There was also a civilian or at least someone who looked like he was a civilian. Parker's secretary ushered us in. He made no comment. None was necessary.

Parker said, "OK. Let's do intro's." He named names and the guilty party nodded,"Colonel Barkley and Major Denver—Royal Marines." They both looked to be in their early thirties—short, muscular, crew cut, deep tan. They looked like they'd just stepped off the plane from Saudi Arabia or some other dangerous, hot, sunny area. "And this is the assistant to the Under-Minister for Defense Rupert Cavor." He looked like he'd just burrowed out of the depths of Whitehall or someplace—not tanned, tall, or thin.

"And this is our contractor."

Barkley asked, "Does the contractor have a name?"

"Not for you. It's too dangerous to everyone for you to know it."

"You can call me Jim. What brings you gentlemen here?"

They all looked at each other trying to decide who got to do the talking. Finally Cavor spoke, "OK. The port authority was doing a random search of a freighter outside the Port of London and they found some radioactivity. They traced it to a container on the freighter. It was labeled 'crankcases'. When they broke it open, they found a suspicious canister that turned out to have the components of a nuclear device in it."

I gasped.

Barkley smiled and said, "Oh, yes. And it was big—enough to kill thousands in the open."

'OK. What has that got to do with us?"

"Well, we interrogated the crew and didn't get much, but the Purser slipped a name—at least we think it was a name. It didn't mean anything to anybody. MI5, FBI, CIA, InterPol, even the KGB—oh, yeh, they don't call it the KGB but that's what it is—didn't have an idea—nothing.'

"Then, out of desperation, we passed it to the SAS."

"Gee, that really makes me feel good about the SAS," Parker said sarcastically.

I nodded and interrupted, "It was Tom Riddle."

Denver gasped and said, "Tom is his first name?"

Cavor asked, "OK, everyone at SAS knows Riddle. How do you know him?"

I looked over at Parker and asked, "Well, do I open the bag?"

He frowned and said, "Sure. You gave them his first name, you might as well open the bag completely for them."

I thought briefly, "I'm not going to unload the brief case completely, but plenty enough."

I looked at the three of them hoping that they'd think I was sizing them up. Actually, I was stalling for time to think. "Tom Riddle is probably the ultimate terrorist on the face of the Earth."

"How do we not know about him?"

"I don't think that it would be good to give you that, although if Parker wants me to, I will." I glanced at him.

"You're the expert here."

Cavor asked, "Then the weapon was to be delivered to him?"

I had to laugh.

Cavor asked, "What's the joke?"

Parker was smiling, "I think that Jim means that the weapon is not being delivered to him, but is intended by someone to kill him."

"Yes, I think so." I said. "My bet is that somebody knows about the M.O.M. and thinks that Riddle would be there. And they don't much care whether they kill a few innocents in London into the deal."

Cavor's mouth dropped. "But why would terrorists want to kill another terrorist?"

"Well besides jealousy, I can think of a couple of reasons, but I don't think that it's a terrorist organization that's doing this. I assume that you analyzed the weapon, where it was likely manufactured, how it got out of their arsenal. Now you give up some of your secrets."

Cavor interrupted," We don't have to give you anything."

"You're right. I think our business is done." I said and rose from my seat.

Cavor's mouth dropped, "Do you know who you're talking to?"

"Sure, but you don't know whom you're talking to."

"And I want to know."

I headed for the door.

Cavor shouted, "You can't leave. Stop him, Parker."

"He's right. We're done with you. It's been nice meeting you."

Barkley spoke up, "Don't be stupid, Cavor. They know a lot more than we do. We need their help. Apparently, they don't need ours."

Parker smiled and drawled, "Yes. And don't think that your contacts outrank ours. Jim and I were in to see the PM last week."

Cavor's face turned beet red. He was apparently trying to come up with some good reason that he had more pull than we have. He gave up. His face turned from beet red to a normal blush. "OK." He hesitated a minute and then said, "The bomb was manufactured by the Israeli's. We've been talking to them on the highest levels.

"The official line is that the bomb was stolen by Israeli right wing extremists who were going to blackmail the Israeli government to get them to allow settlers to expand their settlements on the West Bank."

I asked, "But the real story is…"

He frowned at me. "The real story is that there was no theft. An Israeli security team was going to move the bomb close to a certain department store in downtown London and start a fake blackmail scheme. The government, our government, would quickly evacuate that part of London and when the evacuation was complete enough, BANG. For some reason that the Israeli's wouldn't explain to us, they expected that this group in the department store probably wouldn't pay enough attention to realize that something unusual was going on, and the bomb would catch lots of them and maybe even Riddle, whoever he is."

I decided to nudge them a bit, "You don't know the right questions to ask. Had you, they might have let slip some information."

"OK, Parker, what are the right questions."

I glanced over at Parker. He didn't have anything to say. So, I improvised. "I know the right questions. If you want them asked, I have to ask them." Cavor was close to the end of his short fuse. He started pacing up and down in the small room, staring through his shoes. "All right. All my people have to be there. I'll be there. You'll give me your questions in advance."

I shook my head slowly, "It's been nice…"

"All right, bloody all right," came out through gritted teeth. "You've got to share all the answers—and what they really mean—with us."

Parker stared at Cavor for several minutes. "I don't think that we can promise that. We will promise to give you everything that we can that won't compromise your life—and ours.

"COMPROMISE MY LIFE. What are you bloody thinking?"

I interrupted, "I'm thinking that there are things that we could tell you that would make you a prime target for Riddle and his buddies. And believe me, you don't want to be on their hit list."

"But I have security."

I rolled my eyes. Cavor said, "What are you rolling your eyes for?"

"Look, I don't care how many bloody body guards that you've got. If they want you, you'd better get into a witness protection program and a good one or prepare yourself for torture, the likes of which you can't possibly imagine.

That seemed to get his attention. "You're kidding... Aren't you?"

"I wish I were. I met a couple who had been tortured by these people. They were the next best thing to catatonic."

"Shit. But, people at my pay grade aren't tortured, they're ransomed... Aren't they?"

"Look. These people make the IRA look like the operators of a 'Mystery Tour'." He seemed unconvinced.

"Look. Why do you think the Israeli's are willing to risk going to nuclear war with us and kill a couple of hundred thousands of people?"

A little tick wavered in his left cheek. "Well, the Israeli's are crazy, aren't they?"

"They're daring and willing to gamble big to get a big gain." Parker said.

I said, "The truth is that they're scared shitless by the little that they do know. And I almost certainly know a whole lot more than they do."

Cavor plopped down on a chair—for the first time that day. "OK. No preconditions."

"Good, set up a meeting with the Israeli's that you've been negotiating with. Soon."

"Where? Here?" Cavor was looking around the room.

Parker thought for a while and then said. "Let's meet at a football game. Next Saturday. I'll get the tickets. We'll just be some old school chums getting together for a game and dinner at the pub afterwards."

"But the Israeli's?"

"We'll meet them at the pub afterwards. Let's make it the "Green Man'".

"You can get tickets?"

"I have contacts."

I nodded. "I've been to a couple of games with him. He always seems to be able to get good seats."

'I can't guarantee that we can put a meeting together that quickly."

"Oh, I think that they'll be anxious to get together with us if they think that we know more than they do."

□

The Green Man was crowded. As a matter of fact, if it had been any more crowded, I'd have been in the men's room. We were standing there, waiting for a table. We'd been promised one within one and a half hours. Barkley had arrived a half-hour after we did. He was accompanied by two men. One was short with short dark black hair and was called, "Elud" of Israeli security. The other was an undersecretary in the consulate—David.

David asked, "You can't be serious. Everyone here can hear us."

"Everyone could hear us, but no one will. Everyone here has got their own concerns, and all we have to do is keep our talk light-toned."

Elud said, "Go ahead."

"Your government has decided to risk all-out nuclear war. I know why, but I don't know the details. Let's trade details."

I looked at him for a while as he glanced around the room. He finally said, "Give us something that proves you really know that much."

"I'll give you one word—disapparation."

"What?"

"Oh, you don't know it by that name, but you know what I'm talking about."

"I don't think so." But he glanced to the side for a moment—to the left and up.

"You've seen it, haven't you? Someone materializes out of nowhere."

He kept a straight face and then said, "How is it done?"

"I don't know. We have lots of video of it, but you saw something much more than disapparation."

"One of our agents died on the way to a 'meet'. It doesn't matter what about. He appears to have wandered in on a firefight. We had set up video to record the meet. Several people materialized out of nowhere, and there was some sort of fight, but we couldn't figure out what sort of weapons they were using. The people who had materialized suddenly disappeared, and our man seems to have gotten in the way of some sort of energy beam. He died instantly. Our people who were videoing, verify what happened. I've seen the video, but I'm not sure I believe it still."

"Oh, you should. I've seen it more times than you'd believe. We have tons of video. How did you find your target for your 'device'?"

"We started hacking into the security videos of London, looking for more instances of these 'disapparations'. We didn't get very many good videos, but we did get a pattern. The vast majority were happening within a couple of blocks of the department store ..."

"We know it." I volunteered. "Why did you decide that it had to be destroyed?"

"We tried to capture some of these people. They kept on showing up at the same address. We tried all sorts of snatch schemes but we just ended up with lots of dead agents."

"I'm sorry. You really should have come to us first. By the way you were lucky."

"Lucky!"

"Yes. They might have decided to snatch your people rather than just kill them." I decided to ask the Question, "What's your theory about them?"

"Aliens."

"Not far from the truth."

"Shit." David closed his eyes and then opened them and asked, "You mean real, live, people from another planet?"

"No."

"What do you mean, then?"

"I mean people who are genetically significantly different from us. People who..."

Elud interrupted excitedly, "People who have very advanced technology."

"Bingo. Their technology is so advanced that I don't, and nobody that we've consulted has the slightest idea how it works. Everything they do seems to have staggeringly advanced intelligence embedded in it."

"Give me an example."

"I already have. Disapparation. You've got video of it. You've got people who've seen it in person. Think about it. Really think about. Our physics consultants have said it's theoretically possible, but just the technology of the ways that they can imagine doing it are almost impossibly difficult."

I hesitated and went on, "What if you materialize inside a wall or a foot below the surface of the ground? Your targeting has to be at least as good as the military versions of GPS. Think about that. Our GPS requires a system of dozens of low altitude satellites. The GPS receiver has to do calculations that take into account General Relativity. Do these guys have systems of satellites? No. Do they have electronics-packed GPS systems? Do they have giant databases of all possible target locations? No. I've seen then disapparate inside buildings and in forests. I'm not sure that even military capable GPS's are good enough for that. They don't have any instrumentalities for accomplishing any of this. "

David had been leaning back taking this all in. Then he asked the 64 thousand dollar question. "How do you know all this about them?"

Parker said, "That's not on the table for discussion."

I looked over to see if I could read how serious he was. No dice, so I went ahead and said my piece. "No, I think this is something that they deserve to know. How can they really take us seriously, if they don't know how I speak so confidently?"

Parker rolled his eyes and shook his head, but he didn't object further.

"I used to live among them—for quite some time. Years."

Elud sneered, "How could you possibly convince them that you were a fellow alien?"

"I didn't. They knew perfectly well that I was a Mugg... uh, normal. They aren't all bad guys. They have their Winston Churchill's and Neville Chamberlains; their Einsteins, and unfortunately, their Adolf Hitlers and a lot of pretty average people as well.

"They hired me to do some pretty bland work for them, and I lived with them. I was hired by somebody who was one of the Churchill's—a truly great man."

"Why did you leave?" It was David's question.

"He died. And, not totally coincidentally, the Adolf Hitler look-alike, Riddle, took on a great deal of power. I probably would have disappeared, never to be seen again if I hadn't disappeared on my own."

There was a long pause. During the pause the hostess came up and took us to our table. After we'd gotten seated, we spent some time pondering the menu. I decided on the grilled salmon. Everyone else discussed at length the strengths of the various menu items.

Finally, after the waitress had taken our order, David asked, "What kind of role would we have if—and remember that I said 'IF'—we get involved with your project?"

I smiled and looked over at Parker. "That's your question." And just then the waitress showed up with the drinks. I had the house ale. Everyone else had mixed drinks.

"Do you know what you want, gents?"

I looked around slowly and asked, "Do we have some gentlemen at the table?"

Everyone frowned at me, which I shrugged off, and we ordered.

After she left, Parker said, "We assign you surveillance targets. We see how the relationship works out and perhaps, and remember that I said 'perhaps', you get invited into planning sessions."

"Come on. Our resources are far too good to be sent out on minor errands."

I entered the fray, "Look, you seem to me to not have shown very good judgment so far. I can't believe that you were ready to pull out the nukes —even for several agents killed. You've got to level with us if you want to have a role of anything more than being errand-boys."

Elud half rose from his chair and was restrained by David with a glance.

"What really happened? Something more than what you've told us. You didn't succeed in kidnapping one or more of them—did you?"

I looked from one of them to the other. Neither said anything. I took a chance. "You did, didn't you? You somehow rendered one of them unconscious and took them someplace and when they regained consciousness..."

David looked straight at me. "There were two actually. One of them came to before the other. They were handcuffed to chairs and we'd searched and stripped them of weapons."

□□

Gaspard watched the monitor showing the interrogation room. The two of them had been immobilized by tranc gun, and they had been immediately whisked away to the safe house. They had been tied to the chairs very securely, and the contents of their pockets removed. Each had a strange sort of short ornate wooden pointer in their pockets. They seemed harmless. Quick examination revealed no hidden chambers, but there was no point in taking chances. Two of his best interrogators were in the room. They were just waiting for the two to regain consciousness to start on them.

There were a couple of guards outside. They were taping everything. He'd decided that there were going to be no mistakes, no chances taken. These characters had way too many things about them that couldn't be explained easily to allow for chance, for slip-ups. The guards were fully armed, wearing Kevlar body armor and had orders to shoot to kill at the first sign of trouble.

He watched the monitor. One of them seemed to be coming around. He leaned forward, as though that would give him a better view. That one shook his head a couple of times, as though to clear it. Then he surveyed the room. The interrogators had noticed and were speaking. "Well, in case you're wondering where you are, forget it. You'll never know." Then something very strange happened. One of the wooden pointers leaped from a table in the corner of the room and flew across the room to the one who had just awakened. The interrogator gaped for a second and then drew his gun out of his jacket. But before he could say anything, the man disappeared.

Gaspard leaped up and thumbed the intercom button. He started to say, "Get out of there—now!" But before he could finish the command, three men materialized in the center of the room and swung around the room with those wooden rods pointing in their hands. One of his interrogators, the one with the gun already out raised it and pumped off a shot that seemed to hit one of the men in the upper arm, and then the interrogators fell soundlessly.

Gaspard motioned silently to the other man in the Control Room to follow him. They both drew their guns and thumbed off the safeties. As they rushed out of the room, they heard a short burst of gunfire from the monitor. The guards in the hall must have gone in and started firing.

Gaspard and the other ran down the hallway and down the stairs to the main floor where the makeshift interrogation room was. They saw one of the guards slumped on the floor with one of his legs extending into the doorway, as though he had been blown back by an explosion or gunshot. They became cautious as they approached the door, slowing and becoming as silent as they could. When they reached the guard, Gaspard took two hand grenades from the bandolier on the guards shoulder and signaled the other to do so also. They took a deep breath and in unison each pulled a pin from a grenade waited two seconds, and then in unison, tossed them through the open door at different angles. They both immediately dropped face-down to the floor, feet toward the open door. After two seconds that seemed like an eternity, there was a flash and a deafening roar that was accompanied by the door being blasted through the doorway. They got up and with drawn guns entered the door one at a time. Gaspard went 2nd.

What they saw was a smoked-filled room with no sign of life. There were only three bodies in the room. They all seemed to be his men.

Gaspard took thirty seconds to survey the scene and said, "Come on. We've got to get help for this. Call the other safe house. Tell them to get us back-up. At least a dozen men. We need to remove three bodies that need autopsies. We need people to quickly remove all signs we were here. We need serious firepower. We've got to get out of here now. I don't want those clowns returning with friends while we're here without support."

They left the building and got into Gaspard's car. They drove about a mile away and waited for help. The hours slowly tolled on. The night was cool, and the time was hard. Then two panel Lorries drove around a corner and pulled up beside Gaspard's car. The side doors opened and two men climbed out—one from each Lorrie. They came to the car and exchanged a few words of recognition. Then Gaspard and Ouimette entered the Lorries.

Gaspard spoke to the leader in his Lorrie. "We've got to move quickly, it will be light soon. We've got to clean up the safe house quickly. Drive there and park around the corner, and I'll give you orders."

They drove there, the other Lorie following them closely. They all moved into the Lorie that Gaspard was in, and he started.

"OK. Here's the layout of the building." He had a white board and began drawing the floor plan on it as he spoke. "The interrogation room is here on the first floor. There were 4 bodies there—all ours—when we left."

The leader of the support team interrupted, "Do you mean that you think that they may be gone?"

"I don't know. The opposition knows where we are. I don't know what to expect. That's why a security team is along. We may have a heavy welcome.

"We have to assume that there are hostiles in there, and only after you've swept the building will I send in the cleanup team. Our priorities are:

1. Remove or destroy all evidence that we were here.
2. Remove bodies so that they may be autopsied.
3. Recover as much of the data in the computers and video tapes that we can.

"The security team goes in first. It breaks up into groups of 2 to sweep the building. After you've proved the building is clean, immediately set up demolition charges so that we can level the building if necessary—remotely.

"Then break into three teams, one will guard cleanup group 1 that will recover the bodies—however many there are. The 2nd will guard group two that recovers data and as much of our equipment as possible. The 3rd provides general security and lookout for problems.

248

"All security teams should be prepared for hostiles to appear anywhere with zero warning. Just because you're in a room with only one entrance, don't assume that hostiles will come through that entrance.

One of the security team exclaimed, "What are you bleeding talking about? If there's only one entrance, then that's where hostiles have to come in."

"No, it's not. Look. We don't have time to argue this. If you just accept what I tell you, it may save your life.

"As soon as you give the 'all clear', I send in the cleanup groups. You've got to move quickly, but thoroughly. I don't intend on demolishing the building except as a last resort.

"Questions?"

Everyone looked at each other, then one of the security team asked, "If the hostiles can pop out of a wall, that means that we've got to keep our eyes everywhere?"

"Right." There was a brief silence. Then the security team leader said, "Radio silence until I declare the building clear. Teams divide into pairs. The leaders of each team carries the video. Get your gear and assemble in five minutes."

They all left the lorry, and the monitors in the lorry started to come alive with images from the transmitters on the leaders' helmets. It was eerie how silently the dozen men moved off, the images accompanied by no sound. They crossed the street and rounded the corner. Everyone was clad in black and seemed to melt into the building walls when they stopped before rounding the corner. They quickly entered the building, and the monitors showed interior views. Pairs stopped in front of doors and listened at the door for a moment before one silently opened it and entered the room. After a moment the first signaled for the other—with camera to enter. The rooms were uniformly empty and silent—as a church on a weekday night.

Finally teams entered the interrogation room and the Control Room. Nothing had changed in either as far as Gaspard could tell. Finally, the leader broke radio silence. "Building clear, send in the cleanup groups. I'm taking the general security role."

Gaspard nodded to the other men in the Lorry. They ran out and down the street with none of the care that the security team had used. The leader of the team that entered the interrogation room commented, "You made a real mess in here. Get those bodies into bags, and let's get out of here." There wasn't a whole piece of furniture left, and the walls were scorched and torn by the shrapnel. The bodies were all amazingly whole. There were lots of wounds, but very little blood. One of the men commented on that and said, "Bloody spooky. I've never seen such mayhem without any blood."

"Can it and keep going. I don't think there's going to be much of anything for the data boys to get, but that's their lookout."

The security team in that room was silent and constantly moving, constantly having firearms raised, and constantly scanning the field of view.

They had bagged two of the bodies and were ready to take them out. The security team leader called Gaspard, "We're ready for you to pick up two of our friends."

"Yes, I see. Check for unfriendly eyes outside, and we'll pull the lorry up when it's clear." The security team leader walked out to the main door and scanned the area. He radioed the team member upstairs and asked for a report from that vantage point.

"I don't see anyone."

"Come ahead quickly." The lorry pulled out into the street and pulled up to the main entrance quickly. Two pairs of men carried two body bags out to the lorry, tossed them in and ran back into the building. The whole maneuver had taken 15 seconds. It was repeated about 5 minutes later when the 2nd pair of bodies came out of the building. That time the entire team that had been removing bodies came and entered the lorry. It drove off to the safe house where the medical examiners were.

Gaspard radioed into the security team, "How much time to clear out the rest of the stuff?"

"I've just moved upstairs. You had lots of equipment. I think that it'll be about another ten minutes before we've got the rack-mounted electronics disassembled and stowed. Then there's a lot of miscellaneous stuff in this room. Then there's the interrogation room. It'll take some time to clear it out."

Gaspard voice was taut. "Look, it doesn't matter if you break every damn piece. We're living on borrowed time here. The people who attacked us will be back and probably pretty damn soon. I don't want to be here when they arrive, and you REALLY don't want to be here when they arrive."

"Come on, I don't want to get into a fire fight, but they don't stand much chance against my boys."

"Don't kid yourself. We managed to get in a single punch. I was lucky to get out with my life. I don't understand why they haven't returned already. You've got to move and move a damn site faster than you are."

"You're serious."

"Do you think so? Of course, I'm serious. Don't waste our time with chatter. Get moving."

The security team leader turned off his radio and said to the room. "We've got to get out of here really quickly. It doesn't matter if that equipment ever works again. Just break it down, pack it, and we're out of here."

The team speeded up noticeably. They yanked cables, unscrewed mounting screws and tossed the equipment in bags that looked suspiciously like body bags. They worked with a quiet determination and speed that was almost manic.

The first bags were full, and two men carried them out as quickly as they could. The 2nd lorry was driven up three times to accept equipment from the upstairs room. Then the operation moved to the interrogation room. Everyone was obviously hurrying. The general spirit of deliberate speed was contributing to a feeling just short of panic. In the interrogation room it was obvious even without bodies that lots of bad things had happened in the room, and the team began to feel that they were definitely living on borrowed time while they were in the room. The leader urged them on occasionally with the repeated, "Let's go, les go, les go." The last repetitions almost blended into a single long word. His security team had mostly moved down to the main floor, and the two men patrolling on the 2nd floor were not happy in the least. They hadn't said anything when they were given the assignment, but it was clear—even in the dark—that they weren't happy to be up stairs by themselves. They patrolled the hall quickly, almost back to back as they silently walked, staying close to the interior wall and stopping occasionally to crouch and listen for sounds. They had opened all room doors and took turns checking each room as they reached it. They kept their radio transmitters on but remained absolutely silent.

Meanwhile downstairs the cleanup team carefully sifted through the rubble, looking for anything other than fragments of walls and furniture. They finally decided that they'd gotten everything, including bullets and shrapnel dug out of walls, floor and ceiling.

The security team leader thumbed on his transmitter and said. "We're finished. Get all the explosives and let's get out of here."

The last of the teams collapsed onto the floor of the lorry, and they sped off. Gaspard asked, "Everything is clear?"

"It's clean. Nothing to prove that it wasn't simple vandalism back there."

"Good. Everyone gets a commendation for tonight. Everybody gets moved out of the London area and re-assigned as soon as we can manage. This evening didn't happen."

"They didn't have any weapons, right?" I asked.

"Well, no. That was strange. Anyway when the one came to, he was groggy and took a minute or two to look around and figure out where he was. We were ready to start interrogation when. . ."

I interrupted, "He looked over to a table where you had stacked his valuables. One of them flew through the air to him, and when he had it in his hand, he disappeared."

"Yes."

"You found a short wooden baton in his pocket but it seemed to be harmless. No threat to the Masud interrogators with their tools of interrogation.

"So, you were getting ready to interrogate the other when the first disappeared, and then two or three others appeared in the room."

Elud snarled and said through gritted teeth, "Yes, they appeared, and people started dropping over dead. The people observing the interrogation remotely, sent in heavily armed guards."

"Oise's or something like it, I suppose?"

"Yes, something like. One of them got some rounds off, before he died. Then, control blew the room up—the backup team tossed a couple of hand grenades in, and when they went off, we lost the cameras."

"Did you kill any of them?"

"No."

Then I asked THE question, "They disapparated. Did they take any of your people along?"

"No."

"Are you absolutely sure?"

"Yes. We ID'ed all the corpses. They were all ours and everybody was accounted for."

"Great! This is why we can't trust you. Did you evacuate the 'safe house' or wherever you were keeping these aliens?"

"Immediately. We aren't that stupid."

"I wonder. OK. Here's what you're going to do. You can't trust the survivors of that team any more. They need to be transferred to the opposite side of the globe and kept out of sight."

"What are you talking about? That's a good team. We're planning on keeping them together."

"Absolutely no way. They may already be turned. You have no idea how easily these aliens can get people to work for them. If you're thinking of keeping them on here or anywhere with access to other intelligence people, you're not working with us."

The exasperation was building on the other side of the table. Their faces were getting red. Parker kept his cool and said, "I know that he can be pretty arrogant at times, but you've got to trust his judgment. He knows these people a whole lot better than anyone else in the world. He's saved our asses a couple of times already. He's right. If you don't follow his advice when he's this definite, you're not working with us."

Just then the waitress became apparent. I don't know how long she'd been waiting for the little discussion to end, but she came forward then with our plates. After she left, the conversation continued on a cooler basis.

Elud hesitated and then went on softly, "After we cleaned up the safe house and started reviewing the tapes, we picked up a comment one of the aliens had said, 'Riddle'll have their hides when he hears about this.'"

"One other question. Where did you spot these 'aliens' first?"

Elud hesitated again and said, "We picked the most prosaic, normal suburb we could find for a safe house. The street's called Grimauld Place. We started noticing that people just seemed to appear from nowhere there. We investigated and, well, you now know the rest."

It was my turn to hesitate. Should I open that bag?

I went on. "All right. You want to participate. You start as junior partners. You get to do surveillance on locations that we assign you. You can start with your current surveillance. We need reports on a daily basis. We'll give you some additional assignments shortly."

"Come on. You've got to give us more than that! We give you reports and you don't give us anything"

"Oh, you'll have plenty once you start surveillance of the places we'll give you." That seemed to placate Elud a little.

We finished the meal without further discussion.

On the way back to the office, Parker and I discussed the events of the evening. Parker asked, "Do you really know that location, Grimauld Place? Or were you just shamming?"

"I know it. It's just something that you don't need to know a lot about. It was, purely coincidentally, a safe house for the Order of the Phoenix until recently. I suppose the Deatheaters found out about it and started staking it out."

"Right." He was smiling because he knew exactly who might have been at that safe house, and it didn't have much to do with hierarchy in the wizarding world.

The next day I went to the street where the Leaky Cauldron was located. I went to an inconspicuous mailbox on the street next to a real mailbox for a real residence in the street. I put an envelope in it addressed to Tom, the barman, at the establishment. It was a drop that we had worked out a few weeks before. Inside the envelope for Tom was the real envelope addressed to whomever I wanted. Tom would collect the 'mail' twice a day and see that it was forwarded to the recipient. Mail going the other way didn't need that sort of elaborate handling. The sender just sent an owl to me.

That afternoon one of those owls appeared outside my office, found the owl flap, and came in politely. I removed the letter from his leg. I kept a bowl of owl treats on my desk for such deliveries. After tipping the owl, I went to my desk and opened the letter. It read in part,

"Dearest Jim, I can get away on Sunday next in the early afternoon. But I'm very concerned about the danger to you of meeting me. The security here is getting tighter and tighter. I'll meet you at the pub that you suggest, but I can only spare a couple of hours. I'm supposedly visiting my sister. She is very kind to co-operate with this subterfuge. I may not be able to arrive promptly, but my intention is to meet you at 13:00. Love, always, M."

I put the letter back into the envelope and locked it into my lower right drawer. I suppose that it's not very good security to keep those letters, but they were one of the few links that I had with Minerva, and I couldn't bear to destroy any of them.

Sunday came, and I took the Tube to the station near the pub. I then hiked up to the Green Man. I arrived at about noon. The pub was not quite empty but it would fill after the game ended around 4pm. The hostess who seated me asked me how long it would be until my guest arrived.

"It will be at least an hour. But you're not busy and I'll provide a really good tip if you just give me a house ale and let me nurse it until she arrives."

"Yes, sir, I'll tell the waitress."

"Thanks."

At 12:50, Minerva scared me half to death by sneaking up and sitting down next to me without a sound and taking my hand. "Did you disapparate there?"

"No, I walked up. You were so deep in thought, I could have been playing a drum and you wouldn't have noticed." I put my hand on her shoulder and drew her head close to mine and we kissed.

"Why did you want to talk?"

"Well, you mean besides the fact that I'm madly in love with you?"

"Well, yes. That hardly counts, does it?"

"Something bad happened, and I wanted to see what you know about it."

"Something 'bad' is always happening these days. I suppose you mean something worse than a few more Muggles and wizards getting killed or sent to Azkaban."

"Yeh. There's a foreign intelligence service that discovered the existence of Deatheaters."

She squelched a gasp. "What happened?"

"Well, they've been doing surveillance on them—sort of like we've been doing."

"Butttt. . ." Minerva knew there was more to the story and she could always read me better than anyone else.

"But they've gone farther. They decided to . . . uh . . . well. They decided to detonate a nuclear weapon outside of the Ministry."

Both of Minerva's hands came to her mouth. "It's not going to happen s ...s...s...soon?"

"No, we stopped them. They would have killed thousands of people, but we stopped them.

"We need to know what Grimauld Place is. Is it still a safe house or what?

Minerva's face contorted, and she pursed her lips and tried to say something.

"Oh, I see. There's some magical reason that you can't answer."

Relief spread over her face.

"I'm sorry, Wendt, but . . .' She trailed off.

"So it must be an Order of the Phoenix thing."

She smiled and shrugged.

"That's OK. You don't need to say anything further. Do you know that that place is being watched by Deatheaters?" Her mouth opened wide and gaped for a while

"OK. OK. I know that you can't say anything." I chuckled once and then again and then I started laughing uncontrollably. I was laughing so hard that I couldn't make a sound. I couldn't breathe, and I couldn't move a muscle. I managed to look over at Minerva, and I could see that she was almost as convulsed as I was. We finally were able to breathe.

"Minerva. I never want to go through that again. Let's see if we can stay away from that topic again."

"You were the one who brought it up." She smiled really widely. "Is there something else we can do? As long as we're here, together?"

I smiled and said, "Let's go. I think that I know a little bed and breakfast near Paddington Station."

"But I've got to get back to school before the night's over."

"Who says that we have to spend the night?"

"Hmmm. Maybe you've got something there."

We walked to the Tube station (a fairly long walk) and to pass the time I asked her how things were at Hogwarts.

"Oh, depressing. You know that Snape is the headmaster?"

"Yeh, you told me sometime. I don't remember when."

"Well, he's brought in the Carrow siblings to be the heads of Ravenclaw."

"Carrows. Hmmmmm. The name is vaguely familiar, but I can't place it."

Minerva made a face. "They were in the raid on Hogwarts last spring."

"Oh, great. I suppose Snape must have gone through hundreds of resumes to find them."

"Don't joke about it. They are hideous. They don't even have any imagination. At least Snape does have one."

"Yes, Snape. Is he teaching any classes or maintaining his dignity in his office?"

"Oh, Snape is teaching his favorite topic."

"Defense Against the Dark Arts? Or has he renamed it 'Defense of the Dark Arts'."

"Very funny. Actually, he's taken an unusual tact with it. Your joke is closer to the truth than you might think. He's lecturing about the dark arts. He's not really teaching them. Oh, he's teaching some minor curses and having students practice them, but the 'Unforgiveable' curses are strictly subjects for lectures and occasionally demonstration—not practice." She paused and gazed off into the distance thoughtfully.

"You know, he reminds me of the imitation 'Mad-Eye' Moody. You know, he performed the curses as demonstration, but, you know, he never really taught the students to do them—even in the advanced classes.

She turned contemplative for a minute, chuckled and said, "It's actually kind of funny. For the advanced classes, he's accepted only Slitherins, well, practically only Slitherins.

"So?" I asked.

"Well, he actually is teaching one 'Unforgiveable' curse to the advanced classes—Crusio." She paused again and chuckled some more.

"Actually, he had students. . . ." She stopped again and laughed out loud for a minute.

"Well."

"Sorry. I really shouldn't laugh. But." She paused to laugh again. This time it was harder and louder. "But, he had them pair up. . . ." She laughed again so hard that she leaned against me—as though she couldn't trust herself to stand on her own—which was OK with me.

"Oh. . . Oh. . . Paired them up and had them practice on each other." With a real effort, she composed herself and went on. "They. . . They. . . Well, half of them ended up in the hospital wing for more than a week."

"You're kidding, surely."

"No. No. That really happened. " She paused thoughtfully again. "As a matter of fact, that weekend Slitherin had a Quidditch match with Hufflepuff. Half of Slitherin's team was in hospital wing. That was a game such as had not been seen at Hogwarts—or maybe anyplace else—in the history of Quidditch."

We had reached the Tube station and were waiting for the train. She said, "I don't see why you insist on traveling by Muggle means, when we could so easily disapparate."

"Well. . . The truth is that I'm afraid that some of my buddies at work will pick us up on the security camera net, and I'll get kidded to death if the guys at work see us together."

"I think that you just want to get me alone in a dark corner of the 'Tube'."

"Yeh. I hadn't thought of that. Good idea. But what happened at the Quidditch game?"

"Well, you know those games typically start at 1 PM. Anyway. . ."

The students were filling up the stands pretty morosely. There had been very little to laugh about during the term so far. Hufflepuff came, hoping, rather than expecting to have a little fun. They really didn't expect much because Slytherin has always had a strong team. And Hufflepuff, well

Hufflepuff had never had a reputation in the long history of Hogwart's for having a strong Quidditch team.

The announcer was a Ravenclaw. McGonagall had made a policy that every game would be announced by someone from one of the other houses that weren't competing. The announcer was introducing the teams.

". . . And that was the Hufflepuff team. The Slytherin team has a few changes for this game. It appears that some of the Slytherin's had a few . . . uh . . . accidents. In particular, the two 7th year Slytherin beaters— Gregory Goyle and Vincent Crabb . . . uh . . . accidentally cursed each other. They are recovering in the hospital wing. They are being replaced by 3rd year beaters Peggy Burris and James Hargrove. The Slytherins are fielding a rooky Seeker as well. 4th year Frank Beam stands in for 6th year Albert Achor. The goalie, 5th year Amber Jones, has been replaced by 4th year Jake Stann. Playing their normal positions are Chasers, Bill Barker and Frank Ball.

"This game between Slytherin and Hufflepuff is normally not a very interesting game, but this year's matchup seems to have to potential to be quite entertaining, what with the change in lineups.

"We've had the coin toss, and the Slytherin's are defending the South goals. . . The whistle has blown, and they're airborne.

"The Slytherin's chaser has won the tossup, and they're heading down the pitch.

"Oh, the Hufflepuff beater, Jacobs, sent a wicked Quaffle at Jones. She drops the Quaffle as the ball bounces off her left leg. The beater Jackson for Hufflepuff catches the Quaffle and advances it to the Chaser, Pearson. He's got a clear shot at the goal. The Slytherin beaters are trying to get their brooms under control. He completely faked out Stann and scored through the left hoop."

The next hour was a series of plays in which Hufflepuff kept scoring, and Slytherin kept doing nothing.

"And Hufflepuff scores again. The score is now 250 to 20. Won't somebody just catch the snitch? Pearson flies under Stann for another score. 260 to 20. ..

"We are now entering the 4th hour of this game, the score is a record 1180 to 90. We are still praying for somebody, anybody to catch the snitch. There's got to be somebody on a broom who can catch that thing. Please. . ."

"The sun has just set, and I see Professor McGonagall and Headmaster Snape in what appears to be a heated discussion. Maybe they will end this travesty. Oh, yes. The score is now 1210 to 100. Most of the players look like they are about to fall off their brooms, and most of the stands are empty. There are two or three Slitherins left in the stands and maybe half of the HufflePuffs. I think I see a Gryffindor someplace in the stands. Oh, yeah, it's that Luna Lovegood. I can tell by her long blond hair.

"Professor McGonagall is coming up to the stands. Maybe we'll find out what she and the Headmaster were talking about. . . Professor McGonagall what's the ruling about this game. Can we quit now?"

"I'm sorry to have to tell you that Headmaster Snape has ruled that the game will have to continue until someone catches the snitch."

"But, it's going to get dark soon, and no one will be able to see the snitch."

"It's not exactly as if anybody has seen the snitch in broad daylight. But the Headmaster says the players must use lighted wands to continue play."

"But what will the beaters do? They have to hold bats and how will the seeker catch the snitch?"

"Give me the microphone." McGonagall said.

"Attention all players. Headmaster Snape has ruled that the play of this game must continue until the snitch is caught. All players will light their wands to show their positions and light the field. Carry on."

"Well, you heard it. Game play will proceed. We are approaching the 5th hour. This must be some kind of time record for a school game. Isn't it, Professor?"

"Well, I've never seen a game that went anywhere near nightfall at Hogwarts."

"Thank you, Professor McGonagall. Now we return to the play of the game. HufflePuff chaser Bailey has just picked the Quaffle up off the ground where it fell when the pass came up short and is lazily approaching the Slytherin goals. Meanwhile the Slytherin beaters are trying to hold their wands in one hand and their bats in the other and keep their brooms under control with their knees.

"Uh Oh. One of the Slytherin beaters. I think it's Hargrove. He has slipped under his broom and is hanging upside down while trying to hit the ball. He's flying in wide loops trying to get himself turned right side up. LOOK OUT FOR THE GOAL. Sorry folks. That was a near miss. Hargrove almost flew into his center goal. Oh, sorry. In the mean time, HufflePuff's scored again. That's 1230 to 100. Oh, yes. Sorry again. That's actually 1220 to 100.

. . .

"Well, we're now into the 7th hour of this marathon Quidditch game. The score is 1230 to 100. I don't think there's been a score in the last half-hour. Most of the players are just flying in long slow circles over the pitch. No one has the slightest idea where the snitch is, and I think that if this game doesn't end soon, the players are going to drop to the ground and not be able to get up again. OH OH. I see McGonagall and Snape talking again. Could be; could be that we're going to see the end of this awful day.

"Here comes McGonagall. Maybe this is it. Professor McGonagall, what's happening?"

"Well, Mr. Roberts. I'm happy to announce that the Headmaster has agreed to end the game and that the final score stands at HufflePuff 1230; Slytherin 100. Hufflepuff wins."

"Well, you just heard it from the ho... er from the lips of Professor McGonagall. The game's over. Hufflepuff has been declared the winner and we can all finally go back to the castle and get a cold dinner, assuming that there's anything left to eat. I want to congratulate all 15 of you for staying for the full game, and of course, all the players for staying on their brooms for the 6 plus hours of this game."

Minerva and I had just reached the bread & breakfast that I had in mind. We signed in and got our key. We reached our room,. After we'd entered, I pulled Minerva close to me and asked, 'Do you really mean that Snape didn't let them end the game until long after sunset?"

She started laughing again. It was contagious. I could hardly stop myself. I had to let go of her and drop to my knees with the gales of laughter. She had sat down and bent over double with laughter.

"And. And. . . " I gasped for air. "The Slytherin beaters were flying around upside down?"

"Only." She broke out into fresh gasping laughs. "Only." With a struggle she got herself under control and said, "Only one of them. The other one managed to stop his broom dead still and hung there in the air, trying to figure out what to do."

We both had reasonable control again. I came over to sit on the bed next to the chair where she had sat down. I took her left hand in my right and said, "Do you think that we can talk about something that won't threaten to suffocate us?"

She wore the broadest smile that I'd ever seen on her face. "I haven't laughed this hard since. Well, in longer than I want to remember. What do you want to talk about?"

"Oh, I was thinking about how much I enjoy looking at your face."

She turned her head a little sideways and looked out the corner of her eyes at me. "Are you sure that you don't need glasses?"

"You always say that. Yes, I know that I don't need glasses, but I'm beginning to think that you do." Her other hand caressed my left arm gently, stroking the forearm as she turned to face me fully.

We sat there for a bit not saying anything, and then she leaned toward me. I let her lips approach mine, but I held back for a moment while I tried to decide whether I could keep my eyes open while we kissed. I finally decided that if I hadn't figured out how to do that yet, I probably never would. The gentle meeting of lips was never the same. I could never figure out how that could be. It made me want to keep kissing her time after time trying to find that kiss that was just like one we'd had before. I never found that duplicate kiss—no matter how hard I tried.

We, at some point, found ourselves on the bed with my arms around her back and one of my hands caressing her hair. I had not even tried to find the pins that held her hair up. She had had to unbind her hair herself. She had teased me about that, but I couldn't have cared less. I had her in my arms. She snored softly. That was all that I cared about. The shadows on the floor from the lone window in the small room grew longer and longer. The room had only a few pieces of furniture—an old armoire, the bed (of course), one chair, a small desk with a phone. I knew the long shadows meant that Minerva would be leaving shortly. I watched them off and on. I couldn't keep my eyes off the shadows for very long. They counted the minutes I had left with Minerva. How many minutes? How could she sleep heedless of the flow of time, the remorseless, pitiless movement that brought us closer and closer to the end of our time? Our time. Together.

And then surprisingly, there was the disconcerting discontinuity of being suddenly awakened and unsure where I was, when I was. I saw Minerva dressing. She looked around and frowned. "You were so peaceful. I was hoping not to wake you until I had to."

"Yeh, sneak out. That's what you were going to do. Sneak out, before I can kiss you goodbye or . . . something better."

Minerva opened her purse and pulled her robes out.

"I never get over that. I've disapparated with you, taken the miserable floo network with you. By the way, I don't understand what you see in the floo network. You get covered with ash. You get turned inside out."

"What are you talking about?"

"When you pull a complete outfit out of that purse, and God only knows what else you've got in there. Well, it's just so bizarre."

She pulled out her hat. "I suppose that you didn't like that either."

She held out her hand. I got up off the bed, walked over, and took her in my arms. The smile on her face broadened. She said, "I wish we could stay here longer, but I've got to go."

I strengthened my hold on her slightly. "Do you really? You surely wouldn't disapparate with me in your arms. You might have some fancy explaining to do." I smiled a little more broadly.

She laughed and then mouthed the word slowly so that I could read her lips, "Ex-pell-i-a-mus." I flew across the short distance to the bed and landed on my rump on it. She then said, "Toodles" and disapparated. I picked myself up and looked around the room to be sure I'd found all my clothes and all the little odd things that fall out of your pockets when you dis-robe quickly. I hurriedly accounted for everything except my key chain that turned out to have somehow gotten into the space between the hot water radiator and the wall. I wondered how it had gotten there. Then it occurred to me. Minerva must have magiced it there when I wasn't looking.

I walked down the stairs to the small front lobby. The man on duty didn't look up until I came to the desk and announced that I was checking out.

"Where's your fancy lady?"

"She didn't want to be seen leaving with me."

"That's pretty common. Is she married?"

"Yes." I paused momentarily. "To her job."

"Which is?"

"She's a teacher."

"Oh, yeah. The 'eadmaster would probably not like the little tykes to know that she was fooling around."

"Well, they're not little tykes. It's a prep school."

"Even worse. The parents would be unhappy for the example she was setting. How'd you meet her?"

"I was a teacher at her school."

"Even worse. I suppose they 'canned' you for being a bad influence."

"Something like that. The old Headmaster put up with my dalliance, but the new administration didn't like it."

"He was probably one of those old farts who fancied the young ladies himself."

"Not really. He was a good man. He put up with me even though a lot of the staff would like to have seen me gone long ago."

"'e sounds like the kind of guy who'd never retire."

"Yeah. I guess you could say that he died on the job."

"Sorry. BBL."

"Eh?"

"Bloody Bad Luck."

"Yes." I suddenly had a hard time holding back tears. After a moment, I got enough control to say, "Bloody Right. See you."

"Come back some time. I like you. You and your fancy lady are quiet. You leave early enough that I may be able to sell your room again."

"I doubt we will, but I'd like to sometime." I turned, walked out the door, and headed for the Tube.

I arrived about an hour or so after midnight. It was quite dark, and I fumbled with the key. I fit it in the heavy lock on the door to the parking lot. The lock was heavy because it was pretty solid, and it had an RFID reader that verified a chip in my key. I opened the door and walked to the main entrance from the parking lot. I got there and opened the unsecured door. The night guard was waiting. He sat at a large desk. He looked up and asked, "How was your day?"

I nodded to him and kept on walking. I'd gotten about two steps past the desk when I was knocked to the floor from behind. Before I hit the floor I felt the hard muzzle of a large caliber gun in my back. The voice that accompanied it was loud and had a hint of shake in it. "DON'T move. Don't open your mouth." My arms were forced behind my back and cuffs were snapped on my wrists. I was dragged up to my feet and frog marched down the dark hall. A door opened to the right, and I was tossed in. I hadn't hit the floor a second time before a 2nd dis-embodied voice asked, "How many cartridges?"

I smiled and answered, "Three in the clip. One in the chamber. Oh, yeah, two in my right pocket."

There was a pause. "Convince us that you're not imperioused."

I answered, "If I'd been imperioused, would I have skipped the challenge at the door?"

"OK. I buy that."

The door opened behind me, and the 'cuffs were removed. The remover turned me around and exclaimed, "What the shit do you think you're doing? You had me scared to death. I thought we had a real wizard."

"It was just a little impromptu security check to see if you were on the ball."

"Well, just never do that again. I might have killed you. What kind of luck would that have been?"

"Pretty bad for you."

"Yeah, what about you."

"I'd never have known the difference."

"Well, get a good night's sleep."

"Thanks."

Auntie

I was in my office reviewing the plan for getting the wizards out of Azkaban and out of the country when the phone rang. Sally answered, and there proceeded a long series of "yes's" nad "no's" punctuated with a few "Really's". When I could no longer stand the suspense, I finally broke in, "Sally, what the heck is this conversation about?"

She looked over at me, shushed me silently with her finger, and turned away so that I couldn't see her face.

She nodded a couple of times and then put the receiver on her shoulder so that the mouthpiece was covered. She turned to me and said, "Something unusual has happened."

"No, really. I'd never have guessed."

"The more you interrupt, the longer it'll be before you find out what it is."

"OK, OK. You've made your point. Go ahead."

"Well, security is holding a woman in one of the interrogation rooms. She claims that she's looking for you."

"That's impossible." I stopped what I was saying and then thought a moment. Maybe it was possible. I went on, "Me, specifically—by name?"

"That's what the man said."

I thought fast. Then I picked up the phone and dialed Parker's number. When I got through to him, I said, "Look, Parker, have you heard about the person down in the interrogation room?"

He answered, "Sure. Wants to see you. We've been telling her that we've not got the slightest idea who you are."

"Good. Look, this probably isn't a witch, but I think we've got to be really careful. I think you should evacuate the place of everyone except essential security, immediately."

He answered, "I thought about that possibility, but surely something would have happened if she'd been for real."

"Maybe, but we can't take chances. I'm going down to interrogate her. Send a couple of guards up here."

"Noooo, you're not. You're too valuable."

"Look, I'm the only person who can tell you if . . . No, wait a minute are the twins in the building?"

There was a pause on the other end of the line, and then Parker was back on the line. "No, they didn't sign in, but it would be just like them to disapparate in to play a joke on us."

"Then, I'm the only one you've got. Don't argue. Besides, this surely isn't a Deatheater. This just isn't the way they normally play things."

Parker paused again and then answered, "OK. I'm sending up a couple of escorts for you. She's in Interrogation Room Two. Just don't take any chances. If you've got the slightest hint that she's a witch, just kill her."

I hung up and turned to Sally. "We're evacuating the building. Get going." Then I walked over to my desk and dug around in one of the drawers looking for my Glock.

She said, "Not on your life. I want to see this. This should be good. A woman looking for you. Do you have another 'friend' besides McGonagall?"

"This isn't a laughing matter. You're going." I found the Glock. I released the clip and checked that it was loaded. Then I made sure the safety was on, stuck it in my left hip pocket, and started to put on my sports coat.

Sally gasped and said, "You're going to shoot your buns off. And I'm going to be there to see it and pick up the pieces."

I looked up at her and said, "Out of here. I'm not going to shoot my buns, and you're going home."

"Do you want to bet?"

Just then a couple of guards came in, and I told them, "Escort Ms. Harker out of the building and make sure she gets on the Tube. Oh, yes. You don't have to be polite if she gives you any trouble."

One of them rolled his eyes, but my stern face must have convinced him that I meant business. "Yes, sir. Come along miss."

She gave me a poisonous look, and I knew that I was going to pay in some way if I came out of this alive. She went quietly enough—at least while she was in earshot. I ran down the couple of flights of stairs and saw people filing out of the building. That seemed to be going OK anyway. When I reached the interrogation rooms—really just a couple of offices that had never been assigned to anyone—I slowed, took a moment to think about what I was doing, and wondered if it was really the right thing to do. There were several guards in battle dress outside IR #2. One started to challenge me until he saw who I was. Another asked me, "You're not going in there carrying a piece are you?"

"Sure I am. It's either going to be so dangerous in there that it doesn't matter or not dangerous at all." He shrugged. One of the guards was standing beside the door ready to open it for me. I took a deep breath and counted to five slowly, hoping that some brilliant idea would occur to me. Unfortunately, none did. So, I nodded to the guard, and he opened the door slowly. He stood ready to slam it shut if necessary. The other guard had his assault rifle at the ready. I walked in.

The room had a bare table with a couple of chairs. A portly late middle-aged woman sat at the table with a surly expression on her face. There were two men standing back against opposite walls forming a 90 degree angle with her as the vertex. They looked like they were casually waiting for a bus to arrive but, of course, there were no bus routes that stopped here.

The woman turned to me as I entered the room and sneered, "Did they finally get someone who has some authority in to let me see Wendt?"

I studied her for a moment trying to decide what tack to take with her. She seemed to be a completely normal, if unpleasant, housewife from Surrey. I decided to just start asking questions and see where we got.

"What makes you think that this Wendt of yours is here?"

"Oh, I know he's here. Ripper told me." It was then I noticed that she had a short leash at the other end of which was a small bulldog that was sitting at her feet, effectively hidden by the table.

I walked around the table to get a better look at Ripper. It wasn't worth the walk. I decided to take a different tack. "What do you want with this Wendt?"

"Didn't your buddies tell you before you came here?"

"I want you to tell me."

"I'm looking for my brother."

"Wendt's your brother?"

"No, are you daft? My brother's disappeared with his wife and kid and I think that Wendt knows where he is."

I was amazed. Who was this person? Why did she think that I knew where her brother was? I pulled up a chair, fascinated by the bizarre picture that was forming. I asked her, "Who is your brother?"

267

The rigid expression on her face loosened a bit, "Mr. Vernon Dursely. His wife's Penelope and his son's name is Dudley."

I was so surprised that I could hardly suppress the laugh that was bellying up from deep in my insides and struggling to get out. I rose with as much dignity as I could, walked to the door, and opened it. I walked out, and hardly had the door closed behind me when I broke out in a laugh that I couldn't suppress any longer. I laughed so hard that I could not breathe. I was afraid that someone was going to have to perform the Heimlich maneuver on me, but I finally stopped and thought that I could go in again. Then suddenly the laugh forced its way through my clenched jaws again. That happened a couple of more times, and when I finally thought that I had control of myself, I nodded to the guard at the door again. Then I walked back into the room.

Marge was furious, "Don't you ever walk out on me again while I'm talking to you! What do you think you're doing?"

I sat down again and looked at her, seeing her in a new light. Yes, she must be Harry's "Aunt" Marge. I smiled and said, "OK. Your name is?"

She looked like she wouldn't answer but then relented, "Margery Dursely."

I wasn't completely convinced, so I asked, "Can you prove that?"

She looked over at one of the men at the walls and said, "He took my purse."

I glanced over at him, and he nodded and said, "Her ID says that she's Margery Tuttle Dursely. It's a pretty good forgery if it is one."

Margery sniffed loudly and said, "The very idea that I would carry forged papers."

I said to the man, "Go find out if Margery Tuttle Dursely is home or if anyone knows where she is."

He nodded and left the room. One of the guards in full battle gear replaced him. Apparently they hadn't been there when they'd brought Marge to the interrogation room. She was clearly nonplussed by the sight of his automatic weapon. She asked, softening a little more, "What happened to my little Dudley and his family?"

I looked at her quizzically, "You'll have to answer a few more questions before I tell you anything. First, how did you find your way here, and what makes you think that we know anything about the Dursely's—other than you?"

She said, "Several months ago, they all disappeared. No one seems to have seen them go, but one day they were living a normal suburban life at Little Whinging, and the next no one saw a sign of them. His boss called me after a couple of weeks trying to find out why Vernon hadn't been to work. I had no idea that there was any problem with them. I tried to get in touch with them. I finally went to their house and even searched it. It looked like they had packed everything away for a long, long trip, and the house had clearly not been lived in for over a week. None of the neighbors had any idea what had happened to them although they all admitted that they hadn't seen them in all that time nor had they seen anyone leave.

"The next couple of weeks after I'd reported their disappearance to the police, I waited for some word to come, but I didn't hear a word from them. Then, I began nagging the police, but they had no idea where they were. As a matter of fact, if you ask me, I think that they'd given up after the first week."

"So, how did you get the idea that this Wendt had anything to do with their disappearance?"

"Well, I was pretty desperate, and I began to think of all kinds of crazy," she hurried past that word, "ideas about how they might have disappeared. Well, I remembered that they had a nephew staying with them, a Harry Potter, who was a real 'dicey' sort. I thought that he and a gang of his friends from Saint Brutus' might have kidnapped them for their money."

I was having a hard time not laughing when she mentioned Saint Brutus', but I maintained my composure. "OK. Well, assuming that you're right, where does Wendt fit in?"

She squinted her little eyes and looked right and left to indicate that she didn't want to be overheard. "I became the regular little detective, don't you know? I searched their house, especially that Potter's room. There wasn't much left but in a bureau in his room under some old socks I found a letter from this Wendt character."

"Go on."

"Well, it talked about all sorts of spooky things—witches and wizards. I couldn't make much sense of it, but I think it was written in some sort of code that his gang uses to keep people from knowing what they're up to."

"That sounds likely. So, how do you figure that Wendt's here?"

She puffed herself up a bit and went on with her story, proud of how she'd tracked me down. "Well, I looked in the London directory and there are a couple of dozen Wendt's but it was pretty easy ruling most of them out. When I talked with them on the phone, they were all single mothers or old men who had never heard of a Jim Wendt." She paused for effect and then went on. "Except for one who lived in a small rooming house. He never answered the phone and didn't even have an answering machine. I finally went to his apartment and found that he hadn't been there in a couple of months even though he paid the rent regularly.

"I got the landlord to let me into his apartment by claiming that I was his aunt who was terribly worried about him because I'd not heard from him in almost two months. He was reluctant, but he finally accompanied me to Wendt's appartment. The place hadn't been lived in for at least that long, but there were clothes, books, that sort of thing. I managed to pinch a pair of his socks.

"I gave Ripper a whiff of those, and we set off to track him."

I was fascinated. She was just like her bulldog, really tenacious. "But surely there wasn't any trail to follow. He hadn't been to his flat in all those weeks."

"Yes, but I figured that he must still be using the Tube. We went to the nearest Tube station, and I let the dog sniff for him. He didn't get a whiff of him there, but we kept trying Tube stations up and down the line. We finally found one where the Ripper got excited. We tried a couple of Tube stations further down the line, but that was the only one where he really got the scent. We got out at that Tube station and began following the trail."

I concluded, "And that led you to our door?"

"Right you are. Now, if you'll just hand him over."

This all sounded quite plausible. However, I wanted more proof, so I asked, "If you really are related to these Durselys, then you must know what happened on Harry Potter's 13th birthday."

Marge was livid. "I'm telling you that three decent, normal people have gone missing for months, and you want to know what happened at that sniveling little cretin's birthday?"

Something must have happened to my face. There was no one else in the room who had a view of it, but Marge somehow got the idea that her continued existence depended on the answer to that question and answering it quickly. She was flustered as she spoke, "Well, let me see. Yes, his 13th birthday. That would have been 4 years ago. Let me see. Yes, yes, I was there visiting the Durselys that day. Well, nothing happened. We were celebrating—not his birthday—just celebrating being together, and I was saying something about Potter's Mom and Dad." Something further must have happened to my face because her expression clouded, and she hastened on. "Oh, nothing out of the way, just. Well, I really don't remember anything else that day, really. Really. Oh, I don't know."

I was merciless. "You really don't remember anything else that day? Nothing at all!"

She looked worried, "No, really, I don't remember a single thing. I don't even remember staying at their house, though I must have."

"Are you absolutely sure. You don't remember anything else, at all?"

"No, why are you badgering me about that. I don't remember anything."

I relaxed. "OK. Yes, I believe you."

She relaxed too.

"All right. I can tell you a few things.

"First, no one here knows where your brother and his family are."

She started to protest, and my mouth tightened.

"Second, I think that you're right. I think that he's been abducted along with his family."

She sobbed, showing the first real concern for anyone other than herself. She said, "Is that all?"

"No, I suspect that they're still alive, but the people who have them don't intend them to remain that way. They want information from the Dursleys. When they're convinced that there's no more information to be had from them, they'll kill them. Probably the only reason that they're still alive is that their captors think that they might be able to get Harry Potter to exchange his life for theirs."

Marge looked up from her sobs with a strange mixture of sadness and amusement. "You're daft. Why would anyone want Harry Potter? And who would believe that that little piece of. . ." she hesitated when she saw the expression on my face, "that he would give himself up for them?"

I leaned back and tried to study her again to come to an understanding of her. After a while I gave up. She said, "All this is so crazy! What's really going on?"

I tried to appraise her. I finally decided that it couldn't do her any harm to tell her more of the truth. "OK. Here's the truth. Not the whole truth. But enough so you'll have a chance to understand what's going on."

"There's a battle going on right now in England. It's between a group of terrorists and a group of people who oppose them. These terrorists are particularly hard to deal with because they can do real, honest-to-God magic. The leader—no, that's not the right word. It'd be more like the 'key player' for the anti-terrorists is Harry Potter. He's basically all that stands between us and a new dark age where wizards and witches use magic to suppress the non-magicals—Muggles—us—in our society.

"You're certifiable!"

"Look around you. Do you think that everyone you've seen in this building is certifiable—and believe me there are a whole lot more people here than you've seen in your little tour of our building.

"Oh, you can't imagine how much I wish the Weasley twins were here! They would convince you of the reality of magic.

"Well, anyway, the terrorists have the upper hand right now, and Potter has gone to ground. The terrorists would do anything to force Potter out of hiding and kidnapping his only living relatives is something that is right up their alley. That's why I think that they've kidnapped your brother and family."

Some of my intensity must have shaken her certainty of the insanity of what I was telling her. "You've got to do something about it!"

"I wish I could think of something to do about it, but I can't." The other plain clothes officer had re-entered the room silently at some point. I turned, caught his eye, and said, "That's why we've got to put you in some safe place until this is all over. Do you have any ideas?" I asked the plain clothes-man.

"How about one of our maximum security prisons?"

"Not here. It's too close. It's too easy for them to find her."

The security man shook his head and went on, "Then you'll have to talk with Parker or someone further up the line. They have contacts in other countries."

Marge broke in, "Wait a minute. You're not talking about sending me to prison with no charge. You can't do that. This is England!"

The plain clothes-man smiled and said, "Haven't you ever heard of the 'Official Secrets' act, ma'am. We do that every day of the week and twice on Sundays."

I agreed, "Believe me they can do that. Why do you think that I'm here?"

Marge gawked with more white of her eyes showing than I would have thought possible.

"This is crazy. You're all loonies!"

I turned to the plain clothes-man again and said, "You're right, I've got to find Parker. Keep her here until we find a good spot for her." I got up and headed for the door. She leaped up and managed to take a step toward me before the other plain clothes-man had her pinned against the wall.

Ripper had shown his teeth and growled fiercely. The other plain-clothes man had just given it a look that would have frightened me if I'd been the recipient. Ripper just hunkered down and whined with his paws over his head.

None-the-less she got out a squawk and wailed, "You can't do this."

Just then Parker walked in the door, and I brought him up to date on what had been happening. He scratched his head and finally said, "Foreign incarceration, eh? Is Germany far enough away?"

"I don't think so. I want something completely off the continent."

"Hmmm. What about the States?"

"Oh, I don't think that we should burden them with her." I flicked a thumb in her direction.

"I suppose not," Parker agreed. Then he seemed to have an idea, "Oh, wait." his face cleared, and he smiled. "What about our partners?" He was thinking of the Israelis.

"Hey, that's a brilliant idea."

"I think so. I'll get them to come in and take a look. I'd hate to inflict her on them sight unseen."

"Yes, you're right. It wouldn't be fair—even to them."

Just then the door opened, and someone came in. I turned and found that it was Sally. I said, "I thought that you were home."

"I told you I wanted to see this. Have you shot off your buns yet?"

"Don't be that way. Didn't the guards put you on the Tube?"

"Sure they did, and I got off at the first station and turned around and returned. And none too soon I see." She walked over to Marge and asked, "Please introduce us."

"Sure." I turned, walked over between the two, and said, "Sally, this is Marge Dursley, an aunt of Harry Potter."

Marge broke in and said, "What do you mean Harry Potter's aunt. What kind of introduction is that? Who would want to be identified with him!" and she actually noticeably turned up her nose. "Besides, who's ever heard of him? Why isn't he still at St. Brutus'?"

Sally shook her head, laughed, and answered, "I've heard of him. How about you?" she turned to the guard with an AK-47.

He shrugged and said, "Sure. He's the magical kid who's up against the Deatheaters."

Marge squawked and sat down again. I went on, "Marge, this is Sally Harker, my associate."

"Fancy word for secretary." Sally said.

I answered, "Plain word for brilliant collaborator." She stuck her tongue out at me.

"So, you're sure that she's really who she says she is?"

"Yes."

"Then she must be on her way?"

I hesitated, "Well, noooo. She knows way too much to let her back on the street."

"Then what are you going to do?"

"We'll hold her here until we can find some secure place far off where we can put her until the trouble is over."

273

"You can't do that!" Sally said.

Marge contributed, "No, you can't. I won't allow it."

"I just can't take the chance that a Deatheater will come looking for her and get to us. And don't forget that the Deatheaters aren't exactly signatories to the Geneva Convention. They won't think twice about killing her after they've got what they want out of her."

Marge said, "You're crazy, no one would kill an English citizen like that!"

Sally swung around to her and looked at her carefully for a moment. "You're right. We can't let her out on her own. They'd take her apart one piece at a time. But you're not going to keep her in this room until you find a place, are you?"

"Do you have a better idea? Would you like to take her home with you?"

Sally looked back to Marge, turned slightly red, said with a whine in her voice, "Welllll," and she trailed off. Then she went on, "Well, I'll stay here and keep her company."

"That should be interesting. But I do appreciate the offer." I looked back at Margery and then at Sally wondering if she were really serious, "No, would you actually do that? That would be great."

She nodded, and I shrugged. "Well, if you need anything, you have room service right outside."

I left the two of them and went up to the office.

□

The next day I was in the office again when Parker called. He didn't tell me why, but he wanted to see me. When I got to his office, I found my two favorite Israeli's, Gaspard and Elud. Parker had a big smile on his face. "Good, Jim. Our friends are willing to help us with our prisoner. They've agreed to take her to a high security detention center and will interrogate her for us."

Elud said, "There's just one thing that worries me. If she's a witch, how are you keeping her, and how will we keep her no matter how secure our prison is?"

I answered, "Oh, that's easy. She's a squib."

Gaspard asked, "What in the world is a squib? And how does that make a difference?"

"Oh, that's easy. Squibs are non-magical descendants of witches or wizards. Ordinary security should work with her. But one thing. She's wily and a consummate actress. She'll convince you that she knows nothing about magic."

"Don't worry, a few days of interrogation, and we'll change her attitude."

Parker was disturbed by the idea, and I didn't like it much either. So I said, "Look. We're following the Geneva Convention strictly. If we hear the slightest hint that you've done anything that even strains the convention, you're on your own completely—no more cooperation from us."

Elud said, "Well, we're pretty good at conventional interrogation too. We'll get something out of her. And we might just get your principals to approve our methods."

Parker was adamant. "Go ahead and try. But if you'd like to lose some money, I'm taking wagers on it right now—even money."

He turned to me with details, "Jim, we've arranged a flight from RAF Molesworth. They've got an American transport plane that will take them."

"Good. If you don't mind, I'd like to accompany them there—quickly. Can we get a helicopter here to fly us there?"

"Sure. I'll get the helicopter attached to our unit down here. They should be here within an hour at our heliport."

"Thanks. I'll go down and get her ready to go." I left the office accompanied by the Israelis. When we arrived at the Interrogation Room, both Marge and Sally were there. I asked, "Have you had breakfast?"

"Yes, about an hour ago."

"Good. These two gentlemen are ready to escort you, Marge, to your new home away from home. Don't be too hard on them."

Marge looked up and gave me an evil look, but she didn't say anything. She just got up and held out her hands side by side, as though she were about to be handcuffed.

"That won't be necessary. It will be a little while before we're ready to go. Make yourself comfortable."

We all sat or stood in silence until there was a knock on the door, and one of the guards stuck his head in and said, "You're wanted at the heliport."

"Let's go," I said to the room in general. The guard preceded us, followed by Marge and then the rest of us. It was a quiet walk—until we got close to the heliport. The helicopter engine was idling, and the draft from the rotors was blowing up a good bit of dust. Marge quickly looked around and said, "You'll regret this," with a grim look on her face.

I answered, "Not half as much as you will."

I told Sally. "I'm going along, but there's no room for you." I didn't know whether that were true or not, but I didn't want her along on this ride. We got in the helicopter. I recognized the pilot from before. When they gave everyone headphones, I hand-gestured that they shouldn't let her plug into the intercom system on the 'copter. When I got myself plugged in I told the pilot, "It's really good to see you again. You know where we're going?"

"Sure. Molesworth RAF. Are you coming along?"

"Sure."

"Would you like a good ride?"

I knew what he meant by a 'good ride'. I bit my tongue and said, "Sure, the faster the better." He nodded happily.

We got buckled in, and he lifted us up off the ground so fast it took my breath away. I glanced back and saw Marge turning green. One of the Israelis asked over the intercom, "I thought we were following the Convention."

I answered, "Sure, but we're not interrogating here. And what I said still stands, if I hear anything out of line from you guys, you're out—for good."

"OK, OK."

The rest of the flight was punctuated by occasional swooping dips followed by long stretches of seeming supersonic flights at such low altitude that I was convinced we were going to hit something before we got to the air force base. But we didn't. Suddenly, there was a jet that buzzed us at not much higher altitude than we were. I asked the pilot, "What's going on?"

Before he could answer, a voice sounded in my headphones that I didn't recognize, "Blackhawk, identify yourself and take a heading of 040."

The pilot answered with our flight ID and turned the helicopter in a rapid dizzying turn. Then the dis-embodied voice came back on and said, "You're cleared to proceed. Slow to 60 klicks and land at the south end of the main north-south runway. Don't get out of the Blackhawk until you're instructed to."

I asked the pilot, "What's that all about."

"Oh, those Americans have gotten really touchy lately. They check and re-check everyone before you come on any base. And they mean business. A buddy of mine was flying a Harrier to one of their bases a few days ago. He wasn't fast enough answering the challenge, and they shot a few rounds off in his general direction."

"Do you know why the change?"

"I haven't the foggiest. You'd think that they were at war."

"Yeh, wouldn't you." By this time we'd landed, and I could see a truck coming our direction. It arrived, and about a half-dozen armed men in full battle dress leaped out. They weren't shy about pointing their guns at us. Then an officer got out of the truck and said, "Come out one at a time." As we got out he checked us out one at a time—Wendt, Elud, Marge, Gaspard. Marge was really looking green at the gills but didn't say anything.

"Good, we're to put you on a transport, and get you off the ground ASAP. Get in the truck. All but you, Wendt."

I turned to Marge and said, "Good luck. Just remember that I've probably saved your life."

"You'll regret this." She managed to sound pretty intimidating despite the fact that she looked like she was about to wretch.

"I probably will." I turned to the officer. "Make sure that she's treated with respect."

They helped her into the truck, and I got back in the helicopter. As I did, I asked, "Do we have permission to go."

"Permission? I wish you'd never been on the base. Get going."

I got in, buckled up and hooked up my headphones. The pilot asked, "That lady didn't look all that well. Is this some sort of CARE flight?"

"Oh, she always looks like that. Let's go." And I prepared myself for another harrowing ride.

I got back in time for lunch. Sally was waiting for me. She had a pretty stern look on her face. She started in before we'd gotten out of the Cafeteria line and to our table, "You were really hard on Marge. What gives? I thought that you didn't know her before yesterday."

"You're right. I had never met her before yesterday, but it turns out that I had heard about her. I just didn't connect the name until I was in the room with her and started talking with her."

I heard the tension in Sally's voice, "Go on."

"Well, the way I'd heard about her was that I once interrupted a conversation in my English class at Hogwarts. It was some Slytherins who were. . ." Sally interrupted me.

"Slitherings?"

"Slytherins," I corrected, "the school of Hogwarts is a residential school. They have 4 dormitories. Each is named after one of the founders of the school. One was Salazar Slytherin. They have the reputation of being ruthless and turn out lots of dark wizards.

"Anyway, there were three Slytherins talking in class. I gave them detention. When they were serving detention with me, I insisted that they tell me what they were talking about. They took some pride in explaining that they had it on good authority that Harry Potter's aunt was a cruel martinet that made Harry's life miserable when she had the chance. They gave me one example. Apparently, at a family get-together she'd accused Harry's father of being a drunken lay-about and his mother of being a social misfit. They didn't use those terms, of course, especially about Lily Potter, but they were pretty clear.

"I never had the honor of knowing either his father or mother, but I have it on really good authority that his mom was a kind-hearted lady. Now, his dad had his faults. He was no respecter of authority, but he was apparently neither a drunk nor lazy. His last act was giving his life in defense of his wife and son. His wife was just as brave in the defense of Harry. I really wish I'd been able to meet them."

Sally asked, "So, they were both dead when this incident happened?"

"Yes."

She made a large round O with her mouth and said nothing.

I went on, "So, I just 'lost it' over the last two days. I couldn't take out my anger on the Slytherins but I could make Marge's life miserable while she was with us."

"Why didn't you tell her how you felt about her?"

"She wouldn't have understood. She'd just have laughed. Don't you agree?"

"Well, it's hard to judge people in the situation where she was. But, yes, I suppose she did seem pretty, uh, well . . . ."

"Don't try to come up with a description. She's not worth the effort."

We finished lunch mostly in silence.

□□

I thought that would be the last that I heard of Marge Dursley for quite some time, but I was mistaken. It was not a fortnight later that Sally and I found ourselves in Parker's office. David and Elud were both there as well.

Parker looked from one to the other of the four of us and commented, "It seems that there is a problem with Ms. Dursley."

David picked up the narrative immediately. "We decided to assign her to a prisoner of war camp where we keep female terrorists.

I opened my mouth to object, but David forestalled me. He lifted the palm of his hand and said, "Hear me out.

"We did not immediately decide to do that. We kept her under house arrest for a short while as we decided what to do with her. We didn't want

278

to put her in an ordinary prison. For one thing, she could appeal for the equivalent of your habeas corpus.

"We might have kept her under house arrest but . . ." He paused as though trying to come up with the diplomatic way of saying something. "Well, let's be honest. She is quite a 'pill' as you English say."

I commented sourly, "We say that in America too."

David continued. "She made such a nuisance of herself that the staff at the house that we'd chosen insisted that she be moved or they would resign." He paused again as he chose words.

"Israel is a small country. We do not have lots of facilities as you do in England. The only appropriate location seemed to a women's interment camp. We thought that in a population of other women who did not speak English, she would be more . . . uh . . . subdued."

I nodded, "How did that work for you?"

David scratched his head, "I suppose it did not 'work' so well. We underestimated the amount of English that the Palestinians spoke, and we overestimated the Palestinians' toleration of the difficult conditions in the camp. To make a short story even shorter, there was a riot in the camp. The women went on a hunger strike.

"Despite what you English seem to think of us, we are not inhumane. We agreed that she would be moved to another facility. We temporarily— very temporarily—moved her to house arrest again."

I began to see the way the wind was blowing as did Parker who asked, "You want us to take her back, don't you?"

David looked down at his feet. Apparently, he didn't like to admit failure in such a simple task as keeping one Englishwoman in confinement. He didn't have to say anything.

Parker shook his head. He then looked at me, "Do you have any ideas?"

Sally spoke for the first time, "What about our American cousins? Do you think they would take her?"

I hated to admit it, but that seemed to be the next stop for Ms. Dursley. I said, "Well, maybe, Darmstadt Air Base in Germany isn't as bad an idea as I thought at first."

Parker smirked, "I think you were just trying to protect your countrymen from Ms. Dursley. I'll get hold of them immediately."

David smiled for the first time during the meeting. "We'd be grateful if you would." He added hesitantly, "Just how quickly do you suppose that you can arrange for her transfer?"

Parker smiled a broad smile, "Oh, we'll do our best."

David brightened visibly as he said, 'I think I can get her transferred to our embassy in Berlin. They will be happy back in Israel."

Elud then added slyly, "Of course, if it takes too long, we may decide to transfer her to our embassy in London."

Parker growled, "We'll get back with you as quickly as humanly possible."

With that David and Elud left. Parker turned to me and said, "Get on the phone with the base commander at Darmstadt. Tell him that we're sending them a special guest who will be staying much longer than the rest who go through their base. You don't have to mention that she's not a witch."

I nodded and said ruefully, "They'll discover that she is one soon enough."

Christmas

I was in the Cafeteria when the owl landed on my plate and held out its claw. I took the message off and read it. It was from my usual correspondent. It said,

"I hope you're well. Since the term is almost over, and the Christmas holidays are upon us, I would suggest that we meet somewhere convenient and spend some time together. Would you be interested? Reply immediately and end my suspense. All my love, M."

I pulled out my pen and a piece of parchment. I'd started carrying them around for such emergencies. I started my reply quickly and then slowed as I thought about a suggestion to make, "My dearest, I think you've got a brilliant idea. I completely agree. When will you be available? I have an idea about a wonderful place to spend the holidays. You'll just have to remain in suspense as to our destination, but I assure you, you'll enjoy it. I will give you this hint. It's a warm Muggle destination and you should obtain some appropriate Muggle clothing for the trip." I wrapped the message around the owl's claw and sent it on its way.

The place that I had in mind was the Canaries. When I got back to the office, I asked Sally what she knew about the Canaries. She said, "It's a very popular vacation destination—especially in the winter. It's mild most of the year and usually pretty dry. That's why it's popular. I've never been there. If you're thinking of going for the holidays, you'd better get reservations while you can. And be prepared to pay through the nose." Then she reflected and said, "You've got a holiday with your fancy lady, don't you?"

"You know that I can't give you any such privileged information."

"Well, it's part of the EU, so you'll have no trouble getting in with your passport, but does your sweetie have an English passport?"

"A good question, I don't know. She had a fake one a couple of years ago. I don't know if she's still got it."

"Well, she can probably magic her way past customs, eh?"

I thought, "Yes, she could surely, but would she? Or would we have to get some kind of documentation for her?"

"You seem deep in thought."

"Yes, I am."

"And?"

"And."

"And what?"

"And none of your business."

Fortunately, I didn't have to be in suspense long myself. The next day, Minerva answered. Her note read, "I can hardly wait for the end of term. I think I'm worse than my students. They have lost all interest in their subjects and—sadly—so have I. I can't wait to find out what you're planning. Write me immediately and tell me more! All love, M."

I composed this reply, "Beloved, Hurry, yourself. I'll tell you this, I'm planning to take us out of England. Do you have a passport? Do you have any kind of English government issued identification? If you don't, would you consider it to be unethical to 'Confund" a customs agent? Answer swiftest, dearest!"

The reply owl appeared the same day, "My love, bother customs agents, whatever those are. I'll 'confund' an army of customs agents. The last exam is the 22nd and I'll disapparate to my sister's that night. I can see you the next day. Bother grading exams. I don't have to have them graded until a week after Boxing Day."

I immediately replied, "Spend the 23rd getting Muggle togs. Meet me at the Waterloo train station at noon. Be packed. Be ready for adventure. Be ready for fun. Be ready for warmth. Be ready to confund. Forever yours, W."

The last letter that I'd sent by owl post was from my office. Sally was there and asked, "Well, are you finished with your arrangements for your little holiday with your sweetie?"

"Not that it's any of your business, but yes, I've got airline tickets and hotel reservations, AND I've even gotten a week off from Parker."

"How'd you do that? He doesn't strike me as the romantic sort?"

"Oh, I threatened that I'd go complain to the PM."

Sally laughed out loud, "You said you'd go to the PM? You didn't?"

"No, I didn't have to. He was OK with it."

"So, when are you leaving?"

'Christmas Eve."

"Where are you going—the Canaries?"

"Sorry, no can tell."

"Well, then, can I come along?"

"No,"

"Oh, pooh. Why doesn't anybody invite me on a wild vacation?"

"Go get your own vacation. What's wrong with Fred? Talk him into going somewhere."

That was the 20th. Then a few days later, I was standing at the ticket counter at Waterloo. I wasn't in line, and I was beginning to attract some attention. Of course, I wanted to attract one person's attention but that was all. After about ten minutes, she showed up. She was wearing Muggle clothing and it wasn't too gaudy—at least by the standards of wizards. She was wearing a bright green blouse and a white skirt. Her shoes were the same shade of green. She was carrying a matching handbag. I asked her, "I suppose that you've got all your belongings in your handbag?"

"Of course." She stepped up to me and gave me a kiss that was a pretty decent kickoff for a vacation.

"That handbag makes great carry-on luggage."

"Carry-on luggage?"

"You're going to find out Let's go." I took her hand and pulled my carryon bag in the other hand.

"Are we going to get on a train?"

"No, we're going to take a taxi.

"Where did you get the blouse? I like it, but you don't want to stand in the sun wearing that. You'll blind all the onlookers."

"I wanted to make sure that you noticed me."

"I always notice you."

I led her out to the main entrance and hailed a cab. We got in, and I requested Gatwick.

Minerva asked, "What is a 'Gatwick'? Some sort of fancy candle?"

"No. Just wait, and you'll see."

We arrived at Gatwick.

"I still don't know what a Gatwick is."

We walked into the terminal and up to the British Airways counter. I checked us in and got our boarding passes. We got into the security line, and I briefed Minerva on the drill. "You have to put all your belongings on the conveyor so that they can X-ray them to make sure there isn't anything dangerous inside. Then you walk through a metal detector to make sure you're not carrying any sizeable chunk of metal, like a gun on your person.

"What will the X-ray show in your bag?" I asked with a little trepidation.

"Oh, I'll have to use a Confundus charm on the person checking the check-ray. She'll think that she's seeing a lipstick and a couple of condoms."

"You're kidding."

"Just wanted to make sure you were listening."

We got to the head of the line, and I had Minerva go first. She carried her wand like a tiny baton that she whirled as she walked. She apparently confunded the security person at the X-ray silently. When she got to the scanner, the security person asked her to send the wand through the X-ray machine. Of course, the X-ray showed nothing but a wooden stick with a core of a hair from a festral—not that the operator would recognize a festral hair. She walked through the scanner, and the security man passed her through. I went through without issue.

"Why all the security?"

"There are terrorists who sometimes hijack the airplanes."

"Airplanes" Her eyes grew as wide as saucepans, "We're not going to fly in an airplane. You're kidding, right."

"No, I'm not kidding. Why, what's wrong."

"But airplanes fly thousands of feet in the air. What happens if it falls?"

"You know, for someone who flies on brooms in the open, you have a strange fear of flying."

"It's completely different. I'm in complete control of the broom. I know what to expect from it. I can come down quickly anytime I suspect that there may be a problem with the broom, but an airplane has to land at an airport. That's what Gatwick is, isn't it, an *airport?*" She said the word as if she were talking about a field full of land-mines.

"Yes, Gatwick is an airport. Millions of people go through it and either take off on an airplane or have just gotten off one every year, and none of them have been injured or killed."

"Of course, all the dead ones are scattered on the fields between here and wherever they came from."

I took her hand gently and said, "It will really be OK. Just think of the first time that you took me to Hogwarts by floo powder. It can't be worse than that."

"Yes, it can be." But she let me lead her to our departure gate. It had our destination listed, but I think that she was too nervous to notice. We sat down on fake leather chairs and waited for our flight to be called.

I continued my explanation, "They'll announce our flight in a little while. When they do, we have to wait until they call our section of the airplane to board. We'll just go up to that counter, and an employee of the airline will examine your boarding pass. Then they'll let us get on the airplane. There is assigned seating, and we'll put my carry-on luggage in the rack above our seats. Then, we'll have a nice relaxing flight to where we're going."

She gasped as I said 'relaxing flight' and then asked, "Just where are we going?"

"It'll be a pleasant surprise. I promise."

"That's what you promised about this whole trip, and here I find that we're having to *fly in an airplane*."

"It will be great. Please trust me."

She took my other hand in hers, squeezed, and said, "OK. If you say so." She was wearing a wan little smile, but I could see there was still some spunk in the back of her lovely eyes.

They did call our section of the plane, and we walked down the jetway to the plane. She didn't quite notice at first when we'd gotten on the plane, but she realized as soon as she saw the seats. We walked past first class and found our seats near the wing. I offered the window seat but she declined. A few minutes after the last people had gotten on she said, "This is amazing. I'd never believe we were flying."

I had the sad duty to tell her, "Uh. . . We haven't actually taken off yet. They'll announce when we do, and you'll know anyway."

After a few minutes the plane started to back up, and she asked, "Does this airplane fly with people facing backward?"

"No, we're just maneuvering around to get to the place where we take off."

A few minutes later one of the stewardesses was explaining about the safety features of the plane. Minerva took it badly, "What does she mean? Is it so likely that something bad will happen that they have to announce all these emergency thingees before every flight?"

"No, they just want people to be ready for even very unlikely events."

"Well," she smiled, "I need help fastening my seat belt."

"There's nothing I like better than being of service." I reached across her and gently passed the seatbelt across her waist, gently caressing it and her legs as I buckled and fastened it.

"Maybe there are some benefits to flying." She said.

285

By now we had taxied to the end of the runway. We turned onto the runway and waited a moment as the pilot revved the plane's engines. Then he released the brake, and we accelerated down the runway. Minerva said, "Well, this is a little bit like flying a broom. Maybe this won't be so bad." We lifted into the air, and she actually said, "Whee" with glee before she caught herself.

"You see, you're a natural."

"What comes next?"

"Well, after we get up to cruising altitude, probably 15 or 20 minutes, the stewardesses will come through the cabin offering people something to drink and a snack to eat. They figure people will get bored without something in their hands to eat and drink."

She looked out the window and saw the deck of broken clouds quickly descending below with little villages and tiny roads crisscrossing the countryside. She asked, "Would you mind if." And she looked longingly at my seat.

"I suppose so. And here I was hoping to have the window seat."

"Well, if you want. . . "

"No, I wouldn't withhold any pleasure from you, especially if it helps you enjoy your first flight."

We unbuckled and tried to switch seats without getting into the corridor. Finally, we gave up, and she entered the corridor. I quickly switched places with her. As we passed I gave her fanny a quick squeeze, and she returned the pressure elsewhere. She commented, "I could really get to like flying."

Of course, a stewardess quickly came to us as we were completing the maneuver and scolded us for getting up and moving while the fasten seat belt light was still lit. Minerva said, "Oh, I'm sorry ma'am. This is my first flight, and I was so enchanted with the view that I insisted on switching with the gentleman."

The stewardess smiled and said, "That's OK. In the future, please pay attention to the seat belt sign, and don't get up and move around the cabin until it's turned off."

The rest of the flight Minerva had at least half her attention on the view out the window. As the sun set, she kept her eyes glued to the scene. I took the airline magazine out of the pocket and read it toward the end of the flight. After the sun set, Minerva gushed about the view of the sunset, how long it was, and how cozy it was in the airplane with the sunset and the lights in the cabin subdued.

I commented, "Artists call this the 'Golden Hour' because the light is perfect for photography and painting. When you're flying west into the sunset that hour gets stretched out far longer. It's one of the little charms of flying."

Minerva frowned and asked, "I suppose you learned that little tidbit from that little, blonde roommate of yours?"

I rolled my eyes. "She was never my roommate. We just lived in the same boarding house. And she was never my girl friend—far from it."

Minerva sniffed and said, "Boarding House! More like Bordello House if you ask me, and even if she weren't your girl friend, she was certainly trying to be."

There was a twinkle in her eyes that let me know that she was just giving me a hard time. Just to prove that, she really gave me a hard time by reaching her hand between my thighs.

Before long the pilot announced that we had arrived at Tenerife airport. We banked and got a nice view of San Cristobal. We landed without incident other than another "Whee" from Minerva.

We got off the plane and faced our 2nd challenge of the day. The customs people were suspicious of two people traveling with only one piece of carry-on luggage. The customs agent insisted on Minerva opening her handbag. She had to move quickly. She opened it, and before he could look inside, she had grasped the wand inside and silently spoke another Confundus charm. He glanced in the handbag briefly and passed us on after only looking at my passport.

We caught a cab for our hotel and checked in at 11PM on Christmas Eve. We were lucky to find the café of the hotel still open. We had a meal consisting of Gespatcho, salad, chicken paella and flan. We had a small bottle of the house wine. By the end of the meal, which was well after midnight, we stumbled up to our room and barely had hit the sheets before we were sound asleep.

□

The next morning, when we finally got up, it was almost 11 AM. Minerva quickly claimed the bathroom. I decided that I was going to have a wait so I opened up my bag and got out the draft of what the guys at the office were calling "Attack Plan A". I was making notes in the margin when Minerva got out of the bathroom. I stuffed the document into my bag and headed for the shower. Minerva called after me, "What were you reading?"

"Homework. I was grading a paper."

"No, really, what was that?"

I turned back to her as I slipped off my shorts, "I told you. It's homework. I'm grading this one paper. It's a paper about a subject on which I want to ask you some questions. But, I don't want to ruin Christmas day with it, so let's get dressed and get down before lunch is over."

"OK, but I'm not forgetting about it."

"I know," I said absentmindedly as I turned on the shower and waited for the water to heat up. After I got out, I was greeted by Minerva bearing gifts or at least one gift that was wrapped in red paper and a white bow. "Surprise".

I said, "I have an even bigger surprise for you." I rummaged around in my bag and drew out my own wrapped present for her. She took it and said, "Go ahead and open yours first."

I weighed it in my hand and shook it. It faintly rattled. It was about the size and weight of a large paper-back. I said, "Hmmm. It could be a book except for the rattle."

"Just open it!" she begged.

I carefully removed the bow and paper slowly and deliberately to frustrate her. Finally I removed the last layer and revealed a DVD. "This is 'Blade Runner'. How did you know that I wanted this movie?"

"Well, you've only been talking about it for years. I know that you've got a DVD player at your office. And I thought that you would like it."

"How did you know about the DVD player? OH, oh. You've been corresponding with Sally haven't you?" She just smiled.

"Well, open yours."

She ripped the wrappings with a professional rapaciousness that belied her usually gentle demeanor. This revealed a jewelry box at the sight of which her respiration quickened. She slowly opened it revealing a pair of earrings with green stones. She looked into my face and asked, "Peridot?"

"Of course. It's your birthstone, isn't it?"

"They're really, really beautiful, you know." She held them up to the light and then carefully put them through her ear lobes."

"I agree. Lovely." I said, 'Now that they're on your ears."

She said, "Let's go have some lunch. Merry Christmas!" And with that we kissed.

We went down and found that lunch wasn't served until after noon and guests weren't really welcome until at least 1PM. We went for a walk through the town, dropping into the occasional tourist trap. Sometimes we found a store that wasn't "touristy". Minerva was wearing something different from the previous day. She seemed to have packed Muggle clothes for all occasions. She'd pulled out of her handbag just about every kind of clothes you could imagine. She had an evening dress in chartreuse. What it is with witches and wizards and color, I've never figured out. She had jeans. She had a frilly blouse. She had simple tops. You name it. Today she was wearing jeans and a simple blouse. The only thing that she hadn't packed were shorts and bikini's, I think. We ended up eating in the town at a little café with outdoor seating. It wasn't beautiful weather. Most people would have considered it a little cool with temps in the mid 60's. It was just shy of completely overcast with a few rays of sunlight hitting hillsides in the distance.

The next couple of days we did the usual tourist things. One day we rented a car and visited the local national park. We did more window shopping in towns. Minerva fit in just as if she were a Muggle. If you were nearly color-blind, you might think that she was really, really stylish.

On the next to last day, it finally cleared up. We bought a picnic lunch at the hotel and went to the beach. The water was too cool for both of us, but the sun was warm. We sat and read and commented on the news in the *Prophet* or *The Times of London*. It got to be noonish, and we pulled out the picnic hamper and started fiddling with the food. Minerva asked, "How about talking about your homework?"

"What," I couldn't figure out what she meant. Then I realized that she was talking about the draft in which I'd been making notes. "OK. Yes. What I'm reading is a draft of a plan that has a two line title but we lovingly refer to it as 'The A Plan'. Where A stands for Azkaban."

"Azkaban. What are we talking about?" There were some stretch lines around her eyes as she squinted at me.

"Azkaban. We're planning to stage a breakout from there for all inmates."

"You're crazy. No one has ever broken out of Azkaban!" She reflected a second and added, "except for a breakout from within—one person, Black."

"You're forgetting about Riddle breaking all the Deatheaters out a couple of years ago."

"No, I'm not. That was an inside job. The dementors co-operated and made it a snap. There never have been many wizards manning Azkaban. The dementors are enough to prevent breakouts from the inside and are a formidable challenge to breakouts from without."

"You won't have it that easy. You'll have to drive off the dementors, and then you'll have to worry about them getting help, not to mention the fact that there will be Deatheaters running the show there." She was silent for a moment and then her frown broke into the beginnings of a smile, "What's our plan?"

"Well, we're going to bring a team of DA wizards and witches. When we arrive, we'll. . ."

I was interrupted by Minerva. "Just how are you going to get a group of wizards close to it unobserved?"

I laughed, "We're going to approach Azkaban from beneath the North Sea."

She laughed. "You do have a sense of humor. Are they going to swim there with the Bubble-head charm?"

"No, we're going to go by submarine."

She shook her head briefly as if trying to clear her head. "Did you say 'we'? 'We' as in you?"

"Yes. I said 'we' as in 'me.'" There were two minutes of silence.

Minerva looked down and took a deep breath, "You're serious, aren't you?"

"Yes. I am."

"You can't be talked out of this can you?"

"No. You're acting like it's dangerous." I tried to keep it light, but I'm sure that there was tension in my voice.

'Well," Her voice was definitely tense, and her lips compressed as she tried to control herself. "Let's see. You're going in a damn Muggle boat that's underwater to attack Azkaban—Azkaban, which is crawling with dementors that Muggles can't even see. Not to mention the Deatheaters. Not to mention that. . . that. . ." She couldn't finish. She picked up after a few seconds, "No. NO. I'm not worried it's dangerous in the least."

I put my right hand on her left forearm lightly. "I know it's dangerous. If you're going to go against Riddle, it starts dangerous and just gets worse as you go along."

"OK. OK. What happens next? You get close."

"We get close and snipers on the mainland take out the guards on the roof of Azkaban."

"There are guards on the roof?"

"There are now. Is that something new?"

"I suppose so. How do YOU know about guards on the roof?"

"We've had it under occasional surveillance."

"How did you find it? It's unplottable?"

"Well, we knew it was unplottable, but we started looking through satellite photos. We looked and eventually we could see an area where the resolution was miserable and couldn't be made better regardless what we did. We sent a team close to it. We couldn't give them the exact coordinates, but we could give them co-ordinates close to it. We told them to look. They looked and looked and eventually saw."

"But how's that possible?"

"There are Muggles who can resist magic. Not in a large way. They just have to be very determined."

"OK. So, you 'take out' the guards. I suppose that's nice talk for kill?"

"Yes."

"OK. What's next?"

"The sub surfaces and sends a DA team with a few Muggles. They blow the main doors off their hinges with explosives and go in. They repel the dementors and immobilize the guards. They get the prisoners out of Azkaban and disapparate them to the sub. We all sail away and live happily ever after."

"Kind of thin on details after you break in to Azkaban, aren't you?"

"Well, yes, but there aren't that many people whom we could interview who know the interior of Azkaban."

Minerva smiled for the first time in a while. "I can think of one."

"Who are you thinking of?" I almost gagged. Minerva just kept smiling and saying nothing. Then an idea struck me. "There was one DA member who was in Azkaban. It was—what—5 years ago? Yes, five years ago. Haggrid."

"Right. I'm sure he'd be glad to help you break people out of Azkaban." She was practically chortling. "He'd love it."

"You're right. Can you help me find him?"

"I think it oughtn't to be too hard."

I asked her, "Aren't you getting hungry?"

"I thought you'd never ask."

We had the lunch and finished the afternoon with a leisurely walk on the beach. Neither of us talked about Azkaban again that day or that trip. It's too chilling a subject even in the warmth of the Canaries. The next day was cloudier and cooler so we just hung around the hotel room mourning the end of our time together. She wore the bright green blouse again. It didn't seem quite so bright. We took a cab to the airport. It was no longer novel to her. She'd been here before. We didn't say much. The whole flight back we held hands. Somehow it all went too fast.

Haggrid

When we landed at Gatwick, we went through customs and walked to the taxi area. Sally was there. I asked her, "How'd you find out where and when we'd be coming back?

Sally was bright on a dark, cold night, "There has to be some advantage to working for an intelligence organization doesn't there?"

"Oh, well. Where do you want to go, Minerva?"

Minerva was wearing a pair of sunglasses so I couldn't see her eyes. I thought that she was looking a bit severe. She said that she would disapparate herself from here directly to Hogsmead. She softened a little and added, "I'll talk with Haggrid and see if I can get him to help you out." I took her forearm. She turned a little and came into my arms. Then we kissed. She walked down the corridor toward another terminal. I watched as she disappeared around a corner, and I knew that she was standing in Hoggsmead.

Sally opened the door of the car that she'd driven, and I tossed my luggage in. She got in the driver's seat and said, "If I didn't know better, I'd say that your sweetie was unhappy that I'd come to pick you up. And what was this about Haggrid?"

"Well, first, I think you're right. I think that she would prefer that we had muddled along on our own to London."

"Yes, but I've been going crazy without you here. The last weekly staff meeting was pretty awful. Riddle has disappeared, and no one has any idea where he is. No one has any idea of how to find out. And what's that thing about Haggrid? Who is it, assuming that it's a 'who'?"

"Well, I suppose we might as well get down to business. I'd completely forgotten that Haggrid had been in Azkaban for a few months five or six years ago. He's perhaps the only person that we have access to who has actually been inside Azkaban. We need to schedule a meeting, probably a whole day, to have the planning heads available to learn from his experience."

"Haggrid. You've never talked about him. What's he like?"

"Haggrid is—well, he's got to be encountered to be believed. I suppose that I'll have to prepare all of you who will meet him eventually. But I want some time to prepare for that instruction. You could start preparing people for that meeting. Get on their calendars and find a day or two when we could have the meeting. Off-site would be preferable. Look at least a week out. Perhaps two or three would be better."

"OK. I'll get to work on it tomorrow. How was your vacation?"

"It was wonderful! The weather was much better than here, of course. We sun-bathed on the beach. We walked in a national park. We ate well. Even Minerva admitted that the Muggle food was good."

"I suppose that you enjoyed your accommodations?"

"Yes, I suppose we did. And, don't think that you'll get anything more out of me about them or what happened there. I'm not one of your girl friends."

"That was the farthest thing from my mind. But . . . But, if you ever wanted to talk about it . . . "

"I know. I'd have a willing—even an eager—listener in you."

"Well."

We drove on mostly in silence. The land was cold, brown, and covered with leafless trees. The silence was pleasant. We both had thoughts to occupy our minds. I was recalling how completely pleasurable the vacation had been. I have no idea what Sally had to think about, but neither of us felt any uneasiness about the silence, sensing the absorption that the other had with their thoughts.

I eventually asked how Fred and George were doing. Sally replied, "I went to a New Year's Eve party with them at their aunt's. She was not very happy to see me along, but was not unpleasant. I met their mom and dad. His dad's really a pretty nice guy. Did you know that he collects Muggle things?"

"Oh, yes. He's approached me from time to time to help him understand the function of various Muggle artifacts."

"Like what?"

"Well, once he wanted to know what the purpose of a Pez dispenser was."

"A Pez dispenser? What is that?"

"Pez is a kind of candy. It comes in small individually wrapped packages that are dispensed by a, well, dispenser. It used to be very popular."

"Not where I come from."

She dropped me off at the office. She'd borrowed the car from the motor pool. I went up to the office while she dropped off the car. It was close to the end of the working day, so I called down to the motor pool to see if I could catch her before she left. The officer on duty picked up right away and caught Sally before she left. "It's your boss on the phone."

She laughed and asked the officer, "What does he want that is so urgent that it can't wait until I get up there?"

"How should I know?"

She took the phone and said, "Hi."

"Hi. Look, it's close to the end of the work day. Why don't you head on home?"

"Since when do we work on the clock?"

"Look, I try to do you a little favor, and look what I get—resistance is what I get."

"OK. If you don't want me around, I know how to take a hint. See you tomorrow."

I got out the proposal for the attack on Azkaban again, reviewed it for the third time, and wished I had Haggrid's insights.

□

The next day we went over it again, and I had Sally set up a meeting with the department heads for later that day. I had Sally bring in some extra chairs for the crowd that we expected.

When they arrived—Peters, Hall, Jergens, and of course Parker.—we talked about Haggrid. Of course, we didn't come to his name for a while. I started off, "We've found an authority on Azkaban."

Peters practically jumped out of his chair, "Who is it? Why isn't he here?"

Sally said, "Well, first of all, you realize that he's a wizard, and we pretty much have a rule against wizards ever being within 5 miles of the place, let alone actually inside."

Peters was red-faced and apologized, "Sorry, I know. It's just that in all my other operations we've always been able to find somebody who knows the target—frequently somebody who's actually worked there. But this time, we're flying blind—really blind."

I picked up from there, "Yes, you're right, but now we've got somebody. We're trying to set up a meet. It won't be easy. He's a former inmate and is a 'wanted' man right now. The price on his head is probably second only to Potter's."

Parker, always cheerful about money, asked, "How much is this going to cost us?"

"Oh, it will be cheap to get our man. As a matter of fact, I think that he'll talk to us for free. But we've got to set up a safe meeting place for him—and us."

Hall suggested, "There's a hotel with a nice meeting center that we've used before. It's in Cornwall. It's the Rosemundy House in Saint Agnes. They're very co-operative. They've even taken a wing of the hotel and sealed it off for us to use before. We can come in very quietly, cater it ourselves, and leave without any of the staff seeing more than a couple of us."

Parker said, "Oh, yeah. We use that one enough that we get a volume discount. Sounds good. How soon can we get this meeting set up?"

Sally said, "That's the sticking point. We have to find this guy first. He's holed up somewhere in northern Scotland and doesn't want to be found. We think we can find him, but we don't know how long it will take."

Parker said, "Bloody . . . Do we just rent the wing for the next 2 months?"

I gave a mirthless chuckle. "No, just be ready to do it on a day's notice.'

"I suppose I should thank you for this."

"That would be nice."

We went on to discuss who should be there. We decided that the heads plus the team leads for the various teams that would be taking part in the attack should be there. We went over the main areas that we didn't understand about Azkaban. How many wizards were on site? What was the interior of Azkaban like—how many levels, how many cells, how many guards, how many dementors? What protective spells are there?

I said, "One last thing. I don't want him just walking up to the hotel, even if it is remote. We'll need an unmarked truck." I insisted on that.

"You mean like a step van?"

"No, I mean like an army transport."

"But why in the world do you want something that big for one man?" Peters asked.

"He's a big man."

"He'd have to be a giant."

I said, "Well, strictly speaking, he's not a full giant."

Jergens jaw dropped. "You're kidding, right?"

Sally said, "Have you ever known Wendt to kid?"

Jergens just stared for a while.

I said, "OK. That's enough for now."

□□

A couple of days later, I was sitting at my desk jawing with Sally. We normally kept our door open. That was a day that proved the good judgment that was behind that habit. An owl flew into the room. I smiled because the probability was at least 90% that it was from someone very special. Sally said, "I see your fancy lady has sent you a love letter."

I reddened a little and held out my arm to let the owl land on it, but it didn't come. Instead it headed straight for Sally. It landed on her desk and held out its claw for her to remove the parchment. She lifted her eyebrows but reached out and removed the message. She untied it and unrolled it. She smiled and read, "I thought that I'd write to you, Sally, because I just don't think you get enough mail. Down to business." Sally stopped and teased, "I've often wondered what your sweetie's writing style was like."

"Just keep going." I said while I was trying to keep my voice steady.

"OK. Let's see. Oh, yes. Here we are, 'I found Haggrid yesterday and he's agreed to come to you and help you. He can come at any time. You've got to allow me a couple of days to set it up. It's not easy to get away to find him.' Oh, yes, here's a good little bit, 'Maybe, Sally will let you add a personal note to your reply.'"

"You should just hand it over and trot down to Parker's to get the ball rolling so that we can set this meeting up."

"Spoil sport, I was counting on getting to compose an answer."

"We won't have an answer to compose, if you don't get going."

She got up and left. She had this ability to walk directly into Parker's office regardless what was going on there. I knew she'd be back pretty soon with results. I composed a little personal note. I'd gotten to be pretty good at expressing myself in the few words that the small parchments allowed. By the time I'd finished coding all the feelings that I wanted to express in a couple of lines, Sally had returned with reservations.

"A week from today. Is that enough?"

I thought briefly and counted on my fingers—a day for the owl to arrive, say three days to get to Haggrid, two day for miscellaneous delays. It sounded good. "That will be just fine." I added two sentences to the note, rolled it up and asked Sally to tie it to the owl's claw.

"You never have learned to do that properly have you?"

"Well, it's a lot harder when you have large hands." She took the scroll and deftly tied it to the owl's claw.

Seminar

The section heads, the leads of the tactical groups, Sally, some troops for security, and I got into several Hummers and the truck. We drove out just after lunch and arrived about time for dinner. We checked in to the Rosemundy House. We split up into a couple of groups with similar tastes which went off to find places to eat.

After dinner, we went to the meeting room that we were going to use and started setting up. We arranged the chairs and tables into a U. It took a while to find a large bench for Haggrid, but we finally did. We set up a projector and screen. A tech connected a laptop and ran through a few slides as a test. We had a little meeting right then to be ready for tomorrow.

I started the meeting, "Haggrid will arrive tomorrow morning at 9 AM. He'll show up at the woods near Saint Allen on the A30 along the route that we drove through. Sally, a driver, and I will go to pick him up. Do I have a volunteer?"

A bulky soldier who was short but looked like he could lift an elephant, volunteered. He was named Richards.

Richards asked, "Why did you ask for volunteers?"

"Because, Haggrid is like nobody you've ever seen. I want to make sure that you won't be bothered by, well, by an unusually large man. As a matter of fact, all of you need to prepare yourselves for a shock. Haggrid is just BIG. He's as nice a guy as you'd ever meet, but he's a bit much to take the first time you see him.

I turned to the man on the laptop, "Open the image on the desktop named 'Haggrid.jpg' and project it on the screen."

He did so, and there was a picture of Haggrid next to me and Minerva. Everyone gaped. Somebody said, "Is he human?"

I answered, "YES, he's human. He has feelings and everything. I MEAN EVERYONE is to treat him with respect. Is that understood?"

There was a ragged chorus of Yes's. I looked around and tried to catch each one's eye. They all seemed to be answering honestly. I turned to Richards. He looked back and smiled a modest little smile.

We went through the other slides that Sally and I had prepared, discussing what little we knew about the target and a few slides from the department heads with their "canned" questions for Haggrid.

I declared, "Well, I'm on my way to bed. Tomorrow morning comes early." But some were determined to find a good inn to spend some time and money in. That was fine with me, but I was going to bed.

Sally intercepted me and asked, "Wouldn't you like to join a few of us for an hour or so? We'll just find a quiet little pub close by and have a pint."

"Sorry. Tomorrow is a big day, and I need a good night's rest."

She shrugged, "Sorry. I think you'd enjoy it."

"Don't worry. We can do it tomorrow night. Maybe."

She said, "Yes. Maybe."

I went up to my room and watched a little "telly". I watched a documentary about the failure of the Millennium Bridge. There were a structural engineer and a mathematician on the show arguing the virtues of the various theories of its failure. The structural engineer was in favor of the harmonics theory. He showed video of a similar failure of a bridge in Washington State in the United States. It had failed due to wind interacting with the bridge exciting a natural harmonic of the. The mathematician had his own computer simulation that showed that there were no natural harmonics that the bridge possessed that could be excited. If only it had been a live program, I would have been tempted to call in and tell them the real cause of the failure, but it would have been dangerous and really pointless.

I retired early, about 9:30. I had some sort of nightmare in the night, but like so many dreams, if you don't wake up during it and write down notes on it, you'll never remember it. I didn't remember that one.

The next morning my alarm went off at 6:30. I got up, showered, dressed, and went down to the coffee shop. I had a bagel and hot tea for breakfast. I was joined during the meal by Sally and Richards. I asked Sally, "Do you have the clothes for Haggrid?"

"They're in the room that we reserved for him."

"Did you have any trouble getting them?"

"The army was very understanding about making desert camoflage fatigues to your specs—no rank insignia, but I had a really hard time with the boots. I had to go to a private cobbler to get boots the size that you wanted. They seem like boats or maybe battleships. Are you sure you're right about the size? A 22 quintuple E is awfully darn large." She held her hands as far apart as hers arms would allow emphasizing the gargantuan size.

"I'm only afraid that they'll be too small."

Richards wanted to get going. It was only a few minutes past 7 AM, but he was a strong believer in being early. Both Sally and I were not anxious to go out in the cold morning pre-dawn air, but he finally prevailed on us. He asked, "Just where are we going?"

I answered, "It's on the A30 maybe 20 miles back toward London. Haggrid's going to disapparate somewhere in a large stand of trees. We'll all recognize him when we see him. We'll just have to drive up and down and when we catch sight of him, we'll stop and pick him up."

We all got into the cab of the truck and started off back toward the A30. I'd taken the center seat of the bench, which Sally objected to. She thought the center was the warmest place in the cab, and I should be a gentleman and let her have it. I retorted that the person in the center had to sit over the manual transmission, which was uncomfortable. I added, "Anyway, when we pick up Haggrid, we'll both be plenty cold, so you should appreciate the opportunity to get used to it that sitting by the door affords."

She snorted, and we drove on at a sedate 80 KPH. We almost missed the stand of woods the first time. We had almost passed it when I realized that we were just passing it. I asked Richards, "At the next reasonable turning spot, we need to turn around. We just passed the stand of woods."

"I was wondering if that was it," Richards said and added, "How will we recognize him when he shows up?"

Sally and I laughed and she said, "Believe me, there won't be any doubt when he shows up."

After a few minutes, we reached a cross road, which we turned into and then immediately backed out of so that we were going back toward the woods. We passed it slower this time and watched the woods carefully. It was now bright enough that we could see pretty well. We passed it without noticing anyone. We stopped at another cross road and reversed again and headed back toward the woods. We did that a couple of more times.

Then, when we were heading back toward Saint Agnes, we saw what looked like a grizzly bear walk out into the road and wave its hands at us. Richards slowed to a stop and said, "I see what you mean."

Sally jumped out quickly and went up to him and greeted him with a hearty "good morning, Haggrid." I was close behind her and held out my hand to him. I said, "Professor Haggrid, I can't tell you how happy I am to see you." He took my hand in his tremendous mitt. It was more like a tremendous flexible tennis racket than anything else.

"Good morning Professor Wendt." He shook my hand vigorously, and I tried to get out an introduction that sounded something like, "Le-e-et me-e introd-duce Salllly Harker, Haggrid."

He smiled at her and said, "Good to meet you, ma'am."

I tried to take his arm and lead him toward the back of the truck. "Let's get out of the wind. We'll get in the truck and then head for the hotel where we're staying."

We went to the back of the truck and opened the doors. Haggrid had no trouble stepping up into the truck—even though the bed was 4 feet above ground level. Sally reached out her hand to him, and he gently and effortlessly lifted her into the truck. I scrambled up using the bumper as a stepping stone. I closed the door and turned on an overhead light. There were two packing crates in the truck, covered with blankets. I invited Haggrid and Sally to sit, and we all put the blankets over us.

Haggrid asked, "Do we really have to stay in the back?"

"Well, the cab of the truck is really too small for all of us."

Haggrid replied, "I thought that Ms. Sally would prefer to be in the cab and maybe you too, professor."

Sally answered, "I'd much rather be back here with you and Jim."

And I added, "As would I, Haggrid.

"Now, I've got to tell you about what's going to happen when we get to the hotel.

"We've got a room for you. I hope that you would like to take a shower before the meeting."

Haggrid sniffled softly and said, "Ye'r didn't need to do that."

Sally said, "Oh, yes we did. We want the people who are going to talk with you to listen to what you have to say. So we want you to look your best. And we've got some new clothes for you. They're a kind of uniform that the British army wears when they are in the desert."

Haggrid was puzzled, "Why a uniform and why in the world one that you wear in the desert?"

Sally answered, "We thought that you'd look good in that kind of uniform."

"Really?" And he snuffled again.

We bumped along the road jerking unpredictably right and left as we took turns. No one spoke for a while. Then Haggrid said, "But, you're said that you have a hotel room for me. I don't want to stay overnight, I've got to get back to me brother."

I had forgotten about Gorp. I asked, "Where are you two hiding out?"

"Oh, we found a snug little cave up in the mountains. It's dry and has good ventilation so we can have a fire."

"Aren't you afraid of the smoke attracting Deatheaters?" Sally asked.

"Oh, they're not interested in finding us. They just want us to keep out of the way. Neither Gorpee nor me want to go looking for trouble—at least until there's something good to come out of trouble. If there's a revolt against You-Know-Who, we'll be there quick enough."

Sally asked hesitantly, "What do you eat?"

Haggrid smiled broadly, "We don't have any trouble getting food. There's lots of game in the forest. If you're as big as Gorp is, you've got to be able to hunt pretty well to keep yourself fed. I can do very well with the leftovers.

"You know, he's coming along real well. He's gotten to the place where you can understand most of what he says." Haggrid looked down shyly and said, "I almost brought him along. He could have just stayed out here in the woods till I got back."

Nobody said anything. I don't know what Sally was thinking, but I was thanking heaven that he hadn't decided to bring him along. We approached Saint Agnes and slowed down. The driver backed the truck up to the hotel and opened the door of the truck. He'd backed up to the service entrance. I stuck my head out. No one was around. I signaled Haggrid and Sally to come on out. Richards had opened the service door, and we trotted in. I was really happy when we had the door closed behind us. I didn't want the locals getting a glimpse of Haggrid.

Richards commented, "We have the employees cleared out. You ought to be able to go to the service elevator without running into anyone."

We reached the service elevator. When the door opened, Haggrid hesitated. I asked him what the problem was.

"Sorry, Professor. The last time I was in an elevator was at the Ministry of Magic when I was tried for loosing the monster at Hogwarts. I'm just a little shy of elevators." He got in, and we rode up to the 2nd floor where our room was. Sally had the key for the room. She opened the door, and we all went in.

I told Haggrid, "The bathroom's in there. While you're showering, we'll get the uniform that we have for you." He barely fit through the door and when he closed it, he immediately opened it again.

"Where's the candles in here?"

I reached in and flipped the light switch. Haggrid marveled at that and said, "It's just like magic."

Sally excused herself to go get the uniform we had for Haggrid, and I waited for him to get out of the shower. He took his time, and I could hear him humming to himself. Sally got back, and I sent her out of the room to wait in the hall for us. The shower turned off, and after a couple of minutes he opened the door a little and asked for his clothes.

"That's OK Haggrid. Sally's waiting for us outside."

He just reached his enormous hand out of the crack in the door, and I smiled at his modesty. I handed him the uniform. He took long enough getting dressed that I was beginning to wonder if I'd have to ask him if he wanted help. However eventually the door opened. He bent down and entered the main room. The shirt was almost loose but the pants were just about right. I looked him up and down.

He asked, "Well, how do I look?"

"Just fine. I think that you're quite imposing. How do the shoes fit? We really had to guess about them."

"Oh, they're a little long but OK otherwise." He turned around and looked in the floor length mirror on the back of the door. He couldn't see all of himself at one time, but he must have gotten an idea of what he looked like.

"Are you ready?"

A frown creased his face and he said, "I'm not so sure that I am."

"Everyone there is a friend. You'll do fine."

"If you say so, Professor."

I wished that he wouldn't keep calling me Professor. I said, "Look, Haggrid. Neither of us is a professor any more. Let's just stay with names. Call me Wendt if you prefer."

He said, "I'm not sure that I can do that, Profes. . .er . . Wendt. I've had years of practice calling you Professor."

"That's OK. You'll get used to it. Let's go. Sally's waiting for us."

We went out the door and joined Sally. As we walked down the hall, I said, "I want to go in first to get them ready for Haggrid. Would you stay out with him until I'm ready?"

Sally said, "Sure thing, Professor," with a wry smile.

"Don't you start on me."

303

As we walked down the hall and down the stairs, the floor groaned under Haggrid's weight. I'd not thought about the fact that virtually all the rooms at Hogwarts were flagstone and able to bear a tremendous amount of weight. We approached the room, and I had my first doubts about how this would work. It's one thing to see a picture of Haggrid and quite another to have him sprung on you in a moment. I stopped and motioned the two of them to wait there for me. I went on into the room. I closed the door behind me because I didn't want Haggrid to hear what I was about to say.

I went to the open end of the "U" of tables and paced back and forth for a moment to think what I wanted to say. I stopped and turned to face the group. "I'm about to ask Haggrid to come in. He is somewhat imposing. Please be respectful. Remember that he's doing us a great favor coming. It's dangerous for him, but he wants to help us. He's wearing a uniform, which I thought would help him to seem more normal. We'll do introductions before starting." I looked around and found everyone's attention was focused on me. Everyone seemed to be taking it seriously. So I walked to the door, opened it, and signaled for Sally and Haggrid to come in.

Haggrid walked in first. He had to bend so far down entering the door that his face wasn't visible—only his shaggy head of hair. It almost looked like he didn't have a face. I was very afraid of what effect this bizarre appearance would have on the people seeing him for the first time. It seemed to take an age for him to get far enough in so that he could raise his head. When he did so, you could almost think that he brushed his head against the ceiling.

When he turned his face to the group seated around the "U" of tables, Parker got up and started to applaud. Immediately everyone else jumped up and applauded enthusiastically. Haggrid smiled

I waved Haggrid over to the bench in front of the "U" of tables and motioned for everyone to sit. Sally took a chair at the end of the "U" closest to Haggrid. She smiled at him. He noticed and smiled uncertainly back.

I began, "I want to thank you for your enthusiastic welcome. I know that you all are happy that Haggrid's come to help us, but I'm glad that you let him know. First, I want to do introductions. Haggrid, you already know Sally." I pointed at Parker and introduced him as our commander and went around the room. I blessed my lucky stars that I remembered everyone's name, though I didn't remember all their offices. No one objected to being slighted, fortunately.

I went on, "We're all here to learn as much as we can about the prison, Azkaban. Haggrid is the only person who would help us. He's a true authority—having lived there for a couple of months.

"We're prepared to spend the entire day—if Haggrid needs that much time. We're getting a late start, so I think we'll just work through until lunch is served. Then we'll resume in the afternoon and take a break around 2:30. We'll take a break at tea time if we're still going, and then we've arranged a nice supper. So, let's get started. Haggrid, please tell us what you know about Azkaban."

Haggrid seemed to take a deep breath. Then he tried to slick back his hair. Then he opened his mouth as to speak, but nothing came out. The seconds ticked by. Finally someone in the crowd asked, "How many guards are there at Azkaban?"

Haggrid started to answer, "Well, it depends. You see, there are two kinds of guards." He hesitated but before he could answer, someone else asked, "How big is Azkaban?" A bead of sweat broke out on his forehead, and Haggrid stared down at his feet.

I could see that we needed a different way of doing this, so I got up and held a palm out to the group and said, "Wait, wait. We need to give Haggrid the chance to talk about this in his way.

I turned to Haggrid and said, "Haggrid, how would you like to tell us about Azkaban? We have all the time in the world. You think about how you'd like to do it, and we'll be happy to wait to listen."

He looked at me, and I held his eye. He took a couple of minutes thinking and finally said, "Well, Perf. . . er. . . that is Mr. Wendt, I'd like to tell me story, and Azkaban will come out when it does."

I nodded to him, never losing his eye, and I said, "That sounds like a good idea. Everyone will wait for you. You tell the story the way that makes sense to you."

He started almost immediately and was speaking directly to me, but everyone could hear him, "Well, it all started when I was a boy. Me dad was a wizard but," and he took a deep breath and said, "me mum was a giant. I guess I got some of her in me." There was general laughter, and Haggrid seemed to relax. It was the kind of laughter that you laugh with someone, not at them.

Haggrid went on, and now he looked around the room a bit as he talked. "Me dad taught me until I was old enough to go to Hogwarts. I guess there was kind of an argument among the teachers whether I should be allowed to go to Hogwarts, my being part giant and all. But Professor Dumbledore held up for me, and old Professor Tippit who was the Headmaster went along with Dumbledore. Professor Dumbledore was a great man. He believed that everyone deserved a chance or even two chances." At that, Haggrid stopped, and I could see that he might be about to sob. After a minute he said, "Great man, Dumbledore." He paused again and did sob.

Then he went on, "Anyway, me dad died in me 5th year." Haggrid stopped for a minute and struggled to keep his face straight. Then he went on, "I was an orphan sort of then. Me mum had left him a long time before. I never really knew her. That was just the way with giants.

"Anyway, maybe it was just as well. The next year I got into trouble when the Chamber of Secrets was opened, and the monster got out and killed a student. They blamed me because I had a giant spider that I'd raised from an egg. Everyone thought it was the spider that killed the student. So, I was expelled from Hogwarts, but Professor Dumbledore talked Professor Tippit into letting me stay as a groundskeeper. A wonderful man was Professor Dumbledore.

"So, I stayed on and I was happy to be at Hogwarts. I wasn't' allowed to do magic, but I could be there and see all the kids come through. Some of them went on to be great wizards and witches.

"Finally, somebody else opened the Chamber of Secrets again, and kids were attacked. The Ministry of Magic thought that I'd done it again, and the Minister of Magic himself came to arrest me. He took me directly to Azkaban. We disapparated there, and I suddenly found myself standing in front of the gates of the prison.

Haggrid stopped for a breath, and Parker asked, "Professor Haggrid, could I ask you a question?"

Haggrid stared at Parker as if he didn't realize that he'd been addressed. Then a smile crept over his face as he realized that he'd been addressed as "Professor." He nodded and Parker asked, "Just where is Azkaban prison?"

Haggrid thought a minute and said, "I don't rightly know, sir. Azkaban is unplottable. People get there by disapparation. You don't have to know where someplace is to disapparate there, you just have to sort of have a feeling for the look of the place. I don't know how to explain it."

Parker nodded and looked at me. I said, "We can get close. We now know approximately where it is, and that's good enough."

Haggrid went on, "So, there I was at the gates of Azkaban. They opened by themselves, and we walked slowly in. You could feel how awful the place was. On my right as I went in was a large building with several doors. The first door on the right went into the Guard Room. When you are going to stay in the prison, you check in there.

Haggrid chuckled, "They call it the 'Guard Room' and there are wizards there that they call 'guards', but they aren't. The real guards are the dementors. They're what make the place practically impossible to break out of. There was only one man who ever escaped from it without help from the outside, Sirius Black."

"You see, those dementors are so depressing to be around that you just can't think straight, let alone think carefully. I just can't tell you how awful it is to be near them. Try to imagine the worst time of your life. I mean really bad. Something that made you think that you'd never be whole again. Think of the worst time for you." He got up and started to pace back and forth. His brows wrinkled in concentration. Finally, he seemed to have an idea. He asked, "Anyone here, what's the worst day of your life?"

At first no one said anything. Then, someone said, "When my girl friend threw me over for my best mate."

Someone else said, 'You never had a girl friend."

Someone else said, "When my gram died. Someone ran over her and then drove off. They never found the bastard."

The leader of the team that would make the assault on Azkaban, Lieutenant Baier stood up and said quietly, "I was in operation Desert Storm. We were in Kuwait. It was the 2nd day of the action. Kuwait was covered by a thick layer of smoke and haze that barely let any sun in. Even at midday it was like twilight. And at twilight, it was like midnight. Our unit was getting some pretty severe resistance. There was just enough light to know that the sun was up somewhere.

"We spread pretty thin and a counter-assault cut a couple of my mates and me off from the rest of the unit. You couldn't see anything. We hoped that we could sneak past them and re-join the rest of the unit. I had begun to think that we might just do it, when I tripped over something—a body, a dead goat, I don't know what. I went down and made some noise doing it. As soon as I hit ground, a firefight started up. We were pretty close to the Iraqi's I guess. It was all over in a couple of seconds. Before I could do anything, the other three of us had hit the ground, including my best mate whom I'd gone through training with. Our boys were pretty close and drove them back. I guess the Iraqi's figured that all of us on the ground were dead. They just scattered like smoke, and our boys found us.

"I was trying to see if anyone other than I had survived. I was the one who found my mate. I didn't recognize him at first. He had a big chunk of his head missing. No one else survived.

"In that minute that I fell, and the fire-fight started, I thought that I would be dead before it was over. Then, when I discovered that I'd escaped and my buddies hadn't, I felt guilty and hopeless and helpless all at the same time. I hope I never feel like that again.

"I still have dreams about those guys."

Someone said, "What a nightmare!"

"No, not nightmares. I'll have a dream about being with them—going out on the town or something like that. Sometimes they're so real that when I wake up, I'm not sure if they're true or not—not sure if they're still alive or not. Then the reality hits me, and I'm back in the dark in Kuwait. I've let them down, and they're dead."

Everyone was quiet for a minute, and then Haggrid nodded and said, "Yea. That's it. That's what being around dementors is like. Except it's worse. And it just keeps going on and on. It goes on longer than you think it's possible to survive with that much pain."

He stopped as if he were someplace else, and his body was still here. "Some people don't survive it. But it just keeps going on. The minutes turn to hours. Then the hours turn to days and the days to weeks and the weeks turn to months. Eventually years go by. It's strange, but if you ever get out, it somehow seems like the time has been much shorter. You loose track of time, and you can't believe that you've lost as much time as you have." He paused, trying to regain his strength.

It seemed like a good point for a break. We hadn't quite gotten to noon, but I thought that we could have lunch. I interrupted, saying, "Let's break here for lunch." Nobody objected, so I sent Sally for the caterers. They brought in great trays of sandwiches, fresh fruit and vegetables. Haggrid was excited by the prospect and was first in line. He piled his plate high with everything and gulped down sandwiches as if they were bite-size morsels, which they were for him. His gusto brought back the spirits of everyone, and there was a lot of joking about Haggrid's appetite. They kept urging him on to greater feats of gluttony. Finally, everyone had had their fill and resumed their seats.

Haggrid was in good spirits and started off again without any urging. "As I was saying, the 'guards' are really not worth anything. The only thing they guard is themselves from the dementors. When I was there, there were only a few—maybe a dozen or so.

Someone asked how many dementors there were. Haggrid answered, "I don't really know. Certainly dozens." Then he proceeded. "After they checked me out to make sure that I didn't have a wand on me, a guard took me up to my cell. After you pass the guard building, there's a court yard, and the cells are built between the walls of the courtyard and the outside walls. There's an inner row of cells and an outer row. There are at least three or four floors of cells. I don't know how many because I was on the 2nd level.

Parker asked, "When did they let you out of the cells for exercise?"

Haggrid stared at him, dumbfounded for a moment and then simply said, "Never."

I asked about the food.

Haggrid puzzled on that a moment and said, "I guess it was the same every day. I don't remember any difference from day to day. There were two meals a day. It was always a kind of porridge or gruel."

There were a number of similar questions, and then Parker stood up and walked next to Haggrid, where he would command attention. He asked Haggrid, "Has anyone told you why we want to know about Azkaban?"

Haggrid said, "You're planning on breaking people out of Azkaban. You want to know everything about it that you can."

"Right. Is there anything else you can tell us that would help us?"

Haggrid thought and finally said, "Can I ask you a question?"

"Sure."

"Would you tell me what your plan is?"

Parker gestured at me. I nodded and he said, "Go ahead, Wendt.'

I described the basic plan. Haggrid listened and then said, "Do you think that the prisoners will walk out on their own?"

That question took me down a peg. "Since you asked the question, I suppose the answer must be 'no'. Why don't you explain that answer a bit?"

Haggrid stood up again and started to pace. "Explain. What do you mean explain? Anybody in that godforsaken place is beat down to the point that he can hardly eat his own gruel. Some can't even do that. And you expect them to just up and walk out when you open the door of their cells. By the way, at least that should be easy. There's no fancy spells on the locks. Even a Muggle could probably open them. They might as well not even be locked."

"OK." I said, "I suppose that means that we need more men to help get them out of the prison."

Haggrid swung around toward me and spit out, "You're bloody right it does!"

That excited a lot of discussion about just how many men would be needed to evacuate the prisoners. There was a lot of debate because no one really knew how many prisoners there were in Azkaban, or how to find out how many there were.

As we approached tea time, there was general discussion about how we should move the discussion to a nearby pub. There were those who were in favor of having dinner first and those who insisted that dinner should be a part of the pub visit. There was talk of a drinking contest, and the opinion was expressed that maybe the contest should be Haggrid versus the rest of the group. Haggrid seemed to be having a great time. He had almost agreed to a contest, but he was insisting that there should be three groups—himself and two groups consisting of the two halves of the SAS group.

I wasn't sure what to make of it, but it suddenly occurred to me that they had every intention of doing the contest. I interrupted the happy group. "Wait! Wait! Don't tell me that you're actually going to go through with this."

Parker said, "Sure we are."

"But we can't let people see Haggrid here."

Parker rejoined, "Why not? He walks around London, doesn't he?"

"Well, sure. He walks around London, but that's the point. It's normal for him to walk around London. It would be dangerous for him, but it's normal. It's not normal for him to walk around St. Agnes. He'll be noticed, and people—even wizards—are bound to hear about it. Then the Deatheaters might get interested, and that wouldn't be good for us.

Someone said, "Oh, he won't be noticed among us. He's wearing a uniform, isn't he? How will they know the difference?"

I echoed weakly, "He won't be noticed among you." And then louder, "He won't be noticed among you lot! You're crazy. Of course, he'll be noticed."

Parker said, "Not in a group of boisterous soldiers."

I could see that I'd lost the argument, so I just asked, "Who's buying?"

We left the hotel, walked down the street, and found a large pub with high ceilings. It was not very busy, and I just sat in a corner and ordered a Stella Artois and was surprised that they actually had it in stock. Everyone else was having pints of the local draught. The drinking contest never got off the ground, but everyone was drinking liberally. I ordered lots of fish and chips. I don't know how much, but I said, "Enough for fifty."

The bartender wondered where we had the rest of the army hid. I told him not to worry. It would all be gone. The food started coming and everyone was having a roaring good time. I think Haggrid started a song about Odo the Hero. Everyone in the bar was singing along or at least making noises as though they knew the lyrics. Then suddenly Haggrid became very silent, and he came over to me. He said, "I completely forgot meself. Me brother is all by himself. I've got to go right now."

"Haggrid, are you sure. Everyone is having a great time. Wouldn't you like to stay the night?"

"No, I couldn't."

"We've got a room for you."

Haggrid was teetering on the brink of deciding to stay, but he stuck with his intention.

"No, sir. I can't do that. I'll just go outside and look for a dark corner to disapparate from."

"OK, but I want to come out with you and see you off."

Haggrid headed for the door. I followed, and we stepped outside. We had only gone a few steps when I heard someone behind us. I turned and found Sally hurrying over to join us. She said, "You're not leaving without me."

Haggrid kicked the ground and turned a shade of pink. He tried to say something a couple of times but seemed to have something caught in his throat. Finally I said, "Haggrid wants to go back to his brother before it gets too late.'

Sally said, "Of course, Haggrid, you've got to go. Say hi to Gorp for us."

He promised to, and we found a quiet street with no one visible on it. He said, "Goodbye. This was the most fun I've had in a long time. Say goodbye to everyone for me."

Sally said, "Of course, we will." She impulsively went to him, threw her arms as far around him as they would go, and almost whispered, "Please don't get into trouble."

He sniffed once and twisted and disappeared simultaneously with a faint pop of collapsing air. We walked back to the pub silently, each with his own thoughts.

Everyone thought that Haggrid had gone to the loo or something and were disappointed that he'd sneaked off. The party sort of broke up then, and we went back to the inn.

The Ohio

The three of us were being driven in a Hum-Vee to the US Naval Base at Parris Island in Georgia. George was complaining about the bumpy ride. "Why did we have to drive again? Couldn't we just," and he formed the word "pop" silently with his mouth. "It'd be so much faster . . . if you just, you know."

Fred said, "But just think of the last time you tried disapparating across London. You ended up in the . . ."

George broke in and laughed. "We don't need to go into those details just now."

"Oh, but I thought it was so funny when you came out of the men's room in the Leaky Caldron covered in. . . "

Again George broke in and laughed. "Yeh, yeh. Just remember the time that. . ."

The driver broke in. "I really enjoy these reminiscences, but we're coming up to the gate, and we've got to get us all into the base without getting some of us in the brig. Let's just concentrate on looking mostly harmless."

□

The car stopped at the Guard Post, and the MP looked like he was there for real business. Rather than dress gear, he had fatigues on that bulged with more than just muscles. I was betting that he had armor under the fatigues. He wasn't wearing a helmet, but I bet there was one just inside the door of the Guard Post. He had a buddy who was wearing a helmet and was carrying some kind of assault rifle. Guard #1 was talking to the driver. He was saying, "Sir, I need to see ID for your passengers."

Fred heard that and asked George, "You bring your Hogwarts' prefect badge?"

"Oh, Oh! I left it in my other robes."

The driver was polite but firm. "Please get in touch with the base commander and ask about a Mr. Wendt and party."

Guard #1 said, "Please turn your car so it faces 90 right. Then you all get out and lean against the car, hands above heads."

George said, "That wasn't very friendly."

Fred answered, "They certainly weren't," as he got out and put his hands over his head. Guard #2 motioned him to emulate George, the driver, and me. He was pointing his assault rifle at us and looked like he would take pleasure in using it. Guard #1 was in the guard box on the phone. His free hand had an automatic pointed pointedly at us. His eyes were concentrating on us but scanned the neighborhood occasionally.

Finally after what seemed two or three hours, Guard #1 put down the phone and said to Guard #2, "Get ID from Wendt. Who's Wendt?"

I lifted my hand. Guard #2 asked, "Where's your wallet?"

"Right rear."

He backed away. He laid his gun flat against the wall of the Guard Post and walked back.

"Spread your feet. Lean further in, both hands flat on the vehicle." I followed instructions. He worked my wallet out. He then said, "Turn around and let me see your face." I did. When I did, I saw that Guard #1 had my wallet and was looking me over. Guard #2 had his gun back and was definitely looking unhappy.

Guard #1 said, "OK. You guys look OK. They're expecting you at the Commander's Office. Just drive straight down the road and . . ."

Our driver said, "Yeh, yeah. I know. I've been there before."

He got back in the car as did the rest of us. We were all a little shaken as Guard #1 gave us a little salute. We cruised down the street, making a couple of turns.

I asked our driver, Gaven, "Hey, is it usually this hard to get in the base?"

"No, I've never seen it locked down so tight. Those guys at the gate weren't regular MPs. I don't know, but they looked like a couple of Navy Seals that I know slightly."

We arrived at a building, and we all walked in the main entrance and found a little greeting party waiting for us—more Seals. We went up a couple of flights of stairs. George and Fred were exchanging glances. I saw one reach inside his jacket. I said, "Fred. This is not the time."

"Yeh, I guess." He had raised his hands while I was talking. Then I saw that one of our escorts had a gun in Fred's back.

"Fred, just let him have the wand."

The guard said, "Take it out slowly. Raise your hand above your head and don't move."

Fred had raised his hand with his wand. The guard took it. "OK, anybody else have one of these?"

George said, "Yeh, you want my pointy hat too." Then he slowly, ever so slowly pulled out his wand and put it over his head.

We finally reached the office of the base commandant. We went through the door and found two men waiting for us. They were seated. Neither got up. The one behind the big desk said, "I'm the base commander. My name's Jensen. This is Captain James of the USS Ohio. Sorry about the tough reception. But when we heard you were coming, they told us that we needed highest security for you. I didn't think that you'd get caught in it. Please sit down." He indicated a couple of hardwood chairs, which we pulled up and dropped into.

Fred asked, "Could I have my wand back?"

Jenson, "I'll see that you get it back—whatever a "wand" is." He wrote something on a small pad on his desk.

James was thin and looked to be a hair less than 6 feet tall—a little taller than I. He got up and paced to the window. "Gentlemen, look out the window." We got up and walked over beside him. He pointed out the window toward a dock with a submarine that was longer than the dock by a small margin. It was hard to get an idea of size at this distance. There was a good deal of activity on the dock as supplies were lowered into two large ports into the submarine, one at each end. "That's the Ohio. I'm the commander and responsible for its safety. I expect you gentlemen to respect my authority whenever we're below the surface. Above surface, you, Mr. Wendt are the master. Let's keep the distinction clear whenever we're aboard."

"Yes, sir. I hope that our interests are the same."

"Unlikely, but you never know. Special missions with special teams are always problematic—for everyone."

He turned and looked at me eye to eye. I don't know how long we spent staring each other down, but Jensen said to James, "I have sealed orders for you. Here." He had an envelope in hand, which he held out toward James, who took it. He glanced at it and asked, "Not to be opened until we're under weigh?"

"Of course."

"I suggest that you complete your preparations to sail. I understand that there are time constraints that you can discuss with Mr. Wendt when you open your orders."

He turned to me and asked if I had any questions that he could answer.

I smiled, "Yes. If you can point us to a Cafeteria or Mess or whatever you call it here and someplace that we can spend the night until we're ready to set sail?"

"Your escort will get you to the Mess Hall and your quarters." He stood, and addressing us all, he said, "Dismissed". We left the office. Our escort was waiting outside.

James spoke to me, "I'd like to speak with you this evening."

"Sure." I looked at the Fred and George. "We'll all be there at your convenience."

James made a brief grimace when he glanced at them. "Sure. 8 PM." He turned to our silent escorts. "You know where I'm quartered?"

"Yes, sir."

"Good, I'll see you tonight."

He marched down the hall, and George, looking after him, said, "Fred, we've got to do some thinking about this situation."

Our escort made a harrumphing noise, and we all turned to him. "Permission to speak freely, sirs?"

I answered, "Of course."

"Well, sir, I'd really suggest that you not do anything rash on board a ship."

"Thanks. George and Fred will be models of circumspection." I turned to them and said, "Yes?" with raised eyebrows.

"Of course. You know us."

"It's that bad, eh?"

We went on to the Mess Hall, which was pretty good by military standards. I had an eggplant dish that I decided I'd really like to have again. Fred and George mainly played with their food. I had begun to feel like I had become their local parents. However, I decided that they could get as hungry as they liked. Maybe they'd have a better appetite for the next meal.

After the Mess Hall we went to see the Captain. He had a temporary office on the base. We entered an unusually plain and featureless room. It had an old wooden table, a phone, computer, a couple of chairs, an old red leather sofa and a window looking out over the shipyard. We were closer to the submarine.

James got up as we entered and shook hands—even with Fred and George. "Mr. Wendt, I know that we will be reading orders soon, but you

315

know what this is all about, and I don't. I don't like starting a cruise without the faintest idea of what I'm doing. Would you like to comment?"

"Yes. I would like to. I can't tell you much before we leave. But I'll tell you what I can."

He turned from me to look out the window toward the submarine. "You're under orders too?"

"I wrote them."

He turned suddenly toward us. "Really?" He seemed to be genuinely surprised.

"Yes."

"So, you're the planner."

"Yes."

"They don't usually come."

"I had to come. I'll tell you the basics of what we're doing. We're going to the North Sea. We're going to break into a prison and get some people out."

"I was wondering why there were SAS people in your happy little party. By the way. who are you anyway, DIA, CIA, MI5?"

"I'm a consultant."

"What do you consultant on?"

"That's the question, isn't it? I consult on terrorists."

"We're going to break terrorists out of prison?"

"No, the terrorists are running the prison."

"Hmmm."

"And your friends? Consultants too?"

"It's hard to believe, but they are." I paused and I looked at the twins contemplatively, "Although it's easier to see them as terrorist at times."

"Whoa, we poor innocent waifs?" George said and winked at Fred, who winked back.

"I suppose that you've given me everything I'm going to get until we're under weigh?"

"Yes. I'm really sorry Captain. I think you'll understand when we've discussed the details of the problem."

"That's what they all say. I think that we'll be able to get under weigh tomorrow. You'll want to get to bed early. Sunrise tomorrow comes early."

George gasped, "Sunrise."

"Yes. We rise early in the Navy. Mess at 6 AM. If you're not ready we'll be happy to help you rise."

Fred laughed, "Yeh, George. You're such a wuss. I get up at 5."

"Sure you do."

"How would you know?"

"Come on, let's get settled. This may be our last happy evening for quite some time."

I turned to James. "We're at your disposal any time." He grimaced.

"Let's just get through this cruise, and all go our happy ways. See you tomorrow."

We went to our quarters, which turned out to be an otherwise empty barracks. It was pretty much bare except for a couple of bunks with linen. Fred smiled and got out his wand.

"Sorry boys, no magic, remember."

"But this is awful. This is like prison. I thought the camps where we housed the escapees were bare-bones. This is as bad as Azkaban."

"Oh, don't grouse. It's only one night."

Fred nodded, "Yeh. But I'm looking that Captain up after this war is over and . . . ."

"Good. Just keep that happy thought in mind."

The evening passed slowly.

□□

And sunrise came suddenly. The morning sky was red. Was that good or bad? I couldn't remember.

Reveille sounded, and I rolled slowly out of bed. It was going to be a long day. Fred and George were dead to the world. I went to the loo and relieved myself. While I was there I looked around to see if there were a bucket or something I could carry water in. I had to be prepared for anything.

I went back to the bunks where Fred & George were still sawing Z's. I started gently. I shook George's shoulder and said, "George, time." I shook his shoulder more vigorously. "How about you Fred? Time to get up." I went to Fred's bunk and shook his shoulder. They were dead to the world. "Time to get up if you want to eat."

Well, I'd always wanted to do this since George or was it Fred had put me on the ceiling with the *Levicorpus* charm—charming. I went back to the bathroom and found the bucket I'd seen. I filled it with water and slowly, quietly walked back to the bunks. Then I gently called, "Oh, George, Fred. Time to get up."

"You have to the count of three to get up. One . . . Two . . . Three." I slowly raised the bucket and slowly evenly poured the 5 gallons of water onto the two of them. Then I laughed myself silly as the two of them spluttered and slapped themselves awake.

Fred asked, "What are you playing at? Why am I swimming in my bed?!"

George replied, "I always said you'd be the first in our family to drown in your sleep."

Fred said, "Shut your bleeding face." Then he realized that both he and George were wet. "Oh, yeah. We've got to get moving if we want to eat."

"Well, you've got a head start on your showers. Get moving." I said.

All three of us had a cool shower in the bath and headed for the Cafeteria. We got there, and of course, Captain James was already there in uniform looking like he'd been up for an hour. Maybe he had.

We spent a quiet breakfast. Nobody really wanted to talk, even James. As we walked toward the docks, I asked James, "The rest of the team is here?"

"Yep. They've stowed their gear and are already on board waiting for us. We'll board and sail within the hour. Gentleman, welcome to the US Navy."

After we'd boarded and made our way below, James ordered an ensign to take us to our quarters while he went to the bridge to get us out of port. The ensign turned and took us to what he called officer country. Apparently we were to each share a room (if the large closet that I shared with the 2nd officer could be called a "room") with an officer. We tossed our bags into the rooms and were escorted to the Captain's "office" a broom closet with a desk, a bench, a couple of chairs and a 2nd door—to a private bath? An officer who turned out to be the Executive Officer was waiting for us there. He introduced himself as Commander Wainwright.

"Yes, if you go back about 10 generations you find a long tradition of wagon makers in my heritage. That's where my name comes from."

Fred smiled, "If you back about 10,000,000 generations in our family you find weasels and stoats, right George. Our name's Weasley."

George turned to me, "How many generations back do you have to go to find a wendt and what is a wendt anyway?"

I frowned at the two of them. "You just have to go back 1 generation. We're all Wendt's in my family. I hope you'll forgive my two friends their flip attitude."

"I will, but I'd stow it when the Captain's around. He's a stickler for being serious, especially with non-Navy personnel around."

"How long will it take the Captain to get us out of port?"

"Oh, not very long, maybe a half-hour. Now that we're under weigh, he'll get us out past the breakwater and turn the helm over to the 2nd officer. I'm sure he's anxious to open those orders to see just how courteous he has to be to you gentlemen."

We spent the next 10 or 15 minutes getting acquainted—where are you from? How long have you been in the Navy? Have you always lived in England? Etc.

"I've lived there about 10 years. I was originally from . . . "

Wainwright interrupted. "Let me guess. You sound like you've got a Midwest accent."

I couldn't help being a little flip myself. "There is no such thing as a Midwest accent, but I am from Ohio."

"Really. I grew up in Cuyahoga Falls."

"Are you an Indians fan?"

"No, I'm really more of a pro Football fan."

"Original Browns?"

"Well, I was pretty young when they were in town. I'm a current Browns fan."

Fred and George were apparently getting tired of this two sided conversation, so they had a conversation of their own going.

"Who do you think will win the all-England Cup?"

"You know I'm a Chuttley Canons fan."

"Yeh, I know, but who do you think will win the cup?"

"I suppose that you think that the Warwick Warlocks have got a chance?"

"Well more chance than the Canons."

At this Wainwright interrupted them. "I've never heard of those teams. Are they soccer teams?"

Fred and George chimed in together, "Quidditch".

"What? I've never heard of that. You're making all those names up, aren't you? Give me the straight scoop Wendt."

"I'm afraid they're all real. And don't ask me about Quidditch just yet. That has to wait for the Captain to read his orders."

"Our orders have to do with bizarre sports!?" His eyes were as big as half-dollars.

"What's a bizarre sport?" George chimed in.

"Look, your captain ought to be here soon, and things will become clearer—if not more comprehensible."

That sort of spelled the end of the conversation, and we were lucky that the Captain did arrive in a couple of minutes. The silence was beginning to stretch. Wainwright snapped to his feet, and I followed reasonably quickly. Fred and George were mystified by our actions, but it didn't matter because the Captain immediately said, "At ease, be seated."—a superfluous command for Fred and George.

319

"As soon as we get another klick or so out, we'll be submerging. We'll be following a normal routine until we reach the edge of the continental shelf, and then. . . Well, we'll see what's in our orders, and then decide what happens. I hope you've been getting acquainted."

"Yes, sir." Wainwright said but didn't elaborate about Quidditch and other sporting trivia.

The Captain turned his back on us and bent over. "I'm getting the orders out right now. Let's get this suspense over."

Wainwright said, "I'm all for that sir."

I could hear the whir of some mechanical device out of sight, and the Captain straightened and turned around. He sat and handed the thick envelope over to his XO. "Would you inspect the seals?"

"They're intact, sir."

"Good. Go ahead and open it."

Wainwright broke the seals and handed the envelope back to James. James pulled a sheaf of papers out and started to read. He made terse comments as he went. "Usual boiler plate to start. . . make best speed to coordinates near . . . the west coast of Scotland. . . rendezvous with a small SAS team there. . ." He stopped reading aloud. He turned a page, returned to the original page. Turned another page.

"Well you boys have quite a little mission for us. Would you like to explain it in your words to the XO and me?"

I took a deep breath. I'd done this a number of times before, but every time it was different, and every time I had a dry mouth. "If you don't mind, I'd like to give you a good bit of history of this thing. Oh, and before we even start that, I have to ask you a question."

"Shoot."

"Where do you stand on real "magic"?"

Wainwright looked like he wanted to say something, but he seemed to be waiting for the Captain to speak. The Captain stared at me for what seemed like a half-hour but was probably only twenty or thirty seconds. Then he asked, "You don't mean illusionists, the amazing Randy, that sort of thing, right?"

"No, I sometimes wish I were, but no."

"I've never really thought about that question. You wouldn't ask me, if you weren't about to tell me that there is real magic, would you?"

"No, sir."

"And you'd better be dead serious and I do mean 'dead'."

"Yes, sir, I am."

"Then you'd better start off by proving it."

I looked over at Fred and mouthed the words *levicorpus, me*". He asked, "Really?"

I nodded briefly, and then my stomach turned upside down—really upside down, along with the rest of me. My feet were pressing against the ceiling and my head was down slightly below the level of James' desk. Both Wainwright and James got up so fast that you'd have thought that they'd seen a snake under the desk. I'm not sure whom, but somebody hissed, "Shit."

"Ok, Fred, you can let me down."

George said, "Oh, I don't know Fred. He looks pretty good that way. Better than right side up."

Both the twins broke out laughing. I was beginning to get sea sick. "Look, Fred, if you don't get me right side up, you may be cleaning barf off you shirt."

George said, "Spoil-sport." I could see Fred sub-vocalizing the counter curse, and I was suddenly head over heels again. It took me a minute to be able to continue. Both the officers were still standing. "Go ahead, you can sit down. I don't think that we'll have a repetition of that soon."

The Captain regained his composure first. "How do I know that wasn't a trick?"

George said, "Oh, yeah. We snuck in last night and set up invisible trip wires to hoist Wendt to the ceiling."

Wainwright said, "You know that we've had this ship locked down even tighter than the standard requirements for ships carrying live nukes. There's no way anyone could have got in here and set anything up without. . . well" He hesitated and then said," . . . 'magic'."

"Yes, I know." He turned to Fred, "Could you do that again—to me?"

George broke in, "why does Fred get all the fun?"

James turned to him. "You do it then."

George, who was more of a showman than Fred, flourished his wand totally needlessly and said, *Levicorpus*. And the Captain was heels over head.

I immediately said, "Put him down, now."

But James said, "No, wait a minute." He grabbed onto the desk and tried to pull himself down. He didn't move in the slightest.

George asked, "Can I pull you knickers up? I'll do it for free." I stared at George and he continued, "Or not."

Finally James asked, "Please put me down."

When he was upright, but not sitting, he said, "OK, there's real magic. I'll give you that for the moment." He paused and looked over at Wainwright. He had a firm set to his jaw, and even though I only saw his face in profile, I had the feeling that I wouldn't have liked the stare that he gave Wainwright.

Wainwright gave a small, almost imperceptible negative shake of his head, and James' scowl turned into a frown. "If anything funny has been going on here. . . ." He left it hanging on the air.

Wainwright said, "Your reputation is well-known and well-deserved."

"Yes, but if there were, it would go a lot better for the 'perps' if they came forward now." The final word had a soft emphasis that no one could miss. Even Fred and George looked serious for once.

"What has that got to do with anything?" James had turned suddenly toward me ,and I was surprised into dumbfounded silence.

I found my voice and said dully, "What?"

"What's the significance of magic in this situation?"

I smiled. This question, at least, I could answer. "Well, let me give you the 50,000 foot view. I'm sure we'll talk intimate details later, but for now, this is the 'big' picture.

"I have to start with a little history, so please bear with me. About a couple of centuries ago, there was a great conference of wizards and witches. The outcome of that conference was an international agreement that wizards and witches would 'disappear' from the 'muggling' world. . . ." James' eyes narrowed.

"'Muggle' is the wizard word for non-magical humans."

"Figures."

"Anyway. There was an agreement to keep the existence of magic and wizards secret. It was the only real example of a conspiracy where a secret was actually effectively kept for generations. It was not as hard as you think. Wizards have various capabilities that make it, if not easy, then at least possible. They can modify people's memories. They can cast spells that 'repel' Muggles, so that they can't approach a place.

"Like all people, wizards and witches are political. They have 'shadow' governments, and the head of each Muggle government is made aware of the existence of magic and the magic 'shadow' government.

"Unfortunately, also like Muggles, there are Adolf Hitlers among wizards as well. People who want to rule the wizarding and even Muggle world and don't much care how they do it.

"There has been a coup recently that overthrew the English Wizard government. The person who is now in real control, as opposed to the nominal head of government, is someone who makes Adolf Hitler seem like Shirley Temple Black.

"He is currently solidifying his power and either killing or putting in prison anyone who opposes him." I paused for breath.

"And our mission is to take this madman on?" I thought I saw a slightly upturned corner of a lip on James' face, but I couldn't be sure.

"Fortunately no—at least not directly. Our mission is the very first real offensive against him, though. We're going to attack the wizarding prison where he's putting his political opponents. We intend to free them. We hope they'll help us."

"Does this 'Hitler' have a name?"

"Yes, it's Tom Riddle. He has a self-chosen title, which I don't dare repeat, but he styles himself a 'Lord'. You will never hear me say it, and I hope you never see it written because saying the title is extremely dangerous—not only for the speaker but for all around him."

"Hmmm." We were silent for a moment, and Wainwright asked, "Tell me about this prison. How are you going to attack it?"

Fred piped up here. "We've been giving that a lot of thought. There are three hazards that we have to get past."

George broke in, "Yeh. First and worst are the giant blancmanges."

"I suppose that's some witching word for mermaids or something." Wainwright suggested.

Fred couldn't help laughing. George turned to him sharply,"Now, you've gone and given it away. I was hoping I could string him along for a while." I could see that James was losing his temper, so I broke in, "Go ahead Fred."

"Well, yes. After the blancmanges, we first have to get past the simple repelling charms. Mostly, they keep Muggles away, but they can affect unwary wizards as well. We know what we're up against, and we are not worried by them. It will be important to get some SAS Muggles past them, but I'm not really worried about that either."

George chimed in, "After the blancmanges and the repelling spells, the next most hazardous barrier are the wizards. I have to admit that I'm impressed by this ship. Anything this big and made of so much iron shouldn't be floating. And it absolutely drives me bonkers to think that we're going to be voluntarily sinking this ship to cross the 'big pond'. Even this ship wouldn't stand a chance against a couple of good wizards, and there are at least a dozen powerful wizards guarding Azkaban."

James broke in, "Azkaban?"

Fred answered, "The wizard prison we're going to break into. As vile a place as exists on the face of the earth."

I had to speak at this point. "They're right. It makes Buchenwald, the Gulag Archipelago, the Hanoi Hilton, and Andersonville Prison all seem like resorts."

George continued, "The third and worst hazard is the dementors."

Wainwright asked, "dementors?"

I broke in again. "Let me explain."

"dementors are invisible to Muggles. They are implacable, almost indestructible creatures.

"Muggles have absolutely no defense from them. They can fly. They look very vaguely human, but they have the power to destroy mind, spirit, and soul without killing the body. They torture their victims before rendering their bodies empty husks. A 'demented' person doesn't even have the minimum animal instincts. They would die of exposure, starvation, or thirst in the presence of shelter, food, and water.

"I don't know how far they can penetrate water or how fast they can travel underwater, but I sincerely don't want to find out." I looked at the Captain, and James just nodded his head slowly.

Then James asked, "How do we deal with them?"

George answered, "We wizards can drive them off."

I said, "That's why we need wizards stationed with this ship at all times, and we need to have them in the boats that will ferry people to and from Azkaban."

Wainwright said, "Then you expect to drive them away from Azkaban completely."

Fred said, "No, I think they'll hang around and try to attack any undefended humans. As a matter of fact I hope they do."

"Why?" Wainwright's eye's bulged out as he exclaimed the question.

"Probably some of them will go for help. We don't know how fast they can travel when they're in a real hurry, but we have some empirical evidence that they can travel at most about 200 Km/hr. At that speed, we think that we might just have three hours before they could summon serious help."

"What would happen if they did?"

I spoke again, "It's really important that Riddle not find out that Muggles know about him and are opposing him actively. The consequences if he did would be terrifying. First, he'd undoubtedly wreak hideous vengeance on all Muggles. It could be like all-out nuclear war toe to toe with the Chinese. Secondly, and maybe worse, our ability to affect the outcome of this struggle might end. As long as we remain a secret force, we can do some amazing things—we already have done some pretty nifty stuff."

James got out a pipe and began loading it. As he did so, he slowly spoke. I think that he was addressing Wainwright, but I couldn't tell. "What son-of-a-bitch got me this assignment, do you suppose? I think it was the head of the submarine service."

I had an answer for him. "I know who did it."

"How the hell do you know?"

"I was there when it happened." James gazed at me with a mouth agape. He regained his composure.

"It wasn't who you think. It was the Secretary of the Navy. He wanted somebody who was. . ." I assumed a jutting jaw in imitation of the Navy Secretary, "mule headed and ornery enough to go into Hell on a bet.

"The Head of your service didn't want to let you go."

"I'm surprised he didn't want to get rid of me."

"Oh, no. You're far too valuable to him as an ace in the hole just in case something really bad happens. He figures you're kind of safe on a nuclear missile sub. You wouldn't think of using a thermo-nuclear missile without really good reason."

"Damn right." That was Wainwright.

"OK. Get out of here. I've wasted enough time with you. Wainwright, make sure they find their way to their quarters, and get us down to cruising depth and speed as quickly as you can."

We left without a word.

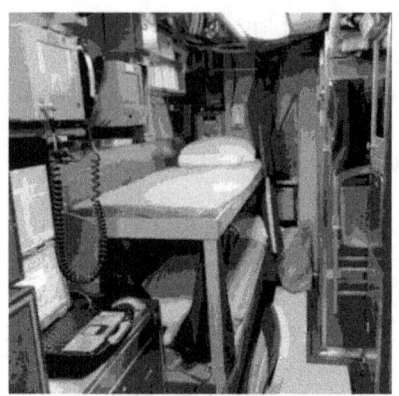

Mess

We spent a couple of hours in our quarters getting to know the two or three cubic meters that had been allotted to us. I unpacked the few things that I could get into my duffle—a couple of changes of clothes and a couple of books. I was reading *Master and Commander*. It seemed as though being on the surface was a more interesting life than silently moving without sensation of motion through the depths of the sea. It was eerie not hearing anything except an occasional groan whose cause you really didn't want to understand. I was intrigued with the adventures of Dr. Maturin and Capt. Aubrey. I didn't notice when Wainwright had entered the cubby-hole that we were going to be calling home.

He had sat down at the little desk the room had. He asked me, "Are you a fan of Aubrey?"

Startled, I looked up and noticed him for the first time. "I'm more of a fan of Maturin, but Aubrey is an amazing character."

"I like him too. Is that your first book in the series?"

"Actually, not. The first that I read was *The Golden Ocean*."

"Do you normally start series in the middle?"

"Well, come to think of it, I don't think that I've ever started a lengthy series in the middle. When I read James Bond, it was *Goldfinger* that I read first. It wasn't the best in the series, but I'd just seen the movie. I was really impressed by it."

"Is that why you started with Aubrey—the movie?"

"No, I sometimes read audio-books—from the library. That was the only one the library had in at the time. Actually, it's gotten to the point that I don't care whether I start with the first book any more. The later books are a better guide to whether the author has staying power. I'm not sure that I'd start with the first any more.

"What are you reading?" I asked.

Wainwright opened a drawer in the desk-let. He pulled out a book and turned the cover so that I could see it. It was science fiction. I didn't recognize the author. "Turtledove. I don't recognize the name. But I only read the classic sci-fi authors. What's the story about?"

"It's an alternate history. Suppose the south had won the Civil War?"

"There's a horror story for you."

Wainwright smiled, "You're a Yankee."

"Well, I am, but seriously, is there a good end?"

Wainwright frowned, "Don't you mean a good ending?"

"No, I mean, suppose slaveholders win. Is that a good end?"

"Everyone has some virtue. The Southern generals were good men, mostly."

"Tom Riddle wants to be a slave master. What do you think the end will be if he wins?"

"Not nice, I suppose."

"You can't even begin to imagine."

Wainwright turned fully toward me and seemed to be sizing me up. "And you don't have to imagine."

"No. I've seen.

"I've seen a little slice of it. I met? Saw? Observed? I don't know. There isn't a good word for it. Anyway, I know a couple who opposed Riddle. They were tortured until they went insane. Nearly catatonic for a long time, and now . . . . I don't know. You could actually have a sort of conversation with them, but you wouldn't come away thinking that there was much *there* there.

"I haven't seen a lot more, but what I have seen makes me willing to do some pretty awful things to prevent it. I suppose I've got to do some soul-searching."

"What do you mean by pretty awful?"

"The really awful thing is that I can't give you a good example. You don't 'need to know'."

"Thank you for saving me from that.

"By the way, it's almost dinner time. Let's go down to the Mess."

The Mess turned out to be the largest room I'd seen in the ship. You could actually squeeze sixty or seventy people into it. It had functional furniture—tables, chairs, and so forth. There were already some crew there, and more came along with Fred & George, some SAS, and wizards. The kitchen opened and people got in line. They had all come over to our table, got up en masse, and joined the line. Wainwright came with us. There were a couple of choices of entrees and side dishes. The steamed broccoli and carrots looked good. Looked. Good.

Back at the table, Wainwright encouraged conversation by beginning one with Fred. "Do you want to explain Quidditch?"

Fred's face brightened, and he kicked off into a spirited description of the game,"It's the best game in the world.

"You have two teams—each with 7 players. The game is played completely in the air. Everyone rides brooms. Skillful flying is one of the most important pre-requisites for a premium Quidditch player.

George, "That let you out from the off, didn't it?"

Wainwright waggled an index finger at them, "Now, now boys, let's play fair. You can bicker after you've explained your game to me."

Fred continued. "Each team has two beaters (the most important players)."

I chimed in, "Guess what position Fred and George played."

"It would be a wild guess, but . . . 'Beater'." Wainwright answered.

"Bingo."

Fred went on, "There are three chasers, a goalie, and the seeker.

"The object of the game is scoring points by either putting the Quaffle through one of the three rings of your opponent or capturing the 'Snitch'. The ultimate objective is capturing the Snitch. The moment it's captured, the game ends.

"Beaters are called that because their job is to use their bats to 'beat' the two Bludgers at the opposing team and cause as much mayhem as possible."

Wainwright laughed and said, "You two were naturals for Beaters."

Fred went on undeterred, "The Chasers try to get the Quaffle and throw it through the opponents' hoops. The Goalie tries to prevent scores from being made against their team. Finally the Seeker tries to find and capture the Snitch." Fred paused from this explanation to catch his breath.

Wainwright used the pause to ask, "How does scoring work?"

"Each goal is worth 10 points, and the capture of the Snitch is worth 150."

Wainwright thought for a second and asked, "That's strange. Why are the scores multiples of 10 rather than multiples of 1. It sounds kind of like the inventor of the game thought that small scores would not be as exciting as large scores."

Fred was dumbfounded for a moment. "I never thought of it that way. Yeh, you're right. Goals could be 1 point and catching the Snitch could be 15 and everything would play just the same."

Wainwright came back immediately, "And if a team fell far behind, catching the Snitch would be the last thing they'd want to do. They'd want to get closer on points before they caught the Snitch."

"Yes, as a matter of fact the last World Cup was won by the Irish even though the Bulgarians had caught the Snitch."

"Why'd he do it?"

"Catch the Snitch?"

"Yes, it must have been a guaranteed a loss."

"Well, the thinking was that the Bulgarians weren't going to catch up. They would just keep falling farther and farther behind, and it was sort of a mercy to end it. And there's a certain glamor about catching the Snitch that saved some pride for the Bulgarians."

"I don't know that I'd say it's the world's best game, but I will admit that it's the most unique. I can't think of another where you can achieve the main objective and lose."

George enthused, "Yeh. It's a great game, but you can't appreciate it until you've seen it in action—everyone flying at top speed, dodging other bodies, Bludgers, the hoops, the stand . . ."

Wainwright broke in, "The crowds."

"You've seen it haven't you? How else would you know about dodging the crowds in the stands?

"Oh, just a lucky guess. No, I've never seen a Quidditch game."

"Really."

Fred asked, "OK, what's your favorite game?"

Wainwright thought for a minute. "I'd have to say Baseball."

"What's Baseball?"

"It's a game that has everything. Every play is begun by the defense. It has man against man. The pitcher versus the batter, the catcher versus the runner, the batter versus the fielder. It's sort of like your Cricket. It's also one man against nine. It's a thinking man's game. Every play is full of thought but can happen in an instant, in the twinkling of an eye."

Fred was losing his patience with this lyrical description, "Come on, man. A play that happens in the twinkling of an eye can't be full of thought!"

"Yes, it can. Every play begins with a pitch by the pitcher to the batter. But before that pitch each player is thinking about the play. There are 3 bases that a batter can be safe at after he hits the ball. Hand me that salt and pepper over there," he indicated the salt and pepper shakers at the center of the table. "And hand me a sugar and saccharine bag." He laid them out in a rough square with the salt and pepper at two opposite corners and the sugar and artificial sweetener at the other corners.

Fred interrupted, "What's saccharine?"

Somebody else who had drifted over and was looking over our shoulders asked, "You don't know what saccharine is?"

Fred said, "No. Why should I?"

"Have you been living under a rock all your life?"

I could tell that Fred was a little steamed. "Well, do you know what a Quaffle is?"

"No."

"Well, there you are." Fred ended triumphantly.

I answered Fred's original question. "Saccharine is a substitute for sugar."

"Why do you need a substitute for sugar when I see you have sugar on the table?"

"Well, some people don't want the calories that are in sugar. Saccharine doesn't have calories."

"Well, that's as clear as mud. What are calories?" At this point, the kibitzer rolled his eyes (fortunately behind Fred).

I went on, "Calories are a measure of the energy that a food contains. Some people eat too many calories and gain weight."

"Fat"

"Yes. Saccharine lets them have the taste of sugar without the calories."

"Why don't they just use a reducing cha . . ." Fred thought better of what he was about to say and cut off.

The kibitzer asked, "A reducing what?"

I filled in, "He means a reducing diet."

"Yeh, that's it." Fred quickly added.

Wainwright started up again. "I've got to do this properly. The sugar is called home plate. The salt is 1st base. The saccharine is 2nd base, and the pepper is 3rd base. The batter stands at home plate. The pitcher stands in the center of the diamond."

George asked, "What diamond! I don't see a diamond anywhere."

"I mean the figure formed by the 4 bases."

"I thought you said there were 3 bases, mate."

"Well, I'm including home plate as a base."

"You mean 4th base?"

"No. Well, you can call it 4th base if you like.

"Anyway, the batter stands at home plate." Wainwright paused for a question. Fred looked up and said, "Yeh, I know what you mean."

The pitcher throws the ball at home plate. There's a catcher behind home plate who catches the ball."

Fred looked at George and said, "The keeper." And George nodded sagely.

"The batter at home plate tries to hit the ball."

George to Fred, "A beater."

"Yeh."

"If the beater, I mean the hitter, hits the ball fair, he runs for 1st base. Meanwhile the outfielders who are beyond the bases try to catch the ball on the fly, which would put the batter out."

"Chasers," George said.

"Well, maybe. Anyway, if the 'chasers' can't catch the ball on the fly, they try to throw it to one of the men playing the bases so that they can touch the runner with the ball away from one of the bases or 'force' him out by touching a base that he has to go to before he gets there."

"What's the object of the game?"

"I'm getting to that. The object is to run around the diamond, touching all the bases in order without being 'forced' out or 'tagged' out. Every player who does that scores one point for his team."

"After all that effort, you only get one measly point?" asked George. "In Quidditch, the least that you can score are ten points."

Wainwright replied, "You've got scoring inflation in that game, Mister."

"You were going to explain to us where the thinking comes in."

"Yes. For example, let's take a simple situation. Suppose that there's a runner at 1st base. The 2nd basemen and shortstop (defensive player who plays close to 2nd base) are thinking about the following things:

1. What do I do if the man on first decides to steal (Actually that's easy and they probably don't think too much about that.)
2. What do I do if the batter hits the ball to one of the basemen?
3. What do I do if the batter hits the ball to an outfielder?
4. What do I do if the hit-and-run is on?

George interrupted. "This is beginning to sound interesting. Who gets hit in the 'hit-and-run'?"

"Nobody. The hit-and-run is a set play where the batter tries to hit the ball no matter how poorly the pitcher throws it, and the runner at 1st base starts to run immediately on the pitch.

Then there's the 'run-and-hit', where . . "

George interrupted, "You already told us about that."

"No, I didn't."

"Sure you did. You distinctly said 'hit-and-run'."

"Right."

"Right." Fred agreed.

"Right." George agreed.

"So, as I was saying, the 'run-and-hit'."

"But we all agreed that you just told us about that."

"No, I just told you about the hit-and-run."

"Right?"

"Right."

"So, the 'run-and-hit' is . . . ."

"You just told about that."

"No, I didn't."

Fred, interrupted, "Blimey. You said, 'run-and-hit', right?"

"The second time right."

"And you said 'hit-and-run' the first time, right?"

"Right."

"What the bloody hell is the difference between the 'hit-and-run' and the 'run-and-hit?'"

"It's all the difference in the world. In the 'hit-and-run', the manager decides when to hit at anything and send the runner running. In the 'run-and-hit', the runner decides to run, and then the batter is obligated to try his best to hit the ball."

"The batter isn't always trying his best to hit the ball?" George asked reasonably.

"Well, yes. But if he gets a bad pitch, he doesn't have to try to hit it. He only gets 3 tries, and if he misses them all, he's out. Well, he's usually out."

"And you think that this is a thinking man's game? It seems more like a madman's game."

"Well, you have to see it to appreciate it."

"It sounds like it could be a real laugh, eh George?"

"Riiiiiight-o Fred."

At that point, we subsided to eating. After the meal, the next shift came through, and an officer asked all the 'special forces' to remain until after the next shift ate. Then we'd have orientation to life on the ship.

All of us at our table stayed there. After the shift, the duty officer went to the small podium at one end of the Mess Hall. He again asked the 'special forces' to remain. The room mostly emptied, and the duty officer began.

"Many of you may know some of these details. But a reminder is worthwhile even for the wise old heads in the room. We have lots of rules on submarines. We'll not cover them all, but the really important ones:

- The first 3 laws are that the Captain is the executive officer to God. Whenever he gives an order to jump, your first and only question is 'how high?'

- The next law is that the XO has the keys to the kingdom. Whenever he gives an order to jump, your first and only question is (followed by a pause which was answered by the company, 'How high?')
- The next law is that the lowest seaman ranks above all of you. If a seaman gives you an order to jump, (Fred and George interrupted here and said in unison, 'How high?')

"Ah, I see that we have a couple of wise guys here. You two," Fred and George looked around pretending to see who he was talking to. "Give me twenty."

Fred said, "Twenty what? Twenty seconds?"

"Let's make it thirty. On the deck, one-handed—pushups."

George, "Are you kidding. I haven't done a pushup since, well, I guess I actually haven't done one." He glanced over at me, looking for some support. I gave him a quick shake, "no."

"Let's just make it a round forty."

Fred and George made it to the deck in record time and did their best to provide forty pushups.

Everyone else was as silent as the grave. They finally struggled up on their 40th and the duty officer kept going. "OK. Now, this ship will be running silent through the entire cruise. That means no loud sounds, no arguments, no friendly disagreements.

"You all have had 'buddies' assigned. They'll show you the ropes: Where the heads are. When meals are. Where you can go and where you can't. Generally, stay away from the fore (front of the boat) and the aft (rear of the boat). That's where the weapons are, and the Engine Room is. Also, stay away from the upper decks in the middle. The bridge is there."

Fred looked over at George, and I just knew that a comment was coming, but miraculously it didn't.

The duty officer went on, "Mr. Wendt, do you want to say anything."

I walked up to the front of the room and took a deep breath. "Yes, thanks. Gentlemen. We are guests on this ship. We need to afford the crew the respect that they deserve. Please cooperate in every way that you can. Fred, George, I'd like you two to be on behavior better than your best."

"Yes, sir." They said in unison.

The duty officer came back to the front and told us that he would take us on a tour of the ship. We moved forward to the Torpedo Room. He showed us a torpedo close up. Fred had a question, "Just what does this thing do?"

"Are you looking to do some more push-ups?"

I intervened this time. "Sir, he's being straight with you. He's really never heard of a torpedo before."

The duty officer looked doubtful but went on, "Torpedoes are the anti-ship weapon of the submarine. They carry a warhead of ½ ton of high explosive. They are a small submarine in themselves. They have a guidance computer," George interrupted, "What?"

The officer looked close to meting out push-ups, but he held his peace.

I answered. "Computers are machines that can think in a simple way. They can detect ships, figure a course to intercept, and then explode to destroy the ship."

George whistled, "Nifty. That's almost as good as the Marauder's Map."

"The what?" It was the duty officer's time for a question.

I answered, "It doesn't matter. It's like a complex computer that can track people over a limited range. I'll explain later."

He went on, "Take a look at the warhead end of this." He pointed at a brief message scribbled in a distorted curve around the hemispherical front end of the torpedo, "Dear John." He went on, "This is the last time any of you will be in this room. And if we ever find any of you here again, you'll be going out of one of those tubes."

The duty officer went on with details of the shipboard life. He talked about the "head" and showers and what bulkheads were and what "silent running" was all about. At that point I could see Fred and George were struggling to hold comments in, and I actually felt sorry for them—which was a really strange feeling. He finished by taking us on a tour of the rest of the ship. It was a strange motley group of men who followed single file. There were a handful of Brits in khaki and a dozen wizards in a variety of civilian Muggle garb which might almost be mistaken for normal—that is normal if you lived in Los Angeles. There were shorts of various lengths and a few pair of slacks that were being trod on by their heels.

We went from the forward compartment and walked toward the rear of the ship. We went through a number of compartments. At each one he gave the length of the chamber. After a couple of them, I decided that I ought to try memorizing them. After several compartments we went into a very large compartment. It had vertical tubes. Of course, I knew where we were and what these were as I suppose did half of the party. The rest were gawking.

Fred asked, "What do you suppose those things are for—vertical tropedo's?"

George answered, "No, you mugg . . er. These are . . . Well, I don't know what they are."

The duty officer shook his head. "This, gentlemen, is Armageddon."

George couldn't resist, "Is that some kind of arm rest?"

The duty officer said, "I'll pretend I didn't hear that." He then glanced over at me.

I said, "The reference is to a location in the Middle East, a place where great battles were fought in history. The Bible says the last great battle will be fought there."

The duty officer walked over to one of the tubes and touched it gently. "This tube contains a weapon that could destroy all of London. Good bye Piccadilly, Good bye Leicester Square. No more Nelson memorial. No more King's Cross station. 221B Baker Street gone forever—all in an instant, in the twinkling of an eye.

"Together these tubes could kill half of the people in Europe."

Fred and George gulped in unison. "Why would anyone build something like this?"

Our guide said, "I don't know. But I would think that you might know something about that. Why else would you be here?"

Everyone was quiet for a while.

"Needless to say, this is the only time you will ever be here as well."

George said in a hollow voice, "Who would ever want to return here?"

We went on and came to the Engine Room. The duty officer commented, "This is the power supply that runs this ship, makes the lights glow, the propellers turn, the computers compute. This is probably the most dangerous room in the ship. The power that drives generators here is the same one that could destroy a city, and we have it going continuously here." He pointed into a large steel cylinder of which we only saw the top. "Inside that steel vessel is invisible death. If it breaks out, we would never feel anything, but we'd all be dead in a few days.

"There's only one important room that we haven't been in—the Conning Tower—the Control Room of this ship. It's small and we could never all fit in it at once anyway. Maybe later you'll get to see it. It's at the top of the ship. The Captain spends most of his time there. We're going to return to the Mess Hall where you'll rejoin your mentors. You'll only have them for a couple of days. Make sure you learn well from them. There will be a test later."

Everyone laughed.

"Questions?"

One of the SAS troops asked, "How long will it be before we reach our destination?"

"Nine or ten days, depending on how hard we are trying to avoid detection."

All the wizards gave a sigh.

"Oh, life on the ship is not so bad. Just keep your noses clean, and we'll all get along just fine." He directed another significant look toward George (or Fred).

Fred asked, "Sir, not meaning any disrespect, but is there something wrong?, I've been smelling something strange since I got on the ship?"

"Oh, that's just the smell of dozens of men confined in a small area for months on end."

"Months?"

"Don't worry, by the time you've been on board a couple of weeks you'll not even notice it."

Another of the SAS asked if there was some way to keep fit on board.

"We've got a small gym with weights and elliptical exercise equipment. Have your mentor show it to you."

After a moment of silence, "Any other questions? Questions, anyone? No questions? Then you're dismissed."

On the way back to the Mess Hall, I asked the SAS officer who had the exercise question, "Do you know how to use, what was it, an elliptical something?"

"Yes, sir."

"Would you mind giving me some training on it sometime?"

"It'd be my "f"ing pleasure to do something normal for a change. I'll find it and then take you there before breakfast for a good workout."

"Yeh, thanks." I wasn't so sure that I wanted what he would call a good workout, but I did want to keep myself in jogging trim.

There's not much to do on a sub if you're just a passenger. So, I actually spent a fair amount of time in the little gym over the next couple of days.

Fun on the Run

The next day, I was in the cabin I shared with the Executive Officer when there was a rap on the door. I said, "Enter."

Fred, George and Rupert Shin filled up what little room was left. Fred opened the conversation, "We've been thinking."

I couldn't help myself and replied, "Now, how many times have I told you lads to not play with sharp toys."

George: "Yeh, well with Fred it's more of a blunt instrument."

Rupert interrupted, "Look, here's the thing. How could those things that Muggle said about destroying London be true? If they really had that much power, they should be able to make chutney of He Who Must Not Be Named. Why are we sneaking around? We should just get them to destroy him."

I took a deep breath. How did you explain to a wizard the "magic" of modern science? I started slowly. "Look, you've got the wrong idea about this. Muggle 'science' is nothing like wizard magic.

"Yes, they both have great power, but they're different. Muggle 'science' is raw power. Yes, we can destroy a whole city at our whim. But we can't direct that power intelligently. We can't aim it precisely. We can't direct them at one person. We can only kill millions of people. We could only make ourselves as evil as Tom Riddle.

"By the way," I had begun to warm to my subject. "As long as you're in my command, you'll never call him 'He Who Must Not Be Named' or his other pet titles. To us, he's just plain Tom Riddle. OR, I've begun thinking about calling him Tommy Lad. He doesn't begin to deserve to be called Lord anything.

"You see magic has great power, but you don't appreciate its real amazing abilities because you're so used to it. You don't see the staggering intelligence that stands behind it. I can't begin to imagine how strange it is.

"Think." I looked at the three of them and they didn't get it. "Don't you realize how hard even the simplest spell is!

"Look! I've been working with some brilliant people trying to get our version of 'magic'—computers—to recognize Riddle and a few of his top lieutenants. You can't imagine how incredibly hard that is. The youngest child can recognize him or any number of people without the least thought. You don't even have to have magic to do that! But try to devise a computer program to do that. Try to get a computer to recognize a person —any person—and distinguish him from a light pole. It breaks the head of the smartest Muggles to do that! But magic! The simplest spells can do things far more complex than that.

"You drop a glass of water, and it breaks. You flick your wand and say, '*Repairo* and *voila!*' The glass reconstructs itself as though nothing had happened to it! I can't even begin to imagine how to instruct a computer to do that.

"Doesn't it scare you to death! Aren't you scared silly that magic can do such difficult things without any conscious thought on your part! That's what scares me! When I first saw real magic, I didn't think too much about it either, but then it began to sink in what's really going on.

"Fred, George, your dad's thought about it. Didn't he once say that you shouldn't trust anything that could think if you didn't know where it kept its brains? Well, where does magic keep its brains? Everything that you can do with magic requires tons of brains—more than we all have together. Where are those brains? How do you know that those brains aren't going to turn their attention to something else? Forget about making chutney of us. If they just turn their brains elsewhere, what happens to all magic and all wizards?"

They had all been staring at the floor during my tirade, and George looked up, "Well, , , if you're going to look on the dark side of everything . . ."

I was forced to laugh. "You're right. There's nothing we can do about that issue but hope that the world doesn't turn really crazy before we get finished.

"But that's why we can't turn this staggering Muggle power against Riddle. We can't begin to aim it!"

Rupert just said, "Yeh, I guess you're right—about it all."

Just then there was a knock on the door. I was standing closest to the door, so I opened it. It was one of the lieutenants. "Gentlemen, we have a

338

little exercise for you. The XO wants you to learn your way around the ship."

It sounded pretty innocent. We stepped outside,and we discovered that he had several black cloths in his hand. "Please tie these around your head so that your eyes are covered."

George asked, "What's going on?"

"The XO thinks that you ought to be able to find your way around without a guide in case the power's out. What we're going to do is this: You're going to put the blind folds on, and I'm going to give you a destination to go to. Then, we're all going to walk there."

Fred, "Sounds easy. You're going to tell us which way to go, yes?"

"No, I'm along just to make sure you don't walk into the Torpedo Room."

No one was anxious to start, but we all did. I took one quick look around to be sure that I knew which way I was pointed. The officer, Higgins, made sure that we couldn't see anything and got us going. The first thing that happened was that I fell over George or maybe it was Fred. Rupert did a little better. He got started off, and then we heard a sharp, "Ow!" It turned out that he had headed for a hatch, but had forgotten to bend down to go through it.

"Well, gentlemen, I think that you should maybe hold hands and get going." We managed to find each other, took hands, and let Rupert lead us. He got through the first hatch.

"Didn't you gentlemen memorize where the hatches to other decks are?"

I was ready to tell him what he could memorize. We ended up on our hands and knees feeling our way around.

The lieutenant said, "Mr. Weasley."

George suddenly lost his sense of humor.

"I was thinking that you could take the lead, Mr. Weasley."

George said, "I don't suppose you mean Fred?"

"No, you Mr. Weasley."

The lieutenant must have reordered us with George in the lead. He led us for a while without incident, and then I heard a shout of "What the . . .?" Apparently, George had hit some obstacle. We later learned that he had hit his head on the bulkhead when he tried stepping through a hatch. Before we were finished, we'd all had a shot at the blind leading the blind.

When we'd finally stopped and took off the blindfolds we found that we were at the forward head. I decided that I was going to take a few walking tours of the ship without blindfolds. We staggered back to the Mess Hall and talked over the adventure of the last half hour.

Fred said, "I was hoping that one of you had a good idea where we were going."

George, "Why the heck does the Captain put us through all this?"

Rupert, "I think that he's got the idea that we might actually have to fight Deatheaters in this ship, and he wants us to know it better than anyone in the crew."

I agreed. "Yes, there's an expression called 'fighting the ship.'"

George, "That does it, I am absolutely not fighting this ship. It's way too big. We're not in the same weight class at all."

I laughed. I was glad that George was keeping his sense of humor. "What that means is using the ship in a fight, but you have to know the ship inside and out to really do that. We're learning the ship inside and . . ."

Fred interrupted, "I'm NOT going to learn the outside of this ship."

I added, "I hope not. Although there was this disciplinary practice called 'keel-hauling' that I wouldn't entirely rule out in your case."

"Well, I'm going to know this ship without having to bump my head against every bulk-head in it."

There was general agreement about that. After lunch we went exploring in the ship, going everywhere that wasn't locked down. Fred commented that he was glad the ladders didn't have a habit of moving every now and then like the stairs at Hogwarts.

Later that night at evening mess, I found the XO and asked if I could talk with him in our joint quarters. Wainwright agreed. Later that night in our cabin I asked, "How long before we reach our destination?"

He got out his pipe, slowly cleaned it, and loaded it. "I suppose that I could claim that was privileged information but it isn't to you. The last course check that I did gave us a little over 6 days."

"Do you think that we'll be ready by the time we get there?"

"Oh, this crew is ready now. What about your lot?"

The Missile Room

I was surprised one morning to hear the public address system to boom out, "Mr. Wendt, Mr. Wendt. Report to the captain's cabin on the double." I was rather surprised, but I broke out into a trot. I supposed that "on the double" meant at least a trot. I climbed a deck and found my way to the officers' quarters. The captain's cabin was near the XO's and mine, but I rarely saw him even by chance entering or leaving his cabin. The door was closed. I hesitated a moment and took a calming breath (calming, hell) and knocked.

I recognized the Captain's voice, "Enter." I opened the door and tried to stride in confidently. I'd only been in the cabin once, and it was pretty much as I remembered. The XO was even sitting in the same seat that he sat in when I was last here. The only real change from the last time was that George and Fred weren't there.

"Mr. Wendt, we need to have a little talk." The Captain was relaxed, even leaning back a bit in his chair. The XO didn't look particularly relaxed. The Captain continued.

"Our last talk in this cabin got me to thinking." He hesitated, and I thought about asking him what he was thinking about. I glanced at the XO, and he seemed to be willing me to hold my piece. Perhaps he was, and perhaps it was just a Zen sense I felt. I waited. After a moment he continued.

"In a couple of weeks we're going to be fighting this ship against an enemy that I don't understand in the slightest. That frightens me. Should it?"

"I think it should."

"Good. I've particularly been thinking of what you call the "Imperial Curse", is it?"

"No, sir. It's called the *'Imperious Curse'*."

"Right. Do I understand correctly, that if I and my crew were subjected to that curse we might be forced to do anything that the Deatheater wanted?"

"Before I answer that, I'd like you to agree to let me bring in George and Fred to amplify on my answer."

He frowned but he didn't look over to the XO for even an instant. "Ageed."

"Then, yes, that's the gist of it."

"For example, could my XO and I be forced to take this key?" He pulled the chain with his "dog" tags out. There was a small odd-shaped key on it. "And the XO could be forced to take his key. We could be forced to put them in their locks. Then we would have to turn them simultaneously and press the firing button for one or more of those Gems in the Death Locker."

I'd never heard that term before, but it was perfectly obvious what he was talking about. "Yes. That's the idea. Now, theoretically, it's possible to resist the *Imperious Curse*. As a matter of fact I know someone who actually has done it."

He went on, "Shit. The damage someone could do with this ship! Thank God, they're none of them pointed at the US or Britain and thank God no one on this ship knows how to reprogram them. It's not simple to go through the firing sequence. Could someone force us to go through a long series of complex acts against our will?

"Honestly, I don't know for sure, but I think they could. I think that they wouldn't even consider using this ship. They would think that it was beneath their dignity to use a 'Muggle' weapon like a submarine."

The Captain looked at me as though I were stark raving mad. "You're crazy. This is the most powerful single weapon in the world. Why wouldn't they want to use it!" He finished by pounding his desk.

"Sir, I understand that there is a statue in the courtyard of the Ministry of Magic that appears to be a man sitting on a throne. Closer inspection reveals that the throne is actually composed of hundreds of people. The people of the throne are Muggles. How could someone with such an attitude toward Muggles even think of using a Muggle tool?"

The Captain shrugged. He looked over at Wainwright. "What do you think, XO?"

"I think that you don't call the chief engineer up here with the intention of not trusting his judgment. We have a couple of dozen wizards on board and one Muggle who has lived with them for years. When we submerged on this mission not a week ago, neither you nor I realized that there were real wizards and that we were Muggles. Whom can we trust if not Mr. Wendt?"

The Captain said, "I don't doubt his judgment of ninety-nine out of one hundred wizards, maybe even nine hundred ninety-nine out of one thousand. But I don't trust his or my judgment of the one thousandth."

I re-iterated, "It's really time to call Fred and George."

"Not yet. Is there any limit on how long this curse lasts?"

"Again, I'm not sure. It does wear off in time, but the time is measured at least in days, probably in weeks, maybe in months."

"Could one of us be trained to resist it, or better, both of us?"

"Like I said, theoretically, yes."

"But …"

"But, it's virtually impossible. The only person I know who succeeded was an exceptional wizard with a tremendous will power who had trained for weeks to do it. If you're thinking that you or the XO could train yourselves before this mission to resist the *Imperious Curse*, forget it. I think it's impossible on such short notice, maybe even impossible with any amount of training."

He frowned again. He picked up the phone handset on his deck, punched a couple of numbers and when someone apparently answered he said, "Send the word for the two Mr. Weasleys to the Captain's cabin." He hesitated a moment and then hung up the receiver. I heard the call for the two Mr. Weasleys go out over the public address system and a mild tap on the door a couple of minutes later. They apparently had been standing nearby or had trotted as well as I could.

"Enter."

The two walked in with heads held a bit low as if they were expecting a "pranging", but what they got was quite civil. "Gentlemen, please take a seat. Mr. Wendt has a few questions for you. Will you please answer them succinctly?"

They answered in unison, "Yes, sir."

I looked over at them and asked, "Let's suppose that the crew of this ship were put under the *Imperious Curse*. Could they be forced to fire the torpedos?"

Fred and George were acting amazingly in sync. They were usually fighting each other verbally. "You bet."

"At a ship full of people."

More soberly, "Yes."

"Knowing they would kill hundreds or thousands of Muggles?"

They looked at each other before answering. Fred took the lead, "I'm sure of it. The things that an experienced wizard like Barty Crouch did were scary."

The Captain broke in, "Could you train me to resist the *Imperious Curse*."

George answered, "In a couple of months maybe. I don't know. You are a Muggle." He added quickly, "No offense implied."

The Captain said graciously, "None taken."

"I'd like you to demonstrate the *"Imperious Curse."*"

I broke in, "Can either of you perform the 'Imperious'?"

George answered, "Yes. Fred and I have been practicing on each other, trying to train ourselves to resist it."

Fred asked, "Who should we perform it on? Mr. Wainwright?"

The Captain shook his head. "No. Me."

Fred took a long breath. In the moment of silence the Captain continued, "I'd like to try to resist it. What can you tell me about how to do that?"

"Well... I don't know what to say. Neither Fred or I have been able to."

"Well then, what does it feel like when the 'Imperious' is put on you."

George, "That is easy, at least. The feeling is one of utter relaxation. You feel that you don't have a worry in the world."

"Well then, give me a moment to prepare, and then I'll nod when I'm ready."

"OK. What do you want me to command you to do?"

The Captain thought for a moment and then said, "Moon the XO."

The Captain seemed to be meditating for a moment and then nodded.

Fred, pulled his wand from his sleeve and soundlessly spoke the curse.

The Captain for 10 seconds that seemed to last an eternity sat motionless. Then, he climbed on top of the desk, pointed his rear end at the XO, and lowered his trousers. Then he seemed to become aware of what had happened. He rapidly pulled his pants up and got down off the table. He sat for a moment thinking. Then he simply said, "Dismissed."

When the Captain gives an order with no obvious recipient, everyone had better take it as directed specifically at them. We all quickly rose, and Fred was already out the door when he said, "Not you, XO. Let's talk."

Fred, George, and I were half-way down the companionway before anyone spoke. Fred asked, "What do you think the Captain's thinking about?"

"I haven't the slightest idea what he's thinking, and that really scares me."

George looked over and smiled. "I've never seen a time when you didn't have an idea. Come on. What's going on back in the Captains cabin?"

"Oh, I know what's happening. They're trying to decide what to do if a 'wheel comes off' our scheme."

"'A wheel comes off?' What are you talking about?"

"Oh, it's an old Muggle saying. For thousands of years Muggles have been transporting things by cars and carts and wagons. You can't image what kind of havoc ensues when a wheel drops off a car if you're going at 100 klicks/hour. If you're in the car, and you're not wearing a seat belt, you may fly out the window. That's an unpleasant experience, let me assure you."

"Can't you levitate the thing or something?"

"No. Anyway, they're trying to figure out what to do if 'a wheel comes off' of this operation, and all you wizards are killed or captured. We'd be at the mercy of the Deatheaters."

"OOH, ooh, I know what happens. You're SQL." Said Fred.

"Where did you ever hear that? I've never heard either a Muggle or a wizard use that phrase."

"Oh, I've been talking with some of the sailors."

I thought a minute. "Are you sure it wasn't SOL?"

George interjected, "You know, it might just have been SOL."

"Well, the upper brass don't believe in SOL." I told them.

"What do they believe in?"

"In the Navy, good planning. They're trying to plan something to prevent being SOL. And I've no idea what they'll come up with."

George asked, "But surely you can find out. You've got pull with them."

"I'll ask Wainwright, but I doubt he'll say anything. For that situation, I think that they want the fewest number of people to know what they've got up their sleeves. You know that anything that an Imperioused person knows the Imperiouser will know shortly too."

"Well, you work on him. And, you know, what if we were to Imp..."

"Don't you even think of that! I'll see what we can get out of him."

I then went to the gym to work out, and I don't know where the Weasley's went.

The next couple of days were the hardest I've ever spent. There was nothing much we could do—other than wait and worry.

Planning

The Captain had called a meeting to review the attack plan. The Weasley's, Wainwright, and the Lieutenant in command of the SAS forces all were present in the Wardroom. We each had a copy of the notebook that I'd help write along with the Weasleys. We sat down. The ranking officer interrupted the conversation, "Captain in the Wardroom." We all stood immediately to attention.

"At ease. Let's get started."

I'd conducted these before, but I'd always been the highest ranking person in the room.

I began, "Let's just go sequentially through the mainline of the plan assuming that everything happens by the book. Then we'll take the main branches where thing go off-plan.

"OK, the Captain delivers us to our objective, which is just a set of coordinates off the coast of Scotland. The moon is just short of new. We come near the surface and raise the radio mast. We make contact with the SAS snipers."

"What happens if we can't make contact?" That was the Captain's question. We were off my plan already.

"OK, the book says turn to page 115." I couldn't remember what the plan said for this in detail. Page 115 said, "The ship orbits the target coordinates for up to 3 hours, trying to make contact. If there is no contact, crash dive and proceed at flank speed to the fallback coordinates. If contact is made, but the ground team can't start the mission, remain at the fallback coordinates until the SAS team is ready. If contact is made, and the ground team can proceed, return to page 7."

Back on page 7, the next step was for the sniper team to kill the guards. At this point we had an interruption from George, "Look, I've never liked this idea about killing the guards without warning."

The Captain was strangely silent. I glanced over to make sure he didn't have anything to say. No word from him, so I improvised, "I don't like it either, but we've been over this a lot of times. Nobody likes this less than I do, but unless you or someone comes up with a better idea, we're stuck with it."

Wainwright asked, "What about magic. Can you guys stun someone from 1500 meters?"

Fred was gloomy, "No. And we can't fly up to get closer because Azkaban has spells that prevent unauthorized disapparation, flying, and probably a bunch of other things we don't know about."

Wainwright mumbled, "Great."

The Captain asked, "It's pitch black when we're going to do this. Can wizards see in pitch black?"

"No", I answered. There were probably special exceptions, but this wasn't the time for it. "So, what are you getting at?"

"Blasting in the door will alert everyone, what does it matter if the guards find out the same time as everyone else."

I thought quickly. We'd talked about this. George answered, "If the guards on the roof are still working, they would light up the grounds and . . ."

"And we'd lose the only real advantage we have over wizards—being able to see in the dark." I went on, "that would make it really dangerous for the people on the ground."

Fred said, "I know the wizards we've got with us. I'm sure that they'd accept the additional danger to avoid killing people without warning."

I asked, "Even Deatheaters?"

"Yeh, even Deatheaters, especially Deatheaters. Aren't we any better than them?"

The SAS officer, O'Brian, cut in, "Look that's fine for your men, but I'm not going to lead my men into more danger than they have to be in." There was a hard edge to his voice that I didn't entirely like. The Captain swung swiftly around and looked hard at him. O'Brian seemed to understand that he was on the edge with the last absolute monarch, and his face softened and seemed to sink back into itself.

I went on. "Besides that, there's a much bigger issue. If we aren't completely successful, the Deatheaters are going to know that Muggles are aware of them and fighting back. That's not good for anyone—Muggles, Wizard resistance—we're all in big trouble, especially innocent Muggles if that happens.

"We can't take any chances. So . . ." I let it hang. No one else spoke for a long minute, and then I went on, "Let's get on with it."

We worked through getting the troops out to the island that Azkaban is built on. Then the ascent of the rock face, demolition of the main entrance, and so on.

Waveguide

One morning I was in the wardroom reading the latest edition of *Scientific American* that I had been able to bring when I packed. It was at least a month behind the latest edition, but it was the best that I could do. The intercom turned on, and I heard an announcement that seemed to say, "Mr. Wendt, Mr. Wendt, report to the con immediately." I could have sworn that I heard my name. And I had. The announcement was repeated, "Mr. Wendt, Mr. Wendt, report to the con."

I knew that I didn't have to rush, but there were two reasons that I did. First, the captain of any ship is an imposing figure. Even if you aren't technically in his command, there is such universal deference to the captain on any ship that you begin to feel it and respect it. Second, there was a certain air of urgency in the voice over the intercom that I detected or thought that I'd detected. So, I trotted. It's hard to do on a submarine. It turns into a kind of sideways fast step. Anyway I was trying to get up to the con as quickly as I could. As I entered a companionway, I saw George and Fred.

Fred asked, "What fire are you off to?"

"You must have heard the announcement. I'm supposed to report to the con."

"Sure, we heard it, but when was the last time that you moved fast?" George asked.

Fred responded, "Don't you remember?"

"Was it when we set his pants on fire in 3rd year?"

"No, nooo. It was when we materialized the habaneras in his stew in 4th year."

I was moving again. "Just don't let it happen again."

I was panting slightly when I reached the Bridge. "Mr. Wendt reporting, sir."

The Captain was looking over the chart table. He turned and said to me. "Thank you, Mr. Wendt. Please accompany Mr. Wainwright and me on a little tour of the ship."

"Yes, sir."

He led the way back down the companionway, and we walked silently down to the lower decks and then on to the forward compartments. We kept going and going, and then the Captain stopped, turned to us, and said, "You and Mr. Wainwright will stay here for a few minutes." He went on to the forward Torpedo Room. We couldn't hear precisely what was said there, except for the crisp, "Captain on the deck" as he entered the Torpedo Room.

After several minutes lazed by, we saw the crew troop out of the Torpedo Room. After they had left the compartment that we were in, Wainwright led me into the Torpedo Room.

Wainwright hung back, closed the bulkhead, and dogged it shut. It was beginning to seem ominous, or maybe I should say more ominous.

The Captain turned to me and asked, "Do you remember the conversation that we had about the Unforgettable curses? You know, the Impervious, the Cruciotus."

I had a hard time trying to keep a straight face. "Yes."

"Mr. Wainwright and I have been thinking about how to defend ourselves from them."

"But, it's not pos…"

The Captain cut me off. "I know. I know, but we had an idea that we want to show you."

He looked at Wainwright, who palmed something small and handed it to me, "Take a look."

It was a simple plastic box with a button on it. It was about 3 cm on a side, roughly cubical. "OK, I give up. What is it?"

Wainwright answered me indirectly. "The real danger is that a Deatheater would get control of this ship and crew. It would be a terrible weapon that could kill millions of innocent people."

"Agreed. So, what does this remote control, control?" I figured that it must be a remote.

Wainwright pulled a low stool over next to the business end of a torpedo. "Climb up there and look on the other side of that 'torp.'"

I climbed and grabbed hold of the warhead so that I could support myself as I stretched around the cylinder of destruction. The other side of the warhead had a small box on it roughly the same size as the one in my hand. I looked for a long moment in stunned silence and then said, "That's a detonator, isn't it!"

"Yes."

"And this is the button that sets it off."

"Right again. Push it."

"You've got to be kidding. I'm not ready for the afterlife quite yet."

"It's OK. Nothing will happen."

Hesitantly, I pushed the button. It lit and flashed.

Wainwright went on, "You have about 20 seconds to push the button. If you don't the thing goes bang."

I quickly pushed it while it was still flashing, and the flashing stopped. "Well, that will take 10 years off you. So, your idea is that if something bad happens, like one of you gets Imperioused, then I'm supposed to push this button and… what exactly will happen when that detonates?"

"Well, there's another detonator on the warhead opposite this one. When they go off. Well, there will probably be one or two others go off at the same time even though the book says that they shouldn't. Anyway, one of those would make a pretty good hole in an aircraft carrier. On this ship, the entire Torpedo Room would be obliterated and probably a good bit of the next compartment or two. This end of the ship would flood with water, and the ship would point its nose straight down and we would be on a voyage to the bottom of the sea."

"And you expect me to commit suicide?"

"To keep this ship out of the hands of Deatheaters—yes. And besides, it might not be suicide for you. You'd be in the conning tower—pretty far away from harm's way. Where we'd be would be in shallow water—well above crush depth. You and maybe half of the crew could escape the ship through emergency hatches."

The Captain added. "We expect to use this anyway ourselves. We don't even have one for you. It's strictly against regs to give a non-officer a means of scuttling the ship."

"But then, why show me all this?"

"It's just in case we're … uh … incapacitated. Then you need to know that we carry these next to our dog tags."

"You do realize that if you're Imperioused, you wouldn't want to cooperate with me blowing this ship to 'kingdom come'."

"We're counting on you to be persistent."

"Right… By the way, just a little technical question. With all this metal around here, how does this transmitter work? Wouldn't it be shielded?"

Wainwright answered. "Good question. We had to think hard on that one. We finally realized that there's a natural transmission mechanism in the ship. There're a couple of conduits that carry the data cables and power lines through the ship. They form a kind of natural wave guide that lets radio transmit up and down them. The access ports are covered by clear plastic. The radio waves escape through those. But here's the catch. You have to open one and put the transmitter inside when you push the button. Here, I'll show you where the access port is." He walked over to the wall near a table with a couple of computer monitors on it and sure enough, there was an oval clear plastic window in the wall

I said, "Look. This seems really well thought out, but I'd really like to include Fred and George in this discussion. They might think of something critical to this really working. "

The Captain said, "No can do. We need something up our sleeve that no wizard knows about—something that can give us the upper hand in an extreme emergency."

"I don't think that I'd call blowing yourself to bits as having the upper hand."

Wainwright said, "Don't be a bad sport. You can't have your way all the time. By the way, is there any way that those two jokers could find out about this?"

"Not if I don't tell them."

"They can't Imperious you?"

"They could but they wouldn't."

"And you wouldn't tell them?"

"No."

"Then you're dismissed."

"Thanks."

I headed back for the Wardroom where I'd left my *Scientific American* but with lots of nagging doubts that I just couldn't forget.

The Island

The four men had been working their way across the rock strewn ascent toward the cliffs that overlooked the dark tower. They were still three kilometers away and the sun had gone down about a half hour earlier. They stopped and took the nap sacks off their backs. It was dark, but a sharp-eyed observer would have seen them take out several long thin objects. They didn't speak a word.

The lieutenant quickly assembled his rifle and attached the sniper scope. He knew that his team was very close to finished with their rifles. They were all wearing night vision goggles. He signaled that they needed to start moving. As they approached the cliff, he assigned them their locations. He would take the center as the other three fanned out to take up positions that gave them very different sight lines to the tower. He picked his spot. He rested the rifle on a rock that gave him a good sight line to one of the guards on the tower. He removed the goggles and looked through the sniper scope. He had a good view of the top parapet of the tower and the three guards pacing there. He turned on his radio, "D1 to team. Pick your targets. D4 is backup if any of us miss, the man's yours."

"D2. I've got the middle height one."

"D3. I've got the short one."

"D1. That leaves me with the heavy one."

He looked through the scope and put the crosshairs on the heavy-set tall one. He watched his movements. He picked a spot that his man favored to make the target spot for his crosshairs. Now, it was waiting. He had waited for days before. But this time should be short.

After 42 minutes, radio silence was broken.

"O to D1."

"Go."

"Blackberry jam"

"Oat Bran bread."

"Are you ready to execute?"

D1, "Sound off."

"D2, ready."

"D3, ready."

"D4, ready."

"D1, ready."

O, "X at will."

D1, "On the count of 3. Anyone not ready sound off." He took a deep breath, as he knew the others were. He put the crosshairs on the target. He started a slow count, "D1, One… Two… Three." He heard the three muffled pops, his own fairly loud in his ears. The others were much quieter but audible to anyone listening for them. All three atop the tower slipped below view.

"D1 to O. Finished."

"D1 to team. Give it 5 minutes to make sure that no one shows up on the tower, then go to your staging point."

The time went slowly. No one showed up. Six minutes went by, and he silently backed off from the cliff and started back. He joined the others and took the rear point. He wasn't going to be ambushed from behind.

He had this feeling that there was somebody behind him. It was spooky. He'd been on several missions, but he'd never had such a feeling of hair on the back of his neck standing up before. He was constantly scanning the horizon for … what? That was it. What was he looking for? He didn't know. In all his other missions he had an idea what he might be up against if things went "south". Here, he had no idea what to expect— and that was an idea that he didn't like at all.

They were almost to the staging point. He recognized the large rock in the shelter of which they'd hid early in the evening. He tripped over something. He didn't completely lose his balance, but he stumbled. Was there something more than a small rock that had tripped him? Had he felt something on his ankle? He decided to leap to the side. He raised his sidearm and flicked the safety off as he fell to the ground on his side. He was ready to fire where his feet had been. The other three all swung around and had their guns up and pointed in the same general direction that he had. Nobody saw anything unusual.

He signaled to the others to go on to the staging point. He stayed back there, keeping his eyes mobile, prepared.

When they got there, he said, "Let's make this quick. I want to get out of here." Jason, asked, "Do you want to jog to the HumV?" He thought about it a moment as they quickly dis-assembled the rifles, slung the knap sacks on their backs, and started off. He took the rear again and had his service pistol out on safety—just in case. He finally decided that he should stick to the plan. "No. Let's concentrate on stealth." He hoped it was a good decision.

In another half-hour, they reached the road that was little more than a cow path. In the barren fields there was practically no cover, so they'd simply left it parked on the road. They were all extra careful checking the vehicle for booby traps, trip wires, anything out of the ordinary. They finally decided that no one had not been meddled with it. Somehow, he was convinced that if it had been meddled with they'd have no way of knowing.

He took the wheel, and Jason took shotgun, literally. He pulled a shotgun from beneath the passenger seat. The others had their service pistols out and were scanning the rear as the engine turned over and purred. He didn't switch on the lights. Instead he used the night vision goggles. He slowly accelerated down the road. They had decided to run without lights for at least 10 Km before turning them on. They could only travel at about 60 klicks per hour without headlights. They finally passed that point, and he decided to turn on the lights just before rounding a curve. He took off his goggles and switched on the headlights. He immediately speeded up to 100 Km/hr. That was as fast as the HumV could manage on a road like this, but it wasn't fast enough for him. Even at that speed it was pretty quiet. He could see the lights of a farm house up ahead.

He kept going past it at full speed, and the road changed character. It was now really paved, and he dialed it up a notch to 120. He knew they were only a few minutes from a small town, and he'd have to slow down shortly, but it felt good to be putting two Km behind him every minute. He only wished it could be more.

They slowed to 45 for the crossroads of the town. After they passed it, he speeded up, and they all started talking at once. Somehow, passing obvious habitation had changed the game. They were now in the "real" world, where they could depend on machines and bullets to work if they had to. Jason started talking about the World Cup and for the first time he felt like he might just get to see it. They wanted to put another 100 Km behind them before they stopped for the night. He thought they might just improvise and push on another 200 Km.

The Conference

The Mess had been cleared, and the small group was sitting at the table. The various group leaders were reporting on the drill. The Captain was dressing them down for their inefficiencies. He turned his attention to me, "What was your evaluation of the drill?"

I looked around the group. "Well, the wizards had trouble with the rolling ship. Getting down to the rafts took a half-hour. We want that to take less time than 10 minutes. It was even harder and longer for them to ascend the cliff. We'll all be dead, if it takes that long when we really attack Azkaban. The snipers were perfectly on schedule. Once the team finally got up to the building everything went pretty much according to plan. I think that only one defender would have had time to disapparate. That would sink us too, but it was a lot less disastrous than the rest. The prisoners got down to the rafts almost as fast as we planned and up to the deck of the sub from the rafts. All in all, we just have to shave an hour off the operation."

"And where do you think that hour's going to come from?"

'Practice?"

"Tomorrow night at the same time. This time there'll be serious discipline for people who cost us time."

Fred said, "Just because I fell in the sea is no reason to punish me. It was its own punishment. Believe me. I have no intention of ending up in the water again."

The Captain just frowned at Fred, and it was clear that he was unhappy.

George asked me, "What do you think the Captain means by 'serious discipline'?"

I looked at George as though he were a moron, which I thought he was. "I don't want to ever have the slightest idea what he means."

The brothers said, "Oh, yeah."

The next morning at 7 AM, I was in the Weasley's cabin rolling them out of bunks. "Rise and shine. Your day's begun."

"Oh, give us a break! The sun's not up yet."

"Right you are. Just the perfect time to practice mounting and dismounting the ship. No breakfast for you two until you're perfect."

Once they got dressed, we found the duty officer and had him assign us a couple of seamen. We wanted them to help us get a couple of rafts out and the netting over the side so that they could practice climbing up and down. It was dark when we started. All of the wizards on the team had to practice, time after time, climbing and descending the side of the sub on the net. I timed them, and they were finally getting close to the time that we'd set aside for it. We took a couple of breaks during the practice, and during the last of those, Fred challenged me to do better than he had.

"I'm not going to be going to the island"

"But you find it pretty easy to stand up here and criticize us." George said.

"I'm encouraging you."

One of the other wizards said, "It'd encourage me to see you try it."

I finally relented, "OK. I'll do it now." Fortunately, it was beginning to become light. I grabbed the top rung of the net and went over the side. I caught a rung and let myself down. I tried not to look down or think about the cold water underneath. I got into the rhythm of the swing of the net and got down to the raft in decent time. A seaman clapped me on the back and said, "Good job."

Then I turned around and started up. It was not so hard going up. I was getting used to the sway of the netting. As I approached the top and began to pat myself on the back for doing a pretty good job of it, something happened. The next rung that I was putting my right foot on seemed to dissolve just as I started to put weight on it. Caught unawares, I slipped, and in slow motion felt my grip on other rungs slip away. I fell and landed in the drink. A seaman grabbed me immediately and pulled me out. The water was bitter cold. It was lucky he grabbed me right away. Even so, I was drenched. One of the seaman accompanied me up the side again. This time we got to the top OK. The wizards on the deck were laughing hilariously.

I said, "I saw that, whichever one of you did it."

Everyone showed mock surprise and laughed the harder. I went below to find dry clothes and some warmth. George reported later. "It went fine.

We ended up having pretty good times. I think we'll be ready tonight when we go through the dry run again."

"I hope so. Let's go down to the Mess and get some tea."

In the mess, there were a scattering of off-duty seaman and the XO. I sat down at his table. He greeted us and asked, "Well, Wendt, I hear that you're a great swimmer."

"That's what you hear is it?"

"Sure, everyone was really impressed by your dive off the deck. I wish I'd been there to see it."

'I'll have to arrange a repeat performance some day."

"You're really becoming a favorite of the crew. The scuttle-butt is that there isn't anything that you won't do for a buck."

"Oh, why do they think that I took that dive?"

"Everyone figures someone bet you that you wouldn't jump in the drink, and you won the bet."

I looked over at George and asked, "Did anyone encourage that story?"

"If you're thinking of me, I'm completely innocent."

"Right."

We talked about the weather, and what it would be like when we arrived at Azkaban. The XO figured that if the drill went perfectly tonight, we'd ship out the next day and arrive in the neighborhood the next night. We'd spend a day prepping, and that night, we'd go ahead with the operation. However, he added, "That assumes all the planets line up right, and nobody sneezes."

George asked, "I didn't know you guys used astrology?"

The XO laughed and said, "It's just a figure of speech. No, we don't use astrology."

We finished our tea in silence, and I suggested that we get a nap before the evening. George wasn't interested in that, but I went back to my room and caught a nap. It's amazingly easy to do that because after a few days, you lose your sense of time, and numbers on a watch are just that—numbers.

That evening, we assembled on the deck. The wizards were wearing dark wet suits and had pouches slung over their backs that contained equipment, including wands, I supposed. I had night vision binoculars. The XO was there with his stop-watch. He gave the signal,and the Naval marines went over the side, inflated the rafts, and signaled silently for the wizards to go. As a matter of fact, the deck was as quiet as though I were standing alone in the middle of a remote desert. I checked my stop-watch occasionally and found that everything was moving a lot more smoothly–

within our schedule. The motorized rafts were away and on their way to the lighthouse that we'd chosen for the exercise. I watched them with my binoculars. Everything was going smoothly.

They arrived at the rocky edge of the shore and deployed the net to climb the steep, almost cliff-like shore. The XO broke the silence, "I don't get it. They could disapparate up to the lighthouse level without all the effort. Why don't they?"

I shook my head, "No one's sure just where the limit of the anti-disapparation spell is. We don't want to take chances. We practice the worst possibility."

Riddle

The Bridge was lit by subdued light. There were several monitors set up above the head levels of most of the crew. One showed a dark seascape with an indistinct dark shape. I knew that it was a large raft with several sailors, a couple of my guys and, in particular, George. Another screen showed a similar view but no low dark shape. Instead another dark vertical form showed.

The 3rd camera showed a scene on the outside of the sub. I saw a profile of the prow of the boat with a couple of dark shapes outlined in green that must have been sailors and maybe a few of my men. The 4th camera showed nothing but black.

It was deadly silent on the Bridge. There were a few people paying attention to the screens but the rest were paying attention to their stations. The Captain and the 2nd officer were on the Bridge watching the screens. One of the screens began to show details—a dark tower outlined in green. The tower kept growing in size and rising higher. There were rough shapes showing up—I knew they were rocks on the island the tower was on. We watched as figures started to climb the rocks. They stopped at the top. A speaker somewhere on the Bridge came alive, "Echo 1 to O. We're ready."

The Captain picked up a mike and keyed it. He said, "O to Echo 1. Ready. Over. O to D1. Ready."

"D1. Ready. All targets in scope. Over."

The Captain looked around the Bridge. #2 nodded. "O to all teams, execute."

"D1 to O. Complete."

The screen at the upper right showed a wildly bouncing scene. Then the camera was above the rocks and the tower was fairly clear with a large door showing clearly. Then a couple of SAS people ran up to the door, and they placed something on the hinges of the doors. The camera backed away and pointed toward the ground, while the SAS people ran around the tower. Then there was a flash of light, and the camera pointed toward the doorway. The doors had been blown clear of the hinges, and there were a couple of dozen men in dark robes running into the brightly lit interior of the tower. There were flashes of light visible through the door.

Then suddenly there was a flash of light in the conning tower. I swung around and saw a preternaturally thing figure in dark robes. It took me a couple of seconds to realize what had happened. The dark red eyes of the figure were pointing at the Captain. I started to shout, but one of the sailors on the Bridge unslung the assault rifle that he carried over his shoulder and raised it rapidly toward Riddle. He turned swiftly toward the sailor and shouted "Avra Kadavra." A beam of green light shot from his hand, not from his wand, and hit the sailor, who shouted. Then it hit me what Riddle was doing. He had pointed his wand at the Captain. I swung around toward the Captain and saw him pull his dog tags from under his blouse. I shouted, "No." There was a flash of light, and I realized that Riddle had disapparated. I started to run toward the Captain. I saw him squeeze something on the chain from his neck. I started counting seconds.

Someone hit me from the side. "Don't move." I swung and kicked at the same time and caught him in the knee. He dropped, and I spun loose from his grip. I was up to 5 seconds. I ran around the chart table. The Captain backed away toward the monitors. He brought his fists up and prepared to fight me. Another officer said, "Stop or I fire."

I shouted, "He's triggered a bomb." Then I rushed the Captain. No explosion sounded so I guess they couldn't quite believe that I was a real threat. 10. I went at the Captain. He struck out. I parried the blow. It fell mostly on my right forearm. I kicked at his groin, but he jumped backwards. 15. I came at him again, and he threw a punch that got past my block and caught me on the side of my head. I dropped to my knees and tried to roll away. He was on top of me, and I rolled again. He hit his head on the chart table and seemed stunned for a second. What was the count? At least 20. I dived at him as he got up, and then there was a shudder that shook the ship followed a tenth of a second later by a loud explosion. The lights went out, and there was a shout.

Someone shouted for emergency lights, and the Bridge was lit in dim red. There was something funny about my feet. They were sliding on the deck, and I realized that the sub was tilting downward at the fore. In a few seconds I was practically standing on the side of the chart table. The executive officer in the Engine Room was shouting over the intercom, "What's going on at the Bridge?"

The 2nd officer picked up the Captain's mike and said, "I don't know."

I shouted, "The forward Torpedo Room exploded."

The 2nd officer asked, "Did you hear that Mr. Wainright?"

"Yes."

"Blow the ballast."

"Yes sir."

Someone on the Bridge shouted, "100 Meters and sinking."

The 2nd officer said, "Wainwright, give me full reverse. All the power you can squeeze out of that reactor."

Someone else reported "150 meters and sinking."

Wainwright said, "We're giving you everything we've got. Are you blowing ballast?"

The 2nd officer looked over at one of the stations. The man shook his head, "We've lost the forward ballast tanks. Some of the midships are blowing, some aren't. The aft ones are all blowing."

"200 meters and sinking."

The 2nd officer shouted. "Somebody find out what compartments are still with us."

"225 meters and sinking."

Wainwright reported over the intercom, "The reactor has reached full power and we're pushing it for 115%."

"250 meters and sinking."

"Fuck, just push the reactor till it breaks."

I asked, "What's crush depth?"

Someone answered, "300 meters." The intervals between depth announcements were getting longer.

"275 meters and sinking."

I looked at the 2nd officer, and he shook his head negatively. "I don't know that we're going to make it."

"290 meters and sinking."

The ship had been groaning with the pressure. Now it sounded like some great pair of hands were twisting the ship. Otherwise, the ship was silent.

"300 meters and steady."

"290 meters and rising."

Then there was a wrenching groan.

"250 meters and rising." Another groan shook the ship. Then I saw a seam open in the metal wall of the Bridge. Water sprayed in and . . .

Then I heard Mr. Wainwright saying something, and someone was shaking my shoulder. "Wake up. Wake up." The room was brightly lit, and it was my cabin.

"You were dreaming."

I said shakily, "Yes, it was a nightmare."

"It must have been a doozy."

"Yeh."

"Want to talk about it?"

"No, that's all right."

"It helps."

"No, that's all right. I'm heading down to the mess."

I walked down the companionway and finally reached the mess.

It was empty. I got a cup of coffee and sat down in the corner, hoping that no one would come in while I was sitting there. I spent the next 15 minutes thinking about how real the creaking and groaning was in the last minutes of that dream. I had been sweating when I fell out of the bunk.

I didn't notice what happened next. Fred and George sat down next to me. I don't know how long they were there, but I eventually realized they were sitting there.

"A knut for your thoughts." George said.

"Oh, no thoughts. I'm just scared shitless."

"You?!"

"Sure. I dreamed the ship sank."

"Is that all? I'm convinced the ship sank every night." Said Fred.

"Shit. Don't try to cheer me up."

"You said it, I won't. Right, George?"

"Oh, definitely, Fred."

"Have something to eat, and you'll feel better."

I absently took the chocolate bar that he handed me. I took a bite and washed it down with some coffee.

Fred said, "You should go down to the gym and . . ."

I didn't hear the end of the sentence because my insides seemed to turn inside out, and I had all that I could do to keep from vomiting on the table. I jumped up and ran for the head. I almost made it to the head.

George, "That was clever how you got him to eat that Puking Pastile."

"It'll keep his mind off the ship sinking."

I lost all the contents of my stomach. Most of it I lost in the head. So, I wouldn't have to do a lot of cleaning up outside the head. I spent about 5 minutes dry retching and got good enough control to struggle out of the head. Fred was waiting for me, wand in hand. He had just cleaned up the mess, and then he handed me the antidote. "I just hate to see someone suffering. Especially an innocent Muggle."

I squeezed my shirt out in the sink in the head after rinsing it in water. "Sure. I'm going to get you one of these days. You'll have forgotten complete about it, and just when you are expecting it not at all, something will happen."

"Yes, you believe that if it gives you comfort."

We walked back toward the mess, today appropriately named. George was still there sipping on his coffee. We sat down.

"I suppose I should thank you for that. It did take my mind off my troubles."

No one had anything to say. We sat there for a while in silence. Then I noticed that it wasn't perfectly silent. There was a thrumming noise in the background. I thought about it and then realized what we were hearing. "Fred, do you hear that?"

"What?"

"I think it's the engine."

"Sure. . . I hear it. Thrumming. So what?"

"That's what stands between us and sinking to the bottom."

"Not that again!"

"No, this is different. The way that submarines work, you have to have power—power to pump water out of the ballast tanks, power to drive the ship forward or back, down or … up. The thrumming is the reactor driving the drive train, the pumps, you name it on this ship."

Nobody said anything. We all just sat staring at the table or the deck or the coffee in our cups.

George asked, "Do you have any exploding snaps?"

"No."

"No."

"How about a game of cards. Anybody got some cards?"

I answered, "I have a deck in my stuff."

"Why don't you get it? It's got to better than staring at the deck."

"Sure". I got up and headed for my cabin.

Flank Speed

We were all in the Wardroom again—the leads of the various teams with the Captain and the XO. The Captain spoke, "You all know your jobs. You know the time frames you have to do them in. Does anyone have any doubts that they can do them in the time you've got?"

Nobody said anything. The Captain repeated, "Anyone?"

You could have heard a pin drop. No one was looking at the Captain. Typical hunker down syndrome. Finally, the Captain said, "If anyone has doubts, there's no problem. We can reschedule and practice more. But if anyone has doubts, screws up, and ruins this op for us, I'll personally see to it that your career in the Navy or the SAS is over.

"Now, who has no doubts?" No one raised a hand. "Then we'll go back to the light house and practice more."

Fred looked up and said, 'I'm ready. I don't have any doubts."

The commander of the SAS said, "No doubts."

Slowly around the table everyone else repeated that. Finally, the Captain looked at me, "I haven't heard from you."

"I'm all in."

"Then what are we all so dour about? Now, Wendt, let's go over this. What's our main risk in this operation?" We'd been over it a couple of dozen times, but I humored him.

"The main problem is the dementors. The guards we can immobilize. The staff likewise. But the dementors we can only keep at bay. If they decide to go for help, we'll have dozens of Deatheaters here in a couple of hours. Then it's all over. Even if we fight our way out, if any of them survive, they'd know that we were Muggles."

"How much time—exactly—do we have?"

I looked over to the Weasleys. "How long do we have? Exactly?"

Fred and George looked at each other. Fred said, "Well, no one knows how fast dementors can travel, but I'd guess they could make 150 Kilometers per hour, maybe a little more. What do you think?" He looked the question at George.

George stroked his chin as if considering carefully, "I'd agree, perhaps closer to 200."

I added, "So, it's basically how long it takes the dementors to get to the Ministry and summon help."

I added, "That would be two hours, perhaps 2 and a half."

"Then, you all have to be done in 2 hours. If you aren't back by then, we're leaving without you. You're all wizards, you can disapparate. No one will suspect you had help. No one will try to interrogate you."

The room had turned quiet again. Slowly everyone got up and left, one by one. Even Fred and George left separately.

□

The rest of the day dragged on. When underwater, your sense of time is distorted. Or maybe I was just so nervous that time dragged and dragged on. Anyway, we finally were at the time that the clock said was sunset. We went to the Wardroom again. The XO was there. He started immediately as soon as we had all arrived. "We just checked the weather. It's a great night for us. The moon is hours away from rising, it's overcast and will be pitch black within an hour. If you all give the go-ahead, we'll cruise in close and start the operation. This time everyone gave the "thumbs up", and the XO sent us to our stations.

My station was in the conning tower. I went up with the XO, and he nodded to the Captain, who ordered the helmsman to approach our action station.

The helmsman reported that we had arrived on station. The Captain ordered, "Come to periscope depth." The helmsman reported that we were at periscope depth. "Up periscope." The periscope went up, the Captain looked around and said, "Put it on the monitor." And then everyone could see the view. "Contact the sniper team."

He took the radio man's headphones and said, 'Are you on station and ready?"

"Good. Stay on the air. I'll check my teams." He took off the headset and asked the XO to check the boarding party. The XO got on the intercom to the missile room where the boarding party was preparing.

"The boarding party's ready."

The Captain went to the periscope and adjusted it. He rotated the field of view up and magnified until the upper half of the prison filled the screen. We could see the top of the prison and occasionally what might have been a head and shoulders appear over the parapet. He put on the headset again and said, "Execute."

There wasn't much to see. At that moment there was one head sticking above the parapet and an instant after the Captain had spoken, it abruptly disappeared. A moment later the Captain nodded his head and said, "Keep a sharp watch on the prison and the air around it. We want as much of a warning as possible if anything—anything—happens that you don't understand." There was a moment of silence, and he nodded his head again and said, "Good."

The Captain turned to the XO and said, "Surface and launch the boarding party. The XO relayed the command to the helm, and I could barely hear or feel our ascent to the surface. The Captain took the periscope and swung it around. The monitor showed the deck of the sub. Almost immediately two hatches opened and the boarding party swarmed out. The rafts were deployed over the side, and everyone scrambled down as though it were 2nd nature. The rafts were away. He followed them with the periscope as they sailed toward the rock that Azkaban was built on. The progress seemed painfully slow. Every passing second seemed like it might be our last.

Finally, the boarding party reached the rock, and nets were thrown up to the main surface. We could barely see small figures working up the nets. The Captain asked, "Are we getting a radio feed from the boarding party."

The radio man nodded, and the Captain said, "Put it on the intercom here."

There was a low crackle but nothing else to indicate that the speakers were on. As we waited and watched, we saw the party spreading out around the main door. Then suddenly there was a flash of light, then sound and the speakers announced, "Door blown."

□□

George was standing beside one of the SAS. He wasn't sure which one. Fred was on the other side of the door. Another SAS was placing what they called a "shaped charge", although he really didn't understand what was "shaped" about it—or a charge, for that matter. The SAS who was placing the charges nodded and everyone knew to retreat around the curve of the wall. The SAS who had placed the charge held his fingers and thumb up showing "Five", then there were four fingers, three, two, one, and there was a loud thunderclap that shook the ground. Fred and George rounded the curve of the door first as planned, and they quickly scanned the debris-filled hall. No one appeared. They entered and signaled for the SAS with the explosives to follow them. Immediately inside the door and to the right was a smaller door that led to the Guard Post. The SAS placed a couple of charges on the door at what they assured him in the training were critical spots. They ran back a couple of paces from the door and there was another, smaller explosion. They could see splinters flying everywhere, and they cautiously rounded the edges of the door, wands extended and firing curses into the smoky debris-littered room. No one seemed to be moving. They entered cautiously and found a couple of bloody bodies, pierced by hundreds of splinters. George shook his head and went back out.

Everyone was plastered against the walls of the hall. They were proceeding toward the quarters of the staff. They took a left turn at the intersection of another corridor. As they did, there was movement. People leaving a door pulled their wands up, but the hall was filled with "petrificus totalis" curses. The wizards dropped. Almost immediately, there was a feeling of chill that penetrated to everyone's bones. Fred, George, and everyone knew that dementors had entered the corridor. Six wands turned and six patronuses flew out. The dementors scattered almost immediately.

The wizards searched the corridor for doors, systematically threw them open, and stunned any occupants. Despite the explosions, some seemed to not have heard and had hardly gotten up when they were cursed and collapsed.

Fred led one party down a corridor, unlocking doors as they went. The first one he reached, he pushed his head through and said, "This is a jail break, let's go." The wizard sleeping on the cot rubbed his eyes sleepily and said, "Is this some new kind of torture?"

Fred said, "No, we're breaking out. Get moving."

The prisoner shook his head and asked, "What did you say?"

"I said, 'Get moving.'

"What is the problem here?" Fred mused to himself. Another wizard came up.

"It's the reaction to the dementors. It takes some time to recover."

They started to help the prisoners up and out.

In the conning tower, the XO had a pair of earphones on. He was listening to the officer on the deck. The officer said, "Captain, the wizards on the deck report that dementors have flown off."

The Captain said, "XO, start the timer. We have two hours to get out of here."

George had gone down a different corridor and had started releasing prisoners and getting them organized to get out of the prison. The next door that George opened had a family behind it—a mother, father, and a young boy. He urged them out and gently took the boy by the shoulders, but he resisted moving. George looked up at the father who had sunken eyes and looked like he needed as much help as the boy.

George got down on his knees and faced the boy. He said, "My name's George. What's yours?"

The boy looked confused but said with a slight stutter, "Ron."

George involuntarily smiled and said, "You know, I've got a brother whose name is Ron." The smile seemed to encourage the boy who smiled a little smile that barely broke the straight line of his mouth. George asked, "Would you like to leave here?"

The boy looked up at his dad who nodded. "Yes, please."

George picked up the boy and said, "What are we waiting for? Let's go." He started to walk off, and the parents moved too. George urged other prisoners who were standing but not showing much initiative to move to follow the quartet. He walked off at a moderate pace. They navigated through the cavernous prison. They reached the main entrance and walked outside. He found that there were several other wizards with small groups of prisoners. George asked the group in general, "Are we ready to go?"

Everyone agreed and George went on. "I'll try disapparating to the ship with these 4 and then return. If it goes OK, Everyone should go, one at a time." He made sure that the father and mother had a good grip on his arm and he did the weird twist that sent them all into disapparation. They suddenly dropped to the deck of the Ohio. Several seamen ran up and put firm hands on them.

The CPO on the deck said, "OK. Ma'am, sir, please come over here. We need to get into the ship as quickly as we can. The mother reached out for Ron, and George handed him to her saying, "It's going to be OK. These are good people, you can trust them." Then he disapparated and re-appeared in front of Azkaban. He looked around quickly. There were more people there—both wizards and former prisoners. He saw Fred and said, "Go ahead, bro. The first group's in the sub."

The XO announced, "The CPO says the first group is in the ship. George was the first over. The rest are starting to come."

The Captain asked, "How much time?"

"We've got an hour and a half."

"What's your estimate for total time left?"

The XO turned to the radio man. "Get me someone in the boarding party."

"Aye." He switched frequencies and made contact. He handed the headset to the XO.

The XO said, "Find out how many prisoners are left."

The Lieutenant commanding the boarding party signaled to Fred who was about to go back in to get more people out. Fred came over. "Fred, how many more people are there to get to the ship?"

Fred made a face and said, "How should I know?"

"Make a good guess."

"Oh, I don't know." He stopped talking to think. There were four levels. There were about 50 cells on each level. Say 2 people per cell. "I'd guess a total of maybe 300 or 350."

"How many have we transferred so far? I'd guess about a dozen or so."

"You're probably about right. OK. Get going and see if you can pick it up. We don't have enough time to get everyone over at this rate."

Lieutenant Stevens keyed the mike and spoke to the XO, "We've transferred about a dozen. I make our current rate to be about 2 per minute. At that rate, I'd say a minimum of two and a half hour to finish."

The XO repeated to the conning tower. The Captain said, "You know we've only got 90 minutes left. We've got to at least double that rate. Get them cracking."

The XO passed the word, and Stevens spoke a silent curse. Then he passed the word on to the wizards.

Back on the sub, the Captain signaled to me to follow him. We went to a corner of the Bridge. He asked me, "You heard that. What do we do when we have to leave in 85 minutes if there are still people in Azkaban? I don't have an idea that I like."

My heart sunk, and I looked down.

The Captain persisted, "Come on. What are our options?"

I looked up into his face so he'd know that I was listening and thinking. I took a minute to review the possibilities:

"Ok, here are the options that I see. First, we could push the two hour limit a little."

"And when there are still people left?"

I didn't have to refer to the Attack Plan A book. I knew what it said. I'd help pen it. "We could leave them. None of the prisoners know that Muggles are involved or where the people are disapparating." I hesitated to let that sink in. "That would be crappy."

"Agreed. More options?"

Here we left the plan. The plan didn't have another option. I thought hard. Back in the Warehouse we weren't faced with decisions affecting a hundred or more people that we could actually see in front of our eyes. We hadn't thought hard about it. Now I was thinking hard. "We could go and leave volunteer wizards to keep evacuating people by disapparation to someplace within a couple of hundred miles until the Deatheaters come. We might get the rest off."

"Others?"

I thought and thought. But I couldn't think of any other options. "You've got me. I don't have any other options. What about you?"

He shook his head. He turned and signaled the XO over to join us. When he arrived, he said, "Mr. Wendt and I have been thinking. We may have to leave some prisoners behind, possibly with volunteer wizards to evacuate them to someplace other than this ship."

The XO nodded and said, "I thought it was going to be something like this."

The Captain said, "Get me on the line with Fred or George. We need to get them ready for this possibility."

The XO went back to radioman and talked with Stevens. He then signaled the Captain to join him. He went over, took the headphones and said, "Fred, if you guys don't get all the prisoners over her in," He looked up at the XO, who said, "70 minutes."

The Captain went on, "70 minutes, we're going to have to leave. See if there are any wizards who will volunteer to stay and keep evacuating prisoners to somewhere else if it comes to that."

Fred said something forceful because I saw the Captain recoil from the headphones. Then he said, "Mister, we're leaving in 70 minutes whether you're ready or not. Just speed things up, and we won't have to do something that nobody's going to like."

The XO started giving reports every 10 minutes, such as, "We've got 120 into the ship. Estimated 200 more. Estimated 50 left when we submerge."

When the time got down to 30 minutes, the report was, "Ninety left. Estimate 30 left behind when we submerge."

At 5 minutes, the report was "35 left. 5 minutes. 20 left behind"

The Captain ordered the helmsman, "Prepare to submerge in 5 minutes. Flank speed. Down bubble 25 degrees."

I signaled to the Captain. He stared for a minute, and then came over to me. I whispered, "You've got to give them a little extra time. What about 20 minutes?"

He stared hard at me and said nothing. Finally he said, "10 minutes."

I countered, "15 minutes." With a hopeful smile.

"Mr. Wendt. I don't negotiate." I opened my mouth to say something (I didn't know what), but he anticipated me, "Say a single word, and it will be 5 minutes." I nodded. The Captain returned to his normal station, and the helmsman looked up to him. He said, "Ten more minutes."

"Aye, sir." The helmsman smiled and turned back to his controls. The XO relayed the reprieve to the boarding party and said, "In 6 minutes, you're coming back. Have the wizards transport you and be sure you don't leave anything including the rafts."

Stevens caught George and said, "We've got to go in 5 minutes. You get your volunteers together."

George said, "Bloody hell. We're almost done. we've only got twenty or so."

"This is one you can't win. The Captain's going to submerge on schedule. Don't waste time."

George thought a second. "As soon as the next wizards return from the sub, you get them to take you back. Fred and I'll finish with the few people left."

On the Bridge we watched the boarding party of Muggles return to the ship with a couple of wizards, and the wizards went down into the ship. Then George and Fred returned with eight more people. They disapparated. The XO talked to the CPO on the deck, "Button up. We've only got 1 minute to submerge." There was a hesitation and the XO said, "That's an order, mister." The CPO climbed down into the hold and the hatches closed.

The helmsman looked up to the Captain who nodded to him and said, "Execute your orders."

The XO got on the intercom and said, "Rig for emergency dive."

We felt the immediate response as the engines revved, and the ship tilted down at what seemed like 45 degrees. Everyone grabbed something. You could hear the ship groan. The sonar man looked up at the Captain and asked, "Sir, do you really want to keep this up, we're cavitating?"

The Captain shook his head, "I know. I know. I might as well have written in bold letters the 'Ohio is here'. Anyone who has two hydrophones and cares to drop them in the North Sea will know exactly where Captain James and the Ohio are."

I glanced quizzically at the XO. He signaled me over next to him. He told me, "Cavitation happens when you drive the screws too hard. They form bubbles that make lots of noise. Noise that sonar can pick up."

"Oh." And then I added, "I don't think the Deatheaters have hydrophones."

"Probably not."

The helmsman reported, "Depth 100 meters. 100 meters below us."

The Captain waited another few seconds and said, "Come to 5 degrees down bubble and level at 150 meters. Maintain flank speed." The tilt decreased to the point that I didn't feel like I was about to fall on the bulkhead.

The XO picked up a phone and dialed the missile room. "How is everyone down there?" He listened for a minute and then actually began to laugh.

The Captain snapped, "Perhaps you'd like to share the joke with us, Mr. Wainwright?"

The XO wiped the smile off his face with some effort and with more effort kept a straight face, reporting, "The CPO in the missile room reports that they've taken on some seawater."

"Didn't the seaman lock down the hatch securely? Is somebody on report?"

The XO suppressed a smirk, "No, sir. There were a couple of people who came on board after we submerged. George and Fred disapparated with nine prisoners <u>after</u> we submerged. They apparently picked up some water disapparating through the North Sea and the hull. It seems they got the last of the prisoners onboard with that final stunt."

The Captain could hardly help laughing himself. But he managed to turn to me and order me down to the missile room to welcome our guests.

The Unbreakable Oath

I trotted down to the missile room. The XO came with me. We arrived and found a chaotic scene. It was wall-to-wall people. Most people were sitting on the deck. There were a few standing. Everyone seemed to be eating. The XO asked a CPO, Mr. Calabrese, why everyone was eating.

We should have anticipated his answer, "These people are starving. They only fed these people twice a day, and it was only thin gruel. I had the cooks start a meal. These are just snacks until they've got something ready."

"Very good."

In the mean time, I'd spotted Fred and George. They were toweling off along with about a dozen people. I went up to them and got swatted with a wet towel for my trouble. "How did you get soaked?"

Fred looked up from drying his feet and said, "What kind of a prat are you? We went through about 30 feet of water! Do you think we wouldn't get a little wet?"

George added, "It was a pretty darn good job of disapparating to hit a moving target moving under the water at about 50 miles an hour."

Wainwright said, "We were only going about 25 knots."

"Well, you try disapparating at a moving target and then tell me that it was a piece of cake. You're lucky that we didn't end up splynched or sticking out of a bulkhead."

"OK. OK. Let's get down to business. We've got to get these people an explanation and so forth."

Fred said, "Give us a mo' to get dry, and we're ready."

I asked the CPO if there were a P.A. somewhere I could use. He led the XO and me and the Weasleys to the side of the room and pulled a mike off the wall. "Here you go." I looked at the Weasleys. They seemed to be as dry as they were going to get without a change of clothes. I picked up the mike and started.

"Hello. Hello. Hello." The noise dropped some, and then it was pretty quiet. There was still a baby crying, but that couldn't be helped. I went on, "I'm going to tell you what this is about, who rescued you, what comes next, and so on. You can ask questions after I've finished.

"First, we're working with the Order of the Phoenix to fight Riddle."

Someone toward the back of the room called out, "Who the bloody Hell is Riddle?" There was general laughter as people got the pun.

I answered, "Tom Riddle is the real name of the wizard that you may know as the Dark Lord. We always use his real name. For one thing, Deatheaters know it when you use his chosen name, Lord etc. and can trace you. Please never use that name again, if you don't want a quick trip back to Azkaban." There was a collective in-drawn breath.

"Now, we broke you out of Azkaban not only because it's the right thing to do, but because we want you help us fight Riddle. You've got two choices right now. You can help us, or we'll drop you off someplace far away and out of the way.

"If you've been looking around, you may have an idea of whose ship this is. It belongs to the United States Navy, and we'll thank you never to mention that fact to anyone. We'll be doing more about that later. You've probably also figured out that most of the people on this ship are Muggles. Yes, they know about wizards, and we want to keep it that way. They've put themselves in a lot of danger for your benefit, and we aren't out of the woods yet by a long shot.

"We're all going to be on this ship for about a week or so. The crew will help you find places to sleep. We'll eat in shifts. They'll show you where you can use the loo and shower.

Some joker in the crowd asked, "What's the smell?"

"I'm afraid everything is the smell. You'll be part of it shortly. The good news is that you'll get used to it—sort of—and you won't notice it much in a couple of days. Just be patient until then.

"I see that most of you have already had something to eat. We'll have a regular meal ready shortly, and you can all have some decent food. If you need anything, just ask one of the Muggles in uniform or me. They'll be glad to help you in any way possible. Now, any questions?"

Someone in the back shouted out, "Where are we going?"

"Sorry, I can't tell you that just yet. But you'll know shortly."

"Why are the Muggles helping us" a belligerent someone in the front row asked.

"I'll have the 2nd in command of this ship, the Executive Officer, Mr. Wainwright answer that."

He stepped up and didn't take the mike. His voice was carrying and everyone seemed to instinctively quiet when he started to speak. "Well, first, we're Americans. We have a tradition of helping out when natural disaster strikes. When there's a tsunami or an earthquake or a terrible storm, you can count on our being there. If you don't know that, then you've been keeping your head in the sand." He paused for emphasis, and not seeing any objections, including from the jerk in the front row, he went on. "And this Riddle seems like pretty much a natural disaster to me.

"Second, he's a threat to us as well. We would be pretty stupid to keep our heads in the sand and think that he's only your problem.

"Third, I'm an all-round nice guy." That got a few laughs. Then he said, "Which brings us to our next topic." And he turned the meeting back over to me.

I went on "Now, we have a ticklish subject that I always leave till last. I say, 'Always', because I've given this speech more than a couple of times. I leave it to last because I have a sacrifice to ask of each of you. You are here because of the risk that every crew member of this ship has taken on your behalf. I think that you owe them the consideration to ensure that your presence doesn't endanger them more. The best and really only way that you can ensure that is to promise that you won't reveal anything that has happened during your escape or while you are under the protection of the Order of the Phoenix." There was a groan from the audience. They knew what was coming, and I'd heard it often enough to not be surprised nor skip a beat in my oft-repeated speech. "So, I'm going to ask each of you to make that promise in the form of the Unbreakable Oath. There are a dozen wizards here who will administer that oath in pairs. We won't require young children or anyone who can't understand the consequences of the Unbreakable Oath to take it. However, older children and all adults will have to."

There were the usual objections. One short wiry wizard with a long white beard asked the toughest questions, "What if someone uses Veritas serum on you. You won't be able to keep from breaking the oath then."

Fred fielded that question, "Veritas serum doesn't work against the Unbreakable Oath."

The old guy came right back, "How about the *Imperious Curse*."

Fred took a deep breath and said, "The *Imperious Curse* can be resisted if you've trained yourself, but the Unbreakable Oath doesn't protect you from that precisely because it is possible to resist."

The old guy shot right back, "That's crazy. Nobody can resist the *Imperious Curse*."

George broke in. "Yes, I've seen it done. Harry Potter did."

He didn't give up, 'Well, sure, bloody Harry Potter. But I'm talking about real people, not the 'Chosen One'."

I could see that George was about to shoot something back. I kicked his shin, and he relented. The rest of our wizards came forward and began to set up to administer the oath, when someone else said, "I'm not going to take it."

I couldn't see who had said that, but almost immediately there were shouts of agreement. I said, "OK. Whoever doesn't want to take the oath come up here where I can see you."

Reluctantly, several men came up. They had a surly look. I walked up to them and said, "If you're not taking the oath then... " I was stuck.

Wainwright walked up and said, "Mr. Wendt, go up to the Bridge and tell the Captain that we need to go back to Azkaban. We have a few people that we need to drop there."

"Wait, wait. What are you talking about?" The guy who was objecting to taking the oath said hurriedly.

I said, "Yes, you are going back. You either take the oath, or we take you back."

Wainwright put his hand on my shoulder and said, "No time. You just get up to the Bridge and have him go back to Azkaban. Get going." And he turned me around.

I agreed. I started walking off briskly.

"OK. OK. I'll do it. I'll take the oath."

"What about the rest of you? Anyone else going back to Azkaban?" Wainwright could convince you of his seriousness without anything more than his way of smiling. It was totally unnerving. It was like he knew a private joke that only he understood, and the butt of the joke was you.

No one else said anything. Fred and George started with the spokesman of the resistors. Fred took his hand and said, "Repeat after me." The guy didn't look happy but he didn't object. Fred went on, "Do you swear that you will never tell anyone what has happened since you were released from Azkaban." Fred paused and waited for the wizard to say it. He grimaced, and Wainwright cleared his throat.

"I swear." But George urged him on as the lines of magic force swirled around Fred and his joined arms. "Yes, yes. I swear that I will never tell anyone what has happened since I was released from Azkaban."

George went on, "Or anything that you see, hear, or learn while you are under the protection of the Order of the Phoenix."

He paused, looked up and saw the expression on the XO's face and went on," Or anything that I see, hear, or learn while I am under the protection of the Order of the Phoenix."

George continued, "Or anyone associated with them. Nor, will you communicate to anyone this information by any means: writing, telepathic or any other until the overthrow of Tom Riddle.."

Another grimace accompanied the repeated, "anyone associated with them. Nor will I communicate to anyone this information by any means, writing, telepathic or any other until the over throw of Tom Riddle."

The oath finished, George summoned the next wizard forward and I started to leave for the cabin the XO and I shared. The XO caught my eye and signaled to follow him with his hand. I followed him out of the missile room, and he turned to me and said, "Wendt, come with me. We need to talk."

"OK. What about?"

"Let's go to the torp room at the other end of the ship." I frowned but followed him. It took us several minutes to get there. He was utterly silent the whole walk. We finally arrived and crossed the bulkhead. Wainwright dismissed the crewmen there and closed the hatch behind them.

He leaned on a torpedo and said, "Those wizards who didn't want to take the oath—we can't let them go their own way. I've seen lots of men like that—in the brig." It was a statement, not a question.

I answered, "You're wrong. We've got to let anyone who wants to part from us, do so."

"I know that you want to keep your promise, but it's really too dangerous to do so. How can you trust everyone to keep silent, even with your 'Unbreakable Oath'?"

"Oh, believe me that oath is a magical contract. There's no breaking it."

"How can you be so sure? What happens if you break it, do you die?" He said it with a smile.

"Magical contracts aren't like Muggle ones. If you break the terms, you do die."

"Really?"

"Yes."

"But even if you die, what if you're tortured, you might still break your oath."

"No, if you started to break your oath, you'd die in the act."

"But you might give enough information away to hurt us."

"No, I don't think so. In the same second that you started to act, you'd die."

"Still, that moment might be enough for disaster."

"I don't think so. You know there have been some studies of physiology lately. Even before a person realizes that he's made a decision to do something, the decision is completed—a fraction of a second before. With that determination, he will die—even before he has begun."

"But, surely it's possible to over-rule or out magic the magic contract."

"Perhaps, but I don't think there's a wizard alive who can do it. Only once in my life did I see a magical contract in play. It was a couple of years ago. It was part of a competition at Hogwarts. There was a student, Harry Potter, who was entered in it by connivance. It was a very dangerous competition, and students two years older than he were forbidden to compete."

"So, he tried to get out and couldn't?"

"No, the greatest wizard of the age, Professor Dumbledore, didn't dare to try to negate the magical contract."

"But the contract was fooled in some way, otherwise this Potter wouldn't have been in the competition."

"Yes, but the thing that was fooled—actually 'confunded'—was not the contract. It was an object, called the Goblet of Fire. You see magical contracts are not objects themselves. No one really has an idea how to attack them."

"I suppose that I have to accept your word, but I really wish we didn't have to put these magical contracts to the test."

"We really need to be straight-up and honest with the Wizards and Witches. Otherwise, we'll be no better than Riddle."

"I knew that you were going to say that." Wainwright made a face himself but shook it off, and we left the Torpedo Room.

The Ohio Film Festival

The next few days in the sub were hard. The next day I went down to the closest "head" and found a line of a dozen people outside waiting to get in. By the time my turn came up I was hopping from foot to foot. We tried various ideas for relieving the problem. Finally, a brilliant seaman with a computer had the idea of assigning times for every "head" to everyone on the ship once every three hours. This allowed for about two minutes for each person each time. Of course, most of the time, people didn't need to use their time slot. People started trading time slots—sometimes even. They sometimes sold their slots. By the time we reached South Carolina, there was a hot market in "head slots" as they'd come to calling them.

The Mess was always crowded either with people eating or with people just trying to find a place to sit.

There were lots of witches in the group, and there were probably more females on the ship than there ever had been in history. There were a number of friendships that developed between seamen and passengers. How they managed to get a couple of minutes alone to talk I could never make out, but apparently people can be very inventive with sufficient incentive.

The Captain was never far from the Bridge in the best of times, but now he never ventured out of the conning tower. There began to be a rumor that the position of Captain was really just a myth and that there wasn't really anyone who filled that position. Actually, he had given up his cabin to a family of four with two young children.

Since no wizard from Azkaban had actually seen the Captain, the crewmen began making up all sorts of exaggerations about him. He was 6 foot 10 inches tall (since there was no room or passage in the sub that was that tall, it was particularly funny to the seamen). He was almost inhumanly strong. He sometimes picked up crewmen with one hand when he was angry with them and shook them like a toy doll. He had the "evil eye" and had been known to freeze sailors in mid-stride with his stare. Fred and George encouraged these myths and even invented a few themselves.

□

On the second day out, when people's patience had reached its thinnest point, and there was always the feeling that a fight might break out somewhere, Wainwright took me aside. He asked me up to the Bridge. He had given up our cabin to another family with young kids.

"Wendt, I got an idea. I want to see what you think of it."

"Sure, Wain, shoot."

"We have a decent library of films on DVD and we can show them on a good-sized projection screen in the mess. Do you think it would help morale for our passengers?"

I didn't need to think long, "It's worth a try. I suppose you've got to have the agreement of the Captain."

"Don't worry, I'll get it. In the mean time, go see CPO Johnson in the galley. He has access to the DVD library. Pick out some good ones but hold on to them until you get the word from me."

I nodded and left for the galley. I got there and found the CPO up to his ears in preparing for the next meal shift. When I told him what I wanted, he just said, "Do it. The DVD library is in one of the storage locker at the back of the mess. Here's the key." He handed me a small key. "Pick what you like. The DVD player and the controls for the projector are in the same locker." And with that I became the owner of an underwater movie theater. I squeezed into the back of the Mess and tried several lockers before I found the one that the key fit.

Inside the locker, there must have been two hundred DVD's. I started working through the titles. They all seemed to be in alphabetical order. I decided that the best movies would be comedies—at least to start with. So, I began pulling out good comedy titles. There was a collection of Abbott and Costello skits; *It's A Mad, Mad, Mad, Mad, World; Duck Soup; Planes, Trains and Automobiles*. That seemed like a good start to me.

Then I started to figure out how to play them. As I was doing that the XO came on the intercom. "Attention all guests. Mr. Wendt is showing movies in the Mess Hall. The people currently eating will see the first movie and can stay through additional movies until the next meal shift arrives. Enjoy!"

There was a hubbub that erupted. Fortunately, I figured enough out about the projection equipment enough that I could speak through a mike that was in the locker with the equipment. "I know that most of you don't know what a movie is. The best way is to just watch and LISTEN to find out. Quiet is much appreciated, but you don't stay quiet, you'll be ejected from the Mess Hall even if you've not finished your meal."

With that word, the room quieted considerably, and I had a few minutes to figure out how the DVD player and projector worked. After about ten minutes CPO Johnson came out and showed me how. Then, *Abbott and Costello* started up. The first skit was greeted pretty much by stunned silence, but once the crowd began to get the rhythm of their shtick, the laughter came fast and loud. It was amazing how funny the "Who's on First" skit was to people who knew absolutely nothing about baseball.

By the end of the day, I'd had to pull out a couple of more comedy films and nearly every wizard on the boat had seen at least one film. After the last film ended, and I announced that we were done for the day. There were groans and even a few threats. I announced that there would be more films the next day and anyone who wasn't happy didn't need to see any of them.

That "night" I dragged myself up to the Bridge and asked Wainwright where I could sleep. His answer was, "Anyplace you can find a spot." He quickly added, "Except the Bridge," as he saw me eyeing an empty piece of floor behind the chart table.

□□

The next day at breakfast, I took up my station at the back of the Mess Hall and announced the subject for the day—Westerns. Of course, someone shouted out the question, "What's a Western?" I explained in one hundred words or less about settling the Western part of the United States, and the films that had been made about that.

The library was heavy on John Wayne, so I had pulled out *The Searchers, The Man Who Shot Liberty Valance, Rio Bravo,* and *True Grit.* I worked into the lineup between Wayne masterpieces a collection of episodes from the TV series, *Maverick, Gunsmoke,* and *The Virginian.* They weren't quite as popular as the comedies.

At the end of the day, the wizards had gotten the idea that I was showing movies by theme. They wanted to know what the next day would be. My answer was, "It won't be as much fun if you know. Good evening."

The next day, I had a hard time finding romantic comedies, but there were several—*When Harry Met Sally, Sleepless in Seattle,* and *You've Got Mail.* That was about it, but I threw in the *The Burbs* because it was sort of a romantic comedy. To finish, I then fell back on straight comedies such as *The Return of the Pink Panther.*

By this time, there was a pool going to try to guess the category that I'd choose for the next day. Many people tried to get me to reveal it. Of course, since most wizards had never seen a movie before, they had a hard time coming up with real categories. I heard about some wizards betting hundreds of galleons that the next theme would be movies about the Goblins of Gringotts or Aurors. I think the masterminds behind the pool were the Weasleys, but I never could prove it.

The next day, I decided on Musicals. There weren't a whole lot, but there were some very good ones. We had *The Music Man,* which I suppose I could have shown as a romantic comedy, but I wanted to save it for the musicals. There were *Fiddler on the Roof, My Fair Lady,* and *The Wizard of Oz.* I guess that most of the wizards thought that was a straight comedy. At least they thought the ideas about wizards, magic, and witches were hilarious. I finished up with *The Sound of Music.*

Something happened in that movie that I didn't expect. In the scene where the Von Trapp family was singing in the music competition, and they sung, "*So Long, Farewell*", there were some people who started singing along. It became pretty loud. Just then, the public address system had an announcement from the XO, "Mr. Wendt to the Bridge on the double."

I did my best to get up there quickly. It wasn't easy with the ship as crowded as it was. When I arrived, I was greeted by a Captain who was obviously on the verge of keel-hauling someone, "What is that noise, Mr. Wendt. We are trying to run quietly. They can hear that in the Kremlin."

Just then, there was a shout that made the ship wring. The Captain was too angry to speak. That was lucky. It allowed me to get in an explanation. "With respect, Captain. We're watching the movie, *The Sound of Music.* The story is about a family who are trying to escape from the terror of a Germany ruled by Adolph Hitler and the Nazis. Don't you think that might mean something to this boat-load of people?"

He stared at me for what seemed to be an hour. Eventually, he just said, "Try to keep the noise from the Mess to a low roar from now on. And no more *Sound of Music.*"

I assured him that I would and returned to the Mess Hall, happy that it was the last movie of the day. My plan was to do Science Fiction the next day. It was good plan. The movies I had in mind were, *The Day the Earth*

Stood Still, 2001: A Space Odyssey, Star Wars, The Empire Strikes Back, and *Return of the Jed*i. That would have filled the day and more. But something else happened that I didn't expect.

When I was cueing up the first, there was a chant that started up softly and quickly grew louder, "We want *Sound of Music*".

I went on the mike and said, "We did that yesterday." The response was that no one in the room had seen it, and they wanted to. I mentally flipped a coin and decided to show it again. It went pretty much like before, but I found that some people were singing along during some of the songs. Some people must have been repeats from before because they seemed to know "Edelweiss" pretty well, and when the "*So Long*" song came up, it was a full throated chorus that sang. Then the end came. I found out what happened when the shout had happened the last time. As the von Trapps crossed the frontier to Switzerland and freedom there was a spontaneous Huzzah! I sort of joined in too.

At that point, a hand took my shoulder, and I turned to discover the XO. He signaled me to follow him. When we were in the Galley, he said, "The Captain sent me down to chastise you." He hesitated and said, "I just can't do it. Go ahead and show your next film. I'll deal with the Captain."

I went on with the first sci-fi movie and we struggled on through the rest, but I had to show the *Sound of Music* again before the day was over.

⬚⬚⬚

The next day, was to be cartoon day, but I really didn't have any choice. I didn't even try to talk them into seeing *Fantasia* first. As I was cueing up *The Sound of Music,* the Captain appeared out of the Galley, and I thought that I might just be swimming the rest of the way to America.

As the opening credits for the *Sound of Music* came up he said, "Well, Mr. Wendt, I see that you blatantly defy my edicts." He looked around. The crowd was absolutely still, and when the first song started, the crowd sang in perfect unison with it. The Captain just shook his head and said, "Carry on, Mr. Wendt."

The Captain actually stayed for the entire film. He shouted with everyone else when the von Trapps reached Switzerland. When I cued up *Fantasia,* he watched it a bit and said, "I'm on the way to the Bridge if anyone wants me." As many of the crew as could snuck in during some of the showings. They were calling it The Ohio Film Festival.

Trafalger

We had finished *Fantasia,* and I had cued up a disc of *Looney Tunes.* It confounded the wizards and witches. It was so unlike anything they'd seen that they were at first dumbfounded and watched the first in total silence. Then the second started. It featured Foghorn Leghorn. The combination of bizarre Southern US accent and the unusual cast of characters with no clear good guy or bad guy struck their funny bones, and before it was over, the crowd was laughing like loons.

Just as the next cartoon started, the klaxon sounded, and the Captain made an announcement. "Rig for silent running. Mr. Wendt, the Weasleys, report to the Bridge ASAP."

For a moment, I was stunned and just let the cartoon roll, but the CPO in charge of the galley came up and killed the power to the DVD. Almost as soon as the power went off, there were grumblings from the crowd.

The CPO took me by the shoulders and shook me, "What are you doing, we've got to get this crowd quiet. You heard the Captain!" All this was said in a stage whisper.

I nodded and switched to the mike. The CPO seemed about to speak again, but I motioned to him for silence. I spun down the volume on the mike and announced, "Please, attention. The Captain has called for silent running. That means that everyone has to be absolutely quiet. No talking unless absolutely necessary, and even then only in a whisper. It's terribly important. No crying babies, no whining. Our lives depend on it. Please pass the word to anyone that hasn't heard this" I hoped I hadn't laid it on too thick, but the CPO didn't correct anything I'd said.

I turned off the power on the mike, but the CPO interrupted and whispered, "Get to the Bridge right away."

It was hard to hurry on this sub, loaded with people as it was, but I made pretty good time. When I reached the Bridge, the twins were there already. I heard the end of a conversation between the Captain and the sonar man.

"Captain, it's a Trafalgar class boat—an attack sub. I'm sure of it."

The Captain swore under his breath, "What are they doing shadowing us? Why would the Brits be following us now?" At that moment, he noticed that the twins and I had arrived. He turned to us, "What's this all about?"

The twins just shrugged, but a thought occurred to me. "Captain, an awful thought just occurred to me. Suppose the Deatheaters figured that the Azkaban lot had escaped by submarine. Suppose they decided to take over a British sub and pursue us." I turned to the twins, "Could an imperioused Captain and a few top crew members run a boat like this?"

Fred nodded, "Don't see any reason why not."

The Captain nodded too, "Yes. If they had the XO and the Captain and maybe a couple of senior officers, they could claim that a rogue captain of a missile sub had to be tracked down and destroyed."

The XO shook his head, "But how would they know which sub to follow?

The Captain replied, "There are only a couple of missile subs in the North Atlantic at any time. Most are in the North Pacific and the Arctic. If they had a hint that it was American, that would make it easier still."

The Captain delivered a decision, "Then we've got to assume that they're here to kill us. What are our options?"

I was pretty sure that he knew what they were, but he wanted everyone on the Bridge to hear this from the XO, who obliged, "Well, we're too far from our port to try to outrun a Trafalgar class sub. We could surface and try to signal for help, but unless there happened to be somebody close, they'd sink our ship, and we'd be sitting ducks in life boats. We could try to engage them."

The Captain broke in, "That would be last ditch, desperation stuff."

The XO went on, "We could try to find a thermocline that we could hide under. But even that would be a long shot."

The Captain turned to the sonar officer, "Have we got anything?"

"Yes, sir. It's not a strong one, but we could go down another three hundred feet and get under it."

The Captain nodded, "Make it so." The XO gave instructions for a gentle dive below the thermocline. The Captain went back to sonar, "How far would you estimate the Trafalgar is?"

He shook his head, "Probably within fifty klicks."

The XO announced that we were under the thermocline. The Captain said, "Slow to stop." Then he told the sonar officer, "If he seems to be closing, let us know."

We all took the best resting position that we could find. I sat on the deck and the Weasleys leaned against a bulkhead. And we waited. I glanced at my watch to see when the wait started. It went on for one hour, then two. I began to wish that I'd stopped to pick up a magazine from my things, but it was too late now.

"Captain, I think he's started using active sonar," the sonar officer whispered. "But he's above the thermocline." The Captain didn't comment.

There was another lengthy wait, and then the sonar officer announced, "He's under the thermocline, pinging."

The Captain started giving orders, "Come above the thermocline. Engineering, come to 50%. XO, get two torpedoes in the tubes fore and aft. Sonar, when he breaks through the thermocline start pinging him."

We didn't have to wait long for that. "He's through the thermocline. Three thousand meters and closing."

The Captain shouted, "Have we got a firing solution yet?"

Someone responded, "Not yet."

The XO reported, "Torpedoes in the tubes, flooded and armed."

"Torpedo fired."

The Captain nodded, "Emergency dive. Get below the thermocline!"

The ship tilted down and everyone grabbed what they could. The Sonar officer reported, "Missed." And then the ship rocked and the world filled with a crash that made me think it was over.

The Captain shouted, "Firing solution?"

"Not yet."

Sonar reported "He's trying to close."

The Captain ordered, "Flank speed, come around and show him that he can get too close."

The ship groaned under the strain of a tight turn. We tilted toward the right as we banked into the turn. The Captain said, "Don't we have a damn firing solution yet?"

"Working"

Sonar reported, "We're less than three hundred meters and closing."

The Captain ordered, "Make sure we miss him. When we're ten seconds past him, fire aft torpedo."

There was about half a minute while we waited to find out if we would ram the Trafalgar or not. Then Sonar said, "Just passed him."

The Captain ordered, "Give it ten seconds and fire. I don't care if you don't have a damn firing solution." I started counting down from ten.

At four, a giant grabbed the sub and shook us like a dishrag. I said to the Weasleys, "It's been nice knowing you."

They said in unison, "Yeh."

Meanwhile the Captain had called for a damage report. They started coming in, "Aft Torpedo Room, minor leak."

"Foreward Torpedo Room, clear."

"Missile room, clear"

And so on. Then the report from Sonar that made us cheer, "The Trafalgar's dead in the water."

The Captain demanded, "We didn't fire, did we?"

"No sir."

"Then what happened?"

The XO said, "I think that we got help from our side. The Brits must have reported that THEY had a rogue sub, and when the Trafalgar started pinging us like crazy, our side located them and fired on them."

The Captain agreed, "Yeh, we're close enough to our ports that they could get a lot of air support out here pretty fast."

The XO asked for orders, and the Captain gave them, "OK. We'll let our guys rescue anyone who survived from the Trafalgar. Resume course as before. Let's just stay under the thermocline as long as we can—as long as we've got it."

□

As predicted, by the time we neared port, no one could smell anything unusual, and the passengers seemed to assume that somehow we had cleared the air of the odors—perhaps by magic.

Later, the Captain summoned me to the Bridge. He was there with the XO. He started off with a welcome statement, "We're within about 10 to 20 hours of port. They're putting together a convoy at our base to take you to your base. What time of day do you want to arrive?"

I had begun thinking about that some myself. I didn't want anyone to learn anything more about where we were than absolutely necessary, so I said, "I'd like to arrive after full dark, then unload everyone and get us on the way by convoy so that we can arrive in the very early morning hours."

"OK. That's easy. We'll slow down a little and get there about 7PM tomorrow. Do you want them to eat on the sub or after getting off?"

"We'll eat the evening meal before arriving, please. How long will it take us to get loaded into the convoy and on the way? "

"I'd say about 2 hours."

"And probably another 5 hours to get to our base. That would put us there about 2 or 3 AM. That's OK. They'll be good and tired, and we can let them sleep in. The transition to camp life will be less intimidating that way. I hope."

The Captain leaned back against the chart table and seemed to relax a little. "I have to admit that I really thought that this would be a tragedy— maybe one where we'd lose the ship. You did a good job. I wish you luck. I've got a feeling we'll all need it. But I'm not sad at all to get you all off the ship and on to somebody else's watch."

I was glad we were parting on decent terms. "For my part, I want to thank you for all the help you've been. You may end up being one of the unsung heroes of this crazy war that I hope nobody ever learns about."

"Yeh. Just see that I am a hero—of the winning side. Dismissed." There was no doubt in my mind that this was the last I'd seen of the Captain. I was being dismissed from his ship or at least his presence forever.

A few hours later I assembled all the former prisoners for a final discussion before we landed. The scene in the missile room looked much as it had on the first day after the breakout from Azkaban. The aisles and every available square cm. had people standing or sitting on it. I didn't use the public address system this time.

"Wizards, witches, and kids, we're about a day away from arriving at the port where we'll land. There will be trucks waiting for us to take us to the base where most of you will be staying as long as this war goes on. We'll land at night because it's safer for everyone the fewer people know about your arrival or where you're going. We'll travel through much of the night. Eat a hearty meal tomorrow evening. Your next meal will be breakfast the next day. No more midnight snacks in the Mess." There was a laugh at that, which sounded genuine. Someone asked what trucks were.

"Trucks are like very large cars or automobiles. Does anyone not know what an auto is?"

No one said anything.

"The next day, we'll give people an opportunity to choose whether they will stay at the base and aid us with the resistance to Riddle or not. What questions do you have?"

There was a moment of silence, and then someone asked, "Will we have our own beds then?"

"Yes. You'll have your own bed, and married couples, especially those with children, will have small cabins. We call them portables."

Some wizard said, "Hurray!" and there was general laughter.

Someone else asked, "Will we be able to contact relatives? Friends?"

I was sorry to have to say, "I'm sorry. Not until the war is over. I know that's a real hardship. When the knowledge that Azkaban has had a breakout hits the news, your relatives and friends will probably assume or, at least, fear the worst. I really wish that we could do something to relieve their concerns, but to do that would be to endanger them and you and everyone at our base and the whole anti-Riddle movement."

There were some whispered conversations but no one seemed to be truly angry.

"If there are no more questions, you can go back to all your very interesting activities. But I promise you in a couple of days, you'll have much more interesting things to do."

People slowly broke apart and went elsewhere.

The Camp

The Ohio pulled into the dock at 7:10 PM. The XO had the crew escorting small groups of people up to the deck and then onto the dock. They then walked down the short dock to a parking lot where unmarked marine transport trucks were waiting. Everyone was assigned to one by name. Of course, they had to hurry up to get there in order to wait.

When Fred, George, and I walked off the dock, we were met by Beth and Sally. Sally's greeting of Fred was very enthusiastic. After a few minutes, she hugged me and said, "Boss, I can't tell you how happy I am that you're OK. Nobody would tell us anything about what was happening with you lot."

I replied, "It's just what you expect with the military, and really, just what I wanted. Sorry." Just then, a marine in battle fatigues with a rifle slung over his shoulders came up and interrupted us.

He said, "Mr. Wendt. The base commander's compliments, sir. We're ready to leave."

"Fine, where do you want us?"

"Follow me." He led us to a Hummer close to the front of the trucks. We got in, the five of us in the back. There was a major in the front with the driver. We took off. Ahead of us were a couple of other Hummers. As we drove through the main gate, I thought I heard a helicopter rev its engines and take off.

I stuck my head into the front compartment and asked, "Pardon me fellows, what're your names?"

The driver was Albert and the Major with him was Will. I asked Will, "Did I hear a helicopter just take off?"

"Yes, sir. There are actually three that are taking off. They're escorts for us. They're scouting the route for trouble and flying cover."

Beth said, "I told them we could just disapparate these people to the base but your Sally insisted on going by ground—stubborn Muggle."

Sally answered, "I told you that we couldn't take a chance of people at the sea base seeing that kind of magic—stubborn witch. If we have to take them off the base and out of town anyway, we might as well drive them the rest of the way." Both women looked at me hoping for vindication of their position.

I said, "First, she's not 'my' Sally. She's her own 'Sally'. Second, I always stand behind my people's decisions. You should know that. She made the decision, and that's all there is to it. What I'm more interested in is what will happen tomorrow morning after breakfast. Do we have things to keep these people busy while they're getting used to the camp?"

Beth perked up a little, "Sure. People will have to get assigned permanently to quarters. In the afternoon there will be a Quidditch game, and we'll start assigning duties—KP, maintenance, training for able-bodied recruits for the DA. Right, George."

George looked a little worried and said, "Oh, yea. Right away."

I asked, "How have things been going on the base?"

Beth said, "Things have been going pretty well. George and Fred have been organizing defensive magic classes and drills. We've got several people who have been doing the drilling while they've been away.

"We've completely taken over operation of the kitchens, and we now are nearly self-sufficient. We grow vegetables and raise chickens for eggs and meat. We use magic, of course, to increase the supply.

"Our only real problem is wands. We want all the people in the DA to have wands of their own. As a matter of fact they really can't borrow wands, although we've had to do that a good bit while people are learning spells. We've been quietly buying wands in small quantities. But it's difficult because the wizard who will have the wand has to be present to test them when they're bought. We can't exactly have the wand-makers go on house calls here. So we take the wizards one at a time to wand makers in various cities. It's really an arduous process if you're trying to keep it quiet about where all these wizards are coming from.

I said that I understood. "You just have to do the best that you can. Have you got enough galleons to buy all the wands that you need?"

"That's not a problem. We've got lots of dollars and the local Gringotts is quite happy to exchange dollars for galleons. The American government is quite willing to co-operate and supply us with dollars—probably due to your influence."

"Well, we try to be helpful when we can." I said.

Beth winked slyly and said, "You could be more helpful if you wanted to, I think."

"No comment."

Sally grinned and said, "I hope not."

George said, "Well, we've got a long boring trip ahead of us. You and your Muggle 'auto's'."

Fred said, "Oh, I don't know, bro. I think it might be an interesting trip."

Sally said, "Not until you've had a proper shower, bro. It's way too odorous here."

There was a radio in the Hummer. Someone was calling us. The voice said, "Mug Air One to Mug command."

The major answered, "Mug Air command, What's up. Over."

"Major, we've got a situation about 50 klicks up the road. There's two semi's off the road along with two highway patrol cars and an ambulance. At least, that's what it looks like. Over."

"Keep your eyes on the scene and keep your radio transmitting. I'm going to call the highway patrol and find out what's happening. Over."

Major Will pulled out a cell phone and placed the call. His side of the conversation went like this:

"Please let me talk with the commandant.

"Yes, Yes, I'm Major Will. He's expecting a call.

"Yes, it's Will. I need a little help. Is there a ligit accident on I-26 near. . ." He hesitated and the driver pulled out a map and pointed to a spot on it. "Oh, near I-95?"

There was a long hesitation and finally, "Thanks. Listen. You'd better get hold of those officers. The accident may not be as real as it seems. Also, please get everyone and everything at the accident scene off the highway and berm."

There was another pause and Will answered, "Yes, we could leave the road at the next exit and use secondary highways, but that may be what somebody wants us to do.

"Thanks again." He hung up.

Then Will asked his driver, "How far away is that accident?"

The driver thought a moment and said, "About 10 minutes."

"Let's get ready." Will got on the radio and said, "Mug command to all Mug units. In approximately nine minutes, we'll begin passing an apparent accident site. There are two semis, two real highway patrol cruisers, and an ambulance. Assume all of those vehicles hide a heavily armed assault force. Mug Air One and Two, be prepared to fill them with 20 mm. cannon fire. Mug Air Three stay alert at our back. Everyone else, watch both sides of the road. What's going on up at the accident site? Over."

"This is Mug Air One, they seem to be moving the patrol cruisers and the ambulance completely off the road. Over."

"Good. Stay alert."

Will asked, "How much time?"

The driver answered, "Four minutes."

The hummer had gotten very quiet. Not even Beth had anything to say. The minutes ticked on, and finally we rounded a curve. At a point where the broken woods came close to the highway on both sides, were the trucks, the cars, and the ambulance. We approached seemingly slowly, but I glanced at the speedometer, and it read 60. The two armored vehicles ahead of us reached it first and passed uneventfully. Then we were beside it. Everyone except Sally was looking to the right. I noticed that Sally was looking to the left. There was an old black Volvo coming the opposite direction. It passed. We passed, and nothing had happened. I released a breath that I didn't realize I had been holding. We turned around and watched as the rest of the convoy passed the accident site. We got confirmation from the rear helicopter that everyone had passed safely. Slowly the tension in the hummer relented.

Then, Beth asked, "Well, tell us what happened. You obviously broke everyone out of Azkaban. Was it easy?"

George said, "It was terribly hard. We had to learn to be Seals."

Beth and Sally said together, "Seals? You mean like the aquatic mammals?"

Fred answered, "No. No. I mean the military group called Seals. They're an elite force that operate on the seas."

"They are bloody tough too," Added George.

"Yeh. We had to climb rock walls 20 feet high without magic."

"And we climbed down the side of subs and bounced on the rolling seas."

"And we fought dementors."

"And Deatheater guards."

I said, "And you rescued over three hundred innocent wizards and witches."

Beth said, "I'm sure you were there somewhere, Jim."

I looked over at her and found her gazing at me while she toyed with a loose curl. "Well, yes. I was standing on the Bridge listening to reports of what was happening next to the Captain and the XO. Very boring."

She said, "I'll bet it wasn't that boring. I wish I'd been there."

"You can be there at our next dangerous operation."

"Which will be. . . What?"

"You've got me. I don't have any idea. When it happens, I'll try to include you."

By this time we had reached I-20 and took it west. The rest of the trip was uneventful and boring. We pulled up at the main gate of the base. The doors swung sideways, and we drove in. It had started raining lightly, almost misting—a cool raw mist, all the same. There were wizards who greeted us and led us to the main Mess Hall. It was crowded, but unlike on the sub, everyone could sit, and you could see everyone.

□

I walked up to the small stage at one end of the hall and stood beside the podium. I gave a short speech, "Listen up everyone. It's late and everyone wants to get to bed, I'm sure. I'm know I do. We'll arrange sleeping quarters better tomorrow, but for now, if you're a single man, follow the wizard on your left to the men's barracks. If you're a single witch, follow the witch to your right. If you're married, follow the witch here behind me. Tonight, you can sleep in. We'll have brunch in this dining hall at 10AM. Don't let the bugle call in the morning interrupt your sleep. See you tomorrow."

We watched everyone file out to make sure that everyone found the right dormitory. Then we all went to the base commander's quarters. It was an old Victorian home with a large porch that went around two sides of the building. It had a large living room and office on opposite sides of the entry hall. At the back was a dining room behind which was the kitchen. There were four bedrooms upstairs. There was a grand stairway in the middle of the entry hall that went upstairs and in the back of the kitchen there was another stairway that went up and down to the basement.

The camp Commander, Beth, took us upstairs and pointed out our bedrooms. One was occupied by a guest from the Quartermaster's Office of the Air Force who was there to inspect the base. Beth pointed that out, and then said, "Fred and Sally can stay in this bedroom", indicating one that was at the head of the stairs.

Fred looked non-plussed and said, "Are you sure that Sally would be interested in sharing a room with me?"

Beth answered, "Don't trifle with me. Sally, do you object?"

"No, ma'am."

She indicated another bedroom and said, "George you can share that with Jim if you want." She hesitated an instant and then said, 'Perhaps Jim would prefer a different roommate."

That caught me a little by surprise, but I tried to come up with a good reply. Finally I settled for, "I would prefer a different roommate from George—who wouldn't? But, I really think that it's my duty to hold up his morale. So, George, you're stuck with me, eh what?"

George came back instantly, "Oh, I don't want to stand in the way of true love. Feel free to sleep with whomever you like."

I would have kicked him if I could have done it surreptitiously, but I just smiled and said, 'I'll share with you."

We separated, and I got to bed as quickly as I could, barely hesitating to brush my teeth.

□□

The next morning I was wakened momentarily by the 6 AM bugle. George didn't even pause in his snore. I was back to sleep in moments and then awakened at 9AM. George was still asleep. I kicked him a good one to wake him up and get back for the gibe of the previous evening. I took a quick shower and went downstairs to the kitchen where I made myself some hot water for tea. Other people started showing up. Apparently the quartermaster had gotten up with the bugle and was off for the day to whatever he was doing. Beth and Sally were already up and sharing coffee over the small table in the kitchen. I joined them.

I had asked them to show up at 9:30 at the Mess Hall so that we could go over the presentations that we were doing after brunch. George eventually got down just as we were leaving for the Mess Hall. He reluctantly joined us, based on the promise that there would be hot coffee there. We arrived, found a table and sat. I told them that I wanted everyone to practice the first paragraph of their speeches. I got frowns from everyone except Beth and Fred, who wasn't there yet.

I stood up and said, "Witches and Wizards, welcome to camp Dumbledore! I hope you've enjoyed brunch. We're going to be doing a lot of important things today and at least one happy surprise, which I will let a later speaker tell you about.

"The things that we have to do today are very important. They are: everyone finds a job to do for the base; everyone gets better clothes today; everyone has the chance to sign up for the DA; Everyone will have the chance to move on somewhere else; and everyone gets to have some fun!

I looked to Beth, who jumped up and took the low stage. She was bright and cheery, as though she hadn't been up the previous night past 2 AM. She started off, "This base is a co-operative. Everyone contributes in some way to our well-being. Everyone, including me, does some manual labor for the common good. I work on the Sunday breakfast crew."

George leaned over to me and said in a whisper, "Why am I not surprised by that?"

She got down from the stage and pointed to George, who said, "Where the bloody hell is my brother?

Then he said, "Who here wants to give the Deatheaters what for?" He waited a minute, pantomiming being knocked back by the tumultuous response, and then he said, "Great! The DA wants you! If you know how to wave a wand and aren't a squib, you too can fight the Deatheaters with the best of them! All you need is a little training up."

He curved a finger at Sally, who got up and patted Fred, who had just arrived, on the rear as she passed him. Beth cautioned, "None of that when you give your talk today!"

Sally answered with an even air of innocence and somehow at the same time smugness, "Why, I don't know what you're talking about!"

She went on with her talk, "Who here would like some clothes that actually fit? And are clean? Then you'll want to visit the commissary this afternoon in your free time after signing up for the DA. We've got robes, hats, shoes, socks, and other necessaries."

She blew a kiss at Fred, who said, "The entertainment is a secret, so I'm not saying anything till my turn for real."

The new camp residents had started filtering in, so I just said, "It's almost time for brunch. I'll hold my next speech for real, too."

By 10 sharp everyone had arrived. As a matter of fact they were all there well before 10—they were hungry.

So, I got up, made my little speech, ending with, "Everyone form a line to the entrance to the kitchen. In the memory of Dumbledore, I just want to say a word before we share our meal." Everyone got quiet, and I said, "'Oddment'. OK. Everyone, get in line, dig in, and enjoy brunch." There was general pandemonium but George was quiet. I asked what the problem was.

He answered, "I just had forgotten that funny habit of Dumbledore of playing around with the common phrases that people use. I don't think that I'll ever be able to be in the Great Hall again without being a little sad."

"I know. I don't think that anyone who ever had a meal there that Dumbledore presided over will ever think that the Great Hall is quite so great again." We got in line at the end of the line. I told George that I really liked being at the end of food lines. He made a face at me, and we waited.

The meal was one of the most appreciated that I'd seen. The meals on the Ohio were wholesome and filling, but were only that. I'd gotten used to much better fare when I was at Hogwarts, and I think that most wizards and witches ate better than most Muggles. This was a meal prepared by magic. It was nearly as good as that of Hogwarts. As a matter of fact, it was perhaps better than some. I commented to George, "When you were at school, you had no idea how well you ate. This meal brings to my mind the meals at Hogwarts."

George commented through a bread pudding, "Right. I haven't eaten nearly as well since I left Hogwarts. Even mom's wasn't better." He added quickly, "And I never said that."

Finally, everyone seemed to be reaching the limits of avarice. I got up and announced that we had a number of announcements to make. I introduced Beth to the crowd and surprised them with the announcement that she was the base commander. She took the podium, laid out the rules of the base, and announced the requirement to sign up for work assignments.

She went on, "We've set up several tables around the dining hall. Each has a different kind of work assignment available. We've got tables for the mess, for camp upkeep—exterior, for camp upkeep—interior, for guard duty. Please don't leave the Mess Hall without signing up. As a matter of fact, you won't be able to until you've made a commitment.

"And now, I want to introduce Sally Harker, who will talk to you about clothing."

Sally got up to the podium and said, 'I must ask your forbearance because I'm not a witch. I'm sure that you are tired of the naval uniform that many of you had to borrow. We have a commissary on the base where you can get clothes that are more appropriate to witches and wizards. You all have a credit there. You can go and choose clothes and pay for them from that credit. But as time goes on, you will earn credit there from your duties, and you may use the credit however you like. Eventually when the war is over and you're able to return to your homes, the credit will be converted to galleons, and you may collect them or have them credited to your account at Gringott's or wherever you do your banking. I'm afraid we can't do that now so long as Riddle is in command. You'll have free time after we finish here to purchase clothes and other necessities.

"And now, I want to introduce George Weasley. Many of you know him as one of the proprietors of Weasley Wizard Weazes. Others will remember him from Hogwarts and the dramatic exit that he and his brother, whom you will meet later, made from Hogwarts when it was under the headmistress, Dolores Umbridge. George will talk about the DA."

George walked up to the stage, leaned rakishly against the podium and began, "How many people here wish they could give a Deatheater 'what for'?"

Nearly everyone stood up and shouted something. Fortunately, no one could hear individual words over the tumult. George motioned for quiet and went on, "That's what I like to see. How many of you are good at hexes and counter-curses?"

The response was much less tumultuous. As a matter of fact, only a few people stood up.

"Well, we can turn you from a nervous novice to a confident curser. The DA is always looking for a few good men and," he quickly added, "more than a few good women. We can train you to fight with the best. . . er. . . worst Deatheaters. To show you what I mean, I've asked a couple of our trainees to come up and give an exhibition in dueling."

Two short men came up on the stage. George instructed them, "Go to opposite ends of the stage and attempt to disarm and immobilize your opponent. The first to do so wins." The two shook hands and went to opposite ends of the stage. George went on, "At the count of three, begin your curses. One. Two." He paused a count of two seconds for dramatic purposes and then said, "Three!"

With that a silent battle began. I recognized that they were using silent curses as the best wizards do. Flashes of every shade of the rainbow scattered off the walls, the podium, and shields that the duelers created and dropped almost too quickly for the eye to follow. They dodged, jumped and rolled about the stage. Finally, one of the opponent's wands flew out of his hand and into the audience. Shortly thereafter he fell to a "petrificus totalis" curse. George congratulated the winner, who was applauded soundly by the crowd.

George said, "You too can duel just like these two. Just sign up at the DA table at the end of the hall."

Beth shouted out, "Just don't think that will get you out of chores."

George then said, "Finally, all work and no play would make Jack and Jill pretty dull. So, we've arranged a little entertainment for the evening. And here's my brother Fred to tell you all about it. By the way, Mom always liked me better."

Fred took the stage and said, "No, she didn't. You just thought she did because she could never tell us apart.

"Now, I'm here to tell you that we've arranged something really special for you. Tonight, at 7PM we're going to have a Quidditch match between a team drawn from the Base staff and the All-stars of the civilians. The game will be under the lights.

"The base staff team consists of yours truly and my brother George at Beater," George stood and raised his right hand in a fist and received a scattering of applause. "At Seeker we have our very own base Commander, Beth Lawson." She stood with both hands up showing victory signs.

"At Keeper, we have the Keeper of Keys and Grounds, Mr. Troy Regan." He stood up and shook his giant ring of keys.

"At Chaser, we have Rachel Grogan, Anthony Tusci, and Joan Ficus. They're the dieticians in charge of breakfast, lunch and dinner." Two of the three stood. Fred said, "Anthony is back in the kitchen cleaning up after the delicious brunch we just enjoyed."

"We'll introduce the base All-stars at the game tonight. So, without any further wasting of time, I'll dismiss you to sign up for base duties and the DA. Then you can look to togs and give yourselves a self-guided tour of the base. Dinner is at 5 PM and don't forget to come to the game at 7 PM."

Beth came back up to the stage and interrupted everyone getting up. She said, "Before everyone sets out to sign up, I want to give you an opportunity to ask questions."

Everyone settled down, and a burly man in the center of the room stood up and asked, "None of us has wands. How can we be part of the DA without wands?"

Beth asked Fred to field that question. He stood up and answered where he was, "Very perceptive. You're right. You'll need a wand. We do have access to wands, and if you sign up for the DA, you'll move to the front of the list to get one. There are local wand makers whom we meet with on a weekly basis for wands. We have to be pretty careful and not take lots of wands off the market. People would begin to get suspicious otherwise. So, we use lesser wand makers and don't buy lots at one time. They're not Olivander wands, but they're quite serviceable. The duel you just saw was using two wands obtained from them."

Somebody else asked, "Can we get access to news? I want to find out what's happening in England. I want to know what's happening with my friends and relatives."

Beth took that one. "Yes. We bring in the *Prophet*. They're usually several days old by the time they get here, but they are complete. You see all the news that your friends in England see. I'm sorry that we can't get you anything decent." There were some laughs.

Someone else stood up and asked, "When do you think that the DA will see action?"

I stood and took that question. I said, "I wish I knew. We're building our strength and waiting for a clear opening to act. We already have acted in breaking you lot out of Azkaban. That was planned, and we had a rough idea when we wanted to do that. But, we don't have a plan for our next move. We won't act simply to show that we can act. As a matter of fact, we want to stay secret and hidden until we can act decisively. We've tried to convince the Deatheaters that it was a small force that overcame a small and complacent group of guards at Azkaban. And, so far, we think we've succeeded.

"As I've already said, I don't even know what our next action will be. I believe that Harry Potter is the key and our best bet is to stay vigilant, ready, and prepared to support Potter in whatever he does whenever he does it. Unfortunately, we have no idea where Potter is or what he's up to or even the slightest idea of how to get in touch with him. So, we're as much in the dark as you are."

No one else stood up, and Beth dismissed us all again. This time it stuck. There were long queues that built up around the various tables scattered around the Mess Hall.

⬚
⬚⬚

I snagged Beth before she could leave and asked her, "This guy from the Quartermaster's Office. Is he for real and what's he doing?"

Beth looked around quickly, "He's legit OK. But he's a real nuisance."

I asked the sixty-four thousand dollar question, "Does he know about magic."

She looked at me as if I had just gotten out of a loony bin, "How could he not know?"

"Well, if he were just looking at the books and stayed in the office, he might not catch on."

"Well, they told him before he came." She said with a little bite in her tongue.

"Did he believe it?"

"I guess. I have to admit that I'm not sure. He just got here yesterday, and he has been spending a lot of time in the office."

"I'd like to meet him and see why he's here."

"Be my guest. He's been talking about taking a tour of the camp. I've not had time for it, and I'm a little afraid to send him around with a wizard. A Muggle is just what I've needed."

"That's what I'm here for. Lead me to him."

She cracked a small smile and said, "Just remember that you asked for it."

"Thanks."

We walked to the Camp Office, which was World War II era. I walked in and found a bare-bones office building with wood floors and window air conditioners still in place. We went through the Front Office and went to a back room where the glorified accountant was sitting at an old mahogany desk with a computer on it with the accountant staring at it in rapt attention. We walked in, but he didn't notice. Beth "uhummed" loudly, and he looked up and said, "Ms. Lawson, I didn't notice you."

She said, "Captain Jameson, this is. . . " She hesitated as if trying to decide whether to tell him my real authority and position. She finally said, "Mr. Wendt. He's in charge on the English side of this operation."

Jameson stood and reached a hand across the desk to shake. I said, "Pleased to meet you. Beth tells me that you are here on a sort of inspection tour."

He answered, "Yes, that's true. The Air Force wants to make sure that its base is not being misused or its money for that matter."

I asked, "Has Beth been co-operating?"

"Ms. Lawson has been very co-operative with the books—which seem to be in fine shape, but she's been a little reluctant to show me around so that I can inspect the physical camp."

"That's where I come in. Beth has been very busy preparing for the group of refugees that came in late last night. Since I'm here, and I probably know the camp well enough to give you a good tour, why don't I do it?"

Jameson seemed to be stumped by that. His mouth hung slightly open, and he seemed to be struggling a little to answer. Finally, he said, "Yes, yes. That would be fine." He ran his hand through his hair and said, "I don't see any reason not to tour with you. That's provided that you can get us into everywhere on camp."

I turned to Beth and asked, "Do we still have the open door policy?"

She shrugged and said, "Sure."

I answered, "Yes, I can get us into anyplace—except the lady's loo. We've always had a policy here that nothing is locked. You see, almost everyone here are refugees with no money and practically no possessions. The few possessions that they do have are either things that only have sentimental value to them or that they got from the camp store. We've never had a problem with thievery."

Jameson squinted at me and turned to Beth for confirmation. She said, "It's just as Jim says. We've never needed locks."

Jameson shook his head but said, "OK. Let's go."

I led him out the front door, and we walked out of the office toward the Mess Hall. "I think we'll visit the Mess Hall first. But before we go there, I've got a question for you."

"Shoot."

"Just where do you stand on 'magic'?"

"Do you mean, 'Do I believe that magic is possible?'"

"No, I mean, 'Do you believe that almost everyone here—as a matter of fact—everyone except you and me and my personal assistant are wizards or witches?"

He stopped walking and thought a second, "I've seen a lot of unusual things in the Quartermaster's Office. I've seen people try to pull all sorts of scams on the Air Force, but I've never seen anything like a few of the things that I've seen since I arrived here this morning."

I prompted, "But?"

"But, I don't know that I'm convinced that it's magic rather than some sort of 'conjurer's trick'."

I looked up in the air, hoping for inspiration. "Then do you think that you could tolerate some really shocking things? That is, without panicking?"

"I think so." He said uncertainly.

"OK. Then you're ready for the tour. We'll go lots of places that will have some pretty bizarre things going on. I just want to make sure that I won't have to pick you up off the ground more than once or twice."

He seemed to be losing his temper. "Just get on with it. I'll be OK."

"Fine. Then we'll go to the Mess Hall and start the tour there."

"Good. Food is one of the biggest items on your books."

We walked on to the Mess Hall. We went in the main door and found that there were some witches cleaning up after lunch. Mops and sponges were flying around through the air without any apparent human direction. Jameson swallowed hard. I looked at him and he said, "You weren't kidding."

"Oh, you've not seen anything yet." We walked across the hall and entered the kitchen. The kitchen had all the usual things that you expect in kitchens—piles of shining stainless steel pots and pans, mixers, prep tables, ovens, and on and on. What you didn't normally see in kitchens were them sailing through the air. A couple of times we were almost hit by pans on the fly.

One of the cooks came up to us and said to me, "Mr. Wendt—long time, no see. I hear that you've been having some adventures."

"Yes, I have. Louis, let me introduce you to Mr. Jameson, Captain in the United States Air Force. Captain Jameson, this is Louis Lamb. He used to be a chef at the Leaky Caldron."

Louis said, "Glad to meet you, Captain Jameson." He shook his hand. Then Louis turned to me and said, "You know what we need?" But he didn't give me a chance to answer, he just continued after an instantaneous pause, "We need more wands. Do you know that they took half the few wands that we had last week. How they expect us to come up with meals without wands I don't know. You know, Napoleon said that an army travels on its stomach. So, how can we feed those stomachs without wands."

I answered, "You've got me, Louis. I don't know."

Jameson volunteered, "You could do it the Muggle way."

Louis looked at him in alarm, "Don't be gross." He turned to me, "I'm not kidding. I don't know what we're going to do to cook for these additional mouths we've got."

"I'm sorry, Louis. The DA needs those wands. We're doing our best to get more wands, but it's not easy for us to buy so many wands without drawing attention to ourselves.

"And you know its going to get worse before it gets better. We've got a whole lot more recruits for the DA now."

We went on with our inspection tour, and when we were out of the kitchen, Jameson asked, "What is this DA?"

"Oh, it's an acronym. It stands for 'Dumbledore's Army'. Dumbledore was the head of an organization that fought Riddle from the very beginning."

"I see."

We crossed the Parade Ground and headed for one of the Wizard's barracks. I said, "We're going to see a typical Wizard's barracks. I think it's pretty much like typical Air Force enlisted men's barracks. The barracks are named after the houses of Hogwarts School. This one is named Huffelpuff." We went in and found a few wizards. One pair was practicing disarming each other with the *Expeliamus* spell. Another couple was sharing a copy of the *Prophet*. As we passed them, Jameson took special note of the front page.

He said, "I could have sworn that that picture moved," as he rubbed his eyes.

"Oh, I'm sure it did. That's Wizard photos for you. I don't know how they manage it, but somehow they have five or ten seconds of video captured and it loops in the photo. What's even stranger and rarer is that the photos sometimes are not captured video, but the people in the images seem to have their own life. Spooky."

Jameson shuddered and agreed.

We kept walking, and I steered us toward the Gymnasium. As we walked, I said, "I don't know what's going on in there today, but a lot of the time there's dueling practice."

Jameson replied, "I am afraid to ask what that is."

"You've already seen a little of that in the dorm that we visited, but it would largely be more of the same."

"How bad could that be? Sure, let's look in."

We walked up to the main door and found a hand-made sign, "Advanced Dueling.3PM to 5PM." We walked in and found George doing a little instruction. He was saying, ". . . so what we're going to do is combine all the basic elements that we've already practiced—silent spells, disapparation, and the usual spells—*expelliamus, petrificus totalis*, etc. This is a free-for-all. The only rule is that you can only do spells inside this Gymnasium. Questions?"

"Does that mean that we can disapparate out of the Gymnasium?"

George smiled and said, "Ten points for Gryffindor. What is the only rule for this game?"

The questioner answered, "All spells must be in this gym. So that means we can disapparate in and out?"

George answered, "Right for out but wrong for in. Now, we're going to divide up into two teams. I've got a bag here." He lifted up a paper bag. "There are jerseys in here, colored green and purple. Everyone pulls one out at random. The people with all the same color jerseys are on the same team. They've been enchanted so that if a spell hits them, they turn red. As soon as your jersey turns red, you're out of the game. The last team standing wins. Any other questions?"

No one said anything. George held the bag up and the players came up and each took a jersey out. Eventually there were none left. George said, "OK. I'm the referee. Anyone breaking the rule will have his jersey turn red. Everyone pick a spot." He hesitated as people moved around randomly. Then he said, "When I blow the whistle, we start. If I blow the whistle a second time, the game's over." He then blew the whistle.

We were standing in the entrance, and what followed was truly bizarre. People started disappearing and reappearing at random places. It would have been silent if it had not been for the sound of spells hitting the walls of the Gym. Someone would appear right next to someone else and use a curse against him. Sometimes someone would appear right next to another wizard who disappeared at the same time.

I looked over at Jameson and found his mouth gaping open. I almost laughed, but especially after what happened next, I was glad I didn't.

No one spoke, there were occasional grunts as people got hit by a spell and their jerseys turned red. Then I heard a grunt next to me. An errant spell had hit Jameson and propelled him out the door and onto his back. It was an *expelliamus*, I think. He was petrified or worse. I went to him and helped him up. I said, "Sorry, it should have occurred to me that one of us might be hit."

He groaned a little as he got up and said, "That's OK. It didn't occur to me either. But let's get out of the line of fire."

He hobbled off, and I asked him, "You look like you could use some first-aid. Should we go to the clinic?"

Jameson was still hobbling. He said, "Well, I suppose I ought to see it anyway. But tell me there are real doctors there."

"Sorry. There're a couple of healers. They're really pretty good."

Jameson nodded silently, and we hobbled over to the clinic. We walked in and found no one in the Waiting Room. The receptionist, a flaming red-head asked us, "What's the issue? A spell that's stuck? "

Jameson said, "We were at the Gym. They were doing dueling practice, and I got knocked to the ground by a spell. My right hip feels like something's out of line."

She said, "The healer will be with you in a few minutes. There's somebody who got cursed with a 'numb-tongue' curse, and now he can hardly talk or even eat.' She shook her head and said, "Childish pranks."

We had to wait almost a half-hour. The patient before us left and thanked the healer as he left,"Thad u ery mush. I . . tall vedder ready."

The healer patted him on the forearm and said, "You should be fine by dinner tonight. You shouldn't miss the Quidditch game." She added brightly. Then she turned to us and asked, "Which of you has a problem." She was one of those blonds who have a little gray in their hair, but you have to be looking at just the right angle to see it. Otherwise she was of indefinite age. She could have been in her thirties or her fifties.

Jameson put his hand up and said, "Do you mind if Wendt comes in with me."

The healer clicked her tongue and said, "Not afraid of the healer are you?"

I interrupted, "This is the first time Captain Jameson has seen a healer."

She looked at him closer and said, "Yes, I see that you're a Muggle. Well, you're lucky we don't have any of those Muggle 'witch-doctors' here."

Jameson's mouth compressed so that he didn't seem to have any lips. He finally asked, "What's your name?"

"Janice." Then she asked, "What's the problem?"

"I was knocked onto my keester by a *spelleramus* thing, and my right hip has been bothering me ever since."

She looked at him a moment and then said, "Let down your drawers."

Jameson asked, "Pardon me?"

"I said, let your drawers down."

"You mean my pants."

"Of course, I mean your pants. What's the problem? Are you shy?"

Jameson frowned but lowered his pants and bent over as the healer motioned him to bend over the examination table. She lowered his underpants, took out her wand, and gently traced it over his right buttocks. Jameson jumped and said, "What are you doing!"

"I'm examining your hip. " She hesitated, "Hmmm. Hmmm."

Jameson asked, 'What's going on?"

"Oh, be quiet and let me concentrate." She hesitated, and then announced, "You don't have a broken hip or any cracked bones." She started kneading his hip gently, and he yelped, "What are you doing?"

She went on, "Don't be such a sissy. I think the muscle's just got a deep bruise." She walked over to a cabinet with glass doors.

Jameson asked, "Can I get up now."

"Just stay where you are." She got a small glass bottle out of the cabinet. She walked over behind Jameson, opened the jar, dipped a little bit of salve out of the bottle, and spread it over his hip.

Jameson whistled, "Wow, that feels a lot better."

"Yes. You can get dressed, and I've got some instructions for you."

Jameson got himself to his feet and buttoned up. When he had himself turned to the healer, she said, "You feel pretty good now, but you're not as good as you feel. The muscles still have to heal. It'll take a couple of days, so go easy on the hip."

"Yes, ma'am. But what was that crack about 'witch-doctors'?"

"I mean that Muggle 'doctors' use all sorts of crazy techniques. Like surgery. Imagine cutting people to pieces to fix something."

Jameson's lips were compressing again, and he said, "Doctors base their treatments on sound science."

Janice said, "What do you mean 'sound science'?"

Jameson's mouth hung open, and he didn't say anything. Then Janice asked, "Well, what would your 'doctors' have done with this injury of yours—cut you open to see whether you had a broken bone?"

"No. They'd have taken an X-ray."

"What's an X-ray?"

"It's like a photo but with X-rays."

"Like I asked, what are x-rays."

I interrupted and said, "X-rays are a form of light but the wave-length of the light is much shorter than ordinary light. They penetrate flesh but not bone."

They both looked at me as if they'd forgotten that I was in the room. She said, "Well, just be careful." And then as a last minute thought, "Oh, are you going to the Quidditch game tonight?"

The question caught him by surprise. He answered, "I guess so." Then more confidently, "Sure, I'll be there." He looked at me questioningly.

I said, "Right."

Jameson asked, "Are you going?"

"I wouldn't miss it. Should be a lot of fun." She examined her patent leather shoes and said, "Maybe I'll see you there."

Jameson quickly said, "Sounds like fun. Would you give me some help with the game? I've never seen a Quidditch game before."

She smiled and said, "You've never lived until you've seen Quidditch. I'd be pleased to introduce you to the game. Oh, and you can use this ointment twice a day until the soreness goes away." She handed the small jar to him, placing it carefully in his hand and closing his fingers about it.

"What is it?"

She was offhand, as though everyone had heard of it, "Oh, it's just oil of merlap."

Jameson said, 'Streptomycin."

She said, "What?"

Jameson said, 'Nothing, just another example of technical jargon."

We left, and since it was getting close to the early dinner, I suggested that we go to the Mess Hall. We arrived and found that a fair number of the new residents had arrived there as well. We sat and talked about the inspection tour. Jameson was satisfied that everything was being run adequately. He said the accounts were in good order, and he hadn't seen any signs of mismanagement. I offered the opinion that Beth was one of the best managers that I'd known. While we talked, the rest of the camp seemed to have arrived for dinner.

After a while George and Fred showed up and took the podium. Fred used the *sonorus* spell to amplify his voice and announced, "Ladies and

Gentlemen, we have two special treats tonight. Dinner will be delivered to your tables as it is at Hogwarts by disapparition rather than your having to stand in line for it. And second, as promised earlier, at 7PM, we will have the Quidditch Championship of Camp Dumbledore. As Dumbledore would have said, 'And now for a brief word—art—please dig in." And with that serving platters of food appeared at the various tables in the dining hall.

The sudden appearance of a tureen of soup at our table rather startled Jameson, and he whispered to me, "Is this safe?"

I whispered back, "It's at least as safe as the food on the USS Ohio. I can tell you from experience." We were closest to the soup, so we dished out soup for the rest of the table. I didn't know any of the wizards and witches at our table, so we went around the table introducing ourselves by giving our first name, where we came from, and our former occupation. There were a couple of Ministry of Magic wizards and witches, a barmaid, two farmers, and us at the table. When Jameson's turn came, he announced his name and said, "I come from Eire, Pennsylvania."

One of the witches asked, "And what did you used to be?"

Jameson replied, "I used to be a baby, but I am in the United States Air Force. I'm a glorified accountant.'

She replied, "I was wondering what the fancy get-up was. So, are you a wizard?"

"I'm afraid not. As a matter of fact this is the first time that I've met wizards and . . uh . . witches—is that right?"

"Yes, dear, we're witches." She said with amusement in her voice.

One of the former ministry wizards asked if Jameson had ever seen a Quidditch game before. Another witch replied, "Of course, not. He's never met wizards before, how would he have seen Quidditch?"

Jameson said, "You're right. I've never seen Quidditch before. I've heard it's exciting, and I'm looking forward to it."

Everyone at the table agreed that Quidditch was indeed an exciting game worth seeing. At the end of the meal, people started to leave the tables, and I suggested to Jameson that we could head over to the Quidditch field and get good seats. He agreed. I noticed as we left the Mess Hall that he sent his gaze more than once over toward the clinic, but he didn't say anything. We arrived at the field after about a ten minute walk. It was the only new building in the camp.

As we approached the stands, Jameson asked, "Those are strange stands. Aren't they unusually high? And there don't seem to be any seats close to field level. That seems strange."

I replied, "You're right, it would be strange for Muggle games, but Quidditch is played in the air, and the seats are at a level that allow for a good view. They're at about the average height of play." We arrived and walked up the several levels of stairs to get to the seating. I picked a good central spot. Only a few people had showed up yet, so we had a good choice of seats.

Jameson speculated, "I wonder when Janice—that is, the healer will show up? She wants to get a good seat." After a moment's silence, he said, "We should save a seat for her shouldn't we? She did say that she'd join us, didn't she?"

"Yes, I'm sure she'll join us, and I think that YOU should save her a seat."

"Of course, you could save her a seat."

"Oh, I think you'd do a better job of it." He looked at me curiously, but I just smiled. It was a cool evening, but probably typical for late February. People started trickling into the stands and then came in larger numbers. Jameson had to shoo off several people who tried to sit near to him. We were only about 10 minutes from game time. The field lights had just come on, and Jameson was showing real signs of nervousness.

Finally, he noticed the healer climb up to the seating level of the stands. Jameson stood up and waved at her, and she gratified him by noticing him almost immediately and climbed up to our level. She came down our row and looked like she was going to sit by me. Jameson said, "Miss Janice, I saved you a seat over here."

She said, "Just call me Janice please now that we're away from my office. Thanks very much for saving a seat for me. I'll join you with Mr. Wendt's permission."

I smiled and said, "Of course." I rose to allow her to pass easily. She sat down next to him.

He immediately started asking her questions, such as "Did you have other patients after we left?", "Did you get any dinner?", "Do you have a favorite team?" She answered all his questions and asked a few of her own, such as: "How was dinner at the Mess Hall?", "How's your hip feeling?" etc.

He declared that his hip never felt better. Meanwhile the teams walked out onto the pitch and were joined by the referee. They took to the air. Neither Jameson or Janice were paying much attention to what was going on. As a matter of fact, I think that Jameson didn't even realize that the players had mounted their brooms and taken the air, because he happened to look out over the field for a change. Then he suddenly realized that the teams were in the air, and the game had started. He gasped.

Janice asked him, "What happened? Is your hip bothering you again?"

Jameson said, "No. My hip is fine. It's just that the teams are flying!"

"Yes, of course they are. That's what Quidditch teams do, dear boy."

He laughed nervously and said, "Yes, I guess that's what the game's about." Then he went on, "Shit! I never imagined that it would be anything like this. I mean, this is like an aerial dogfight—except that there are no airplanes, just people flying around like there was no tomorrow."

He was right. The bodies seemed to be flying at abandon with no order. He had a hard time for a while, trying to both watch the game and the healer's face. And she was very loquacious, describing the game in great detail to his rapt attention. But she occasionally called attention to the game. For example, at one point, one of the players swooped into a hard dive, immediately followed by an opponent. Janice pointed out to the field and said, "Do you see that?"

"You mean the two players in a dive? Yes."

"That's probably a 'Wronsky feint'."

"What's that?"

"The object of the game is to catch the golden snitch. Sometimes one 'seeker' will pretend to have seen the snitch in an attempt to lure the other 'seeker' into a disastrous dive. The other seeker can't afford to take the chance that the first hasn't seen it. The seeker doing the Wronsky Feint pulls up at the last minute and hopes that the other can't respond as quickly."

Jameson stared at the players a second and asked, "Why did you think it was this Wrong Feint thing?"

"It's too early in the game for the snitch to be found for real."

"But you can't know for sure?"

"No, you can't know for sure."

"Hmmm. That's like a game we call 'chicken'."

"'Chicken?'"

"Sure. Only we play it with cars. The two players drive their cars at each other and the first one to swerve to avoid a collision is the looser."

"Sounds like a stupid game."

"So does the Wrong-way Feint."

She laughed and smiled. They both smiled.

Meanwhile somebody sat down next to me. I turned and saw that Sally had taken the spot next to me. She asked, "OK. I see that the healer has a new fan."

"Yea, I guess so." I glanced over, and they were paying absolutely no attention to the game. "George and Fred seem to be in fine form. I can't remember ever seeing them so accurate with the blodger."

412

"Oh, you know, you can take the boy away from the blodger but you can't take the blodger out of the boy—or something like that. Their favorite part of running the training program of this camp is Quidditch."

"It's good to see fine young men enjoying their work."

"I just wish I could see the fine young men a little more often."

"Yea, I know what you mean. I have my own favorite person I'd like to see more often."

The game ended 250—180. The camp all-stars won, although the management team was well up on points when the snitch was caught. We all retired a little early. There was an extra free bedroom in the camp commander's house that night. At least I thought there was an extra bedroom. The next morning when I got up, the captain's room was occupied by the Captain.

Over breakfast there was a dispute about how quickly we had to get back to London. Sally wanted to stay a couple of days, "to make sure the new residents adjusted OK." I reluctantly agreed, but I had Sally book a flight for me to London as quickly as she could.

Beth came up and joined us for breakfast. She was looking very serious. We soon found out why. She said, "What did you tell that Captain when you gave him the tour of the camp? He seems to think that there's a lot more research he needs to do here."

I answered, "Nothing. He seemed to be quite satisfied with the camp. As a matter of fact he said so."

"Well then, what the heck does he want to hang around for?"

Sally laughed and then suppressed it quickly. She said, "What he wants to investigate is the state of medical care on the camp."

"Oh, yeah, I heard that he was injured slightly and ended up in the clinic. Was he angry about that little accident?"

Sally laughed again and said, "No. No. What he really wants to investigate is the state of the medical staff—not the medical facilities."

The light finally dawned for Beth, "Oh, you mean the hea . . . , that is Janice?"

"Sure."

"Is it mutual?"

Sally said, "If it isn't, they sure had me fooled." She turned to me, and I said, "Yep. I'd say they both have a bad case."

Beth said, "Well, what do you know? I always thought that she was pretty hard-boiled. So she's not the completely dedicated healer that we all thought we knew?"

"I've got to get back to the home office. Sally's going to get me a flight out of Atlanta. I hope later today."

413

Beth asked, "Do you really have to leave so quickly. It'd be nice to have someone who can talk about the bigger picture with authority if questions come up from the new recruits."

I grimaced. "I'm sorry. Fred and George are good at talking with authority whether they have it or not."

She grimaced, "Yeh, talk. But you know what's going on, and it shows in the way you talk about it."

"Sorry, I've got to go. There's a big presentation by the 'Boy Genius' about the Deatheater network and I need to be there."

"But you can always read it later."

"Sure, but if I'm not there, those guys begin to get 'ideears'" I pronounced it like a Bostonian would. "and if I don't head those ideears off before they get to the pass, there'll be hell to pay."

"Sure." She laughed.

Sally made the reservations, and I was in the air that afternoon.

Graph Theory

My red-eye flight arrived at Heathrow at 8AM. Nobody was waiting for me. I had a carry-on with a couple of changes of clothes. I took the Tube to the office. I got there about 11AM. I dragged myself into the quarters behind the office and dropped off to a fitful sleep. I woke up about 2 PM and worked for a while. I got to bed that night around midnight and was up around 7 AM, which was not too bad, considering that I was not a morning person. I checked through emails. I discovered that they'd rescheduled the weekly meeting for this morning at 8AM. Well, I'd not have any trouble making that. I showered, dressed, stumbled down to the Cafeteria for breakfast, and showed up in the Conference Room at about 7:45AM.

The Boy Genius was early as usual and had already set out presentations at every place around the table. I started to scan through it for interesting things and found plenty. I was engrossed and didn't notice all the section chiefs come in. Tarkin was looking over my shoulder when I noticed him. He asked, "Have you got a Playboy buried in there?"

"What do you know about Playboys?"

"Oh, I keep track of your American perversions, or should I say diversions."

"You should say," I hesitated, looking for a good word and finally settled for, "nothing."

Parker chided us, "Boys, boys. It's time to put down your toy pistols and get to work."

He went on, "Our guest speaker today is Nicolas, who is going to talk today about what we know about the Deatheater organization from video analysis."

415

The Boy Genius stood up and corrected Parker, "Actually, these results come only partly from video analysis. The main contribution comes from graph theory."

Jergens asked, "What do you mean by 'graph theory'?"

The B.G. said, "It's really pretty simple. As a matter of fact some of you do it all the time, though not with the mathematical rigor that we applied to this study.

"Graph Theory is just the analysis of connections between different nodes in a network. The network might be the set of post offices in London." He paused pregnantly, "Or it might be the network of Deatheaters." He went to the white board and drew a series of small circles on the board and started writing initials in them.

"Let's say that this one is Tom Riddle (TR) and this one, Severus Snape (SS) and this one, Draco Malfois (DR), etc." He kept drawing circles and filling them in with initials. Then he started drawing straight lines connecting them. "OK. Each line represents a meeting between the two. This is a sample of what the real graph looks like. You can see that there are lots more lines connecting Riddle with some Deatheaters than others. Based on the frequency of contact, we determine the working 'cells' of the Deatheaters.

"But what's more interesting is that we can develop a hierarchy of the Deatheaters and others." He erased the white board and then drew another picture with seven concentric rings. He laughed and then said, "The seven circles of hell.

"The innermost circle is occupied by only one person—Riddle. The next one out is his closest circle of Deatheaters. You will recognize Snape, the two Malfois's—father and son—and Belatrix Lestrange and a few others whose names you probably don't know." He wrote names inside the 2nd circle.

"The third circle is occupied by the common everyday Deatheater—people like Waxly and the twins Carrow and so on."

"The next circle out is one that we call the 'fellow travelers'. They are people who don't rise (or fall) to the notice of Riddle. They are Deatheater wannabe's. I only remember a few names myself. They do things to get themselves noticed by the Deatheaters and, of course, Riddle.

"The fifth circle contains those that we call the commercials. They will do anything for a galleon. Because the Deatheaters have gold, they work for them. You find people like the 'Snatchers' in there.

"The sixth circle contains common ordinary people who just want to get along and not get into trouble. This ring is very big, of course.

"The seventh circle contains people who oppose Riddle—mainly the Order of the Phoenix and the DA."

Someone asked, "Where are us Muggles?"

The B.G.'s answer was "We don't make it on this chart, and we're glad that we don't.

"Now, the interesting thing about these results is that we developed them without any reference to Ms. M.'s contribution of evidence from the Order of the Phoenix about the identity and friends of the Deatheaters. Basically, the two lists are nearly completely consistent.

"These facts bring us to the idea that we now have a very nearly complete list of the Deatheaters and fellow travelers and their relative importance in the organization.

Parker asked, "How many people are in each ring?"

"There are 7 in the 2nd ring, 52 in the third ring, about 300—more or less—in the 4th ring.

Everyone around the table was quiet for a while. Then Tarkin spoke up, "This means that we could target all those people in the first three rings, certainly. And we could even do a pretty good job of covering the 4th ring if we needed to. Without most of those people, the organization would collapse."

That comment brought a lot of conversation, or I should say babble. Finally Parker brought the meeting to order, "Are you proposing doing that, Tarkin?"

"Wellllll," he drew the word out, "the idea had occurred to me."

I said, "It would be pointless without getting Riddle. Sure, his organization would be set back for several years, maybe even decades, but that's all. He'd need to re-build it. And that would be the only time we could pull that trick. We're the first people he'd take out after that happened. And don't think that an operation that large could be kept completely secret. It'd have to be completely secret for us to survive."

Tarkin came back quickly enough that I knew that he'd anticipated that objection. "But, IF, and I do say, 'IF', Riddle were out of the picture, we could do that couldn't we?"

"Yes, theoretically. We'd have to have all their routes laid out and be prepared to strike in a coordinated way everywhere they were at once. Just to be sure to get everyone in the 2nd and 3rd rings, we'd probably have to have hundreds of teams pre-positioned, ready to act on a moment's notice."

"That's a lot of teams," Parker said. "But we should make contingency plans and maybe put out a few teams to practice. We'd see how feasible it would actually be—maybe we'd do the 2nd circle, eh."

Tarkin said, "My boys would love to have something to do for a change. Yes. We'll do it." You could almost see him mentally rubbing his hands in anticipation.

Parker turned to me and said, "Why don't you do some thinking about it as well. It'd be good if we could use wizard teams for this, don't you think."

I said, "Yes, sir. I'll definitely think about it and talk with the DA about it. We'll see what we can come up with."

"Well," Parker went on, "get moving." Then we all left the Conference Room.

I went back to my office and thought. It just wasn't the same without Sally to bounce ideas off of. But I finally picked up the phone and dialed the number that I knew best. It was 3PM London time. It was 9 AM in Georgia. Beth should be in her office. The phone rang twice and was answered by Beth's personal assistant. She recognized my voice and immediately put me through to Beth.

The first thing she said was, "What's the weather like?"

"Oh, highs in the 40's, lows around freezing."

"Well, go ahead."

"I need to talk with the Weasleys—and you as well. Can we set up a conference call for tomorrow morning your time." There was a hesitation on the other end of the line, and then Beth said, "Sure. I don't have anything scheduled tomorrow, and the Weasleys have a couple of hours starting at 10 AM. What do you think?"

"Sure. Sounds OK. I can make time. Use your conference phone."

"No problem. What's the subject?"

"I'm not ready to give it to you. I've got to think more about it. Sorry."

"Oh, that's OK. Just don't make it too scary. I heard from the highway patrol, you know. They wanted to know what you were expecting on that last run with the Azkaban refugees."

"I don't know. I never know what to expect. I can't believe that the Deatheaters won't find out about us sometime."

"You've taken so many precautions. It'll be OK."

"Anyway, it's not scary the way you think of scary. It's. Well, it's." I couldn't quite say it. "You'll see what it is. And it's not Deatheaters descending on the camp."

□

I had all day and all night to think through what I would say. I needed all that time and more. I'd gotten tired of fighting everyone—fighting the Deatheaters even though they didn't have the slightest idea that I still existed; tired of fighting the SAS desire to find a solution in the death of their enemies, and I suppose, my own desire to trade a death for a death of the people that I loved who were gone. I suppose it was the time shift and jet lag, but it was hard to know.

The next morning, I got up at a more or less normal time. I ate more normally, and I was able to think. I planned the next step that I would take this afternoon at the conference call.

I placed my call a half-hour in advance. I wanted to talk to Beth. She answered the phone and was surprised to hear my voice, "Is my clock wrong or is yours. I can't believe it's off by ½ hour."

"No, it's not off."

"Do you want me to try to get the Weasleys in for the call now?"

"No, I want to talk to you first. Look, I don't like the turn things are taking here, and I'm trying to find a way out of it. Here's what's happened. The B.G. has . ."

Beth interrupted me, "B.G. Is that some department that I've never heard of?"

"No. I guess I've never talked to you about him by that name. It stands for 'Boy Genius'. "

"Oh. Is that your nickname for Brahms?"

"Yea. I guess I've always been overawed by his intellectual abilities, and I compensate by making up a disparaging nickname for him. Anyway, he just keeps on being a genius. I won't give you the long technical details, but he thinks that he's figured out who all the Deatheaters are and a pretty darn high percentage of the Deatheater sympathizers."

"So, you could capture them after Potter's dealt with Riddle?"

"Well, that would be a good idea, but it's not THE idea."

"And THE idea is?" she asked with some tremor in her voice.

"THE idea is that they could just execute them. Send out sniper teams to pick them off as soon as Riddle's gone."

"Do you have another idea—I hope?"

"Well, not a particularly good one. But it's the best that I've come up with so far. I toyed with the idea of resigning. Of course, I'd sit out the rest of this crazy war in the brig—the same way I started it.

"But I've got another idea that I think is better."

419

I took a deep breath and plunged on, "Well, my idea is that we can be ready to put our own troops in and arrest them—at least some of them—before the death squads move in."

"That sounds feasible. And you are making this call to try to set that up?"

"That's the general idea, but I don't want to tell the Weasleys what the nut cases back at my office are dreaming up. Who knows what they'd do. So, I'm going to set up to be ready to respond quickly if it looks like Riddle is leaving the scene."

"And that's what we're going to talk about?"

"Yep. I hope you'll have your thinking cap on as usual."

"Anything for the boss."

"Right."

"Well, they should be along in a few minutes. Do you want a report as long as we have a little time?"

"Sure."

She talked about how the new recruits were doing. Things were going along pretty well. Our numbers in the DA had almost doubled, so there was a lot of general confusion. There were disputes in the dorms that were difficult to prevent. You put lots of people who don't know each other in a big room, and there are bound to be problems as they learn how to get along. However, it was nothing that hadn't happened before, and this time around we had lots of old hands to leaven the newbie's. The shortage of wands had suddenly gotten much worse with lots of recruits for the DA without any wands. They simply had to sit and watch while those with wands learned and got better.

Eventually I heard people enter the room, and Beth said, "Boys, the boss is on the line a little early. He's on the speakerphone. Mind your manners."

George said, "Oh sure. You're just kidding us. He hasn't called yet."

I set him straight on that by saying, "Just sit down and shut up."

Fred said, "Yep. No one could mimic that whiny complaining style."

I went on, unperturbed, "The reason that I called this meeting was to talk about an idea that I've had. I got it while watching that amazing dueling drill that I saw the last time that I was there."

Fred laughed, "You mean the one where the Muggle got knocked off his feet. I think it was all a ploy to get into the clinic to get introduced to Janice."

I said, "That reminds me. Is the Captain still there? And how are you Sally?"

Sally answered, "The Captain leaves tomorrow. He'd milked just about all he could out of the situation. And I'm just fine thank you."

"Are you thinking of coming back to London sometime or have you decided to become an American citizen?"

"My well-deserved vacation is about to end as well."

"Back to business. The advanced dueling that I saw made me think that we have a pretty effective fighting force, and we should be preparing to use it.

George asked, "Have you got another operation in mind already?"

"Nothing specific, but I think that we should be prepared to move it quickly when the opportunity comes. Now, I want you to put on your thinking caps. What's the fastest way that you could get a group of 300 DA to England on short notice? Think big. Don't worry about how feasible it is. We'll worry about that later. I just want ideas now—lots of ideas."

George said, "Well, that's easy. If we're talking magic ways, you've got port keys, floo network, flying carpets, brooms, uh. I think that's about it. What about you Fred? Got any other ideas?"

Fred said, "You've taken all the easy ideas. You could always pull that trick that that rat Malfoy did with the twinned vanishing cabinets. I can't think of anything else."

I asked Beth, "Beth, you got any other ideas?"

I could almost see her do that distinctive head shake that she used when she was being negative. It was a very slow horizontal rotation of her head one way and then back once. She said, "They've pretty much covered it."

"OK. Then let's take those and critique them."

Fred said, "Well, there are the non-starters—flying, either carpet or broom. That's slow. They only can go a little above 200 K/hr—tops. That would take more than a day—if you could stay alert and not get into trouble flying continuously."

George added, "Floo network is out. The Ministry of Magic watches that like a hawk for the likes of us. We could move around outside England—maybe. But getting in that way would be a one-way trip to Azkaban."

Beth said, "The vanishing cabinet pairs is theoretically possible, but I didn't know that there was such a possibility. Are you saying that someone actually found a pair of twinned cabinets that you could use to travel from one to the other?"

I said, "Yes. That's the way that Deatheaters got into Hogwarts the night that Dumbledore died. If I could get hold of that brat Malfoy, I can't tell you what I wouldn't do to him."

Beth asked, "What about those two vanishing cabinets. Maybe they could be used for something good?"

George answered, "One's still at Hogwarts—I suppose in the Room of Requirement still. That would be the easy one to get hold of. And that wouldn't be too easy at that. With Snape and the Carow twins running the show there, it wouldn't be easy at all. But, of course, we've got Ginny there still and a good number of the old DA. They could probably pull it off if we really needed them to."

Fred picked up the thread, "The real problem is that the other one is in Borgan and Bourke's—right in the heart of Deatheaterland. I don't think that we could get it."

Beth asked, "And nobody knows of another pair like that?"

Fred and George said, in unison, "Not on your life."

I said, "What about port keys. They can be prepared in advance and used at need. You could use one and it could shuttle back and forth may 8 or ten people at a time."

Fred said, "Or, you turn a bus, like the night bus into a port key and shuttle sixty or seventy at a time. But it wouldn't do you any good."

George said, "Port keys are really strong magic that stands out like a sore thumb. You could maybe use one once and have time to get away before the Deatheaters arrived, but not more than once."

Fred added, "And maybe not even once."

Beth summed up, "Then that's it. There's no magical way to do what you want to."

I said, "OK. Then let's talk Muggle ways. How about this? We have a C-5A transport plane ready in a closed hangar at an Air Force base within apparition range of you. There must be dozens of Air Force bases that close. It has a dedicated crew that is constantly on alert. They keep it flight ready at all times. They occasionally take it out on drills—more about that in a minute.

"When the need arises, you get everyone together and disapparate to that hanger. The crew flies you across the Atlantic, and when you get over England, you disapparate directly from the plane to wherever you're going to. How long would that take? Is it feasible?"

Fred said, "Oh, we could probably get people together and disapparate to the pranger within an hour."

George said, "Hanger, you twit, not pranger."

Fred said, "Oh, I just prefer the sound of that word—pranger, pranger pranger. Try saying it ten times quickly."

I interrupted them, "However you say it, it would probably take about seven hours to fly to England. That means that total time would be about eight hours."

George said, "Yea. I suppose that's about right. It wouldn't take any time to disapparate from the plane to wherever in England we were going."

I asked, "Anyone have a better idea?"

No one said anything, so I said, "In that case, let's get started on setting this up. Beth, talk to the Air Force people and see if you can get a dedicated spare hangar someplace that we can use with a C-5A and crew.

"Fred and George, we need you to start doing drills practicing the routine. As soon as we've got a plane and hangar, start having groups disapparate to the hangar and then eventually taking the plane up with you in it."

Fred said, "Wait one minute. Has anyone ever tried disapparating from a moving plane and landing anywhere? Do we know it's even possible without killing yourself?"

I said, "That sounds just like the kind of hare-brained stunt that you two love to do. You should try it out first to see if it is feasible."

Sally finally had something to say, "Now, wait one minute yourself. I'm not having these boys experiment with hare-brained schemes."

George said, "Oh, it sounds like a lot of fun. How fast do airplanes fly?"

Sally said, "Up to 1000 km per hour. That's one km. every 4 seconds."

Fred said, "OH."

I said, "But airplanes can fly much slower. I'll bet that the pilot can almost stall and be going very slow—maybe only thirty or forty miles per hour."

Sally said sarcastically, "Yeah. That's almost nothing."

"Well, if worst comes to worst, the pilots can land it at a military base and when they're on the ground and stopped they can disapparate."

"That's better." George agreed.

I asked, "Any other issues?"

No answers, so I said, "Well then everybody has an assignment. So toddle off."

Sally asked, "What about me?"

'You have the most important assignment."

"Which is?

"Get back here as soon as you can!"

Owls

Sally and I attended our first bi-weekly status meeting since she'd gotten back. I didn't know what was on the docket for the meeting. I only knew that Peters was doing a presentation. We arrived at the Conference Room, and Parker worked through the current status of what was going on. The Americans had balked at turning over a hanger AND a C-5A transport plane AND its crew and support team to us indefinitely, but eventually had given in once the British Exchequer had agreed to put up the exorbitant fees.

The base that they'd chosen was in Ohio—Wright Patterson. Apparently there were a number of closed hangars that contained exotic planes with exotic missions, and ours might be lost among the rest. There had been a couple of drills where small groups of wizards had disapparated into the hangar and boarded the transport. They were preparing for a live mission where the wizards would not only board the plane, but they'd take off and fly a short mission.

There was a brief report about how a couple of sniper teams had been put together and were shadowing the inner circle of Deatheaters.

Then, Major Peters was given the floor, and he made his presentation.

He began with a review of how our intelligence operations had been going. "We've gotten to be good tracing movements of the Deatheaters and have begun to get to the point where we can anticipate their moves a lot of the time.

"However, there's an aspect of intelligence that we don't have any kind of handle on yet. Anyone—what is it?"

There were not many people raising their hands with suggestions. Finally, someone said, "We usually can intercept enemy messages and decode them. I haven't heard of a single bit of traffic intercepted and decoded.

Peters jumped on that, "Right-O. We're ignorant of their intentions—completely ignorant. I want to change that.

"How do Deatheaters communicate?"

I had an answer, "Well, there are several means—letters carried by owls, direct message by *Patronus*, signals on magical talismans. There are probably other ways, but I just don't know them."

Peters asked, "But mostly they communicate by owl, right?"

"Yes, you're right. I think a lot of messages between Deatheaters go by owl. So?"

"I think we should intercept owls going from Deatheaters."

I asked, "Really? How are you going to do that?"

Peters smiled happily, "We've done experiments. We've released owls with messages and followed them by helicopter. After they were out of sight of the people who released the owl, we snared them with nets. We recovered the owl, removed the message, copied it, and then re-released them."

"What was your success rate?"

"In the final trials, we had 95% success rate."

"Did you? OK. I see a few problems.

"First, ordinary owls are not the same thing as owls used as post owls. They're clever, and I think you wouldn't have as much success as you think you would.

"Second, what will you do after you've captured the owl and removed the message. By the way, that's not so easy as you might think it would be. Any way, you've got the message and read it. What then."

"What do you mean, what do I do then—why nothing."

"So, you're not going to send the message on?"

"Well, of course, we'll do that."

"And you don't think that the wizards will realize that the message has been tampered with?"

"Sure. We can reseal messages just as it was before."

"Yes, resealed so that the Muggles can't tell the difference, but so that wizards can't tell the difference? I'm not so sure."

"Well, that's what we have our own wizards for. Surely they can do it?" The last sentence ended with a rising inflection. It seemed like what started as a statement ended as question.

"I don't know. Maybe they can. This would be a job for the Weasleys."

"Then would you get hold of them and see what can be done?"

"Of course. But don't expect miracles." We went on to other topics, and after the meeting Sally and I went back to our office.

Sally was happy. "Well, when are you going to call the Weasleys?"

"Oh, you should decide. You know their schedule a lot better than I do. Or at least one of their schedules better."

With a quick call she arranged for us to call in the late afternoon.

This time everyone was in Beth's office when we called. I started the conversation, "There's this stupid idea that we can intercept owls carrying messages for the Deatheaters, remove them, read them, then re-seal, and send the owl on its way.

"Oh, yes. One last thing. The recipient of this message must not suspect that it's been intercepted and read. What do you think?"

There was a hesitation and then Fred said, "What do you think, bro? We could stun the owl and remove the message. The tricky part would be opening it without leaving traces."

George said, "You could duplicate it, don't you think?"

Fred asked, "But would the duplicate include the ink on the parchment?"

Beth asked, "I think that it would probably work if you were really careful with the "diviso" spell. What do you think?"

George said, "If you're right, we wouldn't even have to remove the parchment from the owl's leg. Then we just send it on its way."

Beth asked, "But isn't there a spell that will find the use of spells on an object?"

Fred, "We need to experiment. We've got to find some owls, practice intercepting them, and see if we can duplicate the message. Then see if we can figure out if its been intercepted."

I put in, "To do that test, you need to randomly pick owls to intercept and not intercept. Then your results will be unbiased."

Beth said, "Yes, good catch. We'll have to find a bunch of owls that we can experiment with."

I asked, "How soon do you think you can do that?"

George said, "How about a couple of weeks?"

I asked Beth, "Sound reasonable? Can we get owls for this experiment quickly?"

She answered, "I think so."

"Then make it so."

Sally asked, "Would you mind if Fred and I talked a little on company time?"

Beth's voice brightened audibly, "That would be fine with me."

I said, "I've no problem with it. I'll just leave the room and go talk to Parker."

She said, "Thanks."

I left and walked, not to Parker's office, but down to the B.G.'s office. We went to the lab and watched the monitors showing the most interesting things going on in front of our networked video monitors. Actually not much was happening.

The next day Sally and I were in the office when an owl appeared flying through the door. It landed on my desk, and I pulled the message off. When I broke the seal and unrolled it, I discovered the following message,

"Dearest, dearest, we have the entire week of Easter off. So, I have a small proposal for you."

I wrote an answer on the very same parchment—"Lucky you. Being the loyal employee that you are, no doubt you're spending your vacation grading term papers. All my love xoxoxoxox."

Just before we left for the day another owl flew into the office. Its parchment said, "You're not the only one who can plan a mystery vacation. Take the week of Easter off, and I'll take you someplace exciting and out of the way. Yours, M."

I quickly scrawled a reply, "I'll get that vacation even if I have to quit.. Yours Forever, oooooooo". I sent the owl scooting immediately—except that I had a hard time tying the scrap of parchment onto the owl's claw. Finally, Sally did it for me with a "tch, tch, tch., why so nervous?"

The next morning there was a reply for me waiting in the office when Sally and I went in. It said, "On Palm Sunday at noon, walk from King's Cross Station down Northdown Street with your suitcase. Love, M."

I returned the note with the answer, "D'accord."

The next couple of weeks were either the most boring, slow moving weeks or the most delightful depending on the time of day. Finally, Palm Sunday arrived, and I made my way to Kings Cross. It was a sunny day and seemed warm if you could stand in the sun. I walked along Northdown street and had gone about a block when I suddenly noticed that there was an arm looped through my arm. I didn't look over but said, "I was wondering when you'd arrive." I hadn't heard a pop, so she must have disapparated somewhere else and snuck up on me.

I turned and immediately my lips met hers. They stuck for a while, and she said, "Hardly a word of welcome. One would wonder if you are happy to see me." I still had my arms around her back.

I said, "I'll show you if I'm happy to see you." But she twisted away and said, "We don't have time to waste on that. Come on, and let's find an alley in the shade."

I complained, "Waste?" But she was having none of it for the moment. She led me down an alley and said, "Brace yourself." Before I had a chance to "brace myself", my stomach turned inside out. It was good that I had planned ahead and not eaten breakfast.

Easter

We were standing on a street in a modest-sized town. The street was narrow. As we rounded a corner, I saw that the building that was next to us was The **Leauses Bed & Breakfast.** Minerva said, "I've already checked in here, so come along, hubby."

"I wish. I wondered why you didn't have a handbag with you. I suppose you left it in our room. By the way, who am I?" We were still arm in arm as we walked in.

The lady in the front room asked, "Is that your husband Mrs. Dursley?"

I left Minerva and walked up to her, offered my hand, and said, "Yes. I'm Dursley, Vernon Dursley. And you are?"

She looked down at the name-tag on her right breast and said, "Penny, sir."

I turned to Minerva and said, "Come Petunia." She smiled and took my arm again. We walked out of the room. We took the stairs up to the 2nd floor where our room was. It was a very pleasant room at the corner of the building with windows on two exterior walls. The room was dominated by a short four-poster bed. There was an armoire and a chest of drawers. I put my carry-on bag down and started to unpack.

"Petunia, this seems extremely pleasant. Where are we? Or do I have to figure it out for myself?"

Minerva chuckled, "Well, Vernon, I think it should continue to be a mystery tour. I'd like to know how quickly you can figure out where we are without asking someone."

"Petunia, let's go for a walk in the neighborhood."

"Very well, Vernon."

We proceeded to take a walk around the neighborhood. We went down Victoria Road to London Road and turned left, which took us to Sheep

Street where we were forced to turn. As we went, we kept our eyes open for somewhere to eat later. We decided that we'd try the Waggon & Horses later. It was a pleasant walk even though it was cool in the shade. The time slipped by while we strolled, and we hardly noticed that the sun was getting close to the horizon when we began to get hungry.

The Waggon turned out to be a pub without much in the way of food, so we inquired for a place for a good meal. The barmaid suggested the Friar Tuck Fish Bar. Somewhat dubiously we followed directions and arrived at a pleasant, sit-down restaurant. Despite the uninviting name, it turned out to be a good standard fish & chips meal. To show our thanks for the good tip, we went back to the Waggon and had a pint.

By this time, we were feeling the effects of the long walk and good meal and ale. So, we happily walked back to our B&B. It turned out that there were several other guests in the Common Room. We spent just enough time to introduce ourselves and excuse ourselves to go up to our room. It had been a really good day, and we had forgotten our troubles. This little out-of-the-way town with its small shops, unhurried citizens, and good food seemed like it was in another universe from the one that we came from. It was really easy when we got to our room to slip into bed and talk happily in each others arms. There was no urgency in the world —even to enjoy each other's bodies. There was all the time in the world, and we talked on about school. We remembered when it had been a school with books and the pursuit of truth. Finally we were content to merely be together.

We were more tired than either of us believed, and I found myself nodding with Minerva tucked under my arm. It was nearly midnight. I turned off the reading light, and we both slept.

The next morning, Minerva's expansive yawn awakened me, and we enjoyed a half-hour of conjugal exercise. We showered and went down to the Common Room, not caring one whit whether there was breakfast waiting for us or not. We found in fact that we had almost missed breakfast. We were the only ones at the table. However, our hosts joined us, bringing eggs, kippers, toast, marmalade and butter. We talked about our vacation and plans.

The wife, Joanne, asked if we'd slept well. I answered, "Yes, very well. Almost too well. We came near to missing the breakfast."

Minerva added that the bed was very comfortable. "We read for quite a while in bed. That's a luxury that we rarely have, isn't it, Vernon?"

"Petunia, I can't remember the last time that we spent so much time in bed, not sleeping."

"Now, Vernon, you'll give these people the wrong idea."

"I just meant that it was very comfortable and suitable for all sorts of activities."

Minerva kicked me under the table. I retaliated by slipping off the shoe on my right foot and caressing the inside of her calf with it. That got me another kick.

The husband asked, "How did you two get together?"

I looked at him and said, "We're both teachers. Petunia was my 'mentor' I guess you'd say. She was the reason that I made it through the first year at school. Right, dear?"

She said, "Yes, Vernon, I think you'd never have made it without me."

"Truer words never spoken. After a while, though, our talk in the mentoring sessions was less about how to control the classroom and teach students and more about how 'wonderful' the world was. We never really talked much about what made the world 'wonderful', but we eventually figured out that it was being together."

Joanne said, "But wasn't the . . uh . . difference in your . . . uh . ."

Minerva immediately put in, "Ages? Yes, we have a few years between us, but it never seemed to make much difference. My greater years of teaching made me a good mentor, and then Vernon was teaching me."

"Petunia, you're far too generous with me. I think you knew more about teaching when you were my age than I'll ever know. I've gotten to the point where I can do a lesson plan and run a classroom without losing control most days, but I've never been able to avoid having my favorites —and probably making it clear in class who they were." I looked over at Minerva and said, "You'll always be my favorite teacher and my love."

Our eyes locked for a while that seemed only an instant but cleared throats across the table interrupted us. We looked back, and I said, "Sorry. It's just been a while since we, well, had any time for anything other than lesson plans, faculty meetings, so forth."

Joanne smiled and said that she understood all too well. We slowly enjoyed breakfast, and we talked about trivial things—the weather and their kids, who were now out of the house and married. They were in London and Cambridge. The daughter was an assistant manager at a bank and the son was an assistant professor at Cambridge—French literature. We talked about music. Which band was better, Pink Floyd or the "Stones". I suddenly realized that I and they were talking and that Minerva was being very quiet. It had happened before. Only I was the one who had been silent as the wizards and witches talked about the Weird Sisters and Quidditch and Celestine Warbucks.

It had been good to talk with someone who wasn't military intelligence, who shared my secret, and lived under that same threat every day. These people didn't know anything about the war. Our hosts were blissfully ignorant of all the bad things that were going on. They could talk happily and easily about planning a trip to London next weekend and talked about the strange disasters that had been going on—the failure of the Millennium Bridge so soon after its opening and the hurricane that had wandered so far from the tropics.

I forced myself to include Minerva. "We will never agree about the Rock & Roll top band and we're boring Petunia to tears. Can you suggest some interesting things to see in the area?"

"There's the Royal Agricultural College." Joanne's husband Dan said.

Joanne enthused, "They've got a museum, and there are lots of interesting little streets with the cutest shops." She was looking expectantly at Minerva. "I know you'd enjoy that."

Minerva smiled and thanked her. Dan suggested that for one or two days we might do a hire car and see some of the neighboring towns.

I said, "This town is so pleasant and your B&B as well that I wouldn't be surprised if we just settled in for our vacation right here." They seemed to be pleased by that, but Dan still assured me that if we wanted to drive to Tetbury or Stroud that we could hire a car here in Cirencester.

I thanked them for the suggestion, but we ended up deciding to take a morning walking tour.

After we'd gotten out of sight of the B&B, Minerva asked me, "Do you want to go to any of those places they mentioned. We could forget about the hire car and just disapparate there."

"I meant what I said. I really like it here. We'll probably be getting bored by the end of the week but for now I think that I'm perfectly happy being here with you."

"What an interesting co-incidence. Me too."

We walked leisurely through the town, stopping here and there at shops and having a lunch. The cool early spring sun was just warm enough to make for bracing walks between shops. Thus the days passed, and we didn't get bored. We walked and shopped, or actually, we pretended to shop. And when we got tired of that we stayed at the B&B and read.

When Minerva started to do lesson plans, I knew that the vacation had been long enough. I suggested to her that it was probably the end of the vacation. She was taken aback, but she reflected a minute and said, "I suppose that you're right. It's just been so wonderful to be out from under all the war against Riddle and wondering when they'd come to send me to Azkaban—or worse—that I've not wanted this to end." She smiled and added, "I know that it sounds like the only thing I enjoyed about it was being lost—beyond the reach of the Deatheaters, but really it wouldn't have been good if you hadn't been here."

"Let's check out."

So we went downstairs and found Joanne. We explained that we were going to check out. We knew that it was a day early. We were just ready to go back—to work and the everyday.

She protested, "I hope that you haven't gotten tired of being with us."

Minerva said, "No, no. It's just that eventually you know when it's over, and this just happens to be the time."

Joanne nodded and said, "I know. People reach that point. It happens fairly often but, well, we've really enjoyed having you with us. You are a good example to us. After a while the 'special' of a marriage seems to seep away. I can tell that hasn't happened with you two. Dan and I have really enjoyed your being here. I hope you might think of returning here some time. Or at least recommending us to some of your friends, Petunia."

Minerva smiled and said, 'We'll always remember this place with a lot of fondness, and maybe with luck, some future spring break we'll be back."

There was a little moistness around one of Joanne's eyes as she said, "Then it's good-bye Vernon. Do come back."

"Petunia said it. With some luck we will." We had already packed, and so we just had to go back up to our room, grab our bags, and take one last look to be sure that we hadn't left something. When we got back to the main floor, Joanne asked, "Do you need me to call you a cab or something."

Minerva said, "No, thanks. We're catching the bus. Don't worry about us. Good bye."

We all said good bye. Then, we left the front door and started walking. After rounding a corner, Minerva put her free arm through my free arm and said, "Thank God, I don't have to hear you call me Petunia one more time."

"You know, Vernon gets old pretty quickly too." She looked up and down the street. I knew that she was preparing for disapparation. I gritted my teeth, and it happened. I didn't recognize the neighborhood at first, but Minerva led the way. I realized that we were about a block from Paddington Station. I asked her, "Why not King's Cross?"

"I just thought it would be nice to have some variety." She put her free arm around my back and I pulled her up to kiss me. It was short. She started to back away and then stopped. "How have things been going?"

"You know that I can't tell you details?"

"I know."

"Well, then, we've had some breaks." I thought about it. I so much wanted to tell her about Azkaban, but if she didn't know that there'd been a breakout, it would be dangerous for her to know about it and dangerous for us for her to know about it.

She sighed, "Nothing more that you can share?" Her face wrinkled in worry lines.

"Nothing."

She nodded and backed clear of my arms.

I asked, "What if I don't let you go?"

"You really don't want to find out what a witch can do in that situation." However, she was smiling. I can't help smiling when she does that.

"OK. I guess there's no way to know when we'll see each other again."

She shook her head and threw her arms around me again, and we had a good kiss. I let go. She stepped back and mouthed, "I love you." And then she was gone.

I found the entrance to the Tube station and headed back to the office. It was Good Friday. I wanted to know what was good about it.

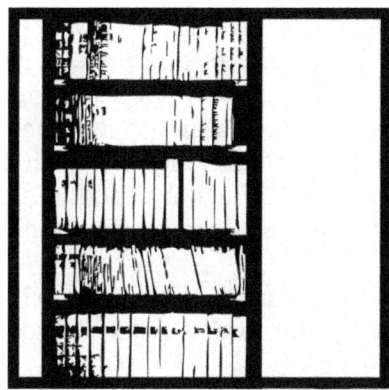

The Last Battle

Sally and I were in the office, having just returned from lunch when the phone rang. She and I had been having a competition to see who could answer the phone first. It was her opinion that she was a secretary (albeit an executive, high-paid one) and thus should answer the phone. While on the other hand, I maintained that she was an executive (forget the secretary) and it's up for grabs. This time I won. I stuck out my tongue at her and said, "Yes." That was something that she was trying to cure me of. She thought that she should answer and say, "Office of Jim Wendt." I maintained that anyone who could reach me on this phone bloody well knew that there were only two people who might answer the phone, and they could figure out for themselves who it was. Her position was that they might have made a wrong number and should know that they hadn't reached oh, say the Cafeteria.

Anyway, I won and answered, "Yes."

The voice on the other end said, "This is the duty officer at the Situation Room. There's something going on here that I think you should see.

I answered, "You couldn't mention what it is?"

"I'd rather you saw than have to convince you that I'm not crazy."

"OK. We'll be right down." I looked over at Sally. She was still on the phone and hung up after I did. "What do you think's up?" I asked.

"I don't have the slightest idea. With these crazy wizards how can you know?" We both liked to walk briskly, which was actually another area of competition between us. This time we were practically going at a run.

The Situation Room was nothing special on the outside. There was a guard permanently on duty with an assault rifle slung over his right shoulder. He gave us a small nod and opened the door for us. Inside, it wasn't that imposing either. Except that there were half a dozen projection screens on the wall. There were rows of desks with 2 or 3 monitors on each. The lighting was subdued, but not so much so that you couldn't comfortably read or write. There were about 8 people in the room at the moment. The duty officer came over and had us sit at an empty table. He pointed up to the main center screen and said, "Cue up the video." In a moment, we were looking at a London street view. It looked perfectly normal.

I said, "OK. Is this what you called us down for?"

The duty officer said, "Just wait a minute. Look carefully just above the line of buildings on the left."

Almost immediately a large shape appeared over the buildings. It was apparently a large bird, but it was almost immediately clear that it was way too large for a bird. The duty officer had the frame frozen and then played in slow motion.

He said, "Zoom in." As the shape became larger and fuzzier, I realized what I was looking at. My jaw must have dropped noticeably. The duty officer said, "Now's that something you don't see every day."

I stared in disbelief, "Believe it or not one day I actually saw four of those—at school.

"Yes. That's a dragon." As I said that, the dragon wheeled and turned slightly and I saw it in profile.

He smiled as I realized something about the dragon. "Right, it appears to have three people on its back."

"Oh, my God, do you suppose those three are. . ." I let it hang.

"While you were on the way down we tried to identify them, but it's only a security video camera. We're lucky to have gotten a good enough image to know for sure that there are people riding it."

Sally asked, "How long ago was this. Do we have any idea where that dragon is now?"

One of the people on the watch said, "We've got a feed from Heathrow Air Control. They're still tracking it on radar. They're getting a little concerned about it because they can't get anyone on what they think of as a plane to answer them or turn on their transponder. I think they're gong to get Military Air Traffic Control involved shortly."

I said, "OK. We need to get there first. Get us connected to whatever Military Air Traffic Control would be tracking them."

He started talking softly into his headset. In a minute, he spoke up and said, "I've got the Military Air Traffic Control center on. The commanding officer is Major Bishop. I'm putting it on the speakerphone. . . . now."

436

We all waited a minute for someone to say something. Then Bishop spoke, "Who is speaking for you. "

I answered, "I am. My name's Wendt, and I'm commanding Operation Red Rover at the moment."

"What's your rank?"

"I'm a civilian contractor, but I have authority to run it whenever the commanding officer is not on site."

"Who's the ranking officer at the moment?"

"I told you that I am, and if you don't stop talking and start listening, the PM is going to hear about it."

I could hear someone in the background faintly. I thought he said, "Sir, they are transmitting scrambled, and we're using the current code to unscramble. This has to be 'Red Rover'."

Bishop spoke again, "Go ahead."

"You should be tracking an 'unidentified' near London."

He spoke softly, and I couldn't make it out. Then he resumed, "Yes. North of London. No transponder. Going slow. Maybe 125 knots."

"That's it. Please transfer control to the 'Red Rover' Air Control."

"What are you talking about 'control'? We don't have control of that flight. We haven't established comm with them!"

"Doesn't matter. Contact 'Red Rover' Air Control and transfer control. Do it now."

"Yes sir."

We broke contact, and I said to the communications person. "Get us in touch with 'Red Rover' Air Control."

In a few minutes they were on the conference phone. "This is commander Stark in command of 'Red Rover' Air Control. What's up?"

I answered, "You should be hearing from another Military Air Command control to transfer an unidentified to your control. I want you to get a couple of fighters in the air to intercept it and follow it as quickly as possible. How quickly can you intercept it?"

There was muted talk that I couldn't make out. Then the commander was speaking again. "We're tracking it now. We can have interceptors in the air and intercept it in." There was a pause and he went on, "fifteen maybe twenty minutes. They'll be in the air in five."

"Good. I want to be able to listen to the traffic with them and give them instructions. Is that possible?"

"Possible, but. I don't know if that's a good idea."

"Look. I know you've all been trained in what this is all about but you've not got the full picture. I need the information AND control in real time."

The invisible man sighed and said, "Right. You've got it. Just stay on this frequency. You'll hear everything and can talk whenever you like."

"Thanks, Commander."

We had a few minutes to talk. Sally asked "What do you think this is about?"

I thought a minute, and she asked, "Wendt?"

"I'm thinking. Just give me a couple of minutes, OK."

I knew that everyone was waiting for me to say something—anything, so I did. "Let's suppose that the three people on that dragon are Potter, Grainger and Weasley."

Someone in the room asked "Fred or George."

I couldn't suppress a chuckle. 'Oh, that's just the sort of thing they would do, but I think that it's probably their brother Ron if it's a Weasley.

"Anyway, if it is them, then where did they find a dragon in the middle of London? And what in the world are they doing riding a dragon? That's pretty cheeky even for Potter."

Sally thought a moment. "Where exactly did you spot that dragon first?"

The officer of the watch asked one of the other men where the camera was. He brought a map of London up on one of the screens and put a red X on it. Sally looked at it and nodded. "I think that's pretty close to the 'Leaky Cauldron'."

"You're thinking that it came from 'Diagon Alley'?"

"Yep."

I said, "I didn't know that anybody kept dragons—even in Nocturne Alley. Where do you think it came from?"

Sally snapped her fingers and said, "Assuming that Potter didn't ride it into Diagon Alley, the place that is big enough there to house a dragon is Gringotts. What do you think?"

"I'd agree with you. I know that Gringotts has some really large underground chambers. Maybe they had a dragon down there. But what in the world would Gringotts be doing with a dragon, and why would Potter want it?" We both pondered for a while.

I said, "Of course, there's another possibility."

She asked, "Yes."

"Maybe it's Deatheaters."

"Could be."

In the mean time the interceptors had gotten into the air, and we were hearing the chatter with them.

I asked, "Do you have radar contact with the unidentified?"

One of the pilots answered, "We prefer bogey. And yes, we're tracking it. We should intercept in eight minutes. Do you have instructions when we do intercept."

"Yes, do you have any kind of camera onboard that we can use to see what you're seeing?"

"Yes sir. We each have a gun camera. There's nothing to see right now. But if anything interesting shows up, we can turn them on."

"Good. When you get close, I want to see what that thing is. So don't get any closer than necessary to get a clear view. Then we'll probably just want you to follow it."

"Yes, sir. We should be in visual range within 5 minutes. But it's pretty cloudy up here. We may need to get pretty close to get a good look."

"Do your best."

We had a nervous couple of minutes. Then the pilot spoke. "We're about 1 klick out and I'm beginning to get a hazy view every now and then. In another minute we'll be about a couple of hundred meters out.

"Woa! What the heck is that thing?"

"Get that camera going. We need to see what you're seeing."

A minute later we had a fuzzy view of mostly clouds on one of the screens but breaks in the clouds showed us brief views of the dragon. "Get in closer. We need a better view."

The camera moved closer, and then suddenly the clouds broke and gave us a clear view of the dragon. There were clearly three people riding the dragon. I still couldn't tell who they were. "Get stills of that and try to identify the riders."

One of the men in our situation room said, "Yes, sir. Already on it."

Then I addressed the pilots, "Pilots, you can back off. But stay within a klick of them, and if you lose them on radar, then move in to maintain visual contact."

"Thank you sir. It makes me nervous being too close to that."

"What kind of armaments are you carrying?"

"We've got some heat seeking missiles and a cannon."

"Good. I don't think the heat seekers will be any good, but the cannon could be. Don't waste your time with the missiles if it comes to that."

"Yes, sir."

"For the time being we'll hope that it doesn't come to that."

The minutes stretched out and grew longer and longer. Finally, the Boy Genius burst into the room, "I've got it. A positive identification of Weasley and 80+% probability of Grainger. It's 50-50 on the third. Probably Potter."

"Good going. That's what I thought."

Just then the pilots reported. "The thing's dropping to lower altitude. It's below 500 meters and dropping fairly fast. We're going to have to go down to maintain contact."

There was a lengthy pause and finally one of the pilots asked, "Is that OK?"

I was shocked that he was waiting for approval. "Yes, yes. Go before you lose them."

There was silence for a couple of minutes, and the clouds cleared completely. Apparently, there was clear air below the clouds. We could easily see the dragon gliding down over the forested hills toward a large lake. The riders were still on-board. It looked like the dragon intended to land in the lake. It could only be a few meters above the water when suddenly all three riders jumped off into the lake near the shore. For a moment, I couldn't believe my eyes. Then, I hurried to say, "Did you see that?"

One of the pilots asked, "The people jumping off, yes."

"Keep your camera on them. I want to see what happens with them." The view on the camera whirled around from the dragon and moved more slowly until it found three people on the shore of the lake.

One of the pilots said, "Look, we're beginning to run low on fuel. We've got to get back to the ship."

I interrupted. "You in Harriers, right?"

"Yes, sir."

"Can one of you land somewhere and wait for reinforcements to arrive?"

There was a pause and then one of them answered, "Yes, there's a clearing near the water line across the lake from them that I think that I can get into. Peterson, go back to base. We need something with longer range, maybe a helicopter."

A voice from the carrier said that they'd have a couple in the air in a few minutes, but that it'd take almost an hour or so before it could arrive on scene. One Harrier landed, and the other was on its way back to the carrier. The helicopter was barely in the air when something happened that changed all our plans. The Harrier's gun camera was focused back on the other side of the lake where the three musketeers were when they suddenly disappeared. It took a minute for us to realize what had happened, then everyone did at once. "They disapparated."

I agreed, "Yes. Everyone can go back to the carrier. We're done here." We broke communications with the carrier, and I was getting ready to return to my office, when the door burst open and one of the Boy Genius' assistants burst in.

"We've got him! Potter disapparated into a place where we have camera surveillance. He's in Hoggsmead!"

I looked over to Sally, and she just stared back.

One of the technicians burst out, "What the bloody hell is he doing there? The place is crawling with Deatheaters."

The B.G.'s assistant pushed someone away from his console and navigated through some control screens until he found the feed that he wanted and put it up on one of the overhead projectors. "There!" he whooped triumphantly. "There's Potter" and then he switched the view to another screen. "And there's Deatheaters closing in." But we could see that Potter and company had suddenly been pulled into a building.

Sally asked how we were getting a video feed from Hogsmeade.

The B.G. said nonchalantly, "We've got several video cameras about a two or so kilometers from the town. They have very, very high magnification.",

I had been pacing the room and hadn't really noticed. But I did notice when I stopped. I stopped because I had an idea. "He's got something. Or he's going there to get something. Something important. That's why he would take such an awful risk."

Sally said, "I think you're right, but what can we do?"

Parker had come in at some point, and we hadn't even noticed him. I asked him, "What are you doing here?"

"I figured something big must be going on, and I wanted to be in on it. AND I've got an idea of something that we can do. We have a Royal Marine unit permanently stationed there." He turned to somebody at a console, "Get hold of their commander. We need to get them onto high alert." In a minute there was a crackly voice on the conference phone.

"This is Major Dan Ryan, sir."

Parker ran the conversation, "Major Ryan, you're now on highest alert until the end of this incident. We've got intelligence that Potter and companions are holed up somewhere in Hoggsmead. Get some live eyes on the town and watch for Deatheater movements. Station a couple of snipers overlooking the town. I want to be able to pick off anyone I don't like the looks of. Pick up surveillance of the forest. I want to know when a mouse moves there. We'll control this operation from here."

"Yes, sir. We'll have a video feed from the sniper position to you, and we'll add a couple of patrols in the forest. We'll keep audio feeds open at all times from the patrols."

"Sounds good."

Parker sat down and said, "Get comfortable. We'll probably be doing a good bit of waiting."

I looked around and asked Sally, "Do you want to go home. We'll call you if anything interesting happens."

"Are you kidding? Not when things are just beginning to get interesting."

For the next half-hour the monitors were all from various cameras outside Hoggsmead and Hogswarts. Nothing much happened, and there was very little sound coming from the live feeds from the patrols.

Then, a barely heard whisper said, "We're sending video through now."

It took a while to recognize what we were looking at. It had gotten thoroughly dark by then, and at first it just looked like a surreal painting made in various shades of green, but gradually we got the context. There were trees, and then a flood of light that overwhelmed the camera for a few seconds. It auto-adjusted, and we could see pretty clearly a clearing in the forest with a large group of hooded Deatheaters. In the center of the group was someone who was instantly recognizable from his tall, thin, sinuous form and the weird eyes, which looked bizarre even from a distance in a poorly lit scene. It was Riddle. Everyone in the room froze. Parker slowly rose and said, "Shit. This is the closest that Potter and Riddle have been in years. I think something big is happening." He looked at me.

I nodded and said, "Yeh. This could be it. . . The final battle. We've got to get moving. Get hold of the Americans. We need the plane."

Parker nodded. "And we should mobilize our other assets. Get us the PM on the hot line, and get our base on the line."

Our base in Georgia was the first to come online. Both Weasleys were there, and they were both on the phone. "OK. Fred. I've got the conference phone working. I think."

Fred said, "No you don't. I can see the little light flashing. That happens when. . . When. . ."

I broke in, "You've got it right. We can hear you both. Now listen carefully."

The two said in unison, "We always listen carefully."

Fred said, "We just don't always pay attention."

"This is serious. We need to get the DA moving. We need them over to the air base immediately and in the air. Both Potter and Riddle are in or close to Hoggsmead."

"No, shit. Yes, sir. We've been drilling this. We should be able to get everyone to disapparate over to the air base within ½ hour. Can you have a plane ready by then?"

Parker answered, "It'll be ready before you are. Get moving."

Meanwhile connection to the PM was made. He said, "The wife and I were watching a movie. I hope this is important."

I said, "This is Wendt. This may be IT. Potter and Riddle are both at Hogwarts right now. We need to. . ." I couldn't finish the sentence. Blair broke in first.

"Don't tell me 'attack plan R'. Oh, go ahead and tell me. I know that's it."

"You're right."

"Are you absolutely sure?"

"Yes, we are. Everybody's in the situation room monitoring the, well, the situation. We've mobilized the DA."

He sounded forlorn, "Is Parker there?"

"Yes, sir. I agree. This feels like the real thing."

"I'll get in touch with the Americans. I just hope that they balk. But you know, they never do when the chips are down."

"Yes, sir."

"Nothing can happen for a while—at least with our forces. I'll finish the movie, and then give me hourly status calls."

"Yes, sir." Then he hung up.

"He's right. We'll just have to wait and see what develops", I said.

And he was right. Nothing happened for a while. I even went up to my office to get a magazine. When I got back down, I just stared at the first page of an article that I'd been trying to read for 15 minutes. I finally just laid it down. I looked around and didn't see Sally. Then I realized that she was leaning on the arm of the chair that I was sitting on. When I looked up at her, she said, "Sorry, I'd forgotten you were here." We had all been staring at the monitors. There was pretty much no change in them, except that more and more people kept showing up at the clearing where Riddle was.

Finally, Ryan called. "Sir, one patrol has noticed some Giants entering the forest. They're going at a trot and must be making 15 or 20 miles per hour. They seem to be heading for the clearing where Riddle is."

Parker commented, "I think that he must be waiting for them to arrive. Then something will happen."

Shortly after that we got a call from a Wright-Pat air force base commander. "This is Major General Bullock." He spoke laconically with a southern accent, "I'm to report that the B1B is off the ground and has reached cruise altitude and speed. It should be arriving in your airspace in approximately." He hesitated, "Y'all, my adjutant tells me that it should be about 5 ½ hours. I sure hope y'all know what you're doing. That thing is 'packing'."

Parker looked at me and then said, "Yes, we sure hope so too. Thanks for your quick response. We owe you one."

Bullock drawled, "You owe me several. But I'll be happy if y'all send them back fully armed."

I added, "Amen."

Bullock finished, "Godspeed to y'all." And the line went dead.

I asked Parker, "Does our unit up at Hogwarts have anything that would be effective against Giants?"

Parker asked Ryan, "Do you have those special bazooka shells?"

"Yes, sir. Do you think they'd be effective against giants?"

I asked, "What's special about them?"

Parker answered, "Well, we took the design for the special explosives that you requested for the assault on Azkaban and we applied the principles to rocket-born munitions. They have absolutely no electronics or even electrical circuits. That meant that we couldn't have timer fuses so that meant that we couldn't delay explosion the fraction of a second that it takes a shell to penetrate armor. We compromised and traded explosive in the warhead for propellant in the rocket. The idea is that we get the rocket traveling so fast that it at least partially penetrates the armor before exploding. Our tests show that while it's not as effective at armor piercing as munitions with electronic fuses, the design is pretty effective at attacking armor. The result is small warhead, and high-speed propulsion. That makes it rather like a large dum-dum bullet."

Ryan said, "I see. It makes a bazooka sort of a gun for giants."

Parker answered, "Well, that wasn't our design intention, but that's the way that it's worked out. Yes. If a general battle breaks out, Ryan, I want us to use those bazooka rounds against the giants."

He answered, "Yes, sir. What about against Deatheaters?"

Parker looked at me, "Yes. If there is a general battle, use your snipers against the Deatheaters, but only on our command. And for goodness sake, whatever you do, don't fire on Riddle. We have to let Potter deal with him if possible."

"What if Potter's killed, sir?"

"Well, we have something else in mind in case that happens. As a matter of fact, if that happens, I want you and your troops to stand down, take whatever cover you can, and just observe."

"Will do, if possible."

We spent the next couple of hours waiting. The B1B arrived on station and we gave them their instructions. Then we got a call from the Weasleys:

"We're over England and we're ready to deploy by disapparation directly from the airplane. What are we doing?"

"OK." I said, "Here's the situation. The Deatheaters are in the Forbidden forest, and I think that they're preparing to attack Hogwarts. Potter, your brother, and Hermione are there somewhere, we believe. I know that you can't disapparate directly into Hogwarts, so I guess you'll have to go into Hoggsmead and work your way into Hogwarts as best you can. We've got some Muggle troops—not many—stationed at the edge of the woods. They're mainly observers, but if a general battle starts, they'll support you as best they can. There are Giants in the woods with the Deatheaters, but we think that we have a weapon that will be effective against them.

"Got it." George said. I suddenly realized that I could tell Fred from George by voice. That was strange. I don't think that even his mother could.

He went on, "We'll scout out the town first and see what they know. Then we'll try to get in without revealing ourselves. There may yet be a hidden way in."

I looked over at Parker, "Any other suggestions?"

He shook his head, "None."

I said to George, "Go ahead. That's all that we've got. Keep in touch and let us know what's happening."

"Right."

Just then, Sally squeezed forward and said, "Is Fred there?"

His voice sounded, "Sure. Is that Sally?"

She answered, "Yes. Fred, just be careful. Right?"

Fred answered, "You know I'm always careful."

Sally had tension in her voice, "No, I'm serious." Her teeth gritted and she forced between her teeth, "Fred, you know I. . . I. . ."

Fred returned quickly, "I know. I do too."

"Yes, I know. I just wasn't sure that you knew."

Parker interrupted, "This is not the way to go into battle. Now get going."

Sally sobbed once, and then her face stiffened although her upper lip quivered a little.

We could hear George giving the commands to start people disapparating, and then it was very quiet. I said, "Well, everyone's in place. How much longer do you suppose?"

Parker shook his head, "Dawn, maybe." Then he said, "George, are you OK? Did everyone make it?" There was no answer. Parker repeated several times and shook his head, "What do you suppose happened?"

Sally sobbed again and stifled it. I said, "I'm not too surprised. Electronics just don't work close to large concentrations of magic. Hoggsmead has got too many wizards in it. We're probably not going to hear anything from the DA until after everything's over."

Parker grunted. "I just don't like it."

"None of us do." Sally answered in that stiff, stifled voice that she'd been using all night.

It started much sooner than that. Ryan came back on the line to report that the Deatheaters and giants were moving. It took them about a half-hour to get into position and then all hell broke loose.

Paratroopers

Fred pushed the button that stopped the 'phone'. He said to George, "Wouldn't Dad be proud of us if he could see us now. He always wanted us to follow in his footsteps as collectors of Muggle junk."

George laughed and said, "Right. Let's get going. Where is that siren thingee that we use to wake up the camp?" He searched on the desk in the base commander's office. Finally he noticed the large red button on the wall behind the desk. As soon as he saw it, he leaped for it, but Fred, noticing the movement and being closer, got there first and hit the button.

Fred let go almost immediately, "Whoever invented that thing must have been related to a banshee. It would wake ghosts."

"Right. We'd better get out on the Parade Ground to get the DA organized and moving." With that both men disappeared with a whoomp as the surrounding air rushed in to replace the vacuum that they'd left. They instantly appeared on the Parade Ground in a small but growing group of men who either disapparated or ran up from adjoining fields or buildings.

"OK. Listen up." George said, "This is not a drill. Everybody in the DA get your wands and cloaks and meet back here in ten minutes. I don't know the details but something big is up." The air shimmered as men and women who'd come out to see what had happened disapparated. A few without wands ran off.

Fred commented, "We'd better get going too. I don't want to leave without my cloak."

The last stragglers were disapparating in before fifteen minutes were up. There were a good number of women in their number. Some were in the DA. Others were there to see friends, parents, siblings, lovers off. There were more than a few intense embraces. No one seemed to pay much attention to the fact that there were a couple of hundred people in close proximity.

Finally George pointed his wand at his throat, said, *"Sonorus"*, and spoke, "Settle down, everyone. We're going to disapparate to the aeroplace in just five minutes. Before we leave, I have a few words to say." In the background, a few people could hear Fred say, "Oddment, piebald, eckeltricity."

George pretended not to pay attention and went on, "We just heard that Riddle, Potter, and a bunch of Deatheaters have shown up near Hogswarts. This is probably the last duel between Riddle and Potter. But there will be plenty of Deatheaters to keep us busy. This will probably be the biggest fight that wizards will see in our lifetimes. Potter needs our support, but I don't want anyone to go into this fight unwillingly or half-heartedly. So, if you aren't sure about doing this, just don't disapparate, and there will be no questions asked; no recriminations. We don't have much time, but are there any questions?"

Everyone looked at each other for a minute, but no one spoke. No one raised a hand.

"Then, you all know where to disapparate to. On the count of three. One. Two. Three."

There was a whoosh as over two hundred bodies disappeared.

At an Air Force base about three hundred sixty miles away, a couple of sentries were walking the base fence. Suddenly, there were a lot of men standing where no one had been a second before on the tarmac. One guard turned to the other and said, "I've seen that before, and it's broad daylight, but when they do that, it always spooks me out."

The other answered, "Yeh. It's just not natural. It doesn't seem so spooky when you see that on Star Trek on TV, but in real life, it's completely different."

On the tarmac, there was a giant military C-5A transport. They had landed close to it, but they were still a couple of hundred feet away. Everyone broke into a run. They quickly filed into it. When everyone was in, and they were preparing for flight, Fred got on the intercom and said, "Welcome everyone to the inaugural flight of the DA Express bound for Hogwarts. Please strap yourself in. We may be in for a bumpy ride. For those of you who haven't flown in a pairlane before, please observe the following rules: don't throw up on your neighbor when we drop a couple of thousand feet un-expectedly. No jokes about Muggle transportation. Flight time to Hogwarts will be approximately . . uh . . six hours. Prepare to disapparate directly to Hoggsmead when we arrive over England. There will be an in-flight meal served by your lovely hosts."

Just then the plane's engines revved, and the plane began moving down the tarmac. There were muffled gulps throughout the plane. It slowed and turned onto the takeoff runway. As it slowed someone asked, "Are we there yet." Then the engines stirred again, and the plane began speeding down the runway. They lifted slowly into the air, and there were a number of gasps. At least one person said, "I don't think this thing is going to make it."

George said, "Who said that? One more word, and we'll throw you overboard. Just relax and enjoy the flight."

One of the DA said, "Easy for you to say. You've been in these aerioplanes lots of times."

George answered, "Yes, we have, and we've lived to tell the tale. I can't believe my ears. Muggles get on these things hundreds of times, and none of them are such wusses. How is it that they are perfectly happy, and you are all such sniveling trolls?"

No one said much of anything for quite a while. Everyone was grasping the arms of their seats or pacing around. After a while, one of the flight crew came back carrying large paper bags. One of them said, "Is anyone back here hungry?"

No one said anything for a second, and then there were some grumbled, "Yeah's."

"OK. Come on up. We've got lots of MRE's."

Somebody asked, "What's an MRE?"

The answer was, "You goober, Meals Ready to Eat. Don't waste our time. If you're not hungry, we'll just take them back up front."

That set off a general rush. People unbuckled and squeezed forward between other bodies as quickly as they could. But the first people who got the MRE's were grumbling, "What kind of meal is this?"

The disgusted airman had to shout to get everyone's attention. "OK. Listen up." He picked up an MRE package and said, "Pay attention. This," he held up the MRE package, "Is the outside package. You tear it open like this. Then inside you have a variety of food in individual wrappers. You've got your Beef Stew, your crackers, your peanut butter, your raisins, your," He hesitated as he read the wrapper, "your Toaster Pastry, Strawberry, your oatmeal cookie, and your beverage tube, Orange. You could have a pretty good picnic with this.

"You can heat the stew with your FRH. Oh, yeah. That's Fireless Ration Heater. Just mix the bag of saltwater to make it heat."

Almost immediately there were shouts of pain. "What the bloody H. This thing's hot. What kind of black magic is this?"

The airman said, "Right. Be careful. That's hazardous material you've got there. It's not any old wizard who can use it safely."

Someone in the back shouted. "Anything a Muggle can do, I can do," followed immediately by a yelp of pain.

After a while, the hubbub decreased, and most of the DA were getting a decent meal. The view out the windows was getting dark as they approached the eastern Atlantic.

Fred asked George, "Look, bro, we've been talking about disapparating from a moving plane for a long time, but we've never tried it. Do you have any last minute ideas about doing it?"

"I figure that it's just like doing it standing still. To be honest, I've been kind of reluctant to try it and haven't pushed to get a chance."

"Yeh, that's the way I feel. Only now, we're going to have to just do it and hope that everything comes out all right. What do you think will happen?"

"Well, either of two things. We either land, and everything's OK or . . ."

"Yeh, it's that OR that I'm worried about. What do you figure the OR is?"

"Well, OR we land going at the speed of this airplane."

"Which would be?"

George gulped and said, "I don't really know. Let's go up front and ask the pirate, uh, I mean pilot."

Fred said, "Sure." But neither got up. They just stared at each other. Finally, Fred slowly got up. George followed him, and they walked laboriously toward the cockpit at the front of the plane. When they got there, one of the crewmen looked at them and asked, "What's up? You two look like you've just lost your best friend."

Fred looked over at George and said, "Could be."

George asked, "How fast is this aereoplane flying?"

The co-pilot looked around and stared him in the face. Then he said, "Why?"

Fred said, "Oh, just curious."

The co-pilot glanced down at the instruments and said, "About 600 knots."

George asked, "And that would be what in miles per hour?"

"Oh, I don't know, maybe about 650 miles per hour."

Both Fred and George's eyes bugged out, and they shouted in unison, "650 miles per hour?"

"Sure 650 miles per hour, what's the big deal?"

They turned around, didn't say another word, and trudged back to their seats. When they got there Fred asked, "Why didn't we try this out first—on you?"

"On me? Why not you?"

"What would I look like if it didn't work, but you've got the . . .. the " and he pointed at his ear.

"Yeh, yeh, I know. I already have a part or two missing."

"Well, it just makes sense."

"Right-O."

There was nothing to do now but wait. The flight droned on and on. Some people tried to get some sleep, but they weren't having much luck. Finally, one of the flight officers came back and said to George, "We've got a call up front for you two."

They went forward to the cabin. The first officer handed a headphone and mike to George. They showed him how to put it on and work the mike. He spoke to it and turned to Fred, "It's our boss. He says that we're over England now and we can disapparate any time that we want to."

"Great. Let's get going."

George took off the heaphones and said to the Captain of the plane, "Could you guys kind of slow down a good bit. It'd help us a lot."

The Captain shrugged, "How much?"

Fred smiled a stiff smile and said, "Not a lot—maybe to about twenty miles per hour?"

The Captain choked and said, "You're crazy. That's below stall speed."

The co-pilot, who'd been listening to the conversation said, "You really want to have a slow ground speed. Right?"

Fred said, "Yeh, I guess."

The co-pilot nodded and said to the Captain, "We could go up to where the jet stream is strongest and head into the wind. Then, we throttle down so that we're pretty slow—maybe a little below stall speed, let them go and then we can speed up."

The pilot frowned. "Well, we knew the job was dangerous when we took it. Yeh, let's try it." He turned to Fred and George, "Go on back and get ready to go. We'll come on the intercom and tell you when you can go. But, you've got to get out quickly, and then we'll throttle up and try to save the plane."

They went back to the main cabin, rounded up people, and told them that they could Disapparate when the pilot announced they could. They had discussed precisely where to go earlier. George gave the final talk, "OK. We're ready to go. Anybody who doesn't want to, doesn't have to. We're going to Hoggsmead. We'll Disapparate just outside of town to the east. We'll meet behind the Three Broomsticks and try to decide how to get into Hogswart's then."

Somebody in the back said, "Why don't we get the owner of the Hoggshead to let us meet there. He's a bit crusty but he's not bad."

Just then the Captain came on the public address system. "Time to go. Good luck!"

Fred said, "OK. Let's go. On the count of three. One Two." And then he and everyone else disappeared from the plane and re-appeared just outside Hoggsmead. A few lit wands, and they assembled behind the Hogshead. They knocked on the door, and they heard the owner ranting as he approached the door and opened it, "I thought that I got rid of you stupid Deatheaters!" He looked around and whistled. What the heck are all of you doing here?"

Fred said, "You remember us Abeforth. Harry Potter is somewhere around here. We're looking for him. We're here to help him."

Abeforth lit his wand so that he could see who was there. "Well, I suppose you're not a Deatheater, Fred."

"Yes, we want to find our way into Hogwarts. We figure Potter's there."

Abeforth took a long look at him, then said, "Are you all planning to get yourselves killed tonight?"

Fred said, "Maybe. Maybe, it'll be Deatheaters who will be on the short end of this stick."

"That never happens in this world, in my experience.

"But, if you want to find Potter, I can help you with that. He's in Hogswarts. I can help you get there too. Come on in. There's a passage from here to Hogswarts."

George said, "I knew there must be another passage that we didn't know about. Where is it?"

"Come in, gentlemen. Throw yourselves over the cliff."

They trouped in to the Hogshead, row on row of Dumbledore's Army into Dumbledore's tavern. The barkeep took them to a painting that magically connected to another painting inside Hogwarts. They trooped through one at a time and showed up in Hogwarts.

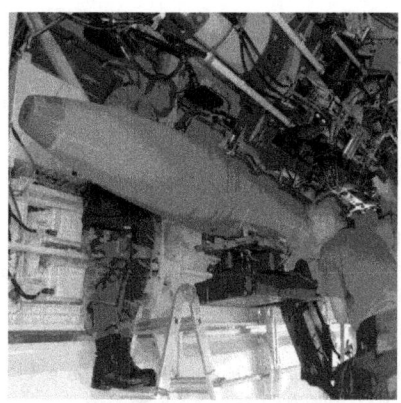

Dear John

The taller man was standing on a short ladder with his head obscured because it was sticking into the open bomb bay of the airplane. The shorter one was standing on the tarmac below, looking up into the bomb bay, and speaking. "You're going to get us into more trouble than I can imagine. You can't just paint on those bombs."

The taller man answered, "You don't have very much imagination. Sure I can Jake. There's nothing lewd, lascivious, or even laconic about what I painted. It doesn't cover sensors or antennae or anything functional."

Jake answered, "What does that mean anyway, Roland?"

Roland told him, "I saw an old classic black comedy last night on DVD, Dr. Strangelove. There's a USAF bomber in it with two thermonuclear devices. They have little greetings painted on them. The same ones that I just finished painting here."

Jake read one greeting, "'Hi, there.'" And then he read the other, "'Dear John'".

"Right you are. Those are two."

"What do they mean?"

"It's a statement about the stupidity of war. Actually, the whole film is."

Just then an officer ran up to them. He was a captain and was carrying a thick manila envelope. He said, as he jogged the last couple of yards, "You two are supposed to get into the air pronto. These are your orders. Get moving."

Jake asked, "What's happened? Has war been declared?"

"I don't know anything about that. Just the two of you get in the air. I don't think the top brass were planning on the three of us jawing."

Roland climbed down from the bomb bay and said, "We were just examining our payload. Everything seems in order. Let's get going Jake." They climbed the ladder on the other side of the plane and got in. They got the engines spinning and got clearance to taxi to the runway. The takeoff was quick and uneventful.

They went up to 30,000 and flew out over the Atlantic. When they were over international waters, Jake asked, "What's this all about?"

Roland answered, "You're the man with the orders, open them and find out."

Jake looked at the envelope for a minute and then said, "Right." He broke the seal on the envelope and pulled out the CD-ROM in its sleeve. He slid it into the CD-ROM drive in the computer at the co-pilot's station. The PC screen showed a file folder with several PDF's in it. He opened up one that was labeled Mission Profile. He started to scan the profile. Slowly, his jaw dropped, and he turned to look at Roland.

Roland was getting impatient, "OK. What's it say?"

Jake's voice broke as he started out. "This isn't a drill or a training mission. This is the real thing. We're to set our cruising altitude to 52,000 feet and cruise at maximum speed. I haven't looked up the coordinates, but I can tell that it's somewhere in northern Europe. When we get there, we're to prepare to deploy our nuclear weapons on command. It's got command frequencies and code strings too, of course."

"Well, come on, put them in the computer, and let's find out where we're going."

Jake keyed in the coordinates and put in a couple of commands. When the map reset to the new location he whistled, "We're about to go to nuclear war toe to toe with the Brits."

"And you say that I've got too much of a sense of humor."

"No, I don't have a sense of humor, and I've entered the coordinates a 2nd time. They're on the northern coast of Scotland.:

"Come on, be serious. What's on the northern coast of Scotland?"

"I'll look." Jake adjusted the scale of the map and zoomed in on the coordinates. "Well, in this case, nothing. There are some fjords and a few small towns but "

"They call them 'Lochs'. What about military bases?"

"I'm telling you, there's nothing. Zilch, zero, nada for dozens of miles."

Jake brightened and said, "This has got to be a training exercises, we don't have an offensive weapons officer. Or a defensive weapons officer for that matter."

Roland said, "You know perfectly well that *you* are the offensive weapons officer if we lose him in action. You're it for this mission."

"Great."

"How much cruise time do we have after we arrive?"

"Well, at our current rate of consumption, we can get there and have maybe an hour cruise time if we're careful. But don't worry. They've thought of that. We're supposed to rendezvous with a tanker about an hour out from the target."

"Well, let's set the autopilot on, and I'd like to have a look at those orders for myself."

A half hour later, Roland leaned back in his seat. "I can't see any loopholes. I think this is for real. Did you notice that they said that we'd be under RAF control once we arrive in British territory? Is there some kind of revolution going on in Scotland? No, 'can' that. That's crazy."

"And did you notice that we're to orbit the real target once we arrive. And wait for orders. Since I'm the weapons officer, I'd better get going setting up the cruise missile targeting computers. By the way, did you notice that these aren't standard nukes? I don't think that there's been a warhead larger than one megaton in the arsenal for decades, but these are 20 mega-tonners. We've got to be sure that we stand off at least 50 klicks when we light them off. I suppose that's why we have to orbit so far out."

Roland said, "Yes, I noticed that. Did you read the fine print? We have to stay on station even after we've fired the first one."

"Yeh, sure. Just to make sure it actually detonates, so that we can light up the other one if it doesn't."

"Noooo. Even if it goes off, we're to stay on station until we're released. And be prepared to fire the other one on the same target. Also, even after we're given the 'Go Code', we're to hold off firing until we're over the sea."

"No shit?"

"Look for yourself."

"Well, I'll be a son of a . . . ."

"Yes, you probably are. What the heck kind of mission is this? What's our target? It must be some kind of super-hardened underground site."

"I don't think so. Look at the fusing on the warheads. They're to detonate at 1 KM altitude. The things fly in at treetop level and then have to climb at the last minute to a klick before detonating. That's a formula for wide-spread devastation; it's the way you'd attack a large city if you wanted to kill everything in it. But there's not a city up there in the middle of nowhere."

"Maybe we'd better phone home for verification of orders."

"I think the orders call for radio silence except with the tanker until we are contacted by RAF."

"Well, we've got another three hours to stew until we get that."

Roland thought to himself. "It's a good thing we've got an autopilot. I'm not sure that I could maintain concentration waiting to find out what this is all about."

The refueling went smoothly, and the crew of the tanker had no idea that this was anything other than a training exercise. They avoided Ireland and were approaching the coast when RAF control contacted them on the control frequency. The voice on the radio didn't sound British exactly or at least had a strange accent. After exchanging countersigns, it went on,

"Look, I'm not an officer in the RAF or USAF. But I do have operational control of this mission from this point on. I don't have the technical lingo, so bear with me. Have you reached your target?"

"Yes, sir. We just started orbiting the target and are at the stand-off distance for firing our munitions."

"What's the delay from your releasing the missiles until impact?"

Roland looked at Jake. Jake answered, "My estimate is about five minutes."

The voice answered, "OOH. That's longer than I was hoping. I wanted it to be less than a minute. That makes it tricky. Things could be happening at the target very quickly. Five minutes could be the difference between them getting away or not."

Roland answered, "Sir, surely, if they don't know it's coming, they can't get away that quickly. Not from weapons this size."

"I'm afraid they can." A pause. "Well, we can't do anything about that. We have to be ready to act at a second's notice."

"Yes, sir. We're ready when you are."

"Well, frankly, I really hope you guys can go home without having fired anything. Just sit tight, and we'll see what happens."

"Yes, sir."

After the radio transmitter was shut off, Jake said, "Well, curious-er and cruious-er. I hope we all know what we're doing."

"Me too."

The Death of Potter

We were watching things in the Control Room. The cameras that our Royal Marines had were not great on resolution and showed things in that eerie green and black illumination that makes you feel like it's Halloween even when it's a beautiful star-filled night. There were occasional reports from Ryan, but what it came down to was that the Deatheaters were advancing on Hogwarts. Then the Deatheaters started the assault. It was really hard to tell what was going on. There were flashes of light all over the place—most showing against the dark walls of Hogwarts. It wasn't clear where the fire was coming from—except that it was obviously being caused by the Deatheaters. They kept advancing on Hogwarts, and then some returning fire began. The Deatheaters took cover, and the fireworks really started.

There was some fire that was coming from obvious sources. There were a couple of catapults that had been set up by several Giants. These were firing huge stones at the castle. Some were beginning to hit.

Ryan finally spoke up at that, "Parker, is there anything we can do about this. We could knock off a bunch of these Deatheaters before they knew what hit them."

He asked, "You mean your snipers."

"Yes, sir."

"Are you able to get close enough to fire on them safely?"

"We've got a couple of men up forward. It's not easy to move in with all this magic flying around, but we've got a couple of stout lads who can move against it. They're set up and ready to go on your order."

Parker looked over at me and asked with his eyes.

I said, "I don't like the idea for a couple of reasons. One, this is really a wizard fight, and we don't want to interfere if we can avoid it.

"Second, there's the whole thing about Potter and Riddle. We don't want to interfere with that confrontation happening if it's going to happen. We just don't know what will happen if we stick our noses into this.

"Finally" and I had to think a minute to come up with a 'finally'. In the mean time Sally interrupted. "And, finally, I've got a bad feeling about interfering."

I expected him to be miffed about Sally butting in, but he seemed to be OK with it. He just stared at her and then said nothing. He turned around and started pacing. Ryan asked "What about it?"

Parker just shook his head—not that Ryan could see it—and said, "Not now. We'll get back with you when we want you to do something."

So, for the time being we kept watching and hoping that something good would happen for our side. And nothing did. The Deatheaters kept advancing, and the Royal Marines and we kept watching. Ryan asked again.

"I know Ryan. We're following the situation."

Then Ryan appealed to me. "Wendt, this just keeps going worse and worse. Can't we at least knock out some of their Giants?" By now there were lots of holes appearing in the castle, and it looked inevitable that the defenses would fall.

I was not comfortable with saying, "Just wait, and let's see what happens." So, I didn't say it. I just shrugged and lifted my eyebrows.

Just then, Ryan broke in. "Listen, you've got to listen to this." But he didn't have to say anything. Riddle was making an announcement. It was so loud that I didn't think that Ryan would have needed a mike to pick it up. Riddle was giving them an ultimatum. Give up Potter or we'll take him and give no quarter.

Ryan asked, "Orders?"

Parker said, "We'll be back with you shortly."

He killed the mike and asked, "What do we do now?"

"I think it's up to Potter. If he doesn't go out, we'll have a renewed battle, and I don't see that we're in any different place than we were a minute ago."

"And if he does?"

"Well, then maybe we have the big duel that everyone in the wizarding world thinks is inevitable, and who knows what will happen from that?"

"OK. We wait." Parker turned on the mike again and said, "We're waiting to see what Potter does. Keep an eye on the Deatheaters."

Just then, there was an interruption. A tech said, "There's a call coming in from the RAF. The B1's just arrived on station."

I said, "Get us contact with them. We've got to start controlling them as well."

He got us in touch, and I gave them instructions. Then, I had the tech shut off the contact and I said to Parker. "It's good timing. They're in place if we need them." I heard a strange strangled sound, and I looked around to see Sally stifling a sob. I said to her softly, "I sure hope we don't have to do anything either."

Parker asked, "OK if we have to do something, how do we know when we do it?"

I opened the mike to Ryan, "What's Riddle and company doing?"

"They've retreated back into the forest. They seem to be headed back to their original rendezvous point."

"Can you get close enough so that we can see what happens there?"

"Sure. But I don't think the cameras will work that close. We'll have to depend on commentary by the scouts."

I was surprised, "The radios work, but the cameras don't?"

"Yes, sir. We've been stationed up here for a couple of months now. We've had plenty of time to experiment. It seems like the simpler the technology, the closer you can get it to magical folk, and it still works. Cameras can't get closer than a klick or so. Radios can get into maybe 100 meters. Hand grenades work right next to magic."

I was incredulous. "You've used hand grenades on wizards?"

"Not exactly. We took a couple of hand grenades and removed the explosives. Just left the detonators. Then we took turns tossing them at the wall of one of the buildings of Hogsmeade. They all went off even if they were right up against the wall."

"Hmmm. OK. That's good to know. Well then, get scouts in where they can see what's going on, but still transmit out of the forest."

"Yes, sir." Ryan closed the circuit.

Then we waited. There was very little to see. Then we could see on one of the monitors that one of the doors of the castle opened, and a figure silhouetted against the light inside appeared. It left the castle and walked out toward the forest.

Parker clicked the mike on and said, "Can you see the figure walking away from the castle?"

"Yes, sir."

"Can you get us a better view of it? Good enough to tell who it is?"

"I'll try."

After a couple of minutes the view from that monitor started to jiggle as though it were moving. And indeed it was. The view slowly got closer and better. Parker asked me, "Could that be Potter?"

459

I couldn't tell who it was, but I couldn't exclude the possibility that it was Potter. "I don't know. It might be."

"Who else would be walking as bold as brass right toward the forest and Riddle?"

"Got me. Who do you think?"

Parker made a face at me and didn't say anything. The camera continued to follow its course as it approached the trees. Finally, it disappeared just before entering the forest. Parker asked Ryan, "You got anyone close enough in the forest to ID that bloke?"

Parker was obviously losing his temper. He was slipping into an east London accent. Ryan came back. "I've got somebody headed his way. I'll let you know shortly."

Then an unfamiliar voice came on the circuit. "This is Hathaway. It's hard to tell without night vision goggles but I think that it's Potter. I could make out a scar on his forehead before he disappeared. It's got to be him."

Ryan started to say something, but Parker interrupted, "You try to keep close to him and give us a running comment on what's happening."

Hathaway came back on, "He's disappeared. What do I do?"

From then on, there were brief whispered comments, "He was going toward Riddles' location when I lost him. Maybe he put on his cloak."

Parker, "Great! Just keep going toward Riddle. Don't get too close. Keep up the comments."

He got within viewing range of Riddle and the Deatheaters and stopped. "I'm not getting any closer. I can see things just fine here." Then a little later, "Blimey. He just appeared out of nowhere. Those Deatheaters sure looked scared."

"This is strange. He's not doing anything to defend himself." "I can't make out what they're saying, but they're talking."

There was silence for a while. Somebody had moved a camera pretty close, but the forest was too thick to see anything worth while. Then the scout said, "It's over. Looks like Potter's dead."

Parker took off his cap and threw it to the floor. "Bloody Hell! That's it." He didn't say anything for a minute. He just paced back and forth for that minute. Then he looked around. The rest of us weren't doing anything —swearing, stomping, pacing. We were just lost. We'd worked so long and hard to reach this moment, and it was all over with a simple word. We couldn't even see what happened. I felt stunned.

Parker quietly said to a tech. "Get me in touch with the plane." After a minute he went on, "Here's the 'Go Code'" and he read out a string of numbers. "Proceed to execute."

You Kill with Your Mind

The radio activated. Roland answered the call. "Yes, sir."

The radio answered with a 'Go Code' and the orders to execute. Roland looked over at Jake. "OK. This is what all the fancy training is about. Let's get going. What do the orders say about launch?"

Jake browsed through the pages on the laptop monitor, "Yes, yes. OK. Here's the deal, Roland. We have to be over the sea when we launch. They want the missile to be flying in from the sea. How soon can we launch?"

Roland looked out the cockpit window and at the map on the monitor in front of him. "Give us about 5 maybe 6 minutes, and we'll be in position. That enough time for you?"

Jake had been keying some last minute commands into the cruise missile computer through his laptop keyboard. "Just a minute. We'll be ready. I've almost got the final commands in."

Roland said, "You know how I've trained you. You need to keep your concentration. You kill."

Jake interrupted, "I know. You kill with your mind. You have to think the missile down their throats."

"You just be sure you do that, Mister."

"Yes, sir." He had finished with his command entry and was checking it—slowly, methodically, all the time in the world. At last, he said with finality, "It's going down their throats."

Roland whistled, "Any time. We just crossed the beach. We're over the ocean."

Jake squeezed the firing trigger, and they both felt the jolt as the explosive bolts fired and separated the missile from the larger missile that their plane had become. They both watched the engine fire to life on the cruise missile; the wings fold out, and the missile bank sharply to take a new heading that ran it toward the Loch that flowed into the sea. "How long to detonation?" Roland asked.

Jake answered, "Four minutes, thirty seconds until it reaches the target coordinates and maybe another 20 or so seconds for it to climb to detonation altitude." They both watched it as it dropped down to a couple of dozen meters above the water level. Jake watched the camera view from the cruise missile as it skimmed over the water and then climbed suddenly as it approached a hill. It was like riding a roller coaster that was traveling at 600 klicks per hour. He gulped convulsively as the view shifted rapidly.

Whom do you trust?

In the Control Room, I finally woke up. I looked around and realized that there was a nuclear weapon about to detonate and kill a lot of people that I cared about, not to mention a lot of innocent people and maybe the last hope for defeating Riddle.

So, I stuck my neck out and said, "Parker, we've got to stop that bomb from exploding."

"What are you talking about? Potter's dead. He was our last hope. We don't have any choice."

"How long before the cruise missile reaches the detonation point?"

One of the pilots responded, "It's 4 minutes 30 seconds from detonation."

I went on, "Can you disarm it or re-program the target or something before it goes off?"

I later found out that it was Jake who answered again, "Yes, we can change the 'Go Code' at any time, and it won't detonate because it has the wrong code."

Parker strode over to where I was standing and stuck his nose into my face and said, "Are you crazy. This is our chance. All the Deatheaters are there. We're not going to stop it without a bloody good reason."

I answered, "Look we don't have much time. Potter wasn't our only chance."

"What are you talking about? It was always 'Potter this' and 'Potter that'."

"No," I shouted, "Potter was only the person that everybody thought would put an end to Riddle. That was mostly because he'd survived so many attacks by Riddle, but we don't know that Potter is the be-all and end-all of Riddle."

"Well, who's going to do it if Potter doesn't? And we know where Riddle is now. After tonight we might not get another sure shot at him."

I was desperate, "How much time?"

"Three minutes, 15 seconds."

I went on, "Look, Parker, there's a whole army that we've put together for this battle. One of them might do it for Riddle."

Sally stirred and added, "And there are other great wizards there too. Most of Hogwarts' instructors are really good wizards in their own right, and we don't know how many others might be showing up."

Parker started to pace back and forth, looking down at his feet. I added, "Look, we've got another bomb on the plane if we abort the first."

Parker kept his head down and said, "I'm thinking. I'm thinking."

I asked again, "How much time?"

"Two minutes and 35 seconds." Jake had apparently gotten tired of being asked how much time was left. He started a countdown punctuated by counts at 10 second intervals. "Two minutes 20 seconds."

Parker asked, "How long to fire up that other cruise missile if it comes to that?"

The other pilot said, "We could do it in two or three minutes if we could fire from any point in our orbit around the target."

"Two minutes 10 seconds."

Parker answered, "Yes, yes. Anyplace is fine."

In the meantime one of the techs had gotten a video feed from the missile on one of the screens. At first it was hard to tell what we were seeing, but shortly as the missile bobbed up and down following the contours of the ground we got occasional large views. You could tell that it was a view from the missile, and we got a feel for the lay of the land. Once we got that understanding, the view became disturbing. You began to feel that you were on the missile, bobbing and weaving like a roller coaster ride. More than one person averted his eyes from that screen with a slight green tinge on their face that didn't come from the green tinge of the monitor views.

"One minute 50 seconds," intoned the voice that I'd begun to think of as the voice of doom.

Parker was still pacing. I prodded him. "What's your decision? If you don't make one pretty soon it's going to be taken out of your hands."

Parker just muttered, "Why did I ever leave the football game?"

"One minute 30 seconds." I'd missed one of the countdowns.

I couldn't stand the tension. I found that I'd begun pacing, myself. "Come on, Parker. Do the right thing."

Parker looked up at me and shouted, "What makes you think that you know the 'right' thing?"

"One minute 20 seconds."

"Look, if we do this, there's no going back."

I looked over at Sally. She shook her head and then said, "If I could think of anything, don't you think that I would say something." Then after a strained moment, she added, "Fred's there."

"One minute 10 seconds."

I looked around desperately and noticed the 'Boy Genius'. "Brahms?" I looked at him imploringly.

He looked down at the floor and muttered, "I'm all for blowing the bastard to Kingdom-Come."

"One minute." I glanced up at the video monitor that showed the missile's-eye view. It suddenly topped a hill or low mountain and I got a broad view of a long lake and what must be the castle at the end of it.

"Fifty seconds."

I pointed at the screen and shouted, "Look at the screen. You can see the castle. There's no time. Stop it! While you still can!"

"Forty seconds."

Parker looked up. Something in the scene transfixed his gaze. His mouth dropped open.

Sally asked, "Should we cover our eyes or look away?"

"Thirty seconds."

Somebody said, "No need. The blast will destroy the camera before it sends an image."

Parker said softly, "Turn it off." And then he repeated louder, "Defuse it."

There wasn't a "Twenty seconds" count intoned, but Jake said, "'Go Code' changed and verified."

Then he resumed the count, "Ten,,, Nine,,, Eight,,, Seven,,," I noticed that Sally had grasped my right arm at the elbow, "Six,,, Five,,, Four,,, Three,,," No one seemed totally convinced that the bomb wasn't going to go off. "Two,,, One,,, " The castle was now looming fairly large in the distance. The missile was clearly over the lake. "Zero." The view of the missile kept rolling forward. The castle grew and then disappeared on the left side of the missile. In the last instants before it passed the castle, I thought that I could see figures on the ground in front of the castle. It kept rolling along for another few minutes and then suddenly the trees seemed to leap up at the missile and the video feed went blank.

Jake said, "I dumped the missile. It has the range to reach heavily populated areas. The casing is supposed to withstand impact in situations like this but why take a chance?"

Roland said, "Good job, Jake."

I said, "Stay alert out there. We may need you yet, before this night's over."

I asked, "Ryan, anything going on there in the woods?"

"Yes, sir. The Deatheaters seem to be headed out of the woods. They've got Haggrid carrying Potter's body, and they seem to be heading toward the castle."

"Keep on them. We may yet need you"

"Yes, sir."

The tension in the room gradually dissipated. I noticed that everyone had been standing and had begun to sit on the edge of tables or even on the backs of chairs. Parker and I stayed on our feet pacing in small circles, never taking our eyes from the screens that now showed the castle and the main group of Deatheaters with Riddle and Haggrid headed toward the castle.

The group finally cleared the forest, and we got the first really clear view of them. Whoever was controlling one of the cameras zoomed in on Haggrid and Potter. It was really clear that it was Potter. I heard a low growl, but couldn't identify who in the room had made it. Shortly it became clear. Ryan's low growl changed into a tightly controlled whisper into his mike, "Awaiting orders, sir."

Parker was taken by surprise by the request from the otherwise well-controlled officer. Parker looked about to say something, then he turned to me with a questioning look in his eyes. I shook my head. Parker turned back to the screen, "Carry on as you were."

The "Yes, sir," returned a little too snappily. We watch the screen as the Deatheaters reached the castle. We were all numb and hardly realized what was happening. Suddenly Sally's voice sounded, and I only slowly realized what she was saying. "Who *is* that young man who just killed the snake?" I woke up and really looked at the main screen.

"That's Longbottom. My God, he's killed Riddle's snake."

Then we were all struck speechless by the sight of Potter rising. There was a gasp from everyone. Parker's mouth dropped, and mine probably had too. If we were numb before, we were alive now, listening and watching with the most rapt attention. We could hardly comprehend that there was a duel about to happen again. It was all over almost before we had realized that it had begun. Potter was standing and Riddle was not.

Parker was the first to speak. "Is this really over?" He gestured about him at the assembled people, the screens, the forces visible on the screens. "That's all there was to it? Somehow I expected a titanic struggle with lightning flashing about and streams of, oh I don't know, magic forces scattered everywhere. And what happens? Nothing."

I asked, "You'd think that you'd preferred that we'd had to spray bullets around and kill most of the people."

Parker answered, "No, I. I just wasn't prepared for it all to end so quickly." He trailed off, not knowing quite where to go with it.

Someone was tugging on my arm. I looked around to see Sally urgently tugging at me. I followed her out of the room. Inside, there was a tumult going on. People were shouting and jumping up and down, but all the hubbub was receding as we walked away. Sally looked into my face with a tight constrained grimace on hers. She said urgently, "Find out what happened to Fred, please." There was real pleading in her eyes. "Can you send some soldiers in?"

I looked at her, my heart rent at her pain. I was about to say the hardest thing I had ever had to say in my life. "I can't. The wizards must never know how close they were to death and danger at our hands."

She gasped and was silent for a moment, trying to compose herself. Finally she said, "It doesn't matter." She sobbed for a moment quietly, "I know that he's dead."

Of course, we didn't know that, but I couldn't say the obvious. We didn't know that. She would probably be with him in a few days. She guessed what I was thinking and said, "I know. You think that Fred may be perfectly well for all we know. I know better. He's dead. I don't know how I know, but I know.

"Go on back in and celebrate. I'm going home."

I took her arm and said, "Don't. You shouldn't be alone. Stay. Come up to the office." She looked at me for a long moment and then said, "Sure."

We walked slowly up to our office. She sat at her desk, and I pulled up a chair next to her desk. Neither of us said anything for a time that seemed to stretch on to eternity. Finally she said, "You're a good friend. I think I'm OK. I'll go home now."

"I'll go with you." I said. She demurred, but I insisted. She was too tired to resist. We left, and I found a cab. We arrived at her flat. She fumbled with the keys at the door and dropped them. I picked up the keys, unlocked the door, and opened it for her. Then I handed her the keys. She paused on the threshold and was about to speak. I intervened and said to her, "Good night. You don't need to come in to work tomorrow, but if you'd like to have lunch, I'm at your disposal." She smiled a wan smile and said goodnight. She closed the door, and I left.

Minerva

The next couple of days at work flew rapidly. There were lots of loose ends to tie up. The accounting was horrendous. We had to figure out what was left of the current year's budget, what we still had to spend to close down operations, and what we could return to the exchequer. There was wrangling with the Americans about what they would charge us for one B1B bomber's transatlantic flight, the recovery of the nuclear-armed cruise missile, the decommissioning of the base in Georgia. At one point, I was afraid that I would have to travel back to the States to take part in it, but that eventuality wasn't necessary.

After some wrangling, we worked out a deal with the main countries involved: UK, US, Germany, and France. They were all NATO members. We talked them all into considering their costs to be part of their NATO contributions. It was almost a win-win.

In one meeting in Parker's office, the US representative had been complaining about the lack of contributions from France. At one point, in exasperation, he exclaimed, "You fro . . . uh . . . French have never held up your end of the NATO treaty. Now, you want to count passively sitting by on the sidelines letting trains go through while the Brits and Germans and we took real risks! We almost lost a nuclear submarine!"

Parker agreed heatedly, "We really did lose a nuclear submarine. What in the world did you contribute?"

The French delegate blustered. He was rattled enough that his normal urbane English slipped up a bit, "We risked lots. Who knows what would have happened if ze Riddle had found out that we arranged special trains and cleared ze tracks and so on. That was not that easy to do while keeping the arrangements secret." He hesitated and then added, "And what did you Germans contribute anyway? You just let the Americans use their airbase that they were paying you for anyway. Humpf."

The German just sat stoically and shook his head sadly. Then, he slapped his head and laughed. When asked what was so funny he said, "You've no idea how much torture we endured from that Englishwoman that the American foisted off on us. What was her name? Dirkley? Dunstan?"

I smiled myself and supplied the name, "Dursley."

"Oh, yes, I give you Marge." I turned to the French delegate and said, "I defy you to spend an evening with her sometime."

The French delegate just sniffed and maintained his hauteur.

□

Sally had come back to work after only a day off. She decided that work was a good way to find relief from her grief at times.

I was beginning to work through the accounts when a thought occurred to me. I should really get in touch with my parents. They hadn't heard from me since sometime early the previous year. And maybe that was just a thank you note for Christmas presents.

I wondered how many letters had stacked up in my mailbox at Hogwarts. It occurred to me that they'd probably thrown them all into the fire.

Of course, I couldn't get in touch with my parents after the SAS picked me up. At first I was a prisoner without any privileges. Then when I did have phone privileges I didn't want to try to contact them because I might put them in danger. But now. But now, I should get them on the phone and let them know at least that I was still alive.

That day, I picked up the phone three or four times, but I just couldn't bring myself to dial the numbers. I was afraid that . . . No I was not afraid. I was ashamed. What could I possibly say in that first conversation that would justify to them my not keeping in touch?

The next day Sally started an innocent sounding conversation. She asked, "How are your parents these days?"

I think my face turned as red as a beet. I stammered, "OK. I guess."

She nailed me with her eyes, "You guess? Don't you know?"

I took a deep breath and said, "Well, I've been pretty busy lately and . . ."

She just sniffed. Then she said, "Do you want me to dial their number for you?"

I was trapped. I tried to maintain as much dignity as I could as I said, "No. I'll do it."

470

She had already picked up the phone. I picked up my extension and said, "I'm doing it." She set her handset down. I started to punch the numbers and suddenly realized that I knew the number of the base in Alabama better than I knew my parents' number. But I did remember it. I slowly punched the numbers and listened to the rings.

No one picked up for quite a while. I began to panic. What if they didn't answer? Would I have to endure this torture again when I tried the next time?

Just as I had decided to give up for now, I heard a receiver pick up on the other end of the line. It was Mom! We talked for a while. Of course, it was far easier than I feared.

After I hung up Sally asked, "Well?"

"Well, it went well. They're fine." I hesitated.

Sally asked, "But???"

I still hesitated and a worried look came over her face.

"Well, it was strange. You'll never guess who was there with them." She gave me a frown. I added, "Oh, it's a relative of someone that you know."

Her eyes lifted and there was almost a smile on her face, "Not one of the Weasleys?"

"No, it was the Dursleys?"

Sally actually laughed. "What in the world were they doing there?"

"I don't know. What I'd like to know is how they found my parents." The Dursleys were evidently as determined and bull-doggish as Marge Dursley's Ripper. "That is a story that I would really like to hear."

I sat there musing for a time over that question when another thought occurred to me. Thinking out loud, I asked myself, "I wonder what's happened to their house?"

Sally agreed, "I suppose Marge kept an eye on it until we sent her off to protective custody. That's been over nine months ago."

I agreed, "Yes, maybe we should call in one of the many markers that Parker owes us and have him see about that."

Sally nodded and wrote a note to herself on a post-it note. There was a whiteboard in our office. Sally put reminders for us on post-it notes and stuck them to the white board. Right now, the whiteboard was more post-it note than whiteboard.

□□

One day I was sitting at my desk, getting a spreadsheet of accounts to balance when there was a 'crack' that sounded over my shoulder. I tried to

471

pretend that I hadn't noticed the sound. I casually opened the top right drawer of my desk as though I were looking for a writing instrument or eraser. My fingers closed around the handle of the Glok. I thumbed the safety as quietly as I could and tried to remember if I had a clip with bullets. The weight of the gun argued for bullets. I prepared myself for a sudden movement. I planned to duck as I swung around, pulling the Glok from the drawer and bringing it to bear as quickly as I could.

A strong hand closed on my right wrist then became gentle. A voice said, "I waited and waited for you to invite me to see your office, but you've been obstinate about being a hermit." The voice was perfectly familiar.

I laughed and said, "Never sneak up on me like that. I thought that you were a fugitive Deatheater come to wreak revenge for the death of your leader. You don't know how close you came to being the last casualty of this war."

She smiled. "Not in a million years. I knew perfectly well that you were preparing to do something foolish. You are not much of an actor. It was obvious that you had heard my entrance to your room. Since you didn't turn immediately, you must have been preparing for some unfriendly greeting."

"I suppose you want to have a tour of the place."

"I'd rather have a tour of you." She moved her hand up my arm slowly and circled it around my neck, drawing my head closer to hers. I drew her down into my lap and our lips met. After a moment she asked me to show her the office. I took her by the hand. We left the office and walked down the stairs. We slowly made a circuit of the building. We stopped in the Control Room where the techs were busy taking apart the electronics.

"What in the world is this place?" She asked

I responded, "It's where we work our magic." I pointed up to one of the displays. "We watched the last battle on that screen."

Minerva asked, "The last battle?"

"Yes. Riddle and Potter."

She looked at me with genuine surprise in her eyes. "Truly? How in the world could you possibly have seen that? I don't believe it. Describe the battle."

I inclined my head to the right and asked, "You doubt my word?"

She smiled and said, "The thought had occurred to me."

I proceeded to describe what I'd seen. She was forced to admit that I had details that only an observer could have. As we talked, I took her arm, and we walked on.

She asked, "George told me that there's a young lady who works here who loved Fred. Is that true?"

"Yes, there is. Do you want to meet her?"

"No, but I will—if you want."

"I think that she's in the Cafeteria having a cup of coffee. Let's go see if we can find her."

She was there. I introduced them. Minerva said to Sally, "Do you know that I thought that you were a rival for the affections of my Wendt?"

Sally looked surprised and then said, "I had never thought about it, but I can see why you might think that. No, you've never had a rival for his affections. You should hear what he has to say about you."

Minerva smiled and said, "I would dearly love to hear what he has to say about me to other women." She turned to me and said, "Run along. I think I'll have a cup of coffee with Miss Harker. I'll join you later."

I reluctantly left the two of them together and returned to my office and the spreadsheet. Later that evening over tea after a meal I found her very affectionate indeed. "What can I attribute my good fortune for this evening? Why are you so good to me?" It was rather difficult to really talk coherently. She was running a stocking-clad foot up and down the inside of my left calf.

"Oh, no reason, really. It's just nice to know that your Miss Sally has no designs on you."

"Well, I could have told you that."

"You could have told me no such thing. Men have no idea when women have designs on them."

"And I suppose that women know perfectly well when men have designs on them?"

"Certainly, I knew that first time we disapparated together that you wanted me."

"Do you know that I have designs on you this very second?"

"Of course, I do. You should. I've been helping those designs along as much as I possibly could." She laughed that husky laugh that I find irresistible. I ran a hand along her left cheek and smiled.

Much later she said that she had to leave and disapparated directly from my room. That has never stopped being disconcerting for me—seeing someone present in a room one moment and gone with a "crack" of air collapsing into the empty space that they left behind the next instant.

I worked through the billing spreadsheets and the various forms to account for how we'd spent Her Majesty's money and eventually had reached the end.

As we worked out what would happen with all the people we'd assembled, it shook out this way:

Most of the SAS unit stayed together. I don't know what their next assignment was. It could have been anywhere in the world.

The contractors (besides me, Sally, and the Cafeteria staff) were all the Boy Genius's. He helped them find positions. I later heard that he started a consultancy himself. He probably hired the crème de la crème himself.

The Cafeteria staff scattered, and since they were good, probably found positions around London.

Sally was special. I insisted on writing a glowing letter of recommendation for her. She would have none of it and at our parting, which happened in our office, she hugged me fiercely and whispered in my ear, "I don't want to see you ever again. You will only remind of Fred."

She then broke the embrace, turned quickly, and left without turning back. She strode out the door and slammed it after her. As I heard her footsteps fade in the distance, I mused that she would never call the office that we had just been standing in, "our office." It was always "your office." I never thought of it in any other way than "our office".

Parker called me into his office the last day that I was there.

Parker asked, "You know what this is?"

"Sure, it's an exit interview. What do you want to know?"

"Really? Not much of anything. There's a bunch of bloody foolish questions that I'm supposed to ask you, but it all boils down to this: Do you think that we treated you fairly?"

"Well, besides giving me the boot as soon as you could after I pulled your bacon out of the fire, I guess I don't have anything to complain about."

"You know why we're sacking you?"

"Sure. Your superiors don't want to have the embarrassment of having a Yank responsible for getting you out of your problems."

"That's what it comes down to. Nothing you or I can do about it. This is MY question—what are you going to do now?"

"Oh, I don't know, maybe go on the 'dole'."

"No, I mean really. Be serious."

"I am being serious. What else can I do? Sacked from a job where I can't even ask for a referral because officially I never worked for you.

The next previous job was teaching at a school of 'wizarding'. Who's going to pay any attention to that if I even try to get a reference?"

"Come on."

"Well, maybe I'll see if the Royal Marines have an opening for a contractor."

"You wouldn't."

"Wouldn't I? Why not? What's to prevent me? A sense of loyalty to the good old SAS?"

"Hmmm. Would you really?"

"Yeh, the more I think of it, the better I like the idea."

Parker got up and started to pace back and forth. "I don't like that. I don't like that at all."

"Well, what are you going to do about it?"

"I don't know. But, maybe, maybe, I could see about getting your old job back."

"Maybe I don't want my job back."

"Oh, come on. Let me try. You never know. I'd just hate to see you go over to the Royal Marines. They're such a bunch of rotters. You wouldn't like it at all over there."

"I don't know. They just might be more loyal than the SAS."

"That's unfair. I tried to save your spot. I really tried."

"Well, apparently not as hard as you're ready to try now."

"Just don't make any commitments. I'll be in touch as soon as I know anything. Oh, how do I get in touch with you?"

"You didn't have any trouble finding me a year ago when you found me originally. I'll be around. I've cleaned out my desk, and everything that I value is in this brief case. Amazing how little there is, right?"

"Well, whatever happens, good luck."

"Thanks. Be seeing you." I started out the door and then turned around. "Don't worry, I wouldn't have gone to the Royal Marines."

"Well, I would think not. No one with any pride would."

I closed the door behind me and worked my way out the building. I went through the main entrance and dropped my ID badge at the desk.

"Sorry to see you go, Mr. Wendt,." The guard at the door said as he waved goodbye.

"Me too. I eventually got to like it here. Just don't tell Parker that."

"Yes sir."

I left the building and started to walk down the street when I heard a "crack" behind me. I turned around and found Minerva freshly disapparated there. "Don't you ever disapparate in front of someone?"

"Sorry. I just like to surprise you."

475

We embraced, and I kissed her. In the midst of the kiss, we disapparated. When we had arrived I pushed her back and asked, "Don't you ever travel any other way? I've had enough disapparation to last me a lifetime."

She was not bothered in the least. "You love it and you know it!"

"I only love it (if I do) because it's you. Where are we?"

"Look around."

I did. I immediately recognized the streets of the only purely wizarding village in England. "We're in Hoggsmead."

"Yes. I thought we might spend the night here."

"I won't argue with that. The 'Three Broomsticks?'"

She said, "I was thinking the 'The Hog's Head'."

"'The Hog's Head!' Why in the world would you want to stay there?"

"Oh, it just seems appropriate for the sort of liaison that we're having."

I frowned at her but let her have her way. We entered and got Abeforth to give us a room.

Abeforth stared at me for a minute and said "You figure you saved wizard folk, do you?"

"No, why in the world would you reckon I would?"

"No. It's just that I recon most Muggles would."

"Well, I don't. See you in the morning." We went up to our room. Minerva used the enchanted key. Only a wizard or witch could get it to open the door to our room. It turned out to be not so bad as I had feared. The furniture was old. It looked hand-made and dated back more years than I would speculate on.

Minerva seemed at home there. She managed to get me into bed amazingly quickly considering how tired I was. Her hands were gentle and soft as they hadn't been before. We spent quite a long time in gentle foreplay. I ended the night falling asleep while spooning her. I awoke with the smell of her hair in my face, filling me with a freshness that I hadn't felt in a very long time. She stirred, and I nuzzled her back. She laughed and caressed me. She finally said, "You really are insane."

"Well, yes. But what has that to do with anything?"

"Oh, I've been hoping that you would prove to me that you were sane, and that there was a good explanation for why I let you lead me astray."

I cleared my throat and said, "Who was it who led whom astray?"

"You know what I mean."

I was tempted to tell her that I didn't know what she meant but restrained the temptation. This was too wonderful to take a chance spoiling it. It was the first time that we'd made love without the threat of the Deatheaters dominating our thoughts. She mused, "When are you going to make me an honest woman?"

"How can I make you what you've been all along?"

"Don't be tedious. You know what I mean." She spoke the words with a twinkle in her eyes.

"As soon as you've introduced me to your family as your fiancée."

"I was hoping you'd do that." She said as she yawned.

"Coward."

"You bet. You know my sister has been afraid of this for as long as we've known each other."

"Yes, it's strange. It's OK for us to be lovers, but heaven forbid that we would get married."

She drew little circles on my thigh with her index finger and asked, "What will you do now? Will you leave Hogwarts for the glitter of Piccadilly?"

"What do you mean leave Hogwarts? I was thrown out last summer, and I can't imagine that any Headmaster of Hogwarts would hire me, a Muggle. The only one who would is dead now."

She smiled an arch smile and said, "I can think of one that would."

"Oh, sure. Barnabas the Balmy, I suppose he'd take a Muggle teacher."

"No, I was thinking of the current Headmaster of Hogwarts."

"Don't tell me that they've made Mr. Weasley the Headmaster!"

"You are being intentionally obtuse. You know perfectly well who the Head*mistress* of Hogwarts is."

"Not Rita Skeeter?" She pinched my ear at that.

"OK. OK. You're the new Head*mistress*, right?"

"You bet I am. You'd better believe that your old position is still open and it's yours. That is, unless you've got some better offer."

"Well," I drawled, "there is that offer from that American witch."

She shot me a murderous glance and said, "You really are full of yourself today."

"Yes, yes. I humbly accept. I hope that no one threw away any of my papers while I was gone."

"Oh, there wasn't anyone interested in English Literature while you were gone. But there is one little issue. I'll show you when we go to Hogwarts after breakfast."

"Oh, yes. Breakfast. At the Hogshead. Yes. Hmmm. Perhaps there's a little snack we could get at Hogwarts? Hmmm."

"No, this is a bed and breakfast. We're going to have breakfast here."

Well, I said to myself, "Here's a revolting development," but I hunkered down and prepared myself for a meal to remember or perhaps forget. We went down to the Common Room and took a table. Abeforth came over and said, "You've got a choice for breakfast. Hagus or fried grits."

I looked at the table top, hoping for inspiration. I finally asked, "How did you learn about grits?"

Abeforth answered, "I read about it in a cookbook."

I took a deep breath and said, 'The grits, please."

Minerva stuck her tongue out at me and said, "Coward, I'm having the Hagus, Abeforth, please."

He left. We talked about the work being done on the castle to repair the damage that the recent battle had done. I asked if she thought that they'd be able to open on schedule in the Fall. She smiled sweetly and said, "If we don't, I'll wring those contractors' necks. They're charging us enough for the work."

Our breakfasts came, and I decided that the only way that I could get my grits down was to keep my eyes on a much more pleasant view—namely Minerva's eyes. She may have had the same idea because we spent a great deal of the meal with our eyes locked while we ate. The fried grits were actually not bad. They seemed to have a lot of substance to them and I didn't feel like I'd need to have lunch, I felt so full.

We checked out, and Abeforth presented us with the bill. It was 12 galleons. I suddenly realized that I didn't have any wizarding money with me. "Ooh. Ooh. I don't have anything smaller than a fifty pound note."

Minerva smoothly said, "Don't you remember that you left your galleons with me when you left Hogwarts?"

Actually, I'd forgotten that I had done that for a very good reason. I hadn't done it. I thought I might have a couple of galleons that I'd kept as souvenirs. "Oh, yes. You don't have some of them with you, do you?" She opened her handbag and withdrew a small purse, opened it, and handed me about 25 galleons. All the time Abeforth was standing behind the bar polishing a glass. I turned to him and offered 15 galleons and generously told him to keep the change.

We left the inn, and I commented, "I think that must be the first glass in history that has been polished in the Hogshead."

"You may be right. I always drink butter beer from the bottle when I visit there. The glasses may be purely ornamental."

It was a brisk walk up to the castle. As we approached, it was easy to see the signs of the battle that had been fought there. There were great holes blasted in the walls, and we could see scaffolding where there were workers repairing the walls. The main door was still intact. We entered and found Mr. Filch staring up at the work from the inside. I went over to him and patted him on the back and said, "It will never be the same." He jumped at my touch and whirled around, "Oh, it's you, Mr. Wendt. I thought that we'd never see you again. You know that that Muggle studies teacher last year was tortured to death by Snape. If they'd do that to her, I couldn't imagine what they'd do to you."

I answered, "No, I hadn't heard that. I'm sorry. How have you been?"

"Oh, it was hard last year. Hard. I wondered what they'd do to . . er. . You know that I was never much at fancy magic. Uh. . I was a little worried, what with all the Muggle-born that were being sent to Azkaban and all. Well, I'm just glad that nothing worse happened here at Hogwarts."

"Oh, I think that no one would bother you. You're almost like a part of the school." He looked up silently at one of the gaps in the outer wall.

I smiled and said, "I take your point." We moved along toward the central part of the castle.

Filch called after me, "Wendt."

I turned and said, "Yes."

"I'm glad you're back. There are few enough of us old-timers left."

"Thanks. I agree." I turned back to Minerva and said, "Since when have I been an 'old-timer'?"

She chuckled and said, "He says that to everyone he knows here. I think he actually said that to Kretur the day after the battle."

I frowned trying to remember who that was. Minerva noticed my puzzlement and said, "You remember Kretur, surely. He's one of the house elves. He used to belong to Harry Potter. Potter tried to free him but Kretur stoutly refused to be freed. He insisted on staying indentured to Potter. So Potter assigned him to work here until he could put his affairs in order and take on a household."

I remembered Kretur then. I just couldn't remember the name. "Sure, I remember him. He was always so sullen. Is his temper any better?"

Minerva said, "Yes. I'd forgotten that he had a complete change of disposition during the winter last year. I don't know the details, but somehow Potter won him over. He had spent some of the fall back at Grimauld Place with Potter, Weasley, and Granger. They became reconciled during that time. Somehow Potter convinced him that he wasn't so bad after all. Kretur became positively cheery when he returned to Hogwarts after that fall."

"Hmmm. Kretur. Cheery. Hmmm. I'll believe that when I see it."

"Oh, you'll see it pretty soon, if you ever go down to the kitchens like you used to."

I laughed at the idea of a cheery Kretur as we proceeded toward the wing of the castle where my office was. We arrived, and I opened the door for Minerva. She preceded me, and I followed her into a scene of devastation. There was a gaping hole in one wall and everything in the room was upended and scattered. There were papers everywhere. I said, "Somehow, I don't remember my room being quite this disorderly when I left. Don't tell me the Weasley twins made a return appearance after I left."

Minerva said, "God, I wish they had. I think the last time that I saw them together was. . . " She stopped and tears flowed. She composed herself and said, "I was going to say at their brother Bill's wedding. But then I remembered that they'd been here for the Last Battle. That seems an age and a world away."

I nodded and was silent for a bit. Then I said, "You know, I think that I'd finally developed a complete set of lesson plans for every form here at Hogwart's, and now I suppose I'll have to start again from scratch."

She nodded, and I saw a tear on her cheek. I pulled out a Kleenex and dabbed at the cheek. She raised her hand to mine and patted it. We were quiet for a minute—each with his memories of Fred and George. The two of them would never be together again, joking and jostling each other— except in our memories.

Finally, I said, "I'm going to start organizing here. I'll see if I can re- construct any lesson plans. Why don't you go up and do Headmistress stuff." She started to leave, and I called after her, "What's the password for the stairway up there?"

She called back "Tart to you."

I responded, "Are you keeping with Dumbledore's penchant for names of sweets as passwords?"

She answered, "No."

I set to work sifting through the rubble, putting together the papers that were still legible and deciding what books were still serviceable. I'd made a fair start when Minerva appeared in my doorway. She asked, "Are you never going to get hungry for lunch?"

I looked at my watch and was surprised to see that it was after 13.30. I said, "Those grits really stick to your ribs. I'm not really very hungry even now."

"Well, I'm starved. If you want to have lunch, you'll have to come with me now."

"You don't have to ask twice. Are you having lunches in the Great Hall?"

"Oh, we had lunch over two hours ago for the workers and any staff that are still around, but that's over long ago. We'll have to go down to the kitchens and see what we can scrounge."

"Good enough." We walked down the three flights of stairs that took us to the kitchens. We entered and found the house elves busy cleaning up and seemingly working on a sauce or two for the evening meal.

Minerva took my hand and led me over to an elf who seemed to be in charge. He was wearing a bright vest and a bowler hat. He seemed to be pretty full of himself. He noticed our presence and turned. He bowed deeply to us and welcomed Minerva. She in turn asked me, "Do you recognize the sous chef?"

I looked at him and tried to search my memory. Finally I gave up. "No, who is it? "

The elf answered, "Master Wendt, you don't recognize me?"

"I'm afraid not. I suppose I'm going to be really embarrassed when I find out who you are. Wait, a minute. You aren't Kretur?"

"Yes, sir."

"Well, it's good to see you, indeed. It's good to see some familiar faces around here."

"That's just what Mr. Filch said."

I smiled at him and said, "Let me say that I think that you have much better taste in clothes than Dobbie."

"Yes, sir. I think I do, but I miss him very much."

"I didn't know him very well, but I do too."

"What can we do for you?"

Minerva said, "We didn't have lunch. We were wondering if you might have a sandwich or something left-over from lunch."

"We've nothing left from lunch, but we can put an omelet together for you quickly if you like."

"That would be great," I said, "Would you mind terribly making it with the egg whites only?"

Kretur made a hacking cough and said, "How can you eat such a thing?"

Minerva said, "That's OK. Mr. Wendt has some funny tastes, but I'll have an omelet, too. A normal omelet." She looked at me meaningfully.

I took what I thought she was trying to suggest silently, "Kretur, just this once, you could make me an omelet just as you think is best."

"Yes, madam, sir. It'll be up shortly. Will you take them upstairs?"

"No, Kretur," I said, "I'd like to stay here in the kitchen if it's OK with you—like old times."

"Yes, sir. As you wish."

"Perhaps you could tell us a little of your life after I left Hogwarts?"

Kretur hesitated and stammered. I realized that he didn't want to talk about it or disobey an order—even from a Muggle. So, I said, "That's all right Kretur. I'm looking forward to the omelet. Get to it."

"That was nice of you to let him go. He left Hogwarts and was very silent after his return late in the fall last year." We took chairs around a work table in the kitchen and presently Kretur brought a couple of plates with omelets, toast and some cream cheese and jams. We ate, and I praised the omelet as strongly as I could, "Minerva. This is really the best omelet that I've ever had. And I love the blueberry jam."

Kretur cleared his throat and said, almost to himself, "I picked the blueberries myself."

Minerva said, "I quite agree. Toast, jam, and omelets is an unequaled English breakfast."

"I quite agree." I added.

Kretur turned a pastel shade of beet red and returned to the fireplace, pretending to be working with a sauce. I told Minerva, "I'm concerned about something."

She smiled and then the smile died when she saw the expression on my face, "What are you thinking of?"

"You didn't get all the Deatheaters, did you?"

"No, but we got almost all of them and by far the worst."

"I know, but those who are left will want revenge for the death of their leader."

"I'm sure they will, but that is their lookout. They will have a hard time taking revenge. They'd have to attack the whole of the DA"

I took a deep breath and said, "I think that you're right but they won't go after the whole DA. They'll go after the leaders of the DA."

"You mean Potter, Weasley and Granger. I think they'd have a very hard time with them. As a matter of fact, I almost wish they would try attacking them. There would be an end to them all."

"Yes, if they attacked those three, but what if they went after relatives and friends, so forth."

Minerva laughed, "I'd like to see them go after the Weasley's—especially Ms. Ginny."

"I know, and Potter doesn't have loved ones other than the Weasleys, but . . ." I let it hang.

Minerva frowned, "Yes, there's Ms. Grainger's parents. I see what you mean." She looked down and said, "What can we do about it?"

"We can begin by talking to her and trying to convince her to keep them hidden for a bit longer. Perhaps a year. Six months at the least."

"I see that you're serious about this." She paused and appeared to think. "Yes, I'll send her an owl as soon as I get back to the Headm . . . uh my Office. You know, I don't know if I'll ever get used to the fact that it's my office now. With all those former Headmasters and Headmistresses on the walls it's hard to think that you deserve to be among them."

I smiled for once, "You deserve to be at the head of them."

"You are a flatterer to the end. I can never hope to stand among them as equals."

We finished our meal, and I returned to my office as did Minerva. I continued to work the mess on the floor.

In the evening, we joined the motley crew working on the castle and a few professors in the Great Hall. The cuisine stood in a stark contrast to the condition of the hall.

The next day passed slowly, and I began to wonder if the building would ever be more than a shadow of its former beauty and grandeur.

Passport

I had hardly been back to my office twenty-four hours when I was already well back into the routine of trying to piece together lesson plans. I was sitting at my desk when there was a knock on my door. It was so soft that I wasn't entirely sure that it was a knock. I ignored it, if it really were something .

Then a second knock occurred. I was sure this time that it was a knock. So, I answered, "Yes?" There was no response. I again dropped my head to work on the lesson plans.

Then a third knock sounded. I was getting a little angry. I had never known any—even the most timid student to fail to open the door on their own and come in. I said, "Oh, all right, I'll be there in a second."

I rose quickly, rounded my desk, walked briskly to the door. I swung it wide quickly, ready to give the knocker a piece of my mind for being so timid.

What happened was that a dark shape swept into the room, threw arms around me and said, "I was so sure that you were dead." In that instant, I recognized the voice and with that recognition I identified the perfume that she wore.

"Sinistra, what are you talking about?"

She still held me fiercely and said, "She wouldn't tell me anything about you. Nothing. Were you alive or dead? Did she know anything about you? Nothing."

I guessed that she must be talking about Minerva. I started to disentangle myself from her. She did not resist. Instead, she backed away then kissed me passionately but quickly and was completely out of my arms.

I was dumbfounded for a moment about what to say. She didn't need more of an invitation than that. She quickly closed the door behind her and walked briskly to my poor sofa. It had been damaged during that final battle but was still serviceable if you just wanted a place to rest your feet.

She sat and almost begged me, "Please tell me what happened all this past year." At the same time, she patted a spot beside her.

I temporized by saying, "Let me get you something to drink for your present relief."

She nodded. I realized that I might not actually have anything to offer. I'd not opened the bottom left drawer of my desk where I kept my liquor yet. Maybe there was nothing but broken glass and dried whiskey in it. I opened the drawer and found that there were two bottles. One was an open bottle of everyday Jim Beam. It didn't seem like a good thing to offer her.

To my amazement, the other bottle was Johnny Walker Blue Label. I didn't remember having an unopened bottle of that. Of course, it had been over a year since I'd opened that drawer. While I was fumbling in the drawer, Sinistra asked, "Would you like me to conjure something? Perhaps a couple of glasses of wine?"

I shook my head, "No, I have something better than that." I placed the bottle on the desk and walked over to the bookshelf where I kept my glasses and some miscellaneous cutlery. I opened the drawer and found the broken glass that I'd been looking for before.

I raised my head and said, "Well, perhaps you could at least conjure a couple of shot glasses, and if you happened to have some ice,that would be good too."

Her voice was much brighter. "Nothing easier." With that she waved her wand and a glass floated through the air to her and another to me. I took that glass, complete with two spherical ice cubes, and placed it on the desk. I then opened the Blue Label and went to the sofa. I poured a good shot into her glass. Then I went back to the desk and filled mine.

It seemed churlish to sit behind the desk as I almost always did when she came calling. So, I walked back to the sofa and sat.

She had been waiting for me before sampling her glass. She said, "Thanks." Then she raised it to her lips and tried a sip. I also took a sip from mine.

She hummed and said, "Now that is good. Why have I never had any of that when I've visited before?"

"I save that for very special occasions."

She took another good sip and said, "Please tell me what happened. I was so afraid for you when you disappeared."

"Well, it's a very long story."

She smiled. It was the first real smile that I'd seen from her in over a year. "I'll give you as much time as you could want."

I smiled ruefully, "Well, I'm not going to give you the details but I will give you the fifty thousand foot view. I intend to write about the last year. As a matter of fact, I've been writing about all my time here. Someday, if it's ever published, you can read it."

Her eyelids lowered and she asked, "Is there no way that I can convince you to share your adventures with me —fully?"

I laughed, "Not now. You'll get the *Reader's Digest* version now."

She looked puzzled. I anticipated her question, "*Reader's Digest* is a Muggle magazine that publishes condensations of all sorts of literature.

"For now, this is what I'll tell you. Don't press me for more."

I composed myself and asked, "I'll ask you one question before I get started. What did you know about the break-out from Azkaban?"

She looked puzzled again, "Do you mean the one the year before last when the Deatheaters escaped?"

I shook my head "no."

Her eyes widened and she asked, "There was another?"

I nodded and considered my options. Should I reveal one of the closest held secrets in the War before it was published in the *Prophet* and reputable newspapers? I decided on my course and asked, "Then you've not been in contact with the DA or the Order of the Phoenix?"

She shook her head and said, "I thought that the DA disbanded after Umbrage left Hogwarts. Wasn't that the purpose of the DA?"

I didn't answer that question but asked, "What about the Order?"

She said, "I was never in the Order. When it first formed, I was still a minor and after the return of Riddle, it was hard to . . . well, I was afraid."

She went on, "So, there was another escape from Azkaban. Did you have anything to do with it?"

I insisted on dropping back further in time, "At the end of the school term last year, Minerva *convinced* me to leave Hogwarts and return to America. I fully intended to do that. However, before I could leave the country, a Muggle security service. . ." She was preparing another question. I held up my hand and said, "That is privileged information. I can't tell you which."

I took another sip to give me time to compose what I was going to say. "At first, they had the idea that I might be some kind of Deatheater."

She giggled at that and took another sip. It was the last from her glass. She noticed and said, holding up her empty glass, "May I have another."

I nodded and started to rise. She waved her hand and said, "Asio heavenly liquor." The bottle obediently flew into her outstretched hand which no longer held the glass. She quickly poured herself a generous helping and filled my glass to the rim. I had to take a decent sip just to prevent it from spilling on me. That made her smile.

I went on, "Well, obviously they didn't know much about Deatheaters at the time. They didn't even know the name."

She giggled and said, "Well, I would think not!"

I nodded and continued, "Eventually, they figured out that I was pretty much an innocent bystander. They kept me on because I knew more about magic and the War than anyone else that they had access to."

Her mouth had dropped open, "Then Minerva didn't know what had happened to you. She was as much in the dark as I?"

I decided that I'd pretty much stay silent—neither denying nor confirming any of her guesses as long as I could. Sinistra was going on, "And I thought that she was just being a jealous bitch who wouldn't share anything about you with anyone else who loved you."

I shrugged, hoping she would take that as a sign of ignorance. Sinistra made a guess, "Then you helped this escape from Azkaban by telling people what you knew about it."

That I could nod affirmation to. She went on, "Oh, you were so brave! To take a chance that the Deatheaters would find out and do who-knew-what to you." She reached out and clasp my fore-arm. She squeezed encouragingly, but I stuck to my no comment tack. She gasped and said, "You were lucky to come out alive!"

She was leaning toward me and had almost finished her second shot. I decided that I had to bring this interview to an end. I stood. She stood as well. I guess that she thought that I was about to lead her back to the quarters part of my office because she took a step or two in that direction.

Instead, I allowed her to continue to hold my arm, but I used that attachment to let me drag her slowly toward the door to the hall. "I hope that satisfies your curiosity because that is all I'm going to tell you now."

We reached the door, and she almost begged, "Oh please tell me more of your adventures. I have all the time in the world for you."

I just said, "Not now." I then used my free hand to open the door and nudge her out.

She took one final shot though. She said, "Oh, just remember me. Anytime you would like a favor, there is no one in the world that I'd rather help out than you." She nodded her head vigorously with those words.

I said that I wouldn't forget, and I closed the door, separating her from me.

□

The next day, Minerva entered my humble (oh, sooo humble) office and said, "I've heard of Ms. Grainger."

I looked at her and asked, "'Of' not 'from'?"

Her eyebrows were drawn together over a frown, "Yes. I got an owl from the Weasleys. Apparently, she had been there, and my owl had just missed her there."

"Missed? Do you know where she went?"

"No."

I stood and paced while I thought. Finally I said, "I've got a bad feeling about this. We've got to find her before she reaches her parents, wherever they are. I'm sure that's what her intent is. I'm going to do some research of my own."

I strode to the door and left. Minerva followed me. She asked, "What are you going to do? You look like you're going to walk outside the grounds and disapparate."

"I'm going outside the grounds but not to Disapparate but to use my cell phone. I'm going to call in some debts."

"A cell phone?"

I picked up my pace and left her behind.

Later that day I went up to her office, "You really did make the password 'tart'."

"Well, of course. That's what I said."

We closed the distance between us, and I took her in my arms. We kissed. "I got in touch with my former employer. We talked about Ms. Grainger. He's going to try to discover where she's gone. But in the mean time, I've been thinking. Where would they be?"

"Her parents?"

"Yes. I think they must be out of the country. But where?"

Minerva said, "I think that they aren't fluent in any foreign language. Surely they must be in the English speaking world."

"That would be most of North America, the Republic of Ireland, Australia, New Zealand. Anywhere else?"

"I don't think so. But that's a lot of territory, how would we ever find her?"

"It might not be really hard. We know their approximate age. There can't be a tremendous number of husband and wife dental teams of that age in any of those countries. I've already started inquiries in America with my American 'friends.' Also, I've got my local 'friends' appealing to the Australians and New Zealanders. The Irish might be difficult, but I really doubt that they'd have gone there."

Minerva frowned. I asked, "Yes?"

"They might not both be working. That would be a nice little feature that Hermione might have added to her spell—preventing her Mum from remembering that she was a dentist."

I went back off the grounds to get to someplace that the phone would work and called my contacts. Parker had news. I rushed up to the castle and had the devil of a time finding Minerva. "Minerva, Minerva!" I called as I ran through the castle. The halls echoed with the sound. Finally I found her in the owlery. "Minerva, my buddy Parker has found her."

"Where is she?"

"She's on her way to Australia. She used her own passport to leave the country."

"Wonderful. You can use your cellophane to call her and . . ."

"No, no. She doesn't have a cell phone." I emphasized and spoke slowly the last two words. "We've got to go find her!"

Minerva's mouth opened wide and she was speechless for once. I went on, "We've got to get to the airport immediately so that we can get a flight to Australia."

"But, but. . ."

"But me no 'but's. We've got to get going immediately. Can you disapparate us directly to Heathrow?"

"Sure. Why?"

The question brought me up short. How did I explain? Come to think of it, did I really know that going to Australia by airplane was better than a wizard way. "OK. I can't explain in five minutes, but I think that airplane is the best way to follow Hermione. Do just let me have my way here."

Minerva said, "Well, finally, a definite idea. When do we leave?"

"Right now. Can we go?"

She was speechless again for a moment. "Yes, but I don't have any money with me."

"You won't need money. I've got my credit card. I don't think Gringott's cut it off. We should be able to travel on it for a week or so."

"'Credit cart'? What's that? How many wheels does it have?"

"Sometimes, I think you're making fun of me when you do that."

"Do what?" She smiled with a knowing air.

"You'll see. We've got to leave immediately. Come on, let's get off the grounds so that you can disapparate."

"Now, it's OK to disapparate?" She asked in mock disgust.

"I still hate it, but we've got to do it. We've got to get to the airport as quickly as we can."

We trotted out the main entrance of the castle and got off the grounds as quickly as we could. When we reached the main gate, I took her hand, and my gut felt like someone pulled it inside out. We were standing in a dark corner of what proved to be Heathrow. I led us up to the British Airways desk and went into the queue. We eventually reached an agent, and I started the procedure. I asked her, "We want to get to Melbourne, Australia as quickly as we can. Can you help us?"

She looked at us and asked, "Do you have a preference on route?"

"We'll take whatever gets us there the fastest."

She nodded sagely and started keying on her keyboard. Minerva whispered in my ear, "What's she doing?"

I whispered back in her pearl-like ear, "She's looking up flights and trying to figure out which will get us there the quickest."

"But surely she must consult a book or pamphlet?"

"No, there's a computer that knows all that and will tell her."

Presently the ticket agent smiled and asked, "There are two routes that will get you there pretty quickly. They both go through Chicago. One goes on to Japan and then the Philippines and then to Australia. The other goes through Hawaii and then to Tahiti and then to Australia." She looked slyly at us and said, "Hawaii is very romantic. You'll arrive there in the late afternoon and will stay overnight. You could see the moonlight over Haunama Bay."

I said, "Is that the quickest route?"

"The Japanese route is the fastest. You'll get there about 7 hours earlier than the Hawaiian route, but it's so much less interesting."

"We'll go via Japan."

"What class do you want to fly?"

"We'll fly first class if you can get us two seats together."

She consulted the computer screen again. "Yes. We can do that. How will you pay for the flight?"

I handed her my Gringotts Mastercard. She nodded. I gave her our names, and she worked the computer again. "The total will be 1,525 pounds for the two of you round trip. I suppose you want the earliest available flight?"

"Yes, when does it leave?"

"In two hours."

"Fine. We'll take that." She worked the computer again, and the ticket printer started chattering. She took the tickets apart and stapled them together. Then she added as an afterthought. "You've got your passports with you, don't you?"

I nodded brusquely and said, "Sure."

"Do you have bags to check?"

"No." She looked at us quizzically.

I volunteered, "We're just going to do carry-on's." Her eyebrows rose at that. But she didn't say anything. She handed over the tickets, and I gave Minerva's to her.

"Hold on to that. We'll need it throughout the trip. Let's go to the gate, and we'll pick up some luggage and clothes on the way." We went to the duty-free section and bought a carry-on bag for each of us. Then we found a clothing store and went in.

"Minerva, you'll have to buy some Muggle clothing. And I will as well." I helped her pick some inconspicuous, conservative, but attractive blouses and skirts. We argued over colors. She wanted louder colors than I wanted her to have. "Look, Minerva, we want to not be noticed. I really think a bright purple blouse with a red skirt is going to attract attention."

She laughed and said, "I want to attract your attention."

"You've got it, regardless what you wear, but I don't want to attract the attention of Deatheaters. We're going to stick with dull Muggle-wear." She pouted, but I won the argument. Probably the last I'd win, I reflected. We went on to our gate We arrived about thirty minutes before flight time and we caught the end of boarding. We were among the last who walked down the jetway. She looked around, seeming perplexed. Finally, she asked, "I never understood just why we have to walk down this tunnel? Is the idea that we have to pass a claustrophobia test to prove we can stand being locked up in a long metal tube that's flying 30,000 ft. above the ground?"

"No. But first, it's not 30,000 ft. It's 40,000 ft. And it's really not that bad—at least not in first class."

When we reached the main door to the cabin, the stewardess glanced at my ticket and took my carry-on. She glanced at Minerva's and said, "You two are sitting next to each other?"

Minerva said, "Yes, we are. We're traveling together."

The stewardess looked from one of us to the other. She looked like she wanted to say something, but she didn't. There was a line of people behind us for economy class, and she didn't have a chance. We found our seats, and I asked, Minerva, "Do you want the window seat or the inside?"

"Of course, the inside. I've flown at 300 feet on a broomstick. I don't want to be at 30,000 feet let alone 40,000 feet."

"It's completely different in an airplane. When we flew to the Canaries, you appreciated how beautiful it can be when you're on the edge of space, and you see the clouds laid out below you."

"I'll take the inside seat. The Canaries was only a couple of hours. This is going to go on and on and on. I've seen all the beautiful edge of space I need."

"OK. It's your loss. You'll be sitting there drooling at my seat."

We took our seats. The stewardess went through her pre-flight spiel. Minerva said, "You see! If this were such a wonderful, safe way to travel, why does the woman have to stand up and tell you all the safety things that they've got in the airplane?" She was slurring all her "S"'s she was so upset. She couldn't sit still. We started to taxi down toward the runway. As we speeded up, she gripped the arms of her seat. I took the hand clawing the arm of her seat next to me. "It's going to be OK. You know the Weasley twins flew a number of times, and nothing happened to them."

Minerva shot back, "Well, they were the Weasleys!"

By this time we were in the air. "Now, we've got some talking to do."

"Well, I hope so."

"No, no. This is serious. There are several things that we need to get done. First, there's the passport."

"What passport?"

"Yours."

She closed her eyes and said, "What did I do with that fake passport of mine from before?"

"Well. Let's start making a new one. Here's my passport." I pulled it out of my breast pocket and handed it to her. "See. On the first inner page, there's my photo and . . ."

She interrupted me. She took the passport and looked at the cover. She said, "It's almost a work of art, isn't it? 'United States of America'. The seal of the 'United States of America'." She passed her hands over the seal. "You can feel the seal."

I looked at her and said, "You're right. I've looked at it a hundred times when I traveled, but I never stopped to see."

I went on. "Can you make a copy of it? A copy but different—with your name, your photo, your birthday."

She answered immediately and dismissively, "Of course, am I a witch or not?"

"Oh, you don't understand. It has to be a really good copy. The state department puts in all kinds of special tricks to make US passports unique. I don't know what they all are. You can see a few. Hold the first page up to the light. No, obliquely. Do you see the eagle? That's only the beginning."

She took it and flexed the pages, sniffed it, and she finally said, "I need to tear out part of a page. Is that OK?"

"Yes, of course. It has to be a US passport."

"I can't change it a little to be a UK passport?"

"No. I don't have a British passport. Look, the copy has to be really, really good. We can't guess about the difference between a US and British passport. We have to get it right."

She closed her eyes and pulled her wand out of an inner pocket of her cloak. She kept her eyes closed and passed the wand over the outside of my passport and then, page by page, she passed it over the interior. Finally, she nodded and said something inaudible. She handed back my passport to me and I noticed that there was another passport under it. I opened the both of them. They were identical, as far as I could tell including the torn page from the middle. I asked, "Which one is mine?"

"They both are. I don't know which one is the original. As a matter of fact, they both are."

"Well, great. I have two passports, and you still don't have one."

She shook her head. "Hand one of them to me."

I did. She opened it, took her wand and began to make motions that seemed to be writing. As I watched, my name disappeared. She asked, "What name should I use?"

"Why, yours, of course. If you're going to tell a lie, especially a big fat lie—like that you are a US citizen, you should include as much of the truth as you possibly can. Use your real name, your real birth date." I laughed, "Your real sex."

"What about birthplace?"

"Leave what's on mine. Ohio, USA. And we've got to come up with a reasonable life history for you. It has to be one that is believable, that explains why we're traveling together, and what you were doing in Britain; everything."

"OK. Where was I born—more specifically than 'Ohio, USA'? What do I do for a living? And, most interesting, why are we traveling together?" She put emphasis on the 'are'.

"That's all simple. You were born in Columbus, Ohio. 2150 Fizroy Drive. You went to Ohio State University and majored in English. You got your PHD there and became an associate professor when. . ." Just then the stewardess who had stared at us before came up and sat down in the empty seat across the aisle from us.

She said, "Ma'am, I couldn't help noticing that you seemed kind of nervous. Is this the first time that you've flown?"

Minerva answered instantly and automatically, "No. I've flown lots of times. But never so high."

I tried to make my interruption seem casual, "Now, Minerva. You've flown lots of little planes for short hops, but you've only flown across the Atlantic once before."

"Oh, yes. That's true. I just can't get used to being in the air for so long or so high."

The stewardess said, "Oh, it's just the same. It'll be over before you know it. My name's Sam."

It was Minerva's turn to stare. Sam answered, "That's short for Samantha. You're Minerva McGonagall and", she looked at me, "you're James Wendt. I remember from your tickets. We're not supposed to get too friendly with the guests, but I couldn't help being curious." She looked directly at Minerva. "Are you James' mom?"

Minerva's smile tightened into a rictus. I intervened, "Minerva and I are friends—extremely close friends. We've been, well, it's complicated."

Minerva's turned to me, and her smile softened, "Yes, why don't you tell her about us. You do it sooo well."

I was not very happy at the prospect of having to improvise as I went. I was hoping that the two of us could work out an equally acceptable back story for strangers, like customs agents, but it looked like I'd have to work it out. She'd just have to be happy with it. I kept with my idea that closest to the truth is best for lies. I took a deep breath and said, "Well, it's a long story."

□□

Sam smiled and said, "I love long stories, and there's practically no one else in first class. It's frequently so boring with only a few guests. Don't worry about how long it is."

"OK. I'll give you the long version. I grew up in Ohio. Southern Ohio. I decided to go to The Ohio State University. I'd always liked stories— reading and writing them. So, I decided to major in English literature. Ohio State is better known for football, but they have a decent English Literature department. I know that Ohio University is better, but my family has a tradition of going to OSU, so that's where I went. I had one of the classes in my major taught by Minerva when I was a junior. It was on the early 19th century novel. She is an associate professor there now, and when I went to school there.

"Anyway, I was pretty impressed with the course. She struck me as having a very good grasp of human nature. That's really necessary to be a good writer, and I frankly hoped to do some writing someday as well as teach.

"So, when I became a senior, I decided to change my faculty advisor to her. Nobody objected, and she came up with a good idea for a senior thesis for me." I could see that Sam was preparing to ask a question. I forestalled it, "It doesn't matter what. It was a thesis about a technical issue, and it turned out to be really embarrassing. I really flubbed it up.

"But the critical thing was that Minerva and I—it was Professor McGonagall and I then—spent a lot of time together. She would critique my ideas and suggest research directions. She was patient and considerate. She was always willing to be interrupted when I had what I thought was a great idea. Her patience was saintly."

Here, Minerva interrupted, "You later discovered that my patience was not nearly so saintly as you thought."

I chided, "Let's not get ahead of the story. That's why I'm so good at telling it."

I resumed, "Anyway, I eventually finished the thesis and got a grade and was graduated. I was lucky and got accepted at Stanford University for graduate study. But, I returned to Ohio fairly frequently to visit family and friends. And somehow my friend Minerva was usually available to listen to tales from graduate school and encourage me. I had the occasional girlfriend, but I just didn't have time to be serious with any of them. Somehow, I always tried to look Minerva up (it had become Minerva then that I was away from OSU), and somehow, she always had time for me. I always enjoyed these interludes—usually over lunch or dinner at some campus hole-in-the-wall pizzeria or Italian restaurant.

"Anyway, I eventually got tired of graduate school. I'd received a Master's degree, but I just hadn't the strength to keep going. So, I decided to move to England for a while and take in the same atmosphere that Dickens and Austen and O'Brien had. Maybe I would get re-energized to go back to school and finish my PHD.

"Eventually, I got tired of the odd jobs and found a teaching job at a private residential finishing school in Northern Scotland. At summer breaks and on rare occasions at Christmastime I would return to Ohio and, of course, always look up Minerva.

"Then something awful happened. A college friend died. He was more than a friend. He was my roommate in college. It happened during a term, and I got special permission to take a couple of days off to attend the funeral. It was in Northern Ohio. I didn't even have time to return to my home town. I flew into Port Columbus. As I prepared for the trip, I realized that I was really happy to be going back to Ohio. When I got on the plane for the long flight, I realized something else.

"As the hours of travel passed, I realized the most wonderful part of all my trips to Ohio had been the chance to see Minerva.

"I arrived at JFK airport to change planes for the flight to Port Columbus. I tried calling Minerva from there but didn't get through. I left a message and boarded my flight for Ohio. When I arrived, I rented a car and immediately headed north but not before trying to call Minerva again. Again, no one answered. I was beginning to feel like I'd never see her on this trip. I arrived just in time for the funeral and the wake. I didn't know many of the people who were there, and I longed all the more to see Minerva. It got late, and I stayed the night in Toledo but got up early the next day to head back to Columbus.

"I arrived at her apartment and rang the doorbell and knocked. I used to be a paper boy, and I had a special knock for those occasions when my clients were reluctant to see me. I call it my 'paper boy' knock. I used it, and still no one answered. I started to leave. I actually got in my car and drove away. I rounded the corner to head for the airport since I didn't have anything better to do, but it occurred to me that I should at least leave a note. So I stopped, scrounged in my bag for some paper, and scribbled off a pathetic note about how I was soooo, sooooo sorry that I'd missed Minerva and that I really wanted to see her and talk to her. I drove around the block and pulled up at her apartment building to leave it in her mailbox. But I noticed her car parked in front of the building. My heart racing, I ran up the steps, and rung her bell. She answered. I told her briefly why I was in Ohio and she asked me up."

⊡

Sam interrupted, "So, you confessed your undying love to her and . . ."

I in my turn interrupted, "No, I didn't."

"After all that, you didn't?!"

"No, we talked pleasantly about my trip and what had happened in her life and my life. We talked about the tragedy that early death was, and in short, we talked about everything but what I desperately wanted to. She had a dog, and she suggested that we take the dog for a walk. I was happy for any excuse to spend more time with her, so we went walking. We talked about all sorts of things, but . . ."

Sam interrupted again, "Everything but love."

496

"Right. Finally, I had to leave to catch my plane. I got up to go, and we said goodbye. I backed out the door, and she followed. Then we both stopped and were trying to decide what to do. Sort of simultaneously we both decided to hug the other. We embraced, and I placed the gentlest kiss on her right cheek. I was sure that she hadn't realized that I'd done that."

"How about it, Minerva? Did you realize that he'd kissed you?"

"Of course I did. Any woman would know."

I went on. "But, of course, I didn't realize that. I left and felt on top of the world."

Sam asked, "Why did you feel so great? You screwed up, didn't you?"

"Well, yes, I suppose so, but I'd been with Minerva. And you can't help feeling wonderful when you've spent time with Minerva."

Sam looked exasperated, "So, what happened then?"

"Well, I flew back to England in a kind of transport of ecstasy. That lasted for several days. Then I began to realize that I'd not really communicated with her about what I cared most about. Then came several weeks of agony as I tried to decide what to do. I felt like I needed to do something to let Minerva know how I felt, but I didn't have any good ideas how to do it. Even though I write for a living, I just didn't think that a letter could tell the story. On the other hand, to actually pick up the phone and talk to Minerva was way too scary for me at that point.

"I finally decided that I had to do something, so I spent several days trying to plan out the conversation that I would have with her on the phone. I thought out every conceivable turn the conversation could take. I planned something witty to say in every situation. Then I dithered about calling her. I must have spent two whole days one weekend in front of my telephone trying to decide to go ahead and call her.

"During the week, I must have gone through my speech and all its variations dozens of times. That weekend, I didn't call. Then I decided for sure that I would call the next weekend. I spent several more hours in front of the phone trying to come up with the determination to actually place the call. Finally I picked up the phone and slowly dialed the number. I was both hoping that she'd answer and that she wouldn't' answer. I waited as the rings sounded—one, two, three, I almost decided to hang up then and there. But on the fourth ring, Minerva answered.

Sam asked Minerva, "What did he say?"

She looked at me and I went on, "Well, the one thing that I didn't say was that I loved her. I used every other euphemism known to man to try to say that I loved her, but somehow I couldn't actually bring myself to use the word.

Sam asked, "Did you know what he was trying to say?"

Minerva snorted, "Of course, I did. From that time that we were standing staring at each other in my apartment, I knew that he was in love with me, AND that I was in love with him. It was terrible. I couldn't bring myself to say the words either. We were truly pathetic. Even though neither of us could quite say it, we both knew that the other person knew what we were trying to say. I fumbled some sort of protest that I was too old for him.

"And I said that she was the youngest, freshest, most beautiful woman that I knew.

"But, I wouldn't accept it." Minerva said.

"I finally said that I would never give up. That we had all the time in the world."

Sam sighed. "So, obviously you got together. How did that happen?"

"I didn't give up. I started a writing campaign. I wrote love letter after love letter. Sometimes I wrote three or four a week. Sometimes only one or two, but I never gave up. I sent gifts and cards and was completely dedicated to her. Finally, she called me and told me that she would be willing to spend some time with me in the summer holidays to see if we all felt the same after we'd been together a bit.

"I was in the 7th heaven. I couldn't wait for summer break. I flew to Ohio and we met at the airport. She drove me home. It was a joy for both of us. When I finally returned to England at the end of the summer holiday, we had agreed to get married as soon as we could break it to our relatives and friends.

"That turned out to take more time than we thought possible. The whole next two terms we only saw each other at the Christmas break when I came back to Ohio. At the end of the Spring term, Minerva came over to England to visit me, and we agreed that we would travel to see our friends and relatives together to announce our engagement."

"And all this time the two of you stayed in love and only saw each other for a couple of weeks around Christmas!"

We both answered, "Yes."

I finished up. "So, Minerva came over to England, and now we're on our way to Minerva's sister in Australia, because she's the hardest case of them all. If we can make peace with her, the rest will be a piece of cake."

Sam whistled and said, "That's quite a story. You should write a book."

"Sometimes I think I will. Believe me, I've not told you the half of it."

Minerva glanced at me and said, "That's for sure."

Sam shook herself and said, "I've got to get the next meal ready. Excuse me. I'll come back, and we'll talk some more."

Minerva looked at me for a long time and said, "That's quite a story. It's too bad it isn't true. I almost wish it had happened that way. Did you make that up out of nothing?"

"Not really, the college roommate that I mentioned."

"Yes."

"He was real. He didn't die. The story that I told was his story. Oh, it wasn't a college professor that he fell in love with. But it's close enough to the truth."

"Did it have a happy ending?"

"I guess it depends on what you mean by a happy ending."

"Well, I mean, are he and she happy?"

"The way he tells it, he's as happy as a clam. He's still in love with the lady."

"Buuuut."

"But they're not together. He's still madly in love with her. She's still single. She won't say that she loves him, and she won't say that she doesn't or that she loves someone else."

"What kind of relationship is that?"

"You've got me. I don't understand it, I just tell it the way it is—or at least the way that I hear it. But, you know, I think I understand him as crazy as he is. He loves her, completely, devotedly, for good. He says that just knowing her makes him as happy as it is safe for any man to be."

"I think that somebody's lying."

"Could be. But, I don't think it's him. I know him pretty well. I think he's happy, and he's in love. I don't know about her, but I don't know her anywhere nearly as well as I know my friend."

"Well, I'd like to meet them sometime."

"It's an experience."

"What's up next for us?"

"In a couple of hours we land in Chicago. O'Hare actually. We'll have a couple of hours on the ground, and then we take off for Japan. We'd better catch some sleep whenever we can on this marathon trip."

Sam served us a meal that would almost have been at home in a four start restaurant. Minerva was surprised that you could get such a meal at 40,000 feet or anywhere in a Muggle world. We both tried to get a nap. I was able to nap fitfully. The airplane landed, and we prepared to leave it. We didn't have anything exciting to do in the terminal, so I wasn't especially in a hurry to leave.

Minerva was in something of a hurry. I asked her, "Why the hurry?", as she got her things into her handbag and tried to figure out how to open the latch of the locker over our heads. "Well, we've got to." She hesitated and then said, "Everyone else is in a hurry. Don't we have to get somewhere in a hurry?"

"There's nowhere that we have to go in a big hurry. We'll find the gate that our next plane is at, and then we'll just wait."

"OK. We'll take our time." She sat down and watched as the rest of the passengers left the plane. Then I got up, and we leisurely unloaded our overnight bags from the locker and started to leave the plane.

Sam came up to us and said, "Good luck you two. I hope your sister is willing to accept your boyfriend." She added sub rosa to Minerva, thinking that I wouldn't hear. "You go sister. You deserve a good man."

Minerva was somewhat flustered and said, "Yes, thanks, uh, sister."

We left the plane, and I found a monitor to look up the gate for our next flight. We casually walked down the concourse and shortly had found the gate. We took seats. "You see," I said, "Here we are with plenty of time."

Minerva brought up another topic, "We're going to have to fly to Japan next. Are we going to have trouble with the language? I certainly don't speak Japanese."

"Not at all. In the terminal everyone will speak English." The hour that we had to wait for boarding of the next flight seemed endless. Finally, they called First Class, and we boarded. Minerva had become an old hand, and we boarded easily and found our seats. She even asked for the window seat.

After we'd been in the air a few minutes she said, "Flying is interesting, but how long is this flight?"

"Fourteen hours."

"How do people stand the boredom?"

"Well, there is TV."

"Here? In this plane?"

"Sure. You just pull this screen out of your seat." I demonstrated. I showed her how to turn it on and work the controls. She worked her way through the selections and finally said, "Oh, well. I suppose the music would be all right. But somehow, I just can't get excited about a movie about a 'Terminator'."

"I don't blame you. You know, we could do something revolutionary. We could talk."

She laughed and said, "Or get some sleep. We need it, and 14 hours is a long time to talk—even with someone as scintillating as you."

"Thanks." I showed her how to lower the window shade so that it would be darker and we both tried to catch a nap.

Eventually neither of us could sleep any more. She asked about how I intended to find Hermione Grainger.

"Well, we'll start when we arrive in Melbourne by checking with the car rental companies."

"OK. What are car rental companies?"

"Come on, you know what cars are. A car rental company just let's people rent a car for a few days or a few weeks."

"I'm used to renting houses, but you rent houses for weeks or months not days or weeks."

"It's just like renting a room in an inn."

"I suppose. Still. Nobody rents brooms or flying carpets."

We flew on in quiet for a couple of hours. I read a copy of *The Times* that I'd brought along. Minerva stared out the window at the clouds and views of the surface, which was the great plains of western Canada and the mountains. Slowly the sun sank lower, and we approached nightfall.

It got dark, and we napped a little more. Then Minerva said, "Do you really believe that Hermione's parents are in danger? Is this trip really necessary?"

Her eyes had crinkled in concern, and she showed her age more than I can remember ever seeing her—worried as she was. I shrugged and said, "I don't know. Really. But I think it's likely, and if I'm right, we've got to do this. If I'm wrong, well. If I'm wrong, we'll have had an interesting trip around the world, across the equator, across the International Dateline."

She nodded, sat back in her chair, and looked out the window again at the fading light.

Somehow we finished the long trip, and the airplane landed in the dark. Minerva had fallen asleep looking out the window, and I had to gently nudge her awake as we made preparations for landing. She was disoriented when she woke, and I had to gently remind her where she was. With dawning realization, a frown formed on her lips.

"How much longer do we have?"

"We have to board a flight that will take us to Australia. It will be a couple of hours before that flight and then another twelve hour flight."

She sighed and asked, "Will this trial never end?"

I chuckled, "Probably not."

The plane touched down, and we taxied to our gate. The seemingly interminable wait for people to de-plane went on and on. Most of the passengers were Japanese, speaking Japanese. We finally dragged ourselves up the jetway and looked for the message boards that would tell us how to reach the next gate.

We had to board a shuttle that took us to a different terminal. Minerva asked, "Don't we have to show our passports to travel around on the ground. We're in Japan now, aren't we?"

"Well, technically, no. We're not in Japan. We're in a kind of international zone where anyone can travel without passport."

"Good, the longer that we can put off having to go through that, what do you call it, 'customary uh checkpoint" the better."

"It's Customs, not customary, and it's really not bad. We're just traveling for pleasure."

"Right, pleasure. As if this could ever be pleasant!"

"Now, now. Just keep reminding yourself that this is probably the last time we'll have to do this."

We were both getting tired and touchy. We boarded the next plane and found our increasingly uncomfortable seats. Somehow the leather seats just seem less and less luxurious when you've sat in them over 24 hours, practically in a row. Minerva paid not the slightest attention to the stewardess's instructions and commented, "Everyone has what she's going to say memorized. What's the point?"

All I could do was shrug and say, "I don't know."

The flight was punctuated by a landing in Manila to let off passengers and take them on. Minerva was sleeping through it, and I couldn't bring myself to wake her up. When the stewardess came to check seat belts I put my finger to my lips and said, "She's had a hard trip so far. She's not unbuckled her seat belt since Neruda."

The stewardess just nodded her head and moved on after checking my seat belt. The sun started to approach the horizon, and it was becoming light in the cabin. Minerva squirmed and slowly woke. "I had a dream. I dreamt that I was flying in an airplane, and I could never get off."

"Sorry, that's for real."

"What! Oh, you're kidding."

"Yeah. Actually we're getting close to Melbourne—only a couple of more hours."

"Yeah. That's what you tell all the pretty girls."

"That's what I tell one particularly pretty girl."

Minerva turned to the window again, now that the open miles and miles of ocean spread below us again. Finally the Captain came on to announce our imminent arrival at Melbourne.

Minerva mumbled, "God, I can't believe it."

"Buck up little camper. We're almost ready for the next leg."

"THE WHAT!"

"Well, you didn't think that they'd just be waiting for us at the airport, did you?"

"I suppose not, but couldn't we just get to an inn and catch a little sleep—like a week or two?"

"No, which brings me to the next point. How we follow Ms. Grainger? Do you have any ideas? Is there some magical technique we could use?"

Minerva just stared at me. She finally said, "You mean you don't have an idea?"

"Oh, I have an idea or two, but I wanted to get any cheap and easy ideas that you might have."

"I don't have any ideas. We could find a wizarding community and send her an owl."

"Too slow. It may be too late already."

"OK. Let's hear your idea."

"Well, just hear me out. It involves using the *Imperious Curse* to get people to give us information."

Minerva rolled her eyes. "Oh, yes. That's all we have to do. Use the *Imperious Curse* and get ourselves sent to Azkaban for a couple of years."

"Well, we'd just be doing it to Muggles. You guys modify Muggles memories all the time. What's so different about this?"

She rolled her eyes again and said, "You don't have any other ideas?"

"Well, yes, I do. But I just want to know if we get stuck, would you be willing to use the *Imperious Curse* to keep us going?"

"I suppose so. But only if there's no other choice."

"Agreed."

We spent the rest of the flight in silence, waiting. We landed, and we took our carry-ons and slowly trudged up the jetway. Minerva asked, "OK. You mentioned car rentals. What's going to happen?"

"It's simple, we just go to every car rental and see if we can find someone who remembers Ms. Grainger. Did you bring along a photo?"

She pulled out a black and white photo that included the terrific trio—Potter, Weasley and Grainger. It showed them waving at the photographer. "Is there some way we can get that photo to freeze so that we won't have to explain to Muggles why it's moving?"

Minerva frowned in thought for a moment. She took out her wand, pointed it at the photo, and said, *Suspendo*. The photo froze in an awkward pose with the three seeming to point their fingers at the person viewing the photo. Minerva shrugged and set the photo to moving again and froze it. It stopped at another weird pose with everyone holding their hands palm outward as if they we're signaling the viewer to stop. Finally, she caught a reasonably natural pose, and I applauded.

"Don't be funny. It's not as easy as it seems."

I couldn't help laughing. She frowned and then finally broke out laughing as well. "It was kind of funny."

We landed, and as usual, we took our time and were almost the last out of the plane. We made our way to immigration control and worked our way through the line. I was first and went through the normal checks—are you on business or pleasure—pleasure, how long do you expect to stay— about a week, do you have anything to declare—no.

Minerva came up and fumbled in her handbag for her passport. She finally got it out and presented it. The officer asked her if she were traveling alone, and Minerva said that she was traveling with me. The officer gave me a look and I nodded. He asked, "You have different last names—are you related."

I answered, "No. We're planning on announcing our engagement shortly."

He looked from me to Minerva, then back at me, and continued staring at me for a moment. I smiled innocently, and he finally said, "Have a pleasant stay."

I answered, "Thanks. We hope to." We walked on out past where they inspected luggage. They gave ours a thorough look. One of them noticed Minerva's wand. They asked her to take it out. She did, and they spent 5 minutes inspecting it. One of the officers called over his supervisor who looked at it carefully. Finally the supervisor asked, "Miss McGonagall, what is this?"

She had regained some of her usual verve and answered, "That is a wand."

His mouth opened. He looked ready to say something, but he didn't. Finally, he asked, "Well, what is a wand?"

Minerva was losing her patience. I knew the look on her face immediately. The tightened muscles around the lips, the strictly controlled diction, "Sir, a wand is a piece of wood that has been formed into a thin cylinder. Sometimes, there are decorations as in the case of my wand. Is there a problem?" The tone of her voice said that there had better not be.

He floundered a moment and finally asked, "What do you do with it?"

Her instantaneous answer was, "Sometimes I punish impudent students with it."

504

He looked angry, but he seemed to be at a loss for somewhere to go with the conversation. Finally, he simply said, "Welcome to the country. I hope you enjoy your stay" in a flat voice and motioned us on.

After we'd rounded a corner, I said, "Well, you showed him how impudent students are treated in your classes."

"And I hope he never forgets it."

We found our way to the car rental desks and began at the Hertz desk. We got in line and when our turn came up, the person at the desk asked us what kind of car we wanted. I answered, "I'm not sure whether we need a car or not. We first were wondering if you'd seen this young lady?" Minerva got out her photo, which was obligingly still.

The man looked it over and said, "I've never seen her."

I asked, "Are you sure?"

"It would be hard to miss that crazy hairdo, wouldn't it?"

"I suppose so. She'd probably have been here yesterday. Were you on duty then?"

"Yes, I was."

I looked at Minerva and signaled us to move on. We went to the next desk. It was Avis. We asked the same question. This time the man at the desk asked, "Who are you anyway? Show me your passports."

Minerva answered without batting an eye, "We are friends of the young lady's parents. She's run off from home, and we are trying to help them find her." Minerva showed no signs of complying with the request for passports, and I decided not to either.

Her steely eyes stared the man behind the desk down, and he finally said, "Do you have any proof of that?"

She reached into her handbag as though she were getting her passport out, but instead she drew out her wand. She must have been using the spell silently because I didn't hear her say, "*Imperio*." But the man's attitude changed immediately. He said, "No, ma'am. I haven't seen her."

Minerva stood straighter but slackened her gaze and said, "Thank you." We turned and left. The man said to our receding backs, "Have a nice day."

We went on to the rest of the car rental companies, but none of them had anyone who had seen Ms. Grainger. Minerva turned to me after the last and asked, "What now?"

"We move on to the taxis. This will be harder, I think. You'll probably have to use the *Imperio* curse to get the kind of co-operation that we need."

As we walked out toward the taxi stand, Minerva asked, "There's one thing that I don't understand. Why don't you think that Ms. Grainger hasn't taken an airplane to wherever she's going?"

I had been expecting this question, and I was ready for it, "First, if she'd been going to fly there, she'd almost certainly have made the air reservations for that flight at the same time that she did the rest. She didn't make it then, so she's traveling there some other way."

I wondered about one thing myself, "But I have a question for you?"

"Go ahead."

"Why don't you think that she's disapparating to wherever she's going? It seems like the ideal way to get there. You haven't suggested it, so you must not think that she's disapparated."

Minerva smiled coyly and said, "Come now, you're smart. Why do you think that's she's not disapparating?"

I thought a moment and finally said, "The only reason that I can think of is that she's never been to Australia before. She doesn't know . . . oh. . . the lay of the land."

"It's something like that. You have to be able to visualize where you're going. You have to know what it looks like. I've heard of really great 'disapparitionists' who could look at a photo of where they wanted to go and then disapparate there without having been there before, but I don't believe it. You really have to get the 'feel' of where you're disapparating to in order to do it successfully."

It made sense, but I still had a feeling gnawing at the back of my head that that wasn't quite the whole story. "But what about the Triumphant Trio when they were on the run? Didn't they disapparate to places they'd never been before?"

"Yes, they did, but it was always someplace at random. Whoever was doing the disapparition just pictured a scene in their heads, and they ended up someplace similar to that. It was pretty much at random. When I was a youth. . ."

I interrupted, 'You mean a year or two ago."

Minerva snorted. Then she continued, "There was a game that was popular among young people. Everyone would disapparate somewhere at random. A member of the opposing team would do the disapparating so that the player wouldn't go somewhere they knew. Then they'd have to figure out where they were. They'd leave a galleon magically marked with their identity with someone close to where they were. And then they would return to the 'home base'. They had to tell where they were, and who they'd left the galleon with. The winning team was the one with the fastest returning team member. It was lots of fun. And you'd learn something about places that you'd never been before."

I had an idea. "You know, there could be a new version of that game. It's played with just two players. One does the disapparation at random. The two just vacation wherever they ended up for a few days. With luck that could be a great vacation."

Minerva chuckled and asked, "Isn't that what we're doing?"

"Hmmm. I suppose you might have a point."

We reached the taxi stand, and the first taxi in line pulled up. We got in. The driver asked, "Where to?"

I said, "Just give us a tour of the airport."

"What!"

"We really want to ask you a few questions. Depending on the answers, we may be going someplace, but we'll give you a good tip in any case."

"People have a funny idea of what a good tip is."

I answered, "It depends on the usefulness of your answers, but the minimum tip would be 25 dollars regardless."

"Is that US or Aussy."

"Aussy."

"OK." He said it with a resigned air. "What do you want to know?"

I handed him the photo and asked, "Have you seen this young lady?"

He studied it a moment, uttered a curse, and said, "No."

I said, "Don't be glum. If any cabby that you know has seen her and can help us, we'll reward you as well."

He considered a minute and said, "I'll call the dispatcher and see what I can find." He paused a minute and added, "Do I get to decide how the reward is distributed? How much if we find someone who's seen her?"

I shot back, "$100 minimum. The more information they can provide, the more we'll pay. With lots of useful details, I can see it being $500, maybe more."

He said, "Wait a minute while I call the dispatcher."

We couldn't hear much of the conversation, but he was apparently negotiating a deal. It seemed, he'd get 40% of the reward, the dispatcher 30% and the cabby who had the info, 30%. Then there was a long wait, while we drove around the airport and the cab's meter ran up a charge. I asked, "How long are we going to drive around before we get an answer?"

"However long it takes for the dispatcher to call all the cabbies until he finds one who recognizes her."

"How will he know that he's got the right young lady?"

"The description's pretty unique: younger than 20, long bushy brown hair, bushy eyebrows, English accent. There can't be many of them coming in each day."

"I suppose not." We drove around for another ten minutes. Then the dispatcher called back. The cabbie let us hear this conversation.

"Charlie Lamb picked her up at the airport yesterday morning. How much is it worth to find out where she went?"

The cabbie turned to me, and I said, "We'll pay $400 for that—total. You have to split it up however you decide."

The dispatcher was silent for a couple of minutes and then said, "$600, not a penny less."

"$500 and that's our last offer."

"Done."

I pulled out my wallet and gave the cabbie the $500. He confirmed to the dispatcher that the deal was transacted and the dispatcher said, "He took her directly to the train station. He let her off and watched her go in with her bags. He doesn't know what happened to her after that."

"OK. Take us to the train station. And if you've given us false information, we'll know."

We drove off and I told the cabbie. "Wait for us, and we'll have another fare for you. Leave the meter running while you wait for us."

"Yes, sir." He speeded up, and we were at the train station quicker than I thought we could be. We got out and walked into the station.

Minerva said, "What do you think we're going to do now? She's surely still not here."

"You're right. But with some luck the ticket agents were here yesterday and are on duty again. We'll ask them. I'm afraid we'll have to use the *Imperious Curse* on them."

"Why? Maybe we can bribe them like the cabby."

"No, this will be different. Cabbies have to keep a record of where they take their fares. Ticket agents for trains don't. We'll need the *Imperious* to get them to remember what destination they sold her a ticket for."

"I suppose you're right. But I just don't like doing that."

We had gotten close to the ticket windows. We went up and I got out the picture when we reached the first window. The agent asked where we wanted to go. I said, "Before we get to that, have you seen this young lady before?"

"Are you police?"

"No."

"Private Detective?"

"No."

"Let's see your ID."

I looked over to Minerva. She opened her hand bag and reached her hand in. She didn't even have to take it out of the hand bag. Then the agent said, "May I see the picture?"

"Sure." I handed it over.

He studied it for a minute and then said, "Yes, I've seen her. Yesterday. Late morning."

Minerva asked, "Good. You sold her a ticket?"

"Yes."

"Where was it that she went?"

"Townsville."

"When would she arrive?"

He consulted something behind the desk. Then he said, "Tomorrow early morning."

Minerva said, "Thanks." We went back out to the cab.

I said to the cabbie, "Take us to the nearest car rental agency."

"Why? I can take you anywhere you want to go."

"Can you take us to Townsville?"

"OOOOKay. No, I don't think that's in my area. I'll take you to the Avis rental "

We drove off and in a few minutes had paid our gigantic taxi bill and tip. We had a car rented and had maps that would get us to Townsville. Before we got started, I gave Minerva a course in car safety. "First, you have to understand that you should always wear you seat belt."

"Why?"

"In case of accident, it will keep you from flying through the front window of the car."

"OH, then help me get my seat-belt attached."

I leaned over her, reached across her breast to pull the seatbelt out, and buckled it in while I gazed into her eyes. She asked, "Don't you have to see the seat-belt to do that?"

"No, I don't." I said, as I bent closer, and we kissed deeply.

She finally broke the kiss and asked, "Are we going anywhere?"

"I thought we were."

"Seriously."

"Yes, seriously. Right now." I got back in my seat and buckled up.

She said, "Now, I know what these buckles are for and why they keep you safe when driving—or not driving."

"Yeh, yeh, yeh."

We started off. As soon as we got out of Melbourne, I accelerated to the speed limit and did my usual 10 Km/hr beyond that. Then I sped up a little more.

Minerva said, "Are you sure you know how to drive safely?"

"Sure, I do. This speed is only about the normal driving speed on good highways in rural America."

She gulped and said, "OK. I'll accept that for the moment. How long till we get there?"

"According to my precise calculations, if we maintain this speed and only stop the minimum amount of time for gas, food, and relief, then we'll arrive in 19 hours. That leaves us about 5 hours for sleep."

"Five hours. That's not much."

"It'll be enough."

As the hours went by, we were silently appreciating the beauty of the Australian countryside. It finally became dark. I told Minerva, "You're going to have to talk with me from here on."

"Why? I was hoping to get in a nap."

"Well, I need help to keep from getting in a nap."

"OK. What do you want to talk about?"

"Tell, me about your youth. What were your parents like? How was your sister when you were kids? Did you get along?"

She smiled, "Oh, I don't know. We spent a lot of time irritating each other before we went to Hogwarts, and then at Hogwarts we were in different houses. It's strange. Usually siblings end up in the same house. But this time, the sorting hat put us in different houses. I went to Gryffindor and she went to Ravenclaw. When that happened, we were heartbroken. We had always assumed that we would be in the same house. Then we were apart. But we spent as much time together after that as we could. We sat together at most meals. We took turns sitting at each other's tables. We became good friends.

"Of course, after graduation we went our separate ways. She went to work for the *Prophet,* and I eventually became a teacher at Hogwarts. Now, when you came into my life—that was a real strain on our close relationship. She never did take to you."

"I was/am a Muggle. It's not surprising."

We talked about families and friends, and eventually the hours dragged along. About 10PM we stopped at a motel in Miles. The desk clerk asked us to sign in. We did, and he smiled knowingly. When I asked for a wake up call at 3AM, he was surprised. I paid with cash and told him that we would be leaving directly when he called. Further, we'd not stop at the front desk but would leave the key in the room. We walked up to the room and dropped into the bed exhausted. We dropped off to sleep immediately, and the 3AM call seemed to come almost before our heads hit the pillow. We struggled up and staggered out to the car and got started.

I asked Minerva, "Would you talk to me?"

"Sure. First topic: Why didn't Hermione fly?"

"Were you ready to fly when we arrived yesterday?"

"Well, no."

"And remember, going by train is much easier than driving. You just sit down and let the train go. And another thing, she didn't have any reason to hurry.'

"I suppose."

I added, "Maybe she had—in the back of her mind—the idea that it would be better if people didn't know her final destination."

Finally, the eastern sky began to lighten. Then the sun rose, and we realized that the end to this awful trip would eventually come. I asked Minerva to get the Townville map out and look for the train station.

"How do you find it?"

"There should be a 'key', a 'legend' on the map with the train station."

"Men," She said with disgust.

"What?"

We eventually found it on the map, and I took some directions from the map. The timetable for the train that we'd gotten back in Sydney said that it should be arriving in 30 minutes. We arrived at the station about 5 minutes before it was due. We parked and ran into the station. We had made it! We found the track and reached it about 5 minutes after arrival time. However, we decided that she should be finding her luggage, and we should be able to intercept her immediately after getting off the train. The train was there. But there didn't seem to be much activity. There was no one on the platform. We ran down the length of the train and finally found a conductor. He told us that the train had been 30 minutes early.

We slowly walked back to the station entrance. Minerva asked, "What now?"

"Back to the taxi stand."

Minerva made a face and said, "I don't think I can stand to ask another stranger if she's seen Hermione."

"You wouldn't last a day as a detective. Let's go."

We went to the taxi stand. Minerva resignedly got out her wand. I asked, "Have you seen this young lady."

The cabbie answered the usual, "No."

"Call your dispatcher and ask about her. We'll pay a big tip if you find out where she went."

He put the call through. There was the usual negotiation. I broke in, "Just offer him 30% and the driver 30%."

The dispatcher accepted that and started making calls to the other drivers. They eventually found the driver that had picked her up. "She went to Garden Grove Crescent and Rosencrans. The cabbie just let her off at the corner."

I said to our driver. "Go. Get there in twenty minutes and we'll give you a $300 tip."

"OK. I'll try. What if we get there in 25 minutes?"

"We'll give $200." He took off, and we heard lots of tires squealing for the next 22 minutes."

The cabbie started to object that he should have the full tip. I didn't argue. I just put $300 in his hand, and we got out of the cab. We started scanning the streets for her. Minerva saw her. She was standing in front of a house staring at it. We took off running toward it. We didn't need to. She just stayed there. She noticed us coming and stared at us.

"What in the world are you two doing here?"

I started to answer, but Minerva beat me. "We were concerned for your safety."

Hermione wondered, "Why in the world should you be?"

I said, "There are Deatheaters who escaped. I thought they might like revenge on someone for Riddle's fall. You and your parents were the obvious targets of opportunity."

"Well, as long as you're here, come in with me, and I'll show you how silly your fears are."

I answered, "That would be wonderful. There's no one who would rather be proved wrong than me. But would you let me do the talking at first."

Hermione asked, "Why? They're my parents."

"Look. You think they're your parents. I'm not so sure."

"But you haven't seen them, how can you doubt them."

"Please just humor me for a while."

She looked frustrated, but she said, "OK. Just five minutes."

"OK. Minerva, do the disillusionment charm on Hermione so that we don't get into a family reunion that would be unpredictable. Let's go."

Hermione grabbed Minerva's wand, "Wait one minute. Why do I have to be disillusioned. I did the Obliviate charm on my parents. They won't recognize me when we go in."

I answered, "Yes, they won't. But what about the Deatheaters that may come to the door? I'll bet they'll recognize you."

Hermione was still unhappy but didn't argue further.

Minerva checked for Muggles and, seeing none, she did the disillusionment charm while I got my Mokeskin purse out and pulled out my Glok, checking the magazine for bullets. I put it in my hip pocket with the safety on. Then we walked up the walk to the front door of the house following Minerva. She knocked on the door, and we all waited expectantly. The door was answered almost immediately. I recognized Hermione's dad from the couple of times that he'd visited the school while Hermione had been there. He looked at us and asked what he could do for us.

I spoke first. "Are you Mr. Wilkins?"

"Yes, sir, but what do you want?"

"It's a little involved. Please give us ten minutes of your time, and I'll explain what it's all about."

"Please come in, I'll introduce you to my wife." He led us in and shouted toward the back of the house, "Honey, come on to the front room."

He turned to us and asked us to sit down. I looked around. There was lots that just didn't add up. I said, "This really won't take long. I think that we won't sit." The wife arrived. I went on, "Mrs. Wilkins, Mr. Wilkins let me introduce my associate and me. This," I indicated Minerva, "Is Maude McKay. I am James Wendt.

"I think that the easiest way to start off is to remind you of an incident from a few years ago. You had an occupational accident. You were bitten. The thing is that. . ." I hesitated trying to make my next question as casual sounding as I could manage. "By the way, was that bite on your shin or your ankle?"

He hesitated a second, which I used to glance over in Hermione's general direction. I looked back quickly, and Mr. Wilkins said, "Uh, I'm not sure. It's been several years, I think it was my ankle."

I knew the truth now. My heart was racing, and I attempted to sound as casual as I could. I said, "Oh, it really doesn't matter, anyway. . ." While I was saying that, I casually reached behind my back and into my hip pocket, feeling for the 10mm Glok from my Mokeskin purse. I felt for, found, and flipped the safety to off. I slowly pulled it out of my pocket, trying to shield it from view as long as possible as though I were pulling my wallet out of the pocket. When I couldn't hide it any more I swung it around, intending to point it at the "Wilkins". I heard Hermione shout, "No". I sprung forward, falling as fast as I could, and bringing the gun around to bear on the Wilkins. I hit the ground, and the gun went off. I didn't connect it all at the time, but I had noticed a green jet of light whiz past my head. At the same time I heard someone shout, *"Expeliamus."*

Mrs. Wilkins disappeared before my eyes. I whispered, "Shit" and then noticed that she'd left part of herself behind—a leg severed just below her knee. I looked up to find that "Mr. Wilkins" had been thrown across the room.

I got up holding my gun at the end of my fully extended arm and swung around taking the whole room in, trying to be prepared for "Mrs. Wilkins" disapparating back into the room. Just then Hermione appeared and looked over in my direction. I lowered my gun and flipped the safety on. I told Hermione, "Don't look over where she was. She splynched and left behind one of her calves and a foot."

Hermione sobbed and bent over, dry heaving silently, because she'd apparently not eaten anything in a while. It was strictly dry heaves. I turned to Minerva who had her wand pointed at the other Deatheater. Her throat vibrated, and I think that she'd used a silent curse. She said, "He should be safe now." She turned to me and threw her arms around me. We both had eyes that burned with tears.

I asked, "Are you OK?"

She was sobbing a little but said, "Yes, yes. That other Deatheater almost hit you with 'Avra Kedavra'."

I hadn't heard it, so she must have done it silently. I asked, "How do you know it was a killing curse?"

"I've seen it too many times to forget what it looks like."

Hermione's sobs slowed, and she said, "My mom and dad."

"Those two must have been following you and disapparated into the house just before you arrived. Your standing outside in indecision gave them time to, uh, impersonate them. I don't think that they would have killed them—at least not right away. They must be around here someplace. Let's look."

Minerva said, "I'll take up stairs. Stay with Hermione and search down here."

I nodded and flipped the safety back off and said to Hermione, "Come on. Let's find them."

I walked into the next room, which was a dining room. Hermione asked, "How can you be so sure that they're alive?"

"Those Deatheaters wanted revenge. They must have intended to torture you all in view of each other and kill one at a time. They wouldn't have killed them unless they had no other choice."

"Maybe," Was all that Hermione could say.

There was nowhere to hide two people in the dining room, so we went on to the kitchen. There was a walk-in pantry. I told Hermione to have her wand at the ready and let me open it up. I walked over slowly and as silently as I could with my Glock at the ready. I arrived at the door, leaned against the wall next to the door and tried to turn the knob and swing the door open in one fluid movement. It didn't work. It was a jerky and slow movement rather than a swift smooth operation, but it didn't matter. Both Hermione's parents were sitting with their legs spread on the floor and their backs against the pantry shelves. I signaled to Hermione to come over. She looked, pulled her wand out, and silently spoke a spell. The two of her parents shuddered and shook their heads as if trying to shake off a fly. They looked up at us.

I said, "I'm sorry that we have to meet this way, but you're safe now. Let us help you up, and we'll explain what happened."

They were clearly bewildered. We helped them to chairs around the kitchen table. I said to Hermione, "Go get Minerva, and I'll start explaining to them." She hesitated and then left.

I turned to the real Wilkins and said, "I know that you're probably in shock. You've had a pretty bad morning. Let me explain to you what happened.

"The two people who attacked you are criminals. They used Taizers to stun you. They were trying to set a trap for us. You had a close escape. They would have killed you after they no longer needed you."

Mr. Grainger seemed to have been following my explanation pretty well. He asked, "Why us? I'm just a dentist."

"It's because of a young lady, Hermione. I know that you probably don't remember her, but you're related. They were trying to get revenge on her for helping break up their terrorist plans. She'll be able to explain your relationship a lot better than I can. I'm just a consultant for the English MI5. She should be back in a minute with my associate. Can I get something for you to drink? A glass of water?"

Mrs. Grainger was making sense of it now, "No. I'm OK—really. You know, the name seems familiar to me, but I just can't place the relationship."

Just then Hermione and Minerva came in. Hermione said, "I think I can reverse the spell that I used, but it would be easier if the two of you left the room for a while."

I said, "Sure. Come on Minerva." I took her hand and led her out. Then I asked, "What are we going to do about those?" I pointed at the limb and the Deatheater.

Minerva said, "Don't worry. I don't teach transmogrification for nothing. I'll change the body parts and blood to a bone. I'm not sure how to get hold of the Ministry of Magic. We could send an owl, but I don't know where the nearest wizard post office is here."

"I can help with that." I pulled my cell phone out of my pocket. I dialed the cell phone number of Parker. "It must be early evening back in London. I'll have him get hold of the PM who can contact the Minster of Magic, who can get someone here. Maybe yet today." Parker answered the phone, and I explained the situation.

He answered, "I can help you, but I can't just ring up the PM in the middle of the night. I should be able to get in touch with him tomorrow morning. Say 12 hours. I don't know how long it will take him to get in touch with the Minister of Magic. Just hang tight there, and we should have you some help within 24 hours."

"OK. Here's where we're located." I gave him the address.

He whistled and said, "When you go globe trotting you don't fool around, do you?"

"Just get us some help."

"OK. I'll get on it first thing tomorrow."

We hung up. We waited to hear what had been happening in the kitchen. While we were waiting I started to think about next steps. "Minerva, do you think that other Deatheaters might come while we're waiting for the cavalry?"

"Waiting for what?"

"Oh, never mind, it's an American expression for 'help'. What do you think?"

"I think it's possible—if those two weren't working alone. How soon will it be before help arrives?"

"Parker thought that word would filter its way to the MM within 12 hours. I guess it depends on how urgent they think helping us is."

"Oh, we have friends in the ministry. I think that as soon as they get word, they'll set up a port key, and they'll send some Aurors within an hour or two."

"So, it could be before the night's over?"

"I think so."

"And until then we're on our own?"

"Right."

Minerva was staring at my gun and said, "You don't think that you'll need that again, do you?"

"I'd rather have it and not need it than need it and not have it. I'd have your wand close to hand, if I were you."

"Thanks for the encouragement." She said wryly.

"Any time."

Then we waited. Finally after a slow eternity, Hermione and her parents came into the room. They were still looking pretty dazed. I asked, "How are you two holding up."

Mr. Grainger said, "Not too badly considering that we've had our memories erased, been attacked by Deatheaters, had our memories returned, and discovered that we're not who we . . uh .. always thought we were."

Hermione's face contorted in some kind of mask of discomfort, "Dad, I only did what I thought was best."

"Oh, I know. It's just all a bit much to take in at one sitting."

I took a deep breath and said, "Just one other thing. I'm not sure that we're out of the woods, so to speak, yet. I think that there could be other Deatheaters around and we may be visited again before the day's through."

He wore a pained expression on his face. He asked, "What can we do to defend ourselves?"

I said, "You're in the presence of two of the most accomplished witches in Europe here. We're not defenseless while they're around. And I still have my Glock. But we have to be ready for anything. They could disapparate into this room at any time. Then we'd be in for a serious fire-fight. If that happened, the best thing to do would be to hit the floor and look for cover."

Hermione started to say, "Don't be melodramatic.", when her mother stood up and looking behind the sofa noticed the immobilized Deatheater. She gasped, and Minerva realized what she'd seen. She said, "That's just a petrified Deatheater. He's perfectly safe."

Mrs. Grainger gave a stifled laugh and said, "It wasn't his safety I was concerned about." Her slightly hysterical laughter merged into a real laugh that we all shared. That seemed to relieve the tension in the room some and she went on. "Can you tell us how you two decided to follow our daughter? I gather that she wasn't in on that at all."

Minerva looked to me. I said, "Well, I thought that the Deatheaters who had escaped the battle would want to do something about revenge. And, frankly, your daughter was one of the three who were mainly responsible for Riddle's death."

Mrs. Grainger asked, "But why Hermione, why not Potter or even Ron?"

"Well, think about it from the Deatheater perspective. Potter is a formidable wizard. He defeated Riddle. No Deatheater would want to take

517

him on in anything like a fair fight. Ron might not be quite such a formidable wizard." Hermione frowned at me. I went on, "But he has lots of family—all of whom are not to be trifled with. And then there was Hermione and you. You aren't wizards, so you represent a much smaller threat to a gang of Deatheaters, just the kind of odds that they like."

"So, you think that we could have more visitors?" asked Hermione.

"Oh, we'll have visitors for sure. It could be Deatheaters, but for sure, there will be Ministry of Magic wizards. We expect them before tonight's over."

"So, we're just going to sit here and wait for . . . whoever shows up."

I smiled a wan smile, "Yes. It basically amounts to that. We wait and hope that our friends come before any enemies do." With that silence slowly closed in on the room. There was some desultory conversation about having something to eat. The ladies went out to the kitchen to throw some late lunch together and Mr. Grainger and I waited in the living room with the incapacitated Deatheater.

The ladies returned with sandwiches, coffee and some fruit—apples, grapes and bananas. It was mostly a quiet meal. After a while Hermione started filling her parents (and us) in on what happened to her during their "lost year". Most of it I didn't know, and I'm pretty sure that Minerva didn't know either. We knew some of it, of course: the raid on the Weasley's at Bill's wedding, the raid on the Ministry of Magic when some Muggle-born had been freed from captivity. We knew about the latter from our connections with the Order of the Phoenix. Come to think of it, that incident had eventually even been reported in the *Prophet*, when they were trying to prove the perfidy of Potter.

That had kept us busy through most of the afternoon, but finally the ladies had declared that it was time to start preparing dinner. It was to be a banquet. That would keep them all busy for the rest of the afternoon. Of course, that left Mr. Grainger and me in idleness with nothing to do but worry about possible Deatheaters who might be on the way, so I decided to start a non-dangerous conversation. "Mr. Grainger, you know, I have never learned your first name. I hope you won't consider me to be nosy if I ask you it."

"Not at all, it's Gregory. I know yours already, of course."

"What do you like to be called by acquaintances?"

"Well. First, you're not exactly in the acquaintance category. Someone who saves your life is at least on a first name basis. I like Greg, agreed?" He held out his hand, and I shook it.

"That suits. I like James although everyone wants to call me Jim." I started off on a conversation of introduction. "How did you get into dentistry and so forth?" We had almost begun to forget the threat that we lived under when the doorbell rang. Both he and I leaped up. I had my Glok out with safety off. The ladies ran into the living room.

I strode rapidly toward the ladies and said in a stage whisper. "Minerva, you and Mrs.Grainger go to the back door. This may be a feint. Hermione, take station behind the sofa beside our guest and be prepared to use your wand. I'll go behind that recliner. Greg, open the door and be ready to drop to the floor if you see a wand or anything that isn't innocuous. I'd hate to hit you if the firing starts." I grabbed Minerva, pulled her over toward me, planted a swift kiss on her mouth, and let her go. Everyone went to their places, and the doorbell rang again. I nodded to Greg, and he went to the door and opened it.

The half of the conversation that I heard went like this: "Oh, it's you. Thanks. Mind the step as you go." He closed the door and was holding a small package and several letters. He said, "It was the postman. All's clear."

I asked, "Do you recognize all the people who sent you mail?"

He said, "Yes, there's the power company, the water company, a flyer from a department store and the package is from the Random House book club. That would be my wife's."

She came forward and took the package. Minerva immediately came to her and said, "Please don't open that—even if you're expecting a package. We need to be sure that it isn't cursed." She turned to Hermione and said to her, "Come here."

Minerva took the package to the kitchen, took a table knife from the silver drawer and gently slit the tape holding the package closed. She gingerly worked the package open and turned it upside down so that the book inside fell out. I started to say something, and she shushed me. Then she said to Hermione, "Come with your wand. I'm going to try some spells to see if I can discover any curses." She and Hermione bent over the book and spoke some spells. I think that I heard, "*Speciallis revelio.*" Also, there were several that I didn't recognize.

Meanwhile, Mrs. Grainger came over to me and whispered into my ear, "Is this really necessary?"

I whispered back, "I think so. Two years ago we had a student who had a package, touched a cursed necklace with her mittened hand, and nearly died. Surely, you remember. It was Katy Bell."

She nodded. "Yes, I'd forgotten. Or rather, I tried to put it out of my mind. There were so many incidents at Hogwarts that were very dangerous, you know."

"Yes, I agree." I would have said more, but Minerva had just announced that she thought that the book was harmless and was about to pick it up.

I interrupted, "Wait! Wait! I'll do that. And I'll do that a lot more safely than you will."

She turned and made a face at me, "And just how will you do that more safely than I?"

"I'll use the standard technique that electricians use when dealing with electric wires that might be 'hot'. I'll touch it very briefly with the back of a finger. You see, electricity will make your muscles convulse. If you touch a 'live' wire with your hand in any way your muscles will spasm and your hand could contract to grasp it. You might not be able to release it. I think curses might be that way as well."

Greg interrupted and said, "Look, as the man of the house, I should take the risk."

I answered, "No, you have been in more than enough danger already."

Hermione said, "Well, if someone doesn't do it, I'm going to right now."

I stepped up and quickly brushed the back of my right hand pinky over the spine of the book. Nothing happened that I could tell. I asked, "Did anyone see anything happen?"

Everyone shook their heads or said a simple, "No." I then picked the book up and brought the cover to my eyes. I then handed it to Mrs. Grainger. She took it and walked back into the living room. I followed her and asked her, "*A Brief History of Time* is unusual reading for a dentist, isn't it?"

"Oh, when I was in school, I thought of going into physics. But, it just seemed that physics wasn't a good career for making money or even getting a job."

"I guess you're right."

"I loved reading about astronomy and astrophysics."

"Well, you can certainly continue that."

She put the book on the bookshelf, and we came back to the kitchen where the ladies shooed us out again. We began to notice how the sky had been darkening. We turned on the TV and caught a news show. There wasn't much going on in the world—so little that there was a piece about the Y2K computer bug. Greg asked me what I thought about that. Was there really danger?

I thought a moment and said, "I'll tell you my private theory. You can dismiss it if you like. And please feel free to declare yourself bored and stop me at any time.

"To start with, the problem is really a problem with history."

Greg interrupted me, "What in the world are you talking about! How could the Y2K bug have anything to do with history?"

I went on unperturbed, warming to the subject, "It's really not so strange as it sounds. Think about what the problem really is. Any system that doesn't use history of some sort wouldn't have a Y2K problem. The problem with Y2K is that with a two digit year, a computer might think that, say, January 5, 2001 is actually January 5, 1901."

"Yes, so?"

"Well, what does a computer care whether the date is January 5, 1901 or January 5, 2001 or even January 5, 3001. It only cares if it has to compare it to another date. Say you have a home mortgage. The interest is calculated as the interest rate times the period of time since the last payment times the principal amount. Well, if the computer thinks that your last payment was December 5, 1999 and then your next payment is January 5, 1900, that makes a big difference in the amount of interest that you have to pay. But, you see, the computer was keeping a history of your payments and it was that history that caused the problem. Now, I defy you to come up with a situation where the absolute date makes any difference. Just situations where you compare dates with historical dates."

Greg sat and thought about it for a few minutes. "What about where a law takes effect, say on January 1, 2000. How does history get involved there?"

"Well, strictly speaking, you're right, but you see the point—you're still comparing 2 dates. Just because the historical date is in the future doesn't make any difference to the argument. In your example, you're comparing the current date with the 'historical' date that the law takes effect."

"Well, maybe. But, I'm not completely convinced. You go ahead with your point though. I'll let you have the point for the sake of argument."

"Fine. Now, the next point to realize is that there is what I'd call a natural scale to history for different systems. For example, the natural scale of history for mortgage payments is one month. The natural scale of history for a stopwatch is one second, or one minute or maybe at the worst a few hours. Other systems have other time scales.

"OK. I guess I get that. So, what?"

"Well, I would say that the problems that you have with a system don't last longer than one or two time scale units. For, example, the stop watch is only inaccurate for a few hours and then, the next time you use it, it's perfectly correct without your having to 'fix' it at all. And it's no serious problem for people using stop watches that they don't work for a few hours around Midnight on Jan. 1, 2000.

"Maybe. Go, ahead. What about my mortgage?. That's serious even if I have only one bad payment to make."

:"OK. But, you see. The scale is 1 month. That means that the mortgage company has one month to fix it—even if they do absolutely nothing before the problem happens. That might mean some sleepless nights for programmers but nothing worse.

"You see, the way I see it, things that will be problems for a long period of time and really have to get fixed just naturally have a lot of time to fix them. The things that are only problems for short periods of time fix themselves naturally, and you just have to live with some inconvenience for a short period of time."

"OK. What about middle scale things. Say, things where the time scale is a week or several days?"

"You've got a point, there will be systems where there would be real disruptions and not much time to fix them, but they're really the exceptions, not the rule. I've spent a little time trying to think of those situations, and I haven't been able to think of a single one. That doesn't mean that they don't exist. It just means that there are a lot fewer than many people think."

Just then, Hermione came into the room and announced that dinner was served. Greg and I walked out and sat at the dinner table, which had been set with their best silver and plates and glasses. I commented, "I hope the food lives up to the setting."

Minerva announced, "You be the judge. I think it's really grand."

It was good. They brought out cheese and some kind of fancy crackers to start. Then Minerva brought out a large tureen of soup. She announced, "Le potage de Pierre".

Greg asked, "What?"

His wife announced, "Or in the King's English, Stone Soup."

I smiled, but Greg was still surprised. He asked, "Don't tell me there's a common garden (so to speak) stone in there?"

His wife laughed and said, "No, silly. It's from the children's tale."

He was still dumbfounded so I felt like I had to hold up the male side of the conversation and said, "There's a great children's story that supposedly comes from the Napoleonic wars. A Fench soldier was trudging home from the Russian front. He'd gotten separated from what little of his unit that was left and stumbled into a small village. He went begging for food but everyone pretended to be as destitute as he was. The villagers were tired of their provisions being stolen by soldiers.

"So, he had this brilliant idea. He offered to treat the town to a large kettle of stone soup. All he asked for was a large kettle, a fire, some water and one stone. The villagers didn't think that there was any harm in admitting that they had a kettle and water. So, he built a fire and put the kettle of water on to boil. He then washed the stone and tossed it into the soup. The water came to a boil, and he decreased the fire so that it was just simmering. Then he casually said that although the stone soup would be just fine, it would be much better if it just had a carrot or two. Well, one of the villagers admitted that he had a couple of carrots. He went to get a large bunch, which the soldier cut up and tossed in the soup. Then after it had simmered for a few minutes he announced that. . ."

Here Greg broke in and said, "It would be excellent but it would be magnifique if it only had a potato or two. And, lo and behold, several potatoes materialized."

"Right."

"I think I can see where this is going, before long he had a soup fit for a King, and the whole village had a roaring good meal."

"That's about the size of it."

"But how does that apply in this case?"

Mrs. Grainger replied, "We started with a stone and threw in everything else we had that would go in a soup."

I asked, "Ma'am, we've not really been formally introduced, I think. I'm Wendt—James Wendt. May I ask your given name?"

She replied, "Why, you were a teacher at Hogwarts, I thought you knew my name."

"Well, I never formally had your daughter in any class, so although I may have seen your name on a roster once or twice, I'm afraid I don't remember it."

She blushed a little and said, "My name's Elizabeth—call me Liddy."

"That's an interesting name. I never have heard Liddy as a nickname for Elizabeth. Libby, Lizzy, Beth, Eliza, but never Liddy."

"Yes, a friend of mine in grade school just started calling me that. I think that it was the closest that she could come to saying the nickname 'Lizzy'. Somehow I liked it better than Lizzy, and I've used it ever since."

We returned thanks and had large portions of stone soup with home-made bread and butter. We finished with fruit—bananas, grapes and some cut-up apple. We were having hot tea and coffee when suddenly there was a series of loud "pop"s, and four wizards appeared from nothingness in the room. It took them a moment to orient themselves and get their wands pointed. In that time Minerva and Hermione had their wands out and pointed. I too was able to get my Glock out with safety off and had it pointed at the one who seemed to be the leader. He said, "OK. Just put those wands down and whatever you've got there Muggle, and everything will be all right."

I said, "How do we know that you're not Deatheaters. I want to see some proof of who you are before we put anything down."

He said, "Look, we've got you outnumbered. Just put them down and we'll sort this all out—unless you want some trouble."

"You look. Whatever happens I know that there's one person who won't be able to walk away from this fight."

That seemed to cause him to hesitate. "How do we know you're not Deatheaters?"

I said, "You go first. What's your proof?"

He replied, "OK. We came by port key to this street. And we've got a port key set to go back to the Ministry of Magic. If you're really Minerva McGonagall then you should be able to check the destination of the port key."

Minerva got up slowly and walked toward him, keeping her wand pointed at him. I switched to another one. He held out a Cracker Jacks box. She pointed the wand toward it and said something I didn't hear, but might have been *Priori Incantato*. It glowed blue for a moment. She said, "OK. I don't think that a Deatheater would have a port key with a destination in the Ministry."

I said, "I know whom I called to get help: a colonel Parker. Does that agree with what you know?"

He agreed, "You're right. You're lucky that they shared that info with me."

We all relaxed and he asked, "Give us a brief account of what happened here."

Minerva filled in the details. When she finished, the Auror asked where the remaining Deatheater was. Minerva led him to the sofa and pointed behind it. He came over, saying, "By the way my name is Albert Harker. He casually pointed over to the other three, one at a time: Paul Bedeker, Tom Randle, and George Speers." He looked over the sofa and "hummed". "The last of the Lestranges—Procyon. I supposed that he was dead—run afoul of Valdemort. We hadn't heard anything of him in a long time."

Paul asked where the leg of our other Deatheater was. Minerva produced the transfigured bone. He gave her thanks.

"When can we use that port key to get home?"

Albert answered, "It's set for about 8 hours from now. Kind of early in the morning. Sorry."

Greg said, "Then I guess we have to invite you to spend the night."

"Invitation accepted."

It was kind of crowded in the three bedroom house. The senior Graingers were in one room, Hermione and Minerva in another, I hogged the 3rd to myself, and the four Aurors had to take the fold-out couch in the living room and whatever they could conjure up. We slept like logs and were up at the crack of dawn. The Graingers made French toast, bacon, OJ for breakfast for all of us.

Over breakfast I asked Hermione about Ron. She said, "I wanted the reunion with my parents to be just us. I didn't want complications of introducing a boyfriend."

"I guess I can understand that." Minerva said with a chuckle. We packed. As the departure moment approached, we said our goodbye's. Hermione and her parents were staying. The rest of us were leaving. The moment arrived, and I felt my insides being dragged out. We fell about a meter to the floor of the main atrium of the Ministry of Magic. It was about 7PM there by the clock.

Indicted

There were several Aurors waiting for us. One of them approached me and asked, "Are you James W. Wendt?"

"Yes." He seemed serious—too serious for my tastes.

"I have a warrant for your arrest. Please come with me."

I have to admit that I was kind of surprised. "What is the charge?"

"You're charged with threatening a witch with deadly force resulting in the witch being splynched and losing a limb as a result."

"Of course, I threatened her with deadly force. She was a Deatheater trying to kill me and every other Muggle in the room."

"Not to mention the witches in the room," Minerva said. She seemed to be as dumbfounded as I was. "What is the meaning of this?"

"I'm just doing my duty ma'am. Here's the warrant. You're free to exam it."

She took a quick glance at it. Then her control left her. "This is preposterous. He's done more to help wizards overcome Riddle than 99% of wizards! You should be thanking him and asking him for his autograph."

I laughed. I couldn't help it. I'd chased a witch half-way around the world to save her life, fought perhaps the last Deatheaters in the world that were not in Azkaban, and I was being charged with being a danger to wizards. When I got my wind I said to Minerva, "Don't worry. This is obviously some overzealous official. We'll get it over with in a hurry."

She looked very doubtful, but let me go after an intense kiss. She said, "I'll be at the Ministry tomorrow morning early to get you out. Don't do anything silly while I'm gone."

"What! You suspect me of doing silly things?"

She frowned at me, and we parted. Minerva walked off to one of the fireplaces connected to the flu network. I saw her disappear in a green flash of smoke. My captor led me away to an elevator. We got in, and he punched the lowest level. Then he turned to me and said, "I hope you don't think that it's anything personal.

"I have a cousin who was freed in the raid on Azkaban. I know you led that raid. How did you do it? The people who escaped couldn't tell anyone. And not just because they had made the unbreakable oath."

"Sorry. I can't tell you. I might need to do that again."

He looked genuinely worried, "Don't joke about that. You're in enough trouble as it is."

We reached the bottom of the elevator shaft, and the door opened. We left and walked down an aisle. At a junction we took the left branch and reached a door where a guard was waiting. He signed a document as a receipt that he'd received me into custody. He took me through the door and down another aisle. We stopped at a door of heavy wood with a small barred window. He unlocked the door and gestured me in.

I asked, "Aren't you going to caution me?"

"What?"

"How about seeing an attorney?"

"No."

"A phone call?"

"What?"

"Never mind. Where's the iron mask?"

"Oh, we don't use those any more."

After I crossed the threshold, he shut the door and locked it. I examined my cell. It was pretty basic. Not awful, just plain. It was clean, there was a basin and water and a toilet. One corner had a cot with a blanket and pillow. I puffed the pillow up and it promptly deflated. I commented to myself, "It looks like I'm going to have lots of opportunity for contemplation." My watch said that it was 8PM. I tried my cell phone. Of course, it didn't work.

□

The next morning, a warder came with a tray. It had a plate with a couple of pieces of dry toast, a small glass of orange juice, an egg sunny side up, and a copy of the *Prophet*. I opened the *Prophet* and looked to see if there were an article about me. Sure enough, there was a 2nd page story about my drawing a 'gun' on an unsuspecting wizard, threatening to kill him, and shooting at him. There was no mention of the fact that the wizard was a Deatheater or that he and his buddy were trying to kill us. I read the rest of the *Prophet* and did the crossword before the door opened. It revealed a guard, who ordered me to go out before him. He said that I had a visitor.

We went to a large room with a plain table and a couple of hard wooden chairs. Seated there were Minerva and a wizard that I didn't recognize. He was wearing an elegant set of robes and a cape over that. He seemed to be in his 40's and his voice was what I'd have to call 'magisterial'. He asked me to tell him my side of the story after Minerva introduced him as one Cyral Jones, a lawyer.

I took my time and went through the whole story leaving nothing out except the occasional displays of public affection. He listened attentively and asked nothing. I was beginning to be unnerved by the absolute silence, but when I finished, he did say something.

"Do you want to get out of here?"

I rolled my eyes and said, "No, I think this might be a nice restful resort. Of course, I want out."

"Then, you'll do exactly as I say and follow my advice."

"What would that advice be?"

"The only chance you have is to plead insanity. You'll maintain absolute silence. You won't talk to the press, and you'll not testify. And most importantly, you won't tell that highly entertaining story to anyone."

I looked at Minerva and asked if she knew that this was going to be his approach. She shrugged and said, "He's the best lawyer that you can find. He's defended and gotten some really unpopular people off."

"Look, I'm not really unpopular, am I?"

"You read the article in the *Prophet*?"

"Yes, so."

"So lots of people believe the *Prophet* and trust the stories in it. You're starting with a big disadvantage."

"I'm starting with the truth. Both you and Hermione were there and are going to testify, right?"

"Well, Mr. Jones is very smart and very successful. I was thinking of following his advice. You know that there are lots of people who think that Muggles didn't help us and could have against Riddle. They'd just as soon that somebody besides wizards has some responsibility for the bad things that have been going on."

"I can't believe it. How can one Deatheater stand up in court against three loyal, law-abiding citizens and win out. This is crazy."

Roberts inserted, "That's the spirit. Just keep talking that way, and everyone will think that you're crazy."

I frowned at him, got up, and started to pace. "This is just not right. I'm not going to sneak out of court claiming to be looney."

I looked to Minerva, "What do you think?"

Minerva looked back with a smile drawn tight across her face. "I just want you back at Hogwarts. But I can't ask you to lie or pretend to be insane when you're about the sanest man left on Earth."

"Thanks," I looked over at Jones, "What rights do I have? I suppose that I have the normal rights of English common law—the right to see the evidence to be brought against me in advance of my trial?"

"No."

"Then maybe, the right to request a continuance of the trial to allow defense witnesses to return to the country for the trial?"

"No."

"The right to a trial before a jury of my peers, at least?"

"Not if you mean by peers, Muggles. As a matter of fact, you don't even have a right to a trial before a jury of wizards."

"What! How can Wizard justice not include a jury?"

"You'll be tried before the Wizengemot, which is definitely not a jury of your peers."

I sat down, feeling defeated. "When is my trial?"

"A trial date has not been set yet, but I think it will be set before more than a day or two has passed. And I expect that date to be before a week is past. You are right that they want to prevent defense witnesses from arriving."

"Great!" I asked Minerva, "Whom do you think that we can get as character witnesses?"

She smiled and said, "I think that we won't have any trouble filling the courtroom with lots of people freed from Azkaban."

"Yes, that sounds good."

The guard advised us that we'd run out of time. Minerva and I leaned across the table simultaneously, fearing that we wouldn't be allowed this public display of affection if we didn't take it immediately and without warning. Our fears were unjustified. The guard harrumphed after a minute, and we graciously took the hint and parted.

The guard conducted me back the way that I'd come. I decided to start a conversation while we walked, "I think you know me, but you have the advantage of me."

He didn't answer immediately as though he had to think whether he wanted to talk with me or not. He decided to talk, "I'm Frank Hammond."

"Where are you from?"

"Leeds."

"Did you ever follow the Leeds United?"

"No, my mum and dad were always Quidditch fans. You see, we were pure-bloods, and we never went in for Muggle sports. We're all Tornados fans."

"How are they doing this year?"

"Oh, I think they have a shot at the all-England cup. Of course, the Hollyhead Harpies are always a threat."

"I'm not English, and when I was a kid, my family were American football fans. So, I had a hard time learning how Quidditch works."

"Never. It's easy as pie. You've got the snitch and the Quaffle. You can score with each. Whoever has the most points wins. Simple."

"But, it seems like the Quaffle is just pointless. If you catch the snitch, you win."

"Well, now there's where the serious Quidditch fans get split from the amateurs. You can have the highest score and never catch the Snitch. Now, you take the last World Cup. The Irish won because they had the best Chasers, who scored rings around the Bulgarians. The Bulgarians just were lucky to end the game by catching the Snitch before the score became really one-sided."

"You sound like you played seriously. Did you play after school?"

"What me? I was OK at Hogwarts and in your odd pickup game, but I never. . . Well, maybe I could've. I was a pretty fair Chaser myself at school. But, my dad wanted me to work for the Ministry, and he helped me get this job."

We arrived at the cell, and I went in. He closed the door, and the lock clanged shut. I got out the *Prophet* and wished that I'd asked Minerva to bring me a book or two.

The next day Frank brought my breakfast. The *Prophet* was open to the sports page. There was a headline circled in pencil—Harpies lose to Tornados 220 to 100. I looked up and found him smiling at me. I gave him a thumbs up, and he left me to my breakfast with the smile still on his face. I read the article and worked on the other Quidditch articles, paying more attention to the sport than I ever had at Hogwarts.

When he arrived with lunch, I asked him who his favorite player on the Tornados was.

"A good question. I think that the seeker is really good, but I really like the Beaters. They can really hamstring the chasers of the other team, which knocks most of their scoring. Yes. Spork and Ballard are really the tops. Now, most people are big fans of Seekers or even Chasers, but for me, give me the good Beater. There's nothing like a Beater to break up the advance of the other team's Chasers! What about you?"

"Well, my own favorite is the Keeper. People don't appreciate how difficult the Keeper's job is. Besides having to intercept the Quaffle, they direct the offense because they have a better overall view of the field of play. They also have a very psychologically difficult position. They tend to take a missed block more to heart than, say, the beaters do for not stopping the advance of the other team's Chasers with the Quaffle."

Frank sat down on the stool opposite the bed and rubbed his hands together. He asked, "Did you see the article on the sports page of the *Prophet* about the Tornado/Harpy game?"

"Sure. It must have been quite a game to see. It lasted over 5 hours with constant change of possession and lots of amazing near misses in the air between Beaters and Chasers."

He warmed to his topic. "Yes, I listened on the radio. That commentator for the Tornadoes is quite a color person. That Lee Jordan may be young, but he's really something."

My eyes popped a bit as I heard the name. "Lee Jordan? Did he just graduate from Hogwarts a year ago?"

"I'm not sure. I think that he probably did, why?"

"He was at Hogwarts while I was teaching there. He was a first year the first year that I taught there."

"You taught at Hogwarts?" he asked with incredulity in his voice.

"Oh, yes. I was there for seven years before I got canned. I taught English and English Literature.

"I saw Jordan graduate. Then, of course, Riddle took power, and he had to go underground."

"Why?"

"Are you kidding? He was part of Dumbledore's Army. The Deatheaters would have thrown him into Azkaban so quickly it would have made your head spin. Didn't you ever listen to 'Potter Watch'?"

"Well, yes, a few times, why?"

"Don't you recognize his voice?"

Frank's forehead wrinkled in concentration as his eyes drifted to the left, trying to remember the sound of Lee's voice, I supposed. "Yeh, Yeh. Come to think of it, it did sound a lot like Jordan's. So, Lee broadcast 'Potter Watch', eh?"

"He sure did. He was lousy at coming up with code names. I'm surprised that everyone didn't figure out who his guests were. Did you know that I was a guest on the show a couple of times?"

"No way! Why were you on the show?"

I suddenly realized that it wouldn't be a good idea to say anything that would implicate the government in the Muggle resistance to Riddle, so I exaggerated my natural diffidence, "Oh, it wasn't anything big. I just made a couple of announcements. I was on mostly as a favor from Jordan. I wanted to do something to resist Riddle, and that was the only thing that we could think of."

Frank furrowed his brows again. "I don't remember hearing your voice, but I could only listen to a few episodes. I probably wasn't listening when you were on."

"How did you ever become a teacher at Hogwarts? I thought only wizards and witches could teach there? That was certainly true when I was there?"

"Oh, Dumbledore wanted to get a good English instructor. Somehow he couldn't find someone who had actually studied English seriously among wizards and witches, so he set out to find one among Muggles. I was the lucky one."

Hank scratched his head and asked, "English, why did he want an English teacher? Hogwarts had never had an English teacher before in hundreds of years. Why would he want one now?"

I had had to answer that question so many times that I had my canned answer ready, "He believed that the purpose of education is not just to fit someone for a career but to help make life meaningful for students. Not just to make life comfortable but to make life a joy. Reading literature challenges one's thinking. That in turn raises the level of the critical abilities of people, and that in turn gives people an appreciation for and love for life that they wouldn't have otherwise."

He shook his head and said, "Well, Dumbledore was a great man even if he wasn't a great Headmaster. You've got to allow him his occasional uh . . craziness." He got up and said, "I've got to go back to my rounds. My lunch break's over."

I got up, showed him to the door, and said, "Come back anytime. Come back at tea time."

He looked at me sideways and said, "Yeh."

That afternoon he did come back at about tea time, but he didn't come to visit me. He came to take me to the visitor's room. Minerva didn't stand on formalities. She strode to me—very business-like—and planted a no-nonsense kiss on my lips, which I returned passionately. While we were still tête-à-tête, she whispered, "I tried to discourage him from coming, but he is not a man to be denied. Of course, you know that already." I was somewhat puzzled until we separated enough for me to see who was behind her. He too strode forward. I was afraid that he was going to kiss me, but instead he clapped me on the back and said, "You just can't seem to stay out of trouble. You'd think that the sterling example Fred and I provided would have had an impression."

I said, "George, you can't know how happy I am to see you."

"Now, now. Don't be sarcastic. I'm here to give you my incomparable legal advice."

"What have I ever done to you to deserve this?"

"You mean what did you ever do FOR me to deserve this?"

"Whatever."

George stepped back a pace and looked me up and down. "Nope. I don't think you've ever looked as good. Prison life must be good for you. It would be a shame to take you away from it, but that's just what I'm going to do."

"We'll see about that." I turned to Minerva, "How did you let him come along?"

"He threatened to come by himself."

"OK. All is forgiven."

George took a chair and invited me to join him at the table. I sat down, and he explained why he came. "Have you been reading the *Prophet*?"

"Yes, I get it daily. I haven't paid a lot of attention to the articles about me. Frankly, I decided that I would just get angry if I tried to read them through."

"Well, you should anyway. They are portraying you as a mad killer, and it was just good luck that it happened to be a Deatheater."

"OK. What do you propose that we do?"

"First, we've got to get all the character witnesses together that we can.

."Then, we've got to find out who are going to be witnesses for the prosecution and find out what we can get against them."

"You mean so that we can impugn their testimony?"

"No, so that we can blackmail them into not testifying."

"You know, George, I'm not sure that you've got the principles of English jurisprudence down quite yet."

We discussed the defense. I told him that we really needed to get ALL the Graingers in to testify. He agreed to try.

Trial

George was waiting in the courtroom when I arrived. He said that Minerva would be down in a couple of minutes. She'd stopped to lobby an old friend in the ministry to put in a good word for me with the Minister of Magic. She arrived, and we kissed briefly. The court started to arrive. Finally the Chief Wizard of the Wizengemott arrived,.and we all stood. Then the trial began. The prosecutor made his opening statement.

"This is a simple case. The defendant threatened to kill not one but two wizards. He also fired a weapon at them. We will show this by the testimony of witnesses and the admission of the defendant himself. The defense will point out that these wizards were Deatheaters. That is completely beyond the point. There should be one justice for all. These were wizards. As a result of the threat, one of the wizards disapparated, splynching, and probably died as a result of the injury. It's illegal to attack wizards with lethal force. It's as simple as that.

"I'll enter, as evidence, the weapon that the defendant used.

"I yield to the defense."

George got up and walked up and down the floor looking at the Wizengemott. Then he began. "The prosecutor has said that this case is simple. He's right. It is simple. These 'wizards' that were threatened, and yes attacked, were Deatheaters. It was their pleasure to torture and kill Muggles. They were in the process of preparing to kill the three Muggles in the house and the two other Witches. Mr. Wendt was defending himself, the other Muggles, and the two decent witches in the house. I'll show this is true by the testimony of the witches, the defendant, the Deatheater that is currently in custody and, if necessary, the other Muggles in the house.

"We will use the Deatheater's wand with the *Priori Incantatus* spell to demonstrate that he used the killing curse that day to prove that it was a case of self defense.

"I'm finished, your honor. "

The judge turned to the prosecution and told him to start.

The prosecutor turned to the judge and said, "The first witness that we will examine is Mr. James Wendt of. . . Hum, we don't know where he resides other than he used to reside at Hogwarts School of Wizarding and Witchcraft."

I swung around on George and demanded, "Object. He can't call me as a witness for the prosecution." George stared at me goggle-eyed and leaped up.

"I object. You can't call my client!"

The judge said calmly, "Over-ruled. The prosecutor can call anyone he likes. Proceed to the stand, Mr. Wendt."

I got up shakily and went to the stand. An officer of the court swore me in, and I took the stand. The prosecutor came up to me and began placidly, "On the date in question, you entered a home that you'd never been in before in Townsville, Australia?"

"Yes, sir."

He went on, "You entered the house and engaged the owners in conversation?"

"No, sir."

"No? You didn't talk with them?"

"No, sir, I did have conversation with two people, but I was suspicious of them from the start. I asked them questions that only the true owners could possibly know. They didn't know the correct answers although they tried to pretend that they did."

"How did you know that they weren't the owners? Specifically, what did you ask them?"

"The Graingers are dentists. I happened. . ."

I was interrupted by the prosecutor, "They are what?"

"Dentists. Dentists are Muggles who are healers for teeth."

"Teeth?" The prosecutor seemed dumbfounded.

"Yes, you know. Most people use them to eat food." There was some laughter from the audience, and George gave me a thumbs-up, which I took as a bad sign.

"I know what teeth are. But, healers for teeth? Surely you're joking."

"Not at all. I've gone to dentists many times. When a tooth is infected, they normally drill a hole in the tooth to remove the infection and then fill it with an alloy of silver."

"I beg that you remember that you are testifying under oath. You are crazy. This can't be true! Teeth! Drilling holes! Filling them with silver!"

"I'm afraid that it is true. Anyway, that has nothing to do with the question that you asked."

The prosecutor was taken aback, but went on. "What did you ask that proved that they were not the owners of the house?"

"I asked whether Mr. Grainger had a work-related injury to his ankle or his calf."

"And the answer was wrong? Which was it?"

"Neither answer was right. And the false Mr. Grainger guessed and necessarily guessed wrong."

"Then you attacked him because he guessed wrong?"

"No, I didn't attack him. I deduced that he was a Deatheater and drew my weapon, hoping to force him to remain while we summoned help. As I was drawing the gun, . . ."

"What did you call it? Gum?"

"No, gun, GUN. You know it rhymes with 'fun'."

"It's a deadly weapon, is it?"

"Yes, it can be a deadly weapon."

"And you fired it."

"No, I did not until the other Deatheater pointed her wand at me and shot the *Avadra Kadavera* curse at me. I dropped as she raised the wan. I was going to return fire, but she disapparated before I could. The weapon discharged by accident when I hit the floor."

"Are you telling me that this witch attacked you unprovoked? That's preposterous!"

"Preposterous or NOT, that is what happened."

"Isn't it true that you pretended that she had fired on you, so that you could attack her?" He leaned over me apparently trying to intimidate me.

"It is not true." I said calmly.

He had been pacing but keeping his gaze steadily on me throughout the examination. Finally, he turned and said under his breath, "Witness dismissed."

At that George leaped up and said, "Your honor, when I was in law school it was the custom to allow defense to examine all witnesses."

The judge nodded, and George asked me, "When you and your companions, Hermione Grainger and Professor McGonagall, arrived at the Grainger house, why did you go there?"

"Professor McGonagall and I feared that Deatheaters would attempt to harm or kill the Muggle parents of Hermione Granger. We traveled as quickly as we could to their home to protect them. We feared that the Deatheaters would follow Ms. Grainger in order to find the sanctuary of her parents and wreak vengeance on them."

"I see. Then you were trying to prevent wizards from being assaulted."

"Objection. Defense council is leading the witness." The prosecutor leaped up and exclaimed.

George was dumbfounded by this one. I signaled for him to bend close to me, and I whispered, "Tell him that I'm a hostile witness because the prosecution called me."

George straightened up and addressed the judge, "The witness is a hostile. The persecution called him."

The judge looked befuddled himself for a moment and then nodded, "Yes, yes. Hostile witness, proceed."

I had to think for a second to remember the question, but I did, "Yes. It was our intention to prevent Deatheaters from unprovoked attacks on Hermione and her parents."

"So, was your idea that the people who answered the door on the day in question could be Deatheaters using Polyjuice potion?"

"Yes, it was."

"How did you test that idea?"

"I'd once heard a story told by Ms. Grainger about her father having been bitten by one of her patients."

The judge intervened at this point and asked, "Mr. Wendt. Was the patient a were-wolf?"

"No, sir. He was something quite dangerous, though—a young boy."

"Proceed. I've been bitten once or twice by nephews."

"Yes, sir. Since the Graingers are dentists, the bite was to the hand or finger, not a leg or ankle. So, I offered the Deatheater two wrong answers. If he were the real Grainger, he'd have corrected me immediately. The fact that he hesitated and then actually chose one of the two that I offered clearly showed that he was not who he pretended to be."

George went on. "Then, knowing that the people were counterfeits, you thought that you and everyone were in danger and brought out your 'gun' as a defense."

"Yes, sir, that's correct."

George turned from me and addressed the judge. "I'm done."

The judge dismissed me, and I got down and walked to the defense table. Minerva, who was sitting at the table patted my forearm and whispered in my ear, "Good job."

The prosecutor called his next witness, the Deatheater. He took the stand and swore to tell the truth. I whispered to George, "How can he possibly call this witness? You'll cut him to ribbons. How can he explain impersonating the Graingers?"

The prosecutor asked him to explain what happened that day. He looked around the courtroom and began. "My friend and I got wind of a mad Muggle and his lover who were trying to find the Graingers and kill them. We followed Ms. Grainger to her parents' home and got there before she did. We explained the situation to the Graingers, and they agreed that it would be safer for them if we impersonated them and met these two crazies. So we used Polyjuice potion to disguise ourselves as them. We were just in time. We had hardly gotten disguised before the doorbell rang. We answered and found Ms. Grainger and the two mad people. They had convinced her that we were Deatheaters and that they had to immediately attack us."

In the middle of this wild story, Minerva had jumped up and seemed to be about to scream at the Deatheater. I grabbed her arm and whispered in her ear, "Don't get excited. George will deal with him."

She definitely didn't whisper when she answered me, "I am NOT excited." Then she sat down.

The prosecutor went on, "How did the attack proceed?"

"The defendant pulled this this . . gum thing with inhuman speed. He shot it at us. I don't know if he hurt my partner. We were convinced that he was about to kill us. My partner disappeared. She disapparated, but she splinched. She," and here he sobbed, "left behind her leg below her knee." He sobbed for a moment and said, "We haven't seen her since. I think she's . . she's . . . dead."

The prosecutor tut-tuttted and then asked, "What happened then?"

"One of the witches put the *Petrificus Totalis* hex on me."

The prosecutor stopped and then said, "Your witness."

George got up, and thanked the prosecutor. He approached the Deatheater and asked, "Your name is Procyon LeStrange?"

"Yes" he answered cautiously as though the answer might somehow trap him.

"Are you a Deatheater?"

He looked over to the prosecutor and then to the judge, "Do I have to answer that?"

The judge answered, "Yes."

He hesitated and said, "I used to be a Deatheater."

George sneered and said, "You stopped being a Deatheater shortly after Tom Riddle died?"

Procyon seemed puzzled for a second and said, "Oh, you mean Lord Voldemort. No, I dropped out long before that."

"Just when did you 'drop out'?" He said the "drop out" with even more sneer.

"About, three months before."

George went over to our desk and shuffled through some papers and picked one up. He returned to the witness stand. "Are you aware that you are still on the wanted list for Deatheaters on the loose?"

Procyon glanced at the sheet and said, "Just because I'm on the list doesn't mean that I'm a Deatheater."

George went on, "Just why did you decide to 'drop out'?"

Procyon looked at the judge, but the judge said, "Just answer."

"Well, I could see that things were going against Lord Voldemort. So, I thought this is the time to get out."

"I see, so you're an opportunist who jumps ship whenever someone else's ship looks better. Why should anyone believe you?"

He answered, "Look, you're twisting my words. I decided that I'd rather not be associated with people like the Deatheaters, and I left."

George asked, "And then you decided that it would be really nice if you helped save a couple of lives rather than killing them?"

The prosecutor jumped up and shouted, "Objection."

George said quietly, "I withdraw the question.

"Now, how did you ever get the addle-brained idea that two respected Hogwarts professors were out to kill a former Hogwart's student and her parents?"

He looked around. "I heard them talking in the Three Broomsticks."

"Was anyone else around who can testify to what you heard?"

"No."

"I see. Just you." He walked along the line of Wizengemott wizards, shook his head, and finally said with disgust, "I'm through with him."

The prosecutor called his next witness. It was one of the Aurors that had come to rescue us. His first question was, "When you arrived at the scene, what did you find?"

"We found pretty much what we expected—a couple of Muggles, Mr. and Mrs. Grainger, Mr. Wendt, Professor McGonagall, Ms. Grainger; the Deatheater, Procyon LeStrange, and the lower left leg of a splynched wizard or witch."

"Did the defendant threaten you?"

"Yes, but it wasn't clear who. . ."

The prosecutor interrupted, "Just answer the question, 'yes' or 'no'."

George objected.

"Sustained. These are your witnesses. You must let them answer fully."

The Auror continued, "It wasn't clear who was a Deatheater and who wasn't. We got that clear, and then it was pretty easy. We took the

Deatheater, Professor McGonagall, and Professor Wendt back to the Ministry where Professor Wendt was arrested."

"Do you have any idea who the splynched magical person was or what happened to him or her?"

"No, the authorities in Australia have tried to locate that person. They've had no luck."

"Can you tell if the defendant's weapon harmed anyone?"

"No, sir. These Muggle weapons are not like wands. There isn't a spell like *Priori Incantatem* to find out what happened with previous uses. We can't even be sure whether the weapon was used at all."

The prosecutor was clearly unhappy with the way the testimony went. He spent some time pacing and apparently trying to come up with further questions. Finally the judge asked him, "Have you any further questions for this witness?"

Finally the prosecutor admitted that he didn't, and George took over the questioning, "Did the defendant attempt to harm you or resist you in any way?"

"After we'd proved that we weren't Deatheaters, he was very helpful."

"Did anyone seem to be disturbed by Professor Wendt's presence or has anyone told you later that they were disturbed but were afraid to admit it?"

"No, sir."

"What was your general impression of Professor Wendt?"

"He seemed to be a calm, sensible person."

"Did you examine the Deatheater's wand?"

"Yes, sir."

"What were the results of the examination?"

"The last spell that it had performed was *Avadra Kedavra*. It didn't kill anyone. The next previous was the *Imperious Curse*. It's was performed on the Muggle, Mrs. Grainger."

"And the one before that?"

"I didn't go that far back in the history. I don't know."

"Thank you. I have no further questions."

The prosecutor called a couple of expert witnesses who testified about Muggle weapons and the difficulty of tracing how they were used. Those were the last prosecution witnesses. The judge decided that it was too late to start with the defense, so everyone was dismissed until the next morning.

□

George started the next morning by calling Minerva. She gave me a wink as she went to the stand and was sworn in. George began with questions about how long she'd known me.

"I've known Professor Wendt for over eight years."

"How did you meet?"

"Professor Dumbledore, the headmaster of Hogwarts at the time, had been looking for someone to teach classes on English Literature. He'd started looking among wizards and witches, but he couldn't find anyone who met his standards. Finally, he decided to advertise in some Muggle newspapers. He interviewed about three or four candidates before Professor Wendt applied. The two of them hit it off pretty well. Most Muggles either can't believe in the reality of magic or are scared silly by it. Professor Wendt was different.

"Professor Wendt was quite willing to teach in a school for wizards and witches. He immediately saw the problem that Professor Dumbledore was trying to remedy—that there isn't adequate training in English literature, composition, and the fine arts. They quickly agreed on a general program of education. I think that Professor Wendt had the job by the end of the first interview.

"But Dumbledore wanted me as the assistant head to interview him as well and come to my own conclusions about him. So, we met and spent a pleasant afternoon discussing education."

"What were your impressions of him?"

"He seemed to be an intelligent, thoughtful, kind, happy sort of person. I was very favorably disposed toward him. I immediately agreed with Dumbledore's choice for the post, and he assigned me the task of being his mentor."

"So, as his mentor, did you spend a lot of time with him?"

"Yes, indeed I did. Both during the school year, before, and—well—after the school year as well.

"What is your opinion of him now?"

"Pretty much the same as when I first met him. Except that I know now that he's very kind, considerate, hard working, and patient with the students and teachers. He's just the sort of person who would make a decent Headmaster—if he were only a wizard."

"Do you think that he would maliciously harm anyone?"

"No. I don't."

"How do you explain his threatening the Deatheaters by bringing out his firearm?"

"It was strictly self-defense. When he asked them a question that had them puzzled, they became suspicious, drew wands, and tried to use the killing curse on him. Luckily they missed."

"So, you were surprised by his arrest?"

"I certainly was. If I could find out who ordered that arrest, I would give them a piece of my mind."

"Thank you very much." Then he addressed the prosecutor, "Your witness."

The prosecutor walked over and put a beneficent expression on his face. "It sounds like you know the defendant very well?"

"Yes, I do. Eight years is enough to learn quite a lot about a person."

"Would you say that you like him?"

"Yes, he's a very likable person."

"As a matter of fact, wouldn't you even go so far as to say that you love him?"

I could see that Minerva was struggling to control her temper, the way her mouth tightened and her eyes shot darts at the prosecutor.

"Come, professor. That's not such a hard question."

Finally she answered calmly, "I was trying to remember just when I fell in love with James. I think it must have been that first time that we traveled together hand in hand through the floo network. There's something about holding hands with someone while you're being turned inside out that results in you either loving him or not."

The prosecutor was somewhat disconcerted by that answer. Finally, he tried again, "Isn't it true that you two are secretly lovers."

I was preparing to hit the floor to avoid the debris from the explosion, but Minerva just looked him straight in the eyes and said, "I only wish that I could say that we are secretly lovers."

He looked puzzled for a moment and then tried again, "I mean, aren't you besotted with him, and one could hardly trust your judgment about him?"

She said, "Sir, I know him better than anyone in the wizarding world. My only wish is that I could say that half of the wizards were as gentle and kind as he is."

Finally, the prosecutor was finished.

George stayed at the defense desk and asked, "May I ask one more question?"

The judge looked at the prosecutor silently, who said, "I have no objection."

The judge nodded, and George asked, "What was Dumbledore's opinion of Professor Wendt?"

The prosecutor immediately objected, "Hear-say!"

The judge said, "I'll allow it. Dumbledore is not available for testimony. Go ahead and answer the question."

Minerva answered, "Dumbledore frequently wished Hogwarts had more teachers like Professor Wendt. He also said that he wished that all Muggles had the tolerance and respect for wizards that Professor Wendt has."

George then called Mr. Filch. Minerva was surprised and whispered to George, "Are you out of your mind? Filch is the last person I'd call!" But George just smiled and said, "I don't think you know Wendt quite as well as you think."

Filch took the stand and George began, "Mr. Filch, what is your occupation?"

"I'm the *Chief Facility Engineer* at Hogwarts"

George was surprised, a bad sign, but went on, "What do you mean Engineer?"

"Oh, I keep the place running. I keep all the lamps trimmed and the candles replaced. I do repairs and keep order. I might say that Hogwarts couldn't run without me."

This gave George pause, and I could see him thinking of some snappy remarks. However, he restrained himself and asked, "How long have you been . . uh. . facility engineer at Hogwarts?"

Filch lifted his nose and said, "CHIEF Facility Engineer to you. Plenty long enough, you, you . . ." and he trailed off.

"I mean were you CHIEF facility engineer when Professor Wendt came to Hogwarts?"

"You bet I was. It was I who showed him the ropes. He wouldn't have gotten anywhere without me. You have to know how to handle these young ruffians. I gave him the benefit of my long years of experience."

"I'm sure you did. So you knew him pretty well."

"I think I was his only real friend at Hogwarts. Oh, the other teachers were nice enough to him, but they didn't respect him because he didn't have any magic. I was the only one who would give him the time of day."

"I see. Then, what did you think of him?"

"He was a grand fellow. We used to spend many an hour in my office telling stories of the old days before Dumbledore became Headmaster. Those were the days. There was no molly coddling of the 'students'. If there were pranks played, we'd string the culprits up by their legs. Oh, yes. I tell you, there's none of that now."

"So, you liked Professor Wendt?"

"Liked him? He's the salt of the earth. You won't find a nicer man than him."

"Thanks. I'm finished."

The prosecutor asked him, "Did you know he's a Muggle?"

Filch did a double-take and bent an evil eye at him, "Muggle. What are you playing at? He's a squib. That's why he doesn't have any magic. Don't you know the difference between a Muggle and a Squib? That shows you how much you know. You're just like all these pre-judgmental people who have it all in against Squibs."

The prosecutor was flustered and finally gave it up as a bad job, "No further questions."

George called Luna Lovegood. She came up to the witness stand wearing her spectre-specs and bright yellow dress that clashed with her long dirty-blonde hair. He asked her, "Ms. Lovegood, how long were you at Hogwarts?"

"For six years and a little. Of course, the Deatheaters kidnapped me, and then Harry Potter rescued me."

"How much of that time did you know Professor Wendt?"

'All of that time. I never had him as a professor. Somehow, he never seemed to teach our class. I can't really blame him. I mean I'm in the class, and then there's that Ronald Weasley. But you know him pretty well."

"Yes. You didn't have him in a course, but what did you think of him?"

"Oh, he was nice. All the students in his classes thought he was kind of strange, but they all liked him. Some of them even told me that he made me seem pretty normal. He didn't care whether you were good at magic. He just cared about how good a student you were. I liked his plays."

"Plays?"

"Oh, yes. He directed a play every term. It was usually Shakespeare. He did 'A Midsummer's Night' and the "Taming of the Shrew." They were funny. But every year, he had a tragedy like *Macbeth* or *Othello*."

"What did you think when you heard that he was charged with an unprovoked attack?"

"I thought they had him mixed up with someone else. Maybe, somebody using polyjuice potion to impersonate him. You know there was that time that Professor Sinistra impersonated him for a joke at the Halloween party. And then. . ."

"Thanks, Ms. Lovegood." He turned toward the prosecution's table, "Your witness."

The prosecutor walked up to her and was about to ask her a question when she asked him one, "You can't really believe that Professor Wendt attacked anyone, do you?" in that airy way that she has that disarms and implies that you're sillier than she is if you disagree. And then right away, she answered her own question, "Oh, of course, you do. That's your job, isn't it? They pay you to not believe him?"

The prosecutor was caught with his mouth open. He slowly closed it and turned to the judge, "No questions."

Then George asked the judge for an early adjournment that day because his next witness would be a lengthy examination. The judge agreed.

□□

The next morning, before the trial resumed, I asked George, "It would help us, wouldn't it if we could get the Graingers to testify? Have you had any luck getting hold of them?"

George shook his head, "No, I've tried everything I can think of. I've sent owls but it would take quite some time to get to Australia or wherever they are."

"And we can't get a delay in the trial to wait for their testimony?"

"No, the judge just won't allow it. He thinks that their testimony would be superfluous."

"What do you think?" I started to say, but the judge entered the court, and the trial resumed promptly. George called his next witness, Haggrid. He came in from the hall outside the court and barely fit through the door. He approached the stand, was sworn in and took the seat. The chair promptly collapsed. He got up and said, "Oh, don't bother getting me a chair, I'll stand."

George began by asking him, "How long have you known Mr. Wendt?"

Haggrid laughed and said, "I've known him as long as he's been at Hogwart's. That would be, oh, eight years."

"What is your opinion of him?"

"What do you mean, my opinion?"

George scratched his head and said, "Oh, do you like him?"

Haggrid laughed and said, "Yes, sir, I do. He was always friendly to me. At first, we both sat together at the teacher's table in the Great Hall at Hogwarts. We were together because we were at the bottom of the heap at Hogwarts—he was new and I, well, I was just the Keeper of Keys and Game. Of course, later I was a teacher. Even then, we usually sat together. He always had something funny to say. I remember once when Dumbledore was giving his usual beginning of term talks, he made a funny comment about Dumbledore's announcement that one of the corridors was quite dangerous and people who wanted to stay alive would stay away from it. He said the best way to keep students away was to require that every student had to visit it at least once before end of term. He was always making jokes like that. Sometimes I had a hard time keeping from laughing at the teacher's table. Sometimes I think he wanted to get me in trouble."

"Do you think that he was violent or had a bad temper?" George asked.

Minerva whispered in my ear, "Haggrid didn't think that blast-ended scrouts were violent." I nodded my agreement.

Haggrid was going on, "No. Wendt is as gentle as a . . as a Thestral. I've never seen him raise his voice to any student, regardless how stupid they were acting. He was always kind to everyone at the school—even the Slytherin's."

"How did he get along with the other teachers at Hogwarts?"

"Oh, he was always respectful and tried to get along with everyone. He even tried to make friends with Professor Snape. I don't know if he ever did, but he occasionally sat near him at the teacher's table."

"What do you think of the claim that he attacked anyone unprovoked?"

"It's codswallop. I can't believe he would attack even the vilest Deatheater unless he was attacked first."

"Thanks, Haggrid."

"The witness is yours," George said to the prosecutor.

The prosecutor was wary after his experience with the other witnesses. He asked Haggrid, "Have you ever seen the defendant away from Hogwarts?"

"Sure. Many's the time that he and I went to Hoggsmead and had a pint at the Three Broomsticks."

"I meant far away from Hogwart's, like London?"

"Sure, we've been to London a lot. Sometimes we'd take the floo network to the Leaky Cauldron."

"No, I meant someplace other than where there are lots of wizards?"

"I don't know, I don't go places where there aren't wizards."

"But do you know if the defendant would go to non-magical places?"

"I don't know. I suppose he had to go someplace on Holiday. I never thought about where he went."

"So, you don't know what he's like around Muggles?"

"Sure, I do. There are lots of Muggle parents of students at Hogwarts. He usually was on the welcome committee when they'd come to visit

Hogwarts. He was always courteous to all of them. I don't understand it, but most Muggles are nervous when they come to Hogwarts. He always seemed to have a way of making them feel comfortable. It was so strange to see how it worked. He'd walk up and talk to the Muggle families. Really, he didn't do hardly any talking, he mostly just listened. It didn't matter much whether they were scared or angry or what. He would just listen and say something, and you could see most of them loosen up, and they'd mostly be OK. Then Professor Dumbledore or McGonagall would come and talk and answer questions, and they'd actually ask some questions. Before he came, the Muggle parents always just stood around and wouldn't ask questions. They'd just hover over their kids and ask them if a Troll had eaten any kids yet. As if that happened every year. I can't remember the last time that a Troll got anyone at Hogwarts."

Haggrid paused and then said," Of course, there was that time a few years ago when a troll did get into Hogwarts, but that didn't really count because Professor Querall let it in."

The prosecutor was dumfounded again. He tried again, "But, you don't really know how he was with Muggles when he was alone with them. I mean when you weren't there or any magical people."

"What do you mean? Of course, I don't know. I'm magical. So, I couldn't have been there when he was with only Muggles. What kind of a ninny do you think I am?" He snorted.

The prosecutor took to pacing up and down during this exchange. He kept pacing after Haggrid's last remark with his attention glued to the floor. Finally, he said, "OK. OK. Suppose. . ." he trailed off trying to think how to proceed. Then he had an inspiration, "Did you ever see him mad?"

Haggrid's turn had come to be stumped. He looked up at the ceiling, seemingly concentrating hard. The prosecutor mistook this as an attempt to hide something. He pressed Haggrid, "Well, what is it? When have you seen him angry? You're under oath, and you have to answer my question."

Haggrid replied, "Wait a minute. I think I've got something. I think I can remember a time. Just give me a minute to think."

I lent next to George and whispered to him, "Let's hope he doesn't try too hard."

But Haggrid's contorted face cleared, and he said, "Wait. Wait. I've got it. Now I remember. Snape and he were walking outside the castle not too far from my house. At first, I couldn't hear what they were saying, just that they were talking. Then their voices were raised, and I heard Wendt say something like this:

"Snape, I know that you and his dad were life-long enemies, but he is his own person. Don't let your hatred for his dad blind you to that fact.

It's unjust not to see him for what he is. He certainly has faults. You, of all people, should realize that everyone has faults. Look at his strengths as well. Above all look for his strengths and develop them. He can overcome the faults that he shares with his father.'

"Then Snape said something like, 'I don't want him to.' And then I didn't hear anything more."

The prosecutor just shook his head and said, "I suppose I'm done."

George called his next witness. It was a surprise witness to everyone, including me. He said as casually as he could manage, "The defense calls Draco Malfoy." There was a little shudder that went through the entire courtroom. Someone opened the door to the anteroom and Draco Malfoy came in. He was wearing all black—a black dress robe with a black shirt and black tie with silver stripes. He approached the witness chair and was sworn in.

As soon as he was seated, George walked over to a position where he could see most of the courtroom at the same time as he saw Draco. He asked Draco, "You are the son of Lucius Malfoy?"

Draco sneered and said, "Of course, I'm the son of Lucius Malfoy. You know that."

The president of the Wizengemott interrupted and said, "The witness will restrain himself to answering the questions and not introduce editorial comments."

Draco rolled his eyes when he turned the other direction so that the judge couldn't see him.

George went on, "What is your current occupation?"

Draco suppressed a laugh and said, "I'm rich."

George, non-plussed, said "And before that?"

Draco couldn't suppress the laugh this time, "What do you mean before that? I've always been rich."

George said, "I mean what were you doing before you were doing nothing?"

Draco's face fell. He looked down at his shoes and said, "I was a Deatheater." A few people in the hall gasped, but I couldn't see how there would be anyone here who didn't suspect that Draco was a Deatheater.

George said, "No, no. I meant before that."

Draco looked up, puzzled, "You mean at Hogwarts?" Minerva shook her head in resignation, and I was beginning to wonder about having George as a barrister.

"Yes, at Hogwarts."

Draco took a moment to realize that he still had a question that he'd not answered. "Oh, yes. I was a student there."

"OK. Did you know the defendant?"

Draco was getting short of temper at the endless conversation that seemed to be going nowhere, "Yes, of course, I did. Everyone knew him. He was the only Muggle at the school."

George went on, "What did you think of him?"

Draco hesitated, thinking, and finally said, "I didn't like him. He was a Muggle, after all. My mates and I would play practical jokes on him." He smiled slightly in remembrance.

"What sort of jokes?"

"Oh, one time we used the *Langlock* curse on him just before he went into one of the classes that he taught. It was really funny seeing him trying to teach that class." Draco broke out into a broad smile. "It was so funny. When he realized what had happened, the first thing he wrote on the blackboard was 'Mr. Malfoy, you'll see me in detention tonight at 7.' Then he did the whole class without saying a word. He wrote his entire lecture on the blackboard. It was the shortest lecture at Hogwarts that I ever had. He finished by having us start a full-scroll report for the rest of the class period."

"And what was the detention that he assigned to you?"

"Oh, it was the same as always—Lines. But his lines were different from the other teachers. The other teachers would always have us do something like, 'It's rude to talk out of turn in class.'"

"And what were his lines then?"

"Oh, I remember the first time that I was in detention with him. He said to me, 'Mr. Malfoy, I believe that detention should be useful for something more than punishing the miscreant. You're going to do lines.' I was so relieved. Some teachers at Hogwarts come up with really awful detentions like the time that Haggrid took Potter, Grainger, Weezilkind and me into the forest with him.

"But his lines were that I had to copy and say aloud as I wrote them a scene from the *Merchant of Venice*."

George paused for emphasis and then asked, "What was it that you had to copy out?"

Draco muttered under his breath, "You heard me." And then he repeated, "Even you've heard of it. *The Merchant of Venice*. You know, Shakespeare."

"Did you always do the same scene?"

"No, we started at the beginning and did one scene at a time until we were finished."

"You eventually did the entire play? You must have been a very naughty boy."

Malfoy said something under his breath that I couldn't hear, but later George related it to me. He said, "As if you never were."

"Yes, we did every scene, and then we started on *The Taming of the Shrew*."

"Did you get through all the plays?"

"Very funny. No, we didn't even finish the *Shrew*."

"Why not?"

"Somehow, it didn't seem funny anymore."

"The *Shrew*?"

"No, you git." With that the judge cautioned Draco again.

Draco looked down at his feet again. "No. Playing tricks on him." He hesitated and said, "I got tired of playing tricks on someone who I kind of liked." His face turned a shade of crimson, and I thought I heard a jerk in his voice.

"Why did you like him?"

Draco's chin seemed glued to his chest and he said softly, "He never seemed to hate me whatever I did. The detentions were more like . . like. . well, like tutoring sessions. He was always asking me questions about what I'd read. He always wanted me to learn something. I don't think that I ever learned in school what he was trying to teach me. It wasn't until I became a Deatheater that I learned what the 'quality of mercy' was."

"Thanks for your testimony. I'm finished." George turned to the prosecutor and said, "Your witness."

The prosecutor walked over to Draco and looked at his ever defiant face for a moment and then walked back to his table. "No questions."

Draco sneered, "Coward!"

Someone at the table asked a whispered question, "Why no questions?." He answered, "You never ask a witness a question when you don't know the answer you're going to get." He looked over at Draco as he walked away from the witness chair. "I have no idea what he'd say if I asked him the question that I really want to ask him."

George said, "The defense rests."

The president of the Wizengemott said, "We'll adjourn now and begin tomorrow at nine with final arguments."

Minerva joined us and asked, "I'm astounded that you could get Malfoy to testify."

George answered, "He was amazingly easy to recruit. I think that he has been going through a real sea change. The death of Riddle and the capture of all the Deatheaters hit him hard. Then, too, I offered to speak in his defense when his case comes up. It's pretty generally known that he was being blackmailed by the real Deatheaters to get him to help them."

I was puzzled by that last. "Blackmailed? How? Why?"

George smiled, "You mean there's something you don't know? His father was on the outs with Riddle because he'd failed Riddle several times. Riddle threatened that he'd kill Draco's family if he didn't become a Deatheater and help kill Dumbledore."

Minerva said, "Really! I didn't know that either."

"Well, you've got to be on the inside to get this sort of information."

I sneered, "It was Potter, wasn't it. He knew about all that and told you."

"No, he told Ron and dear Ron told me. And Fred."

I hadn't noticed Draco come up. When I noticed, he asked, "Could I talk to you for a minute—alone." He glanced at Minerva and George.

I nodded and said, "Sure. My jailers will want me to go soon." I took Minerva by the forearm, dragged her close and kissed her seriously. After we finished, I could see George and Malfoy making faces. Then I was alone with Malfoy. "Go, ahead."

Malfoy looked down again for a second and then looked up at me. "Look, I just wanted you to know that at the end, I wanted to keep having detention. I did play those pranks at the end to get detention with you."

"And you didn't want to admit to your mates that you wanted to be tutored by a Squib?"

He nodded quickly, still reluctant to admit the truth.

I said, "Sorry, I see my guard getting antsy. I've got to go. You can still come back to Hogwarts and finish your last year. I'll be there—maybe. Maybe we can do some real tutoring sessions—the kind where you have to think rather than just parrot the Bard."

His head dropped again, and he was silent, composing himself, I think. Finally, he looked up and said, "I wouldn't have any friends. They'd make life miserable for me. I would've. . ." And his voice broke.

"Well, think about it. You've got all the time in the world. But you'd have more friends than you think you would."

He shook his head and left. My guard came up, and we walked out of the now empty courtroom. As we walked back to my cell, I asked him, 'What do you think? You've been around the courts for a while. How would you rate my chances of getting off?"

He didn't turn toward me, but just answered as he stared down the hall, "I think that you're in a tight spot. I know these people. They are pretty prejudiced against Muggles or, as a matter of fact, even people who aren't pure-bred. You're going to have to have a good summation to get out of this."

I nodded silently. That was pretty much my opinion. I wondered what George would have to say tomorrow. I spent the night trying to come up with some ideas for him. By 2 am, I was hoping to get some sleep, but the best that I could achieve was fitful periods of half-sleep.

When Frank came with my breakfast, I was in a pretty sad state. He asked me if I wanted some company while I had my breakfast. I really was hoping he would stay, so I agreed to his proposal. He asked me how I slept.

I answered, that I'd had a pretty awful night with very little sleep. He said, "Yes, that's what I expected. The guilty ones usually don't have much trouble sleeping the night before the end of their trial. For what it's worth, I believe you. I think those Deatheaters were trying to kill you all. If you'd let them have the chance, you'd be dead now. Well, I've got to make my rounds. I'll be back when it's time for you to head for the court."

"Thanks, Frank. It really matters a lot to me that you believe me. I think that you're a lot closer to the real wizards than that court is."

He left and locked me in. Then the condemned man ate a hearty breakfast of an English muffin and an overcooked egg. Frank came back and said, "Time to go. Don't bother about your gourmet meal. I'll get it later."

As we walked down the hallway I asked him, "What do you think? Are they going to declare me guilty?"

He didn't look back but spoke as we kept walking, "I've given up guessing verdicts. I don't know what's going to happen, and I don't want to know until I've not any choice."

"Thanks. Nothing like an encouraging word for the condemned man."

He sniffed once, "Don't you take anything seriously? I think you'd joke at your own funeral."

"Oh, I do but only the things that I have to take seriously. That'll be coming up shortly." We walked the rest of the way in silence. The court room was very quiet with only a few people there. There had never been many in the audience. George was there and, of course, Minerva. There was Ron Weasley. He averted his head as Minerva, and I snogged. We finally broke, and I took a seat at the defense table. The Chief Wizard entered and announced the rest of the Wizengemott. We all rose as they entered the room. We all took seats.

The President of the Wizengemott rose and said, "The prosecution may summarize."

The prosecutor rose and began, "Ladies and Gentlemen of the Wizengemott, I must begin by making clear what the defendant is accused of and what he is not accused of. The defense will no doubt remind you of all the things that the defendant has not done. But none of those things will be what he is accused of.

"He will tell you that the defendant has not killed anyone, which is true (as far as we know). He will tell you that the defendant has not attacked any innocent wizards or witches, which is true. He will remind you that he has never broken any OTHER wizarding laws. All true.

"However, the defendant is not accused of any of those things. The defendant is completely innocent of all those crimes." He paused a moment and then proceeded.

"However, he is charged with a crime: the crime of unprovoked threatening of a magical person with deadly force. This the defense cannot honestly deny. The defense will claim that it was done in self-defense. But even the defendant admitted that all the action took place in less than 2 seconds—perhaps less than 1 second. Even if wizards that he attacked had attacked him, there was not enough time for him to perceive that an attack on him was under weigh and act to defend himself from that attack. He must have begun his attack before he could have realized that any assailant was attacking him. Therefore he, by his own admission. . ."

"By his own admission, he is guilty of this crime—a crime quite as bad as any that he accuses others of.

"The facts are really simple. They have been laid out most clearly by both the defense and us. There is only one possible interpretation—that he threatened magical persons with deadly force and then actually used a Muggle weapon against them without any provocation." He paused again and concluded simply, "I rest my case."

I looked over at George, and he smiled back. Then he rose and approached the Wizengemott. He looked them up and down as if trying to decide even at this late moment how to begin. "Ladies and Gentlemen of the Wizengemott, I have to thank my worthy opponent. He tries to do both his job and mine. But, I hope he'll excuse me for thinking that I may be able to do my job a little better than he can. You good Witches and Wizards should be careful. Presently, he'll set himself up to do your jobs as well." There was some scattered laughter, including among the Wizengemott.

"To begin with, let me comment that his ideas about how to conduct the defense are a bit off target. I wouldn't think of reminding you about my friend's faultless conduct. I would never tell you about the many services that he has performed for our young wizards and witches at Hogwart's school of Witchcraft and Wizardry. I wouldn't think of telling you of the many accolades from current and former students or their parents.

"But I would remind you that he and the Headmistress of Hogwarts set off to prevent the torture and possible murder of a Hogwart's student and her parents. I would remind you that the Hogwart's student, Hermione Grainger, was instrumental along with Harry Potter, Ron Weasley and other members of the D.A. in ending the reign of terror instituted by Tom Riddle and his Deatheaters. I would remind you that two of those Deatheaters were present in the Grainger household, having rendered the Graingers unconscious, having impersonated them, and having prepared to torture and/or kill all the Graingers plus anyone who got in their way.

"When Professor Wendt realized that the false Graingers were Deatheaters, he attempted to arrest them. They immediately attacked him before he had his weapon in place, and it was only by dodging the first spell that was he able to attempt to defend himself, the real Graingers, and the Hogwarts' Headmistress.

"How do we know that the Deatheaters attacked first? An unimpeachable witness bears witness— Minerva McGonagall.

"So, to summarize, an unimpeachable witnesses testifies that Wendt's actions were in self-defense and that they would probably be dead along with the Graingers without his actions. This is a man who should receive a commendation, not an indictment, let alone a conviction. That commendation would not solely be because of his action during the day in question, but because he was instrumental in opposing and defeating the Deatheaters.

"I rest my case."

Ron was the only person in the room clapping, but then George was his brother. Inwardly, I thought that he'd done a fine job of summing up. It would probably do no good, but it was a fine effort. The Chief Wizard thanked the prosecutor and defense, and then dismissed us while they deliberated. We waited in a small room off the main courtroom.

Ron, George, Minerva, and I waited there. I said to the room in general, "How long do you think this will take?"

George said, "This is just the beginning of my career in law, I don't think that I've had enough experience to tell."

I answered, "Oh, well. Do you know how this works in America?"

Minerva said with a resigned sigh, "No, how does it work?"

George answered at the same time, "No, actually, I've spent as much time in America as I ever want to. I know more than I ever want to know." He made a nice face as he said this.

"Good, I'll tell you. In America, the jury leaves the courtroom and thinks in its own little room while the defendant waits in the courtroom. Interesting, the difference in perspective, eh."

Minerva said, "It almost sounds like the defendant is treated better than the judges—interesting indeed."

"Yes, I wish that your legal system considered it the same way. In America, the defendant is assumed innocent. In that system, with that assumption, the defendant should be treated better."

George said, "Yes, you Americans and your insistence on these trivial details."

I asked, "I wonder if we could get some tea?"

Minerva smiled and said, "Finally something I can do." She pulled her wand out and flicked it. A tea service appeared with a half-dozen cups and saucers and a steaming pot of tea. Then George pulled his out and flicked it and a plate of biscuits appeared. Finally Ron pulled his wand out and flicked it. A stack of coal appeared.

Ron shook his head and said, "That was supposed to be a stack of napkins." He poked the coals with his wand and then flicked his wand again. The coals disappeared. In their place, a stack of serviettes appeared. He said, "Well, these would work wouldn't they?" with a hopeful smile.

George said, "Little brother, it's time that you stepped aside and allowed the talented to take over." He flicked his wand, and a stack of fancy napkins appeared in the place of the hand towels.

We had tea, and I asked Ron in order to make conversation, "Well, Mr. Weasley, uh that is, Ron, what is Harry Potter up to? I thought you two were practically inseparable."

Ron smiled, "Well, we did do a lot of things together, especially this last year. He's probably sick of me. And then, there's Ginny."

"Your sister," I asked.

"Yes. He and she are sort of an 'item'. Actually, they're off to the Lake Counties for a little rest and relaxation "

"I hope they enjoy it."

There was desultory conversation about inconsequentials as we waited for the verdict.

George gave the opinion that the longer the Wizengemott was out considering, the better for the defendant.

Verdict

Finally, my guard came in and announced that there was a verdict. We walked the short distance to the court-room. The court settled down quickly. There were still very few people there. The Chief Wizard rose and spoke.

"The defendant will rise and approach the court."

I did so.

"The verdict is that the defendant is guilty of threatening two magical people with deadly force without provocation. The sentence is. . . ."

I interrupted with much emphasis on the first word, "Most courts allow the accused to make a statement before sentencing."

The Chief Wizard's mouth gaped slowly open, and finally he said, "Very well. But be brief."

I was tempted to smile but didn't', "Brief I will be.

"I have only two points to make.

"First, I acted only out of concern for my friends' safety and my own. When we arrived, I suspected the possibility of Deatheaters using polyjuice potion to impersonate the Graingers.

"Consequently, I tested the Deatheaters who were masquerading as the Graingers to determine if they were real. They failed the test, and I determined to arrest them if possible. To do that I had to draw my firearm and be prepared to disarm them. They drew their wands with the intent to kill me and ultimately everyone in the house. When I saw them drawing their wands, I dropped to the floor and a killing curse just missed me before I could bring my weapon to bear and fire. The weapon fired by accident. I don't know what would have happened if I had fired intentionally, but one disapparated and the other was disabled.

"Second, I've been unpleasantly surprised at the nature of Wizarding law. You are the heirs of almost a thousand years of the most advanced system of law in the world—the English legal system, the Magna Carta, the right of habeas corpus, the right to be judged by a jury of your peers. And you've thrown it all away—for what—a mess of potage.

"You don't allow defendants to know who will testify in advance. You don't require disclosure of evidence in advance. You don't grant reasonable time to prepare defense. You don't protect defendants from having to testify against themselves.

"You should think about what you've made of yourselves.

"I'm finished."

I heard George shout out, "Hear! Hear!" That was all I needed.

The Chief of the Wizengemott rose and said, "The sentence of the court is that the defendant be . . ." He hesitated and then stopped completely. After a moment, he continued, "that the condemned be sentenced to five years of incarceration at the prison of Azkaban. The condemned's sentence will be commuted based on this being his first offense and the extenuating circumstances. He will be remitted to the custodianship of. . ." He hesitated again and, as if seeing her for the first time, said, "Minerva McGonagall, if she is willing to take the responsibility."

Minerva's mouth was gaping wide, and she didn't at first realize that she had been asked a question. The Chief of the Wizengemott asked, "Ms. McGonagall, are you willing to accept this responsibility?"

She seemed to wake up and said, "Of course, I will."

I realized that this was really a win for me. I wondered what could possibly have caused the last minute change of heart. I slowly rotated around to see the rest of the courtroom, and then I saw that there were two people standing in the entrance to the courtroom—Harry Potter and Ginny Weasley. They strode forward and approached me.

Harry said, "It's good to see that the faulty Wizard legal system occasionally delivers justice."

He held out his hand, and I shook it. I was a bit surprised that he'd shown up and said so. He smiled the shy half-smile that he frequently took when he was being impish. He said, "I've been out of contact with the wizarding world for a week. We just saw the *Prophet* yesterday."—as if that explained everything. He went on, "What are we all standing around for?"

I said, "Well, I'm not sure what happens to me now."

Minerva said, "Well, you've been remanded into my custody. I think that you go with me."

Potter said, "Well, that settles it. We're off."

I was still bemused, "Where?"

Potter looked at me as though I were a bit addled, "To the Leaky Cauldron, of course, to celebrate."

"Sounds good to me, but I've got to get my meager possessions from somebody." At that point my favorite jailer came up and said, "Come along to the Property Room, and we'll check your ruck out."

We all went to the Property Room and the wizard in charge looked over a receipt for my goods that Frank handed him. He looked me up and down suspiciously and then went off to the back of the room to rummage around. He finally came back with a small box about the size of a shoebox and handed it to me, "Please check the contents and sign the receipt if it's all there."

I did so, examining my purse to assure my self that it was really my moke-skin purse, "It's all there. Thanks." I signed the receipt, and we were off. We went to the fireplaces in the main atrium, and Minerva took my hand as we entered a fireplace. I gritted my teeth against the experience.

Minerva said, "Don't grit your teeth. The flu network isn't that bad."

My only response was, "Says you."

Then she spoke the name of the Leaky Cauldron and threw some floo powder down. We walked out of the large fireplace of the Leaky Cauldron, no worse for wear—other than having a little ash on us. The rest of the group had arrived first.

I stepped up to the bar and told the barman who was on duty, Tom himself, "A round for the house, whatever they're drinking."

There was a general chorus from the people in the bar, "Fire Whiskey!"

Then I came to my senses and added, "All except Ginny Weasley. She can have butter beer or whatever non-alcoholic she wants."

She came up to me, her face almost as red as her hair, "And why can't I have fire whiskey?"

I spluttered, "Well, you're underage. I'm sorry but. . ."

She interrupted me, "I'll have you know I had my 17th birthday last week!"

I couldn't help smiling at her pride at reaching that august age, "Oh, I beg your pardon. Then it's fire whiskey all around!"

Tom served up the drinks, and we found a large table where the six of us could all sit. I proposed a toast, "To the able counsel who's gotten me out of this pickle! To George!"

Ginny interrupted again with a little less heat, "Don't forget Harry."

I was a bit befuddled by her statement, "I have to confess to being confused. Did you say 'Harry'?"

"Yes, I said 'Harry'. Don't you read the *Prophet*?"

"Well, yes, most days, but I was kind of pre-occupied this morning. I didn't, I confess."

She looked around at the table in general and asked, "Didn't anyone read the *Prophet* this morning?" There was general admission that no one had read the *Prophet*. She snorted, got up and went to the bar where there was a copy of the *Prophet*. She brought it over and stuffed it into my hands, "Look"

I did and read the headline, "Minister of Magic hosts delegation from World Quidditch Federation".

Ginny snorted again, "Further down."

I looked and read the headline she was thinking of, "Harry Potter supports Muggle in trial". There was a column of text about how I was on trial, and Harry Potter had declared that he thought that I was innocent. The byline on the article was Rita Skeeter. I read for a moment, and then said, "This is a bad day for me. I stand corrected again. I think I do owe you a lot of thanks, Mr. Potter." I then displayed the front page for everyone to see.

Minerva said, "I do as well, Mr. Potter. I'd almost lost one of my most beloved professors." Everyone laughed at that.

We had a couple of rounds of drinks. Everyone loosened up and after some discussion of the trial, Potter mentioned that the Dursley's had escaped from Deatheaters, but had disappeared and not yet returned from their own sanctuary wherever it was.

I asked him, "Are you going to visit them for old time's sake, Mr. Potter, if they ever re-appear?"

Potter looked at me as though I'd just grown a third eye. "Well, sir, no. I spent some of the unhappiest times of my life in that home."

"Don't you think that they deserve another chance?"

"No."

I looked at him and held his eye for a minute. He returned my gaze and finally shook his head and said, "No. I don't." I decided not to reveal that the Dursleys were back in England.

Potter turned to talk with George, but I continued to look at him and wondered. I wondered why I'd suggested going to see the Dursley's. I tried to trace back my thought processes. There was something that had bubbled up from my subconscious. What was it? I couldn't put my finger on it. There was something that I remembered. Something I'd seen. Maybe something that I'd heard. But there was some reason that Potter or, or, was it I should visit the Dursley's? I didn't know.

Finally everyone left to deal with their own affairs. The Wizarding world had a lot of recovery to do in the aftermath of Riddle's fall from power. George was getting his business restarted. Harry and Ron had to decide on their next steps. I asked the three young people in the group, "Well, what are you three going to do? I assume that you will be returning to Hogwarts, Ms. Weasley. What about you, Harry and Ron, you could do with rounding out your education. You could take one of my English literature classes. It would do you a world of good."

Ginny said, "Yes, I suppose I'm coming back for my 7th year."

Harry said, "I think that I've learned all the magic that I need. I've been approached by the Ministry Auror office. I think they'll offer me a job."

I answered, "Well, I think you're right about magic, but let me recommend a different school than Hogwarts. I had a friend who went to the University of Chicago. He told me about a first day speech that he'd heard on his first day of classes.

"The speaker said that the value of higher education was not vocational at all. As a matter of fact, you could invest the galleons that you didn't spend on education and get a better return than you would spending them on education. The value of higher education is learning to live well; to appreciate life.

I suggest that you spend a year attending a good liberal arts college.

Harry looked at me and after a pause said, "Maybe you're right, but I've got a pretty good appreciation of life as it is, having come pretty darn close to death a few times. I'll think about it, though."

"How about you, Ron, can I interest you in a year at Hogwarts or even Cambridge?"

Minerva added, "You would, of course, be welcome at Hogwarts, but even Cambridge," she sniffed, "would be good."

Ron shrugged and said, "I think I'll see if I can sneak into the Auror's office with Harry."

With that, we parted. I asked Minerva, "Well, where to now?"

"Let's get back to Hogwart's. We've spent enough time away as it is."

"Suits me. We going by the Express," I asked hopefully.

She made a face and said, "No. We'll go by floo powder. I'm sure that you'd prefer to go by Hogwart's Express, but we can't call out a whole train just because you've got an upset tummy."

I sighed, and we stepped into the fireplace. I took Minerva's hand. "Oh well" I thought, "it will be better than disapparating." Then we squeezed through the continuum and ended up in a cloud of ash at a fireplace. I didn't even know to which we were going. I stepped forward, leading Minerva. We were in the Three Broomsticks.

□

We stopped for a butter beer. It was an unwritten and even unspoken rule of courtesy that if you usee an establishment's fireplace, you should buy something there, so we stopped for a butter beer. We found a quiet corner with a small table that would only accommodate two. Minerva looked at me reflectively as we sat comfortably drinking our beers. She finally asked, "What do you think about George's summation, saying that you had made a critical difference in the fight against Riddle?"

I had been a little uncomfortable with that myself. I started to answer slowly, buying myself time to think out my answer as I went. "Well. I think you could make a case for either of two answers.

"First, the case that I didn't make much difference. It's easy. Nobody doubts that Riddle was defeated by Potter, the rest of the Terrific Trio, and a few other people in the DA, like Longbottom and all the Weasleys. They had absolutely no help from me or any Muggle—no doubt about that. Riddle was the king-pin. With him gone, who was going to bring the Deatheaters back? The first time that Riddle was gone, the organization fell apart and would still have been helpless without the return of Riddle." I stopped for a moment.

Minerva said, "I'm sure glad that you weren't on the prosecution side. You've got me convinced."

"Well, I haven't finished.

"The case that the Muggles and I made a significant difference is pretty strong too. First, suppose that the SAS hadn't been around contributing, what would have happened?"

Minerva smiled and said, "Why don't you tell me?"

"Well, there wouldn't have been much left of the DA. A big chunk of it had been in Azkaban when we liberated the prisoners. We added to it with a number of Muggle-born wizards that had been in Azkaban. We got those people to Hogwarts when it counted—just when the battle was going against the DA. If we hadn't been there, the Deatheaters might have killed Potter before he had a chance to duel with Riddle.

"There would have been at least a couple of very capable leaders ready to take over from Riddle even if he had dueled with Potter and lost. There was Bellatrix Lestrange. There was Lucius Malfoy. The Deatheaters had completely infiltrated the Ministry of Magic

"It could have been a long dark time for Muggles and Wizards alike."

Minerva actually laughed, "I think that you should run for Minister of Magic. You could probably convince people that a Muggle would make a good MOM. But what do you actually think? You've talked a lot about philosophical arguments, but you haven't told me what your gut tells you."

"You're right. Frankly, I'm just thinking about it now.

"I think that the truth is somewhere between the two extremes. Without us, there would have been a long extended battle. I think that the Deatheaters would have fallen eventually, but it wouldn't have happened in one night. It would have dragged on for—who knows?—weeks, months, maybe even years."

Minerva said, "I don't know either. I like your answer, but it's just a little hard for me to tell whether that's because I think that it's good or because I just like the idea that my man made a big difference."

We talked about the upcoming academic year and left the inn to walk up to the castle. As we approached it, there came that nagging thought about the Dursley's. I asked Minerva, "Would you mind taking me into Diagon alley sometime soon?"

"No problem, but what do you want to do there? I really need you working on lesson plans for next year."

"I can't really tell you. Frankly, I'm not sure myself. I have only the haziest idea of what I will accomplish or even what I'll do. And the idea that I have is so crazy, that I just can't admit to you what it is."

Minerva frowned and said, "I suppose that means that I can't be the one to take you there?"

I made a face and said, "When you're right, you're right."

She said, "Hmmmm." and didn't say anything for a long while. Finally, she nodded and said, "Yes, I'll get someone to take you."

□□

The next couple of days passed pleasantly. One day over breakfast in bed, I asked Minerva, "I suppose this idyll has to end when school starts."

She harrumphed and said, "It has to end before most of the staff arrives. You've seen way more of the Headmistress's quarters than is seemly." However, there was a broad smile on her face, and I could tell she was having a hard time restraining laughter.

Later that day, I was bent over a parchment working on a syllabus for the English poets class when there was a knock on the door. I responded, "Come in."

I didn't look up immediately. I was trying to force the quill I was using to finish the page legibly. Finally I looked up and saw Ron Weasley standing over my desk. I was happy to see him, "Does this visit mean that you want to come to Hogwarts for seventh year?"

The looming hulk looked down at his feet and said softly, almost apologetically, "No, sir. Professor McGonagall asked me to accompany you to Diagon Alley." Then he brightened and looked up at me, having gotten the hard part over.

"Good, I was wondering whom she would get to give me a lift there. When do we leave?"

"Right away, sir, if that's OK."

"Of course, it is. Actually, I'm glad she picked you. I never did get to have you in any of my courses, and I'd like to get to know someone who was so much a part of ridding the world of Riddle."

His cheeks turned a little bit red, but he was smiling widely, "I didn't really do that much."

"Modesty can be taken too far. While we're traveling, please tell me about your part in it." I got up and walked around the desk to a point where we were within handshaking range and offered my hand.

"How are we going there? Please don't say disapparating."

Ron's hesitated. "I suppose that we could take the floo network."

I made a face and said, "That would be just fine." We walked down to Hoggsmead and Ron told me about being on the run with Harry. He even told me about abandoning him and re-joining him. He told me about the Snatchers.

I stopped walking and looked at him for a second. When he finally noticed and turned around, I said, "I ran into a group of Snatchers once. Did George tell you about that?"

"No, sir."

"We killed one of them. He was threatening us and nobody knew what would happen. One of the people with us shot him dead."

"What do you mean 'shot' him?"

"It was a Muggle—a soldier. He was along to provide us security. I think he lost his head a little, but who knows how many of us would have ended up dead or in Azkaban if he hadn't. It's bothered me ever since."

"What happened to the other Snatchers? They always traveled in packs."

"Oh, your brothers took them away and . . . well, ask George about that."

"That's funny. He's never said anything about that. Normally he'd brag about that kind of thing."

"Maybe he's not any happier with his part of that day than I am."

We reached the village and went into the Three Broomsticks. We had a quick one and took the floo system to the lobby of Gringotts in Diagon Alley. As we left the lobby I said, "Ron, did Minerv . . Ms. McGonagall tell you anything about this trip?"

"No, just that I was to get you here and return with you."

"OK. I have a little private business that I need to do here, and I'd really like to do that in private. I don't even want anyone to know what shop I go in. Do you have something to occupy you for a while?"

"Not, really."

"Why not go to George's joke shop."

"George doesn't like people—or at least, me—to loiter around if we're not buying."

"I'll tell you what, Ron. I'd like to play a little joke on George. Goodness knows that he's played enough on me. I owe you some money for getting me down here and back. I'd like to throw in a little more to enable you to play a joke on George.

"Would you take your pay plus a little extra I'll throw in for a joke, go in, and make a real nuisance of yourself? You know, ask to be shown everything. Make him open boxes—that sort of thing. Then when he finally looses his temper, buy something expensive with this." I had pulled out my purse and handed Ron a pile of galleons.

Ron goggled and said, "That's way too much."

I looked at his outstretched hands and took some back and said, "How's that."

Ron grinned broadly and said, "You really want me to play a joke on George?"

"Of course."

"Then this is just right." He trotted off toward George's shop, and I watched him go in before entering the shop of Olivander.

The shop was empty of customers. Mr. Olivander approached me and asked, "What in the world can I do for a Muggle?"

I stared at him wide-eyed, "How did you know that I'm a Muggle? Oh, I know, you saw my picture in the *Prophet*."

"Young man, no I did not. I never read that worthless rag if I have a choice. '*The Daily Prophet*'—as if they could tell the future. No, as if they could tell what happened yesterday. Maybe they are right. They're just as good at telling the future as they are at reporting the past.

"No, when any magical person enters this shop, one or usually many wands respond to them. They can't help it. I feel that response. I know it.

When you entered, not a single wand, even my most sensitive registered anything.

"So, you are surely not here to make a purchase. What do you want?"

"Well, in a way, I am here to make a purchase—on behalf of someone else."

"That's a touching idea—a gift, I suppose. But magical wands don't work that way, you can't just walk in and buy any random wand for someone who's not present. It just doesn't work that way. It's really the wand that makes the choice. So, you see, you're on a fool's errand."

I had half-way expected something like that. I said, "Well, I have a rather unusual request. I'd like you to make what we Muggles would call a 'house call'."

"You mean take my wands to someone's house and let them choose there?"

"Yes, I suppose that's it."

"That's very irregular. Is the person infirm or is there any other reason that he can't come to my shop?"

I grimaced at the next thing that I had to say, "Well. No, he's not infirm or sick. But he's, well, maybe. I think he'd be embarrassed to come here." I ended weakly.

He looked at me for a long time before answering. Then he said, "It must have taken you, a Muggle, quite a lot of courage to come to me and ask me such a preposterous request. I can see that you are serious and want to do this person a kindness. Yes, I'll come to him with a selection of wands. Understand that I don't promise that any of them will take to him."

"Oh, I understand. I really appreciate the lengths that you're willing to go."

"Do we leave now? As you can see, the shop's empty. Why not go now?"

"Oh, I've got to make arrangements. I'll send you an owl with the location and a time. If it's not convenient, we can work something out."

"Very well. Actually, I'm rather interested to see this unusual person who'd be embarrassed to come into Olivanders." He looked over my right shoulder as though someone had just entered the store and seemed lost in thought for a moment. "You, know. I wonder. I just wonder."

"What?"

"Oh, nothing, I just had a vagrant thought. Well, I'll be looking for your owl."

"Thanks again. Be seeing you." And I left Olivander's shop.

I wandered over to George's shop. I entered and found George berating Ron, "What are you doing here? I've opened half the boxes in the store for you. Are you going to buy something or not?"

Ron was not intimidated at all. He said, "Patience, brother. I'm just looking for the right thing."

George answered, "Well, you'd better have something in about ten seconds or I'm throwing you out. And it'd better not be a packet of Muggle magic cards!"

Ron grinned widely and said, "Such impatience with paying customers."

"Well, I've not seen any paying customers yet."

Ron walked over to a table that had something that I didn't recognize. He said, "I've decided, I'll take the locket."

"The locket? The locket! You didn't even ask to take the locket out of the case? What are you doing taking the locket?"

'It does show the image of the wearer's true love when she opens it, doesn't it?" Guaranteed?"

"Of course, it does. Double your money back if it doesn't, but you can't afford that!"

"Oh, yes I can."

George was wary, "Let's see the glint of your galleons."

Ron slowly drew his purse from his robes and opened the draw string slightly, "How much did you say it was?"

"Thirty-five. And 5 silver sickles;"

Ron slowly counted out thirty-six galleons and said, "Keep the change brother; I can afford to be generous."

George was struck completely dumb. I'd never seen him without something to say. Ron took the locket from his brother's outstretched hands and walked slowly away. He then noticed me and strode over, "Let's go", he said, "I'll bet Hermione will like this."

"I'll bet she will. Let me tell you, I've never seen George quite so flummoxed. This was worth the trip."

We went to Flourish and Blots and took the floo network back to the Three Broomsticks. I thanked Ron profusely and we parted.

Back at Hogwarts I went to the Headmistress's office but discovered that the password had been changed. I swore under my breath and thought to myself that I understood how Potter felt when he didn't know the password and wanted to see Dumbledore. I decided to go back to her old quarters, with the forlorn hope that there might be a message for me there. I got to the portrait of the fat lady and gave her the password, Quidnunc. She opened the passage for me, and then I had a thought. I turned back to the fat lady and asked, "What's the password to the Headmistress's office?"

She looked at me a second and then said, "Oh, I suppose it's ok, since you two are uh. . . shall we say . . ."

"Just give me the password."

"Oh, all right. It's *mufliato*."

"Thanks a million. By the way, how did you know it?"

"Oh, we all know all the passwords."

"All?' I asked.

The fat lady looked around for an over-hearer and then said, "Yes, all the portraits guarding the house entrances. We will always tell teachers the password to any of the doors."

"Including the Headmistress's?"

"Yes. But the guard of the Headmistress's won't give the password to anyone."

"Why didn't someone tell me this long ago?"

"No one knew since the founders. You're the first to guess it."

I went back to Minerva's office and confidently walked up, gave the password and entered. I walked into her office and found her bent over a scroll. She suddenly looked up, screamed, and then said, "How did you get in here. I didn't give you the new password."

"Oh, that's my little secret."

"I'll bet I can get it out of you this evening."

"Only, if you'll agree to have lunch with me tomorrow at our favorite restaurant."

"Well, only if you'll agree that we can go there by disapparation."

I grimaced as usual and she said, "Don't grimace, either agree or don't."

"Yes, we can go there by disapparation." And I unclenched my teeth with an effort of will.

Big D

When my lunch appointment with Minerva came up at the King's Cross Station, I was trying hard to get up the courage to say what I felt that I had to. It seemed strange to me that after fighting Deatheater for a year, I could face anything, but with the Deatheataers gone it was different. It's one thing to attack your enemy and quite another to tell the person that you love that she's wrong. I stood outside the ladies loo on the main floor. She walked briskly out and said, "Sorry dear that I was so long. You know sometimes we women just can't be rushed."

"No matter how long it takes, the anticipation makes it all worthwhile."

"You are far too polite. I've been trying to find a replacement for Mr. Filch."

"I can't believe that Filch is ready to retire."

"Oh, he's not ready to retire. I wish he were ready to retire. He's getting old, and he's just too frail to keep up with the kids."

"IF you value your life, I wouldn't tell him that."

We went to the restaurant next to the station, named after the station. It had a ragout that I just couldn't resist. We got seated next to a window. I like the view. I began to think that the hostess might have noticed our habits.

The waitress recognized us. "Minerva, is that 'spooky'? or what?" I asked.

"You think it's 'magic'?"

"Very funny. But that brings up a point. Do you think that you'd know a magical person if you'd been with them once or twice?"

"I couldn't be sure. But surely you've got someone specific in mind." I took my heart from my throat and put it in my mouth. Just then the waitress brought the salad that we'd ordered, and my heart went back down into my throat. I thanked her, and she smiled.

Minerva frowned, and I asked her what was wrong. She said, "You forgot to ask the waitress not to put dressing on your salad."

I noticed that there was no salad dressing on the salad or even on the side. "Look, there isn't any salad dressing."

"You need to tip that waitress very well."

"Yeh, I agree."

"But you looked like you were getting to some point?"

"Yeah, there's somebody that I think might be magical, and I'd like to have somebody test him."

"Who is it that you want me to test? And why do you think that he might be magical?"

"I was thinking. . ." I hesitated and then leaped up ahead, "that Dudley Dursley, Harry's cousin, might be."

"Dudley? But why of all people, a dunce like him?"

"Since when did intelligence have anything to do with magic?"

"You're right, but surely the Magic Ministry wouldn't miss something like that."

I smiled, "How does the Ministry decide when there are magical kids in a family?"

Minerva was wary as she said slowly, "Well, it depends on the family. A family with a magical parent is presumed to have magical children. The parents will know if a child of theirs isn't magical.

"On the other hand, with non-magical parents, magic in the home would be a sign that one or more children are magical." With that she hesitated. She continued more slowly, thinking out what she had to say. "Of course, the Dursleys are pretty unique. A non-magical family with an adopted child who is known to be magical. . . Yes, the assumption would be that any magic was done by the known magical child."

I smiled but asked, "What about when Harry was away at school?"

"Well, for one thing, there's always been magic coursing around that house because of Dumbledore's protective spell and the Magic Ministry protective spells."

She went on, "But surely there'd be something unusual that would show up about him? I'm not aware of anything."

"Isn't there? How does someone who's as dumb as a brick get to be the leader of a gang of kids? Follower, yes? Trusted heavy, yeah? But leader? Besides that, the Dursleys were followed by Deatheaters while they were away from England. Somehow they eluded them completely without help. How do you suppose they worked that?"

"You've promised the Dursley's something, haven't you?"

"No, I just had a feeling about it, and as I thought about it, things started to drop into place."

She rolled her eyes, and the waitress showed up with my ragout and Minerva's kidney pie. "I don't see how you eat that stuff." I opined.

"Oh. It's just the most perfect pie you'll ever have."

"Yeah."

She leaned across the table for emphasis and said, "Look, you can't do that. Commit me to something that I don't believe in. Do you think that. . . . Oh, I know that it would seem like the kind thing to do, but why raise hopes for them and then dash them."

"I know. But, it seemed to me that he might just have some magic, and even if he didn't, the mother needed us to take her, them, seriously. I think that whatever happens, she'd like to know for sure—that we've given her that courtesy."

"OK, OK. I'll go down there tomorrow." She hesitated and her eyes looked beyond me for a minute, then cleared and returned to me. "You know, I just had an idea. This could be interesting. I'll get in touch with an expert that I know." She stopped and then continued, "I think that I'll get in touch with him and I'll send an owl to the Dursleys."

I looked down at my plate and said, "Actually, I've already got in touch with someone who should be really good at testing him."

"Really, you've become an expert in magic?"

"Not, me. And I have become an expert at finding magical people whom I really, really want."

She smiled slyly.

"Listen, Minerva, would you mind sending a note by Muggle post to the Dursleys asking for permission to test Dudley. I can post it."

"But surely the boy would like to receive it in the 'normal' way."

"Maybe, but I think the father would prefer something Muggle 'normal'."

"Hmmm. Maybe you're right. You are the expert on Muggles."

"Thanks."

"But it will take us a couple of days for the letter to be delivered."

"I only promised some time next week."

The lines around her mouth that had been tight smoothed and disappeared, "Besides that, it would give me a chance to tell that family what I think of the way they treated Harry."

"I gave them a pretty hard time yesterday. Just don't overdue it."

She laughed. "Is that possible?"

□

The return receipt from the letter that I'd sent the Dursleys had arrived at my old address at the SAS office. The resident wizard had sent an owl to Hogwarts. So, Minerva came down to my office to let me know, "Well, your Muggle office got the return receipt. What are you going to do?"

"If you'll humor me, I'll ask you to go out of the grounds and disapparate me to somewhere that I can call the Dursley's to see when they want us to come."

"Sure, but let's go at lunch. I ought to get something out of this."

We arrived at an alley near Gimmold Place. I was surprised we'd gone so far, "Why'd you bring us almost all the way to London? I could have called from Edinburgh?"

"Now what kind of husbandry would it be to make a, what do you call it, 'long range' call . . . ?"

"That's 'long distance' call."

"It's all the same. They're expensive, aren't they?"

"No, they're not for cell phones. They're all the same."

"I just can't believe that. They're always trying to trick you Muggles into spending money that you don't have."

"OK. OK. I'm going to call the Dursleys—short distance—when should I make the appointment?"

"Tomorrow's Saturday, I think that would be good for everyone." She added, "Including your mystery expert?"

"Yes, including my mystery expert."

I dialed, and the phone rang. Once, twice. . . 6 times and then an answer.

"Dursley's residence."

"This is Mr. Wendt. Are you interested in a meeting to have your son tested?"

There was a long silence on the other end of the wire. Then, a tremulous voice that I barely recognized as Petunia's, "Yes. When?"

"Tomorrow morning?" I looked at Minerva, and she nodded, "Say, 10?"

"10AM, in the morning?"

I smiled, "Yes, in the morning."

"You sure you don't mean the afternoon?"

"I'm sure. But, we could do it in the afternoon, if you prefer." Another long pause.

Then distracted, "Yes, . . yes. 10AM would be fine. Should we all be there?"

I put on mute, "Everyone present for the exam?"

"Yes. They should all know as quickly as possible."

Mute off. "Yes, that would be best."

"You're sure?"

"Yes."

There was a gulp on the other end. Then, silence. "Minerva . . . uh Headmistress McGonagall, the examiner, and I will be there at 10 sharp tomorrow morning. If there has to be any change in plan, call the number on the card that I left you. Any time."

She said in a hollow voice, "Thanks."

"Well, we're committed." Minerva commented.

I smiled and almost laughed.

I went on, "Committed is right. If the Ministry finds out, they'll sack me and probably you too from the school."

"If the Ministry finds out? I thought that it'd be a ministry official who did the exam."

"No, I've got someone special." I smiled—this time for real.

"But, you won't tell me who."

"No. It's more fun that way."

"For whom?"

"For me. If you can drive me crazy every now and then, why can't I drive you crazy a little?"

"Well, because you love me?"

"And what about you?"

"We'll see tomorrow just how crazy everyone is."

□□

After leaving Minerva, I took a chance. I went to the Astronomy Tower, where Sinistra held sway. I walked up the winding steps along the inside wall of the tower. When I reached the top level, I looked around for a desk or some sign of an office. There was a door on the far wall of the circular interior of the tower. I approached it and knocked.

Instantly, Sinistra's voice came through it, "Enter."

I did. She too was concentrating on papers on her desk as I had been. She raised her head, and I rushed into my request so that she wouldn't get the wrong idea. "Sinsistra, I have a favor to ask."

She nodded without saying a word.

I diffidently asked, "Would you mind sending a letter for me by owl post?"

A smile broke across her face, "Of course, I would. But wouldn't you rather have your sweety do it for you?"

I shook my head. "This is special. It's something that I don't want her to know about."

Sinistra hummed appreciatively. "Something special, eh? Like that last time that I posted something for you?"

"Yeh, a bit."

She rose and strode to me and looped her arm through the one that I was using to hold my letter out to her. Her smile had become broader, and she said, "Let's head for the owlery."

I was beginning to regret this already. "OK. And if you insist, you can even read the letter."

Her eyebrows lifted the question, "Really? Intriguing."

I handed her the letter as I disentangled her arm from mine. She didn't pay much attention as she inspected the direction. "Mr. Olivander in Diagon Alley. Curiouser and Curiouser." She flipped the parchment over and her eyebrows raised further. She read aloud, "Tomorrow morning at 10 AM."

She then re-rolled the parchment and said, "10 AM is a strange time for an assignation. Even stranger is one with Olivander. That's THE Olivander, isn't it?"

I shrugged, "There is another?"

She shook her head no. Then we walked silently down the Astronomy Tower and across to the Owlery tower. She didn't even try to loop my arm in hers again—she was that astounded at the brief letter. We arrived at the top of the tower and she said, "You have to pay a fee for this favor."

I grimaced. She had me over a barrel. I didn't have much choice at this late hour. I decided to be a good sport and smiled. "What is your fee?"

She shrugged, "Nothing onerous—just a simple kiss, no more."

I too shrugged and she added, "It must be a real kiss—not a throwaway."

I simply nodded. I took her head between my two hands gently and kissed her full on the lips. I didn't resist in the slightest when she opened her mouth. Then our lips parted.

She called her owl, tied the letter to its leg and sent it on its way.

She said, "You've earned a bigger favor than this. What do you want?"

An errant idea struck me from literature. I simply said, "A single lock of your hair."

She was surprised but she nodded. We walked quietly back to her office. She went in and after a couple of minutes, she came back with a lock of hair coiled in a simple locket.

I thanked her and said, "You know that I can't wear this."

She smiled and said, "Just put it in that Mokeskin purse that I know you have. No one that you don't want to see it ever will."

I nodded and left.

⊡

The next morning, Minerva had toast for breakfast in the Great Hall. The House Elves had a sumptuous meal but neither of us wanted, or at least, could force down more than a piece of dry toast. We went to the front gate at 9:45 and the universe turned itself inside out, which seemed perfectly appropriate for once. We appeared in a back alley next to Privet Drive. We walked around the corner with no sign of hurry. The morning was grey and cloudy but warm. There was no sign of rain, just a dreary day. We arrived at the door at 9:56, but couldn't wait the 4 minutes for the appointed time. I knocked, and after a surprising delay, it was answered by Petunia Dursley. Her face was drawn, and I don't think that she'd had much sleep. She asked us in and had us sit in the sitting room. She left, and Dudley and Mr. Dursley came in. The senior Mr. Dursley was clearly trying to keep his mouth from quivering—I couldn't tell whether from fear or rage.

I said, "I hope the letter came in a satisfactory manor."

Dursley Sr. smiled, "It's good to see that someone knows how to use the Queen's post." Petunia shot him a frown, and he sat down.

Petunia got up and asked if anyone wanted something to drink—OJ, milk, water, tea, coffee?

I said, "I'd like OJ. What about you Minerva. I'm sorry. I'm assuming that everyone knows everyone here."

Dursley Sr. nodded almost imperceptibly.

Then the doorbell rang. We all leaped up as though someone had kicked us in the rear. Dursley Sr. walked to the door and opened it after a moment's hesitation. The old gentleman at the door was dressed in a business suit that was old, beginning to be worn, and obviously (to a Muggle) of a cut that hadn't seen the sunny side of fashionability in quite a long time. But it was immaculately, clean, and neat. I couldn't come up with a guess as to his age and never have no matter how many times I've seen him.

I made introductions, "Our charming hostess is Mrs. Petunia Dursley, the young man is Dudley Dursely, and this is his father Vernon Dursely. We are all honored to have one of the foremost wand-makers in the world as a guest this morning. I appreciate deeply Mr. Olivander's courtesy to us in coming personally to this home."

Mr. Olivander smiled a thin smile and said, "I am always happy to accommodate Ms. McGonagall. And I understand that you have an unusual challenge for me. Shall we begin?"

I interrupted gently. "Wait a moment, sir. I have to make a statement to the younger Mr. Dursley and the rest of his family—with your permission?"

Mr. Olivander turned slightly and gestured toward the now closed door, "I brought some tools of my trade along and left them on the doorstep so that they wouldn't offend. May I bring them in before you begin?"

I turned expectantly to the older Dursley. He stared dully and then, realizing that something was expected of him, he shook his head briefly, and then said, "Oh, yes, of course, I'm sure that we'll . . . ." He faltered and trailed off to nothing. Mr. Olivander took the reply as assent and opened the door himself before I could reach the door. He brought in a large brief case, or perhaps it was a small valise. I wondered what instruments would test for magic.

As he brought it in, I took a deep breathe and began, "Before we begin Mr. Dursley, I want to be sure that you really want to do this exam." I was staring directly at Dudley, but his father broke in, "I'll make the decision for my son. Of course, he wants to take the exam. He'll pass it with flying colors too."

I turned briefly to Dursley Sr., "It's your son's decision, Mr. Dursley. Even by Muggle standards he's an adult, and," I turned my attention to Dudley, "you have the right to make this decision." I turned back to Vernon and let a little of the contempt I felt show in my voice, "This could change his life for ever. He should be the one to choose."

I turned back to Dudley. "Please think carefully. You probably aren't magical, but, you," I repeated with emphasis, "might be magical. Are you prepared for the possibility that you're not magical. There are no re-tests. You either are or aren't."

Dudley looked from me to his Mom. Then he said to her, "What do you want?"

She couldn't hold his gaze but instead turned to me. I said, "Look, Mrs. Dursley, I have no idea if he's magical or not. It really should be his decision. Please prepare for both possibilities if he decides to go ahead. I'm sure that he can take either decision and move on." At the end I turned to him as I said the last sentence. I wanted to make sure that he knew that I was being honest with him when I said that. I said to him, "Yes or no?"

Dudley stared at me for a moment and said, "Go ahead. I want to know." I turned to Olivander. He began speaking in his soft voice that had the slightest drawl, "You must all understand that the most sensitive test of magical ability is the process of a possible wizard finding his wand. The wand chooses the wizard, not the other way around. This is a sensitive test, partly because the wand is like a 'Lizer'."

I interrupted, "A what?!!"

"You know Mr. Wendt, a "Lizer" beam. It amplifies light."

"Oh, you mean a laser."

"Yes, I said it, a Lizer. The wand amplifies and directs the natural magic that all wizards and witches have. But the wand must accept the wizard. Even a powerful wizard like "He-Who-Must-Not-Be-Named" could not force a wand that rejects him to do serious magic. Finding the right wizard for a given wand is an arduous process, but sometimes a wizard finds the right wand quickly. The intuition of a skilled wand maker. . ."

I interrupted, "Like you."

"Yes, if you like, can speed the process quickly. I've brought along a large selection of wands. We don't necessarily need to find the exact right wand. Usually even the completely wrong wand will work some magic. So, let us begin if we are all ready." He passed his gaze over all of us seated together. No one said anything or even moved. "Very well."

He opened his case revealing rows of neatly ordered unmarked oblong boxes. He chose one and handed it to Dudley. Dudley hesitated and then took it from Olivander. He asked, "What do I do?"

"Simply open the box, take the wand gently, but firmly, in your dominant hand and flick it over there toward the door outside." As Dudley opened the box, Olivander commented casually as if he were describing a fine writing instrument. "This is a 10 ½ inch Beech with a core of catgut. It's reasonably stiff but soft."

Dudley flicked it very tentatively. It was too tentative for Olivander, "No, no. You must use authority when you wield the wand. The wand must know that you are to be the master, if it selects you."

Vernon interrupted, "Any wand in its right mind would want to be owned by our Dudders."

Everyone looked over at him with a frown, and he sat back.

Dudley tried again with some force.

"Yes, yes. That's not perfect but that's good enough. We'll try another."

He took the first back and got out another box and commented, "Birch with a core of lion's hair. Quite flexible and easy to direct spells accurately."

Dudley tried flicking it and nothing happened. Over the next half-hour we tried a number of wands from Olivander's seemingly unlimited supply. Nothing happened with any of them. Finally, Minerva said, "I'm sorry Petunia." She reached out and took Mrs. Dursley's left hand in her right. "I know you were hoping . . ." She let the sentence hang and die.

No one but I noticed that Olivander had a puzzled look on his face. "Wait a moment. I'm not finished." He hesitated for a moment that seemed to stretch on and on. Then he seemed to say more to himself than anyone else in the room, "Yes. Yes."

He dug deep in the brief case and slowly drew out an aged box that had clearly yellowed over the years. He seemed to have made his decision internally for he went on briskly, for him, "I must explain the wand before I allow the boy to try it. Please allow an old man a moment of self-pity. When I was a young man, I was conceited. I thought that every wand that I made was for someone in particular. I'm not so sure of that now. But one day, I made a wand that I thought no one would use. It was so peculiar and so against the theory of wand-making that I thought I must be crazy. But I couldn't keep from trying this experiment. The wand that I made was Sandalwood, but it had an Ironwood core." He hesitated, but no one responded with the shocked surprise that he evidently expected. "So, you say . . ." He tried to urge us forward.

Finally, Minerva said, "That does seem very strange. I thought that the theory of wand-making was that the exterior must be wood—probably mundane, but the interior had to be something exotic that reacted with the exterior in some way . . ." I had rarely seen her at a loss for words when discussing magic topics, but she trailed off without finishing her sentence.

Olivander's disgust was veiled, but I thought that I saw exasperation in his eyes, as if we were all total dunces.

"Yes, that's good enough an understanding for our purposes. You can see that this simple-minded theory of wand-making clearly would say that such a wand as I made would not have any power. But, still, I made it and deep in my heart, I felt that there was some use for it. I just had to find the right wizard. Well, I had no idea what kind of a wizard would use such a wand. My intuition had totally failed me, but, I didn't give up. I first tired it on every wizard who entered my shop. None could coax any magic from it. Some were affronted. They thought that I was playing a joke on them. Gradually my intuition allowed me to find the right wand for the right wizard after only two, three, or four tries. Eventually I never tried that wand with any wizard. I finally even forgot that I had made it. But today when I packed my bag, I found it again and decided to pack it."

"I'm frankly more afraid of what we will find if I let you try this wand, young man, than you are. I've not quite decided to let you try it."

Dudley said in a steady voice that was simple, "Please let me try your wand, sir."

That seemed to decide Olivander. He held the box out, and Dudley took it. He opened the box, lifted the wand, and gazed at it for a time, turning it over and over in his hands. "It's beautiful sir."

Then he casually flicked it and . . . did something happen? I couldn't tell. There was no stream of light like the ones I'd occasionally seen when someone used a wand, but I could have sworn something happened. I looked around, but no flower pots had gone flying, no chair levitated, no stream of water issued from the wand. I looked at Minerva. She shook her head and started to speak, "I'm sorry son. I think. . ." But she never finished the sentence.

Mr. Olivander interrupted. "What did you just do?"

Dudley looked around and said, "Did I break the wand?"

"No, young man. You did something with the wand, but I just can't tell what."

Minerva said, "Surely nothing happened, I didn't feel anything. Nothing seems disturbed."

"No, Ms. McGonagall. I know that something happened. I just don't know what."

I tired to remember exactly where I'd seen Dudley point the wand. I couldn't quite remember, but I thought it had been toward the front door to the house. I got up, walked over to it, and started examining it. Then, I noticed it. I couldn't understand why I hadn't seen it the first moment I'd reached the door. I turned and motioned to everyone to come over beside me. When they arrived, I asked, "Do you see it?"

Minerva got exasperated. "Just out with it, Wendt."

"Don't you see the ½ in. hole drilled neatly through the door? It had gone through the brass door knocker on the outside of the door. I lined my eye up with the hole and tried to see what the next object in the line of sight was. It looked like it might just be a lamp pole. We went outside, and I walked over to the lamp pole. The others followed. There was a neat ½ in. hole drilled through it and you could just see inside that a wire had been partially severed. I looked through the hole to sight the next obstacle, if possible. It looked like it might just have caught the edge of the house across the street. We walked across the street and approached the corner of the house. At about the height of the top of my head, there was a neat ½ in hole that barely drilled through the corner of a brick. Sighting through the hole was a stand of trees. We went there and spent about 10 minutes looking for a hole in a tree but couldn't find one. No one had said a word until then. I said, "I don't know, but I've got a feeling that if the line of holes just happened to line up with the moon in its orbit about the earth, there'd be a neat ½ in. hole traversing completely the moon.

We went back to the Dursley's. No one said anything. We all sat for about five minutes before Minerva asked the room in general, "What do we do now?"

I said, "I think we've got to offer Mr. Dudley the right to enter Hogwart's as a 1st year student this fall."

Minerva showed consternation on her face, "But we've never admitted a student so old before. How would he fit in with a class of 11 yr-olds."

Vernon Dursley was indignant for a change, "If my son is entitled to attend Hogwart's, you've got to bloody well let him."

Mrs. Dursley tried to placate, "Now, Vernon, it'd be so hard on the boy."

Dudley kept trying to break in and finally said, "Doesn't anyone care what I want?"

I stared for a second and then woke up. "Of course, it's your decision. Dudley. What do you want to do?"

He took another deep breath, "First, Mr. Olivander," he pronounced the name slowly and carefully, putting extra emphasis on the "O" as if to be sure he got it right. "I can't keep your wand. I don't want to use it. There might have been a person, a kid, in the line of that beam or whatever went out of my wand. I don't want to kill someone."

Olivander looked at Dudley for a long moment. "The wand wouldn't let you hurt someone seriously if you didn't want to. That isn't to say that you might not lose your temper and hurt someone, but I don't think you're someone who loses his temper."

"What planet are you from?" I wondered to myself. But Olivander went on,

"No Mr. Dudley, I can't keep the wand from you. It has chosen you. I would never make another wand if I kept that wand from you. No wand would let me make it. But, you certainly don't have to use it just because you own it. Here." He reached into his valise and pulled out a small soft velvet case. He handed it to Dudley. "Permit me to make this present to you. It is a wand care kit. If you decide never to use it, at least polish the wand gently occasionally. You must treat your wand with respect and care."

Dudley hesitated and then accepted it, "Yes, sir."

He turned to Minerva and went on. "I don't want to study at Hogwarts. I saw the things that wizards do to people. I lived most of my life frightened of Harry. I couldn't let him know, so I had to prove that I wasn't afraid. I did some bad things that I don't like to remember."

I said, "Most wizards aren't mean or vicious. You certainly don't have to be."

"No, I don't want to. But," Here Dudley hesitated again. "You know his friend, the giant."

Minerva frowned quickly and covered up, "Yes, you mean Haggrid."

"Yes, Harry told me that he couldn't do magic because of something bad he did. But he was at Hogwart's."

"Yes, he used to be the gamekeeper. He became a professor a couple of years ago, and he can do magic now."

"Well, I thought that maybe I could be a gamekeeper like Haggrid. I think he was the kind of person that I am. Big, clumsy. Not real smart."

"Haggrid is a wonderful man. Being a gamekeeper was well . . ." She faltered again. And then it struck her what Dudley was asking. "Oh, you want to be the Hogwart's gamekeeper."

"I know that I don't know very much about animals and things, but maybe I could learn."

Minerva's eyes began to glisten. "Oh, Dudley, I'd love to let you try gamekeeping, but we already have one. It's really a very dangerous job. And . . ." She was having a hard time finishing sentences today.

I interrupted, "Wait Minerva. I know a job at Hogwarts that doesn't require any magic, and the guy who's got it now is about as dumb as they come, I'm sure that Dudley could . . ."

"Oh, James, I couldn't replace Filch. It would break his heart."

"Who said anything about 'replace'. I was just thinking that he isn't as young as he was. He could use someone to do the heavy lifting, and he would probably love having someone to give orders to who would actually follow the orders."

Minerva's frown turned half-way into a smile. "Well, you're right. Filch would love it, but would you wish Filch on anyone?"

I answered, "We have to ask Dudley.

"Dudley, there's an apprentice job at Hogwart's. You could learn on the job. You wouldn't have to do any magic. Your boss would be a crusty old man who would love for you to work for him, and you might even get to the point of liking him. What do you think of visiting Hogwart's, meeting Mr. Filch, talking to a few of the teachers?"

Dudley didn't hesitate, "I'll take the job."

I was a little surprised, but I went on, "I can't let you take the job without a chance to look around and decide if you really want to."

"Oh, I'll want to."

"Wait a minute," Vernon had come to life again, "I can't let you take advantage of my son like this. Dudders, they haven't even told you what the pay is. Is there chance for advancement? What's the retirement like?"

Dudley interrupted. "Dad, this is my decision, not yours. I'm going to make it on my own. AFTER I've seen the place, I'll come home, and you can talk to me about it."

Petunia got up and put her right arm about Dudley's shoulder. "Oh, Dudders, I don't know how we'll get on without you."

"Oh, mum. I've heard you and dad arguing about going on vacation by yourselves. I won't be really far away. Harry always came home more often than you wanted."

Her voice caught. She broke into open tears. "And now, I suppose I'll never see him again. You know he always reminded me of his mom, especially his eyes. I hated him for that, but now I wish. . ."

I interrupted again, "Look, Dudley, the Headmistress and I have to leave. We'll get in touch to arrange a tour, and let you meet some students too. By the way, don't pay too much attention to what Mr. Filch tells you about students. Form your own opinions."

Vernon got up first and quickly moved to the door to let us out, which didn't surprise me. I was the last out. He touched my arm and said, "I want to thank you for this. 'Pet' wanted this more than you can imagine. You see she had this idea that she would have liked to uh go to. . ."

"You don't have to say. I know what she was hoping for, and I think I know why. You know you're very lucky. Your son could have been 'normal', and then you'd have to help your wife live with the final death of her dream. I've seen that happen. Really, it happens to everyone sometime, but it's never easy. Good luck."

"Have you ever had a dream die?"

"Sure I have. You have too." He looked like he wanted to say something, but he didn't.

Minerva was waiting for me. "It's really too bad that she wasn't magical."

"Yeh, people always want the craziest things, don't they?"

She looked at me strangely. "Yes, I've never quite understood you."

"But mine are only the simplest, n'est pas?"

About the Author

William Wilkin lived in a small Southern Ohio town until he began his college career. He has a Bachelor's degree in Physics from The Ohio State University and a Master's degree in Physics from The University of Chicago. He had a career in corporate Information Technology and currently lives in Nashville, Tennessee.

He enjoys music, both "serious" and "classic Rock". He reads classic Detective fiction and Science Fiction & Fantasy as well as trying to stay current in Physics.

He began writing seriously about 2005. He has a blog, in-mid-world, where he writes about Science Fiction & Fantasy and remotely related topics.

www.ingramcontent.com/pod-product-compliance
Lightning Source LLC
Chambersburg PA
CBHW061634050726
47502CB00012B/1932